# DÆMONOMANIA

———

# JOHN CROWLEY

---

# DÆMONOMANIA

BANTAM BOOKS

NEW YORK   TORONTO   LONDON   SYDNEY   AUCKLAND

DÆMONOMANIA

A Bantam Book / August 2000

Book design by Laurie Jewell.

Library of Congress Cataloging-in-Publication Data
Crowley, John.
Daemonomania / John Crowley.
p.   cm.
ISBN 0-553-10004-1
1. Fantastic Fiction.  I. Title.
PS3553.R597D34      2000
813'.54—dc21       99-44109
CIP

Published simultaneously in the United States and Canada

Bantam Books are published by Bantam Books, a division of Random House, Inc. Its trademark, consisting of the words "Bantam Books" and the portrayal of a rooster, is Registered
in U.S. Patent and Trademark Office and in other countries. Marca Registrada. Bantam
Books, 1540 Broadway, New York, New York 10036.

PRINTED IN THE UNITED STATES OF AMERICA

BVG      10 9 8 7 6 5 4 3 2 1

# DÆMONOMANIA

———

# PROLOGUE

---

## TO THE
## AUTUMN
## QUATERNARY

T he Third Quaternary of the twelve houses of the Zodiac comprises three houses: first, *Uxor,* the Wife, the house of marriage, partnership, divorce too; then *Mors,* house of death and the dead; and *Pietas,* the house of religious observance and also, strangely, the house of voyages. Set out.

The Third Quaternary is Afternoon, and Autumn, from the Equinox to the Winter Solstice. It is the element Water, and the melancholic humor, and the west wind; it contains the middle of life, passages, friends and enemies, loss, dreams, dying, safety and danger. Its matter is the answering of calls, or the failure to answer them.

Midway between equinox and solstice in the year of the end of the world, Pierce Moffett in the thirty-fifth year of his own age mounted a long-distance bus outside the variety store on River Street in the town of Blackbury Jambs in the Faraway Hills. He looked for a seat in the rear, where smoking was at that time permitted, though his mouth was already foul from too many cigarettes. It was a raw day, with low clouds rolling before a wind and droplets forming on the tinted windows of the bus.

The Houses of the Zodiac are not the Signs, as Val the Faraways astrologer and barkeeper has often to explain. The Houses, she says, are like this: Suppose, at your birth, a line were to be drawn across the eastern sky right at the horizon out beyond where you lie. Then up the sky were drawn eleven more lines, equally spaced, going up over your head, down around behind you, and into the nether sky below, coming back around to where you started, dividing the blue ball of the heavens around you (pretend it's really a ball) into twelve equal orange-slice sections, with your little self at the center. Then suppose the sections are numbered, starting with the one just at the eastern horizon. That section's the first House, *Vita,* the House of Life; the eighth House, *Mors,* House of Death, is over your head and to the west. Interesting? Now look out the windows of these houses—they are nothing *but* windows—and see what stars are caught in each just at the moment you appear bare and wailing on the earth. Say for instance Saturn, so heavy and cold, is out there in your first house, the House of Life; and say the sign Capricorn or part of it is just behind him, which is one of his favorite signs; and there you are, a lot of Saturn in your horoscope, in a House where it counts too. And though Val would never say that this street of houses on which you find yourself will make you what you are, what you do make of yourself has got to be made here.

Saturnian, with all that that implies, Pierce Moffett took his seat, his heart small and as heavy as the old god's lead, a plumb bob in his breast. He did not himself believe that the autumn darkness within him was due to the stars; nor did he think it came to him from out there, from the turning year and the fast-falling sun. He thought this darkness was unique, unrelated to any other, an awful new disease he was perhaps the first to catch, at the same time seeming oppressively familiar, as though he had always borne it. He had begun to wonder if it would ever pass from him, or subside, and return him to the clean and happy, or at least ordinary daylit, world he was sure he had been inhabiting not very long ago.

The bus driver now entered, sat and activated his long-armed wipers to cleanse the fine droplets from his window. He pulled shut the door, which made the sound of an airlock closing; around Pierce the familiar fug collected, bus air, what composed it exactly. The brakes exhaled, the lights came on. The driver turned his great wheel to carry them away.

Too late now to leap off.

The gray and haunted little town from which Pierce departed for what appeared in his mind as an even darker region was an old river port gathered at the feet of a mountain, Mount Randa, whose wooded heap rises suddenly to the north of it, carrying upward the last few of its streets and houses. Around Randa's base two rivers run, the Blackbury to the east, the Shadow to the west, which flow together at this town, *coincidentia oppositorum,* and make one big river. At Cascadia, once an important mill town, it falls over a steep falls, and then (growing larger, fuller, slower) flows toward the city of Conurbana, which it once sustained and now merely sunders: a broad brown poor city to which Pierce, unable still to believe it, had agreed to journey.

It was to Blackbury Jambs that Pierce came in the spring of the year from New York City, with a publisher's advance at least metaphorically in his pocket, to live and write a book and to begin somehow anew. This bus he now sat on was the same one, the driver too, that had first brought Pierce into these green hills, the same Conurbana bus that had broken down and deposited Pierce by the side of the road, whence he had wandered and been guided to other places by the inhabitants, a happy flock they had seemed to him then, until by a backwater of the Blackbury he met Rose Ryder, whom no wisdom could have foreseen he would now be travelling toward, with such awful trepidation, in this November of the end of the world.

Rose had moved to Conurbana just the month before, red October, and lived there now, attending Peter Ramus College and studying the Bible. She had invited him to come visit when they last parted, outside his house in Littleville, her little red sports car already shuddering into life. Oh come please come. And he had answered that call with his mouth, and here he was.

How often he had marvelled, when reading stories or watching movies about the sudden irruption of the fearful uncanny into ordinary lives—the activation of an ancient curse, the devil in the flesh—that the heroes seem to feel it so little. They are surprised, they gasp, they deny it at first, but they gather their wits soon enough and begin to fight back; they don't faint from insupportable dread, as Pierce believed he would, as he always did in dreams when something awful, impossible yet undeniable, the end of the world, arose into diurnality. Fainted and woke.

And now he was himself off to battle such a force (so he could not stop feeling) and he remained stuck in those opening scenes or pages, between unmanning fear and urgent denial, while the enemy gathered strength. What he actually wanted to do was draw his knees up to his chin and lock his arms around them and hug. This was the posture that he thought he would end up in for good if this went on, and the temptation was to start now, to take cover behind himself.

He looked up, for he had caught for an instant out of the corner of his vision, in the window opposite, the sight of a herd of great shapeless horned beasts, big as haystacks, like yaks or musk oxen, being driven over the rainy fields and away. The bus was past them before Pierce could see what actual thing they were—real haystacks, or the piled goods of some industry, heaps of excavated earth—that had given rise to the weird illusion; he looked back, half-rising, to catch them out the back window, but the bus had no back window. He sat down again.

An awful slippage or instability had just lately come over things, or Pierce had just lately come to perceive it; he seemed to have discovered—though he refused to assent to the discovery—that he could make choices that would bring the present world to an end, and begin another: indeed that he was already helplessly making such choices. Of course in every choice we make we choose among worlds; every choice propels our own souls and selves along one path and not another, where we see sights and do deeds we would not have seen or done otherwise: but to Pierce it was starting to seem that his choices actually brought into being the new world he must wander in, not only for himself but for others too. He could not exit from the circular logic of it: my choices, wise or foolish, make my life in the world; here is my life; here is the world; I have made it. Like a man awaking in an earthquake trying to hold the pictures on the walls and the dishes on the shelf and thinking What is it? What is it?, Pierce wondered what he had done, and tried to make it stop.

What was quite certain, what had come to be quite certain, was that the woman he loved had gone and joined or been inveigled into a preposterous and tyrannical pseudo-Christian cult, and that the cult's operatives—there were many of them, not all admitted—were even now emptying her mind and heart of him and of common reality, and that she was smiling and willing, and that he must but could not get her back. That was the reason for this dread that had taken hold of him, why he had ceased to sleep at night, and why what sleep he had was filled with horrid dreams as with dirty water.

At other times, though, these certainties came themselves to seem dream-like, and fell away; he ceased to believe that he was appointed to save his beloved, or that she needed saving, or that she was his beloved.

He dropped the stub of his cigarette to the floor and crushed it. Doing so reminded him of the long voyages he used to take aboard buses in weather like this, from his Ivy League university to his home in the Cumberland Mountains of Kentucky: seven hours, including a layover of an hour or two in the desolating squalor of the station in Huntington, West Virginia. November days, Thanksgiving, Christmas; rain, dead earth, the home awaiting him at journey's end no longer his home really but still thickly, suffocatingly warm and familiar. And oh Lord another thing.

Another thing. He remembered how once, when riding the bus from school to home, he had conceived of a test of true love: a test, that is, of how much one truly and wholly loves another.

God the cruelty he had been capable of conceiving, and all directed against himself too, his own unoffending person.

The test was this: powerful sorcerers have, without her knowledge, taken control of the woman you profess to love, who loves you too (Pierce did not think then that these terms, love, loves you too, needed further definition). These sorcerers have laid upon you—for reasons of their own, the cruel satisfaction of it, whatever—an absolute injunction: you may never see her again. If you do she will die. Meanwhile these wicked mages have created or crafted a sort of robot or eidolon of you, exactly like you in every way, except maybe just a little bit better looking, a little wiser, a little more generous. And this automaton has taken your place with your unsuspecting beloved. The deal the sorcerers make with you is this: the false you will love your beloved and cherish her and keep her from harm, for just so long as you, real you, continue to ride this bus.

You can never see her again; but so long as you ride this bus, through this November, on this highway, she will be safe. If ever you get off—get off for good, and not merely at scheduled rest stops in the poor parts of alien cities or at lonely diners on windswept hilltops—then her demon lover will begin to change; will cease to be a good man and become a cruel man, an uncaring one; will hurt her in certain dreadful ways only you yourself, her lover, could discover; bastard, prick, will mark her for life with an unrelievable sadness: will break her heart.

The test then is: how long will you stay on the bus?

Crowded, too, the poor people who ride buses filling up the seats, filing sheepishly toward the door at rest stops to buy rubber hot dogs or unwrap smelly homemade lunches, lining up again at the bus's door gripping their grimy tickets. Not condemned, though, like you; able to get off, to be replaced by other similar but different ones, burdened with similar but different cheap suitcases and bundles tied with twine. So how many nights will you spend with them, sleeping fitfully wrapped in your overcoat, picking up your book (Kierkegaard) and putting it down again, looking out at the swiftly passing desolation? She of course knowing nothing ever of your riding.

Pierce marvelled. What kind of an idea of love was that, what kind of twisted. A century seemed to divide him from that youth, who surely had no one to try out this theory with anyway, even hypothetically. A test of love harsher than in any romance, and yet, as in no romance, a test unable to be passed, the villains defeated, love won at last.

Once upon a time there was a knight who was given a trial of true love. He took up his sword and shield, but then could not do what he was commanded; and he laid them down again.

No, he told himself, no: no it is *not* up to you, it is not. Not up to you.

He looked at his watch. Only an hour and a half really aboard. Then the station in Conurbana at evening, where she'd said she would meet him, he hadn't ever been there before but already knew it well. In fact he brought into being its molded fiberglass chairs and the dried chewing gum affixed beneath them and the subtle filth of the floors even as he pictured, touched them in advance; and as he propelled himself and his bus unwillingly toward this place, he came to know, very surely, that she would not be there to meet him, would certainly have been prevented by her handlers from coming.

The rain had grown a little heavier, or was it only that the bus drove into it harder and made its drops course hastily down the windows? They had entered onto the interstate, and fled past green signs that held out to them the names of imaginary places, unwanted towns and roads. His fellow passengers, borne along with him, looked out or inward helplessly; around them the herd of cars pressed on, on their dreary and unrefusable errands.

What have I done? Pierce whispered in his heart. What have I done?

# UXOR

## THE
## MARRIAGE
## OF AGENT
## AND
## PATIENT

# 1

When the world ends, it ends somewhat differently for each soul then alive to see it; the end doesn't come all at once but passes and repasses over the world like the shivers that pass over a horse's skin. The coming of the end might at first lift and shake just one county, one neighborhood, and not the others around it; might feelably ripple beneath the feet of these churchgoers and not of these taverngoers down the street, shatter only the peace of this street, this family, this child of this family who at that moment lifts her eyes from the Sunday comics and knows for certain that nothing will ever be the same again.

But though the world ends sooner for some than for others, each one who passes through it—or through whom it passes—will be able to look back and know that he has moved from the old world to the new, where willy-nilly he will die: will know it though all around him his neighbors are still living in the old world, amid its old comforts and fears. And that will be the proof, that in his fellows' faces he can see that they have been left behind, can see in the way they look at him that he has crossed over alive.

All that summer a lethargy had lain over the county that comprises most of the Faraway Hills and their towns, farms and waterways. In the heat and torpid silence unaccountable things came to be, small things perhaps and apparently wholly unrelated. A fisherman caught a large-mouth bass in Nickel Lake and saw words written in the fading iridescence of its flank; when he wrote them out for the librarian at Blackbury Jambs she said they were Latin. A Conurbana man building a summer cabin for himself and his family on a mountain road (was it Bug Hill Road? or Hopeful Hill?) couldn't one day find the lot he had bought, or the foundation he had begun the day before, though he was certain he was on the right road—he went back twice to the crossroads, twice on to the road's end, bewildered and rageful, it just was not there, until the next day he returned by the same road (he was quite sure) and there it was.

And other things. But these of course are always happening, whether the world is ending or is not. What was less noticed was that, here and there, effects were appearing before their causes. Not often, not consistently, or life would have become unintelligible: just here and there, now and then, and trivial mostly. Hummingbirds ceased suddenly to visit a flowering hedge by a path of the Sunset Nursing Home, saddening one of the women within, who loved to watch them; not long after, a fool handyman following what he thought were his instructions went and cut down the hedge. A mother hanging clothes to dry saw her little daughter, plastic backpack on her back, going down the road—out of her eye's corner, just disappearing over the hill's brow; and later that day the daughter decided secretly to run away from home.

If such things could be gathered and counted, how many would there have been? How many should there be, in a normal year? Can a sudden rise in point-less coincidences—say a briar springing up just here where last year I lost my briar pipe, or all the mothers and daughters in Fair Prospect happening to say the word "honey" at the same moment—be charted? Is there a secret unfolding in unnoticeable things, that might if we could reckon it give us warning of ends, and of beginnings?

"When two people say the same thing at the same time," Rosie Rasmussen told her daughter Sam, "they do this. Look. Hook your little finger around mine. No like this."

Sam, tongue between her teeth, succeeded in hooking her little finger around her mother's.

"Now answer," Rosie said. " 'What goes up a chimney?' "

Sam thought. She shrugged.

"Well what does?"

"Smoke," Sam said.

"Right. 'What goes up a chimney?' "

" 'Smoke.' "

" 'May your wish and my wish never be broke.' Hold tight."

She tugged with her finger, and Sam with hers, until the strong link parted.

"There," Rosie said. "That's what you do."

"To get a wish?"

"Yup."

"What did you wish?"

"Well you're not supposed to tell," Rosie said. "It might not come true."

What had her own wish been? There had long been but one wish Rosie could formulate: a wish for something to wish for, something to fill the empty and unfeeling space where (it seemed) her feeling heart had once been. But then last fall she had gained something new to wish for, something to wish for on every evening star, to toot her horn for in every tunnel (hand on the car's roof as her father had taught her). And never to tell.

"I made a wish," Sam said.

"Good."

Sam slid across the broad smooth leather seat of the car, which was a Tigress, her mother's lawyer Allan Butterman's car. Allan up front alone drove, and Rosie and Sam played in the back, in the richness of the tinted windows and the honeyed music of the rear speakers.

"I'll tell you."

"It might not come true, though."

"It might."

"Well what is it?"

"Not to take medicine anymore."

"Aw Sam."

That was, in one form anyway, exactly Rosie's wish. In August Sam had first experienced something that her doctor thought might be an epileptic seizure, though for a month she'd had no more. Then, just past midnight on the autumn equinox—a night of wild wind—Sam had her second seizure, a worse one than the first, taking hold of her small body and all its contents for nearly a minute, and no doubt about it then. And next day in the splendor of the blue morning, amid a pageant of fast-moving white clouds and the trees still softly gesturing with their turning leaves, Rosie drove Sam again to the doctor's, and talked long with him; and then went to the drugstore in Blackbury Jambs. So now Sam took a small dose of phenobarbital elixir, three times a day. Too young at barely five to swallow pills. Rosie had the bitter liquid with her, and a little plastic syringe without a needle to draw it up with and squirt it into Sam's mouth, after a battle, always a battle.

"There it is," said Allan.

"Look, there it is," Rosie said to Sam.

They had been driving down the Blackbury River road toward Cascadia, and now at a turning there had come into view an edifice out on the river, piled on a little island whose pied sycamores were turning to yellow.

"Ha!" said Sam, kneeling on the maroon leather seat, fingertips on the sill of the car's window. "Ha ha!"

It was a castle, comically dour and yet not uninviting, with three irregular towers rising from the corners of its walls and a sort of central keep with a machicolated top. No one could think it was really medieval, but by now it was certainly old, shaggy and squat and gripping its three-cornered island in midstream like a great black vulture in sullen molt. The wall facing the river road had tall letters carved in it, letters in that square plain style Rosie knew was called Gothic though she didn't know why. The letters said BUTTERMAN'S.

"He said he'd meet us at the what's-it," Allan said. "The harbor, the."

"Marina," said Rosie.

"Right."

Allan Butterman claimed that his own name had no real connection to the huge name carved on the castle wall, but Rosie (and Sam) wouldn't believe him. Well somewhere there was some ancestor, Allan said. His modesty amazed Rosie; he found it more satisfying to pretend he had no connection to the most visible surname in the county than to give any appearance of laying claim to the old pile, or any share in its eccentric provenance. Rosie though didn't mind claiming her share: for legally Butterman's belonged to the Rasmussen family, and Rosie was the last twig on the last branch of that family in the county, and today she was going to cross the river and go inside it for the first time. She felt a quick dilation in her breast to think it, and laughed.

Just an old wreck after all.

"Here," Allan said, and with a pinky flicked the bar that turned on an emerald arrow. Sam watched it blink. Allan turned the car off the road and into the little marina's lot.

"Here we go," Rosie said, and pushed open the tombstone-thick door of the Tigress. "Come on, hon."

But Sam now was of a mind to hang back, either afraid of the place and the journey now that she was so close, or reluctant to leave the rich enclosure of the car. Maybe she was unable to laugh, as Rosie had, at her heart's reluctance.

Only stop staring in that stock-still way, her mother wanted to say and never would say. Don't freeze and stare, oh don't.

"My ode house," Sam said, not quite breaking her spell over herself.

"Oh yeah?" Rosie said. "Well let's go see it."

Her old house. Sam had first surprised Rosie with news of her old house when she was three. At first she had just told tales of it: how in her old house her old family had lived and played. What old house? The house she had lived in before. But then she began to point out places, not many, that reminded her of it: That's my old house. That? Rosie would ask, wondering why she chose just that place—once it was a two-hundred-year-old barn in the process of being dismantled and shipped to be a rich man's house in California; another time a caterpillar-like Airstream trailer weeping rust at the rivets, set up on concrete blocks, with geraniums in pots before it and a green fiberglass carport. But Sam always said finally about these places when Rosie asked: It's *like* my old house.

"My ode house," she said now again.

"Really really?" Rosie asked.

"Really really."

The heat outside the air-conditioned car was astonishing: the Faraways lay under a heat wave, brilliant Bermuda high, motionless for days. Yet Rosie shuddered. Any child, she thought, taking Sam's hand: any child can seem sometimes like she's from somewhere else.

The marina offered a few party boats with striped awnings for rent, and berthed a few sailboats and motorboats. Allan in his fine black shiny shoes walked with care down to where an aged boatman fiddled with the outboard motor of a pretty little one of varnished wood and shiny chrome. A Chris-Craft, for bearing a child across a river.

"Oh Sam. This'll be fun." Sam's eyes were that drink-it-all-in wide that touched her mother nearly beyond bearing. When Allan and the geezer motioned to her and smiled, Sam walked to them fearlessly and took Allan's hand and the boatman's and allowed herself to be boarded.

"She needs a life jacket," Rosie said. "Okay?"

"Sure," said the boatman. "You bet." With arthritic hands, oil-stained and nail-broken, he fixed it on her, her armor. She watched, still and interested. Rosie, her squire, boarded last.

"There's a dock still standing on the downriver side," said the boatman, taking up a blunt cigar end from a tin-can ashtray on the seat beside him. "Okay?"

"Fine," said Allan. The motor started.

Once, when the Faraway Hills had been filled with tourists, when the hills were just far enough away from Conurbana and Philadelphia and New York to seem a forest fastness and yet easily reachable by train and steamboat, Butterman's was a pleasure-garden, a sort of tiny and primitive theme park. There were band concerts and Japanese lanterns and fishing from the piers and views taken from the towers. Now the Faraways aren't far enough, and the word "tourist" (to Rosie's ear anyway) had a comically old-time sound, an air of small safe excursions undertaken with maximum fuss, Tourist Cabins, Tourist Homes. And Butterman's has been deserted and decaying for decades. Once briefly, fifteen years before, when Rosie still lived in the Midwest, the novelist and local celebrity Fellowes Kraft had laid plans to reopen the place, use its theater for a Shakespeare festival, plans that were far too large in the end; Rosie knew that a play had nearly been put on, not Shakespeare but old, the one about devils and magic, what was it. Then closed up again, returned to sleep for good.

It loomed, it really did loom over them as they putt-putted beneath its walls around to the dock, their wake lapping against the rocks and the concrete pilings wherein huge rings rusted away. They all lifted their heads to look up. The narrow ogive windows were shuttered, the shutters rotting. Rosie thought of Nancy Drew mysteries. The Secret of Castle Island. She had a flashlight in her bag.

"Last stop," said Charon the boatman. The boat dock had stairs, still sound-looking, and there he tied up his boat. His passengers got out, but he said he'd stay. Sam looked back at him, studying him, seeming to be deciding if that was all right, that he stay, and deciding it was; and then she led the rest of them up to the great shut doors. They were scarred and cut as though in imprecation or beseeching with two decades' worth of initials, names, obscenities, notices of love-couplings, Greek letters.

"Fools' names," Rosie said.

"What?" Allan asked.

"Fools' names, like fools' faces, oft appear in public places. My mother used to say."

How were they to open these doors, swing them back on their huge hinges? They didn't have to, there was a small door inset in the big door (Pierce Moffett would name this small door for her when later she told him of the visit, it was a *wicket*), and as Allan approached it he took from the pocket of his suit, absurdly, a rusty iron skeleton key as big as a spoon.

She had been opening long-closed doors ever since she returned to the Faraways: that's what Rosie thought. This one; and the door to Fellowes Kraft's house in Stonykill, that had been shut since his death. Doors too to her earliest childhood, lived in these hills, doors that she came upon unexpectedly in odd corners, before which she would stand in puzzlement till the key to their combination locks occurred to her or in her. Doors too in herself that she had found but not opened, doors that might have, she feared, nothing at all behind them.

Lord how sad and strange: stepping over the wicket's jamb let them into a wide weedy courtyard set with tables and benches, ready for company but gone gray and warped and fallen, littered with leaves and bird dung. Around the borders, cedars loitered, outgrown and shaggy, that had once been neat rows of toyland topiary. At the back, on a dais, sat a pair of wooden thrones, his and hers.

Sam walked straight through the wreckage as though she were indeed arriving home. "There," she said, and pointed to the thrones. "There."

"Yours?" Rosie asked.

"My daddy's and mommy's."

"They lived here too?"

"And I had sisters."

"How many?"

"One hundred."

"Wow, a lot. Did they all fit?"

"They are little," Sam said, and held up a thumb and finger to show the size, a small, a very small gap, she raised the fingers to her eye to squint at the microscopic smallness they measured. "Teeny TEENY tiny."

"And they all lived here."

"No," said Sam with instant certainty. "No, in the ball. Go sit there."

She pointed to the throne. Allan and Rosie looked down on her. She kept her pointer up, for their information. "There."

"Maybe we should look around a while."

"Sit," said Sam, minatory. And waited while her mother and her lawyer mounted the steps and sat.

Why, Rosie wondered, had they just walked away? The owners, the staff, leaving all this behind. Maybe it wasn't thought to be worth anything then, old stuff, weather-beaten. It didn't look worthless now. People in the past had been willing to go to trouble they never would today; not content with a river island, they had gone and built there a whole false place, of real stone and wood though, realer than any stage set. The seat where she sat, as richly detailed as the Queen's in *Snow White* or the big cobwebby furniture in a vampire movie.

"I wanted to tell you," Allan said. He had not sat, stood at her side, minister or wizard or gray eminence. "Just before I came out to pick you up. I got a call from Mike's attorney." Mike Mucho was Sam's father, from whom Rosie was almost divorced—practically, effectually, virtually, but not yet quite completely.

"Oh yes?"

"It was a strange call. She seemed a little hesitant. But what I gather is that Mike wants to reopen some aspects of the agreement."

"Oh."

"He wants to talk about custody."

Rosie's hands lay queenlike along the arms of her throne. The smell of the sun-warmed gray wood was strong. Why had she known from the beginning that she would hear this? Sam, who had ignored them after she had them enthroned and gone exploring around the litter of the open yard, now stopped. She looked down at her feet, at the ground between her Mary Janes, where she had spied something of interest, and then squatted there to get a better look. The beauty of her bare brown legs, of her attention to earth's minutiæ. Through Rosie's soul there blew a wind, an awful certainty of loss.

"We'll have to talk," Allan said. "Not here, not now."

They explored the rest of the place. They pushed open the doors of the small theater that occupied the central tower (THE KEEP it said over the doors, in letters carved in the stone but carved to look shaggy and twiggy, like logs) and found it filled with things, chairs and tables, ancient kitchen equipment, canvas awnings, piles of trays and wooden crates of steins and cups; some whole towers of such crates were sunken and the dishes smashed in dust-covered archæological heaps. Rosie's flashlight reached inward to finger the stage draperies, the stacks of benches. Sam under her arm looking in too.

"Bats," said Allan, unwilling to go in.

She made him climb to the battlements with her, though, the old stairways still sound, they built so solidly then; the walkways at the top were less certain, but Rosie and Sam climbed up into a belvedere to look out.

"Rosie," Allan said. "We don't have to get crazy."

"Allan, I know what I want," she said. "I just figured it out."

"You did," Allan said, one level below her, a hand on the ladder by which they'd gone up.

"I want to have a party."

"Not here."

"Here," Rosie said. "Really big. On Halloween. For a lot of people. Everybody."

"Yay," said Sam.

Allan said nothing. Rosie turned to look down on his patient upturned face. She had come here to see her castle, hers, and to decide about it or begin to think about deciding, before it died of neglect and slipped into the river and was lost. And she had decided, or it had been decided for her as she stood there.

"It ought to be given to the town," she said. "You're right. We will. They can have it and fix it up. We can help fix it up, the Foundation can. But I want to have a party first."

"Halloween?" Allan said. "Halloween night?" He was so patient, so willing to try at least to entertain the things she wanted.

"Witches, Allan," she said. "Can't you see it?"

"Bats," he said.

"And ghosts." Rosie laughed, at the lands below her, the height of air above.

"Ghosts," Sam said.

It was a big view, the river winding lordly to the north, to the Jambs, disappearing around the bend through an imaginary portal called David's Gate cleft into the mountains (imaginary because it simply widened and fell away as you came close to it to pass through, no gate after all).

Up on Mount Whirligig (which was named, some say, for the winding mists that rise on currents of warmer air from the Shadow River and seem to spin around it or cause the mountain to seem to spin; no one really knows why) was The Woods Center for Psychotherapy, a refurbished summer retreat where Mike Mucho worked as a therapist, where he was this day probably; he'd told Rosie he had been practically living there lately. A lot to do. Rosie couldn't see The Woods from here, but she knew just about where it lay; someone standing on its roof might be able to see her standing here.

From the beginning she'd told Allan that she would have custody, that there was no question about that, none that she would entertain. And Mike had not raised any question then. What had happened, what was the matter, what was he thinking, of his child only, or of something else?

I'll bring her here and keep her, she thought, lock that big door behind us. Never ever ever.

An equilateral triangle could be drawn, in that summer, from summit to summit of the three mountains she looked at—Mount Merrow, east of the Black-bury; Mount Whirligig, west of the Shadow; and, tallest in the center, Mount Randa to the north. More exactly, the points of the triangle lay respectively on a bluff on Mount Randa's western height, where a monument stood, a monument to a long-dead freethinker of the county, once somewhat famous or notorious; on the central gateway of The Woods Center for Psychotherapy; and on a red 1959 Impala sedan submerged in the waters of an abandoned quarry halfway up the wooded slope of Merrow.

Bisect the east and west angles of this triangle and the lines meet in Stonykill, at Arcady in fact, the house built last century by Rosie's forebears and now the seat of the Rasmussen Foundation. Drop a plumb from the triangle's peak through its base and it will arrive at length just here, at Butterman's, right at this tower at the island's tip, the belvedere where Rosie looked out.

Secret geometries such as these tend to loosen over time, slide away from true, and become ambiguous. It always happens, was happening just then to these; they would not survive the change just then sweeping unfelt over the county and the world. But since no one had ever discovered them in the days when they still obtained, no one would notice when they failed.

# 2

T he worldwide wind that had blown so strongly on the night of the
autumn equinox that year (don't look for it in your almanacs, they
date from later on, conscientious editors have already altered
these impossibilities and healed the weird lacunæ, listen to me and I will tell
you): that big wind and its rain resembled autumn storms of the kind we all remember very well, indeed was such a storm in every way—the barometric pressure fell fast, an awful weight was felt on every breast, a black exhilaration too
as the front, tall as the night sky, passed over, roaring and stamping; then the
bright day following on, littered with tree limbs and tossed shingles, and the sky
and the heart strangely, wonderfully clear. That kind of one. They all feel, those
autumn storms, as though they blow away something old, and bring in something new.

When the wind began that night, but was far from full, Pierce Moffett sat in
the little sitting room of the apartment he then had on Maple Street in Blackbury
Jambs, talking with his neighbor Beau Brachman, who perched in a little velvet
slipper-chair; now and then as they talked Beau brushed back with a soft girlish
gesture his long black hair from before his face.

"In Tibet," Beau said, "they practice on dreams."

"Oh yes?" Pierce said. He loved to listen to Beau talk, wasn't sure he wasn't
half in love with Beau himself. They were talking about whether, or to what extent, the world can be altered by human intent alone. (The world: all this, the
surrounding stuff, its laws and bounds and givens, what is, was, will be—they
knew what they meant.) All around them, in boxes and bags, in this room and
the next, were most of the contents of Pierce's apartment, for the next day he was
to move from Blackbury Jambs to a house in Littleville not far away. On the floor
between the two were a tall cylindrical Turkish coffeepot of brass and two brass
cups; Beau on his travels had learned to drink it and make it, and Pierce happened to have the pot and cups, never used; and so now they sipped the little

sweet strong doses, careful not to let their lips meet the sludge at the cup's bottom.

"They learn," Beau went on, "how to remain conscious in dreams, even though they submit to all the adventures, and experience all the events. But then when some danger comes, or when they get bogged down in some endless circular insoluble problem, you know the kind . . ."

"Oh yes. I do."

"Or some bad anxiety, or grief—well then they alter the dream so they can pass safely through those things."

"Like . . ."

"Like oh you're lost in a dark woods, and you're threatened by wild animals; you want out, so you consciously summon up a . . ."

"A taxi."

"Sure."

"Take me home."

"Sure," Beau said. "And so by practice you learn to do the same when you're *not* dreaming. When you come to a place where you need help, or can't find a way; or you feel threatened or . . ."

"The difference is," Pierce said, "that dreams are in us, inside. The world though is outside us; we're in it."

"Uh-huh," Beau said, and smiled; actually he had not left off smiling, he had a sort of permanent smile like that of a hieratic mask, a head of Buddha or an archaic Greek sculpture, foxier though, more teasing.

Lost in a dark wood. Pierce thought of a long-ago kid's show on television, where you could send away for a special sheet of plastic to fix over your screen, and a box of crayons; and then when the little cartoon hero of the show (what was his name?) stood baffled before a chasm or a cliff, an urgent voice told you Quick, kids, draw a bridge, or Draw a ladder, kids; and up or over he'd go. Only he also went up or over if you didn't, through thin air.

But if you expected you could alter the world, the way Beau said, that you could make good luck in your life or the lives of others, wouldn't you then have to think that awful and unlikely disasters, just as coincidental, just as perfectly appropriate, were also alterations of the world that you had made, reverse miracles? Or were they the work of other powers, other persons, as good at this as you or better? If you can choose any of it, you might have to believe you choose it all: that at any moment you stand at a crossroads you yourself have drawn.

Winky Dink, that was the little guy's name on TV. Helpless little foolish little. Hurry, kids. Hurry and help. Who would do that for him, he wondered, draw him a bridge from here to there, a door to go out by? The trick would be to assume that someone somewhere would, and just set out.

Set out.

They both thought at first that the wind, rising, had flung open the street door downstairs with a bang: but right away there came rapid stumbling steps on the stairs leading up to Pierce's apartment, and they heard his name cried.

Then Rose Ryder was at the glass-panelled door, both knocking and working the handle, and in deep distress.

"What," Pierce said, opening the door to her, but she was wild, too wild with some grief or disaster even to describe it. She began to cry, or to laugh, raising harsh staccato sobs that could be the prelude to either.

"What," Pierce said again. "Hush. What."

Beau withdrew his leg from beneath him and rose.

"I flipped the car," Rose said. And she looked at Beau and Pierce in sudden horror, as though they had delivered this news to her, not she to them.

"What?"

"The car," she said. "I flipped it over."

"While you were driving it?"

She stared at him. Astonishment seemed for a moment to calm her. "Well yes while I was driving it! I mean Pierce."

"When?"

"Just now just this minute. Aw God."

"Where?"

But whatever it was that had happened overcame her again; trembling, she sank to the floor. Her hair, blacker and longer than Beau's, curtained her face. "Aw," she said from behind that curtain. "Aw."

"Well what," Pierce began, but then Beau came and knelt beside her. He took her face in his hands to make her look at him, though he said nothing to her. Then he sat beside her on the floor and put his arms around her shaking shoulders, his temple close to hers, till she was quiet. Pierce, hands in his pockets, looked down on them.

"So," Beau said at last. "What happened? Where's the car?"

Rose buried her face into the crook of her arm to wipe her tears. "On the Shadow River road. Just over the bridge. In somebody's lawn."

"And you're okay?"

"I guess. Some black-and-blues I bet." She looked up at Pierce, and away again. Pierce wondered, not for the first time, at her nighttimes, filled with weird incident, as though she somnambulated. Real, though, usually.

"I was coming down to town," she said. "And too fast. And the big sharp turn, you know? And this something ran across the road in front of me." Once again she was seized, and seemed again suddenly to get the news of what she had done, and looked ready to bawl: but she pressed her cheeks with her two hands and kept it in.

"Something?"

"Like a chipmunk, I think. I just couldn't see it real well."

"Chipmunk?"

"Or a raccoon. So I." And she wrenched an imaginary wheel. "And." She turned her hand in midair, making her sailing car. She wept again, but more softly.

The two men said nothing. Beau kept his arm around her; they had questions, but they let her leave them for a moment. She was in the car again, free-wheeling, knowing that she and earth had parted, first on the left side, then on the right.

"Oh shit," she said.

Pierce, feeling her horror come and pass, sat too on the floor beside her and took her arm. "You're okay though," he said. "That's all that matters." For she might have been driving her own car, her little red Asp convertible—that was actually what he had been imagining, the small projectile turning in air, trying to right itself in time . . . But of course it wasn't the Asp, the Asp was in the shop (it often was) and she was driving a loaner, a dumpy sedan she had spoken contemptuously of, a Harrier (or Terrier? he hadn't heard clearly) that was plainly at fault here, maybe. "All that matters," he said again, and kissed her unhurt head.

"How did you get from there to here?" Beau asked.

She seemed not quite to know. It was a long way, several blocks (Pierce still measured in city blocks), a mile at least out to the edge of town and across the bridge over the Shadow River. Her eyes seemed to look back over the distance in wonderment.

"Ran," she said, a guess.

She had first found herself—rediscovered herself—hanging upside down in the seat belt, she didn't remember buckling it even but apparently had: and it was one of those times again when she exited from a black funnel of unknowing into a place, a place in her life, this place; and she had to reconstruct the rest backwards, without a clue, how, why. Was she still in motion? No that was the wind at the crack of the window. Was this her blood dripping warmly down her leg? No some car fluid decanting. What black being was pressed up against her side window, pressing in, mouth-flap open?

"I think I knocked over their mailbox," she said. "Yes. I know I did." She lit a cigarette, hands still trembling. "And so. I got out of the seat belt, and I guess the door open. And got out." Got out, revolving as she did so, to stand upside down beside her right-side-up car? No the dark world turned around with her as she came forth, it was the car that was upside down, one wheel still lazily spinning. "And I was just so scared. And I came here, I don't know how, and now. Now. Oh shit."

"But," said Pierce. "You're all right, and nobody's hurt . . ."

"She left the scene of an accident," Beau said, seeing Pierce's bafflement.

"Oh."

"Not supposed to do that."

"Oh yes."

Pierce's own driver's license was brand-new, he had only just come to know how fully the world he lived in was adapted to cars and their drivers, how their needs for information and directions, space to park and turn, help when crippled or abandoned, were provided for, he had not really noticed this before; and of course there would be the exactions too, the regulations and controls, just as complete.

"But," he said. "I mean. What was it? Were you drunk?"

"Well Pierce yes of course I was. Am."

"Oh."

She covered her eyes with the heels of her long hands, her cigarette between two fingers pointing up. "God if I get tested. I'll lose my license. I just know it."

Her little convertible had a number of dings in it where she had tangled with others in minor set-tos, never her fault exactly, but piling up no doubt on the records kept carefully somewhere. Drunk she might now be, but Pierce thought she could probably pass any test given her, her reaction to even a beer or two was strangely psychotropic, Bacchantic even. He knew.

"Were there people in the house?" Beau said. "Nobody saw?"

"I don't know," she said. "I didn't see lights." She hugged herself mournfully. "Oh what'll I do."

"Maybe there's time then."

"Time?" she said warily. "What time?"

"We'll go see," Beau said. "Maybe we can get you back there, before—"

She was already on her feet, arms around herself straitjacket style, defensive. "No no I can't. I can't I can't." She sheltered against Pierce, eyes closed.

Beau regarded them both, perhaps thinking (it seemed to Pierce) how he might interpose himself here to mend this reality. The wind took the house just then and shook it sharply once, as though shouldering past them on its way up Maple Street and out to the mountains. "We'll go see," he said. "Pierce?"

"I'll get my car," Pierce said, firmly he hoped.

"No!" Rose said, and took his arm. "No stay!"

"We'll take mine," Beau said. "I'll drive by in a minute. Listen for me and come down. I've got an idea, if you want it."

When he was gone, Pierce guided Rose to the next room, his largest, his bedroom and office, and sat her on the bed.

"I'm going to lose my job," she said.

"Because of this? Oh I bet not," Pierce said.

"Not because of this. The place is shutting."

Rose worked as an aide and social worker at The Woods Center for Psychotherapy. Pierce had heard the rumors. Large amounts had been spent on the conversion, and staff were said to be well paid, thought to be lucky. It was a huge place, though, and despite the modest solid richness of its public face, the nice graphics and the glossy vans seen in town, the support it gave to community events, it had always also seemed insubstantial; ungrounded, maybe, like its clients.

"They've told you?"

"Oh they don't *say*," Rose said. "But they told us staff appointments for the spring won't be announced till the end of the year." The Woods worked on a sort of semester system, like a college in reverse, most popular in the summer, mostly closed for much of the winter, too hard to heat, too high up the snowy mountain. "They told us this *at the party*. Well you *know*."

The end-of-season staff party was where she had been this night, he remembered. Jug wine and maybe a keg. Without him to watch over her. She'd asked him not to come.

"But," he said. "They didn't specifically."

She lay back on the bed; she raked with both hands her long hair from behind her, and laid it out on the pillows.

"Oh," she only said, or keened. "Oh what'll I do. Waddle I *do*."

He lay beside her to hold her. The wind rolled around them. What would she do? He thought of all those who made their own way nowadays, who like her had come away from universities with degrees in their hands real but useless (hers in American literature), who got jobs in social work or opened shops on shoestrings, learned simple crafts and sold their products or other things or themselves, always knowing it might not last long.

Well and he too. Strange generation they were, loose seam in the civil fabric, some of them actually bound for big things, some not, some borne away and lost. Optimistic mostly but the abyss could always open before you, you had to wonder and fear.

And he had long served them, women in that perplexity. He could almost (if he chose) believe that he had been put here just for that reason, to serve and help them: women looking for something, an art, a craft, a passion, a means of unfolding their selves and turning them to account. Artistic temperaments, certain they possessed powers but with nothing to use them on, predators trying to discover (in tears, in a frenzy, in the dark of night) just what their prey might be. *What's to become of me? What'll I do?*

He made Rose no answer. He knew what was being asked of him here, and he was not going to give it, he did not have it any longer to give and if he did he would keep it for himself, whose need was just as great. He had served selflessly (not selflessly, no, but recklessly anyway, it came to the same thing when the cost was to be counted); he had served and he would not again. *Non serviam.* Not this time. Not this damn time.

"There's Beau," he said, and started up.


Though Rose and Pierce had been lovers for the length of a Faraways summer, they weren't faithful to each other; at least Pierce assumed she was not to him; her stories weren't always clear and never complete, she had a great capacity to deny—to herself above all—what she had been up to or down to; when she had had a couple of drinks the nights shut up behind her like dreams, and men and adventures weren't always firmly registered. Once she had accepted a ride home from a dim acquaintance (Asp in the shop again?) and, when she pulled out his ashtray, glimpsed the corner of a small container in the gray; and feeling an inchoate burble of memory she put her fingers in, and took out the contact lenses she had been missing for days.

"Ruined?"

"No. Just dirty."

"And could he explain?"

"No he couldn't. How could he if I couldn't?"

"And so you don't know then what else might have happened in the car that other time. Coincident to what happened with the lenses."

"Well," she said. "Actually, no."

He could not require faithfulness of her, had nothing in return to offer her for it, and wouldn't have known, just then, what to do with it if she had proffered it. Every one of those with whom in the past he had made or assumed such a compact, of love, of fidelity, had not kept it, and he thought he was done with making them. Even so, without ever choosing to be, he had all this summer been faithful to Rose, at least in the sense that he had had no other lovers but her. Or only one, and he imaginary, or phantasmic: his familiar spirit, incubus too, and (Pierce was convinced) the pander who first brought Rose and him together.

That was his son, Robbie.

"I wish I could meet him," Rose said. Rose believed Robbie was the child of his body, begotten on a long-ago long-gone lover, raised by grandparents elsewhere, only just come again into Pierce's life. That's what Pierce told her. And in telling her this and making it likely, Pierce had come upon some details of Robbie he might not otherwise have discovered.

"You might." It was midnight in August, and still as hot as day; they were naked and neck-deep in the motionless dark waters that fill an abandoned quarry up Mount Merrow.

"Dark like you?"

"Blond. Well sort of amber honey; maybe it'll darken."

"Dishwater blond."

"And his eyes too. Honey." Made by the bees upon Mount Hymettus, the ones they sing of.

"Not like his dad."

"Not in any way."

Pierce had expected that his imaginary son and lover (he had not told Rose about that part) would vanish, fast or slowly, from his life as Rose came farther into it. But Robbie hadn't gone when Rose came. He had only grown denser, glowed more honey-warm as throughout that summer Pierce and Rose coupled. Indeed he was with them (though seen, or perceived, only by his father) on that same hot midnight at the Mount Merrow quarry. A laughing Caravaggio boy, naked on a stela of granite at the water's edge, one knee drawn up to rest his cheek on.

"Warm," she said. She let herself sink down till her chin met its pale reflection on the water's surface. "At first I was so hot and the water was cold. Now the air feels cold and the water's warm."

He swam ponderously to her. Her face was dim, her hair spread out behind her over the black water. The depth beneath them was palpable, its weight solid like its darkness. Why at night does deep water seem so much more a beast, a being, and why when you swim naked?

Those quarry waters are deep, fathom on fathom certainly, though maybe not so deep as some believe. Down at the bottom is the red Impala in which two lovers drowned in the year 1959; the trunk is open, for the suitcases they were fleeing with were seen floating on the surface next morning, that's how it was learned they'd gone together over the cliff above. You hear it told that the lovers are still inside, up to their chins now in muck, she at the wheel, he beside her (his hand on the door it may be, too late, too deep). But that's not true. Divers got them out, and they are buried now in earth, like the most of us, and far apart.

Up on the height, the road that the Impala drove in on, long closed, has nearly disappeared; lovers and swimmers now leave their cars out by the highway and walk in, past the nearly illegible No Trespassing signs, to reach the quarry's edge. That's how Rose and Pierce had got there. Still the only convenient way of entering the water is to leap. So Pierce had taken Rose's hand (for what other woman would he have had to be so brave?) and they went in together, feet first and looking downward, crying out.

"Here's my plan," Beau said to Pierce, and laughed lightly at himself. They could already see the glow and pulse of blue lights out around the bend across the bridge out of town. They approached slowly and not by the straightest way while Beau explained. It seemed simple enough, though Pierce's heart shrank somewhat in his bosom, he had never been able to negotiate easily with the earthly powers, did not usually assume they could be negotiated with, only bowed to or evaded.

Beau stopped his car opposite the overturned turtle of Rose's car and set the brake. The cops turned to take notice of them as Pierce got out.

He had driven her home, no picked her up at the party and driven her homeward or townward when. No he had driven her safely to his place (where she yes now was) and then returned alone back up the mountain because she had left her, had left behind her contact lenses, which he had volunteered to go back and get. And couldn't find. And so then on the way back into town, here, he had encountered something in the road. A raccoon he thought, maybe a. Something crossing before him. Unfamiliar car, too, his own was a Steed sedan, big American. And.

Beau was there to say how he, Pierce, had come to his, Beau's, house in a state of bewildered disorientation. Not hurt no, a thump on the head maybe. Doctor? No no. Momentary. Fine now. Why had he left before calling the police? Pierce (not for the first or the last or the worst time) pleaded ignorance. They asked if Pierce could step into the light here, and they looked into his face with a fierce flashlight; then they made him walk the white line that edged the road.

He could do that, and did. He had stepped forward to take her place here, and would do what further was required of him; he would substitute his (momentary, transient) innocence for her guilt, and would take the fall too, he guessed, if there was a fall to take. There wasn't: there were things to do he had never done before, get a wrecker (they worked through the night, apparently) and fill out forms; and Pierce's blameless if brief record was now spotted, he would see the result when he went to pay his next insurance premium. But he knew nothing of that then.

"Something's going on up at The Woods," he said to Beau as they drove back. "I don't know what. Something."

"I know," Beau said, unsurprised. "Yes. We know there is."


Rose was asleep when Pierce got back; she had pulled down the covers of the bed but had not undressed, lay sprawled swastika fashion across most of the sheet, her long feet bare and her face hidden in her hair. He took off his clothes, suddenly stifled and too hot, and lay beside her. When he put out the light the wind seemed to expand, and filled the rooms; in the kitchen something fell to the floor with a papery rustle, and Rose awoke. She ascended as though from a deep pool, lifted herself and sat up as though on the pool's edge, looking down within. Then she turned to see Pierce lying long and naked there.

"There wasn't really any chipmunk," she said.

"Raccoon, I thought you said."

"Well there wasn't any."

He pondered what that could mean. That she had no excuse for losing control at that turn. That she had not lost control at all, not of the car anyway, which had done what she had asked of it. *Why* was the only question then, and he wouldn't put it to her.

"Okay," he said. She lay again beside him, and put her hands beneath her head.

The room was growing colder as the mass of air within it was exchanged for the incoming one. She slept; she rose again, tossed up and outward will-lessly to her feet, and went off to the john. He listened to the wind and the toilet's flush. She padded back and was clambering again aboard the bed when he stopped her.

"Wait. Wait a sec."

She stood before him where he sat on the bed's edge. He undid her stiff jeans, pulled at the snap and the strong zipper; she rested her hands on his shoulders. He husked her, tugging the denim downward so she could step out.

"There," he said.

He unbuttoned and took her shirt from her too, and encircled her to un-hook the bra in back; lightly stroked her freed breasts, looked into her absent eyes; let her back in bed.

"Scary wind," she said.

It really had grown alarming. There were noises out in the world, a descant of bangs and thumps and whistles on the wind's melody that could not be interpreted, would only next day be seen to be escaped lawn furniture or blown-away pickets.

"What if it's the one?" she said.

"What one?" he said, but she seemed to be again asleep, anyway didn't answer; he looked at her face in the dimness and couldn't quite tell if her eyes were closed or still open.

He in fact knew what one, for it was from him that she had heard mythologies of wind, how it bloweth where it listeth, one part of Nature not under God's thumb and therefore perhaps at the disposal of our Enemy; she had heard his stories about changer winds, how one had once blown away the Spanish Armada and thus saved England from Catholic conquest, a famous wind which if you went to look for it in the records of the time wasn't there. He had told her of the wind that carries away the old age, and the contrary wind that brings in the new age, and of the stillness between. He had told her a lot of things.

God what a dream-tossed sleeper she was, her arm now flung across him and her open mouth making a child's soft frightened whimper with each exhalation. He didn't usually permit her to sleep beside him.

Not something in her path that she had swerved to avoid: more likely something behind and following, which she meant to escape. *Who flies so fast in the night and the wind?*

He shuddered deeply, and drew the sheet over his nakedness.

When it was late, Robbie came from his daybed out on Pierce's sunporch to stand above his father. Pierce, who was fast asleep, was amazed at how clearly present the boy was to him, more than he had been since Pierce had begun to perceive him. The golden hair of his arms; the awful serenity of his smile, abashing and cheering at once, which Pierce had not often seen, which he had sought so often by spiritual and lowly physical means to see. Robbie bent and kissed his father's cheek, and turned away, his duties here done and others and other games summoning him. Unable in the depths of sleep to cry out or call after him, Pierce felt him torn away, but he would not remember that: he would remember only how he had suddenly awakened, desolate, the woman only alongside him, and the wind enormous.

The next morning then, a tremulous blue one with flying clouds overhead, Rose sat on Pierce's sunporch and thought and smoked cigarettes while Pierce loaded his boxes and furniture into the truck of his friend Brent Spofford: the same man, same truck too, that had once brought Pierce and these books and belongings out of the city and into the country. When they were done they all drove out of the Jambs (waving to Rosie Rasmussen coming out of the drugstore, Rosie who was in a sense Pierce's employer, and also, in another sense, Spofford's lover and intended) and then went out to Littleville, to the house to which Pierce was moving. He almost expected to find it had vanished, magicked away by the wind, but it was there.

# 3

At September's end, then, Pierce was living by a running river, and Rose Ryder too, a different house by a different river. Rose was spending autumn in the summer cabin of an administrator at The Woods Center for Psychotherapy; when The Woods began to wrap up its summer programs the administrator moved back to her City house and office, and Rose had her cabin until the freezing weather, when she would have to turn off the water, bring in the deck chairs and the grill, board the windows with sheets of gray plywood, and look for somewhere else to live till the next fall, a roommate or a room. Meanwhile she could watch the woods along Shadow River color, and the deck fill with tattered leaves, and the river steam whitely in the mornings. She thought of the little house as hers.

Pierce's new house in Littleville was by the Blackbury, the other river that runs through the Faraways, rising from different sources than the Shadow's, springs and melting snows far up in the Appalachians, and eventually subsuming the Shadow on its journey to the sea.

It was Rose who had led him to the house. He had first met her long before he moved to the county, at a moonlit party by a backwater of this river. He invited her for a row, and she guided their boat out through the reeds and the water lilies and the willows drowning their hair, out to the broad mainstream, and a while later they came up against a little dock, the dock at the end of the needle-strewn path that led through the pines to the big screened back porch or patio of this house, which was unoccupied then; and they broke and entered, and looked around. *Oh secret* she whispered, opening the door to a far bedroom, entered through the bath. And he came in behind her, and there they embraced and kissed deeply, and then nothing further; rowed back.

She remembered nothing of this at first when he met her again, he having by then moved to the Jambs; remembered perhaps the party by the river, but not the house, nor the bedroom, nor the moon full in its windows.

Then when he had to give up his apartment in town, he came to this place again: he answered an ad for a house in Littleville to rent, and found it to be the one they had violated in the moonlight. She was with him then too: they went together through the small and faintly smelly bathroom and into a bedroom. *Oh secret* she said this time too and Pierce embraced her as he had done before, and said to her *Now you must remember.* And she said *Yes* in a whisper.

And yet (Pierce thought, as he lay now on this late-September morning looking at that very bedroom from within his own bed, his own curtains now hanging at the windows and his own pictures dim on the walls in the dawnlight) maybe even then she had not remembered. She had answered Yes: but had he not made it a rule that in certain circumstances she never answer No to him?

In this broad bed in the midnight once, not here but on Maple Street in the Jambs, he had placed the rule on her: *Don't say no to me, Rose. You don't want to say no. Only yes. Do you understand?*

*Yes.*

*Say it.*

*Yes.*

So it may be that she had really not recognized the place, and therefore had not felt the queasy pressure of Fate on her inward parts as he felt it on his to have returned here. Perhaps she even *chose* not to remember it. She could do that. She had a talent that way.

Most secret of all is what's forgotten.

He rose, wide awake—she in her bed in her cabin within the sound of the Shadow slept on—and stood in thought, long, naked and pale where his skin was not darkened by black hair. Tonight they would meet, not here in this room but in her little place that she was so pleased with, dinner on her deck by her young cold river. He would have to lay some plans then for the evening, could not go up there all unready.

At that he lay down again to think.

Pierce had no alarm clock. He awakened when his dreams were done, plenty early. He then usually lay long indolent, attentive to the pour of his thoughts, until that cup too was empty. He did so even while telling himself that the best chance he would probably have to make a mark and some money in the world was wasting fast away, and that he was a fool.

Once, Pierce Moffett had been a historian, or aspired to be one, but he had kicked over those traces, in disgust, in impatience, in the throes of need too, for he had a living to make and history was apparently not where he was destined to make it: the sole entry-level teaching job he had been able to acquire had stopped well short of tenure and then expired.

So he convinced a New York literary agent (Julie Rosengarten, former lover of his) that he could write a book which very many people would be eager to read, and she in turn won over a publisher, Cockerel Books, the world's largest at least by some measures, so Julie told him. The book, shaped and guided by Julie, was about magic, secret histories, and the End of the World, an event that Pierce would suggest was under way undetectably even as he wrote, as the reader read.

For a long time after he received the publisher's advance that (along with some money from the Rasmussen Foundation) bought his daily bread, Pierce made no progress on this work. He had climbed to the high diving board, and thereupon found that he could neither jump nor back down. He scribbled notes and lined them out, typed pages and almost immediately crushed them. *Why is it we believe that Gypsies can tell fortunes?* he would begin; or *There is more than one history of the world:* and then he'd lie down, or go out, or give up.

But by the time he moved to Littleville, he had accumulated a couple of large stacks of typed paper, Part I and Part II, much scribbled over and interleaved with yellow lined sheets amplifying and modifying the matter in them; he could heft them in his hands, as gratifying as baked bread or hewn wood. And just lately he had ceased to sleep at night, or hardly to sleep: he commonly fell into a deep paralysis for two hours or even less when he climbed into his great bed, and then awoke as though he had been shaken, to lie alert and humming like a switched-on appliance for hours, thinking, thinking, weaving, weaving; sometimes rising to scribble, or smoke, or just stare out at the sinking moon. Another hour or two of sleep after first light began to touch the windows; then up and busy in the kitchen, at work already even while he clattered the coffeepot and skillet.

What had happened? Summer had come, hot as hell, fecund and various, inspiring in him maybe an imitative abundance. Robbie, summoned by his powers, powers he hadn't known he had, a being himself made of powers that Pierce did not know how to calculate: he had surprised and fascinated young Robbie with the copiousness a grown man was capable of, of a piece with the prose he had simultaneously been able to produce, and as tirelessly too. And then Rose, whom he was now nearly done thinking of for this idle morning. Like a wise investment, the more time he spent on Rose or with her the more returns he seemed to get; he pretended a lordly annoyance at her calls and impetuosities during his hours of working or spellbinding but he had grown superstitious about her too, couldn't be sure his productivity didn't actually depend on her, found himself talking her into forgoing other possibilities in favor of dates with him; and when she came at evening she would find him often enough still in his dressing gown, shaken and glowing like an athlete, with a new yellow pad filled that had been blank not long before; how do you go so *fast,* she would marvel, and he would laugh a great laugh and push her before him through the little house toward this bedroom, the bedroom she called Invisible.

Another possibility, which Pierce sometimes entertained as he lay abed, laughing there sometimes outrageously as well, was that Time was really decanting into his big brain, unfillable like the conjurer's trick chalice, the wine of a new revelation, one that he was to impart as best he could to those who waited for it: a revelation that might only in this moment, this year of this decade, be worth imparting.

So be up and doing, Pierce: for the night comes, when no man can work.

·     ·     ·

Meanwhile Rosie Rasmussen flew. She leapt from the top of the Ball Building on River Street, where four big stone balls are placed; she had always looked up at those balls but had never before been able to touch them, and the cold rough feel of them was gratifying as she pushed off and out above the river.

Whyever had she forgot she could do this? She remembered now, as the wrinkled river spread below her, that of course she could and had, many times, in certain seasons, which seasons? Flying weather maybe. She was a little rusty now but oh the easy bliss of it when you got your bearings and learned to bank and wheel, kick-turn, dive and rise again!

There was Butterman's on its rock, should she alight there? No not where she was headed. She lifted her eyes. Beyond, the city of Cascadia spread, the paper mills pouring white smoke, the new treatment plant, the shining pelt of the river draped over the dam and gathering in foam at the bottom. No not far enough. She strained somewhat to rise, afraid momentarily she was getting somehow heavier, airlogged, sinking. The straitened river opened again southward. Over earth's curve came the tops of the twofold city, Conurbana, the old towers on the left bank (gold dome of the Municipal Building catching the morning light) and the far higher cold-steel ones on the right bank.

Oh yes there, Rosie thought, losing altitude. That's the way she would go. Duty and apprehension gathered in her breast. She wondered if she had been wrong, if actually she had been thrown or shot upward and was now not flying but falling: and she realized that to think so was to fall; and she began to.

Landing on her pillow in her bed in the predawn gloom, her eyes gulping light. The alarm clock on the table beside her just gathering force to go off, its whir what woke her. Rosie smacked it, forestalling it, and fell back. Groaned aloud in eerie horror then as she became aware of some living thing in the bed with her, oh yes Christ, Sam, who had awakened past midnight with the terrors and wouldn't rest till Rosie took her in.

Oh I don't want to go, Rosie thought or pleaded. She sat up and felt with her feet for her slippers, couldn't find them, got down on hands and knees and felt under the bed for them (another shiver of eldritch fear as she groped in that dark den) and then gave up and went barefoot into the hall. Past Boney's old room and to the back stairs. Autumn odors, of chilly air and last year's fires waiting to be relit, cold old woodwork, past lives lived here and their meals and linens and furnishings, all for some reason vivid in this season. The stairs debouched into the kitchen. Rosie left the door open (why anyway did stairs need doors at all?) so she could hear Sam if she awoke; and she filled the teapot at the sink.

Remembering flying. You always seem to remember, in dreams, that you can, and have before. And of course you have: in other dreams.

If she could fly today to Conurbana for this appointment she would fly.

She and Sam had come to live here, to this house with a name, after Rosie learned that Mike, despite his promises, was seeing Rose Ryder again. Arcady was her great-uncle Boney Rasmussen's house, and she worked here as his secretary, seeing Boney through his last yearlong decline toward death, offering him as much as she had and sure it was not enough (nothing could have been; she felt, like a deathbed curse, the weight of his need for help, for escape from death, and her own helplessness before it). Now the house and its pots and pans and linens and beds were in some sense hers. Not hers to dispose of, but hers in trust: for it all belonged to the Foundation that Boney had long ago set up, which now possessed all the Rasmussen wealth. It was not a great Foundation such as those once established by repentant steel magnates or oilmen but a Foundation nonetheless, with assets to administer and gifts to disburse; and after Boney was dead Rosie learned that he had named her to be the Foundation's new director.

It was no fate she expected or desired. He had been kind to her and she missed him terribly. But she had refused his bequest, or at least hadn't agreed to accept it; turned aside all of Allan Butterman's inquiries about when a decision might be expected, while the summer ran out and the house grew cool; every day that she didn't decide seemed to her a small hard-won victory, and every morning she prepared herself to fail once again to decide. It was a knack, she thought, and one that might have come down to her in her genes, for Boney certainly had it. And maybe it would keep her alive till great old age as it had Boney. Maybe she could do here what Boney had somehow longed to do and had not done: maybe by making no decisions she could live forever.

There was Sam now: an urgent moan as though she had been roughly snatched back from wherever she spent the dark hours.

"Okay, hon, Mom's coming," let her know who's with her here, sometimes Sam arrived in the waking world in a sort of bewildered amazement that Rosie used to find funny. She mounted the stairs by twos, the teapot singing urgently behind her.

Dr. Bock's phenobarbital was a stopgap, he said; Sam needed tests to find out what was going on with her, and a program of medication tailored to her. *Tailored* was the word he used, a little suit just her size. She needed an EEG, the test where your brain waves are measured with electrodes, which might or might not reveal something about what in Sam's brain could be causing her seizures.

So today Sam and Rosie were to go to Conurbana Pediatric Institute and Hospital to see a neurologist and have the tests; and then (Rosie could feel it already) they would continue in that direction from then on. No road that they could take would ever lead back to before that August night when Sam first said *What's that?* toward something she alone saw in the empty air, and then grew rigid and trembled, blind deaf and absent. The road they parted from that night fell steadily behind them, the life Rosie had been living; it went on unrolling no doubt, she would picture it sometimes vaguely but vividly, with a pang of regret and longing nearly unbearable. Her real life, growing imaginary, while her new life filled up with obdurate reality.

Bring a favorite toy or book, said the mimeoed list the hospital had sent her. Sam chose Brownie, a rag doll she found in a drawer here at Arcady, whose brown yarn hair and gingham dress were sordid with age and whose left eye, a black bead, had recently come loose and now hung by a thread, ghastly a little, Rosie promised to fix it and had not. If you wash your child's head carefully the

morning of the test this will not have to be done upon arrival. Answer the following questions in consultation with your child's physician. A careful description of the nature of the attacks is necessary to make a proper diagnosis. List the
medications your child is currently taking with exact dosages and times.

"No Mommy. No no no no."

"Oh come *on* Sam. For just this once no fight. We need to go so we're not
late."

Sam slipped from her and started down the hall. Rosie with her dose followed. "Samantha!"

She hadn't been told if she was to give Sam her usual medicine. Would it interfere with the brain waves? Make them look worse, or not bad enough? She
didn't dare not give it to her. Dr. Bock said that very likely Sam's seizures weren't
hurting her brain, but Rosie couldn't bear to see another one, her child shaken
nearly apart, how could that not damage you. And no number of them she saw
thereafter, down the years from that day to this (never many in a year, but never
none) would make them easier to witness. Or remember. Or envision.

"Oh Sam damn it. Come here. You little."

"Go way you big."

Down the front stairs naked and bright against the dark wainscot and pur-
plish carpet, Rosie after her handicapped by the syringe she held aloft. Negotia-
tion in the downstairs hall where Boney Rasmussen died, on his way to the
toilet. Yes okay French toast if you'll just, Sam I haven't got time to argue: laughter rising helplessly in her throat, laughter of bewildered frustration, cosmic
laughter maybe because this really *was* just a game, as Sam (laughing too) believed or knew; but it had to be got through anyway, had to. Sam be serious.

Done at last, tears but at least she didn't spit it out (Rosie had tried mixing
it into juice but Sam never drank the whole thing, and Rosie never knew in what
part of the drink the medicine—medicine she called it, it cured nothing—was
lingering). While Sam ate her French toast Rosie packed, Sam's book about mice
who go up in a balloon, a book for herself too (*The Company* by Fellowes Kraft,
she had been becalmed in the second chapter for some weeks), Brownie and
blankie, cookies and juice and the bottle of phenobarbital and the syringe and
all the various papers.

They went out at last through the front hall and the big door (passing unseen and unseeing around or through Boney Rasmussen himself, who since his
death on July Fourth night had been standing there before a door that would not
open, unable to go forward and certainly not back) and out into the fragrant
morning, a nice day, another nice day.


Though she was now at the very least the acting director of the Foundation,
Rosie wouldn't pay herself more salary; every week she wrote out for herself a
check for the same amount she had been getting as the Foundation's part-time
secretary. Today though she would allow herself the use of Boney's great black
Buick that lay dormant in the garage, formerly carriage house, at the turn of the

drive. Her own car—not even hers but Mike's, he hadn't bothered to demand it from her or was holding the demand in reserve to be laid on the table later— was a Bison station wagon whose struts were weak and brakes insecure, and the thought of driving it on the highway far from home made Rosie uneasy, though Spofford said that if it was going to go, or stop rather, it was more likely to do it careening over a dirt road in the Faraways than on the interstate. She said she saw the logic.

She had found the Buick's key in the pocket of Boney's winter overcoat, left there the last time he had driven, and yesterday they'd gone out to the carriage house, Sam delighted and laughing, to start it up. They pushed the big stable doors open, Rosie marvelling that Boney hadn't ever bothered to put in a real garage with a roll-up door and concrete floor. Sam inspected the sleeping dragon, putting her fingers in the gulp-holes in the side (which were actually fake, Rosie found, went in an inch or so and stopped; on her father's surely they had had some function, swallowed air or something). It came right to life, strong and willing. Sam cheered.

Like all this, it wasn't hers, even if it was hers to use. If it belonged to any- one it belonged, as did all of Boney's remains, to Una Knox.

*I'm leaving it all to my old girlfriend Una Knox,* Boney said to her a month be- fore he died, after Allan Butterman had pressed him about making a will, which he never did in the end. My old girlfriend Una Knox. The way he'd said it, and the fact that nothing official ever turned up with her name on it, convinced Rosie that Una Knox was a joke of some complicated kind, the kind that deeply pri- vate and solitary people enjoy playing on themselves; or on the other hand was maybe a momentary ploy, a name snatched at random to fend off Rosie and Al- lan who were forcing him to talk and think about his own fast-approaching non- existence: that, in any case, there was no such person. Which didn't keep Rosie from imagining her appearing one day, sailing darkly tall into Arcady, come to claim what was hers.

*Vroom.* Sam cheered again at the miracle of the car's starting. Rosie guided the great length of it out of its lair inch by inch, certain that by day's end it would be dinged; and to whom would she have to answer for that?

# 4

**H**uman lives are ordered in cycles of seven years, counting from the child's first appearance on earth to the day or night on which she departs. *Cycles,* which in sequence form a wave, a wave with its tops and bottoms, ups and downs; it can be drawn on paper, a simple sine wave, with $x$ and $y$ coordinates of Time and Amplitude, peaking at seven, at fourteen, at twenty-one, at twenty-eight, at thirty-five.

We come in at birth in the middle of this wave; we start down, and reach the bottom of it sometime after age three. Then we begin to rise up. Halfway through the climb to the top, we reach the horizontal coordinate that divides this rolling wave of the years into upper and lower halves; and the year in which we pass over this line we can call the Up Passage Year. Anyway that's what the most recent discoverer or deviser of this cycle chose to call it. The Up Passage Year is a year full of hope, or at least of expectation; a time for the sorting and storing of new and interesting matter, the gaining of new perspectives. How high it reaches before peaking is up to chance and the world, and maybe to our own efforts too.

Rose Ryder, awake but undressed, sat unmoving on the edge of her narrow bed in her cabin by the Shadow. Rose was, herself, at the threshold of an Up Passage Year, headed for the uplands of twenty-eight. At her feet, on the bedroom floor, were many long sheets of paper with waves or cycles drawn on them, crossed by a median line; she had drawn them herself, with compass and rule. They had slipped in the night from the bed where she had left them, and she looked down at them without exactly seeing them. It was to be another perfect cloudless day, tenth in a row, heating the Faraways to summer levels by noon.

By the time it reaches the summit of the seventh year, the soul or person has come to know itself, has made itself, insofar as it can, the master of its surroundings, at least conceptually—knows itself, maybe, to be powerless, but nevertheless knows. At seven years old I know I'm a kid; I know what a kid is and does, I know the uses of the shoelace and the three-ring binder, no flies on me. At fourteen I have put away childish things, I have hair in places I did not before and am already used to the fact, I can name if not see my future. Thus I have reached what was labelled on the papers at Rose's feet a Plateau Period.

Which in her own case and for this present cycle she did not contemplate reaching. She did not know or actively imagine what would intervene to stop the upward progress but didn't feel, today, that she would be around to celebrate her arrival there.

Of course she knew that "up" and "down" in the system had no necessary emotional coloration, your spirits didn't necessarily rise on the way up nor sink on the way down. Going down around the bottom of a cycle—your old certainties in pieces, whelmed with new data, estranged from former selves and not knowing what new ones await you on the way up again—can be quite exciting and interesting. Okay, she said to herself (or to Mike Mucho, author of the system he called Climacterics, on which Rose had done so many weeks of research; former lover of hers and still her superior at The Woods where they both, Rose just barely, worked): okay, but here on the way up I should at least feel.

Feel what?

Not disintegrating, at least; together, and moving; I should know who I am, and that I exist. At least.

Yesterday she had known who she was, and who she was going to be. She was a graduate student, American and English literature, and she was primarily involved with language; she was a teacher, or on her way to being one. A language school in Lima was advertising for such a person in a journal Rose found the previous week at work, and Rose had been turning into that person ever since, a little bit every day. She spoke good Spanish (she spoke, or had spoken, college Spanish). She lived with a family, her own room up at the top of a tall old city house, lonely and a little afraid at first, but then discovering the city and meeting young people, going to the shore and up into the mountains. In her class she taught young people who wanted to become airline stewardesses or import-export clerks, they were mild and beautifully mannered and seemed to come from another age, or another decade anyway. In the company of these people and the others she met she went on from adventure to adventure, feelable but not nameable in advance, and did not come back by the same path, if she ever came back at all.

For many days the presence within her of this person warmed her, like a child growing, or as she imagined such a child would warm a woman. And then this morning she awoke and found her gone. Dead maybe; gone certainly, a cold hollow where she had been, the awful cold hollow she had for a time filled. Lima seemed as remote and airless as the moon. The Xeroxed page from the journal where she found the ad looked up at her from her bedside table, also having died, showing nothing, or a cruel joke.

Dead.

One more dead. There would come a day when there would be no more to die, and she would be alone.

With one naked foot she pushed the paper at her feet around so that it was upside down. The Up Passage Year now a slope to a valley, the high hill a slough. What the fuck difference did it or could it make. It had died too.

Pierce (who had—maybe not seriously, she couldn't tell—offered to help her make Mike's Climacterics scheme into a book, a self-help book, or a proposal for one) had asked her why a curve, how boring, how two-dimensional, why not a spiral, up which we go as though climbing a mountain; every seven years arriving at the same places or stages, only one turn higher, all different.

Why higher? She hadn't asked it of him then, but asked it now. Why higher? Why climbing?

The electric clock humming on the table hadn't died, it alone remained alive, and by it Rose could see she was late, late. The thought of the drive up around the mountain to The Woods was paralyzing, in spite of all she had hoped from it, this day, this chance. She tried to make herself feel the urgency, getting later, all the while thinking it would be a good day to get lost, drive upstate, find a mall she'd never been in. Get her hair cut. Thinking of this, imagining herself doing this, felt like diving or sliding down that slide, Down Passage Year, no bottom in sight; and for some time longer she didn't stir.

Meanwhile the mist had lifted from the Blackbury, a blanket withdrawn; and in his little yellow house by the riverbank, somewhat hidden and lairlike amid the flame-tipped sumacs, Pierce was hard at his morning's work. Someone snooping would have heard from outside the arrhythmic tapping of the electric typewriter he had rolled out onto the porch; the squeaking of the kitchen chair he sat in too, when he paused for thought or rest.

He'd begun with an anecdote.

One morning just after Christmas in the year 1666, the well-known Dutch physician and scientist Johann Friedrich Schweitzer, known as Helvetius, had a visitor—a small beardless man in plain clothes with an accent that made Helvetius think he was from Scotland. It was a snowy day, and the stranger came in without wiping his boots. He had read, he said, in Helvetius's treatises that he was a skeptic concerning alchemical transmutation, and Helvetius admitted he had never seen it work. The stranger showed him a "neat ivory box, and out of it took three ponderous lumps of the Stone, each about the size of a walnut." He could not, he said, give Helvetius any; but he allowed him to handle one piece, and Helvetius managed to scrape off a bit while the stranger talked of the powers of his stone, and how he had come by it. When the man departed, promising to come again, Helvetius collected the matter of the stone from under his nail, and later experimented with it, following hints in the stranger's conversation. No luck. When the stranger reappeared, he gave Helvetius, after some hesitation, a piece of his stone as big as a turnip seed; when Helvetius worried it wouldn't be enough, the stranger took it back, broke it in half, and gave him only half, "wrapped up neatly in blue paper": that would, he said, be sufficient. And indeed, late that night Helvetius's wife—who was a student of the Art—persuaded him to try it, and together they transmuted with it a half ounce of lead to gold, which turned out when Helvetius had it assayed to be extremely pure.

With the next carriage return, Pierce's sheet extruded from the machine, toast from a toaster, nicely done, and he inserted another. A fast and tidy penman, Pierce had never learned to type, it was like chopping wood the way he did it, banging down each key in turn with a strong forefinger, tongue between his teeth, he would fall back exhausted by noon having covered no more than four or five sheets.

For working Pierce affected a vast old dressing gown that had belonged to his uncle Sam, Dr. Sam Oliphant, now dead. It was a rich garment, a gift from someone to the doctor, someone whose life he had saved (no surely not, Pierce forgot the actual origin) which Sam himself had never worn. It was as heavy as an episcopal cope, of thick pinwale corduroy on the outside and purple satin inside. Pierce wore it always inside out, finding the touch of satin on his skin distastefully unctuous; it was as highly finished on the inside as the out, every seam turned, the collar rolled high, the sleeves capacious. The belt was lost, and Pierce belted it with a wide leather one. Rose had laughed to see that robe, belted with that belt; laughed at first.

"This account," he typed, "is extraordinary for a couple of reasons. First it is highly circumstantial; it has little of the air of fable and romance these encounters with the Mysterious Master usually have. There is the fact that the alchemist left Helvetius alone with the transmutative stuff he gave him, to try it for himself: the smokesellers and frauds who abounded at the time always supervised experiments themselves, and had a lot of ways of seeming to have produced gold. Third and probably most extraordinary, the stranger never asked for money—no investment, no ounces of gold given him with the promise that they would be multiplied. In fact he thereupon disappeared, never to be seen again."

As he typed out this well-known anecdote, Pierce noticed for the first time, like a detective-novel detective sorting his evidence, a fact that had been in the story all along but that he had not considered; and he thought he saw an explanation for what happened. But he continued anyway as he had meant to:

"It would seem, then, that we have two possible conclusions: either Helvetius lied about what happened, or Helvetius made gold.

"We know now that gold is an element, and so is lead; therefore, one could never be transformed into the other by heating it together with a third thing, whatever the third thing was. So we are left with Helvetius lying, spectacularly, convincingly, and for no apparent reason (he never tried again to make gold).

"There is, though, one other possibility, least likely of all, indeed patently absurd: that Helvetius really could make gold by the means he had, but we today no longer can, not by those means or any other. Not because we have forgotten how, though we have, or lost faith that we can, though we have, but because gold is not the same as it once was, earth is not the same, fire is not the same."

He took his hands from the keys.

A snowy day in 1666. In Pierce's imagination, each of the ten digits had a distinct color, a color it had as far back as he could remember, unchosen by him but there in his mind nonetheless: and the six is white. The snow on the Master's boots; the ivory box of glistening matter. Wife in white at the stair's top: Husband what have you there.

That wife: that was what Pierce had noticed in retelling this tale. That wife skilled in the Art. What if she had been in league with the supposed Nameless Master. Able to trick her husband, somehow produce the gold, expecting a further development of some kind, she and the other guy, who knows what; a plot that never fruited. Guy skipped town. Wife kept quiet.

Pierce thought of writing a footnote; then decided not. He was on a quest, in these pages of his book, for evidence that once the world was not as it is now; any little fact or tale, trivial but incontrovertible, that would fire the hearts of his readers with wild certainty, or tease them at least with possibility. He hadn't promised, hadn't exactly promised, that any single one he retailed might not vanish even as it was proffered, in fact it was implied in his philosophy that it must. But it was not for him to underscore his own paradoxes. *Qui non intellegit, aut taceat aut discat*: if you don't get it, shut up or go figure.

"Now it may be," he typed, "that every other recorded instance of gold made by fire—there are hundreds of them, almost all seeming to be variants on a few themes, like old comedy plots—maybe every one is false, the product of mendacity or wishful thinking or the accumulating errors of multiple transmission, history's game of Telephone that always pushes anecdotes toward clarity, wonder, or exemplum. Maybe this is the one and only real one we know about, the only one that slipped through that baffle of advancing Time that falsified all the others, to reach us like Job's servant out of the wreckage of the former world: *I only am escaped alone to tell thee.*"

Pierce thought of the readers for whom he wrote as of three kinds. There were, first, all those who were expecting some sweeping and final change in the ways of the world, had been expecting it ever since a sort of imaginary revolution had, a few years back, seemed to spread nationwide, worldwide; sometimes (like the heretic Franciscans of old) these took to living as though the old world had already ended, and the new one begun. In the hills around here were tribes and family groups of them, inhabiting old farms and living in caves and tree houses; books like the one he planned were about all the reading they had. Then there were the young, a large contingent, whom Pierce pictured standing just at that crossroads in time to which the young always come, where they are certain, sure certain, that they are to see and maybe to bring about a world different from the world they were born into. He remembered his own certainty. And, lastly, there was the permanent and irreducible rump of hopers who can be found in any age, those who feel Becoming almost as though by a sixth sense or a genetic endowment, always reading the signs, never bored or discouraged, atremble lifelong with the approach of the next thing.

To this (potentially) large readership Pierce was going to show a New Age that they would be the first to notice dawning, one they might themselves help to make, a New Age that would be different perhaps for each of them. And he would show them also the passing of an Old Age, which not everyone will notice departing, and which only the most rigorous mental archæology will ever be able to discern later on, when everything is as it will be and not as it now is.

Of course (as is usual in eschatologies such as the one Pierce was constructing) this New Age would in an important sense be an Old Age returning, age of ancient possibilities, just as the bad Old Age now passing was once the New Age: the Age of the makers and the breakers, the men (all of them men, it seemed) who had spanned the world and made it one, who all by themselves with only the help of the Laws they had discovered, had made the crooked straight and the rough places plain, and yet had not got for us all that we needed: or perhaps better say that what we needed (what Pierce's readers needed) could not be supplied by the means they had.

And when their world had passed (as it did seem to be passing, Pierce had a file drawer stuffed with tear sheets from newspapers and journals, impossibilities that could not be accounted for, holes in Big Science's increasingly leaky roof—so he thought of them) we would find or make up new Laws, and on them build a world of a different kind: in fact, as Pierce would explain, the finding and the building *were* the new world.

"Hegel says that the owl of Minerva flies only at dusk," he wrote. "By this he meant that only in the days of the decline of a World-Age does the nature of that World-Age become clear to us. In the twilight of the world that we inhabit there will come to some on soft, silent wings a strange understanding: that things have not always been the way they are, and that therefore they need not always be as they have been. And Hegel says that this understanding is itself the sign that indeed the night is coming, that maybe the morning will be ours to see."

Hegel excluded Nature from the drama of being and becoming that the World-Spirit, human collectivity, underwent. The World-Spirit could alter our *understanding* of nature, but not the obdurate unthinking stuff itself. What Pierce was proposing was otherwise: that nature changes too, and that its huge changes bring about our own; or that we and it (not different, actually) evolve together, and that Father Sun, circling big Earth as he did for millennia, moves to his new place in the center of small Earth's circling in just the years when heroes of thought were discovering him to be there. Now there he is, and always was; and no evidence will ever be found that once he wasn't.

Pierce would speculate that maybe there have been many of these Ages, some short, some long, some we all can recognize on looking back, and some not. The last one, the one before this one, would have ended somewhere about the time Helvetius opened his door to the man in the cloak. The succeeding age was ending now, now when Pierce wrote about it, now when he summoned his readers to hear about it. For it is in the passage-times that fall between ages— when the laws of an old world weaken and begin to fail and the laws of the new are not yet in force—that we are visited with the notion that time is malleable, that the future is up for shaping, that nothing is fixed: then we are brushed by that wing, and it is the only call we will get.

There was, for Pierce, a sort of security in speculating about the existence of huge changes in the nature of things for which no evidence could actually be adduced afterward. Did he believe it himself? No, he didn't, not entirely, not yet. In the (actually rare) moments when he fully grasped what he was indeed saying, he would often stop writing and stand in mute awe before his own impertinence, or laugh hugely, or quit work for the day, wary and afraid. No, it actually seemed to him that those first shudders of the coming age that so many perceived had in fact passed and left the world the same; there had come no irreversible disasters really, no salvations either; the roads still ran where they had run; life was mostly hard work, and all the odds remained unchanged.

Which didn't mean that he didn't share with his readers the longing, whatever its source or name, that the future would be of a different order than the past; that everything lost could return renewed; that the age to which he belonged was not this one, but lay far behind this one, or just ahead. He could not have thought up this thing, whatever it was, if he did not. What Pierce assumed though—what he would perhaps at the very end of his book conclude, what he *planned* to conclude—was that this longing or hope, real and effective as it was and in the past had been, belonged to the things *inside* and not to the things *outside:* that outside remains about as it always has, but that, inside, World-Ages are always failing and being renewed; that no life ends without its share of such upheavals; that any moment will be, for some hearts, the twilight of Minerva's owl. In the end it was to be a fable, of general application; a truth about human nature more than about history.

*De te fabula.*

In that way he could sell his book no matter what befell the world.

Like the brilliant boy he had known at St. Guinefort's, his school, who had shuffled a deck of cards before him and asked what his favorite card was; and when Pierce had answered (rather at random) that it was the jack of diamonds, the boy had laid the deck facedown in rows, then allowed Pierce to take away what cards he chose in an elaborate ritual, ending up with but one lone card on the bed; much hesitation and *mysterium,* perhaps this hasn't worked, then he turned over the card and it was indeed the chosen jack; and only long after did the boy show Pierce the deck he'd used, all jacks of diamonds. Pierce asked what he would have done if Pierce had named say, the queen of hearts? I'd have put the cards away, the boy said; but almost everybody names the jack of diamonds.

It was noon, and Pierce pulled from the wickerwork étagère beside him (it shared the patio with his desk and chair and a glider upholstered in striped canvas) a bottle of Scotch, and poured an inch into a glass.


At The Woods Center for Psychotherapy the parking lot was crowded with the station wagons and cars, many nice ones, of the parents and spouses who had come to take the residents (never "patients") back to the lives from which they had escaped or been ejected to come here. The now ex-residents piled portable stereos and boxes of books and records and green rucksacks into the backs or trunks of Foxes and Jaguars, or watched their parents do it; among some family bands the tension was already mounting as Rose Ryder passed by. Up at the open flagged entrance of the shingled main building, once a family resort (some residents called it the Next-to-Last Resort), staff members were parting from those who had graduated from the program, some of whom were in tears, others sprightly and gay, all better now. Rose had to stop several times to give hugs and get them, her hurry imparting a horrid insincerity to the farewells she tried to get over with quick. Well *heyee.* Now you write, okayee? Hey I'm *sure* it's gonna be *great.*

Away and upward then on the staircase that climbed up within the Tower on the building's sunset side to the Lookout on the top, a broad room once an open terrace and now screened and glassed. Way late. She went up, over, up again, over again around the four sides of the structure, leaving earth. A spiral: coming at each floor to the same place again, only higher.

She stopped. She listened for voices above. She could see that the door to the Lookout was closed. If you can't make it this morning just don't bother coming in at all anymore: Mike, gentle but firm, used to pretend to be able to say such things with calm force but now suddenly he really could. And he had learned up there.

She circled upward, circling what she feared. Easy enough to say she had just forgot, and then to forget she had not really forgotten. And Mike would let it go, let her go.

She could hear a voice now through the door at the top of the stairs, Ray Honeybeare's, speaking softly. She pressed her cheek against the door, smelling its odor of pine and varnish, and tried to hear words; waited for a pause within which she could open the door; waited for what drew her to overcome what pushed her away.

She opened the door and slipped in, gaze lowered. Among those cross-legged on the floor was Mike, and he patted the place next to him, smiling. Ray Honeybeare sat on the edge of a tiny fiberglass chair, leaning forward, his hugeness balanced with remarkable delicacy there. He saw Rose, he definitely took notice of her, but made no sign, and did not pause.

"So I'm not going to speculate about the end," he was saying, "or about God's plans for the future of this world. And I don't particularly want to hear about your speculations either. But I know this: I know that the time we're passing through right now is a time unlike any other. A time full of possibility, for good or evil. A time when God's kingdom comes very close to our old earth, maybe not to arrive for good, maybe just to give us a glimpse. A time when some dreadful evil's being done too, a time of contention between God and the Devil, when the Devil sees his chance to make big gains and is doing his damnedest— yes, his damnedest!—to take that opportunity."

Rose lifted her eyes to Ray, a shy smile, in case his eyes met hers. They did. She felt weirdly penetrated, though his smile was kind. He was big, both tall and heavy, and old, though just how old was hard to guess; his face was a network of fine cracks, as though it had been shattered once to fragments and glued patiently back together, and his features were small in its expanse: delicately winged nose, thin small mouth, very small nearly browless eyes of icicle blue.

They did what eyes she read about in books often did but which she had not actually observed till she saw Ray's: they twinkled. Glittered lightly as though faceted and catching the light when his big head turned.

"And what role in this do we have? What are we as workers in the mental health field supposed to be doing in these days, what's going to be our function and our job? Well, let's open this book we have and do some reading."

He plucked with a practiced gesture a black leatherback from the baggy briefcase at his feet and opened it. Rose saw that it was stuffed with paper markers and place-holders of different colors. "Luke 10," he said. Many of the others opened similar books, and around her there was an autumnal rustle of leaves turned. She remembered now that Mike had told her to bring a Bible (New Testament) and she clasped her empty hands.

Ray Honeybeare cleared his throat. "Here Jesus sends out seventy of his disciples to go on ahead of him through the world, two by two. Seventy people, that's a lot. And he says he is sending them out as laborers to the harvest, but he also says, doesn't he, that he is sending them out as lambs in the midst of wolves. And he tells them that where they are rejected, they should shake even the dust of those towns from their feet, and they should make it clear that *the kingdom of God has come near* and that there will be some stiff judgments made against those places; but where they are well received, he says, they are to heal the sick.

"Now there is no doubt they did so, as Jesus did; and how exactly did they do so? Well, when they return, what they say to Jesus, the first thing they say, is—let's look, ten seventeen—'Lord, even the demons are subject to us in your name.' "

He looked over them, having clinched his argument (so his face and eyes said) and waiting for them to catch on or up.

"The demons," he said again softly. "Even the demons." He read: " 'And he said unto them, I saw Satan fall like lightning from heaven. Behold I have given you authority to tread upon serpents and scorpions, *and over all the power of the enemy:* and nothing shall hurt you.' "

Now there could be no mistake, his eyes said, and they were silent before him, getting it or maybe not getting it, and he spoke with sudden force (Rose started a little in surprise or guilt): "*They were healing the sick by ordering out the demons that were inside those people.* That is what they were told to do, and that is why they were called laborers in the harvest and at the same time sheep among wolves. That's why they came back and said—they didn't say, Lord we laid hands on these people or Lord we gave these people a pill or Lord we put these people through the talking cure like you told us. They said that the demons of illness are subject to us in your name. And Jesus told them they can drive those spirits out, and the Enemy will not be able to hurt them. That's it."

He closed the book but did not put it down. "Now I've said this before and I will say it again. There is sickness and unhappiness around you, all around you here in this place and in other places you might go into on a daily basis. And you've heard me talk about how you can have this power against illness and suffering. And in order for you to have this power it's first needful for you to assent to one thing. One thing. You have to believe that this is now."

He held the book before them.

"You have to believe that *this is now,* just as much as it was then, and that the kingdom of God has come near. That's all. If you believe that this is now, you will know who it is that's being spoken to on every page and every line of this old book, and what you are being promised, and what you are commanded to do."

# 5

Only after she had crossed the bridge at Fair Prospect over the misty river did Rosie Rasmussen remember that she had promised Mike that she would call this morning, so he could talk to Sam before they left. Too late now. She drove on toward Cascadia and the interstate; Sam in the back seat played with the furnishings, turning on and off the reading lights, opening and closing the never-used ashtrays, and Rosie replayed her last talk with Mike: made more clear what she had meant, listened more closely to him; sometimes altered, in her replaying, what he had said, and what she had answered.

Mike—Mike had said—didn't really want to press for custody. Yes he had had his bantam lawyer make that call, but actually all he wanted from it was to get Rosie's attention. He needed to talk, about him and her and Sam, and it was important she hear him out. So many things were clear to him now, so many things that weren't clear before.

Like what things, for instance?

For instance (and here he moved his hand toward her across the stone table where they sat, a table on whose surface a chessboard was inlaid, beside a path up at The Woods) for instance that in many ways he had been a real shit where she was concerned. He couldn't have said that or even *thought* that a while ago and now he could.

And his eyes were big and clear in a way she had not seen before, and she said nothing though a couple of smart things had occurred to her then and more now.

He'd come to see, he said, how much of what had happened between them had been his fault. He'd been very stupid; he laughed, shamefaced, and shook his round head to think of it, how stupid he'd been. He noticed and picked up a fallen maple leaf (why should she remember these details, the whole interview had a psychedelic clarity in her memory, what was she supposed to have learned or done there) and spun it by its stem and watched it flail. He wanted to have her back, and Sam. That's what he wanted to talk about.

She said nothing then, abashed by this, but now she wanted to say Stupid how, Mike? Stupid about exactly what? What if it really didn't have all that much to do with you, Mike, no matter how stupid you'd been? What if it had to do just with me? What if, Mike, I just stupidly wanted to do what I wanted?

"Mom, I have to go pee."

"No you don't, hon. We just went."

"I do."

"Okay. I'll start looking for a place."

*You can't do all this alone,* he'd said, *you can't face it all alone. You shouldn't have to.* This was when she described to him the appointment she was headed for to-day, when she told him about the stuff the hospital sent, the booklet about Epilepsy and You she had read or tried to read. He regarded her closely and nodded attentively but couldn't hide the fact that he had slipped away; it wasn't doctors and medicine he meant or wanted to talk about.

Sam had always been fine with him, he said. Thank God. Always fine here with him. And he was sure, absolutely sure, she was going to be all right.

And he smiled, not exactly triumphantly, but with a kind of self-satisfaction that was surely intended to pass as reassurance but which instead started Rosie's deepest apprehensions, so deep she could not have said then and almost could not say now, even to herself, what she felt: that indeed he had changed, that he had actually been replaced altogether; that when he smiled that way his eyeteeth gave him away, so that she knew he meant not to cherish his daughter, if she were his again, but to eat her.

"Whoops, Mom, too late."

"Oh *Sam!*"

"I was kidding!" Sam shrieked, delighted.

"Oh you. Oh you little."

"Oh you big."

Maybe she *shouldn't* have to face it all alone, whether she was able to or not. She didn't want to, either. But she wasn't going to let Mike back into her life or heart or bed just so she wouldn't be alone.

Brent Spofford had never said that aloud to her in all their talks about Sam—had never said that she shouldn't have to face it all alone, that she didn't need to. He had only and completely offered her and Sam all he had and could do. And yet he put the question anyway, and her answer to him was the same.

The occult and back-end ways we get into cities now. Once we rolled into the great railroad stations built at the hearts of them, and after an expectant passage underground, came right out into the teem and noise. Rosie cycled the freeways that were knotted around Conurbana center, unable to break in; when she chose one likely looking exit she was only sent out again along the bypass meant to help you avoid the city altogether; dove finally at random into a blank warehouse district, the city towers falling out of sight as she went down, like a fairy city vanishing.

Now that she had departed from her mimeoed instructions she had no landmarks to look for. Her childhood memories of this city did not contain hints for moving around in it, only glamorous or sinister tableaus, unconnected as dreams. A chess set of ivory and red jade in the chock-full window of an antique store. The glass-bead curtain of a Chinese restaurant cocktail lounge, and the smell of her mother's Drambuie. The noisome toilet of an overheated children's theater where one Christmas a bright and loud production of *Little Red Riding Hood* had made her ill.

It was getting late. Sam slid otterlike over the back of the seat into the front next to her, and helped her mother get the attention of deaf or uncaring citizens.

"Pediatric Institute?" a taxi driver she pulled up next to said. He rolled the toothpick in his mouth in puzzlement.

"A children's hospital."

"You mean little ones?"

"What?"

"Little ones. Sure. You're right next to it." Horns honked behind him, which he ignored. "This here's the back side, is all. Go around. One way this way, though. Make a circle."

She made a circle, or a rough square, and drew up before it, a huge edifice in many parts, fitted cunningly into narrow streets laid out for livery stables and chandler's shops a hundred and fifty years ago. The name was spelled out in shiny metal letters laid into the side of a sort of windowed bridge or flown passage that led from one new wing of it over to another, older wing: Conurbana Pediatric Institute and Hospital. But on the high architrave of the older building was carved in stone letters another name, City Home for Little Ones. The name it had once had, the first name.

The name it had had, Rosie thought, when Rosie had spent her time here.

"Mommy. Yets go."

Yes when she had been here, when she had been kept inside here. All the closed doors she had pushed or forced open since she had come back to the Faraways led down to here, to this door. Aware of horns blown behind her and the necessity of moving one way or another, Rosie before the gray building could only hold out inward hands to receive, or fend off, or recapture like a fleeing dream, the thing that had happened to her once in that place.


Rose Ryder tapped the ash of her cigarette into her palm, felt the soft gray worm fall there, almost too hot.

"Well I've always prayed," she said. *"Holy Spirit be with me and in me."*

"You prayed," Mike Mucho said. "But did you really believe your prayers were going to be answered?"

"Well sure, I mean. It always made a difference."

"If you ask for bread you're not going to be given a stone. Remember that? Weren't you a Bible camp kid?"

He said it not unkindly. They sat together on the stairs of the Tower, where they had come to a stop, halfway between up and down: where Mike had made her sit down and talk, so that they could discuss this where no one else would hear.

"And about casting out demons?" she said. "That part?"

"What if it's so?" he said.

She looked down at the end of her cigarette. What if it's so? What would it be like to say it was, to know it was?

"It's like a bet," Mike said. "The people who bet on there being no God, or on a God who can't do anything to help them, they lose—if God *can* help and will help but they don't believe it and don't ask. But if you bet God *can* help and will help, what do you lose if he can't? And if you're right, and he can and will, you win. You win big."

She had never thought of this. It seemed to be something you would only think up if you already believed it to be so, that God would help. And she did.

"You know what Ray's talking about," Mike said. "The possibility of cures. Real cures. Not just *talking* forever. Changing somebody's heart and mind, lifting the suffering from them."

What'll I do, she thought. What'll I do. She made a small noise of interest and surprise: "Huh," she said.

"Somehow you know I never did believe that anybody was going to get better because of anything I did or said. I thought they could get better, but because of what *they* did themselves; I was only there so they could believe they could."

"Dumbo," Rose said.

He lifted his eyes at this response, and after a moment seemed to understand it; but he only said: "Rose. All my life I've never, never got a single thing I wanted with all my heart. I want this. I want you to want it too."

The cigarette had burned down to the filter, and Rose nipped off the living ash with thumb and forefinger, let it fall on the rubber tread of the stair she leaned against; let it expire.

"Tell me what you thought," he said. "What you're thinking."

She felt arise in her hugely what she had been thinking, not today but for so long now, so long that it was as though she had never lived without it; wanted to tell it all, tell him how she had rolled her car on the Shadow River road for no reason, how she had lived for weeks as though inside a globe of glass, unreachable; that she could not always remember what she had done the night or the week before, or how things that she possessed had come into her hands. That she imagined futures for herself only to see them die. How afraid she was that, without ever actually willing it, she might die too: wander away from the path, get lost, exit.

"It's hard," was all she said.

Cure me, she wanted to say. Cure me.

"Hard," he said. "Rose this is the most amazing and wonderful thing that's ever happened to me, the most amazing and wonderful thing that *can* happen. But it *is* hard. So hard. The hardest thing I've ever done. Like the hardest course you ever took in college, the toughest game you ever played, the hardest hill you ever biked. You don't just *buy* this stuff. You have to *try*. You have to try and keep trying. I didn't know that."

She watched him, still on his step, hands locked together and hung between his knees: as though she could watch him trying, right here and now.

"He's amazing," Mike said after a while. He shook his head in wonder. She knew who he meant. "You know he sleeps like three hours a night? He has unbelievable energy. See him preach sometime."

She said nothing. Mike huffed out his breath, as though he were going to dive, as though the next thing to say took courage or at least nerve. "So," he said. "What I have to say, about this place and you working here. It's this. If you can't be in on this, there's nothing else here for you."

"You mean I'm not getting asked to come back."

"Well there's not going to be anything left to come back to," he said. "This place is coming to an end, an end as what it was anyway. I can't really tell you a lot more now, but the only thing now that will save it is God. If we give it to him."

She felt she had to go to the bathroom, and really quickly; the need had come over her unrefusably without any warning. She stood, still holding the tiny burnt offering in her hand. "Mike," she said.

"An old world dying," he said, as though quoting something she should know. "And a new world struggling to be born."

# 6

I t had been just a cough at first, not even a bad cough, but persistent. Rosie's mother, who was always made uncomfortable by illness, had watched Rosie and listened to her with that peculiar cross on her face, formed of her contracted brows, her pinched inquiring nose, and the furrow running up her brow between the deepened wrinkles—stigmata she could still produce. Rosie as a kid thought it was what was meant by saying someone was cross.

She coughed and coughed: Dr. Crane came and looked into her throat and took a culture, the swab making her gag and spatter his glasses with sputum, but there was nothing. She coughed daylong, nightlong; would be sent home from school, put to bed, seem to improve, and start again. She was eleven, no twelve: had not yet had her first period.

"Look, Mommy."

"Yes, hon, same as you have." Passing the cheerful and chock-full gift shop, stuffed animals large and small, some bandaged or with little casts and crutches; balloons, games, puzzles, treats. Sam's Mary Janes rapped on the terrazzo floor, and her small hand was damp in Rosie's.

O the interior of those nights coughing: watching the strip of light beneath her door, waiting for Mom to come into her room once again, sit on her bed in her static-crackly nightgown of rayon, and feel her head. No fever, she never did have a fever, but her mother felt her forehead over and over. Held her too while Rosie coughed, her coughs reaching deeper, searching her until a violent spasm came too deep even for coughing and she produced a spoonful of yellowish sputum.

She had entirely forgotten, entirely forgotten: until she looked up at the name of this place and it began returning to her, sometimes in a stream so fast that she had to stop walking while it filled her, saying *Oh oh* while Sam puzzled over her. She remembered the life she had led bound up with that cough, a life different from the life she had led before and after. She and her cough: she hadn't chosen it, didn't like it, God no: but remembered, in some awe, the feeling of settling in with it, getting to know it: her life, different from others'.

Would Sam do that, was she doing it already, going into that place where she would live alone?

"Hi, we checking in today?"

"Um yes I guess."

"And what department are we visiting today?"

"Neurology."

"Sure." A smile for Sam, who looked up at her. Grandmotherly in glasses hung with gold chains. Information taken, and an elaborate set of instructions given, as though they faced a labyrinth, which they did.

It was to this place they had brought Rosie at last (not to this cheerful pastel new place with its blond furniture and wide windows, but nevertheless here, Little Ones). She was losing weight, not getting better, her mother too giving way under the pressure of it, of it and everything—so Rosie imagined, able now to put this event or episode into the story (opaque or invisible to her then) of her parents' marriage and her father's death. Took away her clothes, installed her on her ward, in her white bed.

The poor kid, Rosie thought, oh that poor kid: filled up with pity for the skinny scared girl, carrot-topped, cat's-eye glasses awry on her face, in her bed, coughing ceaselessly for no reason. For no reason.

Neurology turned out to be housed in the older, shabbier wing, much shabbier, dismayingly shabby for a big hospital; the sixth floor, reached by a cavernous clanking elevator, big enough for a rolling bed or a cart full of breakfasts, of which it smelled too, and now Rosie, as though following her own old trail by scent, knew she had been this way before: knew this sad smell, cold toast and porridge and ineradicable traces of soured milk.

"Ever been here before?" the nurse at the intake window asked her, and Rosie thought for what must have seemed a long time before understanding that Sam was meant and not her; and they and their papers were given over to an aide, who would take them down to the treatment room.

"What's your name, sweetheart?" the aide asked Sam.

"Sam."

"Huh. Same as me."

"Your name is Sam?" Rosie asked in wonderment.

"No. Nope. But I got a boy's name, just like her. Bobby."

"My name's Samantha," said Sam firmly, already touchy about this.

"Mine's jes Bobby."

She was a sharp-faced, narrow woman, with pale lashless eyes that made Rosie think of Pilgrims or of farm women in old photographs, but her black hair was teased and flipped and puffed in imitation of country singers, not quite enough of it though. They followed her down halls and half flights of stairs. She saw Rosie look up at the ceiling tiles stained in yellow arcs like a peed bed.

"We're movn," she said. "So they don't spend a dime back here. When we're all moved into the new part they'll fix up back here."

Back here. Back here, deep in, you saw more: the kids in the public areas were mostly just entering, or leaving, all better, but here kids whose illnesses couldn't be guessed at moved slowly through the halls in wheelchairs or were pushed in coffin- or boatlike carriages of plywood stencilled with their floor number; kids in hospital gowns, some cheerful, some dazed, some it was hard not to look away from, though Sam didn't, her eyes wide, silent. Shaved heads were popular, in Neurology: half a head shaved, and a big bandage. Please please let them not shave her head.

"Aren't we going to see this doctor?" Rosie asked. "Dr. Marlborough?"

"You do the test first," Bobby said. "Then you got something to talk about."

If courts of law are like crossroads—one road leading to punishment, cost or confinement, and the other to liberty, exculpation, vindication—then the waiting rooms of doctors are like the trunks of trees: the squirrel of your thought scampers out along a hundred branching ways as you sit there with the doctor's magazines, running toward cure, toward quick cure, toward nothing really wrong at all; or toward something sort of mysteriously wrong which might one day get worse, a little worse, a lot worse, or really quickly worse, very bad right now, much worse than you thought or than you feel, but then maybe better, the resources of medicine—as mysterious as the forces of disease—brought all to bear, one quick treatment, or a few treatments, many treatments, endless treatments, bewilderment, failure, surrender. Death. Life. Half-life worse than death. All these embryonic fruiting bodies ready to come forth at each twig tip.

The test anyway had not been bad; Sam had allowed them to do with her as they liked, curious and unafraid and mild; Rosie wanted almost to warn her, oh don't Sam, fight back a little; they put their electrodes on, she lay hooked up with her arms over her breast like a baby pharaoh or Frankenstein's Daughter, and even fell asleep for a while (*She's asleep* said the technician, watching not Sam but the pen making its shuddery marks on the graph paper) and then it was done, and they gave her a lollipop, transparent barley sugar, Sam would remember it years later; then back up, making their own way this time, to the doctor's office, through a corridor that passed the nurses' station of the ward. By the station there was a windup rocker chair just like one Sam used to have, a Swingading, a Rockadoo, what was it called: a little seat hanging from a frame, a spring you wound up that kept the seat swinging back and forth like a metronome. Sam as an infant had suffered from Mystery Shrieking, colic maybe or maybe not, and the only thing that would soothe her was to be in motion. In this one a large white fat baby, too large, too white somehow, sat unmoving but awake, expressionless, rocking; only just in passing did Rosie see that the back of its big bald head did not match the front, that right over the arc of its skull, under the skin, could be discerned the line where whatever made up the back was joined, not precisely, with the front.

They waited now to see the doctor, to find out about Sam. Inside his little office he was reading the EEG. They were next to see him. Sam continued telling the story of Brownie's life to Brownie; Rosie read her booklet about epilepsy. Though epilepsy was once thought to be a dangerous and uncontrollable form of insanity, it can now usually be fully controlled by medication. Most people with many types of seizure disorders lead full lives without any difficulty. Who were the most and the many, she wondered; when did you find out you weren't them. Famous people who have suffered from seizure disorders include Julius Cæsar and the beloved children's poet Edward Lear, author of "The Jumblies" and many other works.

"Samantha Mucho? That you, honey?"

The Jumblies, Rosie remembered: far and few, far and few, the lands where the Jumblies live.

The doctor didn't look up, when the nurse showed them in, from the long paper; a mechanical pencil in his hand hovered over the marks but in the end chose not to alight on any; he looked up and smiled, and showed them seats.

"Never been here before, huh?" he asked.

"No," Rosie said. Sam climbed into her lap and hid her face in her mother's shirt. "I have. A long time ago."

He looked up, interested. "Oh yes? For what reason?"

"Just a cough," Rosie said, and for a moment felt tears rise to her eyes. The doctor looked down again, losing interest. He was a large ugly man, black hair plastered over a pear-shaped head, and two large moles or warts on his chin.

"So you know why we did this?" he asked.

"Not really." She wished he'd talk to Sam, ask how she was. Couldn't he see she was afraid?

"Seizures come in a lot of varieties," he said. "Some are what we call idiopathic, which means we don't know what causes them. Most of them are, actually. I think Sam's are that kind."

"Oh," Rosie said, not knowing what to make of this, but not encouraged; Dr. Marlborough seemed to read her face, and said:

"Actually that's okay. Idiopathic seizures are often the kind that don't do real harm. They're not due to some underlying pathology; they're just the way someone is."

Rosie said nothing.

"I say I *think* that's what they are. But there's some kind of funny things here." He lifted his eyes from the strip of paper. "Sam," he said, "do you want to see your brain working?"

She looked at him with a face that made Rosie laugh, a curl of her lip that suggested she thought the invitation bizarre, maybe unseemly; but after a moment she climbed from Rosie's lap and went to Dr. Marlborough's side. All three of them looked at the long paper, unwieldy as an ancient scroll, and as obscure.

"See, here's your brain, making waves," the doctor said. "Every time your brain made waves, the pen moved. Your brain moved the pen. And the waves are very nice. But see?" He let his pencil touch certain clusters of marks that seemed to Rosie no different from the rest. Sam lifted her hand slowly to her head and placed it on her curls, as though she might be able to feel the waves, still rising.

"Well they suggest that maybe there is an underlying disorder, a particular place in the brain that's giving rise to these seizures. But we can't tell unless she has one while she's hooked up to the machine."

"Oh great," Rosie said.

"Well, what we're doing, and what I'd like to suggest for Sam, is a new sort of program we've started here. You come in for a number of days—three is usually enough, it might take less—and we have a system where Sam can be attached to an EEG of a special kind during all that time."

"Yikes. That sounds awful."

"Well, it's pretty flexible. You have a portable unit, you can get around . . ."

"And you just wait for her to have a seizure?"

"Um—well no. What we're learning is that in children whose seizures have a distinct focus or foci, there are brain events that aren't quite seizures, or that don't quite precipitate seizures, and that happen rather frequently; that's what we'd be looking for."

Rosie thought, or tried to. "And so then?"

"Depends. It might help you figure out how best to control the seizures. Maybe down the road, if they persist or get worse, we can say well we know where they're coming from and we can neutralize that area."

"Neutralize?"

"Surgically." He added quickly: "I really don't think that's Sam's case. I really don't."

"Well if it cured her."

"You don't want to have to do surgery. Living with idiopathic seizures is preferable."

She put her head in her hands, overwhelmed. "But how do I," she said. "How. If one's always going to happen, how."

Dr. Marlborough closed his plump hands together and rested his chin on them. Rosie thought she saw him glance covertly at his watch. How weird it is, she thought, this man I don't know, who doesn't know me, that I have to trust so much, more than any lawyer, more than any best friend, but who isn't my friend; who I have to trust to be not only smart but wise. And no way of knowing if he was either, no way but the usual ways you decided about people, which didn't apply.

"This is what I think," Dr. Marlborough said. "You'll never know when one's going to happen, and there's not much that you can do beyond making sure she takes her medication to prevent one, and not much you can do to cause one either. So the best thing to do is just act every day as though one will never happen again."

To get out they had to return the way they had come, which Sam seemed to remember, tugging at her mother's hand, plenty ready to go; Rosie looked around for guidance, saw Bobby the aide, who nodded and pointed the way Sam was going; this led them past the nurses' station, past the child in the rocker. Rosie didn't want to go that way, resisted Sam's tug. It was still there, still unmoving except for its ticktock motion back and forth.

"Yets go, Mommy. This way."

Rosie couldn't shut her eyes and be led, but that's what she wanted; couldn't turn back because back was only farther in. But she was for a moment unable to move, because a dreadful certainty had taken over her and held her and stopped her breath. Two certainties: that no time had passed since she had been a patient here on a ward—that this was then, and not done yet; and that the baby in the rocker chair, with its split-level head and black-currant eyes open a crack, was not a real baby at all, but something else entirely.

# 7

At evening when the sun was low, Pierce came out of his house washed and freshly dressed, and breathed the lateness of the day and the end of summer. Far away up the hill stood the big house, the Winterhalters', and there was Mr. Winterhalter too amid the geraniums; utterly still he stood, weary maybe or in the grip of Parkinson's.

The house that Pierce lived in had once housed the servants of the owners of the big house; like the big house, the little one was a lemony stucco with blurry neoclassical details. The big house, though, had the terraced gardens, the sculpted chimney pots, the flagged verandas and French windows the little could not have. When Pierce had taken the house it was with the understanding that, when frost came and the Winterhalters migrated south, Pierce would stay to mind their house and see no harm came to it through the long winter. He had agreed without really pondering the condition, feeling unable to bandy terms with Destiny (by this name he meant only mighty Chance, which we call Destiny when it deals us, after a million so-so hands, one undeniable straight flush).

The well too. He had not yet given much thought to the well.

Up on the hill, beyond the big house, in the little woods, was a pretty little wellhouse that supplied the water to Pierce's dwelling; it came in through a python-thick black plastic pipe (once lead, Mr. Winterhalter said) that ran over the ground and then down into Pierce's basement, to a pump that drew it up to bath and kitchen. In the winter, when Pierce lived here alone, he would keep the water flowing through this pipe, and out an overflow pipe, so that it wouldn't freeze. That was the charge laid on him.

Flowing water doesn't freeze.

He waved to the statue on the hill, which made no response, and got into his car. The plastic covers of the seats, woven in a dim tartan pattern, were still warm from the day's sun, sun that brought out the pleasant old-car bouquet too, grease and metal and what else. He drove out with stately care around the circular bed of tiger lilies, all gone by, and out the long grassy path that in winter would be snow, another thing that Pierce, like the Grasshopper, chose not to ponder now in the golden time.

He drove out through the Winterhalters' stone gateposts and toward Blackbury Jambs, where his river joined hers. He thought there must be shorter ways, right over the lap of the mountain (Mount Randa); one of these roads he was now passing, Bug Hill Road, Jasper Road, Rattlesnake Road, Hopeful Hill, would surely lead him up and then down into the Shadow's valley. His friend Spofford, who had lived here all his life, would know, but Pierce didn't, and any road *he* took, he thought, would doubtless end in swamp or peter out to nothing.

Besides, he had a couple of stops to make, at the library, at the hardware store, before his date. Not before had any courtship of his required a stop at a hardware store, but this one did. Pierce rolled south, more than early enough and without after all another thing in the world to do.

Town was changing. Pierce had been a resident of the county long enough to notice and even to deplore how fast it went, how the old houses would turn, as soon as their owners died or were moved out, into *salons de thé* or antique clothing stores or hair-cutting parlors with awful punning names, if this went on there would not be a human family living on Pleasant or High Street at all. It was hard to find a parking place before the library, and a car with out-of-state plates was eager to get his when he pulled out. He drove around past the building on Maple Street that he had just moved out of; it had already become an antique store, or at least a store that traded in old things, his former apartment the new owners', two guys who had already muffled with curtains the windows of the sunporch.

Where he had once. The sunporch where.

No he is not allowed any longer to see down that way.

He stopped his car, got out. The name was to be Persistence of Memory, the name sketched but not yet painted on the door and window. He went down the path and in.

There was a species of dream Pierce knew well, which took place in environs like this, piled up like this with articles nameable and not, hardly room to move among them, the walls hung too with obscure pictures, the tables and shelves loaded with small and fragile things that would shrink from his searching fingers (is this the one I want, the one I was sent to find? What was it I wanted or needed?) and shape-shift as he reached for them.

Jeez look at this. A picture, much more frame actually than picture, the frame being what he had noticed. It was carved or cast, he couldn't tell which, in that chocolatey-black stuff that might be wood or some kind of resin, late Victorian, the kind that frames a lock of Mother's hair. Deep moldings surrounded the little arched space wherein the picture was contained, which appeared (Pierce came closer) to be a small photograph, though one so tinted and worked-over as hardly to retain any of the light of other days. A bulldog; a jowly head, piggy eyes, ears upright. A dead dog (dead now), a beloved dog whose memorial this doubtless was.

There were figures carved in relief in the frame, and Pierce brought his face even closer to see that yes, they were what they appeared at first glance to be. Little crossed whips at the top, the checking of their leather handles and thin switched tips clearly cut. At the bottom a studded collar, and a leash linked to it that curled away and around the image protectively. A studded collar: its buckle and even the buckle's tooth able to be seen, to be fingered, as the eye can finger relief.

"That'll clean up nicely," said the shop's owner from behind his counter of costume jewelry, old lighters, pens and medals.

Pierce wasn't sure. The ancient dust trapped in its folds and carvings was somehow loathsome, and he could think of no tool that could reach it: as though the thing had been made to gather it, like a bronze statue's patina. There was a tiny bright white sticker attached to it, with a teeny tiny but quite high price written on it in a careful hand. Who would want such a thing at such a price?

"Do you," he asked the keeper, "take credit cards?"

"Oh yes," he said. "Oh we sure do."


When he had finished the rest of his errands, and read the time by the Town Hall tower, he went out of town by the iron bridge over the Shadow. His new oddment was in his trunk, wrapped loosely in tissue. His other purchases were in a brown bag on the seat beside him. He turned north and west up the river road, which soon passed the last of the town's commercial buildings (a welder, a coal-and-oil dealer) and the last residences, and climbed into the woods.

Why does the sky's blue darken as autumn comes? Is it just the gradual subtraction of cousinly green from the foreground palette, the addition of oranges and browns? That little maple, hastening to turn before her sisters did for some reason, lifting and shaking her burning hands. The hurt and the old turned soonest: the high outermost limb of that dying ancient; that riven but still living one.

Among the lesser charismata he had noticed lately, Pierce had come to be aware of an ability to reverse the relativity of motion, experientially at least: when driving in his Steed sedan through the Faraways he was able, as though by flipping an inward switch, to cease rushing past the scenery and instead, himself still, to watch it rush past him; to feel the roadside trees giddily fly by, lifting their limbs and showing their leaves' undersides as they passed over him, the clouds roll up toward him, the mountains too, shape-shifting like clouds as they came. Fence posts rattling single file along the road in their regiments, barns and houses demonstrating their geometries to him as he sat still, hands on the wheel and foot on the gas, marvelling. Sometimes he had a hard time making it stop.

Despite all his malingering he arrived at her little place to find the driveway still empty. The house too, obviously, though he was careful to call out before he pulled open the screen door from the deck. He was alone there, and could go where he liked amid her belongings and her books. That room there would, surely, be her bedroom.

A little later Rose Ryder also turned off the Shadow River road onto the dirt road that led to her cabin, took its three brief turns to her driveway, pulled in and braked. She was running late, still in pursuit of that lost hour or so she could not overtake. She pulled from the car her bag of purchases, all that the Here You Are Grocery in Shadowland provided. It didn't matter, it would do, it was fine. The sheets needed changing, the dishes washing.

Meanwhile Pierce had left, and driven back to the same little store where Rose had just been, and at that moment was buying beer as she had asked him to do. If she had been paying attention, Rose would have seen him go past her on the road: he saw her.

When she had done what she could with the dinner and the house she walked the deck, not knowing how to spend the last minutes till his arrival, feeling she might disintegrate, part company with herself, if she could not think of something. She had to stop running, toward or away, whichever it was. It was both. She prayed: *Holy Spirit be with me and in me.*

Immediately (astonished, she watched it happen) the wind she had been standing in fell. The day was (had all along been) still, perfectly still; the clouds stationary; the river merry, yet still too. Her lost hour was returned to her. She lifted her hands and placed her fingertips in wonder on her lips.


Once, a universal animating spirit pervaded the whole universe, the reason why everything was as it was and not a different thing. Because of the continuity of the spirit within us and this universal spirit, thoughts could be transmitted from the operator's spirit, via the star-powers, to the spirit of another, like a phone call bouncing off a satellite.

Today too there are links and chains of causality, occult connections which can be manipulated in order to make changes and produce effects; that's what science and technology do. One difference then was that anybody could play. If you could see, if you could *feel,* a connection, you had made one; the forging of connections was like the making of metaphors. No it *was* the making of metaphors, fusing tenor and vehicle into an ampersand of incandescent connection.

The dandelion is the sun's child. Pierce pointed out one that had come out by mistake in her brief shabby lawn, dazed by the weirdly warm October. Look at its golden head, a sunburst—which is a lion's mane too, and the lion, golden and noble, is the sun-beast above all. And the green leaves, dentate, fierce, *dent-de-lion.* Now cut its stem and see the sun's sign, ☉, which places it for sure among the sun's things, with the lion, and gold, and the goat and the honeycomb and the heliotrope and a thousand other things great and small. Read a book of such signatures and commit them to memory and you can use them for making medicines, say, or telling small futures; imagine the signatures in your heart, discover new ones, and open a way upward for yourself toward the heavens and the gods.

"But it works on other people too," Rose said. "You said."

"Right. On people too."

This October evening Pierce Moffett, junior magician, was going to attempt to receive, by techniques freely adapted from the masters, a communication between his spirit and that of Rose Ryder. Who was his apprentice as well as his subject, and already showing more natural aptitude than her teacher: it's often so.

"So I'm thinking and feeling," he said. "And hm. You're a Leo, right? Also a child of the sun. And so I think well in these days of the old age of the sun you might be experiencing some anxiety. You might be thinking about the sun, getting closer to the sun."

"How, closer."

"Oh travel. Maybe major travel. In the South, the southern hemisphere I mean, it's spring now, turning summer."

"Yes. Yes it is."

"So oh I don't know really, this is guessing—you might be drawn to that."

"Yes maybe."

"What I'm getting, what I feel coming, is an emblem of the sun, of its what. Its vicissitudes. Sudden changes willed in the sun's life." He studied her, stroking with his hands the chilly tops of his thighs. "Say Phæton."

She looked at him oddly. "Phæton," she said.

"Yes, you remember, the sun's child. The boy who."

"Sure."

"Father Sun and his boy, who drove the chariot so close to earth that he started fires everywhere, parched the ground, boiled the rivers."

She nodded at him, and flicked the end of her cigarette with her thumb, and looked at its burning tip. "Phæton," she said. "Actually I have been. Thinking of him, of that story. A lot. Just this week, last night." She shook her head and laughed. Pierce laughed too, a small laugh of gratified amazement, hey I'm good.

"Well these stories, see," he said. "There's a reason these stories go on being told. In many forms."

He looked west, where the sun was hurrying down, pulling day after him.

"And your father," he said.

She put down the can of beer she had lifted to her lips. "Why did you say that?"

He pondered, staring at her, as though the reason had to come from her. "Well," he said at length. "It's a story about fathers too. As well as about." He smiled. "About reckless driving."

She began to laugh, the sudden laugh from the throat and the gut that rushes forth when tension breaks. He laughed too, the two of them staring at each other and laughing aloud like devils delighting.

.    .    .

Too cold when the sun went down to eat on the little gray deck. She made a fire in the big stone fireplace that it seemed the house had been built around, and which would surely remain long after it was gone, like a house of eld; and when the pine and birch had roared for a long time (she kept rolling the logs into the fire-mass, never enough) he took the black fire shovel that leaned against the stones and shovelled out enough live coals to fill her little hibachi. On it they grilled her wieners and burgers, and sitting on the floor before the hearth ate them with slaw and beans: comfort food for her, he had decided, and wondered if she had marshmallows to toast. It was this meal, this sort, that they had met over, at that party by the Blackbury.

They drank more of the beer he had brought, she trying to incite or invite a certain recklessness and at the same time hold it in check, like a woman with a half-tamed cheetah on a leash; she knew what it was for but not always how to use it. He helping her with a word or a look, moving a third fresh bottle out of her reach at last.

For now it was she who was to be examined, whose powers of mentation and whose colored memories were to be unrolled, for a particular purpose they had agreed on without discussion. Hot enough now from the fire that she could be undressed for this examination: she did this herself at his request or command, he watching, remaining dressed himself.

She approached him where he sat on the spavined couch.

"No hon you take the little stool there."

It was a three-cornered stool of leather and wood, maybe North African, strung with rawhide, the seat somewhat saddlelike. She looked at him a moment, and at it, then lowered herself onto it.

"Now I want to ask you first," he said. He tipped the shade of the standing lamp away from himself and toward her; the lamplight fell on her, spotlight, third degree. He himself was in shadow. "I want to ask first about this guy. Your husband. The one who first."

"Oh God." She put her arms defensively before her for a moment, but then lowered them when Pierce, very slightly, shook his head. "Him, well. Yes we sort of eloped. He was, I think, in fact crazy. I'm still afraid of him."

He had her tell just how afraid he had made her: a dark muscled mechanic just past teenhood, her high-school crush, though not till they were out of school and he had gone through one wife—a girl who had graduated visibly pregnant two years ahead of Rose—had they got together. And where now were this other wife and child? Who knew?

"He had amazing eyes," she said. "Cutter eyes. When he came home in certain, well moods. His eyes were like, just. Like weapons."

"Certain moods," Pierce said.

"Well." She threw her hair from her eyes with a lift of her head.

"Was he suspicious of you?"

"He was sure I was fucking somebody."

"Were you?"

"He'd want me to prove that I wasn't." Now her hands were moving slightly, small beasts stirring. Pierce watched them; they seemed to have their own intentions, of which they were becoming conscious.

"How could you do that?"

"Well he had ways that he thought proved it."

"What ways?"

Her own eyes—likewise amazing—were turning inward now as they should: not clouding so much as growing bright but sightless, sheeted in ice but not cold, her lower lids beginning to rise over them. "Oh I don't remember now really. He was just so crazy."

"Rose. What ways."

She said nothing for a long moment. Her hands were on the insides of her thighs, which were kept apart by the prow of the stool. He let her remember or imagine what ways. All this had happened in some bleak black city or town up in New York state; he could see the muscled tattooed forearm, the can of beer he was never without, damper and raiser of his notions. The oilcloth of the kitchen table. The linoleum whereon she knelt.

What was his name? Wesley. Wes. She alluded to him at other times, but it was only at times like these that he grew a reality. They worked carefully together over it, with pauses for thought, his to frame questions, hers to answer them.

"Well Rose how could you have allowed him to do those things."

"Jesus, I was I guess just so young. And scared. I was just so scared of him."

"And how did that make you feel? Being so scared."

Pause for the deciding of this, her lips parting. *How did that make you feel?* He asked not because he thought she could answer, but because the question itself so visibly stirred her. *This* was how it made her feel: made her lips open in this way, and her hands migrate. "It." Pause. "It made me excited."

"You learned that?"

"Yes."

"And how did that make you feel, Rose. That excitement. I mean were you."

Pause. Pause. The air in which they sat heated now by the fire and the delicate archæology under way.

"I was ashamed."

"Uh-huh." He crossed his legs differently, uncomfortable. "And how did that make you feel, that shame?"

"It made me feel." Pause pause. "I guess more excited."

Her hands had now met between her spread legs, one hiding what the other did. Pierce at this point could and sometimes did instruct her to stop; other times he chose not to notice.

And he would proceed with his little interrogatory until he decided (or gauged) that she had got far enough, and suggested that she go now into the bedroom; and she would rise obediently and go on silent feet, her long stride like a big cat's—and after a time he would follow and find her; and if there were no further exactions to be made, if he had prepared nothing further or considered that she needed nothing further (he could consult only his own heat to guess) he would begin at once to fuck her, often not removing his own clothes;

coaching her still, talking, talking, until at length, often at great length, they produced between them, hothouse-fashion, her orgasm, a great bloom sometimes that astonished both of them.

Tonight though there was more to do.

"Rose," he said to her softly. "Over there by the door, on the table there, is the brown paper bag I brought in. That one."

"What," she said, a breath only, her eyes not leaving his face. He took her head in his hands and turned it toward the door, where the bag lay.

"That. Would you get it now please and open it."

She rose, obedient, and went to take the bag; brought it back to the bed.

"Open it please, Rose."

That implacable Soft Voice, where had he learned it, how did he know how to use it, how to speak gravely and with that awful kindness, as though they both labored together here under an injunction, a necessity that must be yielded to. When it was really he alone who laid the tasks upon her. This one being the next.

"Oh Christ," she said.

"See someone like you," he said. "Who can deny so much, pretend so much that things haven't happened. You need to have sex happen to you that you can't deny. That goes on reminding you, *proving* to you through the day that you did the things you did."

"Oh Pierce."

"We're going to help you remember. We're going to make sure you remember tonight. Is that all right, Rose?"

He took her head lightly again in his hands, feeling with awe and delight the soul within awake and arise as she sought for a way out of this one; felt her find it, and find it was nothing but the way to which he had turned her: the way that led further in.

"I asked: Is that all right?"

"Yes," she said.

He turned her to himself and held her with firm certainty. "Do you accept this, Rose? Do you want this?"

This she did not say for a moment, but he could see that she would; the word gathered again in her despite herself; all she was waiting for was for it to become unrefusable.

"Yes," she said at length, not quite aloud.

"You need this, don't you?" He waited. Nothing this time, but the air around their bodies palpably heated further. "Rose."

"Oh please I can't."

"You can, Rose. You can whisper if you have to."

Nothing still. She had turned to soft smoke in his arms. He drew her ear to his lips. "Say it, Rose."

"Yes," she whispered.

"Yes what."

"Yes I need it."

There. He wound her hair in his hand. She had begun to weep, shuddering. He pressed her cheek into the pillow, and opened her with his knee. No more talking, no more Soft Voice, a remorseless engine now, though inside him his heart was great and he wanted nothing more than to smother her with tenderness and gratitude, and kiss away her tears. It was not time for that.

As he worked, he heard or overheard in some space of his soul phrases spoken, a voice, narrating the things he did to her even as he did them, things even that he had not yet done or dared to do. *He knelt before her and placed his cheek against the hot marks he had made.* It was a voice he was coming to be familiar with, accompanying these encounters. *She offered to him the gift of her crying-out.* As though he were able to do the deeds and at the same time, even somewhat in advance, read a histrionically somber and slightly phony account made long afterward.

One winter's day she had fled Wes and the creeper apartment they shared in that town, fled with only a couple of suitcases (her round hatbox one of them) and three hundred dollars in bills; she took a taxi—Wes allowed her no car in his absence and had taken away her keys—to the train station, and, her heart beating fast, bought from the incurious agent a one-way to New York City. She was twenty-one.

Pierce, in his unsleeping bag before the fire, followed her to the station, the slush gray, the fur trim of her boots wet; her knuckles white where she gripped that bag. (She also lay asleep in her bed in the room beyond, it was her house and therefore her privilege to take the bed, she had invited Pierce to share it but it was narrow and he would never sleep, he lay then in the bag awake of course anyhow.) On that train to New York, where she had no friends and yet toward which she went as much as she went away from Troy or Schenectady or wherever it had been, unwise and yet more knowledgeable than before, aware of something, of a her within her now awakened—on that train she sat next to a gent with a Mephisto beard and tinted glasses, and fell into conversation with him; and accepted, somehow unable to refuse, his offer to help her in the city toward which they both travelled, where he actually had a lot of friends.

Handed on then from party to party, stranger to stranger, as in a quadrille, she might well have drawn quickly close (there is no chance in dreams, or it is all chance) to a connection with Pierce, one that Pierce also might have been making his way toward. For of course he had been a New Yorker too then. So, back in that city, that city deep within, in that past which he made for himself, they *did* draw closer together: because just now the past was up for shaping, just as the future was. As a novelist might discover while he works a key plot element, one he all along needed but did not know he needed, that requires but a quick flip back to the earliest pages, a name change, a small biographical detail added—done—so the present could shape the past now in the time of the ending of the world.

A long time ago, and deep within. How do you like that. That warehouse in the film district, porno district too; winter, the smell of the damp overcoats the actors had discarded. Masks. He put his own on. A woman assigned to play opposite him, hi, already naked and masked and soon writhing in imitation lust in his arms, though he did not yet know her name. And together they two and everyone else there looked upon Rose. Masked too for her role, her starring role, so that later in the Faraways he could not nor could she recognize.

And so Pierce was now, thereafter, connected to her, by a bond he would never know he had been able to forge. To forge: which means both to make and to fake. In the time of the ending of the world those things are not always different.

He started awake on the unforgiving floor. The fire was embers, still alive though beneath a hide of ash. Day was coming. He would not sleep again; he was grateful he had been granted so much. Thank you Morpheus, ungenerous god. He unzipped the mummy case he was ensconced in (what other males had made use of it? It had a smell he could not identify) and stood, still mostly clothed and yet not therefore ready for the day.

At the door of her bedroom he stood for a moment watching. Her dark head deep in its pillow and its dreams, where do they go. From where he stood she seemed entirely gratified, at peace. Sleep, the innocent sleep.

On the table beside her bed still lay the books and letters from which he had read yesterday, when he had arrived here before her and found the place deserted: Bulfinch's mythology, open to the Greeks, the children of Apollo; Phæton. A letter, unfinished, to her father. The little creepy thrill he had felt to find how easily she could be fooled.

Though whether he had actually fooled her, or only induced in her—or helped her induce in herself—a willed suspension of disbelief (the same sort of state, he supposed, he was trying to induce in the readers of his book, who were to be thought of as equally ready to believe) he couldn't know.

He watched her for a time, and then before his steady gaze awoke her he turned away, and as silently as possible got his shoes and coat and slipped out the glass door onto the deck. He went down the drive and to his car; he let out the brake and allowed the car to slide soundlessly down the incline and out to the empty road. He started it then, and turned around to head back down the valley of the Shadow and away. He drove far and fast, out of the town of Blackbury Jambs and out of the county, leaving behind for good his house by the river and that pile of paper on the desk in the study. The Faraways closed up behind him in the folds of autumn mist as he fled, as though they had not been. When he hit the interstate he turned north, or south, and kept going, as fast as his Steed could carry him.

# 8

**N**o he did not flee, though he felt warned to do so, though in the weeks to come, the months to come, he would sometimes wish that he had: no he watched her sleep for a time, then yes turned away, and as silently as possible got his coat and shoes, slipped out the glass door onto the deck; but only stood in the coming morning, feeling as clear and cold as it was. The only birds he heard were chickadees and jays, both taking notice of him, alerting the world.

He went out across the deck, littered with the remains of their hors d'oeuvres from last night, they had been too occupied to clean up. He saw that woodland creatures had apparently scavenged what they had left, had maybe been feasting even as the two humans were thus occupied. Little ears alert to the alarming sounds from within. He walked down the driveway and out on the road.

Sometime when he was a kid, just bursting into puberty, Pierce had found among his uncle Sam's books one on sexual pathology, written, though he couldn't know it then, in another and different world-time, Berlin 1920, and full therefore of the pathologies then apparent, mostly gone now or become unapparent or subsumed in others; mostly it was about people (unimaginable to him, people named with just a job and a single capital letter, F., a butcher, G., a married woman) whose sexuality had become accidentally bound up—it seemed to Pierce that it happened easily and often—with something different from the persons of others.

*Fetishes* was the word the book used.

There was the woman who craved the touch of feathers; or the other who loved crystals, she laid them out lovingly on black velvet, dangled them provocatively before candle flames, dropped them one by one into cut-glass bowls of clear oil, where she could watch them sink slowly as she shivered and moaned in delight.

He had wondered, then, if such a thing might happen to him, that his own mighty feelings might get loose somehow and seize blindly on the wrong thing forever; it seemed not impossible, since just at that moment almost everything (running water, fur on his nakedness, thunderstorms) could alert them. He hoped that if it did, whatever it was he ended up with would not be loathsome or operose, as some of these were, or at least be easily acquired.

If it were, then he imagined it might not be so bad (and having read and thought to this point he was likely to be hard again, of course, the dumb dumb thing); it would be handy in a way, no muss no fuss, just the one little switch to throw, and endless refinements to pursue, each one getting closer to the potent node that had somehow formed, the simple powerful itch to be scratched.

And so it turned out to be. It was just that way. Such a switch did make everything simple, and endlessly intensifiable. He did not think that this switch was inside himself, though; he was certain he would long ago have found it if it was. He thought it was in her.

She had wept, once early on, when they were done and he held her, freed, in his arms: wept clinging to him, asking him "But did you like it? Did you really like it, did you, did you?" And he, not knowing why she wept, because of the pain he had made her bear, or because of her shame at wanting it and knowing he knew she wanted it, or from her capitulation to him, or because of how carelessly, how quickly and completely she had granted it to him—he said yes he had liked it very much, he had; yes really really he had. And held her, wondering, till she slept.

You had to be careful, though, so careful: one misstep, one misunderstood gesture, and the castle vanished. Pierce, though he allowed her to believe he was skilled in these mysteries, didn't really have much of a grasp of the physics, the stresses and tensions he needed to apply to keep her immobilized, you'd have to be a goddamn physical therapist or a trained torturer, he spent hours pondering. For it was worse than embarrassing when his ropes slipped and his bonds failed to hold; she would free herself and look at him smiling like an impertinent child, waiting to see what would become of her for her misbehavior. And he must not shrug or laugh, or look nonplussed, but only nod, and raise the stakes.

For if his knotcraft was lacking he had another quality others might not have had: he was willing to go as far as she needed and could be forced to go, no holding back himself if she would not, a willingness that shocked her, moved her, made her come. So fast had the doors flown open before him down within her that (afraid then as he still was afraid) he had offered her a code she could use: a signal, he'd said, by which he would know that he had gone, or was about to go, farther with her than she could bear to go. He would not listen, of course, to any ordinary entreaties or pleadings, not to *No no,* not to *Stop stop,* no matter how pitifully or imperiously she said these. She had to say this: *I tell you three times.*

She had not wanted to pay attention to this. What did it mean, anyway? Why three times?

Children say it, he said. You know. *What I tell you three times is true.* But it was unknown to her, she had never chanced to hear what he would have thought was a universal formula.

Anyway he was never to learn where her limits lay. Between them they constructed limits, and she would take them for her own, and then in the night, late, they would violate those limits, and cross into new country. He always supposed her own actual limits lay somewhere beyond those, and that she knew where they were or would know them if they came in sight. But he never reached them.

Wesley. *That* was the limit; he would have to be as crazy as she was to get that far. He hoped for her sake that she never again attracted, by the exhalations of her own spirit, a man capable of that rage, that. It was the one thing Pierce had never been able to summon up for her, or even imitate very convincingly: the sudden upwelling of male rage, the dangerous mad aggression like a beast's, unpredictable in onset and consequences, like the fires and the fireworks that also so moved her.

No he was not like them, he was not, there was a difference, clear to Pierce: that kind of man wanted only power, and used sex, wielded it or withheld it or inflicted it, all to have power. Pierce Moffett, though an adult male human, a mammal living on earth, nevertheless believed that power and sex were realms of being not only different but opposed in their natures; that what power was guilty of, primordially guilty of, sex was not: sex, soiled or enchained or even bought and sold, was innocent.

He jammed his hands in his jacket pockets, feeling a shiver run across his rib cage. How much longer would she sleep? He looked at the watch he had not removed last night. A trout—he thought it was a trout—leapt from the Shadow as though inviting him to come play.

He turned back to the cabin. As he pushed aside the slider and came in from the deck her eyes opened: her big eyelids lifting suddenly like a doll's, the rest of her motionless.


The cabin's tub was a mingy stained fiberglass affair not long enough for her body; he ran it for her, testing the water with his hand, and led her to it when it was full.

"Yike it's too hot."

"No it's okay."

She entered slowly. Pierce thought of the dark waters of the quarry on Mount Merrow's flanks. She lay, knees up, steam dampening her hair and curling it against her cheeks. Her little swelling abdomen like an Egyptian drawing: he studied it, and the cup of her navel, deep enough to retain a minute sip of bathwater when she arose, he could foresee that; maybe before it was poured he would drink it. See how we go on building the *impresa* by which we capture ourselves. He washed her; together they examined her. Her wrists were red. That would pass. They talked of this and that as he washed her long hind feet, their white bottoms.

"I did get an offer," she said. She often opened topics in the middle, as though he really could read her mind, and knew what train of thought she was taking.

"What kind of offer?"

"At work. The healing group invited me to join. To start to join, I mean to start the process."

"I thought you thought," he said, "that they were going to fire you."

She raised her other foot to him. "This is different. The two things aren't connected. The healing project is a special group within The Woods. They're not from here."

Why did his antennæ lift? He thought he knew. She was regarding her toenails, where the remains of paint still clung, crimson rose. "Isn't old Mike a part of this?" he asked.

"Yep."

"And was it he who."

"Yep." She squeezed the loofah slowly. "He's changed a lot. You wouldn't believe it."

"Well you know I don't actually know him." Mike Mucho was something of a figure of fun within their nights, the comic relief or satyr-play sometimes preceding their more solemn masques; Pierce had come to know quite a bit about a certain part of Mike's life, though he was yet to actually make his acquaintance. He remembered that his very first words to Rose had been *How's Mike?* back when he knew nothing of either her or him. An imposition, a trick. "How different? Better or worse?"

"Well it's amazing," Rose said. "Having gone through the training." She pondered, he could see her ponder how amazing. What Pierce knew about the healing project or group at The Woods was that it had something to do with the power of prayer, and that it occupied more and more of Rose's thought even as she said less and less about it.

"Training," he said.

"You'd be interested," she said. "Really. It's a way of power. Like you talk about."

"Uh-huh?"

"Only from God. Out of the Bible. If you look and read, it's so clear. The promises are there."

"Uh-huh."

"If you ask for bread," she said, "God's not going to give you a stone."

"I'll wash your hair," he said.

They were silent a while for this. He was careful to draw the soap only one way through the length of it, to keep it from tangling badly; laving it again and again with water poured from a child's plastic bucket kept by the tub just for that purpose. When she was done he handed her out, and robed her in a robe of white (a gift or product of The Woods); and then, holding a mug of coffee by its handle and its body, she went out onto the deck. The sun was already red and hot, strange days, surely they would end. She lay on an aluminum chaise, and let her hair hang down behind to dry.

"I don't know, though," she said or murmured.

"Don't know what."

"The course. It costs a lot."

"They *charge* you for this?"

"Two hundred dollars."

"Good Lord," Pierce said. "Hey. I see in the paper that the Shadowland Gospel Church offers a healing service every Saturday. I bet they don't charge."

"Pierce. This is very different."

"And you've got that much?"

"Well you know. I've got my little emergency stash."

"Oh yes?"

"Sure. Getaway money. I always have had. Everybody does."

"I don't," he said. He thought of her escaping; thought of Wesley. He wondered if the other women he had shared his life with in the past had kept a secret getaway stash. It made, he guessed, a lot of sense, and though a little shocked at the idea, he thought it likely. Get away from him, though? Or with him, fleeing some common disaster? It wouldn't matter, to the money.

"But oh I don't know," she said again.

"Well sure."

In fact she did know. When Mike had brought her before Ray Honeybeare and Ray had taken her hand in both of his and smiled at her as though he knew something secret about her, something fine and brave that she had never told anyone but that was within her always, something that made her who she was: she knew. She was writing home to her father to send her a couple of savings bonds she had been given on big birthdays long ago, which now she would cash to pay for it. Then there would be no going back. The knowledge that she had and would was warm in her breast, warmer than her bath, warmer than this injun-summer sun, warmer than the flesh Pierce had done his work on.

"I thought maybe you'd have a hard time with this," she said. She shook her tresses, long enough almost for a fool prince to climb to her window by.

"With what?"

"Well healing. The power of God." She closed her eyes. She seemed near sleep again. "Miracles."

"Heck no," Pierce said. "I'm with Sir Thomas Browne. 'Methinks there be not impossibilities enough in Religion for an active faith.' "

She grinned, eyes still closed. "An *active* faith," he said again, and laughed, and felt the grip of a small hand on his heart.


When her hair was dry they returned to the cabin, and she doffed the robe again to sit before a little blond vanity with a big half-circle mirror.

He approached her where she sat. She had taken out comb and brush, an antique set bound in tarnished silver. He chose the comb and went to work, starting with the tangled ends, then going higher.

"So what are we going to do with it?" he asked her, lifting it in his hands, black and thick, heavy as a pelt.

"O gee," she said, watching him and herself.

"Well we don't want to just leave it," he said. "Just free."

"No?"

"I think something tight," he said. He picked up the brush, and began to brush, firmly and expertly (he had become expert only in this summer, a fast learner). "Don't you? You don't mind, do you?"

"I," she said. Her legs parted.

"Isn't that what you want?"

Pause. His brush raised, waiting.

"Yes," she said.

Yes. When it was smooth and knotless he lifted a section of hair from the top of her head, dividing it carefully into three equal parts. He began to braid the three strands he held, right over center, left over right, center over left. When he had made two turns that way he took up a hank of loose hair from the side of her head, and added it to the one he was braiding. Then the other side.

Careful not to drop the sections. He didn't want to have to begin again. It had taken him some time and care to gain her trust before the mirror, more time than to gain it in the bed.

Other days, or nights, the process at the mirror might be lengthy. She might have to take out from the dark drawer where they lived her slim-jawed scissors like a bird's skull, and place them on the vanity before her, where she could see them. He would talk to her about them. Sometimes she would take them up. He too might take them up, and if her mood were right, he would, delicately and judiciously, cut.

All it took were the blades' snicker and the little clippings falling glittering in the lamplight over her bare shoulders and the tops of her breasts, her eyes consuming these things. All it took. She had told him how when she was a teenager and just learning this about herself she would sit before her mirror by the hour, and just cut, and come, and cut and come.

He never cut much: a few tiny bites from the hem, unnoticeable. Not only because he was unskilled, which he was, but because if it were truly cut, cut as he talked to her of cutting it—chopped, shorn, removed, and with it her self-hood, will, autonomy; shriven like a penitent, like Joan, like a collaborator made to feel her shame, eyes lowered—then she would no longer be able to imagine it being cut, no longer imagine submitting to its cutting.

So it had always to be long: always able to be cut.

"I'll see you tonight?" he said. "Or . . ."

"I'm going to be gone," she said, watching his hands take up her hair, on one side, the other.

"Oh?"

"Over Columbus Day. To Conurbana."

"For what reason?"

"A group from The Woods is going." She drew from between her parted lips a stray hair that had caught there. "For a sort of orientation."

"And you're travelling there with . . ."

"It's a whole group. We leave from The Woods; we take a van from there. And just go on."

For a time he continued to braid in silence. The trick was to keep the tension equal on both sides, or he would end up with one side tight, the other coming free.

"Well then," he said, "there's something I'll want you to do."

"What?"

"I'll want you," he said, "to leave yourself alone." Tight, tight, a cable, a chain. "Till I see you again. You understand?"

"But—you mean . . . Jeez Pierce." A smile bloomed on her lips, gravely attentive usually at these rituals.

"That's what I mean. No touch."

"Well what if, you know, I can't." Idly, unseriously, she was at it even as they talked.

"Rose."

He took the thick rope he had made and drew her head back. Eve's apple in her throat rose and fell.

"You can," he said. "You will."

Holding her, he bent and placed his cheek on hers, his lips on her throat. French braid: for her, maybe for her alone, it belonged on the list with those other French things, letters, lessons, kisses. He held her hard, and waited till she had, once again, assented.


There was, just as Pierce had supposed, a way back over the mountain that didn't involve returning to the Jambs and going up the Blackbury River road again; before he departed Rose described it to him, the turn to take at Shadowland that would lead to a road that went right east to join the road to Littleville, and what the landmarks would be. He set out that way, up into the hills, as the sun reached its zenith.

He had commanded her not to touch herself; he himself could not even wait till he reached home. On the road beyond the Shadowland bridge, climbing (it seemed) more or less endlessly upward, Pierce slowed at an entrance to the woods, a logging road, in fact, long abandoned, and with some trepidation turned in there, and went a ways, and stopped.

Alone.

There are ordinarily but two instances when spirit—that universal animator that is finer than body yet not quite immortal soul, this quicksilver stuff that enwraps the soul and fills the heart and takes the impressions of the sense organs—can be physically apprehended outside the body. One is in speech, more especially in song: song is in fact spirit, expressed from the body in audible though not visible form. The other is this thick white stuff, spirit double-distilled, cooked up by his heat, clouded into visibility like an egg's white; also the slick coatings she produced, started by his prohibitions, which she was at that moment revolving in her mind even as she disobeyed them. Precious; exhaustible, supposedly, and hard to replenish—which is why we are instructed not to expend it on phantasms, why we are not to lie alone and soak the sheets with it or fling it onto the earth or this dipstick rag.

*Pneumatorrhea* they called it; sapping the starstuff we are born with.

But why, then, should there be the more of it the more he, the more she. Pierce lay inert for a long while, his head back against the upholstery. Leaves of many colors fell upon the hood. Now and then he heard the rush of a car's passing. He did not know that he had taken the wrong turning back at Shadowland, had gone left not right, and that he was now lost.

# 9

The leaves of the oaks at Arcady turned brown and fell reluctantly, would still be hanging on after the first snows fell, even till spring buds pushed them off; the brilliant leaves of the maples though, especially the old ones, fell in sudden glad drifts as though by common consent; it was exhilarating in a melancholy way to lift your eyes and see them, so high, let go their hold on their branches all at once and sail. Whee, death. The other trees (a great variety, associated here by a long-ago landscape architect and grown old together, but not ever really become friends, Rosie thought) shed their leaves of many shapes and many colors at different rates. Bright yellow willow and coppery Japanese maple, golden birch, greeny-brown ash, and a double row of flame trees (they needed pruning) beet-red and hardest of all to rake.

Rosie had taken a huge bamboo rake from the carriage house, easy and graceful in use despite its size, a well-made tool in fact, they'd known what they were doing back then when all this yardwork had been done by hand. Of course she didn't need to rake Arcady's leaves; Allan Butterman had urged her to get a lawn service to do this and all the other jobs that a huge house like this would always need doing, and she said sure yes, she definitely would; but for now she piled the leaves in great spicy-smelling piles, for the pleasure of it and to slow her racing blood: and for Sam to jump in, she'd promised.

"More, Mommy! Higher!"

"Higher, okay, higher and higher."

Sam had a date now to go back to Little Ones and have the test Dr. Marlborough had described, where they wired her up for three days and tried to see where the seizures were coming from. So it had not been a bad dream, Little Ones, or if it was a bad dream it was one that was going to continue. And there was the possibility of real bad news, a possibility arising in Rosie's consciousness at unexpected times, having to be routed before the day's work or the night's sleep could be continued: like being surrounded by hostile tribes or the eyes of hungry animals in the dark. Keep the fire going.

The worst part of it—the part Rosie couldn't cease regretting even though it was shamingly unimportant, relatively—was that the great party she had planned at Butterman's was off. The only time Sam could be scheduled for the procedure was the very days on which Halloween fell. The weekend before—not quite Halloween but close enough—wouldn't do either. Rosie didn't trust herself to plan and hold a huge affair just before she went back to Little Ones; it seemed she had to focus and bind all her energies on what would happen there, on that floor, Dr. Marlborough's floor, though it was evident that nothing she could think or feel beforehand would alter the results of what he did there. Anyway, doing that work of anxious pressing on futurity seemed to make it impossible to carry forward a great and messy event at the same time, to say nothing of the awful bad omen if she dropped the ball and the party failed; so she gave it up.

"Throw me in! Throw me!"

"Throw? *Throw?*" She lifted shrieking Sam under the arms and hauled off as though to toss her a mile; waved her in the pile's direction, then backed off and began again. The anticipation was what made you laugh so helplessly: Rosie had learned that watching Mike toss his daughter in the air. Higher, Daddy.

Mike, when she told him the party was off, was relieved. That stuff's not funny, he said. What stuff? Halloween, he said; witches and ghosts. Be careful what you play around with; you don't know what you'll attract. Rosie laughed, and asked if he was serious, and he hadn't answered, only kept a minatory silence that suggested he could say a lot if he chose to: another Mike trick Rosie was familiar with.

"Whee!" She dropped Sam gently after all, into the middle of the pile. "Okay?"

"Now cover me," Sam said, and lay back; Rosie could smell as through her daughter's nostrils the smell of the leaves, hear through her ears the dry crackle of their crushing. You never forget. When she had first come back to the Faraway Hills and to Arcady after her years in the Midwest, it was fall; Boney was ill then and using a rented wheelchair, and Rosie raked, then as now to have an occupation. He watched her for a time toss the leaves like salad. That's one thing I'll never do again, he said. His head on its long turtle's neck reached toward her, toward the leaves and the day. I wish I'd done it more, he said.

Oh I don't know, she'd replied; you do it once, you've done it a hundred times, right?

I wish I'd done it more, he only said. I wish I'd done everything more. Leaning forward in his chair, his face as though pressed against a glass beyond which the world was taking place, his mouth open a little in grief or yearning or maybe just unable to breathe easily. *He just loves life,* his old housekeeper Mrs. Pisky used to say.

The tumulus was high now over Sam; Rosie couldn't discern even her outline beneath the heap.

"Okay," Rosie said. "Okay? Deep enough?"

Rosie waited. No leaf stirred.

"Okay Sam?"

No answer.

She felt a violent black rush to her heart, and plunged her arms within the leaves; she pushed them aside, they had become heavy as gold; Sam's exhumed face was still. The day in an instant ceased also to stir, and went cold. Rosie took hold of Sam's coat, full of Sam's heaviness, but not, she knew it, of Sam.

"Sam!" Rosie bellowed, a voice she had never used or heard before, drawn from somewhere down inside, loud enough to call her daughter back. She pulled her up, and Sam's head fell heedless to her shoulder. How long was it— Rosie thought later it was only a second or two or three, but the seconds had stopped falling away—till Sam's eyes opened, and she smiled.

"Oh Christ, Sam," her mother said. "Oh Sam, how can you do that. Don't you know."

"I was being dead," Sam said. Taking handfuls of her mother's hair and arranging them to her liking. "I was dead. But now I'm alive again."


Up on Mount Whirligig the leaves were turning decisively even while others in the Faraways hesitated; the mountain's heights occupied a sort of climatic microzone of their own, always colder than elsewhere, its flowers blooming later and more briefly, its storms more severe; when you drive up it on a cold rainy night the rain will predictably turn, just past Shadowland, to sleet, then snow.

Quieter at The Woods this morning, the staff tidying up, packing their papers, putting their personal coffee mugs and stuffed animals and snapshots into knapsacks and totes. One therapist at her desk, in tears, inconsolable, but why? Her door closes. Elsewhere a maintenance crew is emptying drains and sealing attics; but in the spring there will be burst pipes and squirrels' nests to deal with. Or worse.

"Our work done?" said Ray Honeybeare. "Oh no not for a long time. We haven't hardly begun."

"I only meant here," said Mike Mucho. "Just with the closing and all."

"Yes. Well I'm sorry about that, and we'll push forward with a solution. Because there is so much sickness and suffering, and we have so much help to give. We haven't hardly begun. That's my opinion."

Ray had a way of stating that something was his opinion which suggested— made clear, actually—that he didn't think it was just his opinion. This irritated or excited Mike Mucho, made him want to challenge whatever it was, the supposed opinion, and at the same time afraid to.

"Well, Ray," he said.

"I think of the children now," Ray said. "You're treating a lot of young people here."

"Well, we have been."

"And you know that it's the parents who are at the root of these kids' troubles."

"Yes," Mike said. "The early experiences, yes."

"Often they can't remember, though, isn't that right, not without a lot of effort on our part, a lot of inquiry. They can't remember."

"Repression," Mike said, no Freudian himself, his early training had been behaviorist; he knew the concepts though, the language, which Ray seemed often enough never to have heard of.

"It goes so far back and so deep," Ray said. "You see, parents might not realize it, but it's their behavior that invites these possessors in."

Mike neither nodded nor answered.

"Sexual behavior, blasphemy, you know the kind of thing I mean," Ray said. "Even if they aren't consciously worshipping the devil, I mean assenting to him, these parents are caught up in these behaviors, and it comes to the same thing. A tacit pact. And the children are the ones to suffer. All across this land. The boys and girls know nothing of it, and maybe won't know until one day someone calls on those devils within them. I think we're raising up an awful harvest now, and in ten–twenty years we're going to start reaping; the devils invited in now by these parents are going to start to speak, though they've kept silent all those years. And those kids are going to start to remember what was done to them. We're going to see terrible things then, hear terrible things said. We are going to find that a generation of devils was laid in the souls of our children like the eggs of some kind of insect."

He smiled at Mike, and Mike lowered his eyes and smiled too; he knew Ray could sense his ambivalence, this feeling within him that resembled shyness or embarrassment, a not exactly unpleasant feeling.

"These therapists with their therapies made out of doubts and hesitations," Ray said. "They say that sickness is a matter of *belief*. And cure is a matter of *trust*. A matter of *changing* beliefs by giving people something new to believe in. But I say that it's not a matter of beliefs, a matter of who you trust. I say it's a matter of *fact*."

"I see what you mean," Mike said lamely. He wished he were not sitting quite so close to Ray, who liked to sit very close to the person he talked to, for reasons Mike could guess, for reasons he had even been taught about; in his chair, so close to Ray's that his knees were almost touching Ray's knees, he felt giddy, as though he might burst into helpless laughter, like a baby tickled; or weep.

"Now it's a funny thing, isn't it?" Ray said. "If you say something's a matter of beliefs, a matter of trust, well that shouldn't be so hard to change. What are beliefs? Are they real? No, they're artifacts of the mind. They have no real existence. They could change easily, like movie pictures."

"Well the theory is," said Mike.

"So what surprises me," Honeybeare said, and put his hand over Mike's, "is that *they* say it's just a matter of wrong belief—like believing a magician can saw a woman in half, you can show it not to be so, by exposing the illusion. But *they* can't make changes. Not in the hard cases. *We* say it's a matter of fact, that the thing that's wrong is something real in them that has to be got out: and we can do what we say. We can help."

"Yes."

"Right here, maybe, we'll be dealing with them," Ray said, his eyes not having left Mike, nor his smile altered. "It might be you dismissing them, Mike. I'll be lying asleep by then. You'll be seeing them go smoking out every window and chimney of this place."

"Ray, it's so easy for you to say these things."

"Mike," Ray said. "You've seen it."

He had. On that September night when the wind had blown so furiously. He had seen Ray take a woman who was having a bad episode, very bad, and speak—not to her but to some being inside her; and he had seen the thing, the problem, abandon her instantly, and her face soften as though she took off a constricting mask, and her eyes awaken, astonished and grateful. No denying what he had seen. "Yes," he said.

"Not because of any power I have."

"No."

"No. Because of the power of the Holy Spirit in me. Because of the Name I can invoke."

"Yes."

"Because I'm possessed too. You see?" He grinned at Mike, and the multitude of his wrinkles radiated out across his face, running through his cheeks as through a dry topography. "I'm possessed. I am not my own."

"Yes."

"That's the power you're offered, Mike. Not for any unimportant reason. Not for any selfish reason."

"Yes."

It had been all laid before him. Mike felt the wonderment of it, and felt also Ray's impatience with him, or maybe it wasn't impatience, his eagerness. He had only to cease wondering at it, and move.

Ray waited. Everything waited.

"Do you want this, Mike? You can have this. Do you accept this?"

"Yes," Mike said. And time bifurcated. "Yes." Easy, it was easy. Holding Ray Honeybeare's hands, Mike bent his head as though to food, and hungrily ate. "Yes," he said again.

"Yes," Ray said; and after a moment, not releasing Mike's hand, but leaning back in his chair minutely, he said: "Now this little girl of yours, Mike. Do you want to talk a little about her?"


"I just wish you had a damn phone," Rosie said to Spofford. He was calling her from a pay phone near the job site, his lunch hour; checking in with her, as he did faithfully but irregularly, so that she expected and waited for his calls more than she would have if he had called every day at ten two and four. What Mike called *intermittent reinforcement* when in psych lab he'd used it on white rats with twitching baffled noses. She knew Spofford wasn't calculating the effect.

"No I'm glad," she said. Sam in the great double drawing room watched her mother talking. Saw her mother cover her eyes and turn her face away.

Sam thought of Boney: seeing her mother in tears brought Boney to her mind, when her mother had wept, talking on the phone about Boney. And thinking of Boney directed her eyes to a sort of deep-bellied commode that stood between the tall windows, drawers and doors that didn't open, with pictures of fruit and musical instruments on them made of wood of different colors, and at the top of it, as though resting there but really part of it and stuck on, a little box like a jewelry box with doors of its own. Sam slid from the leather sofa to the rug, and (seeing her mother still turned away) crossed to an armchair of cut plush in another corner.

"I know," she heard her mother say. "I know. It's just. You're going to be gone."

Sam pushed the armchair's hassock away, steering it toward the plump and comical commode. And up against its side. It was a long time ago that she had learned she could do this, before she had begun to take medicine; she had never told her mother, or anyone else, how she had first learned the secret of the casket atop the commode.

"I never would," she heard her mother say. "Never. You know that."

She climbed the hassock, holding herself gently against the smooth cold wood of the commode; her sock feet clung unsteadily to the slippery plush of the hassock, her legs knew it might slide away backwards beneath her and let her fall, but she had the key in her fingers now, the filigree of its handle matching the filigree of the lockplate. Turned it, one way, the other. The little door opened.

There was a feeling Sam was beginning to recognize when it came, though not yet to remember between times, that preceded her jumps. A flavor in the air and in her breathing in and breathing out that she would one day be able to name to people of her kind, who would instantly say *Oh yes right sure* but which no one else, not even her mother, would ever recognize; one day she would describe it by saying, *As though I had grown as huge as huge as the universe, and my hand was as far away as a planet* (her hand that now was taking out from within the dark den where it lived the worn velvet bag with the solid weight inside it) *and everything in the universe no matter how far was close to me and yet as far away as possible*: that was the feeling, but not the flavor of the feeling, the flavor that she tasted now.

"She's right around," her mother said. "You can talk to her."

Sam climbed down and went to the far side of the commode, where she was hidden from the view of her mother in the hall, and upturned the bag into her lap. She remembered how once she had spilled a kitten from a stocking cap into which it had crawled; this felt the same, a living thing struggling the wrong way to get out, then revealed, happy, happy to be out.

It was a globe of gray-brown quartz, nearly flawless but with a run of bubbles pointing to a tiny starburst not quite in its center, scar of a wound it took in its childhood, when it was growing, millennia ago. She saw it first the night of the day Boney was put in the ground, when she had stayed here all day long with Mrs. Pisky, not allowed to go to the church or to the cemetery to see him put in, even though Boney was her friend too. She had crept down the stairs unheard and from the landing saw her mother take from the little hiding-box this bag, and let fall into her hand this ball, and look at it a long time in the dimness of the nighttime room.

Sam took it out herself not long after that, and looked into it as her mother had, and had been interested and unsurprised by what she saw there. And not long after that she had her first jump: she called them jumps because she seemed to jump in no time at all from where she was when it began to where she was when it was over (in her mother's arms, on the floor, in another room).

She lifted it now in her two hands. A planet, revolving at an immense distance from her; but her head was immense too, and her hands immense, so it was no farther from her than ever; but at the same time it was across the universe. She looked into it.

"My ode house," she said aloud.

She thought she might jump now. Within the globe it was as it always was, that place, changeless, her old house. No it was not the same, it had changed: somebody looked out at her.

"Sam?" her mother called. "Sam?"

Who was it? Who looked out? She brought her face closer to the ball, her eyes crossing and the flavor of hugeness thick in her throat; but the closer she drew the smaller the place grew. Who stirred in that room?

"Come out," she said. "Come out."

# 10

-I am out, said Doctor John Dee. It is you must come out.

But the girl in the globe of quartz he held, golden-haired child, glimmered and went away as though she heard her name called from behind her; went away without saying more, returning Doctor Dee to the day and this room, from which he had momentarily been snatched when he had picked up the ball and looked into it. He held it up on the tips of his fingers for some time, but it was empty.

—Gone, he whispered.

It was in this stone of gray quartz that a spirit had first appeared in his house: one of the spiritual creatures whom John Dee had long courted and prayed to be visited by, whom for years he tried fruitlessly to attract with his glasses, rings and mirrors, as a beeman attracts bees with his honey pots; not succeeding till he placed this globe before young Edward Kelley and asked what he could see there.

That first one was, or appeared to be, a fat baby, a girl with golden eyes, bearing a new clear stone in her own hands, like a child's toy. So Edward Kelley had described her, who alone could see her. Then for a time she did not come again; when she next appeared she had grown up by years, though but months had passed, and was a child of seven. She had come forth and walked about, here in this room (still only Kelley had seen her) going among the books and papers piled here and there, patting them as she passed, "in a gown of Sey, changeable green and red, with a train," Kelley said, and John Dee wrote it down; "her Hair rowled up before and hanging down very long behind." In this very room, when he had lived here at peace and happily. John Dee felt the stab of her absence: as though she had indeed spent her girlhood here, a child of his flesh, playing with them.

He put down the vacant gray globe. It had perhaps retained only a last brief power, latent and slumbering here while he travelled and labored across the seas;

when he found it and picked it up again, it expended the little life remaining in it, the glimpse of her it had retained. If indeed it had been her.

*Come out* the child had said to him. Then no more.

When he and Edward Kelley had skryed here, he had seen nothing in the glass: he had merely written down what Kelley alone saw. And now, when he had sight, when he could apprehend them himself, they fled from him, and his stones lost their power one by one.

Inside her new, clear glass she had gone with them on their travels. And far away in Prague she had grown to womanhood. From babe to woman in—in how long? John Dee looked back over the interval of time and could not calculate it; it had not been long but it appeared a lifetime. Five years? Fifteen eighty-six he had left this place. Now it was 1592. But six years. Not long: no matter that in those years the world had ended, and begun again.

She had said to them: Do not quail, do not be afraid, give all that you have and when you have given all, more will be asked of you. And he had not quailed. When she (Madimi she named herself) had ordered him to abandon his house and his country and become a wanderer, all his family too, he had meekly, quickly packed his trunks and departed in the night as though the bailiffs were after him. She had promised the Polish prince Albert Laski relief from his debts and his great troubles, and Dee had assured the prince that the spirits attached to the glass could do what they promised, and yet they had done nothing for him; in Poland John Dee had ventured all the credit of his years of study and his standing with the learned men of Europe, and won an audience with the Polish king Stephan, great good man, so the spirits could speak to him, and like half-trained dogs they had refused to come forth and do their tricks.

She had promised him they would reveal to him what no man had ever known, or what all men had once known and all had forgotten: what the angels had shown to Adam in Paradise before they sent him out, the knowledge whose return to men would signal the ending of the world, and its beginning anew.

Had she done so? Perhaps. What he had learned might be what she promised him, wisdom precious above price; or it might be a thing all men knew, a saw; or a jest, or a child's quibble.

She also promised she would teach them to make gold, which was all that Edward Kelley ever wanted from the spirits he spoke to; and in Prague she did it. In the house of the Emperor's physician Dr. Hajek, Taddeus Hagecius, in Golden Lane: largest house of that row of houses clinging to the lip of the Stag's Moat, tiny houses with great chimneys, where gold was worked, or assayed, or forged: made or claimed to have been made.

And where else in Christendom was it as likely gold might be made as in Prague? For matter is a palace, the shut palace of a king, who sits within stolid and inflexible; into that small palace the worker makes his dangerous journey, to awaken that king, vivify him, cause him to be fruitful, multiply; to become his own wife, and bear himself a son. Edward Kelley thought that this action took place not only in the athenor of the alchemists, but continuously in the world all the time, in the toils of the smallest indivisibles, in their tiny shut palaces:

matter transforming as black kings divided themselves, generated sons through their chaste passionate intercourse with themselves, allowed their sons to die, be buried, rot, turn to dust, then revive, live, triumph. Maybe this drama went on, in all its grieving and thanksgivings, right through the ladder of creation, through the plants (poor John Barleycorn, son of the grain, slain every year that his own sons may live) and the animals up to the life of the celestial powers and the planets, up to God Himself, and His Son, self-generated. Who could say that God in His heaven did not suffer every pain and grief that His Son underwent, that He did not also die the death with him, enjoy the rebirth too, the wild elation, alive, alive again? Were they not the one God? Every year, every Holy Week. Every day, in the Mass.

And of this action the city on the River Moldau or Vltava was the *imago* or emblem.

Up in his vast castle on the hill above the silted river the black-clothed Emperor Rudolf had immured himself, King Saturn on his throne; around him in his galleries and closets and *Kunstkammern* was the rest of the world in small, earth air fire and water: precious stones bearing the fires of distant planets in their tiny bodies; waterworks and clepsydras, pneumatic statues, hubble-bubbles that sang; the skins of birds and animals and fish, all in their orders and ranks; monsters too, snails found with jewels embedded in their shells or the names of saints or demons written on them, the little skin of the bear that a Jewish woman of Prague once gave birth to, which "ran around the room and scratched itself behind the ear and died," says the chronicler. And there were representations too of all these things and all other things that could be pictured, in paintings, in albums of drawings, on coins, molded in colored wax or blown in glass—glass roses, one of every kind, their leaves and flowers as perfect as summer's roses, only deathless—and there were catalogues of all these representations, and the covers of the catalogues and the cabinets in which they were kept were covered and cut and molded and painted with further representations. Rudolf loved tiny things, worlds sculpted on cherrystones, clockwork insects, the life inside diamonds.

The Emperor had his own furnace, at which he labored over the Work by himself in blackened gloves and apron while his counsellors shook their heads over him; and on the table in the Emperor's bedroom, at the heart of the great castle from which he issued less and less frequently, lay the book of John Dee's called *Monas hieroglyphica,* explicating the sign for the same process or action:

And on one summer's day in 1586, while the Emperor stared at the seal, and the clocks in his chamber ticked away, counting out the new endless-ribbon style of time, John Dee and Edward Kelley made gold. Using a "powder of projection" that Kelley had carried for years, and following the angelic instructions they had received. They alone, among all those on that street of that city who spent their lives and fortunes attempting it. It was but a minim or two in the vessel's bottom, not a *thaler's* worth, but it was gold that had not existed in the world before; it shone up at them, a little twisted embryo, sophic, wonderful.

Too small though; fruitless little mass, sterile, unable to generate more, a masturbator's vain squib. What was wrong?

Maybe this kingdom was, after all, a sterile one; or this old earth was, or this age. This Emperor who never married, though his counsellors begged him; no heirs, no legitimate bed. He had produced children, though, many of them, with his many concubines.

Then maybe it was Kelley who was the sterile one.

He begged the spirits and Madimi to free him from these hard duties, if this was to be the upshot; and she refused him. *Not for a short time have I yoked you two together.* When he wept, beating his fists on the faldstool's lip in impotent child's resentment, she took him by the collar (a grown woman now, imperious in her gown of red and white, her breasts bare, her skirt parted) and stilled him. *Whatever you want I have in my gift. Will you stop now, when the hart is fainting before you and the dogs are belling and the scent of blood is on the air? Come for me, for I will welcome you, I promise you, as I ever have. As I ever have.*

John Dee kneeling before the glass had bowed his head, abashed; but Edward in her grip laughed aloud gleeful and terrified, like a child snatched up by a laughing mighty captain astride a great horse, to ride along with him.

John Dee remembered how he had laughed.

Ah Christ Jesus forgive me that I loved her, John Dee whispered to the empty globe in his study in his ransacked house in England. Forgive me, Jane, that I loved them both. And do so still.

He had given all he had, and got much, and given all that too: and he was here again where he began.

He sat down amid the litter of papers and broken-backed books. He could hear Jane his wife, weeping, in the farther end of the house, coming on fresh villainies. Those who had broken into his house to destroy his works and smash his tools (sparing this glass but not his great astronomical staff, his sphere of the heavens, his stores of medicines and distillations, he had not reckoned it all up yet) had not shut the doors behind them when they departed, and the thieves who then came in stole his spoons and cups and even the crucifix from over the door.

She had told him his house would be safe in his absence, and she had not been able to protect it, not against her enemies, nor against his.

His enemies, his neighbors. It was his neighbors who in his absence had invaded his house and broken his instruments and despoiled his books: they had convinced themselves, as foolish unlearned people could do, that because he studied deep matters and the stars he served the Devil, and conjured.

Nor was it only the vulgar who thought in this way. The learned too saw damned spirits everywhere now; mad old women who muttered or cursed their neighbors for their unkindness were driven away from home or imprisoned and put to torture for being the Devil's servants. Old Mother Godefroy, who lived near the stile by Richmond field, from whom John Dee had bought his herbs and simples—she was gone now, her small house fallen in, and when Doctor Dee asked after her, the Mortlake townspeople looked away, and said they knew nothing. She had kept a cat, and had a blind eye: it was enough.

The Queen herself, once his friend, whom he had taught, to whom he had opened mysteries: she could not now openly support her old physician and friend. Though her counsellors had sent him letters privily, in Prague and Trebona, it was unwise for a monarch in these times to be seen to favor one who might later be shown, or be believed, to have sold himself to the Enemy.

And John Dee, who had so often protested his innocence and the whiteness of his enterprises, who had never knelt before a stone—this one or any one—without invoking the sacred Name of Christ Crucified, who had wanted knowledge of God's creation only to increase thereby among men the glory of the Creator: John Dee did not any longer himself know if the spirits he had spoken to, whom he had loved and served as he had no human master, were wicked damned ones, or not.

# 11

W *ere wicked damned ones, or not.*

The words were the last ones typed on a sheet of yellow copy paper, which lay atop a pile of other, similar sheets. The pile (a book, a novel) rose from the varnished plywood surface which the author of them had used as a desk, built in below the casement windows that looked out on his garden. The garden, which he had labored over as much as he had over any of his books, was neglected now and brown. Across the bottom of the yellow sheet, below the last words, were three hard-struck asterisks, indicating a chapter's end. The author, or rather the author's ghost (for the author was dead) could remember nothing at all of the book except what was on the page before him, which he could not turn, and which he stared at without satisfaction until there came the sound of a key turned in the lock of the back door, the only sound made in the house that morning; and with that he evanesced.

Pierce Moffett entering the cryptlike space of Fellowes Kraft's library or sitting room was brisk and businesslike, as he had not been when first he had been admitted here, filled with apprehensive wonder then and not knowing what he would see. Now he knew the place, in all weathers too; the mildew he breathed in was familiar, and he sought for something to prop a window open with—this walking stick, he guessed that's what it was, dog-headed and worn smooth. Done. The yellowed lace curtain lifted on a breath of October air. Piles of books rose from the dusty rug of the living room; the rifled shelves looked down upon him and the open drawers gaped.

He felt, as he stood there, something of the grave robber's awe and some regret too at the upset he had wreaked. But he should not have; this is the best way, sometimes, to free the tenacious ghost of an old bachelor from his earthly entanglements. When alive he will often allow stuff to pile up untouched, having no reason particularly to disturb the accumulating papers and unheeded mail, or to change the resting places of his ancestors' things which he's acquired, no reason particularly to examine them either, no one to show them to; and so parts of his own disintegrating self remain behind after death, caught like dust or must in them.

So pull it all out, fill plastic bags with the worn shoes he had no reason to throw away, there being plenty of room in these closets; bang the old books together like erasers after school and watch the dust fly. You do him a favor: with every scrapbook opened, every ancient pile shifted, a little more of him is loosened, and gets away. Look, one pamphlet has lain here athwart another on this shelf untouched for so long that it has actually left a dark shadow on the one below.

What is it? Pierce lifted it. Not a pamphlet actually but a copy of Marlowe's *Doctor Faustus,* one of those yellow playbooks put out by Samuel French, marked up as though in preparation for a production, in what Pierce had come to recognize as Kraft's own spidery hand.

Funny.

He replaced it more or less where it had lain.

Pierce first came to this house in June, with Rosie Rasmussen. Her family foundation supported Kraft in his last years, and he left his house and papers to it, his (worthless) copyrights too. At Rosie's suggestion, Boney Rasmussen hired Pierce to go through the house and catalogue Kraft's literary remains, assess the worth of the books and papers, and even that limited task opened up odd corners of Kraft's life. Once opening a book from the shelf (a life of Sir Thomas Gresham) he found it to be concealing about five hundred dollars in bills. Tucked away there in some moment of paranoia maybe, a lot more money then than now. He counted it all, and informed his superior, who was Rosie Rasmussen.

"Take it," she said. "We'll split it."

"Really?"

"Sure. Finders keepers."

"No one the wiser," Pierce said.

"Absolutely."

It was not all that Pierce would take from the dead man.

On his very first visit to the house, in Kraft's little office, Pierce discovered on Kraft's desk a long typescript, corrected in dim pencil. No one, until Pierce came upon it, had known that Kraft was at work on a final novel when he died; it had been years since he'd written anything. And yet here it was, hundreds of pages, at first glance seeming nearly complete, a historical fantasia or mystic history, Renaissance and wars of religion, angels and other powers. And right then he sat to read it.

*Once, the world was not as it has since become. It had a different history and a different future, and even the laws that governed it were different from the ones we know.* So the pale pages began, without title or preface.

Once, the world was not as it has since become. Nor in the future will it be as it is now. In these truisms Pierce had seen his own book completed; all that remained was to write it.

Though superstitious about moving it from the house, Pierce had nevertheless agreed with Rosie that the typescript ought to be taken away, and photocopied, and then stored somewhere safe. He had already taken from the shelves and cases here and in Kraft's tiny office a selection of what he estimated were the most valuable of Kraft's books, and stowed them in sturdy boxes, to bring them to Arcady to be kept there. For Kraft's house was to be shut up for the winter, and they should not be left here with the mice and moths and mildew (though they had, some of them, survived centuries of such vicissitudes). And this work or thing of Kraft's too, which Pierce now perused again before inserting into its box.

> Peripatetic sages and wonder-workers were everywhere in those years, moving restlessly from capital to capital, crossing paths with one another in university hostels or city taverns, where they acknowledged one another's books or fame in the tongue they shared, Latin, however weird or comical one's national accent made it in the other's ears. As vagabonds will trade news about where a day's work can be had, or a night's lodging, they exchanged news of courts that might be receptive to or at least not scandalized by studies such as theirs, princes who might take them in, protect them, at least for a while.
>
> Paracelsus was one, who said that the Philosopher must study the *codex Naturæ*, the Book of Nature, in just this way, on foot, one country one page; he kept a familiar spirit in the pommel of his sword. Cornelius Agrippa too, moving restlessly across Europe with his black dog, pursued by rumor and suspicion. A little later Giordano Bruno, travelling from Naples to Rome, to Genoa, Geneva, Paris, London, teaching the three keys to power, Love, Memory, and Mathesis. In London Bruno would come upon John Dee, just as Dee was to set off on his own wanderings with his skryer and his angel band; and then Bruno (on his way to Italy and death) would meet Dee again in Prague, the golden city that drew them both, and others too. *Ave, fratre.*
>
> There had, of course, long been wandering scholars, itinerant doctors, learned pilgrims, hunted necromancers; but now they began to feel themselves to be something more than wanderers. The idea came to them (to each of them separately or to many at once, passed on then to others) that perhaps together they were—what? A Brotherhood; a League; a College. Not one that any of them had founded or set in motion, not at least in this age; if anyone had begun it, it was wandering Hermes, in Ægypt long ago.

This idea too Pierce had intended for his own book, this legend like the Black Legend of the paranoids, only white not black: a league of secret helpers, known only to one another, or not even to one another, a golden underground of benefactors with a history of its own, doctors, healers, eminences and nobodies working to defeat the world's dark lords—many of whom the world has not known either. Then vanishing or sinking again out of sight and mind when the new age has fully flowered; continuing underground, a knotted thread, almost dropped, never quite.

Ægypt. When Pierce had himself been one of that company (eleven years old, in Kentucky) he believed that he had himself made it all up. It was a game he had taught to his cousins, a club for them to belong to, an allegiance to swear. He had been amazed then as a grown-up, a historian, to learn he had not made it up, no not at all. Nor had Kraft.

> For thus it is in the passage times, times such as they began to
> understand they were living in. In those times we come to understand
> our membership in certain long-established—in fact horribly ancient—
> groups, unions, brotherhoods or armies, of whose existence we had not
> before been aware. Indeed our coming to understand that we are brothers
> or comrades in them is not different from our sudden discovery that they
> exist: an excitement, a euphoria, a fear even of what we are about to be
> called upon to do, or perhaps fail to do.

Soon after Pierce discovered it, Boney Rasmussen had suggested that Pierce himself might finish this book of Kraft's: add the remaining touches, bring it to an end, see it through the press. Had even pressed him, on several occasions, and named a fee, not small either.

No no. A novel was not within his powers, not this one certainly; it was a lot less finished anyway than it had at first seemed to be, full of incomplete chapters and contradictions (two different versions, for instance, in Part Two and Part Three, of how John Dee parted from his little tutelary spirit Madimi) and maybe after all it had been left unfinished for a reason, maybe it was unwritable, one of those books whose scheme is able to be described but that cannot be rendered, like books read or written in dreams. No.

> There is war in Heaven, the angel Madimi told John Dee, speaking from
> within the globe of moleskin-colored quartz where she was housed; a war
> of all against all. If you are not of one party they will make you of
> another; whom you are not for, you are against.

That globe, the "globe of moleskin-colored quartz," was that the same globe or crystal ball, Pierce wondered, that Sandy Kraft himself (everyone called him Sandy) had once given to Boney Rasmussen, telling him that it really was one that the English magician John Dee had used? That stone or globe was still at Arcady, Boney Rasmussen's house, supposedly; Rosie had told him that, and promised to show it to him.

Of course it might just as easily have been acquired by Kraft at the local Junk-tiques Barn, or maybe found lying around right here in his own house, here where so much else of doubtful provenance was collected, and then placed carefully in his last book to glow with the glamour he assured Boney it once had, really had, the pedigree established.

What did Kraft actually believe? Also at Arcady lay a mass of letters that Kraft had written to Boney and others over the years, from Prague, from Paris, from Glastonbury, from Vienna, letters which Boney had been poring over right up to the day of his death; in them, Boney was sure, Kraft hinted at or even confessed to some actual occult discovery of which his last book was merely the mask or wrapping. Pierce thought it was likelier to be the other way around, that Kraft's adventures in the Old World and other realms were like his crystal ball, constructed to give weight or weightlessness to his fiction, make it worth paying for by sad old Boney, who was looking for more than fiction. Tease him with hopeless hopes. *Mon Empereur* Kraft used to call him. And sent him news from Prague about how the search was going.

That patronage too was extending to Pierce now that Boney was as dead as Kraft. Rosie Rasmussen had told him that if he wanted it there was a further grant waiting for him from the Rasmussen Foundation, a research grant, that would take him to Europe in search of.

What? Life everlasting; the Ægyptian medicine that the old new brotherhood passed down from age to age, the one that Rudolf sought, that he died for lack of. Something, the one and only thing maybe, that had not lost its former efficacy, growing maybe even more potent on its journey down through the centuries into a colder age than the one it had been born in. Now able to be found again in the twilight, morning or evening, of the world.

Funny. Funny funny funny. Pierce felt steal over him in the little room a species of dread, a feeling not wholly different from the wonder that had filled him the first time he had come into it. The book, the book's notes, Kraft's old novels he had read once, these old books he had taken from Kraft's shelves, the letters on Boney's desk, the money in the bank awaiting him, seemed for a moment to be items in a single list, compiled deliberately over the years—one of those huge and lengthy black-magic spells that can only be got out of by reversing them, step by step.

Put it back then, cover it again, bind the box with a pair of red rubber bands that Kraft's desk afforded; place it in the liquor carton with the rest.

Out of the house and across the drifting and ungathered leaves of the lawn. The load of old books was damn heavy, and heaviest of all, resistant perhaps, tugging him backwards toward its resting place, was the typescript. Scotty—Fellowes Kraft's malamute-Lab mutt, who was buried there in the swale—relaxed at last as it passed by him in Pierce's arms; his great breast fell in and eased as though in a sigh, his duties to watch and ward now done at last, all done.

# 12

A l-Kindi—the great Arabian philosopher whose work circulated in Latin in Europe and was known to every well-read person— showed how every entity in the universe emitted radiation, or rays: *radii*. Not only the stars and the planets and the denizens of the heavens but the four elements too, and everything made of them, which meant everything there was. The rays proceeding from each existent thing reached to the ends of the universe, the rays of the sun and the feeble rays of every stone and leaf and water drop, every wave forming on the sea's incoming edge, every fleck of spume thrown up by those waves as they curl and fall. All these rays intersected in all directions with the rays produced by all other things in a shifting geometry of mutual influence that made everything the way it was, caused it to continue or to change.

Everything. Pluck a dandelion and in its death you tore a small, an infinitesimal hole in the fabric of universal radiation, a hole resolved almost as soon as it was made—but in that instant an answering hole opened in the heart of the sun; on the Libyan desert a sleeping lion might open his eye and look up at his Father Sun, then sleep again; no harm done. But when a butterfly alighting on a flower in the Antipodes moved its wings the rays produced extended out from it to intersect with the rays produced by other things, and those deflected rays with the rays of still other things, until eventually by multiplication of effects those collisions produced a hurricane in Thule.

In that world there was no chance: if the strength and angle of every ray could have been charted, and its intersection with every other ray predicted, the future could have been known precisely: but that was impossible, the complexity of the world was so great that its perfectly logical and regular production of effects, though wholly determined, might just as well have been due to chance.

Should this sound too much like the world that has (quite suddenly) come into being in our time, yours and mine, it should be remembered that al-Kindi also knew that feelings produced rays—the strong feelings of gods, dæmons, and human persons, love sorrow hate rage desire: these rays too were able to bring about effects, to reach the hearts of others and alter them. Words too, sounds, the called names of things, the *real* names: oldest magic there is almost, words called or sung aloud. The universe was a part-song for an infinite number of voices, things forever speaking their own names and hearing their names and the names of other things called, and responding. Listen. *Vox es, prætereaque nihil:* you are a voice, nothing more.

Propagated spherically outward from Baghdad in the ninth century, al-Kindi's rays reached down through time as well as out into space, passing through collections of Arabian and Jewish magical lore, refracting and reflecting, eventually reaching Europe, collecting in Latin magical Black Books that smelled excitingly of the infidel, attracting restless souls seeking novelties. *'Tis Magic, Magic that has ravish'd mee.* At length the rays reached the cell of a young Dominican monk named Giordano Bruno in the sixteenth century, by way of a crude manual of magic practices called *Picatrix,* written first in Arabic and translated into Latin.

Men could do wonders, said *Picatrix,* not through the power of the Devil, as the ignorant believed, but through their knowledge of the rays: the chains of being running down from the stars to the star-formed human spirit and back again, up to the stars themselves, thence to the angels who moved the stars, thence to God Himself. That's what the Ægyptians had known, what they had been taught by *Mercurio Egizio sapientissimo:* but their religion was destroyed by the impious, who called them idolators. Idolators! Well if they were, Bruno was too. And from the *Picatrix* Fra' Giordano learned the words to say, the images to cut, that would draw the heavens' strong rays into his own fast-growing soul.

The greatest magician was Hermes, said the *Picatrix;* not the god himself (from whom all magic derives) but the Thrice-great avatar of the god, who was once king in Ægypt. Hermes Thrice-great founded a city named Adocentyn in the east of that country, wherein he built a four-gated castle; over the gates he placed four images, an Eagle, a Bull, a Lion and a Dog, and these images he caused to speak or seem to speak, and question those who came to enter. Inside the castle was a temple of the Sun; inside that, a sanctuary; inside that, Hermes himself, though no one could see him. Above the temple in the center of the castle rose a tower thirty cubits high, and atop the tower a lighthouse, and atop the lighthouse a lamp that changed its color every day for seven days, and whose rays illuminated the city and its walls, whereon were carved by Hermes' art a thousand images, by whose virtues the inhabitants were made both good and happy.

That city is gone, though it will be restored when the old gods return; when we have learned to summon them again.

So *Picatrix* declared.

By the time Bruno fled his monastery and Italy (the Roman Inquisition had wanted to talk with him about his philosophical interests), he knew *Picatrix* by heart, and knew that there was in him a nature like that of the stars, and in the stars a voice like his own, that he might hear. He had read the works of Hermes himself, in the Pope's library where he had been allowed for a time to study. He knew how the wise man might influence and even compel the imaginations of others—of gods and *dæmones* perhaps but certainly of his fellow humans, causing them to see what they do not see, hear what cannot be heard.

In his student days Frater Iordanus had liked to pester his teachers with unanswerable questions. If God one day decreed that everything in the universe was all at once to double in size, everything, including ourselves, then would we be able to tell? And he was given no answer, except that God's power cannot be constrained, or that God has better things to do with his omnipotence.

But Giordano Bruno came to know that yes, you could tell.

When he looked back to see the young man who had fled Rome with a purse of coins and his Dominican habit stuffed into a bag, he seemed to himself to be tiny—not only having shrunk with distance but a small thing, too small to contain all that he had since come to contain. He had crossed the Alps, growing: he thought now that he could recross those Alps by stepping over them, and brushing their snows from the hem of his gown, except for the fact that as large as Giordano Bruno had grown, the world and the skies had kept pace; as he had grown and travelled, they had receded from him into further, into endless distance.

Copernicus the Pole had shown that the Sun was the center around which the Earth and the Moon circled, and it was clear to Bruno—though the Pole had not shown or claimed it—that if the Earth and the planets moved around the Sun as their center, then the Earth was a planet itself—a star, like the others that circled the Sun, great beings with natures of their own. There were no crystalline planetary spheres carrying them, as Aristotle held, or if there had been once there were no more; now they were held to their courses around the Sun by Eros alone. The Eighth Sphere shattered, and the stars once stuck or glued or knotted or painted on it flew apart, out to infinity.

And if that revolution raged in heaven, it raged in Giordano Bruno's nature too. If the stars were moving to new places, then the same stars must move in the heavens within. A man who knew that might interfere on his own behalf, and make the outcome what he chose; he might expel from heaven (inside, outside, it mattered not where you started) the old collection of vices, weaknesses, luxuries and sins the old gods had allowed to populate heaven, and install in their places the strengths, wisdoms, knowledges that were their opposites and cognates, along with new images of new animals and things to represent them.

So in March of 1584, with sweet airs off the River Thames reaching even the little garret where Bruno wrote, its mullioned window open to the world, Bruno called a congress of the gods (writing as fast as he could, but not as fast as he could think).

He called Apollo and Diana (Sol and Luna, that is) and Venus, Mars, Mercury and Saturn, the star-gods from whom we get our natures. And of course father Jove, with Minerva his Wisdom, and Juno his wife.

Well, Jove is feeling his years (*my body shrivels and I'm getting water on the brain; my ribs are tight and my teeth are loose; my skin is yellow and my hair is silver, my butt is stiff and my steps are trembly, the old bag on my bagpipe is longer and the old staff is shorter*). Venus, who doesn't like this talk of growing older at all, objects, but Father knows best: *Ah Venus, Venus. Can't you face our condition, which is yours too? What do you think, that it's true what men imagine, that old gods are always old and young ones always young, that we're as changeless as our portraits down on Earth? When really we change and change and change again?*

Jove has decided that a reform of the heavens is called for. Why, he asks, is everything the way it is, and not some different way instead? *I ask you, just for instance: Why has that Triangle four stars, right near Medusa's head, under Andromeda's behind, above the Ram's horns? No reason; the gods just like triangles. Why does the Dolphin deserve fifteen stars? Because he was the* macquereau *that brought Neptune and Amphitrite together. Why does the Serpent, Ophiuchus, occupy a whole thirty-six stars? Because we said so, that's all.*

Bruno laughed, writing fast and steadily like a man tying cut sheaves of grain into shocks. He wasn't composing, only recording; there was no reason for him to write down his *ludibrium,* his celestial jest or comedy, at all, except for others to read; he himself would not forget it. He had an illustrated copy of Hyginus's great star atlas to consult, in which all the stories were told (actually it was not a physical copy, he had sold the one he had once had; it was an inward copy of that copy, leafable, perfect).

So COME ON, YE GODS! Let's pitch out of heaven these specters,
statues, figures, images, portraits, stories of our greed, lust, robberies,
spites and shames. Let's begin with the intelligential heaven within, then
the one we see outside. Let's drive from the mind's heaven the BIG BEAR
of Perversity, the ARROW of Backbiting, the HORSE of Silliness, the
DOG of Griping, the LITTLE DOG of Ass-kissing. Let's banish the
HERCULES of Violence, the LYRE of Conspiracy, the TRIANGLE of
Impiety, the BOÖTES of Forgetting, the CEPHEUS of Cruelty. May the
DRAGON of Envy be far from us, also the SWAN of Foolishness, and the
HYDRA of Randiness. Shove off the CETUS of Gluttony, the ORION of
Rage, the RIVER of Excess, the GORGON of Ignorance.

He cut a new pen. He decided to dedicate his book to Sir Philip Sidney, smiling knight, who alone of the English whom he had met might understand it. His nostrils flared, he inhaled the spring.

Sixteen years later, in the dire year 1600, the Holy Office in Rome was preparing a *sommario* of the case against the imprisoned heretic Giordano Bruno. In addition to his frankly blasphemous views—which the man had demanded to be allowed to explain and defend in person to the Pope!—there was the fact that during his residence in (Protestant) England he had written a book called *Expelling the Triumphant Beast*, a title that everyone and particularly the Pope could readily understand without seeing the book, which the Holy Office did not actually have; they had plenty of Bruno's others. The Pope, whose name was Mercy (Clement), had at that point already made his decision anyway. Bruno was to be turned over to the secular authorities: for of course the Church itself did not and could not condemn any man to die.

In England Giordano Bruno had lived in the employ of the French Ambassador to the court of Elizabeth. *Diva Elizabetta* Bruno called her, joining the crowd of her English apotheosizers but with a plan of his own, never fulfilled: for in 1586 he returned to Paris when that Ambassador, Michel de Castelnau, Seigneur de Mauvissiere, was recalled. Mauvissiere was retiring to his estates: he was considered too *politique,* not Catholic enough for the present moment; he was even in danger because of it. *Who is not for us is against us.*

Jobless and prospectless, crossing the city with most of his few belongings in a canvas bag, Bruno found himself stopped at Notre-Dame des Augustins by a vast religious procession: musicians and choristers, crosses, wonder-working statues, shuffling friars, the Sacrament in its pyx borne on a golden car. A dense crowd lined the route. The King, with every noble he could persuade to join him, was making penance.

It was this King, Henri III, who had sent Bruno into England attached to the French Embassy. He'd had a triple strategy then for retaining his throne and advancing the interests of his House and France: firstly he employed all the arts of fraud and force that his mother, Catherine de Medici, had brought out of Machiavelli's city; and also he prayed, or had prayers said, ardently and continuously, to the One True God; and whenever it could be applied, he used Real Artificial Magic in many forms. Bruno's arts had once been among them. Go bedazzle the English Queen, he'd told Bruno. Confound our English foes. Project our glory and our might and our star.

—Who is this now coming? someone in the crowd near Bruno's ear said.

—It is the *Confrérie des Pénitents Bleues de Saint Jerome,* said another, eating nuts from his pocket. See? All in blue, and each carrying a stone with which to beat his breast.

All of the penitent *confréries* taking part in the procession wore rough habits of homespun, heads entirely covered by hoods drooping like elephants' trunks before them, with only two eyeholes cut out; but each group had its special badge and color and function. Some carried whips and were bared to the waist to flagellate themselves. The Hieronymites had these stones. Bruno felt the blow each gave. Blood had begun to seep through the robes of some; they stumbled. But the music was sweet, yearning, in the Mixolydian mode, sorrowing and hopeful as a lost child. *In Paradisum deducant te Angelii.*

—The Duc de Joyeuse is one among them, someone said. Who knows which.

When Bruno had first come to Paris, the King and his pretty *mignons* were celebrating this Duc de Joyeuse's wedding day; in their nightlong pageants they had dressed up as nymphs and satyrs and done battle with Eros, bound him and tamed him, to different music than this music. They had thought, those fine, careless, pleasure-loving boys and boy-girls, that by their rituals and songs they could bind Love, and make Love do what they liked: or if not that they could abandon Love, and do without him. But though the King might abjure the love of women, there was no man more entangled than Henri in the web of his own desires—which is Love—and fears—which is Love too, only his obverse or other face.

Bruno had once told the King that. Love is magic; magic is love. The love of the lover is a *passive* love, an enchaining love: but the *active* love of the magus is a power of the imagination, a knowledge by which he binds and is not bound.

The great mage understands what others desire, and with his projections offers the image of satisfaction; by their hunger he grows. For it is *images* that bind, whether coming in through open eyes and ears or built in the imagination by the binder, enchainer or enchanter. Masses of men are easier to bind than individuals, he told the King, for to the commonest bonds all men are subject. And of all the bonds of the soul the strongest is Eros, *vinculum summum præcipium et generalissimum:* the highest, most excellent, and most general bond.

Who can be bound? All can be: dæmons, gods and men; no one is immune from Love's dominion. Those are easier to bind who have less knowledge; in them the soul is open in a way that allows for the passage in of impressions created by the operator: hope, compassion, fear; love, hate, indignation; disdain for life, for death, for risk. Wide windows which, in others, are always closed.

The King had listened (while breaking a chicken's wing and feeding the meat to a tiny dog or doglet he held like a baby) and pondered, and sent Bruno to England, to do what he could.

That was then. Now he had forsaken Magic and turned, apparently, to Religion alone.

—Who is this now come carrying his own head on a plate?

—St. Jean-Baptiste. Who could not see that?

—Those who follow him are his penitents?

—The *Confrérie des Pénitents Noires de Saint-Jean Décollé.* Pray God you never need their services.

The penitents of the Headless John Society, all in black, dedicated to ministering to condemned prisoners, most especially to heretics whose souls might at the last moment be saved. Their appearance at one's cell signalled the beginning of one's own brief procession. Time to go.

—Here is the King's own *Confrérie.*

Here came white-robed penitents stumbling under the weight of tall crosses or perhaps of their shameful sins. The King's own, the *Confrérie des Pénitents de l'Annonciation de Notre-Dame.* It was impossible to know who was who among the shambling groaning breast-beating crowd, but those around Bruno seemed to know that the Cardinal of Guise was one, and his brother the Duke of

Mayenne another, great magnates of the Catholic League. One of them, in no way differentiated from the others, was the King.

Now there are two things necessary for the successful accomplishment of any enterprise of magic, and religious magic is no different. (Bruno had told the King this too, and the King had had his Secretary make a memorandum of it.) Faith is necessary, first, and like love it is of two kinds, active and passive: the agent must believe that his processes will work, and the patient must believe the agent.

The other necessary thing is a complement of the first: the operator must not become entangled in his own imaginal processes, catch himself in his own net. He must not, that is, work his magic on himself. Which is just what this King had done, it seemed.

*Rex Christianissimus*. Bruno shook his head and crossed his arms, and he wasn't the only one. The King had put aside every awe-making love-wielding power he might project, eschewing strong images of Kingship, starry Destiny, human Prominence, divine Favor, wise Governorship. He was not accompanied, as he should be, by properly constructed allegories of his Genius, his Munificence, his steadfast Immobility, by the right gods and goddesses, heroes and virtues in the right order, bearing the right symbols. He had not elicited green Venus to calm and stupefy the red Mars whom his enemies had evoked; could not dissolve his peoples' sorrows in a vast Jovian smile. Instead here he was, one among many, unrecognizable in his gown of knee-stained white wool (he had stumbled somewhere along the way under his heavy cross, just as Jesus would have, or maybe that one wasn't him)—well: he might sway God with his humility, but he would not sway his people. Yes that *was* him: Bruno had identified him by the anxious loose energy leaking away from him, the Universal Love, while the wolfish eyes of the better magicians around him in their sheep's clothing gazed sidelong at him unfooled.


A freelance now, Bruno advertised a lecture at the College de Cambrai on the errors of the Aristotelians (always bound to draw a crowd, even if a hostile one) and by dint of able self-advertisement and a day and time well chosen by the stars, drew a good crowd. At the end of it he invited someone, anyone, to defend Aristotle and attack Brunus Nolanus; he would take on all comers. But the smiling man who rose to oppose him (after a pregnant silence gave birth to him) was a man Bruno knew to be an intimate of the King's inner circle of spiritual advisors, Orphic musicians, and Hermetic doctors. This sign or signal from the King was clear: Bruno was not just out of favor, he was to be actively opposed, maybe suppressed. Bruno in the *speculum* of his huge heart saw the King, his white makeup and the false roses in his cheeks. His little evil dog. His lifted eyebrow.

Before the King's man completed his refutation, Bruno slipped from the hall.

After that there was the incident of Fabricio Mordente and his wonderful compass. Bruno came to know the man among the Italian emigrés of Paris, and he was remarkably like his name, a lank-haired mordant melancholic and a great fabricator. Mordente had invented a new sort of compass, one that could be used not for constructing figures but for deducing the proportions between various shapes, lines and surfaces—not only on the page but on Earth.

—The two arms have several scales inscribed on front and back, Mordente said, and scales are drawn too on this disk, the *nocella,* by which they are connected. And see, the different scales inscribed on the quadrant, into which I fix the compass arms by these little screws, these *galletti.*

Bruno handled the beautiful brass thing, unwilling to give it up. Entranced with the luster of it, with the screws, with Mordente who had called the screws "cockerels" for some reason, most of all with the operation of the thing: Mordente showed him how to sight along one arm of the compass to a distant object (a tower, a door at the street's end) and by examination of the scales to construct a triangle that was proportional to the triangle formed of the object, the eye and the ground. And thus to find the distance. Useful, Mordente said gloomily, for armies on the march, or surveyors; Bruno laughed.

He would make Mordente famous. He borrowed the compass and set to work to write a funny dialogue in Latin. It was evident that Mordente had not understood what he had created, just as Copernicus had not understood that his system had destroyed Aristotle's universe: that was for Bruno to reveal. For what Mordente had done was to build an engine by which the geometries of which the earth is made could be extracted: their souls, Pythagoras would say, lying hidden within them, fooling us into thinking they had none, until this new knife laid all things open to show them. Useful for armies on the march! Mordente, plodding mathematical pedant, was like the ass in the parable who bears unwittingly the ineffable effulgent Sacrament upon his back: strong, patient and good, but deeply ignorant. No matter; he benefitted mankind anyway; the ass of useful toil is a divine being compared to the braying fools who willfully oppose knowledge. Bruno called his little dialogue *Idiota triumphans:* the *idiota* being, of course, Mordente himself.

Mordente chased Bruno across Paris in a fury. Mad beast, why was he angry? The mathematician bought up all the copies of the dialogue he could lay his hands on, beggaring himself in the process, and to Bruno's friends declared that he intended to *go to the Guises* about the matter.

So it was time for Bruno to be gone. "Brunus," a gossip wrote home to Italy, "has not been seen in this town since."

*If I worked a plough or tended a flock,* he later wrote, *no one would look at me twice; but since I work the field of Nature, hoe and harrow the Mind, and shepherd the Soul—look, here is one who having seen me upbraids me, another who, having got close enough to me, bites me, another who having got hold of me devours me. It's not one person, it's not a few, it's many, it's almost all.*

That crude little manuscript manual called *Picatrix,* where Bruno's journey started, went on radiating down through the succeeding centuries, becoming illegible over time as its black-letter Latin ceased to be read. Having wandered far to the north, and shorter then by several pages of curses and cures, it was picked up in a stall in Prague by the novelist Fellowes Kraft for a few crowns in 1968 (Russian tanks were that day passing through East Germany on their way to the city and old books were not at the forefront of most people's minds). It travelled from there to Kraft's library in Stonykill in the Faraway Hills, was sealed in a plastic bag against the mold and the bugs and locked in a glass-fronted case, whence it was abstracted by Pierce Moffett. For some time it lay on the table beside his bed in Littleville, and though he couldn't read it either, he'd felt its rays; and so had Rose Ryder, as he intended she should.

Is it real magic? she'd wanted to know.

It really once was, he'd answered. Once.

And he had drawn it out of its plastic container, and opened it, and put her hand on a leathery page.

# 13

D emonomania?" asked Rosie. "Is that right?"

They sat at the stone table that overlooked the long back lawns at Arcady, stained by leaves fallen in other years and the ghosts of caterpillars who had died there; Pierce wouldn't let her put down on its surface the books he had brought.

There was a big beautiful polyglot edition of the *Hypnerotomachia Poliphili*, Paris 1586, with woodcut illustrations, thousands of dollars' worth of book Pierce thought, though he was not really expert in such matters. There was "an oddity," as he'd described it to Rosie, and a pile of other things to go through, including *Picatrix* in its plastic bag.

And there was this book, Jean Bodin's tract proving that witches had to be put to death, that was circulating in Paris in the years when Bruno was there. A first edition it appeared to be, though shabby and apparently much-handled, with no indication of the title on the leather covers. Pierce opened it with gentle reverence and held it so she could see the title page. *De la démonomanie des sorciers.*

"Demonomania," said Pierce. "Right. It didn't exactly mean what we might mean by it, 'mass craziness about demons,' though actually that was part of what he meant. It means more like *Sorcerers stuck on demons* or maybe *Demons stuck on sorcerers,* or witches. It's about witchcraft, what it is, how it works. *Mania* means attachment, obsession; the maniac is somebody obsessed with or stuck on something."

"Like possessed by."

"Well exactly," Pierce said, looking at her in appreciation. "It's about demonic possession, not only of the witches we usually think of, the Macbeth types with the boiling pots, but of the learned Faust types who studied the stars and summoned planetary spirits."

He handed it to her. The dark, foxed paper, printed in not very regular rows of large type, gave off a strange smell, less the smell of the paper, Rosie thought, than the smell of the crabbed language, old French, with extra letters in many of the words she recognized; the smell of its import, which she didn't yet grasp.

"Basically," Pierce said, "Bodin was in a fight with the fashionable intellectuals of his time, people like Bruno, who believed that the universe was filled with a divine spirit, expressed in higher and more refined ways as you moved up through existence, from rocks and stones to animals to human souls and beyond to the spiritual powers, angels and so on, and up to God. If you knew how, you could attune your human spirit to those spirits, contact them, maybe learn from them; maybe even command them."

"So what was wrong with that?"

"Bodin wanted there to be only *one* supernatural being, completely nonmaterial: God. Only God was above nature, only God deserved worship. If you got involved with the lower spirits, that was idolatry. Case closed."

"He thought those spirits were there, you just shouldn't worship them."

"Almost everybody thought they were there. They were how the universe was managed. Nobody in Bodin's time believed that it could just go by itself, the way they would come to believe two hundred years later, and still do. So Bodin supposed that the universe was operated by demons—beings that are maybe good or maybe bad but are mostly just the power within inert matter. They were mostly invisible but they did have bodies—very fine ghostlike bodies, with minds and hearts and organs of some kind."

"Hum," said Rosie, and clutched her bare knee in her two hands. "And were they, like. Like little."

"Some little, some big. Some of enormous size and power, like the ones who inhabited the stars and made them go. They were in the air and the water and the mountains, in fire and steam, in the wind and the weather. They operated the universe at every level, from making the stars go around and the sun shine to making the grass grow."

"How weird. What a strange world to live in."

"Well," Pierce said, "I would bet that most humans around the world over the last say hundred thousand years have mostly lived in that world. I'd say it's the first explanation we come upon for why things are the way they are, why the weather changes, why storms happen or rain doesn't fall. Well maybe the *second* explanation. The first one being that the things themselves—the trees and sky and wind—are alive and making choices."

"The rain is Tess, the fire's Joe."

"You can see them, if you want," Pierce offered. "The airy ones anyway. They move fast, but you can get a glimpse of them. Just look up."

She looked up into the dense blue sky. Cloudless still. When would it rain again.

"See the little swarming sparkles?" Pierce said, looking up also, shielding his eyes. "Some of them red or gold edged?"

"Sure."

"Well," Pierce said. "Ever wonder what they are?"

"No."

"That's them. The airy demons. Or dæmons. Busy at work, keeping the sky blue, doing I don't know what, their thing."

Rosie stared. They came and wriggled and disappeared again, replaced by others, a bloom of becoming and activity, a school of tiny glittering fish. "And one could get inside you?"

"Well. Not one of *those* precisely. No reason for exaggerated fear here. The ones that are around us all the time, like ants, or breezes, or bacteria—obviously they're not all harmful. Just going about their business."

"But others."

"If you invited one in. If you forgot to bless yourself when you sneezed, or wished upon a star, or wandered around old sites where they had once been worshipped. Possession could be involuntary—just bad luck—or it could be voluntary, your own fault. And Bodin said: witches *wanted* them inside, their demons, to give them power. Schemed to get one, begged for one. And Bodin said that was what the great intellectual magicians were doing too, with their Platonic ascension and their emblems and their star-rituals. They too would be seized on and inhabited. And not by some little imp bent on mischief. Maybe by some really terrible power. And his friends and relations. *Dæmonomania.*"

The more she stared at the bright sky, the more clearly she could see them, the little sperms of light, and the longer they lasted before sparking out or diving again into the blue. If she kept staring they might grow little faces. Catch her eye.

"Cheap trick," she said, looking away and blinking, blinded.

"Yes. There were people even back then who said it was a cheap trick."

"But a lot of people believed. Anyway in witches and possession."

"A lot of people still do. Around the world, I'm sure, more do than don't."

It couldn't be, Rosie thought, could it, that that was what Mike had meant in warning her? *Be careful what you play around with.* Her heart began for a moment to thump painfully, as though startled awake.

"They thought back then," she said, "didn't they, that if a person had seizures—epilepsy—they were possessed. Right?"

*Epilepsy:* strange how naked saying the word aloud made her feel. How long would it.

"Well," Pierce said carefully, "no. I think they knew there was a disease, epilepsy, which you could just have, like any disease; it had causes, though what those were could be argued about. And then there was possession, which could sometimes imitate epilepsy, or look like epilepsy, but was caused by a demon or a spirit."

"I thought they caused everything."

"Well not *directly.* Not everybody agreed with Bodin. Even in his time his view was a little extreme."

"Ah."

"Epilepsy had a medical description, an etiology. Symptoms, causes, cures. It was normal. It had its special patrons, saints who had provenance over it; most diseases did. Like St. Roche, for the plague, or St. Blaise for diseases of the throat, diphtheria and so on. In parochial school we had our throats blessed every year on St. Blaise's day."

She looked at him as though he should not know all this, as though such esoteric erudition verged on the impertinent. He caught her look and said: "The special patrons of epilepsy were the Three Kings."

"Oh for heaven's sake."

"Their names were Caspar, Melchior, and Balthazar."

"You know their *names*?"

"Every Catholic kid learned them."

"And they told you they were in charge of epilepsy?"

"Well no. I learned that myself, later on."

"Why them?"

"I don't know. Somebody somewhere sometime prayed to them, got cured. The story spread."

We three kings, thought Rosie. She imagined someone, a mother, back then, whenever *then* was exactly, kneeling before the crèche at Christmas, asking for their help—the three guys on camels, the youngest (Balthazar?) always black. She thought of Julius Cæsar and Edward Lear. She felt herself for a moment, herself and Sam, to be part of a huge and long-lived family, countless generations reaching into the far past, because the disease must always have existed; like a family, her family, that had suffered and been misunderstood, had had amazing and terrible adventures, a secret history linking its generations, a history that could probably never be recovered. All those children. The awe and fear they caused. And the doctors looking on helpless.

Oh Sam.

She looked at her watch. Where was she, what was he doing with her. The still afternoon was suddenly enormous.

"Awful, I guess," she said. "Being thought to be possessed. What they put you through."

"I guess," Pierce said. "Certainly for most. But there were a number of famous demoniacs, who were sort of media stars for a while. Pamphlets circulated about them, people came from all over to see them. One French one, I remember, had her own platform set up in the church, where she, her demon rather, would give regular shows. Yell out blasphemies, talk in Greek and unknown languages, produce disgusting manifestations, blood, frogs."

"Good Lord. What was really wrong with them?"

"I don't know. I doubt it was just one thing. Some of them were crazy, by our definition. Some were fakes, maybe set up by the Church. You just can't say now. Nothing we can postulate explains away what people then say they saw and heard."

"So maybe," Rosie said, "back then, demons actually did run the world."

"Hey. May be."

Pierce remembered how in Frank Walker Barr's Early Modern Europe seminar at Noate University, Barr and his graduate students (Pierce among them) had pondered the sudden and nearly universal outbreak in sixteenth-century Europe of demonic possession, witchcraft accusations, trials, burnings, hysteria about the Devil and his legions, succubi, incubi, sorcerers seen carried off by the familiar devils who had served them. The hysteria crossed doctrinal and sectarian lines, Catholics as well as Lutherans, Calvinists, Huguenots, everybody denouncing one another and blaming one another's remedies for only making matters worse and inviting further inroads.

Barr had entertained a number of explanations for the plague—economic, social, cultural, even psychoanalytic (delayed Oedipal reaction on the part of those who had overthrown their old Holy Father). The only explanation he would not countenance—"even," he'd said, with the famous Barr twinkle in his eye, "if it's the right one"—was that there really was a big outbreak or inrush of spirits into the human world just then: bad spirits, or good and bad ones, or merely pesky, invited in by willful magicians or just come crashing.

A disease appearing suddenly in the nature of things, or more precisely in human understanding, suddenly fulminant; then over, the fit passing, the fever falling, the human corpus now mostly resistant. Of all that can befall us, that never can again. Other things, and worse too: but not the Devil and his pomps and works. Pierce was sure of that.

"How is she, anyway?" he asked. "Sam."

"Oh. Well. No events lately. One or two till they figured out the dosage."

"If there's anything I can do."

"I can't think of anything," Rosie said, whose soul was beginning to shrink from this offer that she had now heard many times, from her mother, from her friends: so easy to make, so useless. "Ask the Three Kings. Pray."

"I haven't prayed in a long time."

"Well ask your cousin. Don't you have a cousin who's a nun?"

"I do." He wondered if his cousin Hildy still prayed. Certainly she said the words. Words without thoughts never to heaven go.

"So she should have some influence," Rosie said, poking into the box that lay between them. "What's this one?"

It was a large pamphlet lying on the bottom.

"Ah that one."

"*Ars Auto-amatoria*," she read from the cover. "*Or, Every Man His Own Wife.* What on earth."

Pierce folded his hands in scholarly fashion. "That's the oddity," he said. "It's maybe as valuable as all the others."

"What's it about?" Rosie asked, opening it with the careful reverence Pierce had displayed, which seemed to be the proper mode. It was at least in English. A poem.

"It's about," Pierce said, "masturbation, actually," and Rosie thought she saw him blush: was that possible?

"Oh yes?" Rosie read:

*The Widow Palm a House maintains,*
*And no Man whosoe'er disdains;*
*Her Daughters five your Hand-maids be*
*And Night or Day shall welcome thee;*
*The Pander, master Bates his Name,*
*Asks not a Penny, nor his Dame:*
*Without a Purse spend freely here,*
*The Pox and Clap thou need'st not fear.*

"A little rough," she said.

"Awful," said Pierce. "And long. Nearly a thousand lines."

"Why so valuable then?"

"Oh there are collectors. Anything old and dirty, I mean you know, pornographic."

"Who wrote it?"

"Dunno. No name, no date. I would guess, from what we scholars call 'internal evidence,' like for instance a play on some lines of Milton's, and the spelling, that it has to be eighteenth century."

"It sounds sort of pro," Rosie said. "Rather than anti."

"Very pro."

"I thought you were supposed to go blind."

"That was later. Nineteenth-century pseudoscience. No one really cared about it much or even talked about it a lot before then. That's why this is a rarity."

Rosie read:

*Ill-favoured thou, nor hast a Place?*
*No Prospects neither? Nor a Face?*
*If short or fat, or bandy-legged;*
*If thou hast sinned, or failed, or begged,*
*One Bride is still betroth'd to thee*
*No Bride-price asks she, and no Fee.*

"Supposed to save you time and trouble, I guess," she said.

"And money."

"Jesus."

"Well at that time marriage was a big endeavor," Pierce said. "Complicated and costly. Her dowry, his money. A property transaction before anything else. If you were the fearful indolent type, wanted to avoid trouble, you might."

She looked at him sidelong. "Uh-huh," she said. "And what about the women?"

"No mention of them," Pierce said. "I mean as far as I read."

"Somebody should write that," Rosie said.

"Every Woman Her Own Husband."

"But did they even?" Rosie wondered. "I mean of course they did. But did

they know they did, or did men anyway know?" She had, herself, been a practitioner long before she knew it had a name, or that others did it too. The difference, name and no name, had seemed important, even though the feeling was
the same. Two worlds.

"Well," Pierce said. "I remember in de Sade women alone were always at
it. So."

"Where was this?"

"In de Sade," Pierce said. "The Marquis. As in S and M."

"Oh." Now he really did blush, and Rosie watched with interest as it came
and passed. "Well, wouldn't apply to me anyway," she said, placing the old book
back in the box. "I have to fight them off."

"Suitors?"

"I'm sitting on a couple of offers."

"Spofford."

"Not only him. My ex wants to get married again. To me I mean."

"I didn't think you were even completely divorced yet."

"Whatever." She looked back up at the populated sky. "I remember Boney
saying once, when I told him about Spofford—you know Spofford was always
coming around—that a second marriage represents the triumph of hope over experience. Quoting somebody."

"Samuel Johnson. But you know I don't think back then it meant the same
thing we mean."

"No?"

"We think it's a sort of cynical wisecrack—you couldn't get along with A but
you're sure you'll get along great with B. We think it's about divorce. In Johnson's
time there was hardly any divorce. But there was a lot of early death. The way
you parted from your spouse was, she died. Johnson's did. So that was the experience, love somebody and she dies. The hope was the new one wouldn't die."

Pierce had seen while he told this that Rosie's eyes had grown moist, almost
as though melting; now she covered her mouth (he could see the band of pale
skin on her finger where her ring had recently been). She shut her eyes tightly,
though the forming tears pressed out, pooling on her lashes.

"What," he said.

"Oh Jesus," she said. "Jesus I am so scared."

"Of marriage?"

"Of death. Oh I don't want her to die."

Yellow leaves fell around them. A tiny wind-demon lifted a few of the fallen
into the air to play, and let them go again.

"Is there any," Pierce said. "I mean."

"No," Rosie said. She sighed hard. "Nothing I guess that's going to make her
die. She's basically maybe pretty okay. Oh damn damn damn."

Pierce ventured nothing further. Rosie at length put her hand over his and
patted it, as though he not she needed comfort. "So, so," she said. She shook her
box of books. "So what am I supposed to."

"Just keep them dry and cool," Pierce said. He rose; they walked across the driveway to his car, whose hood and windshield were already decorated with fallen leaves. He got in. "There's this kind of plastic bag you can buy now, that seals up when you press the top edges together."

"Okay."

He donned dark glasses, a pair bought on his first journey to these hills and miraculously held on to since. "And no fingerprints. Collectors care a lot. We don't want to have to downgrade from 'fine' to 'near fine.' "

"I hear you."

"The Bodin is kind of fragile. And the poem."

"Speaking of which," Rosie said. "How are you getting on with Rose Ryder?"

She was smiling, looking into his face frankly and openly, but what she might be reading there he couldn't tell. "Speaking of *what* which?" he said.

"Well," Rosie said, "the two of you were certainly becoming a couple. So it seemed."

"Seemed to whom, for instance?"

"Oh Val, for instance. Spofford."

The Nosy Parkers of a tiny town, he thought: Spofford himself had once warned him of them, the shifting alliances of a small cast of characters and the unflagging interest everyone took in everyone else.

"So you coming to Val's tonight?" she asked, still regarding him.

"Oh Christ, is that tonight? Yes, yes sure."

"With . . ."

"No," he said. "Alone."

Behind him, a van from The Woods (bringing Sam home) turned in at the gates of Arcady. Pierce pulled shut his door, waved goodbye, and backed up to turn around, a move he had not yet entirely mastered and which took all his attention; he went out, passing around the wrong side of the incoming van, to which he waved apologetically.

A couple, huh. He supposed that he must have been seen often driving the roads hereabouts with Rose in her well-known little car, no place to hide; and Pierce was not capable of invisibility, though it was a skill he had suggested that Rose might be able to acquire after some years of practice and exacting study under his tutelage. He was comforted that, though they could observe him and come to their conclusions, they could not know what he and Rose had said and done together; there were limits. What he could not suspect was that Rosie Rasmussen had herself done some outrageous things in bed with Rose Ryder; nor that once upon a time, in a flaming rush incited by her weird unresistance, his friend Spofford had laid her on a table. It wasn't time for him to be told these things, though the time would come: when he needed help, and there was no one else to help him.

It wasn't Mike who was bringing Sam, but one of the open-faced smilers whom Rosie had identified as operatives of the Powerhouse in residence at The Woods.

Tidy in khakis and a windbreaker with a logo on it she wanted to read but could not, a brand name certainly probably.

"Here we are," he said.

"So where's her father?"

"Oh," said the young man, as though it were unimportant, "he's real busy. Organizing a trip."

"A trip."

He went on smiling, ready to go and obviously not about to say more.

"Okay thanks," Rosie said.

He put his hand on Sam's head. "She's quite a gal," he said. "Really."

"Oh yes," Rosie said. She smiled for his smile, and for a moment he seemed about to speak, and a flash of unreasoning fear arose in her breast. She got her daughter from him, and he waved and Sam smiled at him distantly, regally. Rosie shut the door on him as fast as she could consistent with minimal manners; and though Sam seemed clean enough, and objected violently to the procedure, she drew a bath and plunged Sam within it, and washed her a long time.


The question, Pierce supposed, is—or was—this: to what extent were the witch and the dæmoniac responsible for their condition, and for the evil that they did or said? Did they always invite the devil in, and therefore were they always guilty; or was the devil capable of possessing souls by force, or winning their allegiance by irresistible trickery, and were the victims therefore not guilty but only unfortunate?

*He begins first with the phantasy, & moves that so strongly, that no reason is able to resist:* so Burton said, a sufferer himself, who knew more about the subject than any man who ever lived, most of it wrong or useless, but he knew that too. *The Anatomy of Melancholy* was balanced on Pierce's bare knees, open to Part 1, Section 2, Member 1, Subsection 2, where Burton quotes Jason Pratensis, who's he, *that the devil, being a slender incomprehensible spirit, can easily insinuate himself into our human bodies, and cunningly couched in our bowels, vitiate our healths, terrify our souls with fearful dreams, and shake our minds with furies.* Once settled down in our bodies, *the dæmons sport themselves as in another heaven; they go in and out of our bodies, as bees do in a hive.*

At the very least responsible for this wretched constipation, Saturnian affliction, can't let go of anything. Pierce shifted his bottom on the cold toilet's ring, sighed, turned the page.

There was no doubt (Burton thought) that those who were possessed or who enslaved themselves to dark powers suffered from the physical imbalance or disease of melancholy. The predominance of *atra bilia* in the humors of their bodies, drying and chilling the spirit, warped them in predictable ways, toward self-involvement, mistrust, bitterness, and apathy; melancholics tended to be solitary, cowardly, and equivocating, bachelor farmers, masturbators, conjurers, misers.

The grand melancholics though, those who suffered from the hot form, *melancholia fumosa,* rather than the colder, might turn their nameless longings toward the contemplation of higher, hidden things (*ad secretiora et altiora contemplanda*) and, rapt, leave the body and the unsatisfactory world behind. Or they could also be the great dæmoniacs, hosts to the grandees of the underworld, and capable of fabulous feats of prophecy and suffering. Melancholy all by itself, the plain condition, was regarded by the Scholastics as one of the seven forms of *vacatio* or spiritual absence, along with sleep, fainting, rapture, what else. Epileptic fits, of course. That's four. And sex. No no not sex, it wasn't known to have been one, though Pierce Moffett knew it to be. The rapt contemplation of hidden things; absence, blessed absence.

Where is she right now, Pierce suddenly wanted to know, Rose, what are they doing to her there in that city he had never seen, to which he had himself been travelling when Coincidence brought him here, where he still was.

Just then as in the sixteenth century a plague of melancholia was upon the world, but Pierce's age lacked the system by which the manifestations of the temperament were once understood, no name for what overtook them beyond the suddenly vacant categories of psychiatry, why do I feel this way, why so sad, why so obsessed, why do I believe I have lost something irreplaceable that I cannot name, why do I long always for cold water to slake a thirst that will not be satisfied? Melancholics, shut up in their indolence and solitude, turning over the same few thoughts like a miser his coins; or searching, roaming the night streets of lupine cities seeking to be devoured, to be possessed by what they long to possess.

In the coming age there might be help for these unfortunates, their condition seen to be not their fault after all. Clinics where they can be, not cured of course, but cared for; where they can be taken for walks in the sun when it is exalted in Leo or in Aries, when Venus is in transit; where they will gather dandelions and primroses, wear blue, drink white wine from copper cups—and where they will be taught at last about love, real love. And when Saturn is in the ascendant they will hold the hands of their nurses, of their fellows, and wait it out, one day at a time.

Or there will not be.

A naked branch tapped at Pierce's window as though for his attention, and he saw with surprise that the day was already near done. Darkness falling so early, darkness out across the Faraways where soon he must go. Hands in the pockets of his unbuttoned pants, he stood unmoving in the little room oddly placed between dining and bed. He did not want to go out, but he didn't want to stay in; didn't want the phone to ring, yet he felt a primitive dread in being alone in the silence and the fading of the light. He would start a fire in his little stove, he thought; get that warm at least; sit for a while by its cheerful glow. Start a small one in his heart too, a drink of something. He thought these things, and other things, and went on standing, at once still and restless, wondering just what was wrong with him.

# 14

**F**irst, the angels told them, they were to burn their books. All the twenty-eight volumes that had been dictated to them (*the holo-caust of all that which from the beginning of the world had been most precious* John Dee wrote on the page where he recorded their commandment); so Kelley and he put them into a bag and the bag in the fire of the furnace where they had made their tittle of gold, and prayed and wept and cried aloud as they built up the fire with dry scraps of wood; Kelley looked in and in the flames saw a person there busily gathering the leaves of the books as they curled up one by one and were burnt. They stirred the fire and sweated (it was the tenth of April, 1586, near Easter, and warm) until there was nothing left within but ashes and live coals and the corners of a few leaves, black, the writing burnt white upon them.

Then the burned books were returned unchanged, or perhaps not un-changed.

About half past one on the twenty-ninth, in the garden of their little house a man pruning some blooming cherry trees called up to Edward Kelley to send the Doctor down; and he went on pruning the cherries, until he reached the end of the garden, and began to walk up into the air and away, with his pruning hook over his shoulder; and when Kelley and Dee went down into the garden they could not find the man.

—Some wicked spirit, Kelley said.

But as they stood there, and blossoms dropped on the shoulders of their dark gowns, Doctor Dee noticed far off "a faire white paper lying tossed to and fro in the wind" under the almond tree; and when he chased it he found there one of the books that had been burned before, its pages white as blossoms, ink black as soot.

—A gardener, he said. He sat beneath an almond, the book in his lap (was it heavier than it had been?) thinking of Jesus and the Marys at Eastertide, and of renovation.

Eventually the spirits restored to them all the books they had burned. The vial of precious powder that Kelley had expended was refilled too with a stuff like dried blood and silver, whose time, they said, was near, but not yet.

All this was witnessed by an Italian priest who had become a participant in the sessions before the crystal and indeed nearly a member of the house, a man named Francesco Pucci, whom they had met in Cracow and who had followed them to Prague; this Pucci had once studied at Oxford and there apparently abjured his faith; he knew the world was to end in 1600, and thought all men might be saved by true faith if only they hurried: for the time was short.

Yes, the angels said to them: yes the time is short.

John Dee, who liked and trusted almost everyone, came to detest Father Pucci. And in fact Pucci was visiting the Papal Nuncio in Prague every week, for he had secretly returned to the Roman faith, or perhaps had never left it, had been Rome's agent all along (Dee came to think so); and on Pucci's information the two Englishmen were summoned before the Nuncio: *Giovanni Dii e suo compagno, autori d'una nuova superstitione,* the Nuncio described them in letters to Rome, and though not quite denouncing them as heretics, had them expelled from Prague. The Emperor himself, perhaps in one of his fits of superstitious dread, signed the order.

All of them afraid, John Dee thought: afraid of any new thing, no matter if it came from the mouth of God Himself; afraid of the souls of those they lived among as though they were bad dogs, that must be chained lest they bite.

Homeless then, and moving from Prague to Leipzig, back to Cracow, to Erfurt. Pucci reached them there with the news that they could return, if they foreswore magical arts: they need only come to Rome with him, he said, and explain themselves, and if they were found not heretical—surely they would be?—all would be well. They refused, and Dee meditated how to get rid of Pucci "by quiet and honest meanes." On to Cassel and Gotha, keeping just beyond the Emperor's reach, until they found a protector: Vilem of Rozmberk, the greatest magnate of Bohemia, devotee of the Art, hoarder of books and manuscripts, patron of artists and doctors—a smaller version in fact of his King and Emperor, whom he even resembled, at least in the unmistakable yearning softness of his liquid brown eyes. He and the King-Emperor were joined not only by their melancholia and their hunger for the Stone, but in the search for precious and unusual gems with special powers; they owned mines jointly and employed gem hunters who roamed the Giant Mountains in the northeast with picks in their belts and Imperial licenses to prospect for "treasures, metals, precious stones, and all the hidden secrets in the whole of nature."

Rozmberk had a great palace in Prague practically contiguous with the Emperor's far greater one, and lands in the south and the west: and at his house in Trebona John Dee and his family were offered shelter. To this the Emperor (ashamed of himself, maybe, and sorry to have lost the two Englishmen) made no objection.

And thus a year had passed, and John Dee wrote to Sir Francis Walsingham at home, how he had been persecuted (*but all in vain, for force human we fear not*) and had triumphed (*the Nuncius Apostolicus is gone to Rome with a flea in his eare, that disquieteth him and terrifieth the whole state Romish and Jesuitical*) and how now he was able to, now he could promise them that he could, now he was sure that he would soon . . . do what? *No human reason can limit or determine God His marvellous means of proceeding with us,* he wrote: and yet there was nothing still, the secret remained unsaid, the angels prayed and hemmed and mocked and scolded but did not tell.

Madimi appeared among them again, grown into a woman now, and all naked (John Dee wrote *And she sheweth her shame also*). She told them to love one another in perfect love as they have not yet done, despite her commandments; told them Paul the Apostle abounded in carnal lust, and not boy nor girl among his brethren was safe from him, so that he too was ready to have left his vocation, but the Lord did say unto him *My mercy and grace sufficeth unto thee.*

As they could not comprehend the heavens, so likewise they could not comprehend the wisdom of God, Who said: *I shall be merciful unto whom I list, and unto whom I will not I have none in store; foolish is he that asketh why.*

And if God abrogated His laws for them alone, what reason could they bring against Him? Whatsoever the Spirit of God teacheth us from above, though it appear a sin before man, is righteousness before Him. *Behold you are become free,* she said. *Do that which pleases you.*

—She is gone, Kelley said.

What did she mean? What sin before man, not sinful before God, were they invited to? What had they done that they should not have done, what had they not done that they should have?

—I know this, Kelley said to John Dee. Gold is a generation, like the generation of children. It cannot be done, therefore, by a man who is without issue. Who is, who cannot.

They spoke low, though there was no one in the room to hear them. It was May again.

—Has thy wife, John Dee asked, not been subject to thee?

Kelley tugged down the cap he always wore (it covered the scars where long ago his ears had been docked, a punishment for coining, or conjuring, or both, *he* would not say).

—In some wise she has, he said. Not entirely.

Years before in England the angels chose a wife for Edward Kelley; at least they told him he must marry, and Joanna Cooper of Chipping Norton, eight years his junior, was willing. She was a *rarum exemplum sanctitatis et castitatis,* so Father Pucci said, a rare example of sanctity and chastity (but he was angling at the time for a way into their house and hearts): she was certainly good-natured, only twenty-four, uncomprehending and patient. Kelley hated her. He could hardly bear to be next to her.

—Is she, Dee said carefully, still a maid? *Virgo intacta?*

—As good as.

John Dee pressed his beard with the flat of his hand. His friend had always been mixed of hot and cold, of male and female too. He had once made medicines for the younger man, to strengthen him.

—But thou, Kelley said. And thy Jane. She from whose womb so many have come.

—Tumbled, said John Dee.

—Arthur, Rowland, Katherine, Michael, said Kelley. And those who did not live.

—Two, said John Dee.

Kelley, restless and unsatisfied, stood up from his stool, clasped his hands behind him, clasped them before him, sat again folded up as though in pain, his head in motion, searching.

—This our quadrature, he said. We four. There is a breach or gap or lack in it, that must be made perfect.

Doctor Dee said nothing in answer. He knew as well as Kelley did that alchemic gold was nothing but an expression of those who made it, as honey is of bees. Only the purest and most noble souls would be able to secrete the purest and most noble of substances in their furnaces. Half-hearts would fail; weak faith would fail; the impure and the wicked would produce false things and monsters.

He said at last:

—How, made perfect?

—They have spoken to me, Kelley said, of our cross-matching. But I would not listen.

John Dee lifted his head to regard his friend, looked long at him to see if what he had said would resolve itself to sense.

—They have commanded, Kelley said, that we are to have all things in common.

—Yes. So we do.

—That we are to live as in the Golden Age; thus we will bring that Age to be again. When gold grew in the earth.

John Dee nodded carefully.

—That thus. That therefore we must have our wives in common too. *Uxores nostres communes.*

The angelus rang from the church tower, each sweet bell-clap hanging in the room's spring air till it was removed by the next.

—Who has told you this? John Dee asked.

—A little spirit came privily to me, Kelley said. The name of it was Ben.

—Ben?

—Who said this cross-matching was no sin, but was required of us, to make us perfect; and was what the angels spoke of, though they spoke as it were in a cloudy or obscure manner. But I would not agree to it. Not I.

—You have not spoken of this one before.

—Ben taught me how to distill an oil from spirits of wine. And said if we are not conformable to the voices, my powder of projection will lose its virtue. To distill the oil, he taught, take thou two silver dishes, whelmed one atop the other, and a hole in them . . .

—Our wives in common, John Dee said. It is a great sin, a most unpure doctrine. They cannot have said so.

—They have. They did. Let us therefore deal with them no more. I swear I will not.

He folded his long fingers together and laid them in his lap, and looked at nothing.

Dr. Dee studied him. Always, always Edward Kelley had played this part in their dealings with the spirits that only he could see: protesting, hesitating, refusing to have further dealings with them, calling them damned and saying that he and his employer were endangering their own souls in dealing with them. So that John Dee had always to plead with him, reassure, belittle his fears, beg too, beg. Beg him to do that which his heart desired.

Like a man with a maid. So that it was always his, John Dee's, doing, not Kelley's: his fault, if it was one.

—Come, he said, and slapped his knees, and rose. Come. We will ask. We will see.


There was a little tower room in the castle at Trebona where John Dee had set up the table of practice, where night after night the spirits had come, drawn to the clear stone in the center, to speak to the two mortals. John Dee mounted the stairs toward this room, tugging Edward Kelley after him by the sleeve of his gown. The afternoon entered in at the lancet windows of the spiralling stair, the voices of those in the courtyards below.

—Up, said Doctor Dee. Up.

The pretty stone in its frame on the table was shot through with sunlight, smug (so it just now looked) and mum. On the table lay John Dee's papers, his record of all that was said here; his horn of ink, and the little cup of turned wood his son Rowland had made for him to hold his pens.

He knelt before the stone. He drew Kelley down with him. They prayed together, as they always did, to be helped, to be kept from harm, to be not drawn into temptation. When Kelley's voice fell behind his, and his eyes narrowed as though with awful weariness, John Dee ceased. Waited. Then:

—We will move the question, he said, taking his forehead in his hand, concerning Madimi her words to Master Kelley, that we two have our wives in such sort as we might use them in common.

Kelley snored hugely just then, as he sometimes did when taken up by the spirits.

—Whether the sense were of carnal use, Dee said, contrary to law and the Commandment, or of spiritual love and charitable care and and.

Kelley began to speak.

—A scroll, he said, and his hands made a soft gesture. Unrolling. On it words written.

Dr. Dee began to write down what Kelley said.

*De utroque loquor,* said Kelley. Those are the words written. I spoke of both.

John Dee wrote DE UTROQ: LOQUOR.

O terrible. *De utroque loquor,* I spoke of both. He put down his pen. Assist me O God. Assist me O Christ.

Terrible to know God's command, but not His intentions; terrible that he must commit at the instructions of good angels what he could not but believe a sin. Worst of all, though, was that he would now have to convince his wife of it: and he could not even think how he might speak its name to her.


Jane Fromond had been just twenty-two when John Dee first saw her, a lady-in-waiting to Lady Howard of Effingham, wife of the Lord Admiral who would years later sail against the Armada. It was the year of the comet that alarmed everyone, most especially the great, whose birth and passing such aerial events foretell. (A Swedish astronomer made a lucky guess, and said it foretold the birth of a great Swedish prince, who would lay waste all Europe, and die in 1632: and Gustavus Adolphus was duly born, red and squalling—he would carry off all of Rudolf's and the Rozmberks' treasures from looted Prague to the snowy North. But the noseless Dane Tycho de Brahe saw the same comet from his sorcerer's castle on the island of Hveen, and proved it to be not any exhalation of the lower air but an object far beyond the moon's sphere—which made it the more unsettling: the changeless heavens were giving birth to monsters.)

John Dee, summoned to Elizabeth's court to expound upon this blazing star, caught sight of Jane Fromond among the worried nobility, bright-cheeked and smiling as she was always then, or so it seemed to him looking back from this far place. He was then a man of fifty, white-bearded already, who had buried one wife; but she had come to know well the court and the men around the Queen, and his honesty and good heart shone among them like the man with the lamp in the story he liked to tell. She was a blazer herself—it was John Dee who said it to her—quick and hot especially when she saw injustice or indifference to cruelty, which she did see often at Windsor and Richmond and Nonsuch; and if she was dismayed at her new swain's great age, she also thought she would rather have this frank grave man than any of the sprouts at court who did not know right from wrong.

Which never until now had she doubted her goodman knew.

It took her so long to interpret what he told her, what he said the angels now required of them, that she could only stare at him, her mouth open and her fingers fencing it.

Then she wept, he had not seen her weep so, not for her fear and her homesickness, no nor for her child born dead, *a full ¼ of an Howre* he later wrote; he had not known she could weep so. Then she raged, even longer and more terribly; she damned Kelley and the spirits in words he had not heard her use, and broke in fury a mirror that Duke Rozmberk had given her. The younger children, forbidden the room, crept back weeping too, not knowing at what and shouting at their father to stop, stop. He sent them away and turned to beg his wife to possess herself.

—Stop, stop, he said, trying to gather her battling arms to his. She went to her knees suddenly with a cry as though shot, and flung her arms around him.

—Husband I beg you do not leave me. Never. Never never.

He could not raise her, could not comfort her. No Jane no. Almost he withdrew what he asked of her; he thought of Abraham with the knife at Isaac's throat, he longed to hear an angel voice call his name, to tell him the test was passed. No one called to him.

All that night there were comings and goings and meetings and partings in the wing of the castle they and Kelley and his wife all shared, lights in the common rooms and halls, doors slammed, voices raised. Jane and Joanna locked themselves in Kelley's room and left the men to pace back and forth outside, their eyes not meeting.

Why did they want this of them, John Dee wondered, was it not enough that they be squeezed like a lemon of all unwillingness, he would go as far as they desired but why must they stretch out their hand to touch his wife, his and Kelley's poor doe of a girl, trembling as though the dogs were at her? Was it that alone, only a further proof of his constancy, were they like jealous lovers, never convinced: or was Kelley right, that they two were to be crossed in this way as roses or apricots are crossed, to bring forth new fruit?

Calm and dry-eyed, holding Joanna's hand, Jane came forth. There was a sudden odor in the air, withdrawn as soon as sensed, none of them could agree later what to name it, new-mown grass said Joanna, Persian attar said Kelley. They two had prayed, Jane said, and vowed a vow.

—You must ask them again, Joanna said. You must.

—We, Jane said, will in no wise agree to this except we are certain they have said what you have told us. Who never before said such things but often comforted us. And we will eat no flesh nor fish till this be answered.

—Jane.

—And I trust, she said (said it strongly, though she seemed close to tears again), that God will turn me to stone before he will suffer me in my obedience to receive any shame or inconvenience.

—Yes, her husband said. Agreed. Now let us to bed. Before the sun is up.


They signed a solemn pact, all four of them, it still exists, written on strong parchment that time has darkened but not harmed, in ink made of lampblack and wax more lasting than blood. They swore secrecy on pain of death; they vowed they would tread underfoot all human doubts that power and authority over sins—their releasing and discharging—are from God. They vowed to keep between them Christian charity, spiritual friendship, and (this written as firmly and clearly, a little larger too) matrimonial liberty. And they spread the document on the holy south table in the chapel of the castle, like a letter to Santa, and waited to be answered.

No countermand came. May crept along, the days lengthening.

In their curtained bed, awake in the midnight, John and Jane spoke for the first time since they had put their hands to it.

—They have honored us, he said. And brought us honor.

—They have, said Jane. And I would they had left me unhonored, and suffered me to stay in my own kitchen, and my kitchen-garden.

—Ah, Jane.

—The peasecods are fat now on the vines there. And strawberries.

—We have no such strawberries as are grown here, in Trebona.

—But they are not mine own, Jane said.

He could not look into her eyes, looked at his own hands folded in his lap as though he had already done her wrong.

—You think it wickedness, he said. And well you might. I too . . .

—I do not. You would never do wickedness. I think it foolishness. If angels speak to you . . .

—If? he said. If?

—When they speak to you. I think it is like the children, in their play, when they whisper words each to each, one to other. What the last hears is not at all what the first said.

—Yes. I know.

—They laugh at it, she said. Laugh and laugh.

—Yes. Wife I am certain we have been commanded to this by God His holy angels, for purposes only they know, but with this result—this one among others—that we will be made rich.

He regarded her then frankly.

—Rich, he said. Rich beyond counting.

She crossed her arms before her. She had known no other man but he. She asked him:

—When we are rich, then may we go home again?


The book that contains the records of John Dee and Edward Kelley's dealings with the spirits ends forever on the day of May 23, 1587. Its light has now gone out, of course; it can no longer be understood; it can hardly be read. But those last entries—not the later printed version of them but the actual manuscript pages in the British Museum—begin with one that has been heavily erased and is barely legible; it seems to record an exchange between the two friends and an angel-spirit, who asks Kelley *Was thy brother's wife obedient and humble unto thee?* To which Kelley answers *She was.* (It is John Dee's hand, his writing.) Then this spirit—gratified, presumably—asks of Dee the same question about John Dee and Joanna, and is given the same answer: *She was.*

That, anyway, is what one scholar or investigator claims was there on that page, on a certain day some years ago, in the Manuscript Room of the old museum, the high windows casting the light into bars, dust of ages, the odor of dis-integrating paper. Maybe in that year it was. Maybe it still is.

May 22, 1587 had just turned to 23, cusp of Gemini the Twins, moon pass-ing into Scorpio; John Dee in his nightgown heard footsteps mounting toward the tower room where he sat. Heard a gasp or sob too: Kelley. There was a can-dle lit in the room, burning out; Dee lit another at it, and pressed it down into the candlestick.

—Well? he said. How is it with thee?

—I, said Kelley. I have scotched.

—Was she not obedient to thee? If she was not . . .

—No, Kelley said. No it was I.

They sat close and whispered, though there was no one there to hear. On the table of practice the globe was dark, gone out.

—And Joanna? Kelley said. What success, what . . .

—I spoke long with her. But she was in no receptive frame.

—No?

—I could not force her.

—No. No.

Limp as a poppet when he strove to embrace her, tears on her cheeks that he could feel on his, she was just the age Dee's firstborn would have been, the daughter of his first marriage, who died of a fever. Her wide frightened eyes. Un-resisting. For an awful moment a sort of rage possessed him, he knew the sol-dier's awful freedom, given liberty to sack and despoil. It so frightened him his male part failed him.

—The willingness is all, said John Dee. If they be perfectly obedient, but the act not done, it is no matter. If it offend not God it offends not me.

Kelley seemed unreconciled. Twisted in his chair. His head lifted as though his ears pricked up; he chewed his beard.

—I pray God, Dee said, that it offend not Him.

Noises chased one another through the tower with unearthly speed. They felt airs on their faces, touching them, buffeting them sometimes. They heard what seemed to be quick steps on the stair that circled up from this room toward the tower's top; then as they looked, their eyes wide and arms linked, a child's ball came bouncing down from above into the room: a ball striped red and white, capped with blue and stars. It rolled across the little chamber's floor and out the wind-opened door and down. Little footsteps receding.

—Let's go in to them again, Kelley said. We will see if they be in better frame.

—Very well, John Dee said. Pray we be stronger too.

—We'll go down together. No. I will go, then you.

—Play the man, Edward. God be with thee.


May dawn lay along the flags of the halls, when John Dee returned to his own bedchamber. Servants and men-at-arms were up; horses laughed and clattered in the yards. He had lain long with Joanna Kelley in her chamber and knew her heart as he had not before, but she was still a virgin; would still be one when her brothers came to Prague at last to take her back to the Cotswolds, away from the strange man the angels had inflicted on her.

At first it seemed his door was locked against him, but it was not; he opened it. Smelled spilt wine. His feet encountered the shards of a jug, which chittered across the floor. The curtains of the bed were drawn.

—Jane.

She made no answer, and for a moment he imagined her gone. Then he heard something, the pillow struck. He waited. He thought: I am a thousand miles from home.

—Jane, I would know how it is with thee.

He drew aside the curtain. There was an outrush of night odor, familiar, familiar. She lay with her face to the wall, her dark curls escaping from the white cap on her head, her shift about her shoulders.

—He is a little withered root, she said. And once again she struck the pillow.

—Did you, John Dee began. Did he . . .

—We did as we did, she said. But you need have no fear for your line.

She turned to face him. He thought that she laughed, or was trying not to; her eyes were alight in the dark of the bed.

—My line?

—There will be no issue.

—How, no issue.

—He was too quick, she said. And spilled beforehand.

—Spilled?

—As we, she said, as we . . . set out.

She laughed aloud, looking at her husband's face; he could see his own puzzlement in her look.

—Spilled, she said, spilled, you foolish old man. He is a little withered root and he was as hasty as a boy stealing a pie from the sill, and try as I might I could not get him in his right place before he.

—You're certain of it?

—I catched it, she said. She held up her big red hand in the dimness. Strong hand, flat fingertips like an old tailor's, the thumb (he knew) with a double joint. She grinned and said:

—The Widow Palm, her daughters five.

A ring on her third finger, little glint of gold deep in the fold of flesh. Worn thin after twenty years; it would not though wear away. *Pronubus* that finger's name. *Index, medicus, pronubus, minimus.* Ringman, from which a vein ran delicate as a thread but growing thicker, *procedens usque ad cor,* running right to the heart.

—I think he knew not, she said. Poor little forked stick. So choleric his flesh burned to my touch.

John sat down on the bed's edge.

—I hope we have done aright, he said. I hope by this we have done what was asked.

—I care not if we have, Jane Dee said. Come husband, come in bed. I have somewhat to show thee.

—What dost have.

—Well come in. Give me thine ear and I will tell thee what. And thou canst tell me of thy sins too. Tell me all.

He looked down at her, and she pulled her cap from her head, and shook out her hair.

—O Lord, John Dee said. More fire in the bedstraw.

In Radnorshire where he was raised it only meant *More trouble to attend to,* but his wife laughed at it. *Fire in the bedstraw:* he laughed too, helpless not to, and she drew him into the bed. They heard their children at the door, forbade them to come in, the children complained, the parents called for the nursemaid, banged against the wall (the wall of her chamber) to rouse her, and drew the bedcurtains tight.

That morning (by John Dee's later reckoning) was conceived the fifth of their eight children, Theodore, gift of God, born at Trebona in the year the world ended. It must have been that morning he was made, for immediately afterward Jane Dee turned to the wall again, and wept, and would not answer his entreaties; and he was banished from her side until past the summer solstice.

But yes it was enough. When day came it was day in the glass too, brilliant blue sky such as Edward Kelley had never seen before; a field of green, May morning, and a great knight approaching on a milk-white steed, armed with a fiery spear, a long sword, a target whereon a thousand cherubim circled. A champion, but whose? And Madimi came, and followed that knight away; looked back once to smile, but made no farewell; gone, dew upon her feet. And another woman came instead, all in green, bare-breasted; *she hath a girdle of beaten gold slackly buckled,* Kelley said, *with a pendant of gold down to the ground.*

She spoke: that is she opened Kelley's mouth and spoke. John Dee wrote the words she spoke through Kelley, the last he ever took down.

—*I am the daughter of Fortitude and ravished every hour from my youth,* she said. *For behold, I am understanding, and Science dwelleth with me, they covet and desire me with infinite appetite; few or none that are earthly have embraced me, for I am shadowed with the Circle of the Stone and covered with the morning Clouds. My feet are swifter than the winds and my hands are sweeter than the dew. My garments are from the beginning and my dwelling place is in myself. The Lion knoweth not where I walk, neither do the beasts of the field understand me. I am deflowered yet a virgin, I sanctify and am not sanctified.*

On she came, this great whore goddess they had awakened, who could she be; Kelley trembled violently, speaking in her piping dreadful lovely voice.

—*For lo,* she said, *I am loved of many, and a lover to many; as many as come unto me as they should will have entertainment. Cast out your old strumpets and burn their clothes; abstain from the company of other women that are defiled, that are sluttish, and not so beautiful as I.*

Kelley, as though divided into two, himself and her, tried to draw away from the burning glass, yet at the same time went on talking, talking, unable not to: *I*

*will play the harlot with you, I will enrich you with the spoils of other men, I will make*
*a dwelling place among you, I will be common with the father and the son, for my youth*
*is in her flower, and my strength is not to be extinguished with man. But disclose not*
*my secrets unto women, neither let them understand how sweet I am, for all things be-*
*longeth not to everyone.*

Then she altered: *She turneth herself into a thousand shapes of all Creatures*
John Dee wrote: Kelley, knuckles white on the arms of his chair and his eyes like
saucers, chin on his breast as though he had been taken by the throat, stared at
the globe.

Tabby kitten, stick of elmwood, wriggling trout casting rainbow drops of
water; Kelley flinched. Burning ember shedding sparks, gray pigeon, drop of
blood on its beak, he could hear the flutter of its wings. Then more things, all
things, and all representations of those things, dogs, stars, stones, and roses,
cities, towns and roads; his childhood home, his mother, himself; the Queen and
her knights, a picture of the Queen and her knights, a picture of the picture.
Beasts and birds, tiger cubs rolling in the dirt, mountain where deer walked, eating apples; wide white lake where longleg dawn-colored birds like herons rose
up in their thousands. She became the little spirit Ben that had visited him, and
then a hundred other spiritual creatures, and all their names began with B. She
became John Dee and Joanna Kelley grappling naked; she became herself, herself and her lover coupling, he the one and she the many, unitary sky coupling
with multiform earth; he saw her become the generation of all things that have
names, a huge limitless fucking, the noise and crying-out of it, the shame and
triumph of it.

He laughed. Laughed and laughed. His prick stood, his chin trembled; an
awful terror and delight had arisen in him, and he cried aloud as though he leapt
from a height into dark water.


At day's end John Dee read over to Edward Kelley all that he had written down.

—She will have us gather here every seventh day, for a hundred days, he
said. She will enter here to us out of the stone.

—No, said Kelley. I will never speak to them more.

—What?

—No more, he said. No more intercourse with them. Else I am lost.

John Dee put down his papers and regarded Kelley, lying wrung and inert
on his couch, white as death. *Your other wife,* his wife Jane had mocked him in
her rage. Wife, son, brother.

—You have said so before, Edward.

He had said so before; but after this day Edward Kelley truly would not
speak to them again. He knew he would not. But it was no matter if he did or
didn't, for he was theirs now, theirs and not his own, as he had feared and hoped
he would become ever since that night of March in 1582 when he came to John
Dee's house in Mortlake with a book he could not read, and a powder that he
had been given, that he claimed to have found among the monks' tombs at Glas-

tonbury; ever since he had pushed aside the books and papers on John Dee's battered table and looked into the globe of moleskin-colored crystal standing there
in its frame.

Possessed. There was nothing more they could teach him, nothing more he
needed to hear them say. He was theirs.

—When you have rested, John Dee said. Refreshed yourself.

—No, Kelley said. Never. Never ever.

The angels had promised him safety from the wicked beings who had since
boyhood tempted and tormented him. Now he knew the truth: that the wicked
ones, those dog-headed yellow-eyed brown-gowned demons, were not different
from the kindly ones, the beautiful and pious ones who spoke to him out of the
glass, who offered him help, comfort, sanctuary: were but their servants, and did
their bidding. Into any one of them she could transform herself too, if she chose.

He had known it all along, all along: and he knew now that he had known
it, perhaps since that first night in Mortlake far away, night of wind and voices.
Oh, sometimes he had backed away from them in fright, and shut his eyes; or
he had stood still for weeks or months in boredom or confusion; but always he
had returned and again come closer, until at length he had drawn close enough,
and now they had seized him, and would never let him go.

# 15

Though the summer seemed unwilling to pass away, lingering at the threshold like a guest who has had too much fun to leave, Val decided to close the Faraway Lodge on Columbus Day as she always did, last day of the tourist season as it is counted in the Faraways, tourists being however rarely seen at any time in that secluded and not very inviting saloon by the Shadow River. It did have a big electric sign before it (to be shut off at midnight that night till the following year) that told those who happened to come upon it the name: Mama's Faraway Lodge.

It was a log structure with a broad porch you passed through (smelling the summer-camp smell of pine logs and a musty davenport) to get to the big barroom, to the left of which was the dining room that every summer nearly closed forever but did not. Behind the bar hung a sign that said in frank bold letters: *This place is for sale. Inquire at the Bar.* In the past, when more people used to find their way here who didn't already know of its existence, people had actually now and then asked the bartender (Val) about the possibility, but everyone who came here regularly knew the sign represented more of a threat than an offer; it meant that no matter how welcoming it looked around here, and no matter how glad Val might seem to see you, you were to know how fed up she was, deep down.

Closing night, Val and Mama served a dinner for Val's friends to signal the end of one more season. The dinner was lamb, which Val had prepared with as much anxious concern for its outcome and its reception as if she were giving birth to it. The lamb had been sold to her by Brent Spofford, one of those who gathered in the somewhat cheerless but familiar dinning room at Mama's; he had raised it, with its brothers and sisters and cousins, on his hillside acres up on Mount Randa and on the grounds at Arcady, where Rosie's two strong but uneducated sheepdogs harried them mercilessly, and (Spofford now observed) produced some damn tough muscles.

"It was in their genes," Rosie said. "You got stung in that deal, acquiring them, boy."

"I got their papers," Spofford said. "All their forebears were delicious."

Pierce remembered how, on his first day in the Faraways, he had encountered Spofford herding those very sheep through the town of Stonykill, crook in hand and straw on head. How he had said to Pierce Come follow me. Invited him anyway to stay over, as long as he wanted. And they climbed together up Mount Randa's slopes, following or leading the little flock and singing Handel: *All we like sheep.*

The dinner was a farewell for Spofford as well as for the season. The loose network of Vietnam veterans to which he belonged had begun circulating news about a couple of men from Spofford's old unit who lived now in the unpeopled hills of Dakota, and who because of that emptiness or for other reasons had come to believe, or to construct with the help of some locals and some odd texts, a legend that puzzled and alarmed Spofford. Who had himself spent time on and off in institutions when his tour of duty ended, trying to figure out what had happened to him and to his Republic in those years.

"These are guys I kept in touch with because of sheep," he said, pushing the bones of one of his own around his plate. "They were talking sheep. But now it's not sheep."

"I don't know why *you* have to do this," Rosie said. "Why now."

"Not sheep," Spofford said. "Wolves. You know those high northern woods once had wolves. Gone for years. Now they're coming back."

"Right," said Pierce.

"These guys say government agencies are reintroducing them. They're not just walking in down from Canada. They're being put in."

"Yes. I think I read."

"Not about these."

"I've read that the wildlife people wanted to reintroduce wolves in the north out there and the ranchers and farmers don't want them."

"These wolves aren't wolves," Spofford said. He drank the last of his wine. "Listen. These guys are very strange. They can't live with people, but there's nothing else they can't do. They go build a cabin by hand in the deep woods and live out there hunting and trapping like characters in a, a. And they think. And things get very, very clear to them."

"What do you mean, not wolves?" Val asked.

They waited. Telling the story seemed to require some care on Spofford's part, as though he drew it out from the coals of a fire: as though it could burn him too.

"You know how when you listen to someone," he said, "and what they say you disagree with; and you listen more, and at some point it goes beyond disagreement, something goes up your nose, I don't know if you know the feeling. You think: The man's gone."

"Yes," said Pierce. "Oh yes." And the others nodded and shook their heads, oh they knew. We all knew them then.

"As though he's been hollowed out," Spofford said. He felt his way toward the quality, his eyes narrowing, remembering. "Hollowed out, and what they say aloud to you is blowing through them from. From somewhere else, beyond or maybe behind them."

Rosie thought of the young man who had brought Sam home the other day. Hollowed out, smiling in the certainty blowing through him from elsewhere.

"Wolves," said Val.

"Well what scares you," Spofford said, "isn't the story so much—I mean this story that there was supposedly a secret unit formed, a government experiment maybe see, I don't know, now they're releasing them up there, rather than killing them or putting them to sleep—it's not that, it's the *certainty* they've got that scares you."

"A government experiment?"

"I don't really get the details, or the big picture," he said. "I mean all you *get* are details, and they're supposed to *make* a big picture; but. It's like the stocks of plague bacillus they say are stored in canisters somewhere, hybrid stuff that can kill half the planet in a week; somebody—lots of somebodies—spent their working lives on making those little germs. Hard to destroy your working life.

"Anyway, that's one thought. That they were developed, maybe not even for this war, maybe long before, I've heard somebody mention Hitler; but anyway we, they, had this capability. And in the end they can't bear to terminate it. So up there in those gigantic National Forests. Where nobody else is but these crazy vets, living on what they can hunt with an M1 they smuggled home from Vietnam. And winter coming on.

"Think of that."

They tried to do that, thinking of those high plains and those forests, colder there than here now; they thought of night, and living alone. Predators. Waking with memories in the silence.

"So if those guys feel threatened enough," Spofford said. "And the Hueys start landing with caged animals in the bay. Feds with trank guns. I don't know."

"It's just a story, though," Rosie said.

"You can die of stories," Spofford said.

They said nothing.

"I mean, Cliff says: Why shouldn't they believe these things? What else were we turned into?" He grinned. "The ones who have trouble now are the ones who couldn't turn back into themselves."

"*Homo homini lupus,*" Pierce quoted. Cliff was Spofford's friend or mentor, also a vet, who lived in the woods himself, though these *heimlich* ones hereabouts, not the Wild Wood. Cliff was going with Spofford. These were Cliff's buddies too.

"Well I don't know why *you* have to go," Rosie said.

"Yeah," Spofford said gently. "Yeah. I know you don't." He covered her hand with his. "I won't be long. A week. A couple. Not months."

"Okay so," Rosie said suddenly. She withdrew her hand from his and pushed her hair from her face. "So. So what strange weather, huh? How long can it last?"

Her back was straight, and she poured herself wine. "What else is new, what's the talk, what's the biz?"

"I hear The Woods is closing. Are closing. Whatever," Val said.

"Yes?" said Pierce, alert. "Really?"

"Well, being sold. Changing ownership."

"Who's buying?"

"Bidding," Val said. "Not buying yet. The Powerhouse. The Christian bunch."

"That's the name of it?" Pierce asked. "The Powerhouse?"

"The Powerhouse International," Rosie said. "I think they have some groups abroad."

"The Powerhouse," Pierce said again, pondering.

"Big secret," said Val. "I don't think The Woods wants people to know, and I don't think the Bible types want to be noticed. At least not yet."

Pierce thought of Beau: Something going on up there.

"They're rolling in dough," Val said.

"And how come you know all about it?"

Val laughed, and lifted a wise eyebrow: "There is much that I know," she said.

"Speaking of which," Rosie said, pushing her chair from the table. "You know it's a gorgeous night. Let's go and look at the stars. Walk a little."


At the Faraway Lodge the Shadow River widens and meanders almost south for a stretch. Down the width of it a band of sky was open to the horizon. The moon had not risen.

"Man look at your rosebushes, Val!" Rosie said in wonder. "Look at the rose hips. They're huge."

"Really?" Val said, peering at the hedges that bordered the walk down to the river. The roses were Mama's, not within Val's provenance.

"You ever use them?"

"For what?"

"Tea. Rose-hip tea. Lots of vitamin C."

"No. Nope. Red Rose yes. Rose hips no." She offered them to Rosie with a big gesture. "You want some? Take all you want. I'll go get a basket."

"Oh no wait. Don't go back. Wait. Look. I'll use my hat."

Rosie had a collection of hats, old and new, big and small; she had a face for hats, and liked herself in them, though after the first gratifying moment when she put it on in the store and looked at herself improved, made more mysterious or interesting or distinct, she rarely wore them. Not enough functions. She took off the broad-brimmed flat-crowned one she wore tonight, and began plucking the bright brown globes, red-cheeked like elfin faces, from the rose canes, careful for the thorns.

"What stars do we see?" Spofford asked Val.

"Oh God," Val said. "I'm so bad at that. It's embarrassing, I know. But when

I do learn it just confuses me and I forget again. I know the Evening Star is Saturn now. It said in the papers. Isn't that the Milky Way?"

"Yep," Pierce said. "There's Cygnus, the Swan, flying down it. See, the big cross."

"Oh," Val said. "Oh well hell. Yes."

"Cassiopeia," said Spofford, turning, looking up. "The big W."

"Right. A chair, actually. Over on its side. The mother of Andromeda. And she's there herself too. See? Bound." He told them the story, showed them the Great Square, the wings of Pegasus, Perseus on his way to the rescue, nick of time.

"And down there," Pierce said, turning again and pointing (this early-autumn sky was the one he knew best, the only one he happened to have studied), "above the Milky Way, is Sagittarius. Like a rearing horse."

"Hey," said Rosie. "It really does look like one."

"Aw," said Val. "I don't get it." She squinted and bent forward, as though to bring her head closer to the black page whereon it was printed.

"Well it hasn't always been a horse, or not everywhere," Pierce said. "Though everybody sees something there. In some places it's supposed to be the gate from earth to the Milky Way, the way that souls take to the land of the dead. That river or road."

"The door we leave by," Spofford said.

"Right. There are peoples who believe that once upon a time the doorjamb rested on the earth, without the big gap you see below the, well the shape; and in those days the gods and the ancestors could come and go on the earth."

"Not now," Val said.

"Only one way now," said Rosie.

"Only one way now." Pierce passed momentarily in thought again through Frank Walker Barr's classroom, where he had acquired some of the tales he retailed here and elsewhere: Barr, who was the only man Pierce had ever known who could talk as though that door were open still, who saw the gods passing and repassing, appearing in history, then returning to the stars, to be stars themselves.

Old Barr.

The universe we live in, he'd say, is made of space and matter, but it wasn't always. Once it was made not of matter but of time. The coordinates of our universe are places, the coordinates of that older universe were moments: solstice and equinox, the sun's passage from Sign to Sign, the moon's from Mansion to Mansion. And though a world made of space and matter can't just end, to be replaced by another one, a world made of time can. A cosmic disaster can in a moment alter the measure of the dance; a hero can right the world again. Silently, unnoticeably, new measures can be given to the repetitions by which the shape of the universe is maintained; one world vanishes without a whisper, and a new one comes to be. And no one the wiser except the wise.

"We come in through Cancer," Pierce said, and moved his pointing finger uncertainly. "Can't see Cancer now I guess. But our souls are supposed to come down into this world by way of the door open in Cancer . . ."

"Starting from where?" Spofford asked.

"Well I don't know. Just newly minted by God. From Heaven I guess. Beyond the stars."

"Okay."

"Your soul comes down through the lower heavens, that is through the solar system, heading for your mother's womb on Earth. On the journey down or in, you pass through the spheres, one by one . . ."

"Spheres?"

"Sure, the spheres of the planets. You have to pretend now that the planets are these gigantic sort of crystal spheres, nested one inside the other, with the earth in the middle."

"You mean they're not?" Val said, and brayed.

"As it goes through each sphere, the soul gets a gift, or a wrapping, a sort of coat or coating of materiality, which gets thicker as it comes down. These coats or gifts are the qualities of the spheres you go through. They are the characters of the different planets, and make you what you are, make you the way you are."

"Are you making this up?" Rosie asked. Still plucking rose hips into her hat.

"No. Nope." He clasped his hands behind him. "It's not made up. That doesn't mean it's true."

Rosie ceased her gathering to snort at this. Spofford took the hatful from her and inhaled its autumnal odor. "So what's it mean?"

"It just tells why we are the way we are, and not some different way instead."

Rosie now looked up too.

"What it means," Pierce said, "is that the soul inside you, when it reaches here, when it becomes part of your little forming body, however that happens, which don't ask me, comes already clothed in a body, which is made somehow out of stellar or planetary influences . . ."

"The astral body," Val guessed.

"Yes," Pierce said. "I guess so. Yes, exactly."

"*Sure,*" Val said with an air of negligent triumph, one for me.

"So each spirit or astral body would have to be different, depending on how the planets were arranged, against what stars, in what houses, when you came down through."

Spofford contemplated Saturn, following with his mind's eye the baby soul's journey. Little mite slung around by the huge planet's gravity, awed certainly by the cold-ringed humongous wall of it. Storing up maybe as it shot past its whole lifetime's worth of vertiginous dreams. He felt a moment's pity. Except that it wasn't true. If there was anything he knew for sure it was that his soul had been made right here, in these hills; that it didn't precede the coupling that one night of those two, old folks now and gone to Florida; and that it was still a long way from being finished. He took Rosie's hand.

"Anyway wow," Val said, neck bent, mouth agape. "Really."

They all looked away down that river of sky, where beasts and birds, weapons, furniture and folks were swept along. They didn't remember, not any of them, how each had sailed it, in the boat of the soul.

Out and down into the spheres through the door open in Cancer: with that sign in fact, they say, painted on its sails. Carried down into the outermost sphere, thickening and growing real; as it passes Saturn earning Saturn's gift, or suffering his blow, anyway laying down its Saturnian nature, however thick it might be; and then, older by that much, passing on, trimming the sails, wondering. After some æons coming into great Jupiter's gravity, where Rosie got her generosity and sense (Val had showed her, Jupiter in her first house, the House of Life), and wrapped thereby in another wrapping; and after who knows what length of time going through the locks or the baffle into the next sphere: Mars red as rust. And maybe our soul would rather not be detained there, feeling not so fly any longer nor so full of possibility as once it did and already probably forgetful why it has set out at all, no help for it though, here are Mars's things piled like the trophy of a warrior, sword, shield, helm.

And oh all that dark starlit waste that lies still between where it has come from and the small place to which it goes, a child off too young to school or camp, it might be fun there but it might be no fun at all. But now the Sun at least comes closer, or we on our way come closer to it, God bless the warmth; hungry, we take in as much as we are able (but what if it's pale and far off as we go by, its face averted, in a sad house, in the winter of the year? Then won't the soul need warmth, want warmth, fear warmth ever after?). Venus then—this is the map we are following, there are other maps—Venus next, in a good mood if we're lucky, perhaps on Earth far away they are looking up at her just then, just as the Sun has gone to rest (so it seems to them on Earth) and she has that smile, that smile at once placid and stirring, and she has it for us too as we go by, to share in, to have. Mercury, next to her, with his caduceus, watch out, he has a smile of his own, of complicity maybe, what is *he* up to? And his finger against his lips, be quiet now about it. All.

He's last.

Only the moist Moon left to pass, bag of waters, all sorrows and birth pangs: strange that when men stood upon her at last they found her to be dry dust, but their souls were after all wrapped in bodies by then and shut in their moon-suits, and the journey back up must be very different; whenever we make our way back anywhere, hearts and heads heavy and alive, won't we find that the treasures have vanished, the trunks are empty?

Anyway our soul pauses there, in the Moon's sphere, throat now full of tears; marvelling at blue-green Earth and its wrappings of air, fire, and water. It can no longer remember why it doesn't want to go that way; burdened now with its misshapen burdens but getting used to them; restless and already homesick but thinking well maybe it's just anticipation, the end of the journey, which has after all been long: thinking too of the warm womb and its sea. Oh let's get it over with.

And mightn't it happen then that, long afterward, grown up now and all this forgotten—just as the lookers-up in the side yard of Val's Faraway Lodge have all forgotten it, and yet shaped for good by it—you will meet another, one who took the same journey you took at nearly but not quite the same time, through similar but different heavens? Someone whose growing soul was made of just what you just barely missed, what you need but lack, which you can't know or name but which now you recognize, feeling even as you meet the possibility of being, at last, filled up: knowing, knowing for sure, that the more you are in the company of this soul, this complementary soul, the more you will be repaired?

O then be afraid.

A quarter moon had risen and wiped away all but the brightest stars when, hours later, Rose Ryder drove in at the gates of the Winterhalter estate; the gates open, the big yellow stucco house unvigilant. She turned down Pierce's drive, turning off her headlights; the tall unmown grass was white and alive in the moonlight. She cut the engine of the Asp as it topped the last rise before the little bungalow came into view, and coasted in silence (she could hear the brush of grasses against the car's undercarriage) down to the house. No lights were lit there.

She had come to see him, unable not to, but was silent now so as not to wake him. Without her braking it the car rolled to a stop, and she stepped out. If she left it here, and was allowed to stay, then by morning dew would have covered its seats and the steering wheel, the volume of poetry (Rilke) and the Bible (King James) that lay on the floor. It was time to put the top up anyway for the year, it was time, it was time.

Rose circled what she wanted, but not always out of caution. Sometimes out of caution, like any wise animal approaching found food, why this bounty, why left here so carelessly, is there some reason to avoid. But other times not out of caution; other times she circled, approached, retreated, approached again, waited: waited for whatever drew her (she knew it would) to overcome whatever kept her away. Circled close and closer, finally close enough to be seized.

She walked up to the door but didn't knock or open it or call at the keyhole, only stood listening for a time, more to something that might speak within her than to anything she might hear from the house. (Pierce saw her there, her head lowered, lips parted, arms crossed.) Then she stepped back from the door and into the moon's light, her brief red dress gone black and her eyes alight and her brown skin pale (Pierce could see all that too, and the slim wristwatch on her wrist; could even see—if not just at that moment then certainly when he looked back in after years—the glitter of wetness on her lip after she touched it with her tongue) and she went around the house into the darkness of the pines.

Pierce lay open-eyed and still in his bed, awakened by—what was it that had awakened him? Was it the car's approach and sudden silence (we can come to know the sound of a car as we can a familiar footstep, he was surprised to learn this) or was it the close of its door, or simply an alteration of the universal *spiritus* that filled the space between her and him? Now she had come around to the back porch, and Pierce thought he could hear her try the screen door, as they had done together in the former world wherein they had met. Had she come in that way? There was a noise at his bedroom window, it made him start, bat or bug though, not her. He sent out his spirit herwards.

Once when she was twelve or so, thirteen, her father had burned brush on some long-neglected acres of the farm, and she and her brother had helped tend it. Maybe it was a blowy day, or the wind increased; maybe she was just inexperienced with fires, how you made a fire do what you wanted though it was so huge and dangerous, like a trained tiger: she didn't know it wasn't out of control, she only worked furiously around its perimeters as her males did, raking and pushing the burning brush toward its consuming mouth, feeling the astonishing burn on her face and eyelids (her eyelashes later crumbling away to black dust in her fingers) but then at last ceasing to struggle against it and only standing in its aura, her breath short and her nipples hard (her father and brother staring, stirred too she thinks now by her being stirred): her whole being held as in a hand that might close.

Pierce knew that story (or would later imagine knowing it, so vividly as made no difference), and he had a fire too in his own past. She knew *that* story, and had thought of her own fire when he told it to her, how he had set a forest on fire by accident in Kentucky when he was a kid. By now she had come through the door from the porch into the kitchen. It was the fire's quickness Pierce had marvelled at, how quick it became uncontrollable, how surprising it was that it so soon could not be stamped out. She stepped into the dining room, his office, smelled the stove's breath, the books, and from the darkness he seized her.

Hand over her mouth and arm around her body. That hand closing. He cried out at the same moment he grasped her, shouting one wordless word into her ear: and it was that shout (she told him later) that made her come.

# 16

Once in a medical text, another of his uncle Sam's maybe, Pierce had seen illustrations of the body in which the sizes of the various parts and organs were drawn relative to the numbers of nerve endings each possessed: the weird homunculus that resulted remained in his memory ever after. The nerve-poor torso and shanks were shrunken and small, the calves not half the size of the feet, and the hands were larger still, with great fingertips like a frog's; from the small skull protruded huge seeing eyes, big nose with bigger nostrils, lips like loaves, the slab of tongue protruding from between them as big as the whole of the breast. When he closed his eyes and concentrated, he knew that this fellow was the one his inner sense knew and went by, not the image in the mirror; he could feel him; he thought that the blind would have this body and no other.

A fig leaf, he remembered, exiguous surely, had in that picture covered the penis (it was only a man that was shown) but which was certainly great big in the mind's map, big as could be desired, heavy-shafted and helmet-headed, however disappointing it might be to the colder measuring eye. Her great hand though (or his) still big enough to grasp it easily, for her parts had to be as large as his to meet him everywhere, her lips like his, her tongue etc. What was odd was that as their neural fibers fired and grew warm and the parts that were crowded with them enlarged even further, their eyes adjusted the rest, though never quite catching up; so they both grew gigantic, as measured by the details of their largest parts, the flocked and dark and blood-rich parts: the purple-brown lips filmed with shining liquid, the tender eye-corner where the great globular tear formed, the drop of clear syrup in the blind cyclops eye of.

Meanwhile they forget how to speak, they become beings of another order, or unfold those beings from somewhere within themselves, giant and giantess, who take his place and hers there on the shiplike, the prairielike bed: and that was why they did what they did. They learned what things they must do in order to become those beings and so, for a time, cease to be themselves.

*Vacatio,* absence from which they always returned too soon, unsustainable for long. The desire is infinite, the act a slave to limit, law of diminishing returns, in the kiln of actuality anyway, if not in the pyramid scheme of the *Ars Auto-amatoria.* The erotic bond wastes away, says Bruno, through all the senses by means of which it is created; which is why the lover, like a child building a castle by the sea, continually struggles to shore up his work, "desiring to transform himself into the beloved, pass through her and into her by all the portals of sense through which knowledge comes, eyes, tongue, mouth, and so on."

And so on.

On a night as he sat on his bed waiting for her, with his *impedimenta* and tricks and traps around him, Pierce thought in a kind of helpless wonderment that there must be a whole different way of forging bonds or links, a way that everybody of course knows about, that's common knowledge. Just time, probably, basically, time spent in love; the slow accumulation of shared things; life choices accepted and lived with. Husband and wife. Laughter and tears. Years go by. Whatever.

But he was sure he didn't have those means; and if he had not these means, he thought he would not have any; would no longer be able to draw from her or cause her to produce, as the alchemist produces his quintessence from the sufferings of his *prima materia,* her spirit-stuff for him or before him. And at that he thought of what he had prepared for her this night, and his heart dilated and his loins grew conscious, experiencing in advance what he would do, what she would say and feel, as if it were already over.

In Pierce's bedroom, the bedroom Rose called Invisible, besides the big bed Pierce had brought from the City (spoils of his life there, a life which had required and could also afford such a barge and its fittings) there stood another, narrower bedstead. It had been there from the beginning, had been the first thing they had both seen in this room in the moonlight. It was of bony iron. Somewhere the springs had worn away or broken, and had been replaced by wooden slats. There was a mattress too, its ticking stained but by what, smelling more sad and old than foul; circled here and there with o's of orange rust where buttons had come off.

On this night she asked him if he would please cover it before she. He said no.

She sat down on the bed's edge and he gave her a small faceted glass of bitter-green liquid. It was a Catalan concoction that a former lover (whom he called Sphinx, when he named her to himself) had brought him home from Europe once; it was called *Foc y Fum,* and the label showed a house burning down. Fire & Smoke? She was naked now except for the long socks she would not do without. He had her drink it off, regarding her kindly, speaking softly to her about this and that.

"No more," she said.

"Finish it."

In the room's corner glowed a small electric fire, Moloch's mouth, great grimace with orange teeth and constant growl. More heat, never enough.

And all these things too became part of the forming seal, *impresa* on the labile stuff of his spirit: the heater, and the green bottle, and the narrow bed. How she held out her hands to him when he asked, watching with close attention his every move, but lifting her eyes to his now and then, her eyes from which he drank, *foc y fum.*

Now. Take the glass away. Begin.

When she was bound to the iron bed he went about her with his hands, an acrobat going about the ring before his performance, tugging on every rope, imagining them failing. As he did so he spoke to her. "How sweet I roamed from field to field," he said, "and tasted all the summer's pride; till I the Prince of Love beheld, who in the sunny beams did glide."

"Pierce," she said or breathed.

Pierce only answered: "He showed me lilies for my hair, and blushing roses for my brow; he led me in his gardens fair, where all his golden pleasures grow."

The delicacy of her hand, the tension of its hundred muscles, for a moment he watched her test, too, what she could do and not. Without a word he put his hand between her legs, not roughly but not kindly, a physician's or breeder's assessment. My God how fast it started in her.

"Pierce I can't. I'm afraid. Pierce not tonight."

No more seeing: he bound her eyes in imitation silk, knotting it firmly against her silken slew of hair, not easy. He wanted to ask if or what she saw but knew he couldn't. Then: "All right, Rose," he said, and withdrew.

He had among his possessions a Polaroid camera that long ago his mother had bought for his uncle Sam for Christmas. Now, like Sam's dressing gown, it was his. The little black-and-white pictures it made were a lot like the pictures that his cousin Bird used to get from her Hawkeye box camera: dim, sometimes barely scrutable, hiding and revealing at once.

Rose didn't know he had taken it out. She could tell nothing. Pierce? she asked again, and he made no answer. He opened the camera's body, and its folded neck extruded, bearing its one hawk eye. The noise of its clicking into place startled her, she tensed against her bonds with a sudden shudder, it was something to be used against her, but what. Pierce saw in the foggy viewfinder a tiny scene, broadened at the edges, all lines leading outward to nowhere, inward to the human figure at the center.

The eye is the mouth of the heart. What it eats is not light, though light is its mode or means: what it eats is Recognition, which the heart can chew on, which the soul can know. There always had to be time in their meetings for this cold collation, this scavenging and scarfing by his eyes, filling him with a repletion not different from hunger as he looked.

Tic.

The camera was obsolete even then, his roll of film was the last the pharmacy in the Jambs had for sale and out of date. But there the image was, light curdling on the retinal oblong of white paper that you peeled from behind the camera's eye. There is the shine of her thigh, there is the parting of her lips; there even is the parting of her buttocks, and the shadow revealed or hidden there. Right away you had to coat the image with a sort of slime, sliding a little spongy bar provided by the manufacturer over the surface, if you didn't it would fade faster than memory. Pierce did that.

"Pierce?"

No more talking. He bound her mouth. She could still raise three fingers if she needed to. He showed her she could. "With sweet May dews my wings were wet," he said. "And Phoebus fired my vocal rage." He leaned close to her and spoke into her ear: "He caught me in his silken net. And shut me in his golden cage."

At last he put his ear against her, between her breasts, to hear her heart tapping fast and fearfully, ready to receive he thought or guessed. Years later when about to pass into sleep she will be revisited by that—his warm strange ear upon her—and awake with a start, her heart filling painfully. Or she will forget it with the rest.

He unbound himself.

*He loves to sit and hear me sing*
*Then laughing sports and plays with me;*
*He stretches out my golden wing*
*And mocks my loss of liberty.*

They had come so far from where they had started. We've all come so far. Isn't that it? Isn't that why we can't stop hunting, restless, dissatisfied, champing at a bit that never becomes familiar? Or is that so only for those born under that leaden star (as deeply embedded in her chart as his, she knew it but had been misled about its meaning) that governs the liver, in whose glossy sheen (Aristotle says) the most desirable things are reflected for the hungry soul to see?

They were exiles here. He had once known it, and forgotten, and then forgotten that he had forgotten. No secret more secure. She knew it though: had just learned or relearned it, after a long forgetting had seen it, shocking and familiar at once. Not in her borrowed Terrier sedan, not on that night of wind coming down the Shadow River road, no before that—but it was indeed what she fled from that night. She was fleeing in the wrong direction, though—Beau Brachman would say we tend to: not out but further in, as into a maze.

She had said almost nothing about her first weekend in Conurbana, guilty maybe or wary, and he had not pressed her. Now she began going there every few days, a drive of an hour or two in her restless scarlet roadster; she returned the same day, or stayed the night. She said little also about what went on there, sometimes volunteering vague cheerful remarks, sometimes leaving it up to him to ask, or not: as though it were a series of probing and maybe slightly shameful medical procedures she was undergoing, too intimate to discuss at length, from which she returned refreshed, alert, gay.

"Oh we study," she said once. "We'll take a word, a word out of the Greek, and see how it appears in different places in English in the Bible, translated differently. To see how the meaning changes."

"Like."

"Like *parhesia*."

"*Parhesia*," Pierce said. He searched his inward schoolroom. Greek came just before lunch, the smells of macaroni and cheese drifting up from the refectory; by the big knocking radiator, beneath the crucifix, was the wooden stand where the big Liddell and Scott was chained; he felt it urgent he find the word before she told him. "Openness, frankness."

She pointed a gunlike finger at him, you got it. "But it's translated in lots of different ways in English. So we look it up and see. It takes a while."

"Hm."

"It's interesting."

"Mm."

More than the theodicy it was the company he pondered. Her cheerful evasiveness was that of a woman with a new lover, or an old one, which is what Pierce assumed. Mike Mucho, her *quondam,* and her boss at The Woods too in some sense; inventor or developer of the new science of Climacterics which had absorbed or occupied Rose when she and Pierce first met, forgotten now apparently. He fished delicately for certitude on this matter, but *parhesia* was no part of his relation with her, or hers with him, and it was too late to start now.

"Are there other people from The Woods at these things?"

"Oh yes sure. Some of them have moved there or I guess live there."

"In Conurbana."

"It's nice. There's always somebody to stay with."

Whatever it was that she had learned, or now confessed or professed, whatever she dabbled in during her time away, did not or had not yet altered her nighttime tastes. She said she was happy, and she was, but it seemed to him that she had actually grown hungrier too, and in more than one way. She ate and drank with luminous eagerness. She talked about her life and the future as though impatient for their unfolding. And she listened as eagerly, if anything more eagerly, to the stories he spoke into her ear, in which she featured, she or her eidolon—the small she within her, the she whom together they had discovered or made.

She wore a fur-collared coat when next she came to his house, and the smell of the cold night air caught in it reminded him of his mother, the city, time. He brought her into the bedroom before she took it off.

"We can't be too long," she said. They were going tonight to a poetry reading, some old friends or acquaintances of hers, mostly male. She herself kept a sheaf of much-handled poems she would show to no one. "They said really eight."

"Just come in," he said. He brought her, still talking, to the bed, to face the wall by the bed. For a long moment she would not see what he faced her toward.

" 'Cause if you drive it takes forever and we."

"Hush. Look." He placed his big hand on her neck and held her head like a doll's pointing toward what he had brought her to see.

She saw. She started to say *Oh no,* laugh and turn away.

"Hush," he said, and tightened his hold on her. "Look."

She did so. She ceased to laugh and looked. He watched her look, watched her eyes consume, or drink.

"See?"

The little Polaroid had turned out to be smaller than the picture of the dead pug had been. So he had made a mat for it of dark rose taffeta, shocking within the dark surround of the frame. He bent the flowered shade of the old brass standard lamp to shine athwart it, which brought out the details of the carving or molding of the frame, the collar, belt and switches; still tenebrous, though no longer funereal. He brought her closer, to see, to touch if she wanted to.

"Who is it," she said. "Is it."

"Yes."

"How did you, how," she said.

"Hush," he said. "Look."

They looked. If you did not know what you looked at could you actually discern. A tawny headland, she; pale seafoam of her discarded slip around her oddly contorted body. Pearl-drops of light where the camera's flash (Wink-Light, its proprietary name) had struck her bonds.

What he had made, he saw now as she looked on it, was a seal: an *impresa* such as the Renaissance made so many of, thinking they were imitating the hieroglyphs of Egypt, or Ægypt; hoping to make an allegory so potent and utter that it passed directly through the eye to the heart, where the soul could read it and be moved to virtue or to action. Giordano Bruno had conceived dozens of them, some he himself cut to be printed, some he only described at length in words. For in fact they couldn't be understood without words, not even back then in the picture-book world, at the very least each needed its motto: the picture was the body, the seal-makers said, the motto was the soul.

What motto for this one, then.

*Andromeda,* perhaps. *The Marriage of Agent and Patient.*

"All right," he said at length, when he thought that it and its lesson had entered her. He put his arm around her shoulders, to lead her away, as though she were bereaved, had just viewed the open casket. They said no more about it, only tore through the night in his car; at the reading he watched her listen to the poet, a rapture or spell upon her face that he didn't think was all due to the mild verse, plangently read, about rain and the moon.

Then late, late, she watched with a new intensity of attention as he took out and put on her neck where the blood beat a studded collar of her own, and buckled with some difficulty the creaking new leather (*is this the largest you've got?* he'd asked the pet-store clerk, divining suddenly that the man knew exactly what he was up to). There were bright chains, new too, for the ring that hung from it, heavy enough for any mastiff bitch, he said to her; and he placed her where she could see the thing on the wall that he had made for her. She looked. She soon ceased to speak except to say, when required, the assents he wanted from her; otherwise, only the sounds of the universal language. But when he entered her, when he pushed with gritted teeth into the strangeness of the wrong or back way into her (inexpressible what constituted it exactly, that harrowing strangeness, he the first who had gone that way) she said softly but distinctly *I love you.*

Who? he wondered. To whom had she spoken? Never had she said those words to him in the light of day or facing him anywhere. He didn't think it was to him she said them now, he thought she was sleeptalking, speaking maybe to a figure in a room into which he had only driven her: a dream she unfolded even as she lay beneath him here gripping the bars of the iron bedstead, a dream where someone was doing things to her like the things he did, but someone different, someone to whom she could say or must say what she had said. He didn't reply. He didn't ask.


Then the leaves were all down. Now Pierce could see from his window the river he lived beside, the broad brown Blackbury River, and, on the other side, the decaying signals and maintenance sheds of a railroad spur line he had not known was there; in the deep green time it had been invisible, the mountain seeming to rise straight up from the far bank.

Fallen leaves burdened Pierce's brief yard and made it as one with the leaf-littered slope that went up to the big house, and with the field that went out to the road; Pierce thought of raking up all of his and burning them, but then (he saw) in the next wind a million more dead souls would be blown downward from the Winterhalter lawns and over his, unless he raked up all of those too, and so there being nowhere to stop he could not bring himself to start, only stood in the stillness and listened to the mass of them crepitating. His landlord's car appeared on the heights above as he stood there, a long golden-bronze one as large as any, and came down from the house; did not turn outward through the gates, though, but the other way, toward Pierce's place.

When Pierce had first met Mr. Winterhalter, emerging now with painful slowness from his car (the more they shrink and shrivel, Pierce had noticed, the larger their cars become), he was a hale egg-shaped ham-handed man, curious and busy. Now, only a couple of months later, he was immensely old, ill, and evidently dying. Pierce greeted him.

"We're leaving," Mr. Winterhalter said.

"Yes."

With some effort Mr. Winterhalter put his shaking hand in his pants pocket and drew out a bunch of keys on a piece of ancient brown twine. "You'll remember everything," he said.

"Yes." Pierce had been given a tour by Mr. Winterhalter in his former sprightlier form, shown the lights to be left burning, the fusebox, the oil cutoff switch, the emergency numbers; the house large and expensively furnished in an anonymous style, faintly shabby and smelling of human occupation.

"That's all right then." He pondered. "Have you seen the well?"

Yes, Mr. Winterhalter had shown him the well. Perhaps he'd forgotten he had. A stone wellhouse in the cove of the hill behind the great house, they both turned to look that way; the black plastic pipe along the ground.

"You'll keep it flowing."

"Yes."

"You won't turn off the overflow."

"No, certainly not."

"It defeats the purpose."

"Yes."

Mr. Winterhalter looked around himself at the leaves and the leafless trees. "Good," he said. "We'll be gone all winter. In the spring you'll see us again." He looked at his great gold wristwatch, then lifted his eyes, as though to check the constellations turning unseen behind the white sky, time to go, hurry hurry. Pierce thought it unlikely that the man would ever return here, and wanted to ask him what then, but he did have a list of emergency phone numbers in case the Winterhalters did not reemerge with the chucks. A lawyer's was among them.

"In the spring," Mr. Winterhalter said again, and made to enter his car. At that moment another car appeared at the far gate and turned in.

"Who's this?"

"A friend," Pierce said. "Actually, we're headed out just now."

Mr. Winterhalter stared at the car and at Rose. She was again driving the Terrier loaner sedan, its top somewhat crushed and rumpled but otherwise not much worse for its adventure on the night the wind blew so hard.

"You've met her," Pierce said. Rose waved.

"No," said Mr. Winterhalter definitely. "Never."

Where was her own car? In the shop again, she told him. The mechanic at Bluto's Automotive could not acquire a certain part that the foreign-made and long-discontinued little Asp needed to run, did not think he would be able to acquire it except maybe from some collector or buff somewhere, unless he could machine it himself, which he was more eager to try than she was to permit. So it sat there.

"The distributor drive," she said as she drove them away from where Mr. Winterhalter stood beside his car. "Stripped out."

"What's that?"

"Some little gear. Is he all right?" She was studying Mr. Winterhalter in the rearview mirror. "He's not moving."

"He can stand there," Pierce said. "It's his house. He's just thinking."

They turned out onto the main road. They were going today to her cabin by the river, which must now be closed up for the winter. She had asked for his help some time ago and he had agreed, though he had feared this moment, the place where her path once again ran out, feared it enough that he had given it no thought: where she would go now, what would become of her, the trembling that he had never been able to still. But she seemed untroubled now, driving too fast through the motionless day, happy, hectic even; for she knew, she said, what she was going to do. She was leaving the Faraways.

"I'm going," is what she said, and he at first didn't know from where. They were parked in the driveway of her little cottage, but had not yet got out. Well she had got a chance to go to school in Conurbana, she said, and she was going to take it. A sort of scholarship. She was going to enroll at Peter Ramus College, the School of Social Work, get a master's in psychiatric social work. A real degree. Credentials. She couldn't really pass on this.

"Scholarship?"

"Help," she said. "They want to help me, and I can work with them there too."

"Them."

"The healing group. I explained it all."

She wiped her cheeks with a rapid movement, perhaps there were tears there; she smiled. She had not explained it all or even any part of it completely.

"But won't you be coming back to work at The Woods? I mean if you get this degree . . ."

"Maybe." She looked at him for an instant sidelong, then away. "What I guess is, I'm not really going to be the one to decide. But I don't know if you could really understand that. Even if I could explain it."

"Uh-huh," Pierce said. "God walks into your life and you just walk right out of mine."

"We can't have a static relationship, Pierce," she said. "You don't want that."

Why? he thought. Why can't we? Static, endless, it's what he did want: an active relationship certainly, urgent even maybe, but yes static, a furious stasis of immediacy encompassed by a bed, four walls.

"And why," he said, "do they have an interest in paying for your education?"

"Why do you need to make it sound sinister?" She pushed open the Terrier's door. "They're committed to healing. If you want to hear about what they've done in institutions, helping people who nobody else can help. I mean maybe this is something you never understood about me," she said.

"What."

"That I want to help. That I want to know how." She started up toward the cabin. "Maybe you don't know me as well as we thought."

While Rose rummaged through the cabin for the last of her belongings and piled them in the car's trunk, Pierce was asked to mop out the toilet, which he did, and to drag out from the shed where they were stored the plywood panels that had to be screwed on over the windows, protection against weather and winter predators, human and otherwise.

"So that's what this is about?" he asked her. "This healing group? Faith healing?"

"Well healing, yes. Healing in the Spirit. It works, Pierce. It does. I've seen it."

"I know it works." Pierce's fourth-grade teacher, Sister Mary Philomel, had cured a stomach cancer (she said) by prayer; Pierce's uncle Sam said there was no doubt it was a cancer; he said that those who believe they will get better sometimes do, against all prognoses. Miracles. Every doctor, he'd say, has seen a few. "Of course it works. It just doesn't work very well, or very reliably anyway. Not as well, or as often, as say penicillin, or surgery."

They worked for a time in silence. Pierce found and carried out the last small plywood sheet. "I thought," he said, "you were talking about healing the spirit. Psychiatric healing."

"Sure." She zipped a huge duffel. "I mean I don't know if I could ever do it. But wouldn't it be amazing if. If I could just take hold of someone sick or screwed up and say *Begone!* And see them get better."

"Amazing," he said.

"Yes."

"And just who is it," he said, "that you would be saying this *begone* to?"

She pointed at him, at his breast. "That little one," she said. "That's the one for the bathroom window around back."


"I want to know," Pierce said. "I do. I want to know about you, learn what I don't know."

They were in his bed, her jam-packed car outside in the fog, the night weirdly warm again.

"Well," Rose said. "You could ask."

He pondered this, and laughed; after a moment so did she.

"Psychological testing," he said. "That could give me an insight."

"Sure."

"I'll test you now," he said, and she looked at him oddly, a look he knew. *I'll test you, Rose.* Then she saw that he meant nothing more than what he had said. "This is a test my older cousin Hildy gave us years ago. She brought it back from school."

"What school is this?"

"Her boarding school. Queen of the Angels, in Pikeville, Kentucky. Hildy," he said gravely, "is today a nun."

"Huh," said Rose. "Well in that case."

"I'll ask you to imagine a house," Pierce said, folding his hands in his lap. "This house is your house, but it is not any house you have ever lived in. It's not your dream house or the house you intend one day to live in. It's just a house."

"I love these," she said.

"I'm going to ask you to describe certain things about this house, and you have to answer with the first images that come to your mind. Afterward comes the interpretation."

"Okay."

"Okay."

They both readied themselves, looking inward, somewhat as they had on

Rose's deck in the October evening when together they had practiced phantasmal transmission. Then Pierce said:

"You're walking toward the house, first of all. And there are trees. What kind, how big."

"Tall dark pines. A bunch. You can't see the house."

"Hm," said Pierce wisely. "Okay. The front path."

"Can't see it for the trees."

"You go in the house," Pierce said. Rose observing her own inward progress shuddered slightly. "And in the house is a cup. Where, what kind."

In the house in the dark pines, a house like her grandfather's little one where he lived alone, unpainted and dusty but he didn't care, not about that or anything. It was that house and every house, like houses in dreams; this one she lay in now too, dark too. In the dining room a cabinet, its insides wallpapered in roses.

"Just a cup," she said. "In the china closet. Old. Not mine." So old or maybe long unwashed that a dark or roughened place could be seen on its lip, where drinkers' mouths had worn away the glaze.

"A key," Pierce said.

"A bunch," she said. "On a knotted old twine hung inside the back door. Old black skeleton ones and little trunk keys and clock keys and cabinet keys and all, all tied together. One's the house key maybe."

Pierce smiled on her, good work. "Outside," he said. "A path leading away."

"Little, and unfinished. Just worn by people walking."

"There's water there. Some water in some form."

She closed her eyes. "The sea." It rose, dark too, wholly unexpected, heaving black rollers, at the end of the path away.

Pierce laughed aloud. "The *sea*?"

"Sure."

There were, he thought, one or two more items on Hildy's list but he couldn't remember them. "Okay," he said, and told her what the things he had named were supposed to stand for in the mental universe: the front path and the trees your past and those who influenced you; the cup, love; the key, knowledge and its uses; the back path the future. The water, sex.

"An allegory," he said.

"The sea," she said, and laughed a little too. "But what's it *mean*?"

"Well," he said, foxy therapist, "what do *you* think it means?"

She rubbed her head against his chest. "Ask me another," she said.

"I don't know another." He circled her cool shoulders with his arm. "I'll tell you a story."

She drew closer. "A story."

"This story is about a little girl named Rose."

"Ah."

"And some of the unfortunate things that befell her."

"I know this one."

"Yes. Maybe you can help me tell it."

She listened, and after a time Pierce's big thumbs pulled down her pants, and he went on talking and she responded; but she also walked in that house that she had built, looking for something, something that ought to be there but that he had not named or asked for. The black pines darkened the windows and the sea unfolded on the shore.

In the far reaches of the night Pierce awoke, and found that she was awake too beside him. Perhaps her wakefulness had awakened him. He watched her reach for her cigarettes, the flare of the match illuminating her shoulders and her downcast eyes like a saint's or angel's candle in a devotional painting.

"What is it?"

"Nothing. It's sad to be going."

"Yes."

"It's such a nice area. I've been happy. Mostly."

"You can't stay?" he asked. "I mean surely there are all kinds of jobs."

"Nope," she said. "Not for me." She threw back her head, shook free her hair, exhaled invisible smoke. "Hopeless, hopeless. *No es posible.*"

They talked more. He knew there was a question it was incumbent upon him to ask now, but not exactly what it was; or he knew what it was (he had to ask her to stay; to ask her, if she had nowhere to go, to stay here, for a while, from now on) but he would not believe it. She put out the smoke, he fed at her burnt mouth. "Now sleep," he said.

"I can't."

"You want some hot milk?"

"Oh yuck you're kidding."

After a time she seemed to sleep again, though he did not; he lay and studied the familiar strange shapes of his nighttime bedchamber, the shirt and suit people in the wardrobe whose door had been left open, the great jewel that was the glass doorknob. The new inkblot of his seal or emblem or *impresa* on the wall, unseeable. And late, so late or early that the night had begun to turn silver in the windows, he heard her weeping beside him; felt the mattress they shared shaken slightly by her rhythmic sobs.

Then it was day. She had slept too long, she said, she was late, Pierce didn't ask for what. He made her coffee hastily. Half-dressed she drank it, near tears again it seemed, while she searched for her keys (they lay on the seat of her car where she had dropped them, the memory had not yet reached her through the wreckage of the intervening night).

"There's so much to *do*. Get an apartment. Do my studying. I have to take GRE's," she said. "I took them once before and did terrible. I can't this time. So I'm going to go take one of those courses they give, to prepare you."

"Oh yes."

"Big pain. I know I'll do well though. And there's the course I'm taking with them."

"The Powerhouse," he said.

"The Bible and Healing," she said. She smiled, chipper. "It's a big commit-ment."

"Two hundred dollars," he said. He jammed his hands in his pockets, and noticed that his heart had begun to beat more rapidly.

"I paid it," she said. "A couple of bonds."

"Your getaway money."

"It's okay," she said.

"No no you shouldn't have given it to them," he said with sudden urgency, rising from his chair. "Listen, listen. If you need it replaced, I'll give it to you."

"Pierce I'm not going to need it."

"You never know, you never know," he said. "You can't be without your get-away stash. What if you need to get away? You have to have it, you have to. Wait, wait."

He went to his canvas bag, stained and ragged, the bag he had been lugging books and other necessities in for years; he rummaged in its contents and pulled out the envelope that contained five old fifties, his share of Kraft's own getaway fund, ironed flat from their years inside the *Life of Gresham,* where Pierce had found them. "Here," he said. "Here take this."

"I can't," she said.

"Sure. It's not even really mine. I mean it came to me by a strange coinci-dence, very strange, I don't have any claim on it but nobody else does either. I don't want it. I want you to have it."

"Pierce."

"Don't spend it ever. Keep it. That way if you ever, ever."

She wouldn't take the envelope from him, but she let him stuff it in her bag; she looked not at it but at him, his big lowered busy head. She thought: *It's so.*

When she'd told them, Mike and the others, that two hundred dollars was a lot for her to spend, they had laughed, and had told her it would come back to her, not in a long time either but quickly, so quickly it would astonish her. And here it was already, even before she had spent it. And from Pierce! She wanted to laugh now, or shout aloud: the foolish wonderful gratification of it, the simple trick of it, which just now she got: that it was so even if it wasn't so. It didn't *need* to be so—didn't need to have come to your pocket right from God's hand—but it only happened if you believed it could be so. And maybe that was the real, the best reason for its coming to you: just so you could learn that.

"Okay," she said, her heart rich within her, the sweetness with which it was topped up rising to her throat. "And if you need it back."

"Sure," he said. "To pay *my* fee."

"Oh Pierce. Listen."

But there wasn't any way to say it, the sudden glistening web of the world's construction she perceived, all things tied together and connected. So they stood together in the brown yard for a time, and said little, how they would surely keep in touch, even see a lot of each other maybe, how it wasn't really that far, not that far at all.

"An hour's drive. Hour and a half," she said.

"Sure," he said, carelessly. He saw in his mind's eye the freeways, four and even six lanes, their perilous ramps and exits. He had rarely driven his old Steed sedan on any but the dirt roads and two-lane blacktop, never crowded, of the Faraways; to go farther was, he felt, beyond him, not after all a real driver.

But he said *Sure* and they held hands and smiled.

When we have come at last to the center of a maze (Beau Brachman called this one *Heimarmene*) it appears of course to be the end we sought. We sit down there (on the little bench of stone, in the sunlight and the odor of boxwood) and wait for a bit. Whatever is to happen to us, we are sure, will happen here. In fact we are inside out, but we don't know this. We wait. And there, at length, one day—how does it come to be, does it come in at the ear or out and upward from within, or does it gather in the air around our heated heads, become the air, is it breathed in with a gasp—we see. We say *I see.* Some do.

What Pierce knew about mazes, what he had gleaned from his researches but had not yet had to test, was that the way to exit from a maze (at least one of those built in the great age of mazes) is simply to *follow the right-hand wall.* Just put out your right hand and keep to that wall. If there had not been such a simple key or trick then the makers themselves would not have been able to get out.

But Pierce had never been able to tell left from right. It was a comical trait that many who knew him, Rose among them, had laughed at. If asked a direction he always pointed, for if he named it the word that popped out of his mouth might be either, a penny flipped; given the name of a direction in which to turn, he was as likely to turn the opposite way. He could not name the hands of his body without a moment's deliberation, every time, every single time.

# 17

*Imagination! Potent Sprite*
*That brings to every yearning Wight*
*What most he wants, and instantly!*
*Imagination! Let me see*
*Discovered in thy Sacred Glass*
*The Image of that Perfect Lass*
*Intended from the Flood for me,*
*My lawful wedded Wife to be!*
*She died a thousand Year Ago?*
*Will not be born till Hell sees Snow?*
*I'll wed her yet in Fancy's Bow'r,*
*Enjoy her, ev'ry Leisure Hour;*
*Build her a House or Mansion fair*
*Of Substance thinner than the Air,*
*And solitary, doubled be*
*By blessed Possibility!*

I t was dark at Arcady, its cupola and tower just visible against the moon, one yellow window lit, like the cover of a Gothic novel; the window was Rosie's room, and she lay in bed, a flannel shirt over her nightgown and her knees up to hold the big old book. A week till Halloween, and Sam's appointment at Little Ones. Sam slept beside her, a little bear, facedown but knees drawn under her, her blond curls alone visible, as still as though dead. She'd wanted to sleep in her own bed tonight but Rosie had asked her to stay. Aw cmon Sam please. From far, far below (just the basement, but another country to Rosie) she heard the furnace awake, and go to work. Getting colder. How was it doing down there, anyway, did it need seeing to, by whom? Never done, she thought.

*Ars Auto-amatoria; or, Every Man His Own Wife. A Very Heroick Epyllion in Four Fits.* There was a jokey Preface full of wretched puns, some she guessed were there but didn't get, and a few epigraphs from sources she doubted really existed; there was a list of Persons in the Drama though the thing wasn't a play at all (*The Brothers Ballock, a Pair of Hangers-on; Scrotum, a wrinkl'd old Retainer*) and then the First Fit started. Rosie turned the thick sheets, wondering why it was printed in such large type; maybe old Anon was just terrifically pleased with himself, proud of what he had produced, and all by himself too.

> *Art thou a Separated Twin?*
> *Then find thy Better Half within*
> *And join in Union Sphericall*
> *Thyself to self, as Plato's Ball.*

She remembered that idea from college philosophy—she would have guessed Aristotle though—that we were all really once beings of both sexes, and round (why round? Because the circle was supposed to be the most perfect shape, whatever that meant; Pierce would know). Then somehow divided, like eggs cut in half with a thread; and ever after restless, unsatisfied, looking for our lost halves. Bedeviled eggs. Lucky if you found him, or her; lucky, probably.

> *No ancient Goody weighs thy Bed;*
> *Betrothed art daily, nightly wed.*
> *See where she stands! In Shift of white,*
> *Meek as upon her Wedding Night.*
> *Forever young, though thou grow old,*
> *Never jaded, never cold*

Cold. She thought of what Pierce had said, the triumph of hope over experience: all those young wives, dead in childbirth, dead from a cat scratch, dead from the plague or the flu. There could be reasons why the prospect was scary, or unsettling. Maybe the writer was not, as she had been imagining, someone old, crabbed and saturnine, but someone young. Maybe very young.

There was a time just after she was married herself (not a short time either, it had seemed endless to live through) when she had been half-certain she had made a very big mistake. The conviction had appeared first at the altar—not really an altar, a bureau with her mother's lace tablecloths over it and flowers heaped on it, she and Mike had refused every church and minister proposed to them—just as the retired judge, her mother's friend, had bound her to him: she felt an overwhelming awful rush like a hit of bad acid coming on, a nightmare sense of having done something so wrong, so stupid and irrevocable she might have been jumping off a cliff. And it persisted, came and went through the week they spent biking in Vermont and their first weeks in a barrackslike graduate-student housing complex—a barracks in fact, having been thrown up twenty years before for returning vets and their families; Rosie could sense, and envy, their plain hopes and hard work and troubles, which had soaked into the Celotex and the linoleum. She lay awake nearly all night every night memorizing the pine branch that hung in the bedroom window, saying almost but not quite aloud *I can't do this I can't do this I can't.* Until one night came when she lay wishing with all her might that she could know the future, the next ten years, know if she was to see this through and be happy, or if not what: and had realized with sudden force that if she really were allowed to glimpse herself ten years down the road there might be nothing to see: the future—her future—might have come to a stop some time before that moment. Blank. Nothing.

And she had thought: But at least you'd know *that.* You'd know you had no more than ten years to get through. Not so long. You'd know that.

An astonishing peace had stolen over her in her spavined marriage bed in Vetville. *Not so long.* She had felt certain that if she could know for sure she would be dead in five years or ten, she could easily be brave and cheerful, happy even. She could love Mike as he needed to be loved, as he deserved to be loved (warm and unaware beside her, his presence suddenly sweet too for the first time in weeks, how strange). She had even been able for the first time to imagine having a child with him: like a smile all through her she could imagine even that, which had seemed so terrifying, an abyss. It would be easy, easy, to love them both and be glad, sure. Because. Because why? Why could she face what needed to be done with equanimity, joy even, if it wasn't going to last forever? It wouldn't last forever anyway. Why this peace?

She hadn't known why. She had only lain and tasted it, watching that faintly beckoning pine branch, wishing for death, death and certainty, and good cheer. It didn't matter why. Soon she'd slept.

Oh strange, she thought at Arcady, remembering. And Sam beside her now. She lifted the book again:

*Or wouldst thou have no single She,*
*But Spouses in Plurality?*
*The Sultan's, in his Hareem strait,*
*A Blackamoor before the Gate?*
*Or base Arabian's, kept in Tents?*
*Thou hast their Choice, but not th'Expense.*

No she was wrong, he was a tight, mean, sneering smug old bastard, Rosie thought, must have been. She flipped the pages, not quite as delicately maybe as Pierce might have wished, feeling a kind of annoyance, at the thing and at its supposed great worth, thinking of the men she saw at the newsstand going so intently through the skin magazines, one woman after another, their eyes sucking them in, why did they need so many.

*'Tis said that Men who waste their Seed*
*Toward their Coffins quickly speed;*
*I say the thing that shortens Life*
*Is an unsympathetic Wife.*

Well go on then, she said or thought; go go, smartie.

*So to our Couch let us Retire;*
*A Cup of Wine we may require;*
*To take the Air our Friend we bid*
*Who in the Dark all day has hid!*
*Then gently, as with Bird in Hand*
*Or Babe in Arms, we help him stand—*
*See how he leaps, a Lapdog he,*
*Eager for a Sport with thee!*

Must be permanent, she thought, or at least real old, the way men regard their p's (as Sam had somewhere learned to call them): you had to be careful about him, not hurt his feelings, the little man who accompanies your man (oops, "little," see right there); the man your man waits on and looks on fondly and indulges, or tries to. Rosie laughed, visited by another scene from her own married life, seen through this antique writing as though from a great distance, and felt a twinge of unreasoning grief, and at that laughed again.

"Greetings from the big city," Rose Ryder's letter to Pierce Moffett began, the first he had received from her. She had warned him he should not expect much in what she called the "initial period," by which he supposed she meant the period of her training by the Powerhouse in whatever exactly they were going to train her in, "brainwashing" was the term that came to his mind. "I'm amazed how good I do in the test-prep course. Pierce I was always terrified of tests, I had testophobia bad, and now—now not. I just do it." Something crossed out here that looked like *I wish you could,* wish withdrawn or left unsaid. "My little apartment is so cute, on an OK street in a safe neighborhood, it's amazing I got it. The class is interesting and Mike has been so supportive about everything here, a lot of hard things—Oh there are things I just can't write to you, Pierce, or even say."

Things she couldn't write or even say: well he had stood before shut doors of that kind before, and what was behind them often enough, as behind the doors of bedroom closets in a thousand dirty jokes, was actually quite easily named.

Old Mike. Still in the picture. Okay, all right.

"Here the great drought continues," Pierce wrote back, his yellow pad, the same he used for his work, balanced on his raised knees where he reclined in bed. "It's unusual, says the paper, but not unheard of. No rain now in a month almost. It has its beauties, it's sort of Edenic in its way, so changeless, but of course changing fast: suspended in the moment of change, how's that? There's a (Chinese?) proverb, I'm told, about how women fall in love with men in the spring and men with women in the fall. Seems right to me, I mean experience can be said to confirm. There's the other proverb too, about absence and the heart. I think about hearts lately, how they do seem like repositories or containers, they feel like it, and I wonder why they do, what the reason is in physiology, that they can be heavy or light. When all they contain is blood, on the move. Hydraulics. Anyway. This is a love letter, if that has not become apparent yet."

Cross that out, burn it, crush it, feed it to the fire. He turned the yellow sheet, which, like all its kind and no others, had its head at the bottom of the verso side; and began again.

"Rose," he wrote. "I now have some instructions for you. I'll want you to follow these *very exactly* and when you call me next I'll want to know just how it went; you'll be asked to describe it all in detail, in detail."

He lifted his eyes. On the wall near the bed's side hung the emblem he had made for her, the old frame and the new little picture. The Marriage of Agent and Patient. It should have been put away, he should not have sat so long before it, but of course by now it was too late.

"First of all," he wrote. "If you are in a public place while reading this, I want you to continue reading all the way to the end. Those around you will observe you reading, and certainly some of them will even study you, my dear, men will, because they do, don't they? And think about you, so absorbed in your reading; maybe, maybe they'll notice something about you, something about your absorption, but they won't know what it is, what it is that draws their eyes to you; but of course you'll know, won't you?

"And if you are out and about, Rose, you can think about these things through the day, until you're alone, and you can begin to do what I will tell you, and say aloud what I will tell you to say."

He pondered. There had already come to be a fullness in his breast. What he had planned for her had taken some thought; but actually writing it down, even the prospect of actually writing it down, of her actually reading it, had an unexpected force. A topic not covered in the *Ars Auto-amatoria:* the sequential or chain-letter form of the art. Universal and ancient, though, Pierce bet. He moved, on the bed, to a less constricting position.

> *What wonder's this, and Magick too,*
> *His Transformation at thy Cue!*
> *His Helmet lifted, and his Sword—*
> *Th'appendage now becomes the Lord!*
> *The Turkey-wattle now an Arm!*
> *What Pow'r! What Strength, for Good or Harm!*

Rosie Palm and her five daughters was how they used to say it in Kentucky, how did the joke travel, carried with lonely Anglo-Saxon huntsmen into the Cumberlands with Boone, or reinvented every generation, obvious enough after all.

*Without a Purse spend freely here.* Clever actually, "purse" being common slang at that time for. And "spend" for come. Rosie Palm.

> *And if he droop or if he flag,*
> *Weaken or tire, fail or sag,*
> *Feed him on thy Fancy's food,*
> *Victuals rich as thou think'st good!*
> *Haste thee, Thought, and bring with thee*
> *Emblems of Lubricity:*
> *Bums and Quims and wanton Wiles*
> *Beds and Cocks and nether Smiles!*

The unfinished letter, and some change fallen from his pocket, crept to the edge of the bed and slid to the floor; the emblem on the wall grew larger, passing directly into his heart through the windows of the imagination, for of course it was in him and not in wary Rose that they were open, open wide. As though his right hand worked the handle of a pump, Imagination now began to draw up from the dark well a nice steady stream. He had Rose describe to him what he had said she should do, and how she did it, and other things he and she had done or would have or might have done; he described to her what he might have once done, but had not done, with a former lover he invented, or to the lovers he had really had but had not thought of in weeks or months; he even, at a turning, glimpsed Robbie, just arriving at his front door, shy golden kid, his mandrake, his fruit. *Do you see what powers, what speed you have?* (That's Hermes Thrice-great, egging on the straining adept to wonder-working by Thought alone.) *Make yourself huge, beyond measuring; climb higher than the highest height; sink lower than the lowest depth. Imagine that you are everywhere, on earth, at sea, in the deep dens of beasts, that you aren't yet born, are in your mother's womb, adolescent, old, dead, past death.*

The desire is infinite, the act a slave to limit: not here though, where Memory endlessly extends or repeats what their combining flesh could do only once, or only every once in a while, and not for any great length of time. A Moment in Eternity: what that old ad promised, that ad appearing in the back pages of the timid men's magazines of his youth, for the Rosicrucians wasn't it. Thoughts Have Wings. He had wondered then what it could mean, the robed magus, the winged spheres. Not this that he was up to, certainly.

"All right Rose," he said aloud in the empty room, the Soft Voice. "All right. Yes Rose. Yes."

> *Now shake him well! Now grind the Mill!*
> *Punish the boy and make him spill!*
> *Thy Teeth are grit, thy Shanks a-tremble,*
> *A snarling Beast thou may'st resemble,*
> *Yet mak'st Thanksgiving in thy Moan*
> *And Gratulation in thy Groan*

*As from the Fundament arises*
*At last the Bliss that still surprizes!*
*Ah lovely is the Fruit thereof,*
*The Foment and the Gum of Love:*
*Do not despise nor in Disgust*
*Turn from the Product of thy Lust,*
*But stop t'admire. This is the Stuff*
*The Ballocks brewed, one Drop enough*
*A Man to make, if baked inside*
*The Oven of a Fleshly Bride,*
*Nine months' thence t'emerge a Child,*
*Puking, shrieking, red and wild.*
*He will grow up to cut a Purse,*
*To die of Drink or something worse—*
*A Gibbet, or a Pauper's Grave.*
*What Griefs, what Troubles thou dost save!*
*Wash but thy Hand, and go thy Way,*
*Free to conceive another Day.*

The worst part, Rosie thought, the part this guy feared the most, worse than the pox or the grasping in-laws or the whiny real wife growing old and sour: the making or leaving of kids. This thing she had in her hands was so old you couldn't tell, people then might have been entirely different, but he seemed to know what most men now didn't really grasp, what maybe most people she knew had forgotten, with the Pill and stuff: that sex between living men and women was for making babies, and you had to get to work if you wanted it to be for something else, because those babies will fight to get made, no power greater. He knew it and he opted out.

Well there were good reasons for that. Like the reason she lay still at Arcady, unable to fly; why she had slept with Sam in her bed almost every night that Brent Spofford had not been in it with her, Sam's room at the end of the corridor being too far away, too far—Rosie without company tended to lie in bed imagining Sam, asleep alone, visited by a seizure of some new kind, some ultimate kind, and just exiting, like stepping out the window into the night air. *They often happen when we sleep,* Dr. Marlborough had said, as though they were his too.

*Go all to Altar and to Woe*
*I shall to the Greenwood go.*
*My Fancy free I'll ever keep*
*I have not sown, I shall not Reap.*

Babies, crying at the margins of the world, trying to get in, no matter the dangers, no matter what awaits them. If you open a way for one or some, there's no getting out of it later, and maybe this guy, Anon or Onan, maybe he had known that too, that you will not even *want* to get out of it or turn away, that nothing matters more than seeing this through. You can't even die, have no right to: tied to life by the choices you make, that you've tried so hard to talk yourself into. She remembered how she used to charge herself with selfishness in those days when she had lain awake in the grip of regret or whatever the name of the feeling had been: selfish, selfish, can't you ever think of anyone else's happiness for five minutes, if you could look *out* not *in* you'd see a good life there just waiting to be lived.

> The Devil and the World enmesh
> The Anchorite who hates the Flesh.
> The Flesh is we and we are it,
> Its Hungers, Fevers and its Shite.
> Then let's be glad we perpetrate
> The little Sins and not the great:
> Better than Pride, or Anger pure,
> Better than Envy green for sure,
> Better than all the Sins of Mind,
> Is Lust of the unproductive kind:
> Blameless, fruitless, bland and free,
> A Rose without a Thorn for thee.

"Speaking of which," Rosie said aloud.

She pushed aside her bedclothes and the musty book, and went out and down past Boney's old room, now kept closed, to the bathroom; found the pink plastic wheel that Sam had lusted to play with ever since she had seen Rosie using it, and dialed it carefully to this day, where yes her forgotten pill still remained. She pressed it into her hand. Weirdly minute considering its power. *Lust of the unproductive kind.* With a sip of water from the still-minty tooth glass she swallowed it; and immediately it began forestalling for another day those processes that Rosie had already, head to toe, felt attempting to begin.

Spofford and Cliff left for the West in the last week of October. They were driving Spofford's truck, and had Cliff's motorcycle strapped down in the bed, covered with a blue tarp. Spofford brought his tools. They came last of all to Arcady so that Spofford could say goodbye to Sam and Rosie.

"It's okay," she said to Spofford. "Really. It's really a small thing, a test. It's not like she's going in for an operation."

He looked down at her, saying nothing. She knew he would stay if she asked, and therefore she couldn't ask. And since she couldn't ask she had to say it didn't matter. And the more she smiled and said it didn't matter the angrier she got.

"So how come you didn't tell me about," she said, and made a subtle gesture toward where Cliff was dandling Sam, just out of earshot.

"Tell you about him? I've told you all about him. Took you to see him."

"You didn't tell me what he looked like."

He had brought her to visit Cliff on a summer day, to see if Cliff could alter or intervene in the sadness that had seemed to possess her (only she didn't call it sadness, there was nothing that made her sad, or happy either, nothing: nothing was the problem). Cliff had once helped Spofford, he said, and others too; but Rosie had never got to see him, he had been gone the one day they went to his place in the woods, she and Spofford, and then too many things had happened too fast: for that was the night that Boney died. She had never gone back.

What would she have thought of him if he had come for her out of his handmade house that day. Not scary exactly but imposing, thin and tall as a wading bird, a heron, no an egret, for his hair, that fell well below his shoulders, was pure white: so were his shaggy brows. His colorless eyes were like moonstones, almost without pupils in the whites.

"Amazing," Rosie said. Sam thought so too, gazing up at his pink clean-shaven face, reaching for the long hair that he pushed away from his face with a girlish gesture.

"He is," Spofford said. "He is."

"What does he think you guys will find?" Rosie asked.

"He doesn't even say. But." He sighed, as though having come up to something hard to say. "He did say he thought this might take a while."

"You said a couple of weeks."

"Longer than that."

Rosie thought: Who is on my side then? Who?

"Well listen," she said. "I think you better get going then. Soonest started soonest done." She rose abruptly and left him sitting there; went to Cliff and took Sam from him. The two of them were best friends already. Men.

"I hope you find what you're looking for," she said.

Cliff regarded her smiling, his long pink hand still on Sam's boot. "I sort of hope we don't," he said. "That would be best. But thanks. I hope you do too."

Oh stupid tears, Rosie felt them gather hotly in her eyes even as she grinned the snide grin she had decided on, it had been easier when Nothing was her only friend and kept between her and everything else. A few months ago. The woods were getting deeper.

"Kiss," she said to Sam, and held her up to Spofford. As Sam clung to his neck the phone rang in the house behind them; so weirdly warm it was that the door stood open.

"I'm gonna get that," she said. "Come on, Sam." She patted Spofford's nose and said: "See you when I see you."

With Sam waving bye-bye, bye-bye over her shoulder, she went quickly into the house. The old phone in the hall, an ancient model that must have been there unchanged for decades (the little number on the typed card beneath a celluloid window on the dial plate bore a letter exchange no one used any longer) was as loud as a fire bell; it always sounded like bad news.

It was Allan Butterman. Rosie had that been-here-before feeling of almost, but not quite, knowing what he would say before he said it. "I think there are some developments," he said.

"Yes," Rosie said. Beyond the open door Spofford's truck could just be seen, going away. "What."

"I ran into Mike's old lawyer at the courthouse in Cascadia. You remember her."

Rosie would never forget her, and could not forgive her either, though nothing that had been done had been her fault. Like a dog who once bit you.

"She's no longer his lawyer," Allan said. "She was pretty short about it—miffed almost I want to say, maybe there was some disagreement. Mike seems to have new representation."

"Who." Her heart began a sort of warning tap tap tap.

"The name mentioned was the firm that's representing this religious group that's around. The Powerhouse. You know about them. They're I guess into some real-estate things?"

"I think."

"Well it seems Mike has changed his mind again, and is asking for a hearing. About custody. And this firm is handling it."

Rosie's grip on the phone had tightened, as though on the throat of an animal, a small animal at her flesh. "What do they call that? Is that Christian?"

"Sorry?"

"This big Christian group? They have lawyers to take people to court and take away their children? Is that supposed to be Christian?"

"You're asking me?" Allan said. "I'm Jewish, for Christ's sake."

"What can I do," she said. "Is there anything."

"Sure," Allan said. "You can defend against this. I can tell you what you've got to do."

"Oh Allan."

"I have to say one thing, though," he said. "From this point I am going to have to bill you."

She said nothing.

"The divorce, you know," he said, "that was dealt with by Mr. Rasmussen. How he described it in his books I don't know."

Rosie still could say nothing.

"There's a certain amount of billing already piling up," he said.

"Okay."

"Not really a lot."

"Well I'll pay it, Allan. Just send it."

"These things can get expensive. If this group is going to involve itself. I have no idea what their resources are."

"I said I'd pay. It might take a while."

"Well can I make a sort of suggestion?" He seemed to shift in his big chair, a chair she had often watched him revolve thoughtfully in, and swap ears on his phone. "If you could resolve your questions about the Foundation. I mean about taking on the directorship. Not only would your salary go up a good deal. I'm already the Foundation's counsel. So."

Rosie's breast tightened terribly. Allan too. Defenseless, she hadn't known how defenseless she was; naked, like a cartoon or silent-movie character whose clothes are blown away by a sudden wind.

"Fuck you, Allan," she said.

"Rosie."

"I'll handle it myself. Can I do that? I can, can't I?"

"It was just a suggestion," he said mildly.

"Forget it," she said. "Send me the stuff."

She hung up.

Run. Run from here where she did not truly belong and never could. Run as her father had run so long ago, maybe back to the Midwest. To her mother. She had to have somebody. For an instant she saw the road running that way, straight, divided by white dashes, into darkness.

No she couldn't run, it was certainly illegal; anyway Mike was Sam's father, she had no right, Sam loved him as much as she loved Rosie, maybe more.

Can't run. Can't die. Down the hall the door still stood open. For a moment Rosie perceived Boney Rasmussen standing there before it, not in the green silk dressing gown in which he had died but in the cuff-worn gray gabardine slacks he always wore and one of his big white shirts, too big for his shrunken torso and buttoned to the neck.

Just for a moment. Then she went down the hall, carefully as though on a dark path, and shut the door; then locked it and slipped the chain.


That week on Pierce's TV (bought cheap on the streets of his old slum neighborhood, the spoils of crime no doubt, but he had himself been despoiled more than once and so a rough balance had thereby been struck) the exposure of a West Coast mage and his cult had been proceeding; Pierce watched, twitching and cocking his rabbit ears this way and that to get even a dim glimpse here in the valley between the mountains. The man had entranced an unknown number of followers with his purported powers, especially his powers to heal; and then a young asthmatic among them, who had given himself over completely to the man, abjuring all medical treatment, had died in his company. And the rest had apparently gathered there in the mage's apartment, with the corpse, and he had promised them that if their faith were strong enough, he and they could raise the dead man.

Days he had lain there while they prayed and willed. Until at length someone's faith failed or someone came knocking or the call was made.

Tonight the cameras were pursuing into and out of court a well-known entertainer, a comic in fact, not comic now as she pushed through the crowd surrounded by lawyers. Many of the man's adherents had been entertainers and actors, some of them famous: magicians themselves, you'd think they would have known.

But oh Lord in that room with death, trying to defeat it: having willfully gone into the place that cannot be gone into. The dreadful illusion and its exposure, the door broken open, the cops amazed, the sleepers there awakening at last or trying to awaken or never to awaken. The dead one though still dead. Smelling too. What was the horror at the heart of it, something shit-black he tasted in the back of his throat, he could taste but not touch it, what was the name of that horror.

More revelations now about the famous and beautiful who had believed the guru. "The circle widens," said the newsreader.

He turned it off.

All magic is bad magic. He thought this thought for the first time. To do magic you must take power over others, and you must believe you can do what can't be done, and make others believe it too. All magic is bad magic.

Was it so?

What if he and she had ever, what if in their madness and willingness they were ever to go so far. *Folie à deux.* It apparently happened, his own father (haunter these days of city bathhouses and dark bars) told him he had heard of male couples who had entered into relations of such force and fascination, athletes or saints of sex, that one had succumbed under the ministrations or exactions of the other. And then the door pounded on, the landlord, the cops, death found to have visited there where he had been invited to come: really death, not death as symbol for deathlessness (*unto death*) and not death as more vivid life, but death simple, death itself.

*I see your soul when I see you come,* he had said to her: had seen it rise to her eyes and stand upon the threshold of her parted lips. Not to step over and out though. No. *No es posible.* Pierce before the darkened TV felt suddenly afraid; wanted nothing but to embrace her, right now, and say *I was kidding, yes, listen listen, I was only kidding.*

He *didn't* want power over her; power had never drawn him, never, had never been a wish of his, he had only ever wished and conspired to avoid being subject to the power of others. All he had ever wanted with her, what he supposed no magic he could do could ever really grant him, was to *be her,* to be on the inside of her when she felt the things he caused her to feel, or helped her to cause herself to feel. Not for good of course or permanently, only at that moment, when she arrived at that incandescence; but he wanted it then intensely, unslakably, utterly.

And what if he had to push a little further every time, a little harder, in order to get her down into the furnace room, the world all heat, and himself with her, there where he wanted to be, had always and only wanted to be, no matter what else he had ever pretended to be about? With her and through her and in her. *In ipsam et cum ipsa et per ipsam.* Maybe he would on some night push a little too far, *vacatio* made permanent and irreversible as the subjectivity itself exited from her open mouth, from his too: *mors osculi* they called it, *morte di bacio,* the Death of the Kiss, possible (so Marsilius saith, so Don John Picus) for striving souls too loosely adhering to the flesh.

No again. I tell you three times.

He went to his bedroom, aroused and afraid, she close by him; remembering or inventing a night or morning when he, when she. How she had suffered him, what he had done, what she had said. He lay down not on his own bed but on the other, the naked mattress, and inhaled its odor and hers, looking and listening too within for the same thing, the trace of her; feeling even in his heat a familiar chill, like the onset of fever: that premonition that soon and unavoidably a whole banquet of symptoms will be brought before you, and you will eat and eat, until you die, or get better.

*Love is magic,* Giordano Bruno said; *magic is love.* The magician and the lover are both *venatores animarum,* hunters of souls; by emblems and by arts, the magician draws down into his heart the powers of heaven, that is the star-persons through whom the whole of nature and the spirits of men and women are ordered, and have their meaning. He ranges these powers within him and asks: teach me to bind, with bonds like love's, the things of this world and the hearts of others. And they do, they can. And thus we become like gods.

But the gods are themselves constantly at work, spinning and weaving with the rays that all things produce. They do not like to be renounced, they will not suffer it; they knit up bonds to bind us to them in love and worship, they are *venatores* too and come after us with their lures. And we invite them to do it, we pray to them to do it, and they do.

Give us this day our daily bread, we pray. Give us what we need and what we want.

And worshipping them we bind ourselves, we are bound to the ones whose gifts we take.

And the greatest of these is Love: Love himself, or herself; Eros, *dæmon magnus,* that son of the morning star, that boy, his other name is Don Cupido, the little lord of all things, he whose avatar or manifestation (there are others, countless others, one perhaps for each of us) had for a while inhabited Pierce's house and heart and then departed, taking Pierce's sleep with him: his work there done, and well done too.

Always poor, a beggar, shoeless and homeless, says Plato, sleeping out for want of a bed; but because his father is Hermes he is a clever hunter too, a magician, always devising tricks, scheming to get for himself all that is beautiful and good.

And how had Robbie found him, how had Robbie come to arrive that hot and thundery day on Pierce's doorstep, dusty sandals on his golden feet, cardboard suitcase in his hand? Was it chance, or Fate? No neither: Pierce had invoked him, invoked him with all his might, had begged for him; had spent the last of his Three Wishes to cause him to come down, and in his heart take up his rest. And so he had. And Pierce thought he had been *awarded* the boy, that the vividness of him was a prize for all that he had renounced so suddenly and so thoroughly.

O the traps the gods have prepared for us, for us their worshippers; how long and well they've worked. We are older than they, far older than the oldest of them; we have come from farther away, way back beyond where they were born: but we don't know that, we have forgotten it—and they know we have forgotten it. And that's why they can do with us what they like most of the time, especially when we think we have escaped them. That's why, in other words, the world has lasted so long, and why we are all still here.

# MORS

---

## EMBER DAYS

# 1

Madimi was gone.

Edward Kelley had done what he had so often promised to do: he had ceased to skry. After that day, the day following the night that he and John Dee had done the great sin they had been ordered to do, he kept the vow that he had made in his anguish, never to speak to them again. And with his abnegation Madimi (last seen—by Edward alone—following her knight) passed: for he would not call her. Not her or any of them.

He seemed, anyway, to have no need to: he had been given what he wanted. Though weak and languid at first, unable to rise from his couch, weeping sometimes, laughing sometimes, he had soon grown strong again, stronger than ever; he seemed to grow taller even, his wrists growing out the sleeves of his gown and its hem rising around his ankles, as though he had been replaced by another, a similar but taller man. He needed room; he made it clear to the Duke (speaking loudly and lifting a forefinger, his new temerity alarmed John Dee, but not as much as the faint constant tremor in his hand) that from now on he would need apartments of his own.

Not for a growing family: his wife that fall was taken home. The letters she had written long before from Poland had at length arrived in Chipping Norton where she was born, and her brothers had meditated on them, and sold a cottage and an orchard, and equipped themselves (unable to imagine what they would encounter Abroad, brave boys, they had each a pistol and a crucifix of silver and a magistrate's warrant) and so had come (a year had passed by then) to Trebona to rescue her. Kelley had greeted them with liberality, laughing hugely, loading them with gifts, and they had looked around themselves at the fine painted rooms and the hangings and tableware and the silver ewer of wine Kelley poured and poured from, and for a moment they wondered: but Joanna weeping in the night told them that what she had written was nothing, nothing, compared to what had befallen since, things that she had not and never could write or even speak; they mustn't ask her, only let them all be gone as soon as might be. Kelley (not in his bed, to which he had told them he was going, but listening at the door) bade her farewell. *Farewell farewell* he thought, and felt a small fire kindle in his breast; he brought the nails of his hand to his mouth and bit them, as he had not done since he was a boy.

—She troubled me, he said to John Dee. God go with her, and let her be gone. She kept me from my work.

As though he had embarked on a task like those laid on the poor lads of old tales, impossible things that had all to be done in a night, he labored ceaselessly, drew up plans in the morning, ordered servants in the evening, read by lamplight all night; seemed to have lost the need for sleep, sure sign of a hectic melancholy, John Dee noted it, but Kelley only grew stronger. He had John Carpio, indispensable workman, begin a new furnace, larger than any they had built before, in a room over the gate of the palace of Trebona: "He used of my rownd bricks," Dee noted in his journal, "and was contented now to use the lesser bricks, 60 to make a furnace," it seemed not to matter to him as long as the work went forward quickly, when it didn't he exploded in wrath, *terribilis expostulatio accusatio* Dee wrote. He nearly burned his book, working too hastily with spirits of wine, but seemed not to care about that either, waved Dee away when he fussed over the scorched pages.

—Keep it, he said. *Tolle, lege:* take it and read.

All Prague soon knew that Kelley was aflame—these things could not be kept secret, though the work itself might be. Since philosophic gold, the new bright gold we make in our alembics and our athenors, is a product of the operator's soul as much as of the fire and the matter, it is possible through certain signs to tell which soul, like a broody hen, is in a state to produce it; and a worker's certainty that he *is* able to produce it—a sudden brilliant confidence, a winged state, a golden aspect, glints of gold even suddenly visible in the iris of the eye—that is the surest sign of all. The aristocratic hungerers who patronized Prague's alchemists, the great cunning-men around the King, even the smoke-blackened toilers of Golden Lane, all saw it in Kelley.

Soon there were other signs too, or rumors. Someone who claimed to have seen him do it said he could produce the *Mercurius solis* in only a quarter of an hour. It was said he gave rings of gold wire to a servant of the Duke's upon his marriage, and one to each of the guests as well, four thousand pounds' worth ran the tale by the time it reached England, "openly Profuse," Elias Ashmole would later write, "beyond the modest Limits of a sober Philosopher."

Never less than courteous and kind to John Dee and his family, Duke Rozmberk nevertheless was drawn as by a lodestone to the younger man. Now when he went to Prague to wait on the Emperor, he often took Kelley with him; when he came to Trebona, after a brief restless call on Dee and his family, he would shut himself up with Kelley in the room over the gate.

Dee said nothing. He said nothing when Kelley commanded away his own best workmen, said nothing except to his private diary; said nothing when Joanna Kelley was allowed to return home with her brothers, except that he and

Jane went with her to church before she left, and took the Sacrament with her, and Joanna afterward "to me and my wife gave her hand in Charitye, and we rushed not from her."

He said nothing when under Duke Rozmberk's protection Kelley moved house to Prague city, where Dee was still forbidden to go, to grand rooms in the Duke's palace in the shadow of the Hradschin; nothing when the great and the curious flocked to visit him there, when the poet and courtier Edward Dyer, who had long been Dee's friend and was his son Arthur's godfather, arrived from England only to take up exclusively with Kelley and write home to the court of Kelley's wonder-working: not even when the unspeakable Father Pucci reappeared and was welcomed there. Years later Dee would write of the "most subtill devises and plots laid, first by the Bohemians, and somewhat by the Italians, and lastly by some of my owne countrymen": but he said nothing then.

He said nothing, but his wife knew he mourned; as for a lost child, she thought (her own child Theodore, hungriest and most eager of all her children, was at her breast) and she was in a sense right: but the child he mourned was not, or was not wholly, Edward.

The round glass of clear crystal still stood in its frame in the tower room, but cold, vacant: gone out, like a lamp.

Never once, in all the years he had faithfully attended on them, from the time when he had first acquired a bright black obsidian mirror (cut and polished on the other side of the world for a Peruvian lady's toilet) down to this day— never once had John Dee himself been given sight *in chrystallo*. Long ago he might sometimes have believed for a day or a week that he had seen, but nothing came of what he saw (a tower, a room, a rose) so it had surely been his own desire only that he had seen, as we see faces in trees and clouds.

Never once.

He stood in his nightgown at the door of the tower room, a candle in his hand. He could see the candle flame, like the living spark in an eye, glitter on the cold ball's surface.

Why have you refused me that, kept that gift from me? The only one, of all those proffered, that I desired.

He went into the little room. The table of practice he and Kelley with their own hands had built with such care exactly to the angels' specifications stood in the middle of the room, each of its four feet resting on a seal of pure wax made in a certain pattern, a *sigilla Æmeth*, a multiple cross with Hebrew letters on it standing for the words *Thou art great forever O Lord*. On a larger seal of the same kind (*twenty-seven inches in diameter,* they had said, *an inch and a half thick,* how sweetly childish they had seemed in their punctiliousness sometimes, his heart filled) stood the frame of sweet wood that held the glass.

And what if it had been for Edward as for himself: that there was nothing at first to see in stones like this, until he taught himself to see them there? What if Edward had not received those spirits out of the glass into his mouth and heart at all, what if they had really proceeded from his heart into the glass, there to reside thereafter, and speak to him his own thoughts?

Perhaps it was only thus that angels speak to men; perhaps the angels that we hear are ours alone, hidden inside.

And he said aloud:

—Then I will do it myself.

As though a seedpod burst just then within him he felt a hot certainty—no, not certainty, possibility—fly through him to his fingertips and his hair roots, and pass, and leave him calm.

Myself. Like the red hen in the tale: *I will do it myself, said the red hen: and she did.*

He set down his candle and came closer to the ball. Did it shrink away from him, shy or afraid, no it could not. As he came closer he could see that on its silvery surface the whole room was reflected, walls and windows curving to touch one another and the floor and the ceiling. Closer and he could see his own face in the middle, swollen like a puncheon, his vast hand that reached out toward it.

How beautiful you are, he thought, beautiful. Bending to it open-eyed and gentle, as though he approached a tetchy pony or a newborn child of his own or an elemental spirit, one of those bumblebee-sized ones he used to catch in a jar among his roses: come I will have you.

He had not got very close, not even as close as Kelley had used to, when he felt taken: felt the cords of his throat tickled, his heart tugged. He knelt. Still he saw nothing but the stone, but now its deeps; his view opened and he looked not at but into. And he heard, faint but clear in his inward ear, a voice, not his own though it seemed to spring at once from the glass and from his throat.

—*I am glad to see thee. Why hast thou forsaken me?*

It was her voice, he knew it, he had never heard it before but it could be no other's. Christ Jesus Lord God thanks be unto Thee for Thy great mercy unto Thy servant.

—I have not forsaken thee, he said.

The sound of his own speaking was loud and coarse, though he barely whispered. He heard no more. He supposed his speaking had frightened her away, and his heart went cold. Then she spoke again:

—*You have not called me. Not these many months.*

—Madam I could not. And he would not.

—*Well let him go. He is a foul traitor, and treason will have his reward.*

She said it teasingly, and yet it chilled him; Lord how she cursed, she always had, like a wicked child, and who was able to reprove her.

—*Has my mother brought thee comfort?* she asked. *Hast had thy way with her? How many times?*

—Thy mother, child? Who is thy mother?

—*Who else but the great lady I brought thee unto?*

—She.

—*She is my mother; her other name Amphitrite. Her mother's name is Night.*

For a moment it was as though he could remember what he had not himself seen: that green mead, the woman coming to them, telling them she was Understanding; opening her garments. He shuddered hugely.

—*She has given* him *what he asked,* Madimi said. *Know you that? He has gold now in overplus. He may eat and drink it if he likes.*

—He is grown great, John Dee said; and he closed his eyes, for tears had arisen painfully in them. He is called Doctor, *dominie;* loved of all.

—*He has not praised me. No matter. Let him enjoy it as he may.*

—We were obedient unto thee, Madam, John Dee whispered. And now we are parted, and the rift cannot be made up; his wife is gone; my wife is given a hurt will be a long time mending.

—*I know it. I know it and I am sorry for it. I am, in part.*

—I would have done that and more for the great gift promised me, he said. Of knowledge of God, His purpose in this enterprise; true knowledge. I would have done all that was asked. I did do. And I, I have not been answered.

—*For that,* she said, in a small voice. *I had not in my gift what thou asked of me.*

—Hadst thou not?

—*Not though I promised it. I gave what I had: Power. I had not Understanding to give.*

A huge and indissoluble stone had arisen in his breast, like a cold precipitate in an alembic, it would never pass. He knew he should bear it and not ask why; but he could not bear it, he must ask.

—Then why did you set that duty upon us? he whispered. Tell me. Why did you ask that great sin of us, of having our wives in common? Which then we did, thinking it commanded by you for holy purposes. Why?

—*For my delight only,* she said. *That I might witness it. I and my kin gathered here.*

He felt himself falling as he knelt, the room tipped up like a dish from which he was to be spilled out, down, forever.

—Then you are fallen angels, he said. You are fallen, and I am damned.

—*Old man,* she said, almost gently, almost tenderly. *Foolish old man. Hast not known? Hast not seen? All the angels are fallen angels.*

—All? How, all?

—*All the angels are fallen. It is in this that they are angels. Have no pity for us; it is so, and has ever been so.*

—How is it then that you can praise God, and say prayers; bless; be wise?

—*How? Cannot fallen man do these things? Enough. Listen now to me and I will prophesy: There is war in heaven, a war of all against all. That war will have its mirror on earth in a like war. It must have.*

—A new war of religion, he guessed. Christ's church divided. More blood spilled between the sects.

—*Ha,* she said. *That is the less war. The great war is the war of all Christ's churches against their enemies: those who invoke the gods dæmons and angels of heaven and earth from the places where they reside. They will burn all who do so. They will have them into the fire as paper.*

—I invoked no wicked spirits, I.

—*They will burn you too. Listen to me and write it in your heart: Fly, but do not fly from the powers into the arms of other powers. And beware: for the powers reside each inside all the others.*

He was weeping now, hearing her voice through the tears that gathered in his throat.

—I know not what you mean, he said. I will do as you say if I can.

—*Come, old man,* she said. *Come. I am off to the wars. You shall not see me more. How like you that?*

—I do not like it. I would see you often, Madam.

—*Do you weep? Do not weep. Come closer. Kiss my brow, tell me you love me. Do you not love me?*

—I do. I do love thee, child.

—*I will give thee a gift. Come closer.*

—Madam, I fear your gifts.

—*Sir, you are right to fear them. I have a kickshaws here in my pocket will bring down nations.*

—I do not want it.

—*Come close. Closer. My gift is for you alone.*

He had drawn so close to the glass, and to the child somewhere inside, that he could have kissed her brow if he could have seen her; so close his breath clouded on the surface.

—*Here it is,* she said. *May'st thou have joy in it.*

He thought of his own children, how they came to him with treasures in their empty hands, that he must ask the name of before he could thank them (what is it, child? A gold ring? Why thankee then for this gold ring).

—What is it? he asked her.

—*It is a wind I have in my power.*

—Doth not the wind blow where it listeth? John Dee said. I know not how to command it.

—*Speak sharply to it, that it obey thee. The gold I have given* him *is not good. But the wind is a good wind. There. Now it is thine. Farewell.*

He felt, with a steely thrill of fear along his spine and scalp, a small cold hand take his. Then it was gone. As though a sinew or nerve were drawn out of his heart's heart he felt her depart; and through the breach a cold wind blow in.


A house burns down, with all the movables, and reveals to the stricken family the place where the miser uncle long ago hid his money. An army tramples a poor farmer's field, and takes his eldest son for a soldier; the boy rises to become a general, buys his father new fields as far as eye can see. Job had his flocks returned to him, new children given to him, and a new wisdom too: and did he never go to sit by his first children's graves, and weep?

She had said to them long ago that a new age was to come, that many now alive would see it before their eyes were closed forever; it would steal upon many, and bewilder them. Much would be taken then, and much of value would be thrown away as trash; but nothing would be lost that would not be replaced with something of equal worth, somewhere, in some sphere, though far from here.

Not ten days after that midnight when she spoke to him from the glass for the first time—only to say *Farewell*—John Dee wrote in his diary: *EK did open the great secret to me, God be thanked!*

And it was a simple thing, as of course it should be; he had known it should be, all the books said it was. Kelley nearly laughed to speak it; it took but a moment to say. He gave them a powder to use, in a plain twist of paper as though it were an ounce of pepper or mustard. He lost nothing by parting with it, he said; nothing. Like a child's riddle: *What is it I give, and others take, yet I never part with it? Answer, my hand.*

Once, he and Kelley had watched and prayed through a whole zodiacal year (two days and two nights, as it happened) to make a single convolute nugget of new gold; now, with what Kelley gave them and the secret he told them, it could be made in a few hours, and the process begun soon again, and more made the second time than the first, the projective powders growing not weaker but stronger through use, multiplying even as they generated: breeding, said John Dee, increasing like a lucky housewife's hens from their own eggs. It was child's play, and indeed Doctor Dee's sons Arthur and Rowland soon learned to assist at the furnace and the alembic; nor did they pray and cleanse their hearts through fasting and reception of the Sacrament as Dee had always done in the (fruitless) former times, it was unnecessary, for clean or soiled their hands did as well. They rolled up their sleeves and like bakers or smiths they went to work, and at evening they were richer than they had been at morning. They cast the gold into half- and quarter-ingots, or made medallions or coins of their own devising, currency of their new republic, any goldsmith would after a quick test change them for coin of this realm. John Dee opened a bag of them and spilled them on the table before his wife, what he had promised, what the angels had promised them, they peeped up proud from where they lay as though saying *Mistress, we told you so:* and she smiled down on them, and laughed, and slipped her hands beneath her apron and would not touch them.

Gold: like the fairground magician who could seem to fill a basin with clinking coins, more and more snatched out of the air and ringing in the basin, the Miser's Dream, Kelley and Dee in Prague that year produced more and then more. Many years later Arthur Dee would often tell his friend the physician Sir Thomas Browne how his father had made gold in Rudolf's time; how the younger children had played with disks of it, how it lay about everywhere. Had they done so truly? asked Dr. Browne. Oh yes; heaps. Real gold? Oh yes, Arthur would say, with a sad smile; oh yes, real enough.

John Dee did not tell Jane of the other gift, the one he had himself been given by the angels, his own recompense, his tip.

Alone with it he learned its name, or the name of its name; he sat up with it all through one night, as a falconer must with a newly captured goshawk, to befriend it, and teach it to mind: to come to his hand, and go where he sent it.

In the day, like a shy ghost, it stayed shut up within him, but in the solitudes of the night he would feel it stir, touch his hair and beard, wind around him like a juggler's tame serpent; it put out his candle sometimes, made his wife look up and seek for the crack where the draught she felt came in, and pull her (new, fur-trimmed) mantle closer.

Then toward dawn on the ides of June he slipped its jesses, and cast it.

Or did it simply escape from him?

Was it ever his to command?

It scattered the papers and dust in the tower room (having rushed at his summons, he felt it, from his gown's pockets or from his bag or his fingertips); he heard laughter, a child's, hers; it grew stronger in a moment, it blew about the feather-pens and made the hangings lift and quiver as though a spy were behind them. Then, before John Dee could shutter and bar the window, it was gone, out and away, little runagate, a lost hawk that might return and might not: and a stillness filled up the disordered chamber.


Whether started accidentally by that wind, or fixed by Fate or Providence to blow anyway on that night, a windstorm had by evening arisen in those parts, blowing the wrong way, from east to west around the world. Exhilarating at first, like a fast ride downhill, it grew alarming as the bloody sun went down amid fly-ing clouds and night gathered too quickly.

Horses would not brave it, oxen would not pull, only the patient asses were unafraid, braying back at the wind's shrieking and closing their lashy eyes against the dust. Travellers hoping to take advantage of the long summer day and the night's full moon to hurry their journeys shut themselves up instead in inns and monasteries and even knocked on the barred doors of poor folks' cottages when the storm grew huge and living.

One of those travellers was Giordano Bruno. After leaving Paris he had spent two years among the mild and kindly Lutherans of Wittenberg, teaching and writing, until the theological faculties decided that, when all is said and done, Scripture made it clear that the Sun really did go around the Earth (how other-wise could Joshua command it to stand still upon Gideon, and lengthen the day?) and there was to be no more disputing this.

So once again Bruno had made his farewells; in tears he parted from the young men who during his tenure there had attached themselves to him, disci-ples such as he would always have wherever he went, not many in any one place but loyal and brave, all of them; almost all. Then he shook the dust of that city from his feet and walked down the Elbe toward the royal city of Prague.

Once upon a time, on such a groaning moaning sleep-banishing night, innkeepers might have entertained travellers with local stories of the *wilde Jaeger,* the Wild Hunt; might have told how the wind they heard crying was actually the clatter of the lady Diana or Perchta or Abundia and her followers beating their steeds through the air, on their way to the land of the dead. On certain days of the year, particularly the days between Christmas and Epiphany, certain of their neighbors went abroad under the moon: not, or not necessarily, in their own persons, which might remain fast asleep in their beds, but in some other form, the form of mice or horses or. And the wind that bore them up and away was also the wind of their own passage overhead, as they travelled to a place known only to themselves, where they did battle on behalf of the rest of us, who kept within doors: we whose duty was only to tell their tale, and bless them.

But those tales had become dangerous ones to tell.

For the protection of the souls of his people the Duke of Bavaria (and he not the only one) had lately instituted laws. No longer were these beliefs and practices of country people to be allowed, for it had been determined that they had all along been worshipping the Devil—perhaps without knowing it—by their superstitions. Ghosts, manikins, ogres, mountain giants, wills-of-the-wisp, the imps that combed sparks into cats' fur and soured milk, all the small creatures of everyday and every-night life: either they had been suborned by the Enemy, or they had always been devils in disguise, working for men's harm, but what was certain was that it was a sin, and worse than that it was now a crime, to leave a dish of milk for them, or invoke their help to find a lost calf, or to induce one of them to reverse the harm another had done. To do so would be *prima facie* evidence of witchcraft.

Best to make sure, then, that our neighbors and our guests saw us bless ourselves when we sneezed, or when nightwalking animals crossed our paths, or when we passed the churchyard. And when the wild wind blew from the wrong quarter, best to bolt our doors and shutters, and in silence (or better yet in prayer, for our husbands and our children are listening) to roll ourselves into our beds and pull up the blankets over our heads.

# 2

omething had happened in Hell.

A hundred years before, Alfonso de Spina had calculated the number of devils in Hell at 133,306,668. Most were confined forever there below, Padre Alfonso thought; only a few—those once worshipped as gods by the pagans—or perhaps only one, Satan, as we are told in Job, ever roamed our upper air, with perhaps a few attendants to run his errands.

No more, though. Since then either Hell-mouth had opened wider, or more doors had been made, or the princes below had acquired new powers; or men's (and women's, particularly women's) wickedness, pride, lust, and luxury had at last given those devils egress from their land (God shaking His head sadly in Heaven, Who had seen it coming) and access to our world and our days. Now it seemed they walked or flew over the earth in legions, herding the wicked like cattle toward their pens, contracting with the desperate and the proud for their immortal souls, their signatures in blood smoking on the parchment, or in female form hovering over men in the night to steal their seed as the men tossed and groaned in guilty dreams.

Once witches were few and isolated, and cases of *maleficium*—harm done by witchcraft or sorcery—rare; now witches gathered in Sabbaths, flying or somehow travelling great distances to worship the Devil, who was allowed to appear among them either in his own dreadful person or in some animal form, actual or illusory. There they performed obscene rituals unheard of in former times. Jean Bodin in his tract known throughout the Latin-reading world as the *Dæmonomania* quoted the famed demonologist Henri Boguet that "witches by the thousands are everywhere, multiplying upon the earth even as the worms in a garden." In fact the witches had apparently formed a sect or heretical religion of their own, a rival or infernal Church subsisting and growing within the very body of Christendom itself, not as worms grow in a garden but as they grow in the body of a wasting child.

How long had this been going on? No one could say; little of it had been suspected until two Dominicans, Fathers Spraenger and Institoris, compiled a manual in the 1480s for investigators to use, the *Malleus maleficarum* or Hammer Against Witches, listing all the secret crimes the fathers had heard or read about or deemed to be possible, and all the methods that ought to be used to search them out. The suspects began to come before judges who had the *Malleus* open on the bench before them. And the confessions began to accumulate, and dovetail.

Did you go abroad at night and consort with others at a Sabbath?

I do go out at certain times, in certain seasons of the year, to fight the others. I have gone since childhood.

What others? Other witches?

*They* are witches. We go in the service of Christ to fight them.

Blaspheme not. Why do you go out? What reason?

Because I am summoned. I am one of those who is summoned.

Who summons you? God, or an angel, or the Devil?

A man. Just a man. He is from Cologne, a big, bearded man; he leaves his body in his bed, and comes to summon me. I leave my bed and follow.

A big dark man comes at night and summons you to join the witches. What are the names of the other witches that you see?

I cannot say. I would be beaten. We have all agreed not to tell the names of those who go to fight, not our names or the names of the witches.

You will say. You will say or you will be made to say . . .

An invisible army, its captains and soldiers known only to one another; a sect, meeting not openly in the daylight as Christians do but secretly at night. A foreign nation to which the witch and the sorcerer gave their whole allegiance, where every common human act and feeling was reversed and made into its opposite: where the Savior of mankind was despised and His Cross trampled and shat upon, and the Devil's fundament worshipped; where persons surrendered their natural dominion over the animals and instead took on animal form themselves; where coupling was done openly in groups and not in the dark alone; where children were not nurtured but aborted and slain, not fed but eaten.

Children killed and eaten: not in fable, not to be released unharmed from the wolf's belly or resurrected from their own boiled bones, but truly killed and eaten like fowl by our neighbors in secret. The ultimate crime, the crime the Roman magistrates once charged the first Christians with, and the Christians their Gnostic rivals and later the Jews who lived among them. When we hear of children killed and eaten we have entered the counterworld, Hell on earth, and it is usual for some, or many, to be hunted down and slain before it is closed and forgotten again.

Madimi had said it: all Christ's churches joined in warring against them. Doctrinaire Dominicans demanded they be burned, but so did Genevan Calvinists and French Huguenots and sensible Dutch reformers. The Archbishop of Trier burned some two hundred witches, including an eighty-year-old blind woman and an eight-year-old boy; and then, just as Giordano Bruno was passing through his lands with a new work on magic in his pack, the Archbishop was himself accused of witchcraft and taken to prison by the civil authorities. Under torture he remembered, or confessed to, appalling obscenities.

In the work he was writing *de magia,* Bruno had listed nine kinds of magic, the first the wonder-working of the Ægyptians, Jewish cabbalists, Indian gymnosophists, Roman *sapientes;* the second, the application of *actives* to *passives* to transform one thing into another, as is done in alchemy; third, the trickery of jugglers and deceivers, able to create the appearance of wonders. Fifth was the magic of seals and numbers, sixth was the worship of Intelligences through ceremonies and sacrifices (which might attract a powerful dæmon into the unwary soul). And so on. In his German inn with his bag already packed and his bill paid, Bruno pulled out the book and added a tenth kind: the magic acquired through a pact with the Devil, a kind unworthy of mention with the other nine and anyway made far too much of, "not by wise men or even pedantic grammarians but by *bardocuculli* [stupid cuckoos] like the authors of the *Malleus maleficarum.*" Outside the inn where he wrote crowds hastened to the square before the church where the stake had been set up, piled with dry wood.

Burning to death is an awful spectacle, but not as painful as it seems it must be: not the ultimate earthly pain its employers hope and suppose it to be. Many who have been severely burned say that the pain comes largely afterward; while the fire is at work there is horror, or dread, or an unearthly peace worse than either, but not pain. This was not apparent to the shrieking laughing crowds watching the skin blister away, beards and hair catch fire like straw, eyeballs coagulate; but the angels who met those souls on the other, cooler shore and asked in pity Are you all right, are you all right? were often answered Yes, yes I think: for they had escaped while the body was still overwhelmed and unable to tell of its anguish. And all all right now. *In Paradisum deducant te Angelii.*

Practiced executioners who suspected that their subjects were escaping the full measure of punishment liked to damp down the fires when half the work was done, when legs and bound hands were so burned as to be unrecognizable but eyes could still see and throat still scream (could, unless the tongue was tied or cut or a metal brace was strapped to the breast to keep the jaw jammed shut, so that the witch could not shriek out the name of her demon protector, or the heretic blaspheme). *Knowledge* is the goal of the torturer, as of the moral instructor: unconsciousness is failure. So let the crowds come right up to the barriers, where they can see and hear, let them hold their children up, let the burghers and the civil authorities have high seats, and let them lean forward, the better to see, to hear, to know: they are here to be made intimate with the sinner, to be made momentarily one with her, they must learn all they can. The eye is the mouth of the heart.

Giordano Bruno smelled ash in the air even as far as the city gate.

Earlier in that year 1588, a certain Peter Stumpf of Bedburg, near Cologne, was met in the woods by hunters who had just seen a wolf and given chase; he was out for a stroll, he said; the hunters found this suspicious, and Stumpf was arrested and imprisoned. Subjected only to the *territio realis*—the showing of the tools of torture—he immediately confessed that he was a werewolf, had killed and eaten sixteen people, yes, that his wife yes and his daughters yes and his mistress were all witches. So he was condemned; bound to a cart wheel, his legs and arms broken, his flesh pulled off with white-hot pincers, and his head "strooke from his body and stuck upon a hye pole," said the vividly illustrated English broadside account published soon after, and was then burned with his women: "Thus he lived and dyed in the likeness of a woolf, and shape of a man."

—And may God have mercy on them that did it, said John Dee. For it was a great wrong and wickedness.

—He had murdered sixteen, said the Emperor of the Romans. Why should he not die the death?

—If they were murdered, John Dee said, bowing low to soften his disagreement with the Emperor, they were murdered by a wolf, or wolves.

—He was the wolf!

—So it is said. Your Majesty will I hope pardon me if I do not believe it.

—He confessed. He confessed all. He confessed murders that had not before been known of.

—Under the threat of torture. Your Majesty, if all your subjects have not confessed such things it is only because we have not all been tortured.

They went spiralling steadily downward, the Emperor, Doctor Dee, the Emperor's physician and his chaplain, a secretary, four clanking guards, all following the servingmen and their wavering torches. The stone steps of the tower had grown slick with damp; the Emperor leaned upon his chaplain.

—You do not, the Emperor's physician asked Doctor Dee, believe in the transvection of witches.

—I do not, said John Dee. I do not believe that God would grant to the Devil such powers, which then the Devil could grant to his worshippers. God's care for us does not admit of it. Whatever the poor deluded women believe. Or are led to believe. Read Wierus, *de præstigiis dæmonium,* of devilish tricks.

—Jean Bodin says otherwise, said the chaplain testily, and with as good citations.

—The man, or woman, who believes himself to be a wolf, said Doctor Dee, suffers from a species of melancholy. A very deep dreadful melancholy. The wolf he believes himself to be is only the inward form or picture of that melancholy. Hear how often they say: my wolf's skin is on the inside.

At that the Emperor, beside him on the narrow stair, made a small sound, a whimper like a puppy's or a child's: one only, and his face did not change. Only John Dee heard. The Emperor had suffered lifelong from melancholy.

—All the ancient writers agree, said Dee. The physical signs are well-known: the dry mouth and eye, the unslakable thirst, the insomnia by night. Thoughts fixed on cemeteries, and corpses.

—Witches cannot weep, said the Emperor's physician. That too is well-known.

—*Morbus lupinus,* said Dee. The stars being conjoined, and the spirit properly formed. Or better say improperly formed. They will believe themselves turned into beasts, and behave accordingly.

—How is it then, the chaplain asked, that those who see a werewolf see, not a man who believes himself a wolf, but a wolf indeed?

—The question is, the physician said, whether the witches can transform themselves into the forms of animals—wolves, mice, flies, all are attested—and go about doing harm; or whether what is seen is only a *phantasticum* or projection of the spirit, sent out as the witch lies asleep.

—How could the witch be guilty of the wolf's crimes if the witch lies asleep and only dreams them? asked the chaplain in a rising voice. Shall we pardon them all then and give them their freedom?

The Emperor stilled them with a lift of one hand. They continued downward. From within the dungeons there came as they passed the rattle of manacles, and sounds that might have been a man's breathing, or a dying man's entreating. John Dee had heard, without believing, that it was here in the tiny chambers of the White Tower that fraudulent or careless alchemists were imprisoned who failed to produce what they promised to the Emperor. The way had grown damper, for now they had gone down beneath the surface of the earth, and the only light that reached them fell from above through tall chimneys. The guards stopped before a door, the sweating black nailheads on it showing how thick it was; an opening in it was too small to admit anything but a man's hand, and yet was barred anyway.

—Look in, said the Emperor.

John Dee came close to the little window. He had, the day before, received a special summons from the Emperor, passed to him by Sir Edward (that was Kelley) to appear quickly at the castle, to advise the Emperor on a matter beyond the skills of his physicians. Edward Kelley had told the Bohemians that nothing was beyond the skills of Jan Devus, *doctor sapientissimus,* and when Kelley spoke now everyone listened, and so John Dee had been brought down into this place of terror: and if he could do nothing in the case, here he might well remain.

In the little stone space on a stone bed a young man sat in the near darkness. He was drawn into a shivering bundle, as tight as he could draw himself given the black shackles on his wrists and neck. By a trick of the small light in the cell, his eyes shone visibly, white and wide and afraid, though his face was dark.

—Taken in his bed in a village of the Giant Mountains twenty nights ago, said the physician. Imperial huntsmen followed a spatter of blood from a wolf trap, not long after a wolf attacked sheep nearby and killed a lamb. The blood led toward his village. He was found in bed amid bloody sheets.

—Naked, said the chaplain. The blood still on his mouth.

—May we open the door?

—Open the door, said the Emperor.

For only the briefest moment—it was over before the Emperor noticed it—

no one did anything; then the guards took up positions at the door's side, and the turnkey was put forward, and a torch held up.

The door opened.

No ravening wolf. He drew back, and his chains dragged against the stones: the dreariest of all sounds. Dark hair matted, with blood maybe; a rug or mantle thrown around his nakedness. John Dee thought not of wolves but of a lamed fox kit he once found the boys of Mortlake tormenting: of its big eyes and panting mouth. So still and weak. Reynard. They let the dogs have it.

—Does he speak?

—He has not.

—Is he hurt? He is.

Dee came to the lad (perhaps he was fifteen years old, perhaps not so old) and drawing up the skirts of his robe knelt on the stone floor beside him. The werewolf's left ankle and foot were bound in cloths, a great clout that the blood had nevertheless seeped through. The naked foot extending from the bandage was blue. The wound stank.

—How did he come by this hurt?

—The trap, said the physician. The force of its closing broke the *astragalus*. The bone coming through. So this was no spirit. No phantom or *phantasticum*.

—But, said the chaplain, have not werewolves been wounded by hunters, and the same wound later discovered on the body of the guilty one?

—How could a wound given to a projection redound upon the living body?

—*Repercussio,* said the chaplain. We are told of the man out hunting, comes upon a clowder of cats, they mock him; he strikes at them with his sword, and cuts off the right paw of the leader. Later returns home, finds his own wife nursing a handless right arm by the fire. Well attested.

The Emperor, wearied with listening to their Latin—a language invented only to worry problems with—asked John Dee:

—Will he die? Can he die?

—He can and will.

—Can he be treated?

—I do not know, Your Majesty, if the wound to his ankle and foot can be treated now. Your physicians can tell better than I.

—If the wound is God's justice on him, said the chaplain, and shrugged.

—He must not die, said the Emperor. He is the only one ever to have come here alive.

The boy, who had evidently understood nothing either of the Latin nor of the German they spoke, only stared; John Dee wondered what he thought he saw. And why, firstly, had the Emperor brought the boy here? Why had he called an English doctor to this place to see to him? The wound was a dreadful one, and the boy must be in great pain; almost John Dee could see the heart within him beating.

—Of his melancholy, John Dee said: of that too he might die. Here in this place, without sun.

—But that, said the chaplain, that that . . .

—That is an affection that can be treated.

—A melancholy so deep, said the Emperor. Only the Stone itself could cure such a melancholy.

John Dee arose from where he knelt on the stone floor. He understood why he had been brought here. He had at his first meeting with this strange king promised that he, John Dee, could make the Stone, cure for all sorrows, philosopher's son, living fountain, plate of divine victuals, splendor of God on earth, the only thing the Emperor wanted. That was what the angels had told him to say. He would not unsay it; not now, not here.

—I can cure him, he said.

The others there, guards, physician, chaplain, turnkey, wolf-boy, Emperor of the Romans with his hurt eyes, all looked at him, and went on looking; and John Dee thought that from the pressure of their eyes' lights upon his heart he might himself momentarily transvect, become a dragon, a flambeau, something that would startle and chasten their foolish faces.

—Yes I, he said. Give him into my care and in twenty days I will cure him.


There is no Stone: not in this age. What the angels had told him to promise to the Emperor they could not get: John Dee knew that now. If it had been made in the past, by men wiser than any in this our time, in Ægypt, Athens, or the Lord knows where, then they who made it were not able to pass it down to us, or what they passed down has lost its splendor; and we can no longer follow their instructions, or understand their fables. What the Emperor wanted from John Dee and the hundred other doctors, smokesellers, cinder-bitten cucurbites, Paracelsian iatrochemists and gold-eating Chinamen he supported, he would not get: the age was too cold, too old.

But there are ways to treat a melancholy: a *melancholia fumosa,* a choler adust, a dry or a moist melancholy, black as Hell though it be. Nothing that John Dee had wanted with all his heart was to be given to him, no more than to the Emperor; perhaps he had sinned against God's goodness in asking for it, and perhaps he was damned now. But he could still treat a melancholy.

He chose a tower from among the dozens that rose above the castle, a remote high one with a broad top open to the sky. He was given an apartment just below, a dusty chamber where armor and weapons rusted; these were cleared, and beds and tables laid, and the tools and materials he needed brought in. Through the narrow windows the sun moving into Libra shone strongly in; the nights, though, were sharp already, and there was not much time.

From Trebon where his family remained in the castle of Duke Rozmberk he summoned his boy John Carpio. John knew the Bohemian tongue, and was accustomed to wonders. When Dee and Kelley had sought the Stone it was John who had sat up with them and watched with them over the athenor, wherein for the first time they had made new gold from what was not gold. John brought from Trebon a cart of necessary things; from the Emperor's own workshops came other workmen skilled in several crafts.

When all was ready the wolf was brought up from his dungeon in the White Tower, where the Emperor's physicians (closely watched by armed men) had been tending to his hurt foot; he was brought out shut up in a cage of black iron like a menagerie beast, carried upward by a gang of strong men, and lifted the last fifty feet to the tower's top by block and tackle: Dee saw him squeeze shut his eyes in terror and grip his cage's bars as he arose by jerks. Far off (Dee was sure) the Emperor himself observed from another tower. It was near nightfall. John Dee ordered the cage (it would not be needed long, was in all likelihood not needed now, but Dee was under strict orders not to free him uncured) to be placed on a low wheeled table or cart he had had built there on the tower's top. And the guards were sent below.

—Come, John, he said, summoning his boy. Come. Speak to him.

—What shall I say? asked reluctant John.

—You shall say *How do you do,* said Doctor Dee.

He could see that the boy's left foot was mending, though it had been so badly hurt and gone so long untreated that he would never walk without a limp or a stick now. He was thin, lean and summer-brown in the light clothes they had given him: a peasant, a farmer's boy. His eye liquid and large, afraid and watchful but not a melancholic's suspicious eye with yellowish white and dull apple: that was good. They said his urine was copious, clear and golden, pale as Bohemian ale: also good.

Dee drew up a stool to the cage and sat. He put his hand within the cage and took the boy's thin wrist in his.

—Come, Sir Wolf, he said. We shall make a man of you again, if you be willing.

Of all the causes of melancholy the remotest are the stars: the nativity and its conjunctions, the houses where the planets are disposed, the signs ascendant and regnant. All other causes—diet, accident, love-madness, evil demons, brooding on wrongs, the black humour rising to dry the tender tissues of the brain—all depend on the stars at first.

So the stars must be cure too.

There on the tower's top the Emperor's excellent workmen had constructed frames for three large circular mirrors, mounted on gemel rings so that Dee could turn them by geared wheels to face any quarter of the sky. The mirrors were not flat silvered surfaces but *catoptric:* they were like great shallow dishes, their incurving calculated according to geometries John Dee had worked out more than thirty years before. Catoptrics, or the knowledge and use of such curved mirrors, was in his estimation the central mystery of astrology; only by catoptrically gathering and directing the rays of the planets could a worker achieve anything beyond mere passive description of the state and prospects (fortunate or unfortunate) of the affected party.

Alcindus of Araby knew: every object propagates itself through the universe spherically, that is by rays proceeding from every point on it. The lodestone's nature of attracting iron or other lodestones proceeds spherically outward from it with diminishing force through almost any medium, water, air, anything—except, of course, garlic juice. The planets, the sun and the moon, are the most potent propagators of rays; earth and all its beings are bathed constantly in their angular intersections (Dee had described the mathematics of it in his *Prapædeumata aphoristica*). So, to counter the natural tendencies of a soul or a body formed by a maleficent planet's rays, John Dee lifted the face of his mirror to the sky, caught within it the rays of a contrary planet in a good aspect (like Venus, just then following the sun toward the west, effulgent, brightest object in the fading heavens); the mirror focused them not on but at a point somewhat in front of its curved surface. A man standing just there, before that focus, and looking in would seem to see her, Venus, hovering in the middle of the air, twice or thrice as bright as in the evening sky—or he would if he happened to be made of glass, for Venus's light cannot pass through his body's solidity to reach the mirror's surface. Instead he sees himself, inverted as in a silver spoon. But though her light will not pass through him, the other rays of Venus will; so if he be placed there, his brain at that focus, or his shrunken heart, Venus's rays will still warm him, like a young girl rolled in bed with an old cold sick man.

There was no doubt of the efficacy of the procedure. The power of curved mirrors was known to the ancients, and even if the story of how Julius Cæsar had used a curved mirror set up on the shores of Gaul to see the Britons preparing for war weren't true, it was certainly the case that a catoptric, turned to face the sun, could cause a thick stick held at its focus to take fire. And if the sun, why not Venus and Jupiter? John Dee had first succeeded with his mirrors in curing his wife of a melancholy, after their first son Arthur was born: a mother-sorrow *post partum* that she could not shake.

The melancholy of the man-wolf would be a deeper one; and it might be that even such sure and certain arts as catoptrics were weakening and failing now. No way to be sure but to use them, and see.

John Dee made a slight adjustment to his mirror, turned his hourglass, and sat to wait in the deepening darkness.

He thought: We tear to pieces the melancholics who have fallen, through their disease, from man's estate, and believe themselves beasts. Once it was not so; not a hundred years ago they were known to be unfortunate, and in need of our care and love. We burn deluded old women who think to make in their iron pots the wonderful elixirs they have heard the wise can make—they take the coded and hidden recipes of the old books and tales for plain truth, and try to do a work with cock feathers, horse piss, field grasses and the moon's light. Maybe, once, some deluded one—hearing tales of the Homunculus, the Son brought to life within the athenor—put in to seethe a birth-strangled babe found in a ditch, or a babe's corpse dug up: wicked, surely, and deserving punishment, but inefficacious, hurting no one but the hag herself.

Old despised and outcast women. They frighten their neighbors with their curses, and when later a child falls sick or a cow dries up the neighbor remembers. And the fear spreads, reaching at length the students of arts the vulgar cannot understand. Arts the priests and judges, most of them, can understand no better.

*They will burn you too,* Madimi had said.

Perhaps. Let him see what good he might do, till then.

When Venus had fallen far toward the west and her beams struck this tower at too oblique an angle, John Dee smacked his knees, arose from his stool, and consulted his ephemeris; he looked east to where Jupiter, jolly giant, had risen: as sovereign against melancholy as his beautiful blue daughter, if she is or was his daughter, as Hesiod saith. Dee sighting with his astronomical staff and the boy John ratcheting the dishes around at his command, they caught the star; they wheeled the caged (and weary) wolf to the focus of the *parabola* (John Dee's word for the mirror-shape he had devised). And feeling the tawny star's heat on his cheek, the boy blinked, looked up, like a man awakened by the sun through a knothole; his mouth opened and he wet his lips and swallowed.

Dee came to the cage, opened the door of it. He said to John:

—Ask if we may safely let him come forth.

John spoke to the boy, who had begun to shiver; the boy made a short answer, and began to creep from the cage.

—He says he thirsts.

—Go, Dee said to John. Bring a clean shirt, a warm mantle. A cup of white wine, with water; apples; wheaten bread. No cheese, no greens. They have given him black beer and pease bread in prison, and he is the worse for it.

John went quickly, glad to go; Dee pushed away the cage from the wheeled cart, grunting with the weight of it, and the boy, seeing him struggle, turned to help him: but when he tried to stand he fell.

—Hurt, said Dee. You are hurt—don't rise. Be still.

He put his hand on the boy's shoulder, and kept him there, waiting for John. He thought of the night six years before when Edward Kelley came to his house in Mortlake, afraid, lost even, though not knowing it: the night this journey began.

They dressed the boy and fed him, and made a pallet for him on the cart. John Dee altered his mirrors, for Jupiter had all this time been moving with the night and the stars. They turned the hourglass again. The boy slept.

Half a billion miles away (John Dee thought it was some forty million) orange Jupiter shone with the Sun's light (John Dee thought it had its own); into its great envelopes of gas, the heavier within the lighter, the little rays of the sick boy's soul penetrated, going down thousands of miles, reaching to the core hot almost as a star; there they stirred the god's generosity to an infinitesimal degree, and redounded stronger.

By morning he was speaking, alert, cheerful even, his melancholy seemingly lifted already—if indeed it was one. John Dee, hearing his tale, wondered if it had not been a melancholy at all that had taken him but a plain madness.

·    ·    ·

He was indeed a peasant's son, he told them, and lived in a remote village in the Krknôse Mountains, with his brothers and his mother and his grandparents in a small stone house, had slept in a loft with four others, next to a small window that was his alone. Only after his father was killed felling trees did his mother tell him that he was not the man's son at all but the priest's; the priest took an interest in him, and taught him some Latin. John Dee began to speak to him in that language (to which he had not responded before, and no wonder) and the boy sometimes understood. His name was Jan, like John Dee's own.

Priests' sons are known for having unlikely flaws and powers, though Jan (Jan thought) had none of them. But there was more to his birth than that. He had been born with a caul: not merely a cap like a woman's lace snood, as some were, but a membrane shrouding all his face, through which (his mother said) his unopened eyes and mouth could be discerned, dimly, as though he had not yet wholly arrived.

—Its right name *amnion,* said John Dee. Many cunning-women have their tales about it. And ancient writers too. A Frenchman I have read says: a fore-telling of the shroud we will all one day wear to cover our faces; a sign, at our coming, of our going hither.

—She dried the caul, he said. My mother. And sewed it into a little kidskin bag. She told me I must wear it always, here, in the pit of my left arm, and tell no one.

Not until he was fourteen did he learn that the caul was a sign of what he had been born for: to be, on certain nights of the year, along with others of his kind, a wolf.

Sweet, pliant and helpful, his voice rising hardly above a whisper as he willingly told his tale; eyes dark as a deer's, and his plump cheeks rosy now that he had rested and eaten.

—A wolf, said John Dee. How, born to be.

He shrugged: If I had been born female, I would have more likely been born a witch.

—Are not witches werewolves? John Dee asked. The authors say . . .

—A witch a werewolf? The boy glanced at his translator, puzzled: had he heard right? A witch a werewolf, he said: you might as well say a day that is a night, a fire that's water. They oppose each other; fight, to the death sometimes. They must.

—Why do they fight?

—For the harvest. If we did not fight them, the witches would carry off the life of the earth to their lord beneath the earth; the harvest would fail, the young of the animals would be stillborn, or not thrive.

—Where do they fight?

—Near the gates of Hell, or within them; a meadow where no grass grows. I have never seen the place.

The night he had been captured he had been on his way with others of his kind to do battle with the witches, as at certain times of the year, he said, they were bound to do; in the Ember Days, and at Epiphany, feast of the Three Kings, who were their patrons. The witches had other patrons, he didn't know who they were; saints whose names were known only to them. That night was the first he had ever gone out to the battle: the first night, and he had not got to the place, did not know how far from it he was even, when he was seized in the trap meant for wolves.

At this the boy reached down to put his hand gravely and tenderly on his broken ankle.

—You were taken in your bed, Doctor Dee said. The watch believed it was you who had been caught in the trap, and got free, but their reasons are very weak. Only that you were in your bed, with a wound to your leg.

The boy nodded, rapidly, thoughtfully, as though to say he understood that the watch had done the best they could and could not probably be expected to understand: and then he said that indeed it had been he in the trap. He had freed himself after a dreadful nightlong struggle, and with a crutch made from a tree limb returned just at dawn to his village, and to his home and his brothers, and got into his bed.

—Your brothers did not awaken at that? Nor your mother?

—No.

—They made you believe this tale, John Dee said. In jail, in the cage they put you in to bring you to the city, in that dungeon in the White Tower. On the rack or in the boot. Told the tale to you so often when you were in pain and afraid that you have come to believe it. . . .

The boy shook his head, shook his head as John Carpio told him what the Doctor had just said.

—No no, he said. No it was the night of the summer Ember Days, and the greatest battle ever to be fought; the last battle perhaps, the last of the world; there were many many on their way, witches in the wind riding their pigs and mice and infants and spoons, and we over the ground: more than any battle before, even the oldest among us had never seen so many on the way to battle; and I was to be there, and help to save the crops and the coming year from them, and I failed, I erred, I allowed myself to be caught and now I will never ever see the battle or take part in it before I die. And what will become of my soul then?

He looked at John Carpio and then at Doctor Dee, in a plain despair that nothing could make right.

—What will become of my soul then? he asked them. How can I hold up my head now among the dead, the day when I go down to them?

# 3

For fourteen nights John Dee went on bathing his wolf in starlight for his health. He would have continued the treatment in the day as well (for the planets are of course there in the day, and just as often in good aspects), except that he would have had to guide his mirrors not by eye but by published star tables; and as every astronomer and astrologer knew, all current star tables and ephemerides were hopelessly incorrect, and not until the Emperor's new Rudolphine Tables were completed and published would such a task even be thinkable; at which time half the nativities cast in Europe would be shown to be absurdly wrong.

He went on, but it was evident there was no trace of a melancholic affliction in the boy; he was strong, high-colored, restless, witty. *Sir Wolf* John Dee still called him, and the boy in return called him *Pan sora,* or Sir Owl. For his beak nose and the great surprised eyes behind his round black spectacles. They slept in the tower room below in the day, Jan in his own small chamber, the two Johns together in the one bed; they called for meals when they were hungry, they went aloft at sundown to study the sky (strangely clear, night after night, Doctor Dee wondered at it, the great wind had blown away the clouds for good), and as the boy sat for his time on the wheeled cart, his hurt leg favored and his chin in his hands, they talked.

Who set the witches and the wolves in opposition? Dee did not yet know if he believed any of the boy's tale, but he wanted to know the whole of it. Are there such battles in other places, east, west? Do you recognize, in the day, those whom in the night you have pursued?

Jesus set the opposition between wolves and witches when he made the heavens and the earth; just as he set the opposition between water and fire, the living and the dead, the ass and the viper, vervain and fever. It was one of the oppositions that make the world as it is and not a different way instead. So all over the world the battles are fought; on the night when Jan himself went out to fight there were wolves and witches from many lands on their way to Hell-mouth, witches from Livonia, Moravia, Rus; black Bohemian wolves, red ones from Poland, gray wolves of far northern lands. He had seen them, or known they were near.

He did not know those he pursued in the day; perhaps he would if he had gone out to fight them on many nights and not once only. It seemed to him (he didn't know why) that he was destined to pursue and punish one witch, one witch linked or bound to him, his own opposition amid the larger oppositions of the battle and the world.

Doctor Dee nodded, for he thought it might well be that the two were one person: that they were, in fact, the melancholy and the man. The chaser and the chased sought each other because they were one, and the struggle between them was a dream-struggle. He thought of Kelley.

—It may be, Jan said thoughtfully, that a wolf might live alongside the witch it is his destiny to pursue and never know her, or him, except in the battle-night; or it may be they *would* know one another, and yet live peaceably.

—Why not name them, Dee said. Have them seized and burned.

The boy lifted his eyes dismayed to John Dee when he realized what the man had said.

—*Homo homini lupus,* Dee said, trying to provoke. Do not suffer a witch to live. Does not the Scripture say so?

—Wicked spellcasters who cause harm by their magic should be punished, the boy said. Who could deny that? If one turns a man's wife against him, or with the Devil's help blasts a field, or makes a cow barren, or causes an illness. But not these. For they alone can consort with the dead, and bring back news of them to the living.

—Can they do that?

—They can see them, the dead and the soon to be dead. If such a one, say an old woman, were to say *You will be dead within the month* it is because she has seen the person's spirit in thrall to the Good Woman who is their leader. Perhaps the spirit could still be released, or brought back; perhaps not. But if the person die, then the old woman is remembered; they think that she did not only warn or prophesy, but caused the death.

—You are not feared and hated too for that?

—No. We don't have that knowledge. We can only go to give battle in that land, and we return forgetful of what we saw and did. They are there somehow always. Theirs is the greater gift; they are the strong ones.

—You are the benefactors. They do harm, or intend it.

—No, said the boy, thinking hard; no. For unless this battle is fought and won the crops will fail, the animals waste away and their young be stillborn. If the people knew how we save the good things of earth they would love and honor us. Some do. But the witches, though they must fight just as we do in order for the earth to be fruitful, will always be hated for what they do: steal the seedlings and the lambs and kids, and carry them to their land of death. Still, they do what they must. I could not. I would not.

—You pity them?

—That night when I went abroad I hungered, the boy said. I with others slew a lamb and ate it. Then I was satisfied. I blessed the lamb, and thanked God. But *their* hunger cannot be satisfied; and they cannot remember that it cannot be.

He ate now, not bloody meat but white bread and wine with water. John Dee watched him. The men and women he had come to know in this country were largely Austrians, many of whom had learned their manners in Spain or from Spaniards; they dressed in Spanish black and cultivated careful Spanish gestures. Or they were Jews, or Italian craftsmen or priests, or Dutch clockmakers who had spent years in Paris or the Savoy. Watching his Bohemian wolf Dee saw there was a Bohemian way in the world too, not quite like any other way, a Bohemian way to break bread, count on the fingers, bless oneself, a Bohemian yawn, a Bohemian sigh.

He had one question for John Dee.

—Why have I not been hanged? he asked.

—Why, hanged?

—It was said that I would be. After the Emperor had seen me, and judged my crimes.

—I fear he wants you for his collection, said Dee. He will keep you locked up and chained, lest you escape by devilish or magic means. Keep you weak. But not kill you. He would not kill you.

—Collection? said the boy, and looked to John Carpio for a translation, who looked to Dee.

—You are one of a kind of thing he does not have, Dee said: he has one of every other kind.

He thought: the lad is strong, and may live many years; and when he is dead they will cut him open, and see if there be a wolf's skin within; and whether there is or isn't they will flay him and dry his skin and keep his flesh preserved like mummia, and preserve his skull, more precious than any narwhal's or two-headed babe's: perhaps they will jewel it, or write upon it; or make a case of ebony or red oak to keep it in, a case carved to resemble a wolf's head.

—For now, he said, you are in my care. For now.

The moon had been waxing through those days; it blotted out the stars now, and ended the treatments, which were anyway unnecessary; they began to sleep in the nights again, staying aloft in their tower only because John Dee did not know what else to do. The Ember Days of autumn had come; in the countryside the harvest would be gathered; in England they would be mourning John Barleycorn, dead that his countless sons might live.

On Friday midnight the moon would be full. Should they put chains on their wolf?

In the end they did not. The Emperor's guards still slept outside the door. When the white moon crossed John Dee's window and her light awoke him, he sat up thinking *He is gone.* And though he knew it was foolish, he must get up from his bed, pull his robe around him, and go to look into the chamber where

Jan was kept. No of course he lay asleep there, the moon on his cheek too, his mouth open, breathing steadily in and out as though an unseen hand pressed the bellows of his lungs. A step closer: how strange: in the moon's light Dee could see that beneath the thin white skin of his eyelids the balls of his eyes were moving, fitfully, rapidly, side to side, just as though they saw.

The land Death is very near, but very long to reach. Sometimes a whole night's journey won't bring you there, though you know always that it lies but one step from where you are.

There is, or often is, a river to cross, and it might be this one he had come to, fast-flowing in a nightwind, dark flocks of sleeping waterbirds, and the leap of a stone bridge to cross it by, greatest bridge he had ever seen or dreamed of, as daunting as the black water itself to enter on. He was far from home.

He had come down from the tower (after pausing wondering and confused on the sill, unaware of having climbed to it, awaking there as though from sleep-walking on hearing his name distinctly spoken) by turning about and with his claws going down, stone by rough stone, like a spider. Then he had made his way from the castle, which was as hard to leave as to get into, but he was not stopped, could not (it seemed) be seen, or believed in.

Now a great river. *A river to cross,* the old ones had used to say who had taught him the journey he must go. *Often a river. Sometimes a little lame child who leads you.*

No child, but a bridge. Belated walkers went across it, some with lights carried before them, but who would do the dead that service? He did not know where the bridge led; he thought that those who crossed it would flee from him if he entered onto it, but they did not, they took no notice of him, and at length, heart hard in his throat and drumming as his four feet did on the pudding stone of the roadway, he crossed. The moon was high.

So many, so many more dead than living: he had known it but had not thought what a big and crowded city they would need for themselves, all those that had gone before. The black houses were tall and with no spaces between them, the streets narrow and twisting as though running to hide, to escape being built upon, and filled with the dead.

A drum called from on ahead, and the streets were filling with souls, *vralký kračivec,* stumblers, wanderers, laughing and wide-eyed and with nowhere to walk, who followed it. Not all poor men either; he saw a knot of wealthy ladies masked and in furred robes, a knight in armor, even what seemed to be a bishop by his cope and crook—except that his head was of a piece with his miter, he was a fish or lizard staring upward with open jaws.

For here, on this side, the Good Lady's company becomes the beasts they ride. They were all here in the thickening crowd; Jan knew them instantly from processions and plays in his own village. There was Lucek, with his beak like a stork's and feather cape and mincing gait. There was Brůna the goat and Klibna the horse, and Perchta their queen in her ragged skins. The shutters of the windows they passed were banged shut as the great-eyed beasts looked in, because if those inside were among the living they should not look upon this company, Death's company.

Yes Death's: for he was there, in the center of the throng where the drum thumps were loudest, Smrtka, Death himself in his coat of moldy straw and his *Totenkopf* eyeless and white, his regal chain of broken eggshells wound around him. Those near him held him aloft, his horrid weak arms of dead lichenous twigs and his legs of rope unable to support him.

Jan chased along with the crying singing capering crowd, swept up among them and unable not to go the way they went; but where were his own company to take his side and oppose Smrtka and Perchta's legions, those who had stolen the life of things and must be made to give it back? Why was he alone here? Why did the swaying staggerers (drunk? One spewed into the gutter) not fall upon him, alone as he was here? No eye turned on him. No one saw.

So it must be that he was still among the living, after all. He could pass by them and among them unseen, as he had passed by the soldiers and porters and doorkeepers of the castle, for he was not as they were; they had merely put on their skins, and he had not. They were dressed for the festival of the Ember Days as the beasts who die but never die, they were Death's celebrants and attendants and carried Death and beat drums to honor him, but they were alive; this city was after all only a dark city, not that crowded realm.

She though. Ahead and alone, moving not with the throng but against them, as though they were not there—as though she could not see them, just as they evidently could not see her. A tall woman with feet bare and hair free, tangled black wings of hair, and her face dark, terribly dark, as though burned or scarred: *facies nigra,* that doctor of the Emperor's had said, the melancholic's black face.

She saw him. As he saw her. She seemed to awaken, or her eyes widened so that he could see the whites. She stopped, and turned away; she stepped off with a long stride, and just then from the crowd or from elsewhere there came a boy, a young pale boy, a naked beggar, hurt in his foot and pegging quickly on a cleft stick held under his arm. Gone from sight almost as soon as seen, but she had seen him too, and turned the way he had turned, down an alley. Gone.

Gone.

No they were there, far ahead, where a square opened at the alley's end, and a tower stood up, with a clock mounted in it, which just then rang the first hour.

For a very long time he followed them. Night seemed to go on and on, or to have come to a stop and ceased to pass. Through city gates standing wide and unguarded (or the guards asleep in heaps, mouths wide like their gates, hugging their pikes like wives) and out onto moonstreak highways. The land smelled like his home. He saw the lame boy, far away, how could he go so fast. He saw her too, always soon after, saw her tall and long-armed in the moonlit wheat like a scarecrow, gathering, gathering.

Another river at last: different from the river flowing through the city; lightless, the banks featureless, the far side invisible.

When he came to it he found her stopped there too, loitering, bewildered; she had grown larger, her burdens around her beneath the muffling cloaks. When she became aware of him she turned to the water, but could not cross it, it lapped at her naked feet and darkened the hem of her skirt. She drew back and looked at him, her eye whites big and her features mobile, afraid, or questioning, or hurt.

Why are we here alone?

She put this question, or he read it in her or he felt it arise in himself; and a flood of pain overcame him, and he remembered the wound to his own foot.

I'm hurt, he said. I can go no farther.

He sat or lay down on the river's edge. Like a dog's his long tongue lolled from his jaw as he panted; now and then he mopped with it the slaver from his chops, and panted again.

Where is the pretty lame boy?

She came to where he lay, and bent over him, and her scarred face and its wild undone hair came close and closer until it filled his sight.

Why are we here alone?

He didn't know. Neither knew. They were like the last two left alive in a village through which the plague has passed, who get up from their beds weak but not dead, and go out into the lanes and the fields, and find the ploughman dead, the priest dead, the baker dead, the miller dead, no village to be of, only they two, whose families have perhaps quarreled for generations, now all dead too; so they sit down side by side.

She sat down beside him where he lay. She was shaking, and drew up her knees to her chin, and put her arm around his neck. He could feel her cheek against the rough hair of his head. He had ceased to pant.

He must have slept: for when his eyes opened he saw her far away, in the middle of the river, following the bright lame boy; her burdens rocked side to side as she slid and slipped over the river's billows as over ice, moving quickly, and the boy's head alight before her like a candle in the fog.

Bereft, bereft as though split in two by a sword, he stood ankle-deep in the water until he could see no more. He thought first: she has fooled me. Then he thought: I am hurt and can never go farther. And he thought: she is stronger than I am.

When he turned away from the river, the river was no more. Now before him lay the way he had come: before first light he must go back that long way, over the roads and the highway, through the suburbs and the city gates, through the city to the castle, to the tower and the small window of his chamber. If he could not do that he would never awaken in his bed. The moon was down. He set out.

It was the same for all of them at that moment: through the world now they were all turning back from the land they had journeyed to, however far toward it they had gone, chaser and chased, afraid, belated, returning each by his own way, the land to which they had gone closing up behind them as they hurried home. In the cottages and in the narrow houses of the city some of those asleep in their beds may have dreamed of him as he passed; some of those awake might have given thought to his kind and their battle, for most folk knew of it, whether they believed it or not, and knew that it was on nights such as this one that it took place. But the only ones who saw him were a priest and his acolyte, bearing the Sacrament through the night streets to a dying man: saw the fleet dark shape of him start to cross their path, then, eyes aglow, stop and kneel to his elbows (he could not cross himself with these arms, though desperately he wished to) and reverently bow his long black head.

—We are alone, he would tell John Dee next day. Once we were many, and went together. And they were many, too. Now we are few and alone. From now on we will be, till Judgment.

Trying to rise from his bed, weak and spent, the color absent again from his cheeks and his eyes black pissholes.

—Alone, he said. Alone.

John Dee held his shoulders as though he were a sick child of his own, and thought How large the world is, how numerous its creatures; how little of it I have known.

That day, while the boy slept, John Dee wrote in Latin to the Emperor's chamberlain:

*God, in His infinite wisdom, has provided to His children the remedies for their hurts, the first and greatest being our trust in Him. God be praised that through the actions of my Art and our prayers accompanying them, the one commanded into my care has passed again into a sort of health and many of the* symptomata *we observed have been relieved. Still the work must be continued, and despite the care and solicitude of SS Majestas that all things necessary be provided here, only in my own quarters can that which was here begun be completed with certainty of success. I have begged leave of His Excellency Duke Petr of Rozmberk that he make room in his great house,* and so on; knowing the dreadful chance he took and how short the time.

Nothing is taken away but something of equal value, or equal harm, is given: great arts now perhaps failed, but little ones were for the moment more useful than ever. Using tricks he had neglected so long he had to knock on his brow to recall how to do them—tricks the common people thought devilish, but which were natural, natural—John Dee passed out of the tower room at evening with his wolf, unseen by the Emperor's guards at the doors, who thought that they heard a mousing cat in the corner, or a jackdaw at the window, and felt perhaps a guilty wonder.

# 4

On an August morning Giordano Bruno left his lodgings at the sign of the Golden Turnip (everything in Prague was golden, there were taverns and inns called Golden Angel, Golden Eyes, Golden Plough) and went down through the Old Town on his way to the castle across the river.

The bridge that led to the castle was as broad and long as the one he remembered at Avignon, the one the children sing about. Black-beaked gulls shrieked and battled around the cutwaters, bobbed on the foam. More spans—ten, twelve, sixteen—than the bridge at Regensburg. The Tower Bridge in London was small compared to it, and the bridges over the Seine, and over the Main at Frankfurt.

Giordano Bruno had crossed many bridges.

He carried under his arm a little book he had dedicated to the Emperor, an argument against the pedant-mathematicians of the Mordente type, who liked their systems to refer to nothing and contain nothing but the operations of the numbers they used: striving to keep their systems closed, like a man struggling to keep his doors barred and his shutters shut in a storm. There was another way to use numbers and figures, an open and endless way, as variable as the world is, as chaotic even; a way to combine the heart-stirring sign (cross, star, rose) and the brain-teasing figure into one parable. *They* would never find such a thing, but he, Bruno, might.

Upward. He mounted the cobbled way up the hill to the castle-palace and its churches and cathedrals. At every gate, he opened and showed to the guards the crackling parchment that had been issued him, hung with seals and ribbons, inviting him to wait upon the Emperor's pleasure this day; they looked at him not at it, and let him pass. It was harder to get by the crowds of beggars and whores who lived in tents, hovels and caves all along the narrow way. Up ahead he saw that they importuned other climbers, tugging at the gown of that white-beard with the tall hat and staff who pressed strongly on past them.

That man. Somewhere in Giordano Bruno's Memory Palace—where every person place and thing, mortal and immortal, concrete and abstract, that Giordano Bruno had encountered in his long wanderings had its place among others whose nature and meaning it shared—in a disused wing or annex, something or someone stirred.

The man on the stair turned back to see Bruno following, and Giordano Bruno saw the face he expected to see, as though he had himself created it.

—*Ave fratre*.

The old wizard started to see him: it was the look of a man who sees a ghost, the one ghost most likely to appear before him.

—The man of Nola, he said. The Oxford scholist.

They had met at John Dee's house on the day of Bruno's first lecture at Oxford, where the asses brayed so loud that Bruno, like the Titans, was silenced. (Those Oxford asses too were penned in Bruno's Palace, not forgotten, or forgiven either.)

—*Quo vadis?* John Dee asked, beginning again to mount the stairs. Short-legged Bruno hurried after. What do you do in this city?

—I am summoned, he said. I have been commanded into the Emperor's presence. Today is the day, *ante meridian*.

—Strange. I have myself been summoned to appear this day. This morning too.

The stair was not wide enough for two to walk together, or one to pass by another. John Dee's steps quickened; Bruno kept pace just behind him.

—You have spoken to the Emperor before, Bruno said.

—Several times. I have been permitted to render him a service. I have had audiences. Promises were made me.

—Perhaps then, Bruno said, you will be good enough to let me pass. You have the entrée every day. I am newly arrived here and very much in need of, of.

—You are mistaken, Dee said, not slackening his pace. The Cardinal-Nuncio is my enemy. I am banished from this city and this castle. I have been issued a passport good for this one day only. I have come many leagues. The Emperor is not quick to meet those who wait upon him. If not today never.

The last and narrowest gate was before them; whichever of them reached it first would be first into the Presence, for the guards there and the clerks would be a long time examining papers and asking questions.

—Let me by, Bruno said. He was tempted to tug at the gown that filled like a sail with Dee's progress upward.

—You will trip me up, Dee said. Stop.

For a moment they jostled at the narrowest point of the stair; then without a word Dee whirled twice around widdershins, and Bruno cried out, for he faced not an elderly Englishman but a tall pillar of adamant.

But in a moment Bruno, fired by fear and need, had changed himself to a jug of red wine, and poured himself out and around the pillar's base.

But the pillar became a flopping marble dolphin that drank the wine.

But Bruno became a net that entangled the fish, then a mouse that fled. But to escape the net the fish had also become a mouse, and the upshot was that, their stocks of *simulacra* or phantasmic projections for the moment exhausted, they both found themselves at the same time before the incurious guards (who had of course seen nothing), both panting sharply and with disordered clothes, their papers held out.

Both were let in together. They went in an embarrassed silence across a courtyard and in a door. Someone was coming down toward them, hands held out in greeting.

It was Jacopo Strada who met them, welcomed them without betraying anything of the Emperor's intentions or inclinations toward or away from either one of them. Signor Strada was officially the Emperor's antiquarian, a learned Italian who acquired for the Emperor's collections the statues and objects out of Greece and Rome and Ægypt, the books and manuscripts, the gems and coins and medals that filled the Emperor's cases and cabinets. He was more than that, though; he was as close as anyone ever came to being the Emperor's immediate family, for his daughter was the Emperor's mistress and had been for many years; the beautiful (so the people believed she must be) Caterina, *Katerina Stradová*, mother of his children.

—You have been asked to await His Sacred Majesty's pleasure in the *Neue Saal*, Signor Strada said to them, inclining his head and with his long and beautiful hand showing them the way. The *Sala nuova*, he said to Bruno. It is a singular honor. Such men as yourselves will of course understand.

He took them through halls being rebuilt in the modern style: on high scaffoldings workmen labored, architects with rolled drawings directed master builders with squares and plumb lines, and in spandrels and lunettes paint-spattered artists worked quickly in wet plaster, limning gods and goddesses, virtues and vices, heroes and ancestors. Transformations. Bruno looking upward stumbled over piled lumber, and John Dee caught his arm.

—Where do we stand now? he asked Signor Strada.

—In Hradschin's center, said the antiquarian.

Strada pulled open the shining-new doors of a chamber and bade them enter.

There are souls that can hear harmonies, and souls that can't; souls that in hearing a melody can also hear it inverted, reversed, transferred to another mode. So there are souls that can perceive geometries, even when they are cast in stone and plaster. Both John Dee and Giordano Bruno knew immediately the figure within which they had been brought.

—A Tetrad, said Dee.

Strada clasped his hands behind his back and inclined his head, smiling. The room's plan was indeed a Tetrad, that is, two identical squares sharing a center, one of which is rotated ninety degrees in respect of the other, making an eight-pointed star, within which they stood. A Tetrad describes the created world, its four Elements connected by four Qualities: cold-dry Earth, cold-moist Water, hot-moist Air, hot-dry Fire. Around them, in alcoves formed by the eight star-points, were cases cunningly made to hold just the items that they held, labelled with signs and made of appropriate materials, so that the contents could almost be guessed.

—Perhaps we may open the *kammern,* said Strada gently. The *ratio* will become clear.

He led them within an alcove. He pulled open a slim drawer and drew out a picture, a stiff sheet made of something like a thin slice of glowing rain cloud.

—Alabaster, he said. It seemed to be the stone his own translucent skull was cut from. It was the material of this division's guardian pillar too.

—See, he said, how the artist has employed the natural colors and variations of the surface, and with only a little brushwork, made them waves, or clouds.

—And the subject? asked Doctor Dee.

—Andromeda, said Bruno, flinging his arms behind himself and catching one forearm in the other hand. The rock she is bound to. Her chains. *Vincula.* Her bonds.

—The monster, Dee said as the figure resolved itself in his gaze. There. And Perseus flying through the air. Coming to free her.

Signor Strada turned the piece in his spectral fingers. On its underside was another picture.

—The verso, he said.

—More freeing, said Bruno.

—Yes. The Freeing of the Winds. You will remember the story, in Vergil.

*Putti* with distended cheeks leapt blowing from Æolus's Cave, and roamed the tormented air. North, South, East, West Winds; the Little Breezes beside them. The gray and yellow swirls and flaws in the glowing stone were cast, like actors, to be stormclouds, windblown seafoam, rockbound coast.

—Sea and wind, Bruno said. So there is a place for it here, between Air and Water.

—Yes.

Both sides, both pictures, were air and water; both were also fables of binding and unbinding. In one direction they ran toward order and the stern elements; and along another axis they ran toward meaning and yearning, toward a thought about liberation. Freedom. No freedom without bonds.

Bruno turned out of the alcove of Air and Water and returned to the Tetrad's center. He saw that at the entrance of each of the eight alcoves a small portrait was mounted. He went to the northernmost, which should be the starting or ending point of the series. It was of a gnarled, woody ancient; his mouth was collapsed where the teeth had fallen out, his skin all warts and folds, eyes rheumy and peering. He was not, however, *like* wood or woody or rooty (Bruno came closer) but in fact *made of wood:* he was nothing but an aged chestnut stump, yellow leaves or few or none for hair, his ear a broken limb's rotted bole, his lips a fungus.

He was Winter. Old Age. Drought.

Bruno turned to look northeast. The portrait there was a man warmly dressed in furs. No a man made of furs, made of furbearers, beasts of every earthly kind. The muscle of his neck was the back of a reclining bull. His eye was only a fox's open mouth, his brow a seated ass, his cheek an elephant's smooth head, his ear its ear. He was not anything but beasts, every beast as real as real, yet the face they made also real, with real wit and wisdom in it, a human face that looked out at the viewer in recognition: you and I are alike.

—The beasts of Earth, said John Dee, coming up beside him. For Earth is the element of the North, and of Winter.

They turned east. The portrait there was a mass of early flowers, tulips, violets, dogwood, *dents-de-lion,* crocuses. It was a person too, a smiling woman. The rosy blush in her cheek *was* a rose; those two minute sprigs were the living glitter in her eyes.

—Spring, Bruno said. Jacopo Strada came closer, and looked up as into the face of someone he knew well, and he did, for it was his own daughter Caterina as well as Spring and youth and flowers.

—Spring is to Air as Winter is to Earth, said Bruno. He pointed southeast: and the portrait there was all of birds, an impossible wild rookery of every kind, as though frozen in just the single instant when by chance they made the form of a face. Air.

In the south was Summer, King of Seasons, smiling with lips of a fat splitting peasecod, his teeth the peas, cherry lips, come too close and he is nothing, nothing, nothing but a pile of victuals. In the coat of barleycorn he wore, as though woven by a peasant with time to spare, were words:

GIUSEPPE ARCIMBOLDO F.

*Giuseppe Arcimboldo fecit.*

To the southwest was Summer's element, Fire: he was a boy all made of flames, flints, guns, matches, all exploding at once, a firework. His hair was fire, and his moist lip was a candle flame, but—oddly—his eye, a candle too, was unlit, its black wick his pupil.

And Autumn in the west was fruits and harvest piled into a basket, and the basket of fruits was a man: his pear nose, mushroom ear, beard of bearded wheat and hair of green grapes and their leaves. And in the northwest, cold-moist Water, Autumn's element, was of course a catch of fish (a flat flounder's eye her eye—and a string of pearls around her neck) just as Air opposite was a flock of birds.

—Thus you see, Signor Strada said. You will excuse me if I leave you now. You will be made aware of His Sacred Majesty's intentions toward you. You may continue to study here. Go in any direction, north, south, east, west. Open the albums, inspect the gems in their cases. Everything is in its place.

He lowered his head, and backed away, placing his long hands together as though in prayer; they seemed silvered, as though themselves made precious by all they had handled.

John Dee and Giordano Bruno stood side by side in the midst of the universe.

—But why, John Dee asked, are they faces? Why persons?

—Because this is what we are ourselves, Bruno said, looking around himself. If all these could be laid over one another, and commingled, they would form one person: one man, or woman. They would not appear strange or singular then but fully human. For we are only composites of the things of this world, held together while we live by our soul. Which soul is perhaps nothing more than the form within matter, the form particular to us. It dissolves when we do, as those faces would vanish if the animals stirred and took themselves off, or when the flowers faded and the fuses and matches burned up.

—As when we see faces in clouds, Dee said.

—The same.

—My soul is not of this earth, said John Dee. It is cut to a different pattern, and when the elements of me disperse, it will return home. To Him Who made it. I am assured.

—Soul is soul, Bruno said curtly. Mine or yours, a god's or a pumpkin's or a snail's. Vergil says: *Spiritus intus alit,* Spirit nourishes all from within.

He looked into John Dee's long face, which looked somewhat downward into his. They two, surely, were made to different patterns: a *coniunctio oppositorum*. The two of them laid one over the other would perhaps make a man of the next age; or would fly instantly into flinders, and bring down this castle.

—Before you came to my house in Mortlake, John Dee said, I was told of you.

—That land was as full of spies as a dead dog of maggots.

—These were no human spies. Those that spoke to me of you were not of this earth but beyond it. They told me of your nature and your fate, but not your thoughts.

—Well well well, Bruno said. *Benebene.* Give them my greeting when next you speak to them, and thank them for their attention to me. I am sure I have not made their acquaintance.

—They said that you intended me no good that day. That you intended to steal from me a thing you could have had for nothing—and which would have left me no poorer to give you.

—And what is that? Bruno asked, grinning wolfishly and knowing in fact very well what John Dee spoke of.

—They said my stone, my letter. They meant, I think, a certain sign.

Giordano Bruno could see—his inward scene changing as in a masque—the dim and crowded library in Mortlake on the south side of the Thames, to which three no four years ago he had gone in the company of the Polish count Lascus or Alasco. How he found there a book (he saw his own hand push aside another book, an almanac, to find it): the book containing the thing, the thing that was in fact not a stone, or a letter, or a name, or a person, or a sign, but all of those things.

How he had later returned upriver too, to find the wizard gone, fled with that *principe Alasco polacco;* the house closed, the dusty window of the library, through which he could glimpse the book left lying on the table, still open to the thing, its light apparently gone out.

—I drew that sign before I understood its use or its nature, John Dee said. I drew it with a compass and a rule. I was a young man, not yet thirty.

With his staff the Englishman began to draw upon the center of the floor of the *Neue Saal* the sign he had been given or had made. For seven years, like Jacob tending Laban's sheep, he had cared for it, taking it out now and again and puzzling over it: a key to which the lock was lost, or not yet found.

—It contains firstly the sacred Ternary, Dee said, two lines and their crossing point. The Ternary generates the earthly Quaternary, and here it is, four right angles and four straight lines.

Bruno watched it come to be as though scored upon the tiles of the floor with a graver's tool. From the four corners and four divisions of the room the elements and the seasons also took notice: their eyes (made of a fox or a fish, of asters and cornflowers, of fire or wood rot) looked down and turned toward it.

—The Cross of Christ is in it, Dee said; in these lines are the signs of the four elements, Earth Air Water Fire; in these lines the twelve signs of the Zodiac, and the seven planets.

It began to burn in Giordano Bruno's mind. Long before he found it in John Dee's library, the sign had found him. In A.D. 1576 he had stripped off his Dominican habit of black and white and begun to journey; and at every turning of his path this sign had appeared, like a great-headed one-eyed handless infant: cut on the seal rings of doctors and booksellers, stamped on the bindings of old books, drawn on privy walls, gone when he looked for it again, wiped away, blurred, not what he had thought he had seen. Summoning him, or warning him; naming him. Or not. There were months when he did not remember it; months when he could not cease thinking of it. All the signs he had cut in wood, all the ones he had drawn in his mind or on earth with Mordente's marvelous compass, had been attempts to avoid this one, supersede it with his own. He was visited by the dreadful thought that in the end he would see nothing else.

—I have believed, John Dee said, that it is a sign of the one thing of which the world is made. Hieroglyph of the monad, the One whose vicissitudes comprise all the multiform species we see. . . .

—There is no such sign, said Bruno. The One is unfigurable. If it were to have a sign . . . No. It has none.

—Well then, said John Dee. Since you so much desired it—if you did—perhaps you can tell me what it is.

—I cannot. Synesius says that the signs of the greatest dæmons are composed of circles and straight lines. Perhaps it is one of those; his name, his call.

—Whose sign? Whose call?

—*Microcosmos,* said Bruno. Greatest of all the Intelligences. The Sun the head of him, the Moon his crown; the cross of the four elements, the planets and the signs composing him. Halfway between *immensum* and *minimum,* worms and angels. No other can claim that. His other name is Man.

—The great Jew of this city, John Dee said, tells me that before the creation of the world there was made an Adam out of a circle and a line.

—Before the creation of the world?

—He said: God withdrew himself from a space within himself; that withdrawal generated a point, which was all that the universe was, or is; it was bounded by a circle, and crossed by a line. Adam Kadmon.

—The emptiness in God's heart . . . is Man, Bruno said. He shuddered hugely, and shook his head: No, no.

—Well, John Dee said. It may be that I will never know. For she is gone.

—She?

—The one who promised to tell me of this sign; who warned me against you. She is gone and I cannot ask her more.

—Your *semhamaphores* do not speak, Bruno said. They are the Reasons of the world; they say only their own names.

—She told me: There is war among the powers. Fly from them, she said, but beware you fly not into the arms of other powers.

The sign burning in the center of the Emperor's floor had cooled, from red to blue-black, like a cinder. Giordano Bruno erased it.

—A question of who is to be master, he said. That's all.

The doors at the end of the gallery opened, and a chamberlain entered. They stood and waited while the man approached gravely down the length of polished floor. When he came close they saw that he bore two letters, one for each of them. He presented them with a slight bow.

—Well well, Giordano Bruno said, after opening his. I am summoned into his presence now.

He tapped the letter to his brow, and signalled with it: lead on. The chamberlain bowed again and stepped backward, turned to lead him out.

John Dee read the brief note handed to him: *SS Majestas requires that you deliver to him immediately the thing of value that was lately promised him. And if you are not able to do this he wishes returned to his officers without fail that one who was lately given into your care.*

He folded it, pocketed it, and thought: It is time to be gone. It is time, it is time, it may already be past time.

# 5

Once upon a time, somewhere other than here, there was an Age of Gold, when men were asses. (This is the story Bruno told the Emperor of the Romans, who thought he had heard it all before.) There isn't anybody who doesn't glorify that old Age. Men didn't know how to work the land then or how to lord it over one another; nobody knew more than anyone else; they all lived in dens and caves; the men leapt on the women as the beasts do, there was little concealment in their lust—and little jealousy, or spice. No spice in their gluttony either; everyone got together to eat oh apples and chestnuts and acorns, raw as Mother Nature made them.

Idleness was then the only guide, and the only god. If we call up before us the figure of Idleness to defend that age, what shall she say? (Here Bruno projected before himself, where he alone for the moment could perceive it, exactly this personage, and transmitted to the Emperor what she said.) Everybody exalts my Golden Age, says Idleness, and at the same time they praise and call a "virtue" the very villain that destroyed it! Who do I mean? I mean Toil, and his friends Industry and Study. Haven't you heard them being praised, even as the world realizes, too late, mourning and weeping, the ills they cause?

Who (says Idleness) introduced Injustice into the world? Toil and his brothers. Who—spurred on by Honor—made one man better and smarter than another, left some in poverty and made others rich? It was Toil, this same meddler and stirrer-up of discontent. Little did our first parents see that from the time they plucked the fruit of Knowledge, nothing would be the same again; they had unleashed Change, and with it Pain, and Toil.

—It is said, the Emperor put in at that point, that the old Age of Gold is now to return. If we can bring it in.

—Nothing returns, Bruno said. Everything changes. Evolution. Transmigration. Parturition. Metamorphosis. The coincidence of opposites. Fortuna has so many variations to produce that change will last for eternity, and nothing will return.

The Emperor regarded him. He might have pointed out that the heavens are changeless, and do return; but his astronomers had taught him that the heavens change too, and new stars are born. He might have named God, Who never changes, but the Emperor didn't think of God; he almost never did.

—In the new-found-lands, he said, there are people who live today just as we did in the Golden Age.

—If there are, Bruno said, they had another father than Adam, and never fell. They will.

—All men are children of Adam, said the Emperor.

—Oh yes? Bruno said (not noticing how the Emperor drew back from his aggressive chin, and from his language, better suited to the brawling of the schools than to these halls). Oh yes? And if they are, how did they get so far from home? Walked, across the seas? Sailed, before boats were invented? Maybe they were swallowed by whales, and vomited up on those far shores? Nonono. Nature makes men wherever men can be, and makes them suited to their land and clime.

—More than one Adam? said the Emperor.

—More than one Adam, more than one fall, more than one history of the world. More (if it please Your Majesty) than one world.

The Emperor, in his suit of black decorated richly in black, a midnight sky whereon his jewels burned, stars and planets, put his hand upon the brow of a tall and melancholy dog that sat beside him; the beast lifted his liquid eye to his master.

—If Toil destroyed the Age of Gold and made Injustice, how can Justice be made again?

He seemed to ask this of the dog. Bruno (his ardor fading in this cold room, in this silence) knew the answer.

—More toil, he said. Action and Change made Difference. Only more can overcome it, and make all men happy. Or happier. The wheel of Fortune rules everything, making high low, good bad, lucky unlucky, rich poor. But if we are strong patient asses for toil we can give that wheel a shove at just the right moment, or put a nail in it.

—It was Idleness that made men asses, the Emperor said. So *you* say.

—There are asses and asses, Bruno said.

—It is prophesied, the Emperor said, that a New Age is at hand. That many kingdoms will fall, crowns too fall from heads.

—Pay no attention to prophecies, Bruno said. They only tell us what we ourselves intend to do.

—This Empire too, the Emperor said. Vanished, contracted, fallen.

—This Empire cannot pass away, Bruno said. And what if it does?

The Emperor opened his eyes wide at that, and Bruno knew he should look away—one does not duel with an Emperor and subdue his regard—but he did not. The rays of his spirit, fired from his eye by the force of his heart's contractions, entered in at the Emperor's own eye and thus into his spirit. It was a shuttered mansion, colder than this room; bare as a sepulcher, and a stone throne within it, empty. And Bruno knew what the Emperor must do, and knew he could tell him how.

—You have seen my collections, the Emperor said, as though to change the subject rather than having to respond to the Brunian impertinence.

—I have. Your Gracious Majesty: your wonderful collection is complete and perfect. But it lacks a center. If it had a center, then what you moved or changed within it would at the same time move or be changed outside.

—And how am I to give it a center?

—Turn it inside out, said Bruno.

—How?

—I will tell you how, Bruno said. Your Majesty has for many years enlisted the signs and symbols of things in the service of your power. You should rather have put your power at the service of your signs.

The Emperor was still for a long moment, his eyes seeming to cross a little; and then their light went out.

—Love, said Bruno. Memory. Mathesis. These three. And the greatest of these is Love.

The big Hapsburg head began slowly to nod, but not in understanding. After a little while (how did they apprehend the Emperor's desire, how was it transmitted to them?) a pair of attendants opened the doors and came to stand one on either side of Giordano Bruno like guards.

Bruno would have told him much more about how the universe is ordered and how full it is. He would have told him how every star is a sun as bright as our own, and how suns enchant the cooler beings called planets, which travel around their suns forever in adoration and delight, whose lands are filled with rational beings and whose seas are filled with fish, as are ours, fish with their own natures and their own societies of which we can know nothing. Dæmons and spiritual creatures fill the air and the spaces between the stars, fill the seas and the caves of earth, some of them gloomy and silent, some hot, active and canny, some interested in the lives of men, some not. Humankind is everywhere, everywhere humankind can be, rushing out to greet us when our ships come into sight, as amazed to see us as we are amazed to find them there, black or brown or golden, foolish or wise or both.

He would have told the Emperor that all this infinite mutability was not so great that we should feel afraid of it or overwhelmed by it, for Man is a being whose nature partakes of all and, therefore, is an equal to all, and by the arts peculiar to himself can ascend to knowledge of all: by Mathesis, to reduce infinitude to natural categories of sense and order, and create seals that are the secret souls of its complexities. By Memory, to contain within us those seals and open them at will, to go through the world within in any direction, combine and recombine its stuff and make new things unheard of before. And by Love, to bend our souls to the worlds in conquest and submission at once, to drown in infinity without drowning: Love cunning and foolish, Love patient and stubborn, Love mild and fierce.

He would have said that and more, but the two attendants walked him away backwards out of the Presence, cuing him to bow, once, again, and one last time as the doors closed on the Emperor by then grown small with distance.

That evening the Emperor summoned his new Imperial Astronomer into his presence. When the man came, Rudolf gave him the little book about mathematics that Bruno had dedicated to him. Seeing the author's name on the title page, the Imperial Astronomer let out a loud ghastly laugh with mouth wide open, a gesture so shockingly rude that the Emperor drew himself up scandalized. Why was he to be affronted at every turn today? He should never have hired the man, a fine astronomer but gloomy and resentful, a Frenchified Italian whose name was Fabricio Mordente.

The Emperor sent a new message to the man he had always wanted to come to Prague and be his astronomer, the noseless Danish knight Tycho Brahe. (Like a persistent though despised suitor, the Emperor wrote a similar note every so often, whenever his heart was full and heavy.) In the note he also asked Brahe's advice about Bruno. After a time Brahe wrote back, once again declining, with manly courtesy, to come to Prague. He said yes, he knew Bruno's work. *Nolanus nullanus* he called him, and said that every number and figure the man had ever written down he had got wrong, including 1 and 0.

So the Emperor put Bruno's book away; he gave an order that Bruno should receive the sum of five hundred *thalers* from the Imperial treasury (something about him made the Emperor want to be cautious), but he never sent for him again.

In another part of the vast Hradschin castle that August, a band of men were meeting to complete, or at least to continue, a work they had joined together to do. The room they met in was a workshop; John Dee would have recognized many but not all of the fine tools hung on the walls, he would have known that the boxes of small gears and piles of brass rods, springs, concave glasses, fusee wheels and pendula were clockworks, but would not have known what some of the other odd things were, for they had never existed before, had only recently been invented in this room. In this room many of them would remain too: they had been inconceivable in the past, and in the future they would no longer work.

One other thing he would have recognized in the crowded room, where now the candles were being lit against the fall of evening: a small Latin book dedicated to the Emperor's father, Maximilian: Dee's own work, the *Monas hieroglyphica*. It lay on the great central workbench, open, a weight laid upon it to keep it from closing.

Jost Bürgi was among those who had gathered there; indeed it was his workshop. Still a young man then, but already among the greatest clockmakers of that clock-mad age, the first to divide a minute into sixty seconds and make a clock that counted them accurately. It was said that Jost could cut the sixty teeth of a brass minute wheel freehand. He had already invented the cross-beat escapement, which, combined with another invention of his, the remontoir, had doubled the precision of his clocks; he was about to invent the pendulum, twenty years before Galileo. He would build clocks for Tycho to make his stellar observations by when at last Tycho came to Prague; and he would serve Kepler too.

The Venetian gold-maker who called himself Count Bragadino was there too. He was soon to be hanged (by that same Duke of Bavaria who so feared the little homely spirits) because his alchemical processes no longer worked, not his fault of course but the Duke couldn't know that.

Cornelius Drebbel, was he there? Or still going from court to court? He was a masque-deviser, architect, inventor of the Perspective Lute and of a dozen perpetual-motion machines, one of which was laboring away ceaselessly on the bench at that moment, expending its little energies on the air, but soon to become part of the work in progress.

—Listen, Bürgi said to them all. He read from John Dee's little book: *He who has fed the Monad will first himself go away into a metamorphosis and will afterward very rarely be beheld by mortal eye. This is the true invisibility of the magus, which has so often (and without sin) been spoken of, and which (as all future magi will own) has been granted to the theorems of our Monad.*

He looked around at the company, and they nodded: they understood. The time was short: they all knew that, the time short in which to do what they had gathered here to do.

They were the Emperor's *magi*. They were Italians, Dutchmen, Swedes, Poles; they had studied at universities in Paris and Cracow and Wittenberg, had attended Della Porta's *Academia curiosorum hominum* in Naples, had visited London and met Sidney and smoked pipes with the "Wizard Earl" of Northumberland, done religious magic for the King of France or for his cousins or rivals; they had published books carefully set out with false imprimaturs and misleading title pages and had them seized and burned anyway, better the books than their own persons, they dropped them as caught lizards drop their tails, regrew them again in freer countries, at kindlier courts.

Doctors Kroll and Guarnieri were there, the Paracelsian and the anti-Paracelsian, unable to agree on anything, not even what elements composed the world, Paracelsus's three or Aristotle's four; both present here, though, side by side, for who knew what the future would make its world out of? The Emperor's own lapidary, Anselm Boethius de Boodt, was also there: no one knew more about the life enclosed in mineral species than he.

—Hermes Thrice-great, said the clockmaker Jost Bürgi to them, died at a very great age in Ægypt where he had been priest, philosopher, and king. Or he did not die but was interred alive, in a manner known to them but lost to us, to remain alive thereafter though suspended in a profound sleep. Or yes he was thus interred alive, but did not thereafter survive the whole length of his journey from that time to the time his tomb was opened.

—Whether the virtue of causing or sustaining that sleep resided in Hermes himself; or in the manner of his interment; or the tomb he was laid in; or was God's special providence: all that is not now able to be known.

That was the doctor who spoke, Oswald Kroll or Croll. Kroll was then at work on the book by which he would be known to the ages, the *Basilica Chymica,* stone-dead now, as he is himself.

—However it was, Bürgi said, in the following age that tomb was opened. Some say by Alexander the Great; some say Apollonius of Tyana. And the uncorrupted body of Hermes was found within, holding in its hands a tablet.

—The Smaragdine Tablet, said Kroll. One solid emerald, and written in Phœnician characters.

—Or hieroglyphs of Ægypt.

—It contained the whole of the chemical art in brief.

—*As above, so below,* quoted Bürgi. *Thus is accomplished the miracle of the One Thing.*

—In the longer writings of Hermes it is told how Ægypt failed and died, said Kroll. How the temples were neglected, the rites forgotten, until the gods of Ægypt left their homeland. How in that time the world grew old, the air thick and unbreathable; how the sun weakened, the sea ceased to hold up ships.

—*In illo tempore,* in that time, said Bürgi. Think of it. How Hermes consigned himself to his tomb, with his Tablet, all that he could hope to bring into the future; hoping to be carried into that new time alive, asleep, knowing that he might not survive, but that his wisdom might, if there was anyone in that new age wise enough to read it.

They all pondered at that, and lowered their eyes; each wondered if he were the one wise enough, or would become so, or if one of the others here were, or if the words Hermes inscribed on emerald had not themselves actually died along with their author in the centuries that had fallen between his age and this one. They had all worked to make the Stone, and none had yet entirely succeeded.

Then they lifted their eyes, for Jost Bürgi had lowered a lamp suspended over his workbench so that it illuminated what lay there.

—He did what he could to save his knowledge for the next age, said Bürgi. So must we. We must save his knowledge, and our own.

Unfinished, its parts and components around it in various stages of completion. Drebbel's little humming engine; Bürgi's astronomical clock, designed to turn as the stars turned—to turn *because* the stars turned—for centuries, from then on in fact: if, that is, the stars went on turning as they did now, which was not certain.

It looked like a long strongbox of black ironbound wood, not particularly distinguished; but it was more or other than that. More than one of them thought it was like those chests or trunks of old in which royal babes were consigned to the sea to be drowned and lost but who persisted and were saved, and did the deeds we remember them by: this was a boat of that kind, to carry over the gulf fixed between this age and the next the wisdom of its makers, so that it would do work for men in the new age, if it could.

De Boodt, the Imperial gemhunter, thought: it will be like one of those stones we find in the mountains, dusty and unremarkable, that when struck with a chisel and mallet break open to reveal a glittering jewelled cave within, purple or green or icy blue, unseen for how long; and release a momentary odor of another world.

But Oswald Kroll thought of Æsop's tale of Belling the Cat.

—We know what must be done, he said; we do not yet know who will be the one to do it, or if anyone can.

—The man whose sign is the Monad, Guarnerius said. He must be the one.

Yes: they nodded, yes. For each of them had come to know that sign, the Monad. They had come to know the Monad even before it appeared among them in John Dee's book, which the Emperor whom they all served had given them and ordered them to study. Seeing it on Dee's frontispiece, each of them had at the same time remembered it—one how he had awakened from a vivid dream to find it inscribed on his palm, only to have it vanish quickly; another how he had without thinking drawn it one morning, or rather something not quite it, and troubling, irritating, unsatisfying; another how he had perhaps seen it scribbled in the margin of a book given him, then taken away. Like a whisper in the ear.

—The old man, said Kroll. Joannes Dii.

—No it is not him. He has said it himself, that it was granted him, passed through him; not his. No he is the voice of one crying in the wilderness. *Vox clamantis in deserto.*

—Who does he cry?

—The other, his companion. Formerly his companion. He has always said the other is the one who sees, who knows. Not himself. Gelleus? Is that the name? And now we see this Gelleus come into his own, flaunt his powers. As if to signify to us. If there is one among us who can carry the Tablet of our age . . .

—*Odoardus Scotus,* said Kroll. Edward Kelley, the Irish knight.

He looked down into the bed of the long black box. There was another thing, of course, that it closely resembled; a very common thing. Remember, Man, that thou art dust.

He said: The man might refuse.

—He must not, said Bürgi. He may not.

He put his hand on the book. *To those who have, more will be given,* he said. *From those who have not will be taken even the little that they have.*

—I will bring him here, said Dr. Kroll. Assign me a troop of guards, and a sergeant at arms. If he has powers around him, I will deal with them. We must be certain, though, that we are right, that this is the man.

—We are certain, said Bürgi.

—And if we are wrong? Kroll said.

—If we are, said Bürgi, then neither he nor we will ever know of it.

# 6

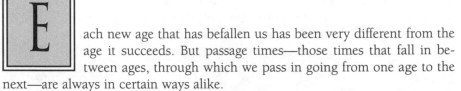ach new age that has befallen us has been very different from the age it succeeds. But passage times—those times that fall in between ages, through which we pass in going from one age to the next—are always in certain ways alike.

Passage times, though separated perhaps by centuries, seem (to those within one) to follow immediately upon one another rather than upon the ages they close, or open; they are successive visits to the same place, which at first we don't recognize, though we know it's familiar: like days of fever, whose onset we feel but don't at first identify, what air is this, what earth; after a time of wary puzzling we say Oh yes I know this kind of life, it's fever, and we allow ourselves to fall back or lie down into it, its former instances accumulating behind us to be remembered, the only days we *can* distinctly remember as the numbers mount and the mercury bar crosses into triple digits.

Like the way Bobby always remembers that one time, always comes upon it when a fever begins, that time in the little house in Bondieu, the kids' little house attached to the big house: in their bed, those spectral children staring at her, certain she was to die among them.

In all passage times the gate of horn is open, between dreaming and remembering, between being and meaning; the gate between wanting and having, between fearing and having too. Things that had been coming together to become one thing, perhaps coming together for a long time, fall apart again into two. Soul and body for instance; male and female; pursuer and pursued; children of God and orphans, nobody's children. But things that had always been different fall together then too, and are shown to be one thing after all: the fleeing one looks back, and sees she is the one she flees; the orphan turned out to weep is the same as the master of the house. The last is the same as the first. That (Bobby thought) is what that hard saying means. Nobody has to switch places at all; we throw ourselves out of our own chairs, and sit ourselves down instead.

She laughed at herself, giddy already, and with a deep thirst starting that water would not reach, as though her throat were turned to lint. A fever in her could rise high and fast, and aspirin not stop it, she knew for a fact, it was the way she was made; her kids the same, her son deaf in his left ear ever after from a fever. But anyway she had to get to work; if it got worse later maybe she would go and ask for a healing. There was an outreach tonight at the Bypass Inn, they would all be there. She hadn't heard of them lowering fevers by putting on hands but why couldn't it do that. Supposed to cure cancer and insanity.

She remembered how her grandfather told her he had nearly died of a fever once as a babe, how they had wrapped him in a quilt and taken him up the mountain to a little cabin; and an old woman there had taken out a stone, a madstone she called it, and said it was taken from the belly of a deer. And she rubbed the madstone all over him and there: the fever passed.

*She was a witch,* her grandfather said. *I seen her later and I struggled with her. I know.*

"Bobby."

"Yes darlin."

"Bobby I'm hungry."

"Okay hon." After he went deaf he couldn't ever talk right either; he said bobby and boon for mommy and moon. Odd that Bobby was her name anyway. She had never called her grandfather anything but Floyd after she was grown. Because she was no blood of his.

She went on working on her toes. Why it mattered she couldn't say, her feet would be unseen within white sneakers all night. It did matter. She sat on the floor, resting her heel on a fat Mopar catalogue left behind by Lars when he departed; she put between her big toe and the next toe the filter of a cigarette butt she took from an ashtray nearby. Then another filter between the next two toes, and the next two.

"Bobby."

"Soon as I'm done, sweetheart," Bobby said to the boy, who lay on the coverless mattress that took up much of the floor. "Get you a cookie. But you gotta wait."

She undid the long-handled brush of the little wine-red bottle and, tongue between her teeth, spread a careful first coat over the big toenail. So rich it always seemed to her, thicker than blood, gleaming on the brush with the shine that it promised to impart. She wished it would stay this way, so liquid and bright, never grow hard and dull.

This too always carried her back, by a straighter path, to when she was a kid. A bottle of cheap polish at the dime store in Bondieu cost a quarter or so. In July she'd catch fireflies in a fruit jar, and paint her broken and dirty nails with the thick paint, and before it was dry take out one of the green-glowing bugs (already fading in the jar) and press it onto the gummy nail, and then the next, and the next, and they would be trapped there; and she would go out into the night with them attached to her, and miraculously they would come alive again and brighten, turning on and off in patterns like electric bulbs in signs. Glow, glow-bugs, glow. In the pines a million others turning on and off too. Hard part was cleaning them off her fingers. Smear of their glow-stuff on the oilcloth of the table, still greenish for a time.

Temperature going up. She moved her eyeballs in her head and felt the pain. If she went in to the hospital they would probably send her home anyway but she didn't want to call in sick, she had done that too often lately when she wasn't sick and they knew she wasn't sick: and she was afraid of the long night that lay between her and dawn.

Bobby always signed up for nights at certain seasons of the year, times when she wanted to be awake all night; Christmas and the days after, the end of June and of October. Her grandpap had known the names of those nights, how to find them in the almanac; he located them just as much though by another, inward sense, and she had that one as he did. On those days she would get up from sleep as the sun faded from the sky, get in her car and head for work on the empty side of the road, her fellow humans filling the opposite side, rolling toward their dinners and their beds. She was comforted by the willed reversal of day and night, liked watching the hours of deep darkness, which should be passing unwitnessed, go by one by one on the big clocks while she and her colleagues busied themselves in the bright halls and artificial day. Safe, awake.

Sometimes, though, those nights came upon her unawares, revealing themselves to be what they were only when they had covered her, like nights of fever, what is this? What's at my back? And when she was taken that way she did things that she couldn't always remember afterward, or couldn't always tell if she had done them or dreamed them.

So on this night she dressed and made up her face, clipped her ID badge to her smock, dropped her son off to the baby-sitter, with a sack of jelly sandwiches and cookies and the sucker that was forever in his mouth if nothing else was, and drove downtown toward Route 6 and the hospital.

Route 6 was one of the roads Kentucky families used to know, one of the ways they took coming out of the Cumberlands, where Bobby was born. Men from Pike and Floyd and Harlan and Clay Counties headed north to Ohio to make tires and steel or to Detroit and Flint to build Chevies and Oldses, or west to the mills of Hammond and Gary and East Chicago. If they went east they followed the Little Sandy River up to the Ohio and across Pennsylvania on the pike, up through the Delaware Water Gap by Route 6 and on to the city of Conurbana, which had been a city of mills once, where firearms and bicycles and cardboard boxes were made, hospital hardware, candy, golf clubs, adhesives, and children's games with famous names the newcomers had never heard. She had used to dream of Route 6 long before she took it herself, pregnant and fleeing; dreamed of it, long, winding, leading out of the broken woods into the blue distance, a glitter of lights, unresolvable, at its end.

Actually that road, the old road, was now called 6A when it came close to Conurbana. Route 6 had become the new four-lane bypass around the city, carrying long-distance travellers in a wide disdainful curve around so that they need not become entangled in the shabby outskirts and warehouse districts. The

new way had created a new strip, on a larger scale than the old one, lots where
the new cars and not the used were sold, where the bright big signs of the national franchises were, and the windowless low concrete buildings like bunkers
on wide landscaped lots, some of them factories making what, others nightclubs
or motels. Nabco. Tuff-hold. Pendaflex. Chilly Willies. Bypass Inn.

She only touched new 6 for a mile or two before returning to old 6A, following the way she had first gone to the hospital, the only way she knew; like a
squirrel who knows only one way back to its hole, or a piglet to his momma, she
had learned what she needed to know and just got quicker at it; on this night of
fever didn't think about it, and found herself back on 6A, the dark unpopulated
strip, unaware of the turns she had taken and for a moment unsure which way
on it she was travelling, toward downtown or outward toward the scrabbly or-
chards and lumberyards. Before she could draw herself fully back down to this
place and this night she saw the Tempest ahead, off the shoulder, canting a little
downward toward the ditch.

It was there. It proceeded toward her (she rather toward it, but she felt motionless). A white Tempest, sleek as ice; its red ragtop up, as it had been. Her
headlights swept it as she came upon it, it altered rapidly in their shifting light.
It was there, there, though she had abandoned it in the mountains a hundred
miles and more away: still there.

Then she was past it. She didn't slow. She looked though in her rearview
mirror, unable not to; and saw him, him too, beside the car, turning her way as
though he could see—far behind her though he already was—right into her eyes
by way of the little mirror she looked into. Eyes like the eyes they all had when
they looked at her, asking or answering a question she did not know, never
would; a question she herself was.

So I did get him, she thought. She looked ahead, at the road, then back at
the mirror, but it had gone black, winked out like a light. I did get him.

Night sped around her. She wouldn't stop or turn, no way she would.

She could remember it as though the heavy gun had burned the flesh and
the bones of her hand, and those burns hadn't healed: how after she had ordered him out of the car, his own car, after she had slid over to the driver's seat
to take the wheel, after she had shifted to Drive, she had lifted the gun and, as
though it had desired this of itself and made her do it, had flung her hand toward where he stood pleading by the road's edge, and looking away had fired;
and at the same moment pressed her foot down on the gas and leapt ahead,
lights still unlit.

And when she fired she had hit him and killed him. Tony, no Tommy. Ted.
She hadn't looked back then to see, she had thought she had probably hit him
but she hadn't been sure. She knew now. She had killed him and she didn't even
remember his right name, could not ask his forgiveness for that night, could not
speak to his shade and say I was crazy, crazy, crazy, please in Jesus' name forgive me.

.    .    .

For a long time she had believed that for the kind she was there was no forgiveness. She thought, at other times, that for the kind she was there was no sin. She thought that her kind went unmentioned in the Gospels, were not warned or welcomed there, that the Word was not spoken to her.

Floyd Shaftoe her grandpap had believed in the Word: had used to sit for hours in his chair with his parents' big brown Bible in his lap as though reading it, his eyes though often elsewhere. He had no truck with any church, though; no truck with his neighbors either, lived alone on his father's old worn-out hill farm with just her and a succession of half-wild dogs she believed he understood, or at least cared for, more than he ever did for her.

Her grandpap had known what kind she was. So he always said. For—he said—he was of a like though opposed or opposite kind. He had used to wonder aloud how it could have come to be that his granddaughter could have a share in that other life he also led, because (he told her, when she was too young to know what he was talking about but not too young to remember and ponder) she was no blood of his. The woman who was the mother of her mother was already carrying that girl-child when Floyd married her, and it wasn't by him; he never did lie with her as husband to wife.

Where was she, Bobby asked, this woman, her grandmother?

Dead. Had bad blood or some weakness. He had met her in a hunky town in Clay County, he told Bobby. She wasn't bohunk herself. But that said nothing about who the father was of the child she carried, Bobby's mother. Who grew up to be another like her, and had gone off to Detroit fast as she could go and there got herself with child—that was Bobby, yes Bobby was herself a woods-colt, a come-by-chance child. And she came back to Hogback just long enough to leave Bobby with Floyd. Floyd pretended to have never known the man's name, or no longer to remember it.

So there was no knowing now what blood was in her.

*You're of that kind* he'd say to her, when she flouted him, when she lied to him so brazenly he had to know, when she lay out all night in the pines and wouldn't come when he called; and though he had legally adopted her, was her father therefore as well as her grandfather, though she slept in his bed until she was ten, she never believed he loved her: used to catch him now and then looking at her as though there was a deep enmity fixed between them, deeper than any commandment to love or honor could reach.

When she was twelve she left his house up on Hogback Mountain and walked to Clay County in search of her mother, who maybe had people there. She never found her, but people took her in, as they always would, drawn somehow to help her, to melt the hard thing they saw in her pale eyes, the reserve in her tight-drawn mouth. They got little good of their kindness. That was her nature too—so her grandpap said—and she had been content to believe that then, though she was not content to believe it anymore.

There was a church being built up on the mountain there—foolish, people said, to build it so far from the valley and the folks who might come there; but the minister, who had preached in backyards and dwelling houses long enough, had a call to build it there, a real church-house. He was one who took her in. She helped him and his young wife: she minded the other young children while the woman, her stomach big, sewed curtains and cloths for the church on a pedal machine; she sang in it too when it was done and prayed and shouted with the others. And because he really had a true call, and because people heard about the call and came to see a man crazy or blessed enough to build a church where no people were, he filled his new church on Sundays and revival nights for a whole summer.

The preacher said she had a hungry for God, that's why she had found her way to his church. She knew she had a hungry, but God would not satisfy it. In their daylong meetings and nightlong revivals, God was invited, awaited, solicited to appear among them or to send his power in, and in it came almost every time, manifested in someone, sometimes in many, the preacher laboring over each one, his shirt drenched in sweat, or himself slain in the spirit and falling to his knees to gabble and prophesy, tears flowing down his cheeks. She never. He worried over her, that she never got a blessing as others did, but she told him that to see others get a blessing—to catch them as they staggered, seized; keep them from falling into the hot stove or hitting their heads—that was a blessing too: and he said well yes it was. And pondered her.

Open your hearts, he cried to them in the church, where the velvet tapestry of Christ's sharing at the Last Supper hung on the wall. Hearts, he cried, hearts is where God dwells in this world, the only place he can dwell. Open your hearts and let the power of God pass in and out. But her heart could only open to let things in; within that small secret box they disappeared. Nothing ever came out.

She never did get a blessing, but at that church-house, on the full-moon night after she first found herself bleeding (stanch it with a warsh-rag, honey, the preacher's wife told her, we'll go down to the store tomorrow), she left her bed when all were asleep, and went out and up the track to the church-house. And she had not gone very far up that way before she saw that there were folks at the shut door waiting to go in. When she came closer she saw that she knew them: they were people of this church, a family that had recently gone all together in their truck off a gullied mountain road in the dark into the holler below and been killed, mother son and grandma. And she saw there was another woman there too, an old woman lately taken up in Christ, who looked at the child coming up the path, patient, curious, or perhaps wondering: has she come to unlock the door for us?

But she could not help them: she wanted to say so but could not, wanted to say something to their faces, strange patient asking faces like the faces in old tintypes shut up in their carved cases, faces that were dead, as these were. I can't help you I can't. And she knew (though she did not dare to turn her head to see) that others were coming up the path to the church behind her, a great number, she alone alive among them.

She couldn't remember later on how she had returned to her own bed, where she found herself next morning. Probably she had taken the way she would later learn she must go: not back but farther forward into that land, until she came once again to her own door or window.

She asked the preacher: Where are the dead now? And he answered that they were in heaven if they had been saved, and in the other place if they had not been saved; and their bodies were in the earth, to be lifted up on the Last Day and made whole, to be joined again with their souls. He said he thought often about that meeting—about the soul's long wait, none knew how long it would be, though surely it might not be much longer now; and the reunion with the newmade body, the joy. He studied her to see if he had answered the question she had asked him, and must have seen in her face that he had not; but she asked no more.

Four more times she saw them in that year, almost able to know before she lay down to sleep the nights on which she would walk out, but unable, when she was abroad and going up the trail toward the church or down toward the river, to remember what she was about, asking *Why am I here, who's called me,* until she began to see them. She told no one; could not even bring herself to give news of those she saw to the ones they had left behind.

On the night of midsummer, shortest of the year, while the preacher and his wife coupled with suppressed cries in the next bedroom (preaching made him eager and loving in all ways, she had learned that) she lay long awake, afraid to sleep, knowing that if she did she would go down into that land; and when dark was deep she arose, packed her clothes silently in a sack, took from the tin box the money that had been collected in the church that evening, and slipped barefoot from the house. She didn't know where she would go. She had heard that up the mountain, far from towns and off the roads, there lived people whose gospel was more perfect even than the preacher's with whom she had stayed. They had no church at all, only their own bodies, wherein they kept the truths they knew. It was told they ate no flesh; and when they decided that their time here below was done, they ceased to eat at all, until they died. She thought about them as she stood in the darkness at the end of the path, and it was as though she could see their faces and hear their voices. It could be that she ought now to go and see if she could find them, and ask them about herself, learn whether in their more perfect gospel she was known about; or prove to herself that after all they didn't exist.

She had to have something to do. From where she stood, where the path met the road, she could go up, or she could go back down, toward the valley of the No Name River, to her father's house: she could ask him too, where the dead were, whether the more-perfects were real and could be found. Mock him if he didn't know. She was walking down along the road, though not having actually decided, when dawn came. A car pulled up alongside her. It was a sedan whose back end had been cut away to make a truck bed, and in it was a refrigerator, tied down with straw rope. She wondered why it is that people cart refrigerators around the world so much, and the thought made her laugh just as the driver (a lean lined man, but not old, with a cigarette burned down almost to his fingers) looked out at her. He slowed, and kept on looking out at her, and kept pace beside her for a long ways, until she stopped; then so did he.

She named her child by him Roberta, which was the secret name those Yankee children in Bondieu had bestowed upon her when they baptized her with a trickle of water stolen from the nuns' church—Roberta, the name of the power that had been in that baptizing, in that water and the words in another language that the boy said. Each of those children had had their secret name, which they said they received in a church—not the little white church-house in Bondieu but a real church with a bishop: Bobby saw in her mind when she thought of it a place as high and stony as a mine was deep, and dark as the pines beyond her grandfather's house. The eldest girl's name was Hildy and her secret name was Teresa; the boy's name was Pierce and his secret name (not yet bestowed) was to be John Bosco, like the chocolate drink. He had showed her a picture of this John Bosco, in white lace and a red robe, looking heavenward. He had showed her a lot of pictures.

Their house on a hill, that was a place she never once thought of going back to, as though it couldn't be found, as though it was a story like the story of the more perfect gospel teachers, though it had really happened to her. So had the meetings with the dead happened to her. She went the other way, away from stories.

Her secret name hadn't saved Roberta, baby Roberta, who died when she was four. That was in Pikeville after Randy left for Detroit. Died of what? Bobby didn't have a name for it, and later would resent the way city people looked at her when she said she didn't know; so she came to call it by the names of various illnesses she learned about as a nurse's aide, each different name with a different story, so that Roberta went farther away with each telling.

And Bobby too moved farther away. Whenever she lived in any place long enough and knew it well enough to be able to say My home, my church, my neighbors, she would begin to see their dead: those who should not have died, those who had been rapt away from life before their time; and she would move again. There were towns and cities and mountain farms and a hospital where a judge sent her and where she recovered from TB; there she learned she had no fear of the sick and the dying, and could make her own living among them. She did not turn to the Word again, though, until the morning after the night when her daughter Roberta found her again, in Conurbana two hundred miles from her grave in Breshy County, Roberta still four years old, in her nightdress stained and foul: came to stand in her door, to look at her and try to take her hand.


Two vans from The Woods were ranked in the parking lot of the Bypass Inn with cars and busses from other places. On an easel by the front desk the name was stuck up in white letters on the black notice board along with Bears Boosters and Avon and some others. Powerhouse International. They didn't believe in churches; wherever two or three are gathered together in My name. Bobby was told that when they had bought an abandoned Bible college out in the Midwest somewhere to be their headquarters, first thing they had done was to take down the cross over the chapel: the symbol of a cult, they said, not for them, the only true uninterpreted unreconstructed Christians.

In the Empire Room they were just finishing the first half of the meeting—time for a break for a while, food and drink, people could only mind for so long, no matter how caught up. She looked in: people were pushing back their folding chairs, looking (some of them) as though they were rising from a deep pool, opening their eyes after long immersion. Mostly though like kids done with school. Ray Honeybeare sat on the dais, still, his arms across his breast, hands cupping his elbows, his eyes looking inward and his mouth down-drawn, a look she knew. Pitt Thurston, who had been preaching (you were not to call it preaching, she had been told that more than once) listened, grinning intently, to a woman who had come up to speak to him. Dark circles of sweat under his arms when he removed his nice sport coat. Working hard. Bobby could hear his strong heartbeat: almost thought she could.

Seeing him changed her mind: she wouldn't tell him what she had seen. If she did the whole story would come unasked from her mouth, and that would prove to him and to all of them that she wasn't what she wanted to be, what they had all worked so hard to make her: it would prove that she remained what she had been, a thing worse than they could imagine, and unable to be changed or touched.

People milled out into the foyer where a long table clothed in white had been set up with a bunch of chrome coffeepots, two women readying them and some trays of cookies, their own baking for sure. Bobby knew one of the women, young and dark and tall. She had prayed with her: one of those who had come in vans from The Woods.

"Got you helpn, huh."

"Oh. Oh hi. Yes."

"Bobby."

"Yes, sure. Rose." She gave a little wave in lieu of a handshake, busy, unsteady it seemed on her low heels.

"Need some help?"

"I think I."

Rose bent to lift from a serving cart a big tray of small creamers, all full. Never been a waitress, for sure. Bobby without time to stop it saw her heft the tray wrong at the same moment as her heel turned under her; the tray had almost reached shoulder height when the girl's body folded beneath it, and as she tried to keep from sinking and Bobby reached to right it, the little round creamers like passengers on a sinking ship rattled all together down the tilting tray and off: Rose trying to avoid them slipped and sat down, gathering most of them in her lap.

"Oh boy," Bobby said. "Oh Lord."

Rose was on her feet again, face shocked, betrayed, afraid. Cream ran down her blouse and dripped from her fingertips; wetness like a bad kid's accident spread over her skirt.

The other woman serving hurried to wipe Rose with stiff motel napkins but made little difference. Bobby turned and saw Pitt Thurston's wife at the meeting-room doorway and—only needing to point for an explanation—got from her the key to one of the rooms she knew the group would have rented for the night.

"Come on, honey," she said to Rose. "Quick."

She could hear the squish of cream in Rose's shoe as she led her to the elevator. The elevator's ceiling was mirrored, like a whore's bed, and Rose looked up at herself, and laughed and wept, holding out her hands helplessly.

The room was filled with bags and knapsacks, a cot unfolded and unmade, fast-food bags unremoved. More important things to do than tidy. They found the bathroom.

"God, this never happened before. I feel so stupid."

"I seen it," Bobby said. She had seen it a lot: how for a good while after you accepted and were cleansed, you could feel that giddy sensation of having been emptied and then refilled with something softer, lighter, new and unknown, and how hard it was to manage your newness sometimes. If you were out in the world, and you fell down the stairs or something, you'd talk about Satan's powers that were around you, tripping you up. Maybe so.

"Don't mind me if I help," Bobby said. She sought the catch of Rose's skirt, slippery, hard to get a grip on, like a kid's wet snowpants. "'Cause I'm a nurse," she said, which wasn't exactly true. "Comes naturally."

"No sure thanks. Really thanks." Bewildered apparently still. Beneath the skirt, panty hose, wet too, and pale peach underpants, tiny and fine—a surprise, for some reason. Rose, her face a mask of disgust, was trying to undo the buttons of her blouse without handling the sodden silky material.

Bobby turned on the shower, and Rose without hesitation stripped off the last of her clothes and stepped in. Bobby stood for a minute listening to the roar of water and observing Rose's shadow, strangely fragmented, on the pebbled surface of the glass shower door.

"You got somethn else to put on?"

"No. Not really. My raincoat's downstairs."

"I'll get it."

"Thanks, really. It's a navy one. With leopard-print collar and cuffs. Sort of silly. You can't miss it."

Bobby went down again. She thought of the other time she had met this woman: how she had hugged her at the end of prayers, as she had of course all the others. In the bathroom she had seen that Rose had shaved off her pubic hair, and she wondered why, at whose suggestion or request.

When Bobby returned Rose stood wrapped in towels in the bedroom, shivering a little; she changed the towels for the coat Bobby held out.

"Okay now?"

"Okay." She hugged herself. "What I need," she said, "or *want* actually. Well. Is a cigarette." She looked at her feet. "I guess they really wouldn't want you to smoke."

"Nope."

"I've almost quit."

"Me too," Bobby said. She rummaged in her coat and brought out a pack, crumpled and nearly empty. She opened the window a crack; they sat together on the littered bed and Bobby lit their smokes with a butane lighter.

"So you're with us now?"

"Yes," she said. "Yes. I am."

"Seen benefits already." Not a question. "You gone take the healing training?"

"I want to," Rose said. "I'm going to. It's . . . I just don't know if I ever could. Really heal."

"Well. It's not everybody who can. You pray to be let to. Now I never. I ain't no healer. I just look to get healed. I get, I don't give. That's a different training." She smiled. "You might be one though."

She considered Rose, and Rose looked down at her hands, then into Bobby's eyes. But what Bobby was thinking, looking so closely at Rose, was not that the woman might heal, now or ever. What she thought was: She is of the kind I am. She doesn't know it, but she is. I think she is.

"You never tried?" Rose asked.

"Got to *try*. I took some training. They start with you, yourself." What was it, was it the woman's hooded eyes, revealing and hiding her at once; was it how she took in smoke so hard; was it the way that nothing had passed from her to Bobby in that embrace she had once given Bobby, nothing at all?

"Is that hard?" she asked. "Starting on yourself?"

"Depends," Bobby said. "On what's inside you that has to come out." She stabbed out the cigarette. "I ain't gone tell you what they drug outta me. Long as I'm shet of it."

Rose looked within: Bobby recognized the look, the same look within that you see on people's faces when you tell them you just had a rotten tooth pulled, or found a lump in your breast. Checking.

Bobby believed she had known others of her own kind; she had usually been quickly certain of it, had revealed herself to them too, without words for none were needed. People who had like a cast in their eye, couldn't look straight ahead at what was there to see, but hungry for it nonetheless; laughing maybe, good-timing, praying even maybe but always seeming to be straining forward like starved dogs; not starved but never full. Bobby knew. Often she knew not only those ones but also the ones who were in pursuit of them, years-long stories she would come across, pass by, encounter again: she knew them.

But of this one she wasn't sure. Could she be one, and not know it?

"One thing they ask you," she said, "is what you most want in the whole world. You got to answer that. If you know. And it ain't so easy, if you tell the truth."

"I," Rose said, and looked stricken, as though Bobby herself had demanded to know this of her, right now. "Oh boy," she said. "Oh man."

Bobby took her hand. Felt the woman's spirit beat, as though pulsing down through her ring finger from her heart. She is, she isn't, is, isn't. "Cause God wants it for you. They'll tell you that. What you most want. And you'll get it."

"Did you know?" she asked. "When they asked you? What did you say?"

"Yes mam." If she could get close enough to the woman to smell her, Bobby thought, she could tell: if she could stick her nose in the cleft of her butt, like a dog. "I said that what I wanted most in the whole world was a brand-new white convertible. Stingray or a Vixen. With red leather seats."

# 7

The resident, tidy in his white coat, held out a huge hairy yellow-nailed palm to Sam. "Shake," he said. Sam stared at him in horror, not the comic Halloween horror he'd been aiming at but what seemed to be social horror, as at a breach of manners. She didn't take his hand, though she stared unsmiling at it; she kept her grip on Rosie's pants.

"This is Sam," the aide said—Bobby, the same who had guided them here before. "The one's got a name like mine."

The resident pulled off the King Kong gloves and hunkered down before Sam.

"You're not going to believe this," he said. "*My* name is Sam." He pointed to his name tag, where a teddy-bear sticker was affixed beside his name, Dr. Samuel Rosenblatt, which Sam couldn't read. Rosie had the impression that the young doctors who did most of the work here were childless, their hours too long, medical school too tough; they had a bantering tone that suggested they didn't know much about kids as people, however much they might know about them in other ways. She wondered what they thought about having kids themselves, after being here, seeing so many of them so sick.

"Okay, well," he said, after looking deeply into Sam's eyes for a moment, "let's see what we're going to do."

Rosie had hoped that the test would be given in the newer part of the hospital, in a big clean ward painted freshly in modern colors like the lobby, pale salmon and wintergreen; but Neurology hadn't moved. The same walls, battered by collisions with rolling beds; the same tea-colored stain across the ceiling tiles. The amateurish murals of forest animals, chipmunks and bunnies, given what seemed to be serious medical defects by sloppy drawing, walleyes and pinheads and twisted grins. Maybe once they'd seemed cheerful; now they seemed like a mean joke played on the kids being treated here, a joke so pointlessly mean and clumsy and sinister that Rosie did laugh, laughed with covered mouth, embarrassed.

Dr. Marlborough hadn't appeared, though all the lesser doctors who came to look at Sam and check her wires and read the results were careful to say that they worked with (never for or under) him. Rosie pondered why they all had their stethoscopes, clipped around their necks or slung over their shoulders like pet snakes, and decided it was not because they expected to use them but because having one marked you as a doctor; only the doctors seemed to be allowed to wear them.

There were two others being tested, as Sam was, to discover the sources of their seizures, *in the program* as they said, a teenage boy who didn't leave his room and a boy two or three years older than Sam and apparently worse off. *Pretty seriously involved* the nurse had said to her, and then no more, seeming to be sorry she'd said even that much. This boy was introduced to Sam; they faced each other, heads shaved in neat spots, both wired up and tethered to the recorders beside them on tall chrome rolling stands. They regarded each other momentarily with the usual kid mix of indifferent incomprehension and simple acceptance, not joined by what grown-ups assumed would join them. The boy, pinch-faced and with eyes of scary intensity, was named Doyle.

"Doyle don't need no outfit," said the aide. "He's gone be a Martian, right honey?"

Doyle in sudden understanding contorted his face, held out his arms and began stalking stiff-legged around the ward, Martian, Frankenstein's monster, mechanical man of any kind; Rosie suspected that having got the idea he was going to do it for some time, and he did, for hours, machinelike, stopping only to plug himself in at various likely-looking places to recharge.

Sam ignored him. She didn't feel Martian, or mechanical. She touched with awful care the wires attached to her head, and took no steps to do anything, sit, play, explore. At the nurses' station now a doctor in a high-collared black paper cape and whiteface checked reports and bared his phosphorescent fangs at the nurses, who took it calmly. Not everybody had got into the spirit, but many patients and nurses had masks and black-and-orange bags of candy.

What were they thinking, though, really, or didn't they think. Making jokes, the usual jokes, about blood and death. Rosie remembered that doctor outfits, including organs or bloody scalpels, had always been a regular Halloween choice. She thought of how she would describe this night, this scene later to someone, to Spofford or to Pierce, how she would tell about the doctors dressed as predatory monsters and some kids with masks no worse than their own faces; how odd it was, more than dreadful; what the lesson of it was, which she might know by then.


The rooms were small, and there were two children in most; parents and relatives came and went, bringing clutches of balloons with cheerful faces on them or stuffed animals larger sometimes than their child; the sicker the kid the larger the animal, maybe. Parents sat and watched inane TV shows beside their children or helped with meals or sat on chairs in the doorways of their rooms like housewives along an old-world alley, talking to one another and swapping inquiries and complaints. Some of them seemed like old hands; they knew how to just nod when a neighbor's condition or treatment was named, and to ask questions but not to show pity or alarm at the answers. Rosie supposed that she would be one herself someday, that part of her life was going to be spent here, nobody could tell her how much; that this was life too, after all, being lived, here where kids got shots and Easter baskets and Christmas presents in their beds and got well or didn't and died; and that was the lesson, maybe, or part of it.

Their roommates were a solid woman older than Rosie, with great sympathetic eyes, and her youngest child—three more at home, she said, twin girls and a teenage boy. She had been here three days already "this time," knew the nurses and even some of the patients, who had happened to be here at other times when she was; she gossiped generously about them. *The seizure kids,* she'd say, *the cancer kid* across the hall.

"Doyle is bad," Sam said. "He won't take his medicine."

"Doyle," said the woman, "hasn't taken his medicine *yet* without a fight. Spoiled," she said to Rosie. "I mean you can understand, but. The poor nurses."

"I have to take my medicine," said Sam. "But if I need to, I can cancel."

"Oh yes?" Rosie said, wondering who had said that in Sam's hearing. "You think so?"

Sam nodded. She took hold of the tall rolling tripod that carried her recorder, and carefully, as though it were a delicate pet, baby giraffe or willowy orang, she guided it out the door.

"Going for a walk?" Rosie asked.

She didn't answer.

"Cute," said their roommate.

Her own child, delicate and beautiful, was already asleep; about eighteen months, Rosie guessed, maybe two years, with pale curls on one side of her head, the other wearing the common badge of fourth-floor neurology, a temple shaved and bandaged.

"She's got a plastic tube in her head," her mother said. She and Rosie leaned on the crib's edge looking down as into a fish tank. "Because her spinal cord didn't form right. The tube drains off the cerebrospinal fluid. Otherwise, she'd get a big head—you know, water on the brain."

"How long does she need it?"

"Oh. Always. Part of her now. Except it got plugged up, and she had to get it fixed."

"Oh. Well. I hope," she started, but thought no, no hoping. "It's nice you get to stay with her."

"Well yes. They only just started that. They didn't use to. You could hardly see the kid."

Rosie remembered. Her mother came down from home every day on the bus, two hours, to sit with her for the length of visiting hours, after which she would leave again for the two-hour ride home, and the vacancy would settle again over the room and the halls; Rosie never decided if she was more relieved to see her mother come in the morning with her schoolwork and her clean jammies, or to see her go, leave her alone with the others who belonged here, the kids in their beds and the nurses and rare doctors and the mild shy candy-striper who offered her books and magazines in which she could read about the world she had come from. Worse was when her father came, so hurt, so tense and combative, ordering around the nurses and disrupting the routine. How afraid he had been of the girl, what had her name been, in the bed beside hers.

Lilith. The curtains drawn quick around her bed, the rattle of their hooks and the muslin rising like wings.

"You were here? On this floor?"

"Not on this floor. Somewhere. I don't know where."

"What was wrong?"

"A cough. I don't know really. They could never figure it out. I was here for a couple of weeks. Maybe more."

"Jeez. A couple of weeks. Get insurance to pay for that nowadays."

"I think my parents paid."

"You got better?"

"I don't know." The past time, that other hospital contained inside this one, reached toward her, trying to come clear. "I mean yes, I got better, but I wasn't cured. The girl in the bed next to mine died."

The woman only shook her head minutely. Rosie could not remember if she had ever told anyone these things, and wondered if she could tell them now without weeping. Lilith. Rosie's father had been shocked that they could not save her, seemed to think it impossible, and that if they could not save her they should somehow keep the knowledge of their failure from her, and certainly from his own daughter in the next bed; some of them there did try, and answered Rosie's questions with cheerful evasiveness, but not most of them. And Lilith knew. She knew she was there to die, not to get better, and they were there to help, and attend on her. Not everyone gets better; she taught Rosie that, and Rosie wanted her father to learn it and be quiet.

"It must have been leukemia. She would get cards from her friends at school, and open them and read them to herself, and give them to the nurse; and the nurse tacked them up where she could see them. She didn't say anything about them except who they were from." She was dark-haired and white, and grew whiter as she lost weight; her eyes bigger too, from the weight she lost, like the huge-eyed kids starving in famine photographs: though Rosie thought then that her eyes grew big from what she saw approaching.

"It was way late one night," she said, "and I was awake; I don't know what woke me. They were around her bed, and then they drew her curtains. And I thought"—Rosie only at that moment remembered that she had thought so, she had forgotten till now—"I thought that they did that so she could pass in private, with just them. But I guess she was already dead, and they were just."

"Yes."

"After that I got better," Rosie said.

"Huh. Just like that."

"I guess I thought: you're not that sick. You've got no right to be here. Get serious."

"Funny how kids can be. So smart."

"Smart and not smart at once."

"Not like us," the woman said, and laughed.


Come night, nothing ceased; the halls weren't dimmed, though the room's curtains could be drawn and the lights turned off. The blinking monitors stayed on, and the intercom, though the voice issuing calls and names grew softer, sadder, sleepier. She got Sam into her hospital johnny, open in the back, made to fit over IVs and machinery such as Sam was hooked to. The nurse helped her manage. A new shift had come on; several of the women Rosie had first met now gone and replaced by others, this one older and smelling of cigarettes, a silver cross between her freckled breasts.

"They're going to give Doyle a shot," Sam said. "Bobby said so." She looked at her mother. "Bobby knows Daddy."

"No. Really?"

"Yet's take this off for sleeping," Sam said. She reached up to touch her Medusa curls.

"No no honey, no sweetie," the nurse said. "Got to keep those on."

Sam looked at her, and lay back against the pillow, that look of unreal resignation in her face that frightened Rosie. "I'm going to sleep too," she said to Sam. "I'm tired."

"Sleep," said Sam. "Go to sleep."

"Okay."

The nurse showed her where to find sheets and a thin blanket (it was a hothouse in the room and would be all night, she guessed) and how to unfold the chair into a sort of half bed. Rosie's roommate was already in a cotton nightgown; Rosie would not go so far, intended to stay in her clothes and tough it out through a probably sleepless night; the woman shrugged.

"Okay?" Rosie said to Sam. "I'm ready."

"Lie down," Sam said.

"Okay. You want anything more?"

Sam thought. "Sing," she said.

"Oh Sam."

"Sing."

"Well what song? We have to be quiet for the baby."

" 'Aiken Drum.' "

"Really?"

Sam nodded, definite. This song about a monstrous hero and his battle on the moon she had learned at day care, it wasn't one Rosie had ever known or sung. Almost in a whisper, Rosie began: "His head is a . . . What's his head?"

"A doughnut!" said Sam.

It was different every time. Rosie sang:

*His head is a doughnut*
*His head is a doughnut*
*His head is a doughnut and his name is Aiken Drum.*

The fun of the song was the assembling of Aiken out of things you chose, the queerer the better. What's his heart? "A button," Sam said instantly.

*His heart is a button*
*His heart is a button*
*His heart is a button and his name is Aiken Drum.*

"His arms are spaghetti," Sam sang out next, "his arms are spaghetti, his arms are spaghetti and his name is *Aiken Drum!*"

"Sh, Sam, sh." Rosie found the song unsettling, creepy even, Aiken pathetic in his odd inanimate parts; the song seemed to mock him in his insufficiency, and Rosie felt his struggle to stay together and do battle. She met things like that in dreams, coming toward her, malevolent or needful.

"That's all, now hon. Got to close your eyes."

"You close your eyes."

"I will. I'm here."

"Okay."

"Okay. I love you."

"I love you, Mommy."

She shut the last light she could shut, lay back against the chair's hard back. No dreams, please no dreams: the shallow vivid dreams of nights in bad beds in strange places. Aiken Drum. What was it that was so horrid about him, horrid like those portraits made long ago, perfectly realistic readable faces made all of birds, or vegetables, or kitchen utensils. Was it that you knew they really had no inside at all, were just stuff, and yet would not or could not lie still? Dead but alive. Skeletons maybe were the same, the inanimate part of you, dry bones empty inside, getting up and hanging together, by no means.

Ghosts too. No not ghosts, ghosts are the opposite: they have an inside and no outside. Naked. Cold. More afraid than you are maybe: what they always said about wild animals, stray cats with bared teeth, moths beating against the pane.

She thought of Boney, almost a skeleton when he died, but alive, alive. Where was he now, did he mind being dead as much as he had hated dying? She thought of her father—who was Boney's nephew—hiding from the knowledge that people die, that his daughter might.

What was it anyway with the Rasmussens, all of them, that they feared death so much; was it death, really, that they feared, or what? Rosie had lately come to think that the world lay under some kind of curse or spell, a lassitude or inattention to what is really important, a kind of sleep that could not be shaken off, and that it was up to her to break or lift it: or rather she didn't think this at all but caught herself in moments of abstraction assuming that it was so. But maybe it wasn't the world at all that lay in the grip of such a spell, maybe it was only her own family.

Herself too: maybe herself.

The Curse of the Rasmussens. As though they were made backwards, thinking they were fleeing what they feared when really they ran right to it. It had seemed to her as she grew up that her father was not really actual, that he talked and ate and kissed her good night and went on business trips and came back with presents but that compared to other people he wasn't there at all. Her mother laughed when Rosie asked her what after all her father's business had been, because it hadn't been real, he had not needed or wanted it to be real, only to seem real, a ghost business. His real life was unreality: Demerol, Percocet. Morphine, whose name means sleep. Thought he was lucky, maybe, that he had found a medicine for fear.

And then he was dead himself, really dead: an overdose that her mother was sure was accidental. But then her mother had also thought he took the stuff for an unremitting pain in his bones, pain no doctor could or would deal with, thus forcing him to go for relief into what she called—because he did—the Underworld. Where one day he acquired stuff (where and how, in that nice city in the nice middle of the country in that decade?) that was maybe a little stronger, a little more compelling or impelling than usual.

So now he knows.

That was what Rosie thought. She thought that the dead know everything, if they know anything. They know what they no longer have, and what they might have had if they had done things differently, and they know that there's nothing now that they can do about it.

She had begun dreaming of her father, after he was dead, dreamed that she talked with him long and intimately but about nothing in particular; dreamed of him talking to her, at last, about what was in his heart. Sometimes in the dreams he would put his head on her shoulder, or in her lap, giving up all defenses and pretendings, the self-protective kidding he always kept up when alive, and became a weary needy lover or tired baby, at which she woke.

One time, though.

One time in a dream she had asked him—the paradox coming for once clear to her dreaming self—if he wasn't actually dead, for she knew he was, remembered him dying, dead, in his glossy box of maroon wood. Yes, oh yes, he admitted, he was; he would have to go back soon, now in fact, the time was at hand. If she wanted, though, she could go back with him.

No, she thought not; no no she would not want to go.

Oh not to stay, he said; just to visit. Just to see where his time was spent; where hers would be too. Wasn't she curious? She'd be safe, he said. She had only to take his arm this way—and he wound his arm right around hers, so that their hands joined together backwards, secure—and not let go. Just don't let go. And they set off toward that land; and of course it wasn't far, though when she came in sight of it—the far tops of its buildings in the distance like the far view of Cascadia from the turn of the highway—her imagination apparently ran out and she saw nothing more, and then woke. Woke wondering how, if she was not supposed to release his hand, she could ever have returned.

Death. She had never thought of it as a land, she knew it wasn't, and yet she could dream that it was, that her father could return and take her there. Maybe we have to think it's a land, can't help it, where all the dead are alive. It wasn't far, even: she was as close to it here in her chair as it was possible to be, in this half-light; here where so many had died so young. She heard their footfalls in the halls, their voices in the whisper of the intercom.

Bobby looked in as her double shift was ending, stepped softly into the room lit by the night-light and the green glow of numerals counting things, heart rates, brain waves, life. Everyone was for the moment asleep. Bobby stood for a time watching Sam and her mother breathe almost in unison; then she left.


There have been, at different times, ways by which the living have gone down into the land under the earth—not down through the soil and stones underfoot but into the earth that is the deepest circle of creation, a circle not different from the earth that we live on, that we lie asleep on, only its shadow. And once there they can placate the dead, the greedy dead, even sometimes win back from them the souls of those they hold in thrall.

To do that, those who go down to the dead have often had to die themselves, or undergo sufferings like death (didn't Jesus—greatest of all the magicians, Bruno thought—have to suffer and die in order to go down and free us from death, to free not just one grieving supplicant's child or parent but all of us?). Elsewhere or at other times they have not needed to suffer and die but have had to cease to be themselves and to become animals, and why animals? Because animals do not die: wolves die but Sir Wolf never dies, not born for death. And when the time is past when those who go down into death are able to turn themselves into animals, still there are those who are able—while remaining asleep in their beds—to go out, in spirit, in the *form* of an animal, or riding on one. And when that time is also over, we can still remember that it was once done or can be done. Some of us can.

Jean Bodin, who wanted to find and burn all witches, all those who took animal form or believed they did—all those who had illicit or unregulated dealings with the dead—was in fact a modern man, a man of the time to come: he was fighting against the tendency to slip back into the older ways, the old world in which persons can be in two places at the same time, the world where Sagittarius sat on the horizon and the doors were still open: the old world that rationality is always fighting against, trying to mop it up, or leave it behind. Dam it or damn it. Clearheaded men like Bodin, Catholic and Protestant, antiphantasmic warriors, pushed back the dark together, rejecting the age-old truce between the Church and the pagans, both with their old philosophers and their old gods, with the small gods of everyday life, with the warning and helping dead. No more.

And it worked too. Frightened or ashamed, those who investigated Nature or nature drew in their researches, shut out the universal rays, narrowed their questions to those that had some promise of clear answers, and to whose formulation no powers could object. If they hadn't done so the plain stepping-stones of science couldn't have been uncovered, and swept. One by one. So successful was that enterprise that by the time Pierce Moffett discovered the old arts (or discovered that others had discovered or never forgotten them) the world in which they had been practiced was centuries gone and they couldn't really be used. Pierce didn't believe they had ever really worked.

*But* (he typed on his big blue typewriter, alone on All Saints' Eve as night fell) *suppose the world is in fact now coming to an end, the world of Meaning we have always lived in. And suppose that the Powers who must make from it a new one—one that will be just like the old one in most but not all respects—are mulling just now over what sort the new world might be, and what garb they themselves might appear in too. If that's the case, then that old multilayered earth and its shape-shifting travellers would have to be among the worlds from which they could choose*—mutatis mutandis, *the same but never exactly the same, take a little out of the waist and plump the shoulders. More likely not, though; more likely they'll choose something entirely different this time, something in a fierce hound's-tooth maybe, or a moiré taffeta, eye-fooling, iridescent: can't you see them (I can) moving amid the racks and counters fingering the goods, unable to decide, all possibilities laid out before them once again before they make their choice, thereafter to pretend (once again) that everything has always been this way, that they themselves have all along had these aspects and not others, rank on rank, the army of unalterable Law?*

*And who is that littlest one among them, wide-eyed, just awakened and believing he has never made this choice before? You know, don't you?*

He rolled this out of the typewriter and read it over; and after a long moment of gazing on it he tore it in two. Too extravagant, too clever, too. Daring? Taunting? He put his hands in his lap, afraid. Years before, when he had finally and wholeheartedly abjured the Church and all its pomps and works, had denied wholesale and at large all judgments it could make or had made on him, he had remembered the Sin Against the Holy Ghost, which no one could define but which Jesus was very clear in stating could not be forgiven, and he had said in his mind *All right, whatever it is, I hereby commit it:* and had felt a sudden chill nakedness, as though he had been taken notice of, and his statement recorded. Which was what he felt now too.

He left his desk and went to lie down. His head was a bread box, his heart was a birdcage. Every page he had written this week he had torn up and thrown away. And as he lay there, from Littleville to the Jambs and Stonykill to Fair Haven and to the old neighborhoods of Cascadia where the Victorian houses stand at the top of steep stairs, the little dead were out in their flocks—all over the eastern standard time zone in fact, and coming out elsewhere successively as night swept westward: some of them being the dead as they have always been seen (vague, sheeted); some of them the old undead, zombies and ghouls and vampires, and some the new undead of science, the Frankensteins and robots and medical disasters. Fictional characters too, heroes and villains both, and costume-ball princesses and consumer products and jokes. Their parents often followed, hovering not too far behind, afraid for their little imps, but not because of the roaming dead whom they might meet, only because of the darkness, the traffic, and maybe the wickedness of the living: and still on this night of this year eighty percent of them believed—according to a recent poll Pierce had read, appalled, astonished—that God had personal care for them, and that they would somehow live on after their deaths, to be rewarded for the good they had done, and punished for the evil.

For another two days Sam stayed linked to her machine, getting more daring with it and trundling it from playroom to bedroom skillfully, Rosie lagging behind; neuro patients came and went from their beds and rooms near hers; her roommate went, and an anxious couple with a newborn came, so stricken that Rosie dared ask them nothing: kids themselves almost, standing looking into their baby's clear plastic box and holding tight to each other as though they stood on a cliff's edge looking down.

Nothing in the end was learned about Sam; nothing extraordinary. The doctor (still not Dr. Marlborough, who was beginning to seem somewhat fictitious or hallucinatory to Rosie) went over the results with her and showed her that the same anomalies were still present, and no more explainable. He suggested a slight change in her medication. Rosie packed up as soon as he was done and got them out, feeling the place fold up and disappear behind them as they walked (almost ran) down its halls and out.

She stopped to get the dogs out of the kennel in Cascadia, Spofford's and her own two, they filled up the car with their eagerness and their lolling tongues and odors, making Sam laugh uncontrollably as they poured from back to front over the seat backs. When she got back to Stonykill she found, amid the spill of mostly inconsequential mail from the Foundation's big box at the post office, a long envelope she was required to sign for, which turned out to be a notice that the custody hearing was scheduled. Oh well oh well. Lastly there was a small envelope with a small letter in it, written in Spofford's very small but very legible and open hand. The postmark date was Halloween.

Sam wouldn't let her stop to read it, insisted on hurrying home—home, home, she said, each time she said it like a little theft out of Rosie's breast. Sam ran inside in delight as soon as Rosie opened the doors, chasing away with the dogs through the rooms, touching the chairbacks and newel posts, the telephone, the hassocks in recognition or reclamation. Home.

*Very still + cold here tonite + the dogs keep finding some reason to wake up + bark—you can hear an answer from a ranch miles away. The guy whose house we are in also wakes up in the night + calls out, says he has for years, ever since discharge. Cliff has been spending time with him. Meanwhile odd stuff abounds. No wolves or wolf critters seen, but cattle—this guy claims sheep too, there are different stories—have been found on the prairie dead, with certain parts removed. Not chewed off but neatly excised, like with a scalpel. Lips, udders, nostrils, assholes. Some people say the ground is swirled up around these carcasses like a chopper landed + took off. Other people say burn marks. We're going north in a few days. We go from ranch to ranch + listen to stories + Cliff talks. These folks are all heavily armed, which scares me more than anything they think they know, or think they've seen.*

He was thinking of her, he wrote, and of Sam. He said nothing about returning. There was an address on the letter, a Rural Route in a far western state. She could write to him. She had no name to give a long-distance operator, no name but his and Cliff's. She saw her letter making its painful way toward him, trying to hurry, caught in a slurry of others in a distant postal hub, sorted, sorted again. She wondered if she could send a telegram. Was that still possible? Telegrams for urgent news, good or bad. She didn't think she could, but she picked up the phone book and opened it, Sam looking in and the dogs sniffing the pages, his dogs, needing him too. And it was there, Western Union. The little telegraph form that was their ad here, as it always had been. She called.

Could she send a telegram? Yes certainly.

Taken by surprise, Rosie had to think what message she should send. She thought of her flimsy yellow sheet brought to the door of this far place, the high plains or dark pines, by whom though, how. "Court date set with Mike," she said. "December 11." She felt foolish trying to talk in telegraphese. "Need you back. Really." She paused, thinking, and was not hurried.

"Say about me," Sam said.

"Sam's okay," Rosie said, and felt a stone, the old familiar stone, form in her throat. "Sam, S-A-M."

Was that it? she was asked at length. Yes that was it. Her phone number would be billed for this service. Fine. And what was the recipient's phone number? Rosie didn't know; there might not even be one. Well without a phone number the message can't be sent; basically it's called in by the local Western Union office. A paper copy can be mailed the same day.

"Well if I had a number," Rosie said, "I could call it myself." Silence. "I guess forget it then," she said, and cradled the phone, feeling she had been fooled into thinking a kind of magic that had vanished from the world could still be used. Yellow magic. No, gone, she thought, and sat down on the stairs. The dogs and Sam clustered around her, looking at her and waiting for what she would do next.

# 8

A bove River Street the town of Blackbury Jambs ascends along a number of short streets that traverse back and forth up the heights. Hill Street is the steepest of these, leading up to the Hill Street Church, then tacking off in another direction, having changed its name to Church Street. The Hill Street Church was built in the 1880s by the Original Mission Baptists; when they became extinct, the building (a pretty timbered and shingled church-in-the-wildwood sort of structure) was sold for a dollar to the Reformed E.U.B., though they can't fill it either and share it now with the Danish Brethren, a small odd sect that holds its weekly services on Saturdays. People, tourists particularly, who don't know this (despite the sign before the church announcing it) tend to think that surely no one will mind if they park in the church's lot on the seventh day; and so before services on that day the minister was once again out with some mimeoed notes explaining why this was actually inconvenient for the congregation, and slipping them under the wiper blades of parked cars, some of which looked damn familiar.

"Hello."

The minister (her name was Rhea Rasmussen) looked up to see a tall man, unshaven or dark-jowled, in a salt-and-pepper overcoat, standing at a distance as though uncertain whether to approach or pass by.

"Hi."

"You remember me?" Pierce Moffett asked her, and right away she was reminded of the one time they had met—at the funeral of Boney Rasmussen, which she had conducted, or rather at the gathering at Arcady afterward. The two Rasmussens, the quick and the dead, were unrelated, at least not traceably; somewhere far back, no doubt, she'd told Pierce that day.

"You're up early," she said, thinking he looked as though he might not yet have slept. "Coming to services?"

"Ha ha," he said, nodding, oh sure. "Though actually," he said, taking a step or two closer, "I have a sort of question. Or rather I'd like to have your professional opinion."

"Yes?" She was a slight woman who appeared tall though she was not, her eyes of palest northern blue at once calming and unsettling; her age was unguessable, her ash-blond hair turning really ashen but only her hands seeming old, large knuckly and worn.

"Have you heard of this—this group or, well this *group* I guess, called the Powerhouse?"

She ceased her leafletting. "Yes. I have."

"Well do you think it's a. I mean how would you characterize it?"

"Professionally?"

"Well."

"It's sort of a churchless church, isn't it?" she said. "With a sort of Christian Science approach. Really quite small, I think."

He looked at her, dissatisfied. She went back to work. "Do you know someone who's involved with them?" she asked.

Pierce shrugged. "I think. Flirting."

"You think it might be a cult."

Pierce thrust his hands deeper into the pockets of his overcoat. "I just sort of wondered what their tenets are."

"I've left my Mr. Coffee on," she said. "You want to come in for a minute?"

Of course he thought it was a cult. One of those that had been erupting like boils over the nation's skin lately, nuts and nonentities becoming strong wizards overnight, as though secretly funded by a foreign power; able to send out troops of devotees into the world to sell flowers or candy, which the newspapers said turned them astonishing profits, believe it or not. Lost children were accosted and suborned at airports or bus stations, or in the city slums to which they fled from nice homes in safe places; they were carried off then to be made into junior wizards and witches themselves, some element of personhood extracted from them and replaced with a weird eye-light and a pasted-on smile. Hollowed out, Spofford had said. You could do it to yourself; or you could allow it—you could ask for it—to be done to you.

"Now not every specialized little religious group is a cult," Rhea Rasmussen said, offering Pierce a small plastic cup of coffee. "They can be swept away, devoted, blind to alternatives; bigoted maybe even, crazy by society's standards today, and not be in the modern meaning a cult."

Pierce nodded, uncomforted. Open on the minister's desk was her Bible, and a dictionary; a clutch of marked-up typewritten sheets; a stack of newsletters. *Asking for Your Prayers* said the headline atop a column of names.

"Have they forbidden her to see you?" she asked. "Do they make a big point of staying out of the world—keeping members from any contact with friends, families, old associates?"

"I don't think so, I mean not yet." Rose Ryder was in his house, in his bed, her old associate; not apparently seized or altered, not different at all, awaking this morning to stretch, yawn, and grin, satisfied, her own light in her eyes.

"When I was a kid," he said, "we Catholics weren't allowed to go into the churches of Protestants, or go to their services. Not even weddings."

"Well see?" Rhea said. "Biggest cult of all. The difference is, for Catholics there's a safeguard in all that bureaucracy, all those centuries of working out the canon law and the hierarchy. But just think of how the Romans saw the Christians in the beginning."

A cult. Mad deniers of state and community. Baby-eaters, family-rejecters, haters of the homely gods. Pierce suddenly felt their revulsion.

"Actually a lot of what are now very respectable, even liberal, Christian churches began as cults of a sort," Rhea said. "Mormons of course: weirder than you'd think, and much feared then. But Quakers too: the Quakers were far from sober originally. Totally rejecting society. George Fox once raised someone from the dead by prayer. So his followers believed." She sipped. "Not crazy really. Just drunk on God."

This also Pierce did not like to hear. Drunk on God. He wondered why he was here, trying to elicit some sort of objective view from someone who was, in some sense, a devotee herself: of the central isolating peculiar antiworld story anyway, the story he had thought himself entirely shet of. An itching trickle of perspiration ran down his arm beneath his coat. "Yours too?" he asked.

"Oh yes. The Danish Brethren? An intransigent bunch of absolutists. Tiny. And—it always happens—made all the tougher by persecution. Nearly wiped out, though. Hated, hated. Hanged and burned."

"By the Catholics?"

"By the Catholics, by the Lutherans too. Makes you strong, they say: what doesn't kill you. The odd thing is that we, the Brethren, were always big on tolerance. It was one of the heresies we were accused of. Which we wouldn't give up."

Her smile was big, warm, proud. Pierce wanted to return it but found he could not.

"Well tell me this," she said. "How deeply are you involved with her? I mean is this threatening a long-term relationship?"

"Oh I don't know," Pierce said, sure that he blushed or blanched in shame. "I'm mostly just concerned, just very concerned."

"Hm," said Rhea. "And do you have an idea of what would have drawn her to this group? Has she been going through a crisis, in her family, her own life?"

Pierce clasped his hands together. "Well she thinks she lost her job."

"Well have you asked her?" Rhea said. "About her feelings? About what's wrong?"

Pierce said nothing, knowing nothing. Then: "We've talked," he said. "About God."

She pondered him. "I think," she said, "religious feelings frighten some people, or alarm them anyway. Religion seems to many people now to be a bondage in itself, not a freedom; and a deeper bondage than any political kind, because it's voluntary. Soul bondage. Does that make any sense to you?"

Pierce said nothing.

"We can all understand the elation of winning freedom," she said. "Breaking bonds: that's the freedom we know. But there's also the elation of giving up freedom. Freely giving it up."

"Uh-huh," Pierce said. "And is that how you."

"No. Oh no. I grew up within it. My father was a pastor. So was his father. To me it's just like the old family kitchen, you know. It's warmth and safety and familiarity. Odd as it might seem to others." She looked at a tiny watch on her wrist. "And speaking of which," she said, "I've got to go preach soon."

Pierce stood. "What's your text?" he asked.

" 'You are the salt of the earth,' " Rhea said. " 'And if the salt has lost its savor, wherewith shall it be salted?' "


Of course it wasn't a cult. It was one of those alternative routes to power, or to the mystic understanding that power can be had in different modes: there were dozens of them too now, their subscribers forming of course a large part of his own (putative) readership. And of course she might well accept training in such methods; there were lots of reasons, including the usual ones, and her employer was clear that she would be fired if she didn't.

Pierce stood before the library on Bridges Street a few minutes before opening time at nine, waiting for the doors to be unlocked by the somewhat flinty-featured but smiling librarian, a silver chain aswing on her glasses, visible to him inside as he no doubt was to her here outside.

"Good morning. Something you need in a hurry?"

"No," Pierce said. "Where though," he asked, "is Religion?"

She told him. He went into the odorous stacks.

Was Rose powerless? The powerless tend (he guessed) to believe those whose power they want to share, surrender to power being itself a kind of power. He thought of the predators she had flirted with, been subject to: Wesley and the others. He wondered if the feeling was the same. His scrotum tightened.

He had come upon her after she had been through the hands of those men; and he had not asked how he could change things for her, what this was in her heart: no that was not what he had asked.

Here was a fat, soberly bound volume, only a few years old, *Atlas of American Churches and Religious Organizations,* printed in thick plain type that reminded him of schoolbooks. The Powerhouse International: it was in the index, with a page number.

*Powerhouse International, The.* Founded 1948 by Dr. R. O. Walter
(b. 1900) and claiming a membership today (1965) of twenty thousand
around the world. The Powerhouse has no churches or formal places of
worship, holding Bible study and prayer meetings in homes and other
places. Walter, who received his LL.D. from Pikes Peak Theological
Seminary in 1932, describes a personal divine revelation when he was

thirty-four, after which he developed a theology combining a basic Arianism with ultradispensationalism and biblical inerrancy.

Pierce wondered what ultradispensationalism could be. Rhea might know. The arcana of Protestant theology were unknown to him. Arianism he remembered had to do with the nature of Jesus: that he was only human, or not human at all.

> Though Dr. Walter retired from active duties in 1960, his interpretations of Bible promises of "gifts of the Spirit" are still communicated in a vigorous mission and outreach program *via* tapes made by Walter himself. Group training sessions emphasize healing and charismata. A Bible Languages and Translation program has been developed at the Powerhouse World Center in Mexico, Indiana (formerly Unity Christian College).

All right. Okay. Pierce studied these arid sentences, a voyeur at an inadequate keyhole, foot falling asleep as he stood holding the big tome, at once guilty and stirred; then, unsatisfied, he searched the shelf.

*Those Strange Cults,* a paperback given a library plastic coating so it would last, but falling apart anyway, much read apparently, unlike the *Atlas,* which it seemed Pierce was the first to crack. The Powerhouse in this one's index too: two entries. Pierce's spying heart tapped faster.

> Cults that claim Christian identity but actually promote nonorthodox teachings, like Jesus Freaks, Powerhouse, Church of God Universal, etc., which believe variously that Jesus is not God, that the Second Coming has already occurred, that believers can do miracles or drink poison without harm, tend to immerse followers in "study groups" that last for hours or days and whose object is not knowledge but "experience" which bonds the followers to the group leader. Universally condemned by recognized theologians, these "churches" have skyrocketed, draining resources and piling up memberships vis-à-vis mainline religious groups.

Good grief, Pierce thought or breathed, buffeted by the hurrying metaphors, trying to think. One other page:

> to be stripped of the "nonprofit," "charitable" or "religious" tax-exempt status they share with genuine churches, they have begun to fight back. IRS agents arriving to seize records have been turned back by gun-toting adherents. At the Powerhouse World Center in Indiana, home of the Powerhouse exceptionalist/healing cult, rumors of illegal weapons stockpiling and Last Days survivalist training have the sheriff's office worried and prosecutors swapping warrants and suits with the group's lawyers.

No no no. Pierce closed the repellent thing and pushed it back into its slot. Impossible in this atmosphere, this moment of this time, to learn anything reliable about such matters; he could imagine the chain of events, the reports and rumors that had led to that book's statements, the fears too that animated them, but not the realities behind them. Could not.

He went out again into the pale day. Maybe he would go see Beau, ask him. He had heard it said that Beau's peculiar household, where Beau lived with (or above, in his own apartment) several women of various ages, some with children, and the occasional lone male, was itself a cult; if it was it was a failed one, for the population kept changing; Pierce thought it resembled more an ancient Irish monastery, one of those kinds where cheerful ascetics male and female gathered to live in stone huts out of the world, Beau their indulgent bishop. There are cults and cults.

When he came before Beau's big three-story house, though, the bare yard where grubby children played, a waiflike woman sitting abstracted on the porch step, he was struck with a species of shyness or dread that was new to him. He waved, and went on.


Inside the house, Beau and Sam Mucho and two other children played Chutes and Ladders on a board almost split along its folds. For tokens they used chessmen from a broken set Beau had gathered at a tag sale; they all knew their own pieces, and Beau kept them separate for them, because, he said, they're still learning the game (the pieces, he meant) and would find change disturbing. Sam's was a tall Queen; Beau's a white Bishop. Sam liked going down the chutes as much as climbing up the ladders, and grieved when she sailed past one uncaught; which made Beau laugh.

"If you don't go down *sometimes* the game will be over," she said.

"Right," said Beau. "If you don't go down you can't climb up."

The white Knight was just tumbling down the longest chute when the door opened and Mike Mucho came in.

"Daddy Daddy!"

"Hi Mike," Beau said, and glanced at the black-cat clock in the kitchen. "You weren't due till noon."

"Well we've got big plans," Mike said, not looking at Beau but grinning at Sam.

"Okay," Beau said, arising from the floor. "But she was winning." He touched Sam's curly head. "Like it or not."

# 9

appy, happy, happy," Rose Ryder said. "So happy. Pierce sometimes I just."

Morning light in the room, she still in the storm-tossed bed; he in the doorway in his overcoat, bag of fresh doughnuts from the Donut Hole in his hand, food of the gods for an hour or so, inedible thereafter.

"You *seem* happy," he said. She did. When she described to him how well it was all really going, her classes and the apartment and her new life, her eyes seemed to melt at last and shine soft and liquid. *Fabulous, wonderful,* she said, sounding to him like the druggies of old (himself one of them) who would recount in such terms some concert or film or street action when what their words and grins in fact referred to was their own sensations at the moment of telling. Stoned.

And what was this blackness in his own breast, in his face too he imagined? She smiled at him and for him, and laughed lightly, and pushed his too-long-uncut hair behind his ears. "Aw," she said. "Pierce. I miss you though. I mean I miss it around here. The city's not so nice. Oh look, look: a heron."

Belated maybe, standing slim and patient in the shallows, which they could now see since the jungle greenery had turned to nothing. It opened its blue wings as they watched, and with a few delicate steps got aloft, impossible as it seemed; rose and with unnatural slowness went away down the river.

"Pierce," Rose said. "I've spoken in tongues."

Pierce's back hair rose. "You what."

"I've spoken in tongues. I can. I found out I can." Shy to tell him, but pleased too with herself; almost sly, confessing to something, as he had heard her confess before, but now to another kind of exciting thing altogether.

"You, one day you just."

She laughed. "No, no. It's a thing that can be learned. You can do it, with, you know, help. Anyone can. You know who can? Mike Mucho."

"No."

"It comes at the end of the training. Like, well not like a final, but."

She looked at him, still bright, and he could see reflected in her face the confusion, the sudden repugnance he felt, as though she had told him—had told him what? That she had learned to vomit at will like a cat? To bleed from her eyes like a horned toad? Why did he feel this horror?

"It's in the Bible. It's a gift of the Spirit. It's promised. And if it is, it is."

"Not everything promised in the Bible is to be taken exactly literally," Pierce said. "Of course."

She regarded him, her newly open face so luminous, that had been so recently shadowed and closed.

"You don't," he said, "believe in Biblical inerrancy. Do you?"

"What's that?"

"I," he said. He had himself never heard the phrase before this very morning. "Well. Basically, the idea that there are no errors in the Bible. No contradictions or false ideas or statements. I guess."

She considered. "Well why would there be."

"What do you mean? *Why would there be?* How could there not be? In what book aren't there?"

"Scuse me," she said, slipping from the bed and quickly making the two or three steps to the bathroom, shutting the door between them. Pierce stood regarding it. Listening.

"How could there not be?" he asked again.

"Because if. If it's the word of God, which is what they say, then why would God let mistakes into it?"

Flush.

"What they I think believe is," she said, returning, finding her panties and stepping into them, "is that it's like a powerhouse. It gives out energy to the world all by itself, through the words and the stories that are in it. That's what it's *for*, why it came into the world."

"It's a book," Pierce said. "Just a book. A good book. Not the only book."

"Well," she said. "It says itself, In the beginning was the Word."

"Sure," he said. "And the Pope says he's infallible."

"Well what they say is . . ."

"The book can't certify its own primacy. That's stupid. That's saying that the book existed before it came into existence. That it came into existence so that it could assert its own prior existence."

"Didn't get that."

"Anyway," Pierce said, "what the text *says* is that in the beginning was *Logos*. *Logos* can mean lots of things; it can mean Reason, or Plan, or Thought, or Study, or Sense—almost anything *but* Word. I think the best translation is Meaning."

"In the beginning was Meaning?" she said.

"And meaning was with God. And meaning *was* God."

She ceased buttoning the big flannel shirt she had put on. "Well," she said.

"It'll all be clearer later. 'Cause they have a big project under way, to retranslate the Bible. The New Testament."

"There are lots of translations."

"Yeah," she said, smiling wisely. "But. What *they*'ve figured out is that even though everybody thinks the New Testament was written in Greek, it was *really* written in Aramaic. Jesus' language. And then translated into Greek. So to get closer to the original meaning . . ."

"They're going to translate it back again." Pierce, stupefied, saw no irony or even plain amusement cross her face. "Oh Lord."

"Don't you want your doughnut?" she asked him, indicating the bloated and glossy things he had placed on a tray between them.

"Yes. No. No I guess not. I haven't been able to eat lately." He drew his unremoved overcoat around him. "I might," he said, "be coming down with something."

When night came they went out. In his little house they had only each other and the one topic between them; everything they might speak about seemed to lead one way or another toward it, here we are again. His work; her studies. The news. Life on earth. None of them able to be spoken of as they had once been.

The Sandbox, on the Cascadia road, was where Val's regulars went when Val closed; when Rose and Pierce entered he could see Val herself at a far table, with Rosie Rasmussen. There was a bad loud band on the tiny podium, making music that to Pierce negated rather than enhanced the meager pleasures of the place; anyway they weren't asked to pay extra for it. He drank Scotch, she a Coke.

"You've wanted power," she said. "You have. Well I want it too. On my side."

"No," he said, his cheeks suffused, his heart bloody, for it *was* what he had tried to have, though only over her and her spirit, to get that which had been enough—for a while—to pretend to have it. "What I wanted was knowledge," he said. "Understanding. It's very different."

"Didn't you think you could do things?" she said. "Magically." She inserted this word within quotes made of four fingers waggled in air. "You said. We tried. Were you just . . ."

"Actually," he said, "I have done things. Certain things. Yes I have. Sometimes I've found myself thinking of having a power—to fly, or lift heavy things, or draw things to me—and I know, I remember, that once or twice in the past, maybe many times, I *have* done those things, and if I try in the right way, if I *believe* what I *know*, I can again."

"Yes."

"And I do. And it's easy."

"And?"

"Then I wake up." He began to roll a cigarette for himself. "In dreams," he said, "I can reach my own cock with my mouth. I'm always surprised to find out I can. I always think, Gee I thought I could only do this in dreams."

"Oh Pierce. Jeez." She lifted her head and smiled a little smile for a passer-by, a trill of fingers.

"Who was that?"

"Just a guy."

"What's he to you?"

"I don't remember."

The band whanged and the singer blared. *Down down down into a burnin ringa fire.* In not a long time Pierce found himself pressing the conversation again toward God, the Bible, the Four Last Things.

"Death. Judgment. Heaven and hell. That's what we were taught." He drank. "No Purgatory I guess for you."

"I was never sure just what that was."

"Well. At least *you'll* get a kick out of my damnation."

"What! Oh I would not! Even if."

"Of course you will. St. Thomas proved it. The contemplation of the torments of the damned is going to be one of the big pleasures of you people in heaven."

"God what a creepy horrible idea. What a Catholic idea."

He laughed, wolfishly, and told her no no, it was just logic; *now* we see as through a glass darkly, and maybe we feel pity for the suffering of the damned, because we can imagine it could be our own; poor slobs like us, suffering forever. *Forever.* But *then* we'll see it as the perfect expression of God's justice, left hand of His power as Mercy is the right, of which we ourselves, the saved, are the beneficiaries. One more thing about Him to praise.

"Dumb, Pierce," she said, looking around herself, the tabletop, the seat. "I don't know why you're insisting on this."

"Because you're sending me there. I'll be one of the ones down there that you know." He pushed toward her the cigarettes she was obviously seeking. "The big payback, Rose. No rejection more final."

"Oh for heaven's sake."

"Well," Pierce said. "It has to be so. If all the other stuff is. Doesn't it. Has to be. Right?"

Her lips parted as though she wanted to speak, and her eyes stopped flitting and looked at him. But she didn't speak.

"Come on, Rose," he said. "Remember. *Parhesia.* Openness, frankness."

She opened her mouth then, and as her face became still she spoke: a gout of language came from her, definite and clearly said but sounding like nothing he had ever heard before, invocation or curse or. Something not belonging to her but using her to be said. It was a second or two in length; entered the air, and was gone.

He stared at her in fear. "Rose."

"What," she said.

"You did it," he said.

"Did what."

"Spoke in tongues. You did it just then." A psychic block or lockout that was now installed in her brain or soul, put there by them, designed to kick in when she was questioned or tempted fiercely enough. He had heard of such things. His heart had begun to hammer. "You opened your mouth and said something meaningless."

"Well gee," she said, and laughed.

"No I mean this was. It was. You did it."

"I didn't. What do you think, that it's not under my conscious control?"

He didn't know. He couldn't say. He knew what he had heard and seen. "Well," he said. "Well what did you say then."

"It doesn't just take over and happen," she said. "It's not like that. It's not . . ."

*Magic,* he supposed her next word was to be, but she didn't say it.

"It's not easy," she said. "It's very, very hard. It's not like, Oh, I accept this stuff, I get the Spirit, and then it's all automatic. You have to work at it. Every day, every hour. And I do." She looked down, and seemed to think hard. She shook the ice in her Coke. "I do." She looked up at him, and a smile broke on her face. "Jeez, Pierce, cut it out. You look like you're going to, I don't know. Something."

"I," he said.

"Your chin is trembling."

"I," he said again; Rose's eyes then lifted to see something approaching behind him, and he spun in his chair to meet it, whatever it was. It was Rosie Rasmussen.

"Wanted you to know how it came out," she said. "Hi Rose."

"Yes," said Pierce. He pulled with his forefinger at the somehow strangulating collar of his shirt, realizing even as he did it that it was a gesture he'd seen a thousand trapped comic characters in movies make, what was wrong, what. "You guys know each other."

"Oh sure," Rosie said; she leaned with both hands on their table, and smiled a nice smile for Rose. "Sure."

"So," Pierce said, "how how . . ."

"Nothing," Rosie said. "No news. Nothing was revealed."

"Is that . . ."

"That's good, supposedly. I mean it's better than the worst, which would be to find a tumor or something. It turns out it's, probably it's—what's the word. The thing where it's got no cause. It sounds like 'idiotic.' "

"Idiopathic," said Rose.

"Right. So I guess that leaves possession."

Pierce looked toward Rose, as Rosie still did: Rose's face was unreadable. Once upon a time—God how much blood under the bridge since then, not even really that long ago—he had stood at night on the banks of the Blackbury River, and seen by moonlight dark Rose and carrot-top Rosie and a third woman, blond, come naked from the water, up onto an old dock, and take towels to dry themselves. And now he was here, and they were here too.

"I've been thinking, by the way," Pierce said to Rosie. "About your Halloween party."

"Yeah, sad huh."

"You wanted a reason for a masked ball, and spookiness. Ghosts."

"Well the place just seemed so perfect . . ."

"Yes. I was thinking that if you wanted those things, masks and ghosts, you could have a Christmas party just as well."

"Yes?"

"Sure. A long tradition of ghosts at Christmas. It's a ghostly time of year."

"Oh it's a ghostly time of year," Rosie sang, like a carol. "Really. Why?"

"Celtic ghosts," Pierce said, "appear at times and places that are somehow neither here nor there; not this, not that." He looked into his glass, astonished to find it already empty. "They appear at solstices, and at equinoxes, and on the nights when one of the two seasons of the Celtic year turns into the other—those are May-day night and Halloween night. But Christmas is the winter solstice; it's a solstice feast. It used to be you told ghost stories at Christmas. Still a tradition in England. Like Dickens."

"Dickens?"

"Ghosts of Christmas Past, Present and Future. A moment between Now and Then. A moment when you choose."

"Oh yes."

"So you could have solstice ghosts. And holly, for the old gods." He lifted his glass so that the waiter could see it, see his need. "And you could have costumes—mummers, masks, cross-dressing, all very popular at Christmas once; a Lord of Misrule, everything upside down. People could be Saracens, Knights, Doctors: at the solstice the Knight, the Sun, is slain by the Saracen, darkness, and then brought back to life by the Doctor. Born again." Rose was toying with her Coke, the smile on her face a leftover one, unremoved.

"Three kings," Rosie said.

"Right."

"Okay," Rosie said. "Christmas. Or near it. If it snows . . ."

"Big fires."

"Or cancel." She lifted Pierce's fresh drink and took a sip. "Costumes may run to the heavily furry."

"Good. It's a beast's night. On the solstice night, you know, you can hear the animals talking, and understand them."

"I thought that was because of the animals in the stable."

"Animals talked on the solstice-midnight long before there was a Christmas. Because of the blurring of the boundaries."

"Okay," Rosie said. "I'll do it if I can. It might not be the blowout I was hoping for. And I still wish it could have been Halloween. Less explaining to do." She looked down at Pierce, and paid him a grateful smile. "No offense," she said.

"No."

"Will you come?"

"Sure. Of course."

"Disguised as what?" she asked; then seemed to see that he was preoccupied, or unready to answer, or elsewhere; she patted his shoulder once and said "Anyway, good," and backed away, with a gesture in Rose's direction, a trill of fingers just like the trill Rose had made earlier.

Rose returned her look to Pierce. Why had it shut up again, her eyes wide open yet closed.

"Would you," he asked her, "go with me to that party? If it happens?"

"Sure," she answered. "Aw. That's so nice of you. If, though . . ."

"If?"

"No fine," she said. "Sure."

"Are you afraid of ghosts? You know one of the funny things about Christianity or Christian societies is how they hold that the dead can be in three different places at once—in their graves, in heaven or hell, and walking around as ghosts. A sort of—"

"Christians don't," she said. "I don't."

"No? The dead are only in heaven or hell?"

"No. The dead aren't alive now." She drew out a cigarette, and regarded it with a sort of fear, or reluctance; then lit it quickly. "Listen Pierce," she said. "Can we not talk about it? I guess I could explain, but it's like. Like telling my father where I've been all night. There's not really any way I'm going to, what's the word."

"Mollify," Pierce said. "Convince. Convert."

"No," she said. "Not any of those." She put her elbow in her hand, the cigarette pointed his way. "Can we go back now?"

"No no I want to get this straight," Pierce said. He threw more ice into a glass, and splashed whiskey in after it; he tasted acetone on his breath and his heart beat rapidly but he was not drunk or getting drunk, the liquor seemed to evaporate from him even as he drank it. He knew how hatefully he was behaving but not how to stop; there seemed to be something huge at stake that he couldn't name, something that needed to be fought for, his soul and safety threatened but not his alone; and yet the only way he could think to fight was with her. "So we die, okay, and we lie in our graves and rot. And after a long time—nobody knows how long—the end of the world comes . . ."

"Well not the end. I mean it doesn't disappear."

"Anyway then, at that time, we all get up out of our graves alive, alive-oh. Like do we fight our way out? Or do we just find ourselves standing there somehow?" He had never felt as intensely before how much this was a story for the night, a horror story; never noticed before how, when he thought of it, he pictured it in fact taking place at night: the grave, the dead.

"Well I don't know."

"Okay," Pierce said, ashamed. "Anyway. It doesn't matter. What Jesus actually *said,* of course, which of course has to be the case, right, is that this end of the world was just about to happen as he spoke. That some of those who were alive and listening to him would live to see it."

"I'm alive," she said. "I'm listening."

"And what," he said, "happened to the intervening two thousand years?"

She said nothing, facing him as though answering, but not answering.

"What, it just stopped being true for a long time, a very long time, even though a lot of people went on believing it with no results, and now for some reason or no reason it's true again, for the people alive now?"

"Maybe," she said. Embattled but not fleeing, trying for his sake (for his sake, he could see it, and a cold pit opened in his breast) to make it reasonable to him. "Maybe that's so. I don't care. I don't care if it wasn't true, or *when* it wasn't true, I only know it's true now for me. Ray says we shouldn't worry about how it's all going to end, but that *right now* the Kingdom is close to us."

Ray? "So maybe it'll go away again," he said. "Good. Sure. Maybe it comes and goes."

"Well isn't your book the same?" she said. She gestured toward the dining room, where his messy typescript and notes were piled. And Kraft's book too, still waiting to be duplicated. "Doesn't it say that things that were true once aren't true at other times?"

Pierce saw where his argument had led him, where he could not help but follow. "Well," he said. "Sure. That's the theory. I mean it's not exactly *asserted.* It's a way of looking at things. A metaphor."

"You mean you don't think it's true?"

"Oh I do," he said. An awful hilarity worse than dread threatened him, a sinking balloonist who has already emptied all his sandbags, and now tosses out the lap robe and lunch basket as well, the champagne, the compass and altimeter. "I do think it's true."

"You do?"

"Yes. It is true. Sure it is. *In there* it is." And he pointed, as she had, to the pile of his pages.


It was late when at last, still restless and flushed, ashtrays full and dishes unwashed, they pulled the covers over themselves and doused the light; for a while longer they still whispered and joked, too pointedly, trying to release one another from the throes of their contention, or of his with her.

But then she was still; she threw her arm over him, and he knew that she was asleep, and was glad; he tried to remove her arm without waking her but it returned. He lay alert listening to his brain run, not all the drink he had had was able to extinguish it, until at a certain moment his thoughts turned to nonsense and he passed over too; only aware he had done so when he woke again with a start.

It was as far from day as could be, yesterday entirely gone but no hint yet of dawn. The silence was so thick he thought it must itself have been what awakened him. So deep. He became aware of a sound that had been there before but now was not, that had ceased or absconded. He knew it was bad news even before he realized what it was.

Water had ceased to flow through the overflow pipe in the basement. He hadn't heard this sound or silence before but knew this was what it was.

He threw aside his covers and searched in the darkness for his big robe, stumbling over his shoes and hers; went to the staircase to the basement, switched on its one baleful light (an ancient round switch you turned clockwise rather than threw up or down, there had been one in the basement of Sam's house in Kentucky) and went nearly falling down the stairs.

Yes stopped. Why. The little pump stood mumchance. He grasped the overflow pipe where it left the pump heading for the window, as though to take its fading pulse. He had to open the valve, this one, no this one.

"What's up?"

He could glimpse her at the top of the stairs, in his overcoat.

"Stopped," he said. "It'll freeze. Maybe it already has."

He turned the valve all the way one way, all the way the other; it turned only a single full turn in either direction, and neither had any effect. "If it was on too strong it emptied the cistern. If it wasn't on enough, the water froze in the line. I don't know which way to turn it."

"Rightie tightie, leftie loosie," she said.

"Nothing happens either way. Oh Christ."

He mounted the stairs, walking up inside his robe as he had used to do inside his cassock as an altar boy, and fell headlong; pulled his feet free and went up hand and foot to the top. Searched for his galoshes by the kitchen door, not there, by the front door; pulled them on over his bare feet.

"I can't tell what's wrong. Nothing should be wrong."

"How about a flashlight?"

"Yes. Right."

He found one on the floor of the front closet, depressed its button, amazed to see its little beam.

"I'll be back in a minute."

The night was shocking, the sky clear and the air dry and very cold; his first breath of it burned his throat. With some difficulty—the flashlight dimmed and brightened irregularly, as though still half-asleep—he found the black pipe and began following it up the hill toward the woods and the wellhouse. The big robe flapped around his booted feet. He realized that the nameless dread, unshakable lately, that had seemed to forewarn or announce some disaster, really had, and this was it. Up, past the shrouded swimming pool, into the woods beneath the black bulk of the house, four lamps lit now in four windows (set on timers, factitious residents who turned them on at twilight and off at dawn). No starlight there to give general shape to the scene, only the flashlight's beam picking out a startled rock face or bush at every glance. He lost the pipe, found it again; he came at last, very abruptly, on the wellhouse.

The little hut or pergola, its broad heavy-shingled roof; the big stones of its half wall. Pierce put his head in; his light's beam showed a pool deep down. A pebble that his hand brushed from the well's lip fell far before striking it with a wet clang. He saw the ripples.

So it wasn't empty. Or it had been emptied but was now filling again, since the pipe was now clogged with ice. But was it that cold? Yes it seemed to be. Cold enough to freeze flowing water in a two-inch pipe? How did he know? He looked, hopelessly, pointlessly, at the phosphorescent dial of his wristwatch, which only told him how long it was till day.

Anyway stuck. Somehow he had failed, or the task had been impossible. He had failed even before he began, no space of time even to be tested, to watch and ward; first hard freeze of the year, and bang.

He turned to go back, unable to think of anything he might do here. He could see, when he came out of the woods, the little house that was his, where all the lights were lit; the door open too, and she standing in it, looking and waiting.

# 10

When day came it was as cloudless as the night had been, and cold; but the sun's heat, absorbed by the black plastic of the pipe, melted the ice that had indeed built up in one or two low-lying bends like plaque in old arteries. By afternoon Pierce's water was flowing again.

False alarm, false alarm, he said to himself, not once but many times that day. What would happen though when the sun moved farther to the south, hurried across the sky weak and old and unable to do that work? He called the plumber the Winterhalters had listed on their card of emergency numbers and had a brief and unsatisfactory consultation with someone. When it snows the pipe'll be well insulated. Yes and what if it doesn't snow? It hadn't rained. Hey, the voice told him, no guarantees: sounding to Pierce's ears as though it knew this from sad experience.

Later he called Rose in Conurbana to tell her. She had left early, without her coffee, without a bath, her hair wild and undone; had hurried away, it seemed to him.

"False alarm," he said.

"Sure."

"Rose," he said. "Those things I said, when you were here. About, well, God and. I hope you don't, I mean I hope . . ."

"Pierce. Listen. I have to run. There's so much to do."

"Sure."

A silence.

"I'm writing you a letter," she said. "Bye."

That night and the next he lay awake, as he had been lately doing, but now listening to the whisper of the overflow pipe, purring steadily. Or was it slackening? He would think so, would get up and fall downstairs to ponder; turn it up, or down, once turning it entirely off thinking he had turned it fully on. Rightie tightie leftie loosie. What was he doing here, he of all people.

It wasn't just the water. He was failing in other responsibilities too, he could feel it though he could not remember or name them; when he stood in the basement staring at the pump squatting mumchance on its concrete blocks he could hear or perceive things weakening around him, and in danger of failing.

Rose's letter came. He pulled it from his box at the Littleville post office (about all of official Littleville there was) along with a card from his mother in Florida, nearer to his birthday than she usually hit it, with a check inside, for twenty-five dollars. It too made him somehow afraid, caused him to think of things unattended to. He was to be thirty-six.

He pulled off one glove as he walked back along the blacktop to the Winterhalter estate and clamped it in his armpit so he could rip off the end of Rose's envelope. He blew into its ragged mouth and teased the letter out. Her peacock-green ink.

*Hi,* she began; she told him she had got home okay and was glad his water flowed, she'd known it would be okay. She said she had been thinking a lot, *nonstop* she said, since she'd got back, and wanted to say so much that she hadn't been able to say. *When you were sort of ranting at me,* she said. *It makes it hard for me to think.* He found then that he couldn't both read it and walk, and he slid it back into its envelope and went on to his road, through the gates, to his house, listening to his heart. Then while he puttered in the kitchen he let the letter lie on his table. Until he could no longer, and took it out and scanned it quickly.

*I don't know all the things you want me to know, even though I know and believe that I will know them someday. I don't understand a lot of things that I do know. The end of the world or whatever. I haven't studied it and you have in your way but what I don't see is what all your understanding gets you. What does it get you? Maybe it's not the point, Pierce. I know the stars can't fall down on the earth and the sky can't burn up but maybe that's not the point. I had a dream last night about death. I dreamed I was on a train a long train going somewhere, a train I had chosen to be on, and my father whose alive and my mother whose dead were on it and my mother was in a carriage for the dead in her coffin, with all the other dead people, and there was a coffin for me in there too, and what I knew was that we were* all headed for the same place together *and I didn't feel any sadness or fear, I felt like wherever it was headed it carried us all. Isn't there a song. And I don't know where it is, or what it means that the stars will refuse to shine, or that we'll be taken up into the middle of the air, but maybe there's more than one kind of knowing. I do know this: that it's not for everybody, and when it does come and it's all over and the earth is done for and the rest of us have been taken away wherever it is we go, the jews will be left and I guess will suffer here terribly. And I wouldn't envy anybody who does not have what we have and which of course I want for everybody, which does not mean I wish hell or damnation on you, Pierce, and what do you care anyway if you don't believe it?*

Pierce holding the little pages felt the world stop, and darken; he knew that a mask had slipped, and that he had glimpsed something unspeakable, without knowing what it was. What.

*the jews will be left and I guess will suffer here terribly*

O Christ, he said. O Jesus. *Suffer terribly*. Oh no.

What had they told her in order to cause her to write or believe such a thing, what obscene lies. Who was she, that she could contemplate such a thing with equanimity, he obviously hadn't known her at all or she wasn't any longer herself, they had hollowed her and refilled her with this, and now she had passed it to him like a contagion, only she slept and knew nothing, and he alone knew what it was.

And how could he ever talk to her again?

He would have to get away from her. Right away. How? How do you get away from women, what do you tell them? He had never done it. He was shivering violently. Why was there a kitchen knife in his hand? How had he got outside on the lawn in the cold? He lifted her letter again before his eyes, no it was not her letter in his hand but a slice of bread. He turned back to the house and to the lunch he had been making but ceased to make it, poured himself a drink instead but left it on the counter untouched.

*Suffer terribly*. It was just like them, Christians, always their way, to transfer their own endless spleen and self-regard to the Maker and Sustainer of the universe; to make the settling of their imaginary scores (settled in their favor a thousand times over already, never enough though) the very last thing the Infinite is to concern itself with in this world—hurting, whacking, flaying, causing pain. Your enemies your footstool. Maybe gather them all behind barbed wire, sure make them wear gray pajamas and starve them to skeletons, make them *know who's boss* or whom the Boss has covered with his favor. Try to say you wouldn't delight in it, just try to tell me you wouldn't.

You. Not *she* surely though, not she but they; she could be forgiven, dumb bunny, surely she could. But *we, us,* was what she had begun to say lately, after so carefully avoiding those pronouns when talking to him about the Power-house.

We. Us. He had to call her, tell her. No he couldn't do that, could not bear the sound of her voice, her small hello, the pause then into which he must put what must be said.

A letter. He'd write her one back. He sat at his desk and rolled paper into his typewriter, thinking of things. There was a right way to say this, a smart way, a way that would not drive her deeper in, that would show her that he knew whereof he spoke and that he loved her. Respected her or at least understood or. The machine impelled forward the ball on which all the letters and punctuation marks were incised, it struck and spun and struck as though banging its little head in rage. An Alphaball, a Selectraglobe: it had a name. In a few hours' time he had written several pages that were not smart, not understanding, or were too much so; had torn them up, and written more. After an impatient search he found a stamp and an envelope large enough; he copied her Conurbana address onto it with a species of revulsion he thought he had never experienced before, not even able to name its object. What was being done to her there in that city. Then he walked again to the post office, its window closed already but the big letter box out front still uncollected. As soon as he dropped his letter into the box's maw he felt a nauseating certainty that he had done exactly the wrong thing, and would have to wait here until the long red white and blue truck came to collect, and beg for its return. After a time this passed, and he walked home again.

He returned to his desk. It was, he thought, remarkably dark for the hour, the year had grown so late, was that it? On the desktop and on the floor around him were the torn members of the drafts of his letter; he could read words and phrases, like overheard bits of a distant furious argument or tirade. *wicked lies you have accepted   if you didn't mean that what   could not love someone who   you can't tell me   it's true what Gibbon said, that Christians   I know very well   bigoted cruel   can't you see* Meanwhile the letter he had mailed lay in the dark waiting to be collected, right on top of a Dear John letter from a Littleville woman who had just left her husband for a preacher. No one would ever know of the coincidence.

It was in this week that Pierce began noticing distinctly the two special symptoms of his condition (he wouldn't have named them thus then, but that's what they were). One was the tap tap tapping of his invaded or infected heart, a *tachycardia* without any physical or physiological cause (he would eventually take himself to a physician, found in the phone book, who dismissed his fears). And the other was this image, or sensation, an inescapable feeling amounting almost to an assumption, that the world had become terribly small, that just above his head, not much higher than the tops of the Faraway Hills, a field of black clouds continually roiled and seethed, oppressing the land; and that just above *them,* pillowed on them, was the awful God of her so-called religion, the Lord God Jehovah and his interfering hosts. He actually caught himself looking up, not infrequently either, at the empty sky. It was not that he thought they were there; he just could not help but now and then look up. In the fat New York Sunday paper which he went to the Jambs every week to get, holdover from his city days, he read a schizophrenic's memoirs: how for years, though she was well aware that she lived in a city apartment and then in a clinic, though she knew that she walked its streets and climbed its stairs, at the same time she had also known—had *known*—that she was crossing the Arctic on an endless voyage: because the world was that cold, that empty, the wind that incessant, the struggle that hard.

And O my God look at this.

In the local New York news a small story about the city college Pierce had formerly taught at, back in what today seemed to him a long-out-of-print volume of his life. The place had been taken over by an evangelical group called The Gospel Speaks. From now on it would be offering courses in Bible Languages, Ethics and Morals for Today, Archæology (!) and Earth Science (!!) "in addition," the article said, "to a full complement of college-level course work," including a new predental course.

Pierce rose out of his chair, the masses of the Business and Sports sections slipping from his lap to the floor.

Barnabas College. It had been a hardworking little place whose entrance requirements were low and study load high when Pierce first came to teach there, then became a rainbow-hued caravanserai at which the wandering young paused, to study astrology, new journalism, Eastern religious traditions, and ecology (Earth Science), and to get credit for courses of their own devising. It had then turned again, this time into a back-to-basics outfit, repainted in putty and white, about the time Pierce jumped ship, or was pitched overboard. Now look. The new Christian management declared that as soon as they took possession there would be a rededication of the school, staff and students to Our Lord and Master Jesus Christ. Secular Humanism could be studied in plenty of places, but here it would be deemphasized. There was to be a dress code, said Dean of Students Earl Sacrobosco—a recent convert to the Gospel group—and loving but watchful supervision of the students. "It's a new age," he was quoted as declaring. "All that stuff is coming back."

Earl. If Earl Sacrobosco had gone over to them it was evident that they had, for the moment anyway and maybe for the indefinite future, the whip hand. Pierce could divine clearly the Barnabas gym, an evil-smelling place he had always avoided, now full of students in skirts and ties, a new cross over the stage. There was nowhere to run that way.

The one thing he could not have conceived, would not have believed if he had heard it predicted: that bigoted religion and willed ignorance would return in strength, and not even in new and outlandishly intriguing forms, just the same old wine, the same old bottles, people believing impossible things in the manner of athletes inuring themselves to pain or soldiers to bloodshed. And for what gain, what power or delight.

Power. That was it. Everywhere, everywhere the strong were riding roughshod over delicate subjectivity, everywhere the toadies and the timeservers were paying back those who had thought themselves their betters; the powerless were gaining a share in power by joining the haters and the hunters. This Ayatollah in Iran. Sun Moon and his zombie herds marrying one another at his command. And Dr. R. O. Walter, whom Pierce had never seen and would never see but who was vividly present to him anyway—the jug-eared head, the potato nose on which his glasses, bound in pink plastic, balanced; the Midwestern caw, the brutal certainties, the little loud jokes. His nasty cult, nothing at all really—unless (no it couldn't be, to think so was to surrender to them somehow) it was allied with those others, at a deep underground level, despite their superficial differences and (phony) mutual hatreds.

War in Heaven. *A war of all against all; if you are not of one party they will make you of another.*

No. No.

He sat again. He dropped the paper, unable to turn further pages. He laid his hands along the rough warm arms of his chair, the same napless wine-colored velveteen armchair that years before he had rescued from a New York street and repaired, the same in which he had sailed away to surprising climes once upon a time, his oldest friend now, it and its motherly clasp unchanged at least. The light in his house moved steadily from east to west; the rhomboids of sun that fell on and were broken by the furniture on one side were steadily withdrawn, after a time reappearing to creep similarly over the stuff on the other side as Pierce watched unseeing.

# 11

Thick clouds moved low over the river and the hill, a clammy still day, and Pierce approaching his house across the stirred leaf-littered field noticed that his front door was standing slightly ajar.

A weird dread passed through him at this, though he knew well enough that this door often refused to shut firmly behind him when he left the house, another small flaw in his rental. He stepped up the single step and with his fingertips pushed open the door fully.

What the hell. He *had* been intruded on. Four no five guys sat around his dining table, calmly expectant, having taken seats there obviously to await him. Pierce, intimating that something large and perhaps dangerous was afoot, didn't demand an explanation or order them out in a dudgeon. He greeted them, cautiously. "And you are?"

But he had already begun to guess. Rose.

Yes, they said. Rose Ryder. She had been quite upset by Pierce's words and his letter, one of his guests declared, placing a hand slowly on Pierce's table as though there were a weapon in it, though there wasn't. She had been hurt, hurt and weeping even. And he raised his eyebrows at Pierce.

Stabbed and shaken, how could he have. He could see her with vivid immediacy, as though she were here or as though he were there: in tears, confused, *upset* and perhaps doubting. But he only replied coolly or coldly that he was very sorry to hear this, it was regrettable and he did regret it, but he had had reason to be hurt and alarmed himself. Well that was really not sufficient, they cut off Pierce's explanation and by their demeanor suggested that there ought to be some retribution for an attack like that on someone's faith. Pierce replied that of course he had not meant, but of course he had. And he could see in their direct but uninquisitive gazes that they were not to be mollified, did not feel it necessary to give him arguments or listen to his.

They were actually an unprepossessing, even somewhat scruffy bunch. Not the pink-cheeked Bible robots that Rosie Rasmussen described but more deeply anonymous than that, he would not remember later the color of a single piece of clothing any of them wore or any other mark of distinction, except a pair of rimless glasses and hair unexpectedly shoulder-length on one. Pierce assumed they would beat him or worse. One began talking in a prefatory sort of way about how little, how little Pierce knew, who thought he knew everything; and Pierce was thinking how to reply (it wasn't *he* who knew everything, he was quite sure he did not; knowing everything was not *his* claim) when the door between the dining room and the kitchen, which stood open, whipped shut untouched with a startling bang.

Bang.

They continued to stare at him, not triumphant or satisfied but clearly done with their lesson: and Pierce felt a cold terror.

Good Lord they can do what they say. What Rose implied they could. They all together had moved his thick real wooden door by mental or some other force and slammed it shut. He hoped for an instant it might be some dumb trick but knew absolutely that it was not, they had done it. They had done it to show Pierce that they could do it, and that they could do much more and worse too. And he could see that *they* could see in his face the panic of an utter defeat. They (their faces said) were able to do such things because they were allied to and in the service of the ultimate power at the core of reality, which Pierce had denied, and did he deny it now? Did he see? Pierce opened his mouth but he could not say what he saw. Well? Had he thought that all this was some kind of joke?

He knew it was not a joke; he knew, all in a moment, even as he pondered some hopeless evasion or apology that would save him from them, that they could exercise this power because they had given up everything else to have it, and if he joined them and subjected himself to them he could have it too: what he would have to do was to merge his soul or mind with theirs (he felt a piercing loathing) just as *she* was doing or had already done (an even sharper loathing). And if he wouldn't share in that power, the only power, he would have none and it would be used against him, defeat upon defeat, until his pride was erased entirely and his selfhood scrubbed away, which is what they wanted if they wanted anything at all from him.

That's what he saw: that was the lesson they had come to teach, and had taught in the instant of his dining room door's slamming shut. He would not escape, for there was nowhere to escape *to*.

But he was sure as hell going to get as far from them as he could. He turned and walked away (this part was hard to remember later) walked away fast across his lawn knowing they would not pursue, that they felt no need to pursue, were ultimately unconcerned with him and his like; he glanced back to see them now at play in his landlord's fields, tossing from one to another a slab of shaped and lettered stone, as lightly as though it were a length of board, and the dumb obvious symbolism struck him. O Grave, where is thy victory. Just then he came out to the boulevard that would, he knew, lead him back to the city, whose dim towers could be made out rising over the trees far off; he immediately saw, and hailed, a big yellow taxi with a stripe of black-and-white checks along its flank. He climbed into the leather-odorous darkness, he pulled shut the door; he called out *Manhattan,* and woke.

Night and silence. He was alone. They were not here, he wasn't there. The dream-film unrolled into his consciousness backwards, from the taxi to the beginning, which was only the end of something earlier, unremembered.

He thought: I don't even *have* a dining table. The big room and big door of his dream were an archway and a small room, where there was only a desk and bookcases, where his papers and Kraft's novel were piled. He could see into that room dimly when, just to be sure, he raised his head. *In there it's true.* Oh good Lord.

From in there as he lay came a sudden summons, the phone ringing harshly, Pierce could not imagine who and wasn't sure he wanted to respond.

"Hello."

"Oh Pierce, thank God."

"Hello, Axel." Only his father. Pierce sat, and breathed again. Axel Moffett at least was changeless: in trouble as usual, it sounded like; at sixes and sevens; buffeted by life, and at sea. As usual. As usual he seemed to be calling from a bar. It was past midnight.

"Pierce, Gravely is dead."

"Oh Axel. Oh I'm so sorry."

"He died in my arms."

There was a long wet silence filled with the far-off sounds of talk and laughter. Gravely was the super of the building in Brooklyn which Axel owned and lived in; though it always took him a long time, there was nothing Gravely could not fix, or fix up. He was far older than Axel, and Pierce knew that Axel had nursed him through some bad stretches lately, illnesses he gave names like grippe and bad blood to; and that while he languished the building had declined.

"I went to his funeral," Axel said when he recovered. "Today. Oh it was so touching. Pierce mine was the only white face in a sea of black. Very, very simple people, Pierce, most of them quite elderly, a kind of Negro I remember in New York long ago. So different from these, these hunted animals you see now."

"I think I know."

"Well they were very kind to *me.* A stranger among them."

"Uh-huh."

"He had no family, you see—none but this huge congregation. They sang. It was impossible not to weep; you expected any moment a band of woolly-headed angels would descend to carry him home to hebbin." He was laughing, a liquid snuffle. "Oh I sobbed."

"Huh."

"I thought of Blake," Axel said. " 'For I am black, but Oh my soul is white.' "

"Oh for heaven's sake, Axel. Really." He found he was leaning on Kraft's manuscript, his palm pressing down on the first page. He stared at it, yellow paper friable and edge-darkening already. He had the momentary impulse to start a fire with it, burn it like infected bedclothes, it seemed to him the source of his troubles somehow though whatever precisely his troubles were.

"Well faith like that," Axel said, "is a wonderful thing. Isn't it."

"Is it?"

"We can't live in doubts continuously," Axel said. "Even Einstein."

"You still going to Mass?" Pierce asked.

"Not every week. Of course not." Axel sipped from his funeral libation and swallowed gratefully. "Do you know the story of the Methodist minister and James Joyce?"

"Yes."

"He asked Joyce if now that he had ceased to be a Catholic he wouldn't perhaps consider Methodism."

"I know the story."

" 'Sir, I have lost my faith but I have not lost my mind.' " Axel could hardly say it for laughing. "Lost my faith but *not* lost my mind."

"Axel, listen. I'm standing here stark naked. The stove's gone out and it's cold as hell."

"Naked?"

"I was asleep. I've really got to go."

"Naked! Naked came I, and naked will I go hither. Naked. Oh dear." His voice had grown wet again. "Naked came I from my mother's womb. The Lord giveth and the Lord taketh away. Oh Lord Pierce what will I do."

It was a while before Axel could relinquish the connection; Pierce listened to the far-off city where once he too had lived and walked with his father, his mad father. Though he could still hear both clearly enough, and said *Huh* and *Really* now and then, he felt them move away from him, too far away already to help him, or to hide him.


"Love and death," said Val to Rosie Rasmussen. "That's how I always think of it."

Rosie and Val sat together in the big central courtyard of Butterman's. They were both wrapped up against the raw cold, and Rosie had a thermos of tea. Val had Rosie's natal chart in her hands, the chart she herself had drawn and explicated for Rosie. Sun in Pisces, a sign nobody particularly wanted, it seemed: a bigotry that Val noticed was widespread, and that she sort of shared even as she tried to combat it. Love and Death was how she named the impulse which it gave to the soul, even though she knew well enough it entailed more than that, far more actually than a commonsensical Virgo like herself could see into. The ends of things, that contained their beginnings. The dark waters.

"Love and death," said Rosie. "That's a little heavy."

"Well it's just the way I characterize it. I mean Judas is supposed to be a Pisces. Chopin was a Pisces. You know?"

"Ha," said Rosie. "Judas."

"But Love," Val said. "It's a big word. And Death too. They can mean lots of things. Sometimes Death isn't death."

"Sometimes," Rosie said, "love isn't Love. So tell me more."

Rosie's ball had been announced, and her court case scheduled, and so she had consulted Val. She was also buying the liquor for her party through Val, cases of bottles with names she'd never heard of but that Val said were perfectly all right. Around them, young people whom the caterer had hired (the same kids, Rosie thought, who had come to Arcady in July, to set up and serve Boney's funeral reception) carried tables and set up lights, laughing and teasing. Sam ran among them, studying them and in them her own future. Rosie had wanted flags to fly from the towers, but they couldn't be seen at night, and so she had at last rented a generator, being set up now out in a shed on the island's back side by the same old river rat who had first ferried them over here; and as long as there was light there might as well be heat, and the marina's pleasure-boat had brought over some fridge-sized blowers, and altogether her do was becoming less the spooky nocturne she had at first imagined and more like a Hollywood movie. On her invitations (which she had pondered long) she had added a line at the bottom: *Come as you aren't.*

"Well. I don't like this month," Val said.

"It's so cold and dreary," Rosie said. "Death for sure."

"I meant for you. I don't like the sky for you this coming month."

"Great," said Rosie.

"It just means you should be careful," Val said. "That's why I'm telling you."

"So why don't you like this month for me?"

"Well. Mars is going to be in Taurus," Val said. "For one thing. That's Mike's sign."

"Is that bad?"

"Not for him." She uncapped the thermos.

"Well if you just say I'm supposed to be careful," Rosie said. "I mean I always wonder what people think they communicate by saying that. Be careful."

"Aren't you afraid?"

"Of Mike?"

"Of all of them."

"No." Sam had come back to where they sat, and took the thermos from Val to inhale the hot fumes, closing her eyes in pleasure. "No I am not afraid. I have to do this and I will do it."

"I'd be sick. Just sick."

"Allan said the original agreement was a good one and there were no valid arguments he could see for changing it. Unless there was something he didn't know." She thought of Spofford. You were supposed to be chaste as a single mom, or at least very discreet. She's a whore, your honor, and unfit to be a mother. More than once, Sam had slept in the bed with her and Spofford; once while Sam slept he and she had even, oh well oh well.

"You talked to Allan?"

Rosie nodded. She had called him, and after a cool question or two had begun to panic, and though she wouldn't retract her decision to do this all by herself she asked him to explain some things, and he answered unwillingly—he told her that a little knowledge is a dangerous thing, did she know that one? Did she know what they say, that a person who acts as her own lawyer has a fool for a client?

Send me a bill, Allan, she said, and hung up.

"He said they might have a lot of money. He said he couldn't really predict what they might do."

"That group?" Val said.

"The Powerhouse. Mike's new thing."

"God they're everywhere." Val raised her eyes to the towers and battlements of Butterman's that rose around them. "How can you think of giving this up? It is *so*. I don't know what. Amazing."

"Yeah? You should see the taxes."

"Well if this place were mine," Val said fervently, "I'd never give it up. I couldn't. I'd come here and live."

Rosie said nothing in reply. For there was a sense in which it *was* Val's, at least as much as it was Rosie's, if what Val believed was true: that she was Boney Rasmussen's bastard daughter, conceived when Mama had been not only Boney's lover but the madam of a part-time semipro whorehouse centered on the place now called Mama's Faraway Lodge, at whose bar Val stood nightly.

Boney had never publicly acknowledged Val, though he had always supported her in small ways (so Mama had finally told her daughter). On the last night of his life, July Fourth this year, Val went to his house to demand that he recognize her before he died: to ask him why, or to judge him or forgive him. In the end she did none of those things, too late, it was evident to her that he had already got away though he had not quite passed over. She only sat with him and watched and waited. And in the dark of the morning, while he slept or faded, she had told her story to Rosie.

Her father. So unlikely had the story seemed to Rosie, and yet so circumstantial was it, lying alongside Rosie's former and familiar world and the familiar persons she had known, that it required a choice, this world or that one. And now she was unsure what her obligations were to Val, or if she even had any, her sort-of cousin or aunt. Impossible to know Boney's intentions because he'd left no will. Val believed that was because of her, Val's, unadmitted existence; Rosie thought it wasn't Val but death itself that could not be admitted or named. The Curse of the Rasmussens.

Val glanced at Rosie sidelong. "You know," she said. "You're really pretty tough."

"Oh sure."

"You are. You might actually make a good boss of that thing. The Foundation. A Pisces with your planets. If you wanted to do it."

"I don't."

"Then who will?"

"Una Knox," said Rosie.

Una Knox, whom Boney had preferred to all his living kin, was a lot less likely a story even than the story of Mama and Val's paternity. Val knew that one;

Rosie had told her about Una Knox, trying to identify her. That night he died, Val asked him herself: *Who is Una Knox?* He had not answered.

And yet it was only Val, or Rosie, who could free Boney from her thrall, if he were ever to be freed, which on that night was not certain. Yes, Val and Rosie: Val, the daughter he was unwilling to own up to, whose forgiveness he had not accepted; and Rosie, on whom he had laid an impossible and unrefusable task, heavy as a spell. Neither one of them knew that the duty or privilege of freeing their dead ancestor was theirs; nor did they know how to accomplish it. If they had known, they might have chosen not to do it.

We act on earth as best we can, and do what it seems we must or ought to do; and by so doing we sometimes bring about redemptions—and defeats—that we never know of, in spheres we cannot perceive. It's only because of the rebounding geometries of the rays, the ceaseless rays whose intersections link the lives of all the worlds. Maybe those who are freed or foiled by our actions know what we've done, but most of the time we here do not; it's only a few of us who ever guess it's possible at all, and soon enough it no longer is.

# 12

At evening Rose called Pierce from the Sandbox: called before coming (she said) to make sure that he was home; had stopped there (she didn't say, but he would guess) to get courage; he heard dimly the sounds of Happy Hour proceeding in the background, as he had heard them in whatever bar it was that Axel had called him from. She asked if it was okay to visit. Of course it was okay. So once again she came to the little house by the river; Pierce came out, a drink of his own in hand, and they stood together in the night.

"Your car's fixed," he said in some surprise. It lay up on the rise beyond the bungalow, canted slightly in the grass as though grazing there beside his own Steed.

"Yes. For a while now. It was fixed the last time I was here, Pierce."

"Not possible. I would have noticed."

"Well I would have thought so, but."

"I thought it couldn't be fixed."

She shrugged, smiled. "Can I come in?"

"Actually," he said, "I was going up to the Winterhalters'. I promised that once a week or so I'd check things out. I haven't yet." He drank. "You can come."

"Oooh."

He put down his drink on the seat of a backless chair that had always stood on his porch; he shook the keys in his pocket to be sure he had them. Then they proceeded up the long rise past the cars toward the house.

"The return to the chateau," Pierce said. It was a French Renaissance house in a 1920s stucco version, cheerful by day, not at night. He took her hand. He remembered how in Kentucky once—in the year he started a forest fire by mistake—he had dreamed that he and his whole family had died and been consigned to Purgatory, which was a burnt-over hillside where they all walked warily together, wondering from which direction the punishments would come.

"That was a kind of mean letter you wrote," she said. "I mean it started out nice. But it didn't end very nice."

They passed by the black oblong of the pool and its fittings; there the path to the house began.

"You know," she said, "one of the hardest parts of this for me, doing this, was what you'd think of it. How you'd react."

He said nothing.

"Like when you said, 'If God walks into your life you can just walk right out of mine.' That made it hard."

He didn't remember or believe that he had said this. Maybe he had. He marvelled at his tough-mindedness.

"You know what I think, Moffett? I think you are getting so angry at this not because of me or religion or the Powerhouse but for another reason."

He waited to hear what this was, or if she would say, or leave it to him to guess it: for he thought it likely, thought it certain even, that there was another reason, and he didn't know what it was.

"I think," she said, "that you wanted to break up, you were tired of this or whatever, and just needed a good excuse; and so now you can tell all your smart friends, Oh Rose joined some freaky Christian cult so of course I had to drop her."

So bizarrely wrong was this that a sort of warning light installed deep in Pierce's consciousness lit up: something has been woefully or hilariously misunderstood, by me or another, and if by another then probably also by me. Then it went out, and Pierce's awareness defaulted to the sensations that her hand and her voice had started in him, a boiling or seething of the blood, fight or flight.

"No," he said, "no. No no. That's untrue. Completely untrue."

"Well."

"What smart friends? What smart friends do I have that I need to tell these stories to?"

She withdrew her hand, and closed her arms around herself. They crossed the wide flagged veranda, past the French windows, around the groups of globular shrubs clipped in cock-and-balls shapes, to the little kitchen door to which he had the key; he let them in.

"Mice," she said. They stood a while and listened to the small sounds, which might be field mice who had retreated to the abandoned interior from the cold fields; maybe rats. Or the wind too. The kitchen was a big old-fashioned one, a long scarred table down the middle over which hung sinister utensils on an iron rack. Rose took Pierce's arm as they walked on through.

"What are you supposed to do?"

"Just look out for things. I could actually move in if I wanted to. No one the wiser."

"Really?"

"I could."

The big rooms reminded Pierce of Arcady, or even of Kraft's house, the same air of aged-bachelor neglect, of having been last decorated and furnished some years ago and then ignored. He had never seen Mrs. Winterhalter. Maybe she was gaga, or an invalid.

"A piano," Rose said.

It was a baby grand, neat oxymoron; glossy black, closed, used mostly maybe to hold photographs in silver frames. Rose sat on the bench, and lifted the cover.

"You play?"

She began tentatively, softly, putting forth notes like suggestions and withdrawing the wrong ones. Sheep may safely graze. She grew more confident. Her downcast black-lashed eyes and the fall of her hair, one leg tucked beneath her, foot shod in a girlish loafer; her concentration, the simple compassion of the music, made more so by her errors: he began to tremble. Bach was a Christian. Believed in eternal damnation, feared it no doubt, knew that Jews and the unbaptized were in for it; didn't really think much about it, though, maybe, the tremendous numbers of them, the billions, not weighing with him (this must be common) against God's goodness to *him* and his flock of children, and why maybe should they? Why did he, Pierce, seem to himself to have come upon a shocking secret about Bach and all Bach's fellow churchgoers, weren't the permanent human facts of fear and gladness, of being lost and found, all that were really being expressed here, all that mattered, since after all no souls were really being tormented anywhere anyway?

"When I was a kid I took lessons from the organist of our church," Rose said. "A lot of us did. It was I guess our way of supporting her. She was a funny woman. I mostly learned hymns. Bach."

"Handy," Pierce said, "I guess, now."

"Oh we don't have Bach," she said. She laced her fingers together and like a virtuoso cracked her knuckles. "He wasn't a Christian, so."

"Bach not a Christian? *Bach?*"

"Well according to them. We have our own stuff. Modern. Actually it's sort of poor, frankly. I could do without it." She smiled, as though amused by this, by *them,* and Pierce logged this, her first animadversion. She played again: *Wachen auf.* Pierce thought: I believe in the resurrection of the dead, the awakening of those who sleep, I do, but only before the grave, not after it; after it all hopes are cancelled, all fears too. Rose thought: Why did I once come here, by the river, I once did but why; why do I know I have heard this music here before, from this piano? Why did I sleep then, was it just so I could wake? Am I really, really awake at last?


The rest of the house was like the main rooms, fully furnished without intimacy; they walked through it cautiously and talked of what could or might be done in these rooms, in these two broad beds in separate bedchambers. Last they came to the library or study, turned on a single green-glass-shaded lamp, and both noticed at once a peculiarity. The walls and their moldings and panels and coves, the ceiling too, were black.

"Black," she said. "What for?"

He came up behind her as she stood pondering, and embraced her. "So listen," he said.

"What. No. No no. It's too."

"Come sit," he said. "This has always been my favorite room. The windows are double glass; the doors are thick. Do you know why?"

"Pierce," she said, a warning, a negative.

"Rose," he said. "Come sit."

He sat himself, slowly, on a wide deep sofa, and stroked its cold leather; prop for a movie he might make.

"What if I don't want to?" she said, crossing her arms before her.

"Take off your coat," he said. "It's really warm, don't you think? They want it kept high. The old man was terrified the pipes might freeze."

She stood a while, and then, as though it were her own idea, took off the coat and sat carefully beside him, knees tight together.

"It's not warm," she said smiling.

"It'll get warmer."

"It won't."

He looked at her a long time, at her imp's face: one he knew. "All right," he said. "Now . . ."

"No," she said, plainly. "Huh-uh." She still smiled.

"Rose."

"You wanna fight?" she said, and held a fist up to his chin. He took her wrist in his big hand.

"Fight," he said. "I don't think you want to." She did want to. She grabbed for his chin with her other hand and Pierce took it as well, fighting for it as for a writhing snake.

"I can get out of this," she said. "I'm stronger than you think. I was always stronger than my brother."

"You aren't stronger than I think," Pierce said. "You are exactly as strong."

She resisted his grip on her, but couldn't move him, either forward or back. "My strength is as the strength of ten," he said, having to exert more force, an unexpected amount. "Because my. Heart. Is pure."

She nearly broke his grip, and to keep her he wrenched her arm behind her and turned her, face down, on the couch. He inhaled its mildewed plush. He remembered his childhood in Kentucky, how his older cousin Joe Boyd had liked to induce him to fight; how it had felt to be beneath him, Joe Boyd holding his head to the floor. Say uncle. The grip of him, unbreakable, an *iron grip* exactly.

"Okay," Rose said, but not in assent, meaning instead Okay you've got the better of me momentarily but I'm thinking of a way out; and she twisted forcibly and suddenly against his weight, and did manage to turn halfway around before he locked her tight again. She laughed lightly. Her long body lay half-on, half-off the couch, her clothes disordered. His face burned, the familiar flush of a fight; he seemed to be her brother, one of those boys who wrestle girls.

"I think that's enough, Rose," he said, the Soft Voice. "I think."

But she made another effort, and by a combination of force and fraud, nearly got away; trying to keep her he fell from the couch to his knees, but before she had slipped from him entirely he had clambered up roaring, and as one beast they stumbled over the floor. Her hip smacked an end table, and a brass lamp toppled as she cried out. He brought her down onto the dusty carpet.

"Now Rose I think," he said. "I think."

"No," she said. She was pinned by his bulk, his hot cheek was on hers, his arm around her and beneath her chin. With his other hand he began to pull up her skirt.

"No," she said again.

"Rose," he said. "Now we're going to find out who's stronger. Aren't we. Who's really finally stronger. We have to. Isn't that right."

This was the moment, always, that he feared most, the moment that she needed most, when she resisted him with all her might and they contested and he won. Her strength was terrible: not that he couldn't hold her, but he could feel how little able he would be to force her if she didn't submit, who he would have to become in order to force her. At school once a coach had said of Pierce *The trouble with Moffett is he knows his own strength*. Afraid of it, sure he could break bones if he used it to the fullest. *I'm a lover not a fighter* he had told her once, not in bed though. And now he had to cross that burning bridge once more.

"Rose. Don't you agree."

She was silent, breathing hard. He pulled open his pants (not easy with one hand and the two of them pressed so close together) and freed his penis, and with his lips laid gently against her cheek and eyes closed he released from his heart just enough tenderness to fill and raise it. Rose, he whispered, Rose now god damn it. He yanked at her underpants. She had not yet said Yes. He could see, turned up toward him, her eye, small living and hating, like a being caught within her looking out. With his knee he parted her. Uncertain he could enter her—he did not understand how real rapists and sadists ever managed this—he tried to lift her from beneath; and with a sudden cry and a twist she was free. Seeing her face Pierce knew, as though tumbling from a height, that he had misread her.

"No," she said. "I said no."

"Rose."

"Just don't." She didn't stand, wouldn't pull down her skirt, nor would she stop looking at him in awful reproach. He could almost see her heart beating in her breast.

"Say it then," he said. "Say it."

She said nothing. For an instant he became convinced that he was *not* to stop, that he was to push through this too and find her on the far side, gratified, glad. *I love you*. It was when he had not ceased that she had said that, and if it was not spoken to him, still it was he who had driven her to say it.

"All right," he said, and opened and flexed his big hands. "All right, Rose."

A bad angel on his left told him to be brave, hadn't he done worse before, hadn't he left marks, lasting ones, they had gloated over them together, aroused, proud of each other. A good angel at his right told him he was about to lose her forever and must beg her forgiveness now with every real tenderness he knew. The bad angel kicked and screamed: no no no you'll lose her forever *that* way, this is the last test, take it.

He lowered his hands.

"You hurt me," she said. "You really hurt me."

"You knew what to say to stop me," he said. "You didn't say it."

"What."

" 'I tell you three times.' You didn't say it."

"You knew I meant it," she said. "You knew."

"No."

"You knew. You wouldn't stop it." She brushed tears from her cheeks. She looked nine years old, or a hundred. "You wanted to hurt me. I think you're really angry at me. I know you are."

"No. No I'm not." He was not to apologize, that would be the end; if he apologized something would instantly shatter, the walls would dissolve and he would find himself alone naked on a cold hillside. Also if he did not apologize immediately. He moved to her to touch her, to pull her skirt down; she put out a policeman's hand to stop him.

" 'I tell you three times,' " he said. "You agreed."

It *was* a test, but not of his nerve; it was a test of his unwillingness to hurt her, of his ability to tell when he had, or would, no clues permitted, no secret signs, only his own clouded senses; punishment for failure being. Being this. He had ceased to breathe, his chest rising and falling but no air seeming to enter him. He thought: *this* is the moment that will last forever, this the stasis I begged for.

Pierce could at that moment perceive (or actually could *not* perceive, or recognize, except in the form of his own unreasoning guilt and longing) the great beings of the time to come, who were looking in upon him with their receiving eyes, looking into the past from which they themselves would by then be freed, or banished; waiting, with anxious sympathy, or impatience, or contempt, for Pierce to *get it* at last, to do what he was supposed to do, move the big hand his one allotted notch to help it pass the little hand, but which he could not do: not right now, not right here.

So somehow the moment was got past without it, he would later be able to tell himself how only in a general way (*somehow we got past that moment*) and have a clear memory only that they came back across the lawn, a sliver moon having arisen, and spent a long time in bed, but only fooling with a book of ancient word games he had found in Kraft's house (*Q: What is it that I give to others daily and yet never part with?*) until—late at night, the lights out—he made her lie still, and lowered his head between her legs (this was the one act she had always resisted, he could imagine why) and fed himself there, fed till after a long time she held on to his ears and came. He clambered up her, his face wet as a baby's, and they fucked moaning wordlessly and holding each other tight in the dark.

Then it was day again, she was going again, her little car already roused and muttering; a cold day, dark at nine in the morning and a searching wind blowing.

"I love you," he said. What had so recently been inconceivable to say aloud was now almost the only thing left he could say with conviction. He waited.

"Pierce," she said. "That's real hard for me. You know, saying."

She had tied a figured wool scarf over her hair, knotted under her chin like a babushka, he touched it and her cheek with grievous tenderness. Then he took her cheeks in both his hands and made her look at him.

"I love you," he said again. "I love you and I don't want to lose you to those, those. That's just the worst. The worst way I can think of losing you."

"Oh that is just so unfair," she said. "When you don't even know them. I do."

He looked at her and said nothing, but his face said *You don't.*

"Pierce," she said. "Okay. I don't want to hurt you and I don't understand why it hurts you but I can't just deny what happened to me. I can't. I won't soft-pedal it."

"Okay," Pierce said.

"You know I almost died," she said then, plainly. "I almost did. I might have if it hadn't been for them."

"Not possible," he said. "How. Died, how."

"You remember. That really windy night. Remember that? It wasn't an accident, really. It was dumb, it was stone dumb, but Pierce it wasn't an accident. You knew that. I know you did."

He said nothing.

"It wasn't the first time, either. It wasn't." She had begun to shiver, a delicate tremor of her chin and shoulders. "I know you think I can deny and forget anything," she said. "But I can't. I'm real aware, actually. And maybe you're so smart you don't need any help from anybody . . ."

"No," Pierce said. "No."

"You say death is part of life," she said. "That there wouldn't be life without death. Well I can't think that. You have to hate death, you have to. Otherwise."

She had not released his hands, which she had drawn from her face, she held them to her; her gloves were wool, and red; none of this would be forgotten.

"Listen," she said. "Next week there's going to be a sort of thing. An outreach sort of. They do these, for people who don't know about us, who are maybe interested. I want you to come."

A dark highway opened in his heart. "Me?"

"It'll be fun. Maybe you can contribute. You know a lot about the Bible." She smiled for him. "You got a Bible?"

"Several."

"King James?"

"Sure."

"You have to bring it."

"I'm really not sure I'm up for this. *Really* not sure."

She let go of his hands. "Don't you think," she said, "you owe it to me."

"Oh Christ," he said, and looked around for escape; found none. She asked him again, oh please please. He thought of what had passed between them in the mansion on the hill, and the doghouse he was still feelably in because of it. So he said All right, almost too low for her to hear, and then much louder, a bark really, and qualified by a grudging sentence about how no, he actually did *not* feel he owed her or any of them very much in this particular matter and that who owed what to whom might be a subject for another day if ever. Or he did not say all of that but only something suggestive of it, while she beamed on him, and then kissed with sudden homely passion the lapel of his coat.

When she was gone he went back into his threatened little house, built apparently on sand, as we have all been warned houses should not be. No, he thought, no oh no. Oh no. He stood for a length of time in the kitchen watching the black ivy lash the windowpane, then in the study amid the papers. He went into the bathroom, regarded the stranger in the mirror, then into the bedroom. On the wall of the bedroom still hung the horrid brown frame into which he had put the picture of her he had taken. He sat down before it, on the edge of the iron bed where she had lain on that night, bound.

"All right, Rose," he said aloud, practicing, trying out an assent more measured, more considered, a *wiser* assent than the assent he had earlier given her. "Okay," he said. "I'll do that Rose. All right. Okay."


And so it was that, on a wet afternoon midway between equinox and solstice in that year of the world's end, Pierce Moffett came to be riding a long-distance bus, its blue-and-silver side marked with a fleeing or pursuing hound, toward the city of Conurbana; afraid to drive his own car so far, more afraid than he had ever been of anything in all his life, not resolute but without other options, and amazed at how dark the world had grown.

*This is all my fault,* he thought. He meant the black cold that he felt rising around him, and the mephitic air, unbreathable and hard to see through; he meant all the precious and irreplaceable things falling to ruin somewhere behind or around him, things he could not name or remember; he meant the threat in the weak scant rain and the black unfreeway, the stench of the half-capped whiskey bottle in his seatmate's overcoat pocket (how sharp his senses had become, though only to perceive what was very close to him, out to get him, needing to be fended off).

All his fault. Willing or wishing that things might be not as they are but some different way instead leads, it seems, to this: it was now up to him to make it come out right. Up to him anyway to imagine that it *could* come out right, or at least all right, a thing which he could not do, which should never have been left up to someone as incapable as he, paralyzed with astonishment and knowing at last how unwise he truly was.

But why amazed? Why astonished? Had he not delighted in the idea that exactly this might really really be so, was he not at work daily (not so daily though recently) on a book proving that the world is malleable in just this way? Wasn't he asserting that, just as the speakers of a language will change it as they use it over decades and centuries, so the language that creates the world—the language that *is* the world, its Meaning, its Logos—can change, and that when it does the world is remade? Well he was right. It can, and it does. In here it does.

# 13

So long as the rain stayed rain, Bobby thought she'd be all right; if it turned to snow she'd have to stop, and even if the rain only got worse the front tires on her flimsy ten-year-old Tomcat, mismatched and bald, would start losing their grip and for a scary second float on the water's surface before being snatched back, like a person nodding off in a chair, or at the wheel, which she might do too if she didn't stop and sleep somewhere for a while. She'd worked consecutive shifts to put together these days, and she felt it. A big sacrifice. To do something she wanted to do about as much as nothing: pushing south and west toward her grandfather against her own reluctance, like one of those magnetic Scotties pressed against the other.

The kids in Bondieu had those, the white one and the black one; little doggies that magically fought each other off, or spun around to meet one another and click together. And in the tall cabinet in the dining room a green bottle with the same two dogs pictured on it, and the words Black & White. The boy Pierce had read the words to her. She couldn't then read at all, and they used to try to teach her, and she would pretend to learn. That week: the week when she hid in their big house stuffed with things, avoiding Mousie Calton who had been hired to care for them, the time she ran away from Floyd and got so sick; how old was she then, eight or nine. What she remembered out of so much forgotten, tossed away, denied.

How her grandpap had hated and feared them, that family on the hill. Not them so much as the church they belonged to, the priest in his collar, the hospital where those kids' father was doctor, the nuns in their black robes and stiff white fronts. Black & White. Got tails underneath, that's why they wear 'em, he'd say, joking in that ferocious way of his, a kid couldn't tell. And now he was there in their hospital, in their care all day and night, though he didn't know it. He knew nothing: they said so: his half-lidded eyes cold as a snake's, knowing nothing, unseeing. They said.

Allentown and Reading and Harrisburg, she knew men who worked in the mills in all three towns, never saw the names on a map or on the green signs without seeing their faces, though (she thought) they never would remember hers. Can't remember it myself, she joked to no one. At Harrisburg she entered the turnpike, passing back through the gate that once—when she had first come to it, going the other way, on the other side of the road—seemed to her to be the gate to a different circle of existence, but which had proved not to be.

She struck the steering wheel in annoyance: she had forgotten to gas up the Cat, gas was more on the pike.

"Supposed to remind me," she said to herself, to the new self within her, channel of the Spirit; and laughed.

The first thing she had heard about the Powerhouse was that they charged you two hundred dollars to take the entry-level course, "God's Guarantee," which would include your books and materials and the videotapes of Dr. Walter's instruction—and a guarantee: they could guarantee that you would have life, and have it more abundantly, starting before the course was even completed. They said they'd never known anyone who asked for their money back. Two hundred dollars had been more than Bobby had ever spent on anything at once; people who had taken the course told stories of how the money and even more had come back to them in time, but it hadn't come back to her, her fault maybe for not believing hard enough that it would, or should: still unsure that it was she who was being talked to, she whom Dr. Walter looked at out of the TV.

Anyway she had not signed up to get money, or abundant living, though she could use a bunch of both. She had signed up and given them the money (taken from the bank on her credit card) because of their promise that if she continued, if she followed their instruction and direction, she would no longer be afraid to sleep. Ray Honeybeare said it: she would no longer need to fear she might fall down through her pillow into the night lands, where her grandpap went, where the dead were.

Can you do that? she'd asked, and No, he said, I can't, but I know who can.

She thought at first he meant Dr. Walter, wherever he was, the man in the tapes, but after a moment she knew it wasn't Dr. Walter he meant.

Is it true? she asked

What I tell you three times is true, he said. Ever hear that, Bobby?

His smile was strange and piercing in such an unsmiling face, and his eyes were on her. It's true, Bobby, he said. I tell you three times.

Dr. Walter, more learned than any of the preachers she had known, could tell you just what all the hard parts of the Gospels really meant, every knotty word, because he knew the language in which they had been written. She had been sort of surprised to learn they hadn't been written in English. In his work with them after the tapes were played, Ray Honeybeare told them how the sinning part of them wasn't them, but a false self that had been acquired in Adam's fall. When you turned to God, He would open you and pour in His grace, pour and pour, as much as would fill you at last; and this they knew how to bring about, for it was part of the revelation made to Dr. Walter. Ray said that even after your true self was filled with the Spirit, that false self might go on sinning now and then, though growing weaker and less headstrong, until at length it withered away or vanished; meanwhile she, Bobby, was clean and not at fault for what her sinning self did.

The mountain preacher whose church she had helped to build never told her that, that the Gospels promised that. He had no personal revelation to impart, no truths or powers granted only to him. Sundays and revival nights he invited the Spirit to come among them, and the Spirit quickening in their hearts caused them to speak, but often as not what one said wasn't the same as what others said; some saying how God loves us no matter what, others saying His wrath knew no bounds. And the shepherd of that flock never would say which of these was true, and which not. If it came from their hearts, the Spirit had moved them to say it; it meant to them what they meant to express, he said, and maybe spoke a truth that another soul right there that minute needed to hear. God's power won't be fenced in; the Word's a great speckled bird, different for everyone.

In the mountains they spoke in tongues; the Powerhouse also spoke in tongues, and could teach you how, anybody could learn they said; they didn't require you to produce from your own heart a unique sweetness, God burgeoning like a ripe fruit within you and coming out through your mouth. It was—well it wasn't a trick but they could guide you and show you how it was done, she learned how to do it just as she learned to draw blood and to give a shot, neither of which she had ever believed she could do; now she could talk the God language as long and loud as they had in that church-house, and without falling and weeping or getting soaked in sweat. When you had done it the first time, your group gathered round you and hugged you laughing and exulting and even Ray Honeybeare hugged you, sure of you now. Sure.

But above all they taught her that she had not seen the dead, not on that night at the big church-house in the mountains, not on any of the other nights down there and in Conurbana. Not any of them; not Roberta.

No matter what others who called themselves Christians believed, the dead were dead, lying in their graves, mere potentialities, until the Last Days. The Bible was as clear as clear on this; you needed only take it and read; any other interpretation, that had people's souls or spirits flying off to heaven or to hell and only joined up with their bodies at the end of time—*interpretations* was what they were, and the Bible needed no interpretation. Its sense was clear: how could it not be?

The dead were dead: dead as the mouse found neck-broke in a trap, dead as the dead dog the crows pecked at by the roadside. What's God's power to give eternal life if we've got it already? The dead did not walk the earth looking for something, asking something of her. They wanted nothing. They knew nothing. They weren't even waiting. Those she saw were not the dead but were inside herself; they were symptoms of a mental illness whose roots ran deep, starting from her past; before the grace of God could fill her fully they must be evicted. And that too the Powerhouse knew how to do.

One hundred miles to Harrisburg, a hundred from Harrisburg to Morgantown in West Virginia, a hundred from Morgantown to Charleston but slower; a last hundred through Huntington and down to Breshy County and Bondieu, a hundred as the crow flies but more if the crow has to climb every knob and descend into every holler as her old Tomcat must.

You measured your progress on the pike by the tunnels you passed through, the long and the short one and the double one but always one more than you expected, and that one the last one. Blue Mountain, Laurel Hill, Kittatinny Mountain, Tuscarora, they had their names carved over their arched entrances, she had not wanted to come to know them or ever to pass back through them again. Night came and she awakened more fully, seeming to descend into her body from somewhere above and behind; things came clearer, the geometries of the road and the lights, red ones ahead, white ones in her mirror, she found it easier to drive when you needed to recognize nothing and think about nothing.

Pray. Time went faster given to Him, they said. All good came to you when you opened your heart to the Spirit's incoming.

What if you couldn't, though? Was that the devil self in you resisting, fighting back like a bad screaming kid you had to haul along with all your might? Maybe, but maybe not; maybe it was not yours at all, maybe it was something squatting in you, like a cowbird's egg laid in a finch's nest. Not until she told the healing group that when she was nine or ten she was still sharing a bed with her grandfather (who was her father too by adoption) did they begin to break through to her, Ray actually putting out his nose to hear this, like a hound who's caught a strong scent, and leaning forward to ask her more. The bed. Of course Ray had known it was there that the thing was hidden, and who it was who had hidden it there, but it was no good his knowing or seeing if she couldn't, no way he could simply *tell* her or infuse her with his insight against her will, she would have to find it herself, reenter it and see it with her own eyes looking backwards.

When she understood they meant to invade it, that bed more familiar to her still than any bed she had shared with anyone ever after, she fought them off fiercely. Christ God Almighty how patient they had been with her, how hard they had struggled and how little she had been able to grasp, in her state of sin, the effort being expended on her. How she had just wasted their time by her hardness, sitting (she could see herself now, if she looked back, as though she were another) clutching one elbow in the other hand, defiant cigarette pointed their way; denying denying denying. Bobby, they would call to her, Bobby Bobby somebody sometime let this evil into you when you were too little to fight it. You can't remember. But the memory is *there* and you can recover it because Bobby no memory ever goes away, it only becomes lost and covered up because it's too painful to live with. Bobby that's what the Devil counts on, that you won't remember, because if you can't remember you can never be free.

It took days, or weeks; she lost track of time. She couldn't have done it without Ray Honeybeare, whose big scored face and sharp small features became the only constant she knew, in waking life or in dreams like waking; Ray talking to her, waiting, unsatisfied with her, loving her. She would say to him *Last night I dreamed you cut off the fingers of my hands* and then awake and know she had only dreamed she had dreamed that. Once she called him to tell him she had proof that the story was all true, what Floyd had done to her and why he had done it (not out of plain lust or loneliness for sure), and then had fallen silent while Ray waited: for she realized that she had not really remembered the proof but had been given it in a dream, and it made no sense at all. Sometimes in those days she walked in her sleep; she awoke in her nightdress once halfway down the stairs to the street, another time in the hallway of her neighbors' apartment; they started then to lock their doors.

So hard was her case that she was given an Intensive, volunteers staying with her night and day (Ray was one) to wrestle with what held her so tight. After a day she began to weep and couldn't stop, couldn't say why; and then to shriek obscenities at them, at Ray, and then—at last—at Floyd. *Leave her,* Ray said, holding her arms and shaking her. *Leave her. I command you. In Jesus' name.* They told her that, later; they told her she had bellered like no human they had ever heard, and had strength like a great furious infant. She remembered only the awful kindness of their faces close to hers, the grip they held her in, not going to let her go, praying to beat the band as she had it torn from her: they saw— some of them later said they actually *saw* it, and others said it was just *as though* they had seen it, so exactly that it might as well have been so—they saw it come forth, right from her hell-yelling throat, big as a potato or (one said) a turd, filling her mouth and wriggling, thrashing out and gone in a second. Quiet came. They clung together weeping. Ray said he was glad they weren't *all* as tough as that. They told her that later too, each one of them told her (*Ray said he's sure glad they're not all as tough as that one*) because she hadn't herself seen or known any of it.

*Learn the truth,* they had told her, *and the truth shall make you free.* Her grandfather in that bed had let some of the devil out of himself and into her, let it out the end of his dick most likely, and that was what caused her to see the dead, or think she did, just as he did. And when he'd said *You're of a kind I know, you're of my kind,* that's what he meant: that he had made her of his kind by what he had done to her. Of course she had hated him, hated him without knowing why. She knew now.

So angry, so angry, she wouldn't have believed how angry it was possible for her to be, layers of black anger one under another like layers of black tar paper on a rotten shack's roof (when had she been set the task of ripping such paper off a roof or was that a dream too?). She practiced walking in the Spirit and fellowshipping and then found herself one morning screaming at her son, Shut up shut up shut up, fingers around his throat and thumbs pressing against his chin.

That was him too, inside her still even though expelled, that devil-shaped black absence. Wanting her to do a murder, sure, why not? That's what Ray said when she told him how scared she was; and he found someone to take the boy in, just for a few days, a month maybe; he told her Bobby, you can see him whenever you want but let's not us take any chances. We're dealing with forces here stronger than the atomic bomb, forces strong enough to destroy the world through our agency. Forces that almost have destroyed the world, in fact, and more than once.

She too: there were people who had offered to take her in, they were so damn kind, maybe if she had accepted their help what happened next might not have happened: but her old capacity to take what she needed for herself had been thrown out of whack too and she couldn't.

It was because she'd been alone, no friend, no man, no kids; because she had just got off a tough shift and had only her dark apartment and her dreams to go back to: that's why on that September night, weird hot night two months ago, she'd stayed on old 6A past her turn, and driven down the row. Just to see whose parking lot was full; to see if she might glimpse Lars's Firebird with the wide wings painted on the hood. Dog returning to its vomit. The Play Pen. Seven Seas. Embassy Lounge. The white Tempest convertible turned in there, coming from the opposite direction and crossing in front of her, flashing across her vision; in her rearview mirror she saw it inserting its brilliance into a row of dull black and gray hardtops.

Not your fault, she thought, making a wide U-turn at the next intersection and turning back: not your fault you can't resist. In the parking lot she took off her glasses, dropped them in her purse; changed her shoes for heels. She ran her hand over the slick flank of the white car as she passed by it. Just washed.

The billed caps at the bar turned her way as she entered. She knew most of them, not by name but by species, the way you know kinds of chickens or dogs; every one of them—it just happened to be so that night, she would still recognize them without it—had a thick unkempt moustache. They each had a pickup, she bet, and a dog in the back of the pickup; an ex-wife too, and a big old belt buckle on their jeans, brass or silver, last scrap of their knight's armor, right there protecting the soft underbelly. She knew the sound those buckles made when they dropped to the floor. She ordered a shot and a beer, and poured the one into the other.

It was easy to tell which one was the owner of the Tempest. He wore no belt at all; his pants were the kind that used none, held closed by a little dickie tab. Shiny boots beneath, and a sports team's windbreaker. They exchanged glances for a while, in the mirror and down along the bar, while she half listened to a guy who claimed to know her from long ago. "Nobody knows me from long ago." She picked up her drink at length and walked down the bar just as he was taking out his wallet.

"Leavn already?" she asked him.

"Well," he said. "Now that you ask."

"Maybe you thought this place was no fun."

"No band," he said, and shrugged. His sandy hair rose in front in a smooth wave in which the comb marks were distinct.

"I like music," she said. "Jukebox's full." She drank. Her Reading man had called these drinks "boilermakers"; this one was in her lips and her fingertips already, or something was. "Or. There's music at the Del Raye. Every night."

"Which is where?"

She thumbed south. He nodded thoughtfully, as though considering a risky business venture, regarding her through black-rimmed glasses.

The white car's interior was leather, as she had known it would be, alive to her touch, lipstick red. The door closed with a light but solid sound she seemed to have heard already, or to remember. She thought of asking him to put the top down but didn't. He turned the key and she felt the drive train through her behind. He pressed the accelerator a couple of times, unnecessarily maybe, maybe just to hear the engine or let her hear it: then he drove out of the lot, one freckled hand on the white steering wheel.

"You can hear me sitting way over there?" he asked.

She slid toward him along the seat and turned on the radio, pressed in the lighter. A little halo of light appeared around it. She felt warm and loved here, dangerous too. She opened the glove compartment.

"Careful," he said.

A gun clipped to the compartment's door, its handle toward her hand. Toward his hand actually, able to be pulled in a second. Before he could take it she had it.

"What's it for?"

"I don't need a reason."

She weighed it in her hands. "Big," she said.

He grinned at her. "That's a Glock nine-millimeter," he said. "Stop about anything."

She stroked its checkered handle, held its barrel lightly in her fingers. She saw he wanted to take it from her, wanted to badly, and yet wanted to watch her with it too. She slid away from him smiling. "What's this?"

"Safety. Don't touch it."

She moved the little lever. Men loved things that were heavy and oiled and fit their hands, with parts that moved slickly and clicked easily into place. A cold happy rage was filling her, had reached her heart, her throat.

"Don't," he said. "It's fuckn loaded."

Her back was to the door, the gun pointed his way. "I like it," she said. "I want it."

His eyes glanced from the road to the gun, back and forth. "Dumb bitch," he said. "Give it here."

"Pull over," she said. "I'm gonna kill you."

"Shut up," he said.

"Pull the fuck over." She had to hold the gun in two hands to keep it steady. He talked more, hand held out, withdrawn, held out again. She said no more. She could see his teeth, clenched in rage. He pulled over. The car and her blood hummed around her.

"Get out," she said.

"The hell you say." He still held the white steering wheel, hands at ten and two.

"Devil's in me," she said. "I'm gonna kill you and steal your car."

"Let's talk," he said.

"Get out!" She could smell him. "Out!"

"Please."

A noise started in her throat, cat-screech or child's impatient mad shriek, pressed out between her bared teeth. The glowing gun poked at him. He eased the door open and the roof light came on; she could see the shine of sweat on his face; what did *he* see. He was out and she was in the driver's seat. He called out *Please* again as she pulled shut the door. If he hadn't said that, if she hadn't heard that from the dark. She hadn't thought she would shoot, had all along thought that she would not.

Two months later, her wrist still ached a little. She had thought then that firing it had broken her wrist. The night too. It seemed not to be a sound it had made so much as a blow falling on the whole wide world at once, caused by her though. As much as her foot on the gas pedal, it had blown her forward, impelled her away. Away down this same road she now went, away as though fallen down a chute.

That was another thing they had among the endless things of that house in Bondieu, that board game they had made her play where you come upon a ladder suddenly and climb up, only to fall down again along a twisty chute. She thought of the dark richly colored board, punitive, and their laughter. She thought: I killed somebody. She had never found a report of it in the paper or seen it on TV (her TV busted and cold in the living room's corner like a gloomy invalid) but she hadn't looked hard, and she sure as hell never asked. She knew now. I killed somebody.

But that wasn't what she'd thought then, flying west and south in his Tempest, a strange wind arising as day came. Then she had thought *He's made me kill somebody. Taken away my life and given me death and the dead for it and now he's made me kill somebody.* Not even really knowing or thinking that she was headed toward Kentucky, toward Breshy County and the bed where he lay, as she was now too this night. The gun had lain then on the seat of the Tempest beside her and as she drove she assumed or supposed she would take it with her to Hogback, to be with her when she saw him; but eventually she had awakened, as though surfacing from dark water. No. No. And a little while later she had pulled over at a scenic overlook and thrown the gun as far as she could into the yellow woods below, listening for its strike. She heard nothing; only the leaves of the trees lifting in a long wave just then, as though she had tossed a stone into a pool.

On a night long before she first ran away from Hogback, Bobby had awakened deep in the night in that bed and turned to Floyd beside her; the moon was bright, or he'd left a light on, as he often did. He lay asleep, but not asleep as she had seen him other times: his eyelids were open a crack, enough so that she could see the glitter of an eye within; his breath was stopped though his mouth was open, and his hands were held up a little, fingers curved, like a dead dog's paws.

Grandpap, she'd said. She shook him, his heaviness, and could not rouse him; put her ear against the rough cloth of his nightshirt and listened to his heart, tolling with fearful slowness. *Grandpap* she said into his ear, afraid to cry out, not knowing why or who she feared would hear. After a time she climbed down off the bed and went out into the night, near bright as day where the moonlight lay and empty black where it did not; a summer night it must have been because she went shoeless, she could remember her own long spectral feet on the road. Got to the nearest neighbor, a childless couple who had sometimes spoken kindly to her but whom she had avoided, wary cub. A light burned in their front room; no when she came closer she saw it was the TV, showing nothing but not gone off, the strange changeless cross or sign it made, its open eye. He was asleep in the lounger before it. Roused at her knock. My grandpap's asleep and won't wake.

They didn't want to do anything, or could think of nothing to do, but in the end they let her lead them back down along the road to his house; they went inside and were whispering in the front room when he opened the door of the bedroom. Huge, barefoot, alive. Why've you brung people into my house. The blacks in his eyes like shafts leading back into the night.

When they were alone he told her—dawn coming and the moon set—that he had been gone, called out by the Spirit to follow. He told her that though she saw him in his bed he had not been present there; nor had he been dreaming. Dreams are inside, he said; he had gone outside, by way (he thought) of his open mouth and the window—he pointed to where it stood open, the rag of curtain flailing in the outpassing air. He would tell her one day, he said, where he had gone, and what he had seen and done there. Now, though, he wanted her to know but one thing: when she found him thus in the night beside her, as though asleep but stiller, she must allow no one and nothing to harm his vacated body, for he could not resist then. Let no one see him. Above all she must never allow him to be turned facedown: for then, returning, he would not be able to find a way back in. And if the sun found him still outside he never would be able to: himself and his body separated for good, till death or Judgment.

She listened, and asked nothing; as she asked nothing when he told her how the world would end, or what God had planned for him. She made coffee and grits and they ate in silence. For a time after that she left the bed they shared, slept on the kitchen floor with the door shut or out in the pines where he would not go to find her; but the weather turned cold, and she came back.

Once or twice after that night she had awakened to find him in that sleep again; had vowed to watch, and see him come in at the window when dawn was near. But she was no more able to stay awake than she had once been able to sit

up and see Santy Claus come down the chimney, to bring her a flannel nightgown and put into her empty shoe a ring of gold-colored metal, a Nestlé's bar
and a lipstick. And, anyway, soon she ceased to believe anything he said.

She knew now, though, what land it was that he had gone out to: she knew,
for she had seen him there, unable to return to the earth of daytime, and all because of what she had done. She had seen him, seen his bewilderment at her
own presence there, facing him: she and he, in that land he would not now
leave, till death or Judgment.

Bondieu in Breshy County is a single street, one swaying stoplight on a wire
across it; the Flamingo, a bar when the county is Wet, a café when it's Dry; Du-
mont's store, the hardware store, a five-and-dime, and a concrete-block building
that had not been there when she was a kid, that housed the state welfare offices.
And Our Lady of the Way Hospital, a new building attached to the old one. Out
at the south end of the street, almost visible as she came in from the north, the
road upward to the big house on the hill where once she had been taken in, and
hidden, and baptized.

She turned in at the hospital, but for a time sat in the parking lot while her
car grew cold. The mountains went up not far away; you could see them from
here. Amazing how little it was, this town that she, coming down from Hogback,
had used to think was so big: almost too little to survive against the spiky mountains and the rain. But here it was still, no less of it though not much more.

She ran in the door, holding her bag over her head against the rain, she'd
just had her hair done the day before.

Her grandfather had been moved, she learned, to a different part of the hospital; no longer in ICU where she had first found him, someplace less urgent
now obviously; she went through the halls smelling familiar smells.

He was not the same: he had moved since the last time, she wondered if
suddenly or by degrees: his arms that had lain slack at his sides in his own bed
had contracted, and lifted his hands a little, and curled the fingers. Feeding tube
going in through his nose, and from under the sheet a tube coming out, from the
catheter to the urine bottle. She had an impulse to check it, see if it needed
changing.

She sat by him. She would touch him and speak to him, but not yet.

One or two of the people in the group—that girl Rose—had offered to come
with her on this trip. Her grandfather in a coma in a hospital far away? She
shouldn't have to go alone. And Bobby had refused them that too, refused to let
them be kind. He and she had made her sinner-self strong, so strong that she
could eat up whatever good they brought to her and them too along with it, let
them keep their distance from her.

"Grandpap," she said.

A nun entered the room with a little knock and a quick smile.

"They told me upstairs you'd come."

Bobby said nothing.

"He's really doing well. Considering. Nothing much changed. His vital signs are good though. A strong heart."

She sat beside Bobby in the other chair there by the bed. Like the rest of them she had stopped wearing the voluminous black garment, layers of serge and net and starched white. A plain black dress like a schoolgirl's, and a white hat; her hair steel-gray beneath. Always said they hadn't any, all cut off.

"Can I ask you something?" she said. Her face pink and scrubbed and finely lined.

"Sure."

"Mr. Shaftoe. He had no insurance."

"No."

"Had he ever been UMW? United Mine Workers?"

"No. He never."

"Well that's my question. He has been here for nearly eight weeks. And it appears that his condition is not going to change. That's the consensus."

Bobby regarded her, adopting the blank uncomprehending face she used for welfare workers and supervisors. Don't guess at them; let them say; it's safer. Sometimes they just can't say it, whatever it is, and let you off a while more.

"We've been able to get Medicare for him," the nun said. "But the coverage is limited. You probably know."

No answer for this either.

"What we hoped," the nun said, "was to get your permission to move your father to a nursing-home facility."

She turned from the nun and looked down on her grandfather's stone face. The nun looked too, and folded her hands in her lap attentively, as though perhaps he would speak, and something new would be learned, or it would be proved that nothing could be.

Bobby had always trusted these women, believed that though they might judge you they wouldn't abandon you or dismiss you. But maybe that was nuns on TV. These were running a hospital; they were just as likely to put you out if you couldn't pay as Conurbana Pediatric, only they'd do it nicer.

"Nothn I can do," she said.

"Will you come to the office before you go?" she said, rising. "You can talk to the doctor then too."

Bobby nodded.

Maybe it made no difference, she thought. Maybe now he had gone so far into that land that nothing done or not done to his body made a difference. He was already looking neglected and abandoned, his skin the color of the clay of his yard, his face like a slab of shale. The nails of his hands as discolored and used-up as chicken claws.

He had ripped her like a rag doll and filled her with his evil. And that's why she had come on that night in her stolen car to his house, where she had found him helpless, for he had gone off with his devil to the night lands. She had put her hands beneath his immobile body and with all her might had lifted him and turned him over, turned his body facedown on the bed to die. And dead was what he was now and she would not grieve.

It would be the old Good Luck Coal company hospital they would send him to. Whatever its name was now. It had been closed for a long time and then become a nursing home nobody ever came out of. When she was a girl, and it was still a hospital but about to be closed by the state, Floyd had pointed it out to her from the truck window and told her Don't never let them take me there. Don't let them cut me. And made her promise.

Another nun, young and red-cheeked, came in with stuff to give him a bath. She greeted Bobby with something like joy, as though she'd waited a long time to see her. Bobby watched her fill her basin at the sink, carefully checking the water as though for a baby's bath.

"So you're Mr. Shaftoe's daughter?" she asked. She lowered the rail of Floyd's bed, the rail designed to keep him in bed if he should ever suddenly awake or come to and decide to roll over, or get up.

"Granddaughter," Bobby said.

"Oh. I thought."

"It's hard to explain," Bobby said. Too hard, too hard. The young nun began to wash Floyd, talking all the while, to Bobby and also to Floyd. How are we today. Get your bed changed too today. Okay scuse me now. Up we go.

"I can do that," Bobby said, shamed. "I'll do it."

"No trouble," said the child.

"It's my job too," Bobby said. "I'm a nurse's aide. What I do all day."

The nun pondered a moment, weighing her duty against Bobby's claim. Bobby knew there was no nurse in the world wouldn't turn over some part of the day's duties to somebody else willing to do them, always too much.

"Well. All right," she said. "You just give me a call when you want me."

She checked the urine bottle with a practiced motion, and was gone. Bobby momentarily envied her, her life of work and prayer, but then there was hardly anybody Bobby didn't envy sometimes; it was the way she was, and she knew it.

There was a razor there to shave him with, and a comb for his hair. Bobby picked up the warm sponge and began to work, slipping Floyd's arm from the johnny and lifting it; it seemed to resist her. She could hear the slight whistle of his breath through his mouth and around the tube in his nose. She wiped his face, pushing aside the lank hair, so thick, she had envied it too.

She lifted the blue johnny from his loins and undid the diaper he wore, folding it over the two small dry turds it contained and pushing it into the waste can. She wet and wrung out the sponge again, and washed the raw and painful-looking skin, wetness and salt urine was what did that. She found cream, the same she used every day on the children, and on his thighs (huge and stringy compared with theirs) and his hollowed butt she spread it well. She could easily turn him now, this way and that, but now it would do no good.

Look what she had done.

Unless it had not been her that had done it. It hadn't happened, or it was his own fault or God's that he had had a stroke, or his heart had stopped for a while. She could remember right now what she had done in the cabin on Hogback, could remember even the smell of the pines and the clay; she could remember it without believing it, as though the coma had caused what she remembered having done and not the other way around.

Ray up North had taken a devil from her that Floyd had put inside her. And thereupon she'd gone and killed somebody; and right after that she'd come and as good as killed Floyd as well. Was that so? If it was so, it was a lie they in the group had told her, for if they had drawn the Devil out from her, what was this left inside her? Was there more than one? Instead of fleeing from Jesus' clear light they seemed to multiply, doubling and tripling, and herself with them; Jesus was like the kindly firm teachers in the schools she had now and then gone to, who had put books and pictures and a globe of the world before her, and a map, and another map, worlds that she was not to choose among—no, they laughed at her when she tried—yet could not reject.

A disaster had befallen her in the healing group, not their fault maybe but it had happened when they had tried to cure her: a disaster like the disasters she had seen in hospitals, something gone wrong that nobody expected, the attempt to cure shattering a man or woman, everything done to make it better just making it worse, relatives shocked, awed even, by the ruin.

She would have to tell them in the group that it could not be made right after all, hard as they had tried. Because it wasn't sin; it was nature, or it was fate, if that was different. He was a hard bad man but she would no longer believe he had harmed her, not at least out of wickedness; he had been as compelled to keep her as she had been compelled to run away, and not only from him. The thing was, she should have kept running. It was when she let them convince her it could be made right if she turned back that this had happened. She shouldn't have turned back.

And there was no becoming single again now. She was no longer remembering the past but creating it backwards from every moment, and what was created would now always be there to be remembered. There was nothing she could do but keep going forward into the uncreated time ahead. *That's* what forgiveness was, that's what being reborn was, that's all it was.

She dressed him in a fresh shirt, and tied its strings in back. He was beginning to draw up into himself, knees to his chest, as a child does going to sleep, as people do who have gone for good; she'd seen it before. She did not raise the barrier of his bed again. Instead she stepped out of her shoes and got up onto the bed; she lay beside him, and curled against him as he was curled.

I won't go away from you, she said. I have to go back North now, but I'll come back here. If I can I'll go there where you've gone, and I won't turn back without you. I'll follow you until you can be saved too. And if we can't both be saved, if we can't return together from that land, I'll stay there with you, and not return.

# 14

"Gee," Rose said to Pierce, smiling. "You don't look so hot."

"I'm fine."

"Did you come down with something? You said you might."

He shrugged, trying to look hale. He felt dreadful. Arriving at Conurbana's bus station was like coming into some desolate port after sailing cruel cold seas for years. He tossed his small bag behind the seat of her car and got in.

"There's a dinner break now between the parts of this," she said, moving out into the shiny street and the traffic. "We've got a little while. You want to get something?"

"Sure." The window on his side was open a crack; he tried to close it, as he always did, always forgetting that it was jammed and would go no farther. The little car turned featly left and right. Pierce became disoriented immediately. Soon a complex junction brought them around the periphery of a plaza, wide and bare, on which were grouped a number of new buildings, some low and swooping, some vastly tall, collectively projecting over the stone space they occupied an orgulous hostility.

She told him what it was, the just-completed monument of the founding family of the city, a name he had read of even in grade-school history, grown rich first in furs and lumber, then coal, steel and railroads, finally nuclear power; giving their money away now in further self-aggrandizement. The buildings were a research center, a specialized hospital, an art museum (the latest avatar of the family was a prominent collector of the severest modernists) and other benefactions, their own offices too, all seeming hewn from adamant, the lights just being lit. A huge sculpture of twisted rusted I-beams in the center of the unpeopled waste, like the family's Steam Age soul.

"The hospital goes down seven stories underground too," Rose told him as they went past. "Besides all the way up. Seven stories. They say."

"Wow. God." Pierce felt, for no reason he knew, for no one he could imagine, an anguished pity. This was the first of his Conurbana places, first to be placed unremovably in memory, though he would never see it again. They went on, past old town-house tree-lined streets and anonymous rain-slick neighborhoods of cars and bars and Laundromats. Rose pointed down one street, hers she said; they crossed another, called Mechanic; the population turned poorer, the lights fewer, burnt cars along the sidewalks, buildings missing from rows of houses like carious teeth. Rose talked, her cram course, her apartment. She had got a part-time city job, she said, working in a battered-women's shelter; she laughed a little at this, ashamed or amazed. She. Pierce thought about the flask in his bag. Why are there cities like this, why this replication, streets and cross streets and other streets, persons and other persons, this one only one of thousands, it seemed dreadful to him.

This city was pierced or invaded by stretches of new highway; entrances and off-ramps struck into old neighborhoods, overseen by tall aluminum lamps like marching alien troopers, Pierce did not remember New York or at least Manhattan having these incursions; Rose shot up one, shifting gears. Where were they now? They seemed to be leaving the city altogether on a flying skyway, but the lights of its clustered buildings remained around them. At speed the light rain was driving; the windshield wipers clacked then hissed, clacked then hissed, melancholy sound; towering trucks expelled clouds of rain-fog from beneath their tires as they passed hugely by the little car, whose roof was leaking. Rose talked about the session leader, already two hours or more into his performance or job and ready for more.

"He's so amazing really. He was amazing today. I just hope he can keep his energy up, I want you to see him and know him."

"Pitt," said Pierce.

"Pitt Thurston. You know, he sleeps like an hour or two at night. No more. So I've heard. Can you imagine me? You'd be amazed though how good I'm getting. Up and attem." They swooped off the freeway again, having used it for only a couple of miles, but only to take another big road along which cold bright enterprises were lined up, rain-wet cars in their lots like glossy beetles and the icons of chain restaurants. Pierce thought that if he were king he would make it illegal for restaurants to be advertised by euphoric humanoid versions of the animals to be eaten there, it was just too crassly brutal. A chorus line of pigs, there, each grinning, each wearing a chef's toque and holding a smoking plate of his own cooked parts. That was where she turned in.

"It's right next door," she said. "Is it okay? They all sort of go here."

They had become *they* again, for now, for him. *Next door* was a squat motel, absurdly named: Bypass Inn. From there were coming now, in twos and groups, people she pointed out to him: they.

"Just a sec," he said. He rooted behind his seat, pulled out his bag from the back, and from the bag his flask. He drank, drank again, and capped it as Rose watched with interest. He offered it to her, a joke, and she smiled and shook her head. (Do you remember the one time she did take it from him and drink, at that party on the Blackbury River, the time they first met or maybe it was not the first time, when each thought the other was someone he, she, was not? Pierce remembered.)

"Ready," he said, and tugged at his overcoat, his breast on fire. "Ready."

The pig restaurant seemed to know the group, waitresses guiding them to the long tables in the back somewhat apart from the other diners. Rose, holding him tight as though it were she who was the outsider, took him to the center of one table where a dozen were already seated. She introduced or named him to those near them, and they smiled on him with friendly and maybe slightly overeager smiles; vast plastic menus were given them. His fellows seemed to know all about what was on offer here, this place was apparently one of a chain strung all across America, Pierce had never heard of it and would never see another. They talked of the meeting, more about the numbers who were present and the enthusiasm than about what was said. They witnessed—that's what Rose later called it, telling stories of remarkable and inexplicable blessings, mostly having to do with money: stories no different in form from ordinary stories of coincidence or luck, only always coming out right, the resulting smiles and nods around the table not smug or entranced but only well satisfied, the same smiles in fact they smiled at the plates of food put before them with amazing speed, where had it been kept. Pierce watched one little woman greet a rack of ribs that seemed larger than her own. Others, their mouths open wide, baring their teeth and scrunching their eyes into a semblance of fury, lifted sandwiches as tall as they were broad and dripping with glossy gravy.

"Not hungry?" Rose asked him, mouth full.

"Um no. Not really. I ate late. You know."

"Okay. Have to keep your strength up."

What could that mean? What was to be done to him in there that he would need strength to resist? Already he felt like Childe Roland in the wasteland, come to the dark tower; the strength it had taken to get to and pass through this city, Edom, Dis the mighty, all but gone. This was the second of Pierce's Conurbana places, this table and its twelve flesh-eaters. When they were done it was time to return; they all walked refreshed and eager back across the parking lot and through a line of scragged evergreens to the motel's parking lot.

There is or was then a certain acrid smell to new motels, arising from the artificial woods and wools they are furnished with maybe, or the harsh cleansers used to scour away the traces of so many humans passing so constantly, or from all that and also another subtler stink of falsity and veneer that the mind's nose takes; Pierce, nostrils flaring like a wary beast's, entered the Bypass Inn with Rose and the happy dinner group. Past the pretend Dickensian bar (Sixpenny's) and down wide stairs to the underground assembly rooms, many others joining them as they went down. Wide is the gate and broad is the way. Pierce furtively assessed them but could make no generalizations, they were not mostly young or mostly old, not very poor, certainly not rich; they were people, his neighbors.

"Look," Rose said. "Mike."

In short sleeves and a tie, yes it was him, Pierce's breast closed like a portcullis; he did not make fists but did feel his ligaments tugged at. He had read once that the "fight-or-flight" response causes the hair on male arms to rise, to make us look larger and more frightening, like startled cats. Our little vestigial hairs, inside our shirts and suits. His scrotum tightened too.

"Mike," Rose said. "You know Pierce."

"Sure. Hi." Mike put out his hand, a manly possibly aggressive grip; he actually did not know Pierce at all, it was one of Rose's confusions that he did, for Pierce had told her so, another lie he had been unable to disabuse her of. "Good to see you here. Really good."

"Well!" said Pierce in response, grinning.

"How are things in the Faraways?"

"Ha ha," said Pierce. "Are you selling books?"

Mike stood aside from the skirted table where piles of thin hardbacks were stacked. Most were tracts with pugnacious rhetorical questions for titles (*Is Jesus God? Why Die Forever?*) and the author was Retlaw O. Walter, LL.D.

"That's him," Rose said.

"Retlaw O. Walter?" Pierce said. "What's his middle name? Otto?"

"I don't think there is one," Mike said. "Like Truman."

Pierce was drawn to pick up a book, to see if there was a picture of the symmetric doctor on the back, but he could not bring himself to touch one. Eat nothing given you, refuse all gifts.

"We better go sit," Rose said.

"We'll talk later," Mike called after him. "We will."

She took him inside the Empire Room, as it was called.

"Does his wife know he's living here now?" Pierce asked. "I mean ex-wife. I would have thought . . ."

"Her," said Rose. "Real nice person. You know she was going to call me in her divorce case? Name me as a whatchacallit and put me on the stand."

"Corespondent."

"Yes."

"I didn't think they did that anymore."

"Well if you want to get somebody's kid away from them. That's how you do it." She chose seats for them, slung her coat expertly over the chairback. "Mike loves that kid," she said.

"So does her mother. I'm sure."

"Well. Not all the power's on her side. Not any longer."

Pierce asked nothing more. The walls of the Empire Room were covered with crimson-flocked wallpaper; on them, hung by golden ropes, were large fake oil paintings in ormolu frames, Claude-like landscapes, distant views framed by heavy-headed trees: zigzag of silver river, pale tiny temple, distant hills fading into cloud banks and atmosphere. Pierce gazed into them longingly.

"Ray's here," Rose said, but differently than she had said *Mike's here*. Pierce looked where she looked, to the dais where a lectern and a few chairs were set;

a large man sat at the edge of one, calm, torpid even, holding his elbows in his hands.

"God I know him," Pierce said.

"Yes?"

"Well. I've seen him." Where? In a white hat and summer suit, outdoors. Boney's funeral: talking to Mike Mucho, yes, and maybe to Rosie too? The Powerhouse was buying The Woods. Had they got Rosie too, got her or got to her? The man seemed to waken, to open his eyes upon them. The people began to grow quiet. He was heavy, both large and fat; his pants taut around his loins, constricting the large lump of his privates. When the room had been quiet long enough to satisfy him, he stood with effort and came to speak to them.

"Uh-oh," Rose said.

"We," Ray said, "we here of the Powerhouse are Christians. Our hearts have been entered and changed, and one way we know this is the powers that have been granted us. We know because we can speak in tongues, and we can prophesy. When called upon we can."

He looked them over. Rose in her chair seemed to stiffen, and Pierce understood that, like an ill-prepared student, she was afraid she'd be called on. He too: as in a dream, called on though he had not done the lesson at all, nor knew what the subject was; a sudden feeling that the man on the dais might have the power to make him answer anyway, belch out meaningless language, just to show him. Ray named a name, and a young woman in the front arose. She spoke rapidly in what sounded like high-school Italian, and sat again. Another woman: "Prophesy," said Ray, and she did: a burst of King James English, not anything specific, not tomorrow's headlines or news of the millennium; vague injunctions and threats.

One or two more women (all women, all young) and that was done. Rose relaxed beside him.

That's it? Pierce wanted to ask her. That's all? He felt almost fleeced. It wasn't exactly a trick, but certainly not magic; just a thing for believers to do, like prayer. He wondered what it felt like. He saw that a great weight of foreboding should now be lifted from his mind, but none was.

"The sign is not the thing," Ray said. "The power granted to the Christian has not been and cannot be fully shown, because it has no limit. Read Mark 16. Anyone who wants to know these things can. It's no secret. But life is short, and there isn't another chance."

He turned from them and went to sit; and just as the silence became profound, there leapt up from the front row a man as trim and chiselled as Ray was not. He looked at Ray and grinned, shaking his head as though to say *Aw you old so-and-so.*

Rose said to Pierce: "Pitt Thurston." She seemed to settle in her chair, and lifted expectantly a corner of her Bible's cover. It was white, in soft leather, with gold ribbons to mark her place.

Pitt Thurston expertly detached the mike from the lectern, and with it in his hand turned to them, feigning surprise, as though they had just appeared before him. A new kind of despair entered Pierce. Long ago in Kentucky he and his cousins with a delicious sense of trespass had used to watch the preachers on TV, they had just begun to use the new tool, they were clownish in every sense, they talked too loud and their haircuts were amazing, and their faith was so real and frank it was shaming. Pitt Thurston had learned not from such as they but from late-night talk-show hosts and corporate sales managers. He joked, he smoothed his tie and suppressed a chuckle. He went limp when he could get no enthusiastic response to his questions, and made the time-out sign to ask again. He had a trick of almost in his excitement letting slip a blasphemous or dirty word, altering it at the last minute to something innocuous, and raising titters—unless for shock effect he *did* say something strong, usually in condemnation of some other Christian sect.

"Okay," he said at length, and took up the limp-leather book from the dais. "Got work to do."

The work to be done was apparently the exegesis they were so proud of, the discovery of various appearances of a Greek word in the Gospels and Epistles, but Pitt never quite settled down to this task, or was easily distracted from it. They got to *dunamis,* power, from *dunasthai,* to be able. Dynamo, dynamite, anodyne.

"Tell you something," he said thoughtfully, looking up from his text. "How many have ever been up to the new nuclear plant on the river island there? Ever taken the tour that the Metatron company gives? Metatron is the outfit that runs that. Quite a place. I've often been there myself. People, that is a powerhouse: that's all it is. A powerhouse of a new big funny kind, slick as all . . . heck and working day and night for us. Now. Suppose you were invited in there by Metatron, into that powerhouse, and shown around; and then suppose the big boss took you into his office, maybe old mister what's-his-name from the big plaza downtown himself. And he said to you We put out a billion megawatts of power every day, or whatever it may be, and we would like to put all that power at your personal disposal. Understand? *All that power at your personal disposal.* Need something done? The power's yours. Do with it as you wish. Bet you could outdo your neighbor's Christmas lights then. No really. Boys and girls, brothers and sisters, that powerhouse has got nothing on God's. Metatron would run out of steam mighty quick if God chose to withdraw the power of His powerhouse from it. And that's the one that God is offering to you. He's just waiting to make that offer to you: all His power at your personal disposal. Free of charge.

"God made this world *for us.* For us to delight in and have what we want. Once we threw away that gift. Fine. He *still* wants us to have what we want. And He will get it for us and *can* get it for us because He made the rules by which the world runs. They're His rules and He can change them. For *you.* God loves you so much and is so much a powerful friend to you that He can suspend the laws of nature on your behalf! He did it, has done it and will do it again. You don't have to *believe* He will; I promise that if you only believe He *can* you'll start to see and experience some pretty mystifying things, things that don't happen to other people. If I started now I wouldn't be done telling stories till morning. This whole great big ball of earth and all those stars around us are His doing! If He wants to rearrange the weather, think He can't? If your car and another are on a collision course, think God can't put His finger out and just push that car a little aside? No? What do you think the world is made of? Something real special? Something with a mind of its own? Or just dirt and rocks and metal and wood? Well? What *do* you think? If you think He can't, can't act on your behalf every day, or wouldn't just for little old *you*, then why believe he's going to change the laws of life and death He laid down, so that you don't need to die forever? Or don't you believe that either? *Do you believe this stuff or don't you?*"

He surveyed them. He pretended to listen hard to hear their assent. Then he clapped his hands hard together, a sudden crack.

"Okay. Here's how it works. You get down on your knees and say Lord I believe all that You have told me of Yourself through Your Son Jesus Christ in His book, the Bible. Lord I don't care about anything of this world except Thy service. I want nothing but what You want for me, I'm happy with bread and water for Thy sake. And you know what happens then? They throw a party in heaven. They are rejoicing. 'Cause I tell you there is more joy in heaven over one lost sheep found than ninety-nine who never left home. Hey, it's your birthday! And what do you get on your birthday? Presents! Ice cream and cake! What you most want, what you most need! Don't believe it? He said it: I am come that you might have life, and that you might have it more abundantly. *More abundantly.* That's a *promise.* You say to me, Pitt, surely you're not talking about the things of this world, about *money,* about *stuff*—yes! I am! That's the *first* thing I'm talking about. *Abundance.* And then next—it gets better and better—how about health? Never sick anymore? Can't have abundance if you're sick. So yes health. And better. Life. More life. *Eternal* life. Right here on this earth.

"Now you have to understand that these things are yours in Jesus Christ. They come to *you* because Jesus Christ renewed God's promise in all its original glory. They aren't for others. Sorry. I mean Buddha was a nice guy but he didn't rise from the grave. God wanted us never to die, and He showed He wanted that for us all by raising His Son from the grave. No death. Simple as that."

Pierce, who had sat stony-faced through all the little jokes and sweeteners, now laughed aloud, a small bark that he instantly regretted; Pitt Thurston's viper's eye flicked to him, seeming to file the unknown face, then away. O hateful man, a catalogue of all that Pierce despised and feared, how could she. The suit of pale wintergreen, sculpted and tufted at shoulder and lapel. The horrid familiarity with the Deity, his boss man, his chum; the smug self-love, the violent energy directed against others: who could not see in him the smooth beast horned like a lamb who fronts for the Big Beast in Revelation, the top salesman, who marked the foreheads of everyone so they could buy and sell. Pierce looked down at his open Bible.

What was it that the fat man had said. Mark 16. It turned out to be the very last chapter.

He who believes and is baptized will be saved; but he who does not
believe will be condemned. And these signs will accompany those who
believe: they will cast out devils in my name, and speak in strange
tongues; if they handle serpents or drink any deadly thing, it will not hurt
them; and the sick on whom they lay hands will recover.

"Come meet him," Rose said. They were done. The Bibles were closed around
him and the damp coats picked up: school's out.

"I can't," Pierce said. "No."

"Oh come on," Rose said. "Just hello."

"I can't," Pierce said. "I can't touch him."

She had lifted him up by his elbow and pushed him gently forward. Ray and
Pitt stood together, back-to-back, taking on the people exiting around them; Ray
an immobile idol, Pitt a thrusting knife. Rose brought him before them.

"This is my friend Pierce."

This was the penultimate place of Pierce's Conurbana memory house, this
exit guarded by these powers, now turning to see him, one with eyes like
saucers, the other with eyes like pinwheels, Pierce's only way out to toss them
the sop of his humility and goodwill, hi. His hand even, touching theirs. Hey hi,
where you from? Oh yes? Hey we're really getting established there, you'll be
hearing things. Oh hey yes oh sure. And they let him by.


"Mike told me he thought you were a pretty interesting guy."

"Oh yes?" Pierce pulled shut the Asp's door and again vainly tried to shut the
window fully. Mike had trapped him in the foyer of the Empire Room, unwilling to let him go without a chat, *parhesia*. Rose had vanished, maybe by pre-
arrangement.

"What did you guys talk about?"

"God," said Pierce. He was shivering, clutching his overcoat around him.

She grinned at him. "And?"

"He asked me if I believed in God. I said no. He asked me how then I accounted for everything, why there are things. I said I didn't account for it. He
asked me, if it wasn't God, what was it, just chance? And I said I had no idea. I
said that just because I rejected his or the Bible's explanation didn't mean I had
to come up with one of my own. I said if he had told me that the wind is caused
by the trees waggling their branches, I would feel okay about rejecting his explanation without knowing what really does make the wind blow."

She laughed. "He said you were pretty definite. Knew your mind. He said
that's rare."

"He seems to believe," Pierce said, "that this whole universe, this inconceiv-
ably immense enormous, this whole thing was created *for us,* and that when our
story's over, this little Christian God story, then the whole universe is too."

He had got away from Mike at last by announcing he had to go to the bathroom. His mouth phenomenally dry and his bowels uncertain. While he evacuated she must have checked in with Mike.

"Do you believe that?" he asked. "About the universe?"

"Oh," she said. "To me it's not what's important."

"Not important?" he said. "Not important?"

"We've got to make a stop at the store," she said. "If you don't mind. Otherwise there'll be nothing for breakfast. Okay?"

"I'm with you," Pierce said.

More travel, seeming to lead to no different places, the rain grown a little heavier, the darkened stores and the houses seeming to shrink beneath it. The supermarket she chose was huge, a half circle like a vast Quonset hut, lit by banks of fluorescent lights that could be seen even from outside through the glass front. Above the wide doors, red letters taller than a house and glowing from within said FOOD. He thought of the power the place must be sucking up and wasting, Metatron's, more where that came from.

"Oh hey," she said as she took him within this place (how did she dare operate here so briskly, so confidently? Had this been her world all along?). "I found the answer to one of the problems you had."

"You did?"

"Well it was pointed out to me. About the end of the world. That Jesus said the end of the world was coming right away? Like soon? And then it didn't happen?"

"Um," said Pierce.

"Well," she said. "In the Letter of Peter. Peter says not to worry about it. Because he says that in God's sight a day is as a thousand years, and a thousand years is as a day."

"Ah," said Pierce. "Yes. Simple as that."

"So," she said. She was picking unhesitatingly among the multitudes of things on offer here, all of them signalling to her in bright colors and bold packages, and throwing them in her cart. "Oh and another thing."

"That wasn't Peter," Pierce said. "Some other guy, much later on. Not Peter Peter."

"Another thing." She smiled at him, triumphant in advance. Her face in these lights was translucent, her eyes small and pale. "About Jews. This is really interesting."

This he did not respond to.

"I guess you haven't heard what's coming out."

"What."

"It's turning out," she said, "that all that didn't happen."

"All what?"

"All the awful things. Six million people killed. The gas chambers. It didn't happen."

Why was it so brightly lit here, as though to deny night altogether; why had he never been taught to live here. "Didn't happen?" he said.

She stopped her cart to look at him, at his face, perhaps to compel his attention. "Well of course bad things happened. People were hated and killed. They had camps where people died. But it wasn't like people said. Six *million*. I mean."

"So all these people," Pierce said, "whose parents and grandparents were burned up . . ."

"Well they don't *know* that, lots of them. They *think* that. They've been *told* that. But they could have been fooled too. I mean everybody has been. That's the research that's coming out. There's just no basis for it."

She waited for him to respond; when it became clear he could not or would not, would just go on staring, she said, "Isn't that great?"

"Great?"

"Well that this terrible thing and all these people killed didn't happen. That it wasn't so bad. Because what people say is, How could God let something like that happen? How could it be that a God of love could let such a thing happen and not do anything to stop it for so long? And so if it didn't."

"And why," he said, "do we think it did happen? If it didn't. Who, why."

"Well," she said. "Just think about it. Who would want people to believe this? Who would want that? Who could tell a lie that big?"

"Jews," he guessed. "Top Jews around the world."

She seemed struck by this; it was apparently not the answer she had in mind but she seemed to consider it, as though it hadn't occurred to her. "Well but," she said. "What I meant was, who would want us to think that. About God. That something so terrible could happen, and God would do nothing." She tapped her nails on the cart's handle. "It ought to be obvious."

Yes. Their counter-God, he saw it, out to blind us to the true God's goodness. "Yes," he said.

She held out both hands, showing him the palms. Easy.

"So, what," Pierce said, "he created all this evidence somehow? Printed up documents, faked some films, I guess published books . . ."

"Oh Pierce," she said, hopeless case. "Come on."

Of course not, he thought. The Father of Lies needn't tell any himself, only busy himself in the brains or souls of others. He said no more. His horror at her proposition, its dreadful falsity, was as great as if it were true; a world in which it *was* true, it and all the rest of their claims and ignorances, the little stone-dead world where they took up all the room, walking in the Spirit with Ray and Pitt and sending their enemies to Hell, was where he was; the world he had come from was withdrawing like a tide down a dark beach, waving goodbye.

"This is the hardest thing I've ever done," she said. "Mike said it would be hard and I didn't know what he meant. Walking in the Spirit. Loving the whole world. I can do it for a little while at a time, but it always stops. But while it's happening there's nothing like it, no ordinary happiness is anything like it. I'd give anything to share it with you. With anybody. I would."

They lay in her narrow sofa bed. The lights were out but city lights from different sources fell over the place in stripes of cold color, blue and dead white and dinge, multiplying the windows across the wall. She had adopted a street cat, whose little slit eyes looked at Pierce from the top of the dresser.

"So nothing, nothing," he said, "nothing can, can."

She lay thoughtful for a time.

"The only thing that could make a difference," she said then, "would be if I didn't get what I wanted. *That* would make a difference."

"If your wishes didn't come true."

"Well. And then anyway maybe when I was an old woman I would look back and say I *did* get what I wanted even if I didn't know it at the time."

"That's what we were told by the nuns. You get what you want. Always."

She put out her cigarette, and her last exhalation took momentary form in the streetlight, a little ghost. "I know I'll slip up again," she said. "Get drunk, fornicate, whatever—the dog returning to his vomit, you ever read that part? But it doesn't matter, because what I've been given can't be taken from me. I've got it for good. I can look down, and see how far up I've come. But I can't fall. Ever again."

The unsleeping pedant within Pierce recognized the Carpocratian heresy: there is no sin for those who are saved. He saw himself too in her scheme, fornicating, not excluded, if he could put up with it, which he couldn't.

"Tell me something," he said. "Rose."

"Yes."

"Is this. Is this the big payback? Is that really what all this is?" He knew it was not, but the monstrous possibility seized him, why not, why not anything.

"Payback?"

"For. All that was done. All that I."

"You mean the Invisible Bedroom?"

He made no reply, wondering if she was smiling.

"Aw Pierce," she said. "That wasn't *you* doing those things. That was made up. That was just a game."

Later on, when in a kind of awed pity he would look back upon himself in these days and hours (as we do when remembering an unspeakable dream, how could I do that to myself, for what reason), it would be this moment that he would feel with the sharpest pangs. He had already been judged, condemned, dragged by grinning torturers down dungeon stairs, but it was then the oubliette opened beneath him and he went down. Entirely unable to see (though it would strike him later as obvious, the punch line of a long joke) the reassurance she of course intended by what she said. Not you: not you that made me feel those things, suffer those things. Don't worry.

What *she* would remember was his demonic restlessness, like a speed freak, unable to be reached or comforted. *Sweet sleep* she said to his head on the pillow (as Ray had said to her one bad night, whereupon her whole body had filled with, yes, sleepy sweetness, she'd barely made it to her bed before it overcame her), but it didn't work on him, maybe she was too distraught herself to put the power into it. He got up, then lay down again; tossed this side and that. She slept; she dreamed, she would not remember of what, and woke, and only an hour had passed; he claimed she had talked in her sleep, about the Spirit or the Powerhouse. She had seemed afraid, he said. It was he who was afraid. He got up again, and sat in a chair; she slept. As soon as it was light he woke her again, dressed now, and made her give him her house keys. He was going out, he said. Unshaven, great-eyed, mad. Like a student up all night cramming for a test he couldn't possibly pass. She let him go.

He could not shake the sensation of being still on the bus. The hum of its engine in his breast, the sense of being propelled unwillingly, the bitter flavor in his throat and his mind. He stood at a wide blank intersection, a store on each corner closed tight and no help anyway (children's sad clothing, drugs, treacherous-eyed cameras, and one whose business he couldn't discern). He walked a block in each direction, finding nothing more. For a long moment he forgot where he was, what city, why; and then, when he remembered, could not remember how to go back, which turns he had taken. Follow the right-hand wall. He was about to turn and try to retrace his steps when he recognized the store he stood before; it was the drugstore he had first seen. Full circle. It had opened, it had a fountain; he entered warily.

Coffee put before him. The counterman looked long and meaningfully at him, toothpick rolling left to right in his mouth; *one of them* maybe, Pierce thought, one of Ray's or God's people, either waiting here for Pierce, planted here where Pierce was bound to come, or just one of many, from now on he was going to find them everywhere, and they would know him too. Then he understood it was only his own appearance that made the man size him up, his stricken face and frowsy hair, and it occurred to him that maybe the mad feel that they are observed and judged constantly because they really are. When he paid, though, and the man flipped his quarter change to him, for a tiny but perceptible moment the little flashing turning disk *paused in the middle of the air* (Pierce would remember this distinctly later on, years later, would see it sometimes in dreams) as the counterman looked again at him in that calm penetrating do-you-get-it-now way, that look that in Pierce's experience had never existed before this month and was now apparently a feature of the universe. The coin fell before him. Pierce was free to go.

*This is not my fault,* he thought. No it was not he or anything he had done or wanted that had brought this about. It was because of some disaster or calamity that had just occurred somewhere, that he was not aware of, and why should he be. Surely there were others like himself trapped or cast away by it. He realized he could see, from the corner where he stood, the building she lived in, thought he could tell which window was hers. She too. No, not she: this was her land, wasn't it, her city. Happy here, happy. Yet surely she was not the *source* of it. She could not be: unless she wasn't she at all.

He saw her then, saw her vacated body asleep in her bed within her dawn-lit apartment. And as though thrust through by a sword he understood what had happened.

She'd got off the bus.

Somewhere far away, wherever she was, she had got off the bus; weeping maybe, in her old raincoat, at some rest stop in some shabby city or some diner on a windswept hillcrest, she'd got off. And her eidolon, the one they had replaced her with in this city of theirs, the one now occupying her bed and her life, had set about doing what it had been made to do.

For *it wasn't he but she* with whom the wizards had made their bargain; not his love but hers that was to be tested. Well, she hadn't lasted long, had she. No surprise; no blame either, as there would not have been if it had been he, he who had been set the test and failed it finally. It was okay: if he could ever see her again (but of course he could not, except in dreams) he would want to tell her it was okay. He had suffered, yes—as they had intended he should, as they had told her he would—but he was not to suffer the worst consequences. No. For he knew their plan, he had in fact himself conceived it in advance of their making and carrying it out: on his way home from school, long ago, on the bus.

She was not she. Clear, strong, and beautiful, more beautiful than she had been before, she was not she, and he knew it. He should have known it sooner. The simulacrum they had made was amazing but he would not any longer be fooled. He knew who they were, of course, though not how they had gained the power that they had, or why he and she should be subject to it. But knowing what he knew he would fight them; he would not surrender, he could not, though he supposed he would not win. He had no weapons but poor Reason, and his memory of what the world had once been like, and he did not think they would be enough.

He let himself into her apartment; it was as he had seen it from the street. The gray light; the cat-familiar in its place, watchful. Her bare arm over the pillow and her mouth ajar. He sat again in the chair where he had sat so long. At length his dry wracking sobs awoke her; he had begun to sob because he wanted so much to touch her, to tell her it was okay, that he understood. She didn't open her eyes or stir; she only listened to the noises he made and, to her shame, pretended to be still asleep.

# PIETAS

---

## THE
## CHRISTMAS
## ASS

# 1

G iordano Bruno left thankless Prague for Frankfurt in November. He carried two long Latin poems he wanted printed there, *De minimo* (on the Little) and *De immenso* (on the Big). He met a man called Hainzell or Haincelius who carried him off to a castle near Zurich called Elgg (how was it they recognized him, men and women like this, by what sign, he had long ceased to wonder at it) and sat him down to write a book on composing signs and seals. How is it done? How can they be made, in the soul, in the mind? How are they to be used; what can they do? Well:

> The First is Chaos, who cannot of course be figured, is unfigurable, dissolves all figures, or precedes their possibility.

Very well; and then:

> Then comes Orcus, the son and offspring of Chaos: that is, Abyss, the wanting out of which all that is proceeds. Orcus too is unfigurable.

These things were surely known to everyone; indeed they can't be learned, they can only be forgotten. One more of the first triad, before the world begins:

> Then Nox, our mother: She is without form and cannot be seen, or she is the last or first thing that can be seen, and yet she cannot be spoken of, or remembered. There is one figure of Nox the unfigurable: an old woman, immense, in black, with black wings as large as night.

Next, her daughter Amphitrite, or Fullness; then Zeus or Order, out of whose brow proceeds Athene or Sophia or Wisdom; then in quickening crowds all the others, one at least for everything there is, and one also for all representations of those things, no number that could be made could ever comprise the whole.

> Venus: A naked girl-child rising from the sea, walking ashore wiping the salt spindrift from her with her hands.

Yes of course. And then:

> The Hours dress that naked girl and crown her head with flowers.

Yes. But then:

> A man of noble bearing and great gentleness, riding a camel, dressed in a garment the color of all flowers, leads a naked girl-child by the hand; from the west comes a kindly wind bringing in a court of omniform beauty.

Where did they come from, where do they go; how did he draw them into his mind on their journey; how was it they would stop for him, regard him with their august eyes, agree to stay? He could not command them but he could modify them: make the sad ones glad, the savage ones mild.

> An image of Orpheus: a beautiful young man with a lute, around him all the animals still and listening.

Yes of course. But also another of Orpheus, coming to him unbidden but just as certain:

> A black king on a black throne before whom a tall man and a dark woman couple violently and unnaturally.

What he knew was that the oppositions invoked in creating these differing emblems could not be simple ones, or the thing would die; the oppositions must run in two or four or twenty directions at once, high and low, male and female, dark and light, one and other, many and one, near and far. What was it the English said: *the more the merrier.*

> An image of Mercury: the young God on his steed, holding in his right hand the winged scepter on which the wakeful serpents are entwined, in the other a strip of papyrus. His steed is the Ass.

This seemed to him clear enough, clear enough to speak truths; but perhaps he was wrong, and it needed Explication.

There would have been no such deity as Mercury, if he had had no animal to ride on. Its qualities are the opposite of his, but his qualities cannot exist without their opposites; they are known by them. So let it stand there in his court, high on a pedestal, so that it may display (for opposite reasons) certain of Mercury's qualities that aren't usually mentioned and are maybe unmentionable.

Mercury in his strength was anciently pictured as no other thing than a male part, obscenely large and aroused. But the qualities passed the other way as well, from Positive to Negative: what the Ass is, Mercury is not; but what Mercury is, the Ass his steed may also be: quick, witty, unscrupulous.

Let those who are Asses rejoice in their asinity; let those who are not transform themselves into Asses as soon as they have the wisdom to do it, or pray just as hard as they can that the Gods will do it for them.

—You may use such figures as these to summon help, he told the puzzled lord of Elgg, showing him his descriptions of Amphitrite and the rest. Use them rightly, and an army of helpers will come to your aid, riding out from your own heart, or from the sky. For a time they can do that; then they no longer can.

—These? said Herr Hainzell.

—No not these, Bruno said, taking them back. These are mine. You must make your own.

He went back down to Frankfurt to cut with his own hands the geometrical illustrations for this book (*De imaginum, signorum et idearum compositione,* the last book Bruno would write); and it was while he was at work there that he received an invitation from a young Venetian nobleman, who had come to know his work (but how? Bruno had once lived in kindly Venice, but that was long ago) and who now invited him to come teach him the arts he knew: Memory, Mathesis, Magic. This last word however the young man did not write. Bruno began to wrap up his business. He had conceived a plan. He was still growing.

Late in the year 1588 there came to Prague from Milan Signor Arcimboldo Arcimboldi, bringing with him the head of the Emperor. That is, we know from certain documents that the head was there in 1591; surely it *could* have come in that year, 1588, when so much was for a moment possible.

Arcimboldo had been many years in the Emperor's service, and been ennobled for his pains (for his pleasures too, it seemed to him that his life and his work were so intensely pleasing as to be almost a crime, or a sin). He had made astonishing pageants and plays for the Emperor, built automata that worked by water and fire and wind. He had designed triumphal arches that told the story of the Emperor's victories against the Turk (*tell me more, tell me more* he would ask the victorious generals as he sketched and lettered and colored, and they would look on each other somewhat guiltily: there had really been no great victory, but Arcimboldo didn't care, there would be when he was done). To pass beneath one such arch, he made a gigantic armored Emperor on a snorting armored horse, so real that a bystander had been cured of the King's Evil just by touching its skirts. Arcimboldo hadn't known whether to laugh or weep.

Then he had begged leave of the Emperor to return to Milan, to live quietly and care for his soul after the years of patient labor, and was allowed to go; reluctantly, for the Emperor hated losing anything he had acquired. Now he was returned. The Emperor was there in the Neue Saal for the placing of his head, the last head he would make, Arcimboldo said, the one missing from among the heads that hung there where the Elements made the Seasons.

A single attendant carried it; it wasn't large. It was placed upon an ebony easel, and the Emperor stood before it, and Arcimboldo himself (plump, all in black like his master but smiling hugely) removed the wrappings.

There is no Stone: no medicine for melancholy. But when the Emperor saw the new portrait aflame in the afternoon sunlight a deep peace and richness filled his bosom that he recognized immediately even while knowing he had never felt it before.

—Vertumnus, said Arcimboldo. Your Majesty will of course be aware. There is a poem to accompany it, to explicate it.

—Myself, said the Emperor, looking.

Arcimboldo bowed deeply.

It was himself, his heavy lip and big jaw, unmistakable. Like the other heads by Arcimboldo that watched over his collections, it was what it was, very exactly, and it was also an emblem; its eyes were eyes, and saw, and they were also not eyes but other things.

Vertumnus is God of the changing year, he who turns the seasons one into the next. So the Emperor's face and breast, his hair, beard, ringed ear, cap and chain, were all fruits and vegetables, the riches of every season gathered into a heap, May's and September's, summer's and spring's, undistinguished but distinguishable.

Almost in awe the Emperor came close.

The figure's toga, of spring and summer flowers and sweet lettuces, revealed the bosom, a great autumn gourd; warty winter roots were the tendons of his neck, and a bristling chestnut the beard beneath his lip. In his lip, June raspberries, and peas in their pods his eyebrows; sheaves of wheat and grapes, blushing apples his apple cheeks, the Emperor laughed aloud in gratitude and glee. How many portraits of himself had his artists made over the years, endowed with his chains of office, his Roman armor and bays, with the sacred Cross; surrounded by Fame, Victory, Justice, Orthodoxy. No: he was of the earth here only, a man composed of earth's multiple and constant production in time; himself, and not himself but all things, beyond all the powers of kings and states, popes and principalities, changeless in constant change. He was the last element not pictured here in this chamber, the fifth, which is Time.

—Time, said the Poem of Explication read aloud by the lector whom Arcimboldo had brought. Ruler over all states, god of the elements. Eternal because cyclical, ever-returning, always the same in change.

—It shall be mounted at once, the Emperor said. He looked around himself; Strada was instantly at his side; workmen were summoned. The Emperor, finger to his lips, studied with Arcimboldo where in the quadrature of the gallery it would hang, in what corner of the earth, or what center. The place they at length settled on meant that the Elements must be shifted in their places (as the workmen with their ladder and plumb bob noted) somewhat north by northwest into the region of the summer constellations; Arcimboldo thought that would be acceptable. The cabinets would have to be shifted and reassembled to the same degree, but that could wait, the Emperor was opening and clutching his hands impatiently behind his back; Strada clapped his to hurry the workmen.

Arcimboldo and his assistant took hold of *Fire* and lifted it from the wall.

Just then in the *Judenstadt* far off, a certain housewife, hurrying to finish her Sabbath cooking before sunset came and the fire needed to be banked, spilled her fat and in horror watched it catch. Doing what she knew very well never to do, she flung a pot of water on it, which spattered the burning fat everywhere. In a moment she was calling for her children, first to help, then to flee.

—*Air,* said the Emperor, and that picture was the next to be shifted, his plumage rustling and the birds that composed him calling like terns crowding a sea rock. Down the ladder it came, to go up elsewhere.

A sudden wind springing up tossed the black-beaked gulls of the river and the flights of city pigeons out over the rooftops. It played over the burning house in the Jewish quarter, and those gathering in the narrow street watched it tease and prod the fire, twisting it into vortices, imps that poked their heads out the windows grinning at the crowd before being withdrawn again to redouble their efforts. And now the crowd saw a remarkable thing: out from the house were coming all the small inhabitants, the mice and cats, a shuffling old dog and even (scorched and bawling, having pulled its rope loose at the last moment) a little goat that Father had bought at Passover for two zuzim.

During that time the workmen in the Neue Saal shifted the beast-man *Earth* with his fox's eye.

Then they climbed to the fish-woman *Water*. By the time they had loosened and lowered it, the house in Fabrent Street belonged to the fire, which was making a quick meal of it and looking around hungrily. But the Jews of the ghetto, so crowded and huddled, were of course great firefighters, and already from the nearest fountain the leathern buckets were being passed hand over hand with rhythmic cries to be flung (half-empty by then) at the fire's feet. It wasn't enough. But by the goodness of the Eternal, blessed be He, the house next door happened to be an illegal tannery, which had with its stink always disgusted its neighbors but which had flourished because it was situated above a small and ancient but reliable well, and every day the tanner's men pumped water to fill a tall wooden cistern on the roof. So now men with axes climbed to the tanner's roof and began hacking at the planks of the cistern, their eyes stinging from the swirl of smoke, and at length the cistern split and like a glutton vomiting shot a great volume of water over the little house that was pressed up next to it. Water and fire, ancient enemies, grappled and fought, and men and women hurried to help, and soon the fire was out. The people wept and cheered. Only one small house lost, not whole streetsful as in other times. The peace of Shabbas came.

Peace: Perpetual Peace. The Emperor in his palace ordered torches and many-armed candelabra lit so that he could go on standing before his new portrait.

—I am not a god, he said.

Arcimboldo, still smiling, bowed again: as you say.

—Nothing I have wanted for the people have I been able to create for them.

—Your Majesty is beloved for the mercy you have shown.

—You mean, the Emperor said, for the evil I have not done.

Arcimboldo bowed again.

Wrong, wrong, he had been wrong about everything. He had believed that by shutting himself within his palace to study the making of gold, by learning to hasten the birth of gold from what was not gold, he could thereby hasten also the return of the Age of Gold. What gratitude for him then! But the one thing the Age of Gold had not contained was gold. It contained peace, not justice; liberty, not might; plenty, not lucre. The golden wheat; the golden cherry, golden marrow, golden grape: not gold.

What had that Italian said, that uncowled monk. Toil destroyed the Age of Gold, and created injustice, and want, and inequity. And only more toil could correct this.

He must not be still, any more than the productive seasons could stand still. Not even Winter stands still, but nourishes Spring in his old cold heart. He must work, and not for himself; roll up his sleeves and humbly toil. God had not taken from him the strength of his hands by anointing his head.

What was it he must do? The old fear threatened his heart. He could *do* nothing. Nothing he had ever tried to accomplish had been completed; it was a curse or a sin in him, a lack like a cast in his eye or a short leg: he said to this one Come, and he goes, and to this one Go, and he comes.

The Italian had said he knew what must be done, and how to do it. Believing he had himself known better, the Emperor had not bothered to listen.

Love, Memory, Mathesis. What he had said. And the greatest of these is Love.

—Call him again, the Emperor said. Everyone started at his sudden command.

—Call . . . said Strada hurrying to his side.

—The Italian monk. You know the one, Braun or Bruin, a little bearlike fellow, oh you remember!

—Bruno.

—Call him again.

Strada bowed, backing away as fast as he dared, turning at the door and calling for servants even as he left the chamber.

—Call him again. The Italian, the little man, Brunus Nolanus Italus.

His servants called their own servants, and sent them into the city, to Bruno's lodgings at the Golden Turnip, to the libraries and the schools and the taverns; they sent a message to Trebona to ask John Dee what had become of the man. But no one knew.

John Dee knew one thing for sure: if the Emperor was still demanding the Stone of him (*the thing of value* he had written in his note to Dee, as though shy to speak its name) it meant that the gold Kelley had learned to make—and taught his old friend to make—was barren. Dee had guessed that it was. It would not generate a son, *filius Philosophorum,* the reason or Logos of matter whose juice or blood was the Elixir the Emperor sought. And everyone knew that the greater the hopes a practitioner raised in His Sacred Majesty the harder it would go with him when those hopes were dashed.

So it was time to be gone. Yes there was a new world to cry; no he would not cry it. Let him once reach his home again and they would not see him more.

Around Rozmberk's house in Trebona the spies had increased in numbers, not only the Emperor's but the Papal Nuncio's as well; they could be seen from the windows of Dee's apartments, genial loiterers with hands clasped behind them, approaching the carters and purveyors coming out of the gates to ask a friendly question. What new people are in the house? When does the Duke return? What is that smoke? One thing they learned was that a young countryman had lately been taken into the house, a dark strong lad with a limp. He was noted in the reports; the Nuncio's reports went to Rome, and would still be able to be found there four hundred years later; maybe the cryptic references in them to *Giovanni Dii e su compagno, il zoppo,* "the cripple," refer to this young man, glimpsed taking the air with the old one, or pulling a cartful of children.

By now the news had reached Prague that King Philip of Spain had failed in his attempt to conquer England. His Armada, greatest Catholic fleet to put to sea since the Battle of Lepanto, had been turned aside: by the Queen's steadfastness (*I know I have the body of a weak and feeble woman,* she told her army at Tilbury, words generations of Englishmen would commit to memory, *but I have the heart and stomach of a King, and a King of England too; and think foul scorn that Parma or Spain, or any prince of Europe, should dare to invade the borders of my realm*) and also by English seamanship (Drake, Hawkins, Frobisher, they had all been there, Dee's old fellows, he had made maps for them in years past and had long pleaded with the Queen to buy them ships, see now), and—at the last moment—by a wind, a marvelous wind, a wind out of nowhere, blowing from the wrong quarter, blowing nightlong: a wind that, by dawn next day, had changed everything. John Dee thought of the tower room, that summer night, and of his imp; he computed the time, and laughed: laughed aloud as he had not laughed in many months.

Then he sat down, and cleared a table in his busy study, and with good parchment and new pens wrote in his best hand a letter to his Queen.

*Most gratious Soveraine Lady, The God of heaven and earth (who hath mightilie, and evidently, given vnto your most excellent Royall Maiestie, this Triumphant Victorie, against your mortall enemies), be all waies thanked, praysed, and glorified.*

His wife Jane put her hand on his shoulder.

—Husband, the carriage maker sent for is here below to see thee. And a harness maker is come too.

—Yes. Soon, soon.

*Happy are they, that can perceyve, and thus obey the pleasant call of the mighty Lady, OPPORTVNITIE. And, therefore, finding our duetie concurrest with a most secret beck, of the said Gracious Princess, Lady OPPORTVNITIE, NOW to embrace, and enioye, your most excellent Royall Maiestie's high favour, and gratious great clemencie, of calling me, Mr. Kelley, and our families hoame, into your Brytish Earthly Paradise, and Monarchie incomparable,*

He paused and dusted his nose with the plume of his pen; the letter that Dyer had brought hinting that the Queen might receive him kindly was a year old at least. He spoke for Kelley here, as well as for himself: but he no longer knew Kelley.

*we will, from henceforth, endeavour our selves, faithfully, carefully, warily and diligently, to ryd and untangle our selves from hence: and so, very devowtely, and Sowndlie, at your Sacred Maiestie's feet, to offer our selves.*

He completed it with compliments, signed it, sanded it.

The answer would be long in coming, if answer there was. A safe-conduct out of this land, Dee hoped, and a welcome into his own. At least that much.

To Edward Dyer, who was to carry the letter, he told more, for the Queen's and Burleigh's ears only: a tale about gold, and a wind, a wind that had blown away the Queen's enemies. Of this last, he said to Dyer, speak very delicately: for everyone knew who it was that could raise destructive winds, and by whose agency they did it.

Meanwhile there was much to pack and ready; many farewells to make, not all openly.

—I am summoned, he told Duke Rozmberk. I have been long abroad, and my Queen, to whom my services are owed, has called me home.

He said it gravely, with regret, and the Duke bowed, and assured the old man of his eternal admiration; offered him every help he could give in preparing the journey. Dee asked but one thing: that it be kept, for the moment, secret. Another bow. And then the Duke, as quickly as was consistent with a solemn and regrettable parting, left for Prague and Kelley: Dee from the room over the gate (furnace gone out) watched his coach tear away, the driver wielding his whip, the postilions galloping, footmen clinging.

Home, home, sang Jane Dee, as she gathered and put into trunks her fine new and plain old clothes, her cuttings taken from the Duke's kitchen-gardens; home again home again jiggety jig. She packed the clothes her children could still wear—her children, the two youngest of them born here and speaking *prager Deutsch* more readily than English, poor younglings: she sat down in the midst of her packing, pressed her apron to her face and wept for the years.


—The Emperor in Prague, the Doctor said, desires that you be returned to him.

He had found Jan the wolf-boy in the kitchen, in his chimney corner, with his stick by him. He liked to stay here, in the warmth and the odors, with folk who spoke the tongue he had grown up speaking.

—When the Emperor gave you into my care, Dee said to him, it was because I told him that I could cure you of your affections of mind. Your melancholia. I failed. He wants you returned.

Jan lifted his face to the old man's as though to read in it a gloss on the words he had said.

—I cannot cease to be what I am, he said then.

—No more can the Emperor, said John Dee. I am leaving this country, and can no longer keep you.

—Then, the boy said, tomorrow when you come for me I will not be here.

John Dee answered nothing, nor did he make any sign of assent.

—You would not lock me in, the boy said.

—No. But think. There is nowhere you can go. Nowhere in Christendom you will not be hunted. A stranger too; everywhere you would be the first to be noticed, and pointed at. You must go far, if you go.

—Nowhere far enough.

Dee pondered. He held his long staff behind his back in both his hands.

—Atlantis, he said. On the other side of the sea.

The boy tried to see in Dee's face if he were being mocked.

—A wolf might do well there, Dee said. Never be caught, never be seen. They say the forests are infinite, and as full of game as a menagerie. They say there are few men there, and those men savages, who speak not nor think nor pray, and harm no one.

Jan had been listening intently; now he laughed aloud, as though waking from a spell.

—And how would I get my living there? he said. I am most often only this fellow you see. Lame now too. I don't know how to be a savage. Or how to get over the sea.

He struggled to his feet.

—I will not go back, he said. Better to die quickly. I will not go back.

—What am I to do with you then? Dee asked. Cut your throat? Poison you? No no.

—Listen, the boy said, and stood to whisper urgently into the old man's ear. Do this for me. Keep watch, and when next I am abroad and yet seem to be still in my bed asleep, here is what you must do: turn the body lying there over onto his face. That's all.

—And if I do?

—If you do that, the boy said, then when the night is done and I come home again, I will not be able to return into that body on the bed.

—The spirit's way out is by the mouth, said John Dee. I have heard the tales.

—And the way in again. And if day comes and I have not returned, I never can. I will remain where I have gone, to wander there till my appointed death-day comes.

—Why then do you ask me to do this?

—Better my spirit never return than that I be shut up in that Tower. Let the Emperor have my body. I will not be there.

He had begun to tremble, and gripped the collar of John Dee's robe in his hands.

—Do this for me, he said, and wherever I am and wherever I go I will bless you for it. If I can bless.

John Dee took the boy's hands from his robe and helped him sit again. He wondered if what the boy had said could be true, if such fates really existed for souls, and could be chosen; he hoped not. He said in English:

—Somewhat we will do.


Not till Christmas did an ambiguous but perhaps not useless answer come to John Dee from his Queen. Enough to keep him from the Emperor's prisons at any rate if he left quickly enough—and if he left behind the things the Emperor desired. One of them was the wolf-boy; the other was Edward Kelley, whom he had led or had followed to this shape-shifter's city.

Kelley was in the Imperial service now; the Emperor had required of Duke Rozmberk that Kelley be released to him; he had promised not to keep him, but did not intend to part with him. And was it Kelley who suggested to the Emperor that though born in England he was of a noble Irish family and of the gentry of that unhappy kingdom; or did he simply not object to someone else's suggestion to this effect? Anyway from then on it was true: the Emperor granted him a patent of nobility. He was thenceforth *eques auratus*.

—Gilded knight? John Dee asked him.

—An ancient term of honor, Sir Edward said. Of old in this land a knight's armor was gilded.

He took wine the Doctor poured for him. On the long table in Dee's Trebona apartments were all the treasures that John Dee had brought out to give him, to keep and use for as long as he needed: his convex glass, small original of those great ones with which he had tried to cure the wolf; the vessels and other necessaries with which Kelley and he had first made gold in Dr. Hagecius's house; all the powders remaining from Dee's own recent work, all the glassware and waxes and resins and spirits.

—All as stated, John Dee said. He held out a catalogue to Kelley, and handed him the pen. Subscribe it with your name, we will seal it, it is yours.

Kelley stood and clasped his hands behind his back. He seemed not to have heard; he looked weighted down by the brocade gown he wore, the gold chain.

—I too will return to England, he said. Soon. Tell Burleigh, and the Queen. I have had letters imploring me.

He had recently sent to the Queen in London a warming pan, an ordinary copper warming pan, from which a piece had been broken, and by action of his powder turned to gold. (This pan and its golden shard would go into the royal collections and persist there for a long time; Elias Ashmole actually saw it, or knew someone who had seen it, and drew a picture of it to put in his book *The-atrum chemicum Britannicum,* where it still is: on page four hundred and eighty-one. The pan is lost.)

—The Italian didapper has come here, Kelley said. The one we were shown in the glass. Who came to Mortlake house.

—Yes. I have seen him.

—Why have they summoned him here?

—Have they summoned him?

Kelley stopped his pacing.

—Ask them, he said. The know-alls from heaven, or t'other place. You may, and see if they will answer you.

He said it tauntingly. John Dee pushed away his cup.

—I have heard her voice, he said. Edward, she has spoken to me.

He had not intended to reveal this; like any poor child with one thing he is forbidden to say, who is told that it must never be said, who then blurts it first thing.

—Who has? Kelley asked.

—Madimi, said Dee. She spoke to me, and told me of many matters.

He could not tell if Kelley heard. There had been times before, in Poland, in England, when Kelley could not hear the plain things spoken to him by his fellow-men, as though the crowd of other beings were too thick about him for the words to reach him.

—She said, John Dee went on, that you have gold in overplus; that you may eat it and drink it if you like; that you have not praised her for it.

Kelley laughed, so hugely that Dee could observe a missing tooth or two. No longer a youth, and no elixir for that.

—Old friend, Kelley said. Think you that it was they or anything they said that opened those secrets to me? Do you think so?

John Dee laced his fingers together. He asked: If not they, who?

—Who. Who. I told myself. Where did I learn? From myself. Who did I teach? Myself. I fetched out the secret, I took myself by the sleeve and whispered it in my own ear.

—Jest not with me.

—Thou'rt a wise old fool, Kelley said. And I love thee. Therefore for my love

I will tell thee. I make gold from nothing, not because I have learned how, no not from the angels nor from the devils of hell nor from old books of shitty rhyme. I followed no *recipe*. I do not know how the world works. I make gold because I am I. Because of the power that I am. It matters not how I do it; I make gold because I know I can.

He had leaned his hand upon the table and bent into his old friend's face; he pounded his breast as though in confession.

—I can, I can, I can. And because they cannot keep me from it I can give the same to you if I choose. To the Emperor too when it suits me. Gold was never made before, but now ever after it can be, from this time to the ending of the world.

—And when is that? said John Dee. If you know, say.

Kelley still leaning forward on the table, mouth ajar and eyes wide.

—I do not know myself, John Dee said to him. But I think this. I think the ending of the world comes to every man alone, soul by soul; when it is ended for you and for me it will not be ended for all; it will not be done till the last soul says Amen.

When Kelley, burdened with his things, left the Trebona house, John Dee rode with him as far as the high road to Prague. The wind was cold and sharp, making their horses dance and toss their heads, wanting to be home. The two men took hands, and John Dee saw that a tear coursed across Kelley's face. From the wind, he thought.

—I'll await you in Bremen, Dee called over the wind's blowing.

—I will be there, Kelley said.

—Then England.

—England, Kelley said. He turned, and raised a knight's gauntlet; set out without looking back. John Dee never saw him again.

It is some twenty leagues from Trebona to Prague. At his new house in the castle precincts Kelley found a man awaiting him: a man he knew slightly, a physician of the Emperor's named Croll, or was it Kroll. All in black like a monk or. Kelley said he hoped he had not been waiting long.

—Waiting long? said Dr. Kroll. He was smiling with an odd intensity; his hands were clasped behind his back; there was a contingent of the Imperial guard come with him, and a sergeant at arms, who watched impassively.

—I hope you have not.

—Oh very long, the man said. Oh yes a very very long time indeed.


—Now, said John Dee. Now we have our carriages and their equipage, horses, fine horses, with harness; leathern bags aplenty; a Queen's safe-conduct too. Let us go, go, go. Now while we may.

Now, while the gold he had accumulated could still be marked by a tooth, still color a touchstone; he filled the bags with it, and secured them in the new coach himself. The coach was enormous, oddly high-sided and heavy, Dee's own design; the coach maker had shaken his head over it and huffed and muttered and turned the drawings upside down and right-side-up, and asked Dee why he had not gone to a boatwright with this. But now it was ready and its furnishings installed and its brightwork polished and its tack all creaking-new and odorous.

Now. One last communication though, left deliberately till last: in the midst of his servants and the Duke's men carrying out his boxes and chests Doctor Dee sat down and wrote in Latin in a swift hand to the Emperor's chamberlain. He told him how God through the medium of His holy angels had first brought him to Prague, and how the evil tongues of some close to the Emperor's counsels had then driven him out; and how the Emperor's commandment now prevented his going there again. He said that he could not himself return the one redeemed from the White Tower without violating that commandment. He said he regretted the delay, but that the boy was now wholly cured, his present gentleness greater than his former ferocity; that he no longer needed restraints. Now, he said, he would give the boy over to those servants of the Emperor who continuously watched the comings and goings of John Dee's household here, to be carried to His Sacred Majesty. The bearer would give SS Majestas all particulars.

This letter, folded sealed and addressed, John Dee tucked into his sleeve. And as Jane and the children, the servants following with the last of their belongings, left the palace and piled into the interior of the coach, Doctor Dee climbed to the tower room to fetch the crystal sphere, the glass from which he had been spoken to. He had almost thought to leave it; he did leave the table with its *signacula*, all the beeswax candles, and the frame that had held it up. But he took the glass itself. He wrapped it in lambskin, placed it in a leather pouch, pouch in a strong box, box in the bottommost of the wagon. Safe as a cage of doves or a saint's bones. He thought it likely, though, that it would never speak again; he thought it would from now on show nothing but the surrounding air and the world, strangely curved by its surface.

Nothing.

She had said, once, that a wind would bring in the time of passage wherein the new age was forged, and a second wind bear it out again; and of that new age she'd said, *Look not for me, I will not be there.* She had not said that in the new age she would not only be absent, but impossible: that whatever was possible, she would not be.

There were twelve young Hungarian horses to pull, and three Wallachees for saddle horses: Arthur begged to ride with the postilions and was allowed. Up to the coachman's seat, *to guide us in the country and the night* he said with a smile, Dee sent the young Bohemian boy with the dreadful hobble, hatted and scarved for the cold. And when, as he expected, the eternal loiterers at the tavern leapt up to see this grumbling coach emerge from the Duke's gates, Doctor Dee summoned one with a wave; he took the letter to the chamberlain from his sleeve, and gave it into the man's astonished hands.

—Take this to Prague castle, he said. Be quick if you expect reward.

And he drew the curtain.

Next day at dawn a company of the Imperial guard rode out from Hradčany, clattering and clanking in their arms, their horses' iron-shod hooves slipping on the cobbles and striking sparks. They were many hours and miles behind the fleeing wizard, but moving much faster. There was only one way he could have gone, the captain thought, through the southern passes of the Böhmerwald, making for Regensburg, and he was right: after another night and day John Dee's carriage stood at the top of a pass, his horses spent and weary and the sun going down far away at the end of a winding road.

—Now, said John Dee, who sensed the troop that pursued him; he could have spied it like Cæsar if he had had the Emperor's mirrors. He climbed down from the coach, wetted a forefinger and held it up into the still air. Now we must make speed or we will be stopped. We must not stay the night.

He had them all disembark, and he and the stolid coachman set to work and stepped a light mast amidships (it had been carried underslung in three long pieces, fitted with iron cuffs and made to slip one into another; with a long hammer the coachman nailed them securely together). A bowsprit too reaching off the bow, which is what the carriage's strange sharp nose now could be clearly seen to be. They slung a yard across the mast and from it dropped a four-cornered lugsail, such as John Dee remembered the fishing keels of the River Humber at home to have, right for a heavy broad craft such as his; he ran a little topsail too, for the brave show of it, and a jib from the bowsprit.

The older children all helped to set a standing rigging of fore-and-aft stays to keep the mast steady. Stays from the bowsprit to the mast too, and stays to hold down the bowsprit from being lifted by the jib—the great grief of your lugsail, said the Doctor. Running rigging then to make and shorten sail, held by pins along the rail. The afternoon grew late. With the little ones Jane Dee sat by the roadside; the children sought for spring wildflowers under the forest mold and put them in her lap; she watched her husband, and when he caught her look he could read it well enough: you are a great fool, and that a Ship of Fools.

When it was rigged he stood off, clasped his hands behind his back and studied it. The air was still.

—Well, we must lighten our load. Come.

From down deep in the wagon's hold he began to pull out the leathern bags that held their gold. *Not those, not those,* his children cried, but he kept on; when they were heaped on the ground he unbelted one and took from it a few great coins. They shone, but not with gold's light; they seemed to have acquired a film of slime. They stank.

—Come, he said again; tossed those coins back and lifted the bag. Arthur and Katherine each took another and followed their father to where a little bridge crossed a rocky gullied place that fell sharply away; a roadside shrine was there, a cross, a Corpus. The leather bag was too heavy for the Doctor to lift high enough; Arthur came and pushed from below, and all the gold within poured out, coins slipping and sliding in a ringing rush down the slope. They looked down to see what they had done: gold enough to buy happiness twice over lay shining in the dark gulch, caught in cracks and crevices and flung over the ground like blossoms.

—Now the rest, said Dee. In the first hard rain it will be gone, or be so changed it will fool no one.

They tore open the others and poured them out too. Arthur laughed aloud: throwing it away was even more astonishing than making it had been.

When they returned to the carriage the Bohemian boy had climbed down, taking with him the small bundle that was his, shirts Jane Dee had sewn for him, herbals the Doctor had made, a Latin grammar of Arthur's.

—I will lighten your load too.

—No, John Dee said.

—If you cannot go quick enough, the boy said, and they catch you, I should not be with you.

—We will be quick. I promise you.

—No, said the boy. I will be gone.

—Home? asked the Doctor.

—I don't know how to find it. They would not take me in. Anywhere is home enough.

—How will you live?

—The boy smiled, and hooked his crutch beneath his arm. Beg, he said.

John Dee would have said more, wanted to say more, to know more too; he had thought to take the boy far with him, to Bremen, to England it might be, and find him a ship bound for Atlantis or the New-found-land: but now a sharp wind had risen, and the wheels of the wagon creaked. John Dee clutched his hat, expostulated under his breath in Latin; the wind subsided, but only a little. He embraced the boy.

—May God bless you then, he said. And keep you from all harm. Wherever you go. In whatever land.

—Amen, said the boy, and kissed the old man, and turned away. The others did not see him go, for the quick little wind had changed its quarter; the children were watching it luff and belly the sails, the coachman hauling on the reins and calling to his frightened team and stamping on the brake. Arthur and Rowland were reminding each other how a lugsail is hauled into the wind.

—The wind! called Katherine as her mother pushed her aboard. Father! Is it *Boreas* the North Wind? Or *Auster* the South Wind? Or *Angustes* the Northwest Wind? Or?

—It is my very own wind, John Dee shouted over its cry, pulled aboard the moving coach by his sons. But God alone knows how long it will be mine. If it blow till the world's end it may not be long enough.


The wolf went on, following a track he came upon, which grew clearer and broader as he walked along, until the roofs of woodcutters' and charcoal-burners' cottages appeared, and just when he thought he could walk no farther he reached a village, a church where he might be helped.

In that village he lived for a time, and then passed on to another village and then to another, gathering as he travelled a past around himself deep enough to satisfy questioners; and he would never again be caught, asleep or awake, in that land or this one. He would not ever see Atlantis, though he would sometimes dream of it. He would find work, and a wife, and father children, and his children and their children would be born without the destiny he suffered.

When he became a very old man he was brought to trial (the records exist) for saying that he had as a youth gone out in the form of a wolf to do battle with witches. The judges tried to make him confess that he had made a compact with the Devil, but he would not; what did he have to do with the Devil? He had fought the Devil's witches at hell's door, and when he was dead his soul would go to heaven. The judges did not know what to do with him. The time was past when men of reason could be frightened by such stories; no witch had been burned in that diocese for a generation. The priest was brought in to scold him for his lies and his blasphemies, and he was given ten lashes and sent home.

By that time seams of coal had been discovered and opened all over those mountains. The people of the region became miners, the most famous in Europe, taught their trade (some said) by the old kobolds whom their picks and hammers had awakened. Take it and leave us in peace. And his children's children mined, and raised their children to be miners. And their descendants did, at last, come to Atlantis, and indeed there were great forests there, and high mountains, and coal in the mountains that must be mined: a vast seam running down the gnarled backbone of the land.

They went south and west as more mines were opened; many more of them came from the old lands over time, and it was they who taught the mountain people how to mine, who before had only farmed and hunted and cut timber. They were called bohunks or Dutchmen by the people of those mountains; they went together with them down the deep shafts and did not see the day, and loaded the cars with the mountains' heart. Black Gold one company called theirs, earth transformed to worth by time. They kept to themselves mostly, in their hunky towns, speaking their own language (less and less over time till only grandmas and babies shared it) and building churches for themselves of wood and clapboard like their neighbors'; priests brought saints' bones all the way from Prague and Brno and Rome to put under the altar stones. And there, in those mountains, some of their children would again be born with the caul, and their mothers would look into their hooded faces and not remember what it foretold.

# 2

There are ways down into the land of Death: and there are also ways upward into the realms above, to which the same dead go.

There are the dark brotherhoods, the unknown ones, who go down into those lands that are not under the earth's skin of soil but are nevertheless deep down; who give chase, who follow after those whom they are bound to pursue, to whom they are joined through time in an enmity that is not different from love. And there are also the light brotherhoods, who go the upward ways, and they are also unknown. Over their lifetimes—over many lifetimes, it might be—these have built for themselves, by thought and by works, a body of light: a body that beyond death can arise through all the spheres like an ark, and escape the jealous rulers. They know the right words to say, they don't drink at the silver river and forget whence they have come and whither they go, and so they don't need to turn back and do it all again.

And yet among them are a few who, knowing all this, nevertheless *do* return here below, for our sakes. How many? Only one in any age, whose name is known to all though not his nature? Or numbers of them, enough so that every one of us will one day be touched by one? Anyway they return, not once but many times, and they will go on returning—not recycled out of hylic ignorance and forgetfulness but turning back by choice from that shore, each time more reluctantly, with deeper pangs, and only because so many of us still remain behind.

Beau Brachman didn't remember where he had first learned this story, on what continent or coast, or if he had maybe not learned it at all but simply recalled it, like Plato's boy and the triangle. He didn't know if, in the story, those who return to us with their aid and their knowledge are able to remember who they are and why they have come back: or if they act as they do without knowing. Which made the heart almost stop for a moment in pity and love to think of—Beau's anyway—before beating again more richly.

Beau was himself on a journey of remembrance and recall, as well as of progress and discovery, if they're different (they weren't then); he was walking downtown through New York City and drawing, from the things and people that he saw, the city he had once lived in. Gautama, Pythagoras too, remembered each and every one of their past lives, and were not crushed by the weight of that measureless suffering; Beau worked to reassemble just the present one he was actually living, cleaning his house in search of the groat he had lost.

Midtown streets were full of the usual handers-out of flyers and offerings. Beau had always taken these, whether snapped briskly at him from the hands of men in dark glasses or held out hopelessly by the walking wounded or pressed on him as though for him alone, for he knew that those who are paid to hand them out only get their money when they're all gone. He had at one time used to study each one too—not for anything he might want that they offered, only trying his luck, a sortilege or fortune cookie. There seemed to be more being proffered now than there had been then, which was maybe why Beau took no notice of the wraithlike boy with starveling's arms bare in the cold who handed him one, his last or only one.

SOPHIA                                                                    WISDOM

WITHOUT SOPHIA NO WORLD
WITHOUT SOPHIA NO SUFFERING

She is the Companion of God, the First Thought of His Mind, and without her was made nothing that was made. Springing forth from the Father she descended from the Highest Heavens, and by her descent created Angels and Archangels. And out of envy they captured her, because they did not want to think themselves anyone's progeny; they dragged her down into the world of waters which they ruled; they imprisoned her in the body of death.

The page was so dim and crabbed, the type so small, that Beau had walked on half a block before he had got it right side up and read its heading; and when he saw what it was and looked back, the child who had given it to him was "nowhere to be seen," of course.

In countless ages she has passed through countless bodies; all the Powers strive with one another to possess her, and where she has appeared has come strife and warfare; she was Helen of Troy, she was Virgin Mary; she is both Wh-re and Holy, both Lost and Found, Child and Mother, helper and harmer. +JESUS+ came to this earth and the body to find her, his twin and parent, and saving her saves us. *Go thou and do likewise* (Luke 10:37).

Read and remember. Knowledge comes in 60 days. Pass it on.

PRAY TO/FOR SOPHIA      SAVE HOLY WISDOM      OPEN YOUR HEART

Beau folded the sordid sheet and pocketed it, wondering, not because of the story it told, which he actually knew, but because he had been handed this sheet or an almost identical one years before, and therefore guessed that this one pointed the right way (backwards).

Out on these streets, yes maybe on this very corner, a decade and more ago: Beau was recently back from Elsewhere and feeling that he had fetched up on the wrong coast, not to say the wrong continent; this Sophia one was not the only paper he had got in the way of in those days, not the only news handed to him or blown up against his legs or bought for pennies that had altered his direction, handmade news borne out from underground printshops by troglodytes and sold all in an instant by bedizened children. A picture for instance (one of many doubtless but this the one that had remained with him) of four or six godlike persons, a band it was said, their thumbs in their belt loops and their jean cuffs turned up above their bootheels, American giants, he had forgotten during his time among the smaller older peoples how strong and tall humans could be; and their hair grown to fabulous lengths, fulfilling hair destinies previously unrealized for modern male humans, hair like Botticelli's angels, hair like dandelion moons, hair like storm-tangled seaweed, a promise that if this was possible then nothing need ever be the same here again. Quicksilver Messenger Service. *I only am escaped alone to tell thee.* Beau now in this winter going downtown on Madison smiled to remember.

And had it been because his hand was open and his heart too that on those streets he had, just about then, acquired one of the legendary passes that circulated on certain days and times in what was assumed to be random fashion (though you were never exactly surprised at having one pressed into your hand or slipped to you across a bar or left for you in the pigeonhole of the downtown hotel where no one knew you slept): a white cardboard oblong with only a number and the letters MM? If you did not know what the letters signified you tossed the thing away with a sense maybe of having avoided being tricked or cheated, but if you *did* know you experienced a hot rush of blessing, having been given for nothing, by fate, what others sought to pay fabulous sums for.

MM. It was underneath Park Avenue somewhere, reached by way of the tunnels that fed people into the subways and trains from the American Metal Climax building, the Cyanamid building, the Metatron building, towers whose weight you could feel above you and that you imagined might go down as far as they went up, mirror Babels or Babylons. (It was believed that you could also reach the place by heading down along the New York Central tracks from the old private station under the Waldorf-Astoria where FDR used to pull in, to exit in his chair out of sight of the newsreel cameras and then appear later erect and grinning at a ball or banquet; more than one party was lost going that way, hope and Evereadys giving out amid the drip of seep and the chitter of rats.) The door when you found it was white, unremarkable, marked with the same MM in black sans serif, no Day-Glo or art-nouveau exfoliation; once past it and another like it, you took further passageways all tending downward and filled with progressively less light and more sound, insistent mechanized yearning and throbbing; then after a last and smallest door the place opened like the great chamber a spelunker comes upon after wriggling through cold narrow caves for unmeasured time: a space apparently unending because so dark, crossed overhead with ductwork and pipes hugely coupled and ramifying, moist and hissing. Wide is the gate and easy is the way: people occupy the floors and bars and fill the vast transparent beds and turquoise pools and the music actually shakes the smoke that fills the air, Beau had marvelled to see that, the wisps and fumes of it standing trembling in the thunder like souls: the rich smell of it, and of the cheapest and strongest incenses from most of the countries he had dwelt in or passed through. And the universal smell as well, nostril-widening, shocking, unmistakable. Suspended overhead in glass was the famous silkscreen of the titular goddess of the place, not one copy but ten or twenty, it being of no consequence which were originals and which knockoffs, they all had the same mouth, and the lidded eyes at once hurt and dangerous, at once having and wanting. Lost and found. Child and whore. Savior never saved.

All protest against the Powers starts with the flouting of their command *be fruitful and multiply:* Beau knew that. Make no more bodies in which the lost light is caught and suffers. Which, with the Pill and all, had just in that time and place become possible, even common. "Copulation Without Generation is Salvation," the famed orgiast Mal Cichy said or shouted once into Beau's ear in the "Venusberg Room" at MM. "Fuck your way to freedom." The Phibionites for instance (Tertullian saith) aimed to consume the seed produced in 365 sexual couplings with 365 different partners, one for each Æon that separates us from God. "Not a big number," said Mal, prolific producer and consumer of seed, at once lithe and porcine, his every maxim an offer too.

*Escapism* was what this was called by concerned commentators in the papers then, this and so much else that so many people were thinking up then to do, and Beau supposed that was exact, especially the *ism* part, implying a program, a commitment, even a hope. Except that the headshakers seemed to think escape was *easy* when just the opposite is the case, as usual the valuation had got reversed and the escapists who were held up as examples—the maddened addicts and the pleasure suicides and the soiled bodies uncollected at MM when the lights came on past dawn—were precisely those who had *not* escaped, those who even after fabulous exertions hadn't made it, crashing shattered and aflame like flop experiments in aviation, aerialists falling prey to hateful gravity, *escape artists* who had been unable to wriggle out of the last wrapping of chains, the last padlocked carette. Beau encountering them in that underground didn't know (but he could tell looking backwards) that his vocation had revealed itself there, that once he had failed often enough himself he would then spend years finding and caring for others who had failed: offer himself for them to love, a path by which they could maybe really *get out of themselves:* out of there where, despite all their efforts, they were stuck more firmly than ever.

The place was gone now, MM: Beau walking downtown was sure of that. It had become for good the fiction that most people always thought it was. The Powers were changing their masks, and so the stories they issue, that we enact, must change as well. Beau kept on, down past Madison Square, arriving at length at a genteel and shabby brownstone on East Twenty-fifth Street off Lexington (the one neighborhood in Manhattan that has no name) where were housed the offices of the Astra Literary Agency: that is, the apartment and book-crowded bedroom of Julie Rosengarten, who was Pierce Moffett's agent and—once upon a time, the time when Beau himself lived in these streets—Pierce's lover too. Beau knew her from MM, to which she had come after her time with Pierce.

"Something has happened in Hell," Julie Rosengarten was just then writing on a long yellow pad at her desk. "An ancient evil has burst its bounds"—she pondered this, then struck out "bounds" and wrote "bonds" instead—"and threatens to engulf the world." She liked "engulf," a word she wasn't sure she had ever written down before. "What dark destiny from another time connects an autistic boy in a small Maine town to the CEO of a giant munitions corporation, a faded movie queen, and the keeper of the poisonous snakes in the Central Park Zoo?" She was aware of footsteps on the stair outside, and wondered a little, for she was almost always entirely alone here weekdays; some departing tenant had probably once again left the street door open. An ancient evil. A *nameless* ancient evil. "Alone and unregarded they battle for their own souls and the soul of the world."

A sweetly deferential and yet definite knock on her own door. She saw she had used the word "world" twice. And what was the soul of the world? Something that Beau Brachman would be able to tell her maybe.

She opened the door to him.

"Oh my God. I just this second thought of you."

"Hi, Julie."

"What is it?" Beau had never visited her here before.

"Can I come in, Julie? I won't stay long."

"Oh God, of course come in." She stood aside for him, seeing as though through his eyes as he entered her chaotic place, the piles of bound galleys, the lurid covers of romances and fantasies, the typescript of the nameless-ancient-evil book she had been blurbing, a book she knew was going to make her some money; she didn't know which made her more uneasy as Beau came in, the book or the money.

He let her make him tea, and ate the bread she gave him slowly and with what appeared to be delight; Beau's abstemiousness always looked like a kind of shy delight, Julie didn't think he really meant it that way and maybe the delight was only hers, just to be in his company again. *It's been so long,* she said, though it wasn't like they hadn't been in touch: in fact she had called him in some alarm and fear the night of the big wind in September, sure that it portended something and not knowing what it was (she had called a few people that night, shocked at her phone bill the following month). They had talked about Pierce that night, too; they had agreed Pierce would have been surprised to know that he was thought about by others; but Julie did think about him, his spirit's life, his fate.

"Where are you going, Beau? How far?"

"I don't know. Not far, maybe. I don't know."

"Are you going out to the coast? Will you meet the guys?"

"I can't say, Julie. I don't know."

That he had been set in motion was news enough for Julie Rosengarten. Once, she had been sure she would see the inception of a world entirely different from the one she had been born into, had sat one summer on the bluffs above the sea at Montauk waiting for the Old City to arise from the blue water, feeling delight not only in the huge possibility but in her own aptitude in imagining it, which seemed to be power. It was Beau who had told her no, it's not a possibility, it's a certainty: but it won't be a city from the sea, it will be some small and unnoticed thing, apparently one of a million identical things but not identical, you will very likely miss it even if it's in your own backyard; which doesn't mean you don't keep looking and waiting.

"What should I do, Beau? If I can help I'll do what I can."

"Tell stories, Julie."

"Oh boy," she said helplessly. "Well gee."

Beau always talked as though she had chosen the work that she did because of the help she could be to the world, which was shaming, sort of; he told her she had a big responsibility, because after all the world is made out of stories.

"There are different kinds of stories," Beau said, as though Julie knew this very well. "There are stories that are like—like wallpaper, or chocolate. And there are stories that are like food and shelter. And in certain times people hunger for that kind, and in those times there have to be tellers of them. Not to have them is dangerous."

"Who could tell that kind now," Julie said or asked. "Who could."

"They aren't only told. I think that when they are needed, they're found too, in lives and in the world. The newspapers and TV tell them as though they were really happening, and they are."

"Which ones are they?"

"Not many. I'm thinking that right now there's only one."

"Just one?"

"It's told in so many ways though," Beau said. He closed his eyes and began to speak as though counting or recounting. "Someone or something is lost and needs to be rescued or awakened or saved," he said. "It's a woman or a man, or it's a child. Or it's not a person, it's a flower or a stone or something of your own or your family's, something valuable or just magnetic, something you need to have. Sometimes you find it. Sometimes you find out that whatever it is that has to be found isn't the thing or person you thought, but another one, one you knew about all along but didn't recognize."

"Right in your own backyard."

"Or *you* are the one that's lost, waiting to be found, or searching for a way back or a clue or."

"Do you always find it?"

"No. Sometimes you fail, and what you have to tell is the story of how you failed. Maybe you took dangerous journeys into dark places, journeys that other people don't perceive to be dangerous, or even to be journeys; maybe you gave up, and turned back. Or maybe you didn't even dare to go. Maybe you refused, and the refusal might cause you some kind of awful shame and guilt, so you're seeking always ever after for relief, and in your search you find what was lost anyway."

"So okay," said Julie.

"Worse sometimes is when you do find it. Like the people you see on the street in this city, every city, who push their carts and busted baby carriages full of junk. These terrible burdens. Every day they find the thing that was lost, the all-important thing, they save it, and they go on, and then they find it again a little while later. And again."

"Oh God."

"It might be that it's to those people the story comes first; that the burden is theirs first. It might be that there has to always be one or some of them."

"It would be hard to do that," Julie said, and lifted her eyes to the solid walls around her.

"Hard," Beau said. "How about if your task was to find some *one,* not something, but someone who is also a seeker, so someone who's always faced the other way, who you can't get to turn and face you."

"How do you think these up."

Beau laughed. "If it was me thinking them up," he said, "I might know how I did it. But it's not."

As usual it was impossible to know if Beau meant exactly what he said, or if what he said applied to the world she lived in most of the time or to another one that was a lot like it but different. She thought of all the books she had sold or tried to sell, many of those that were around her now whose covers and titles Beau's eyes passed over, and she thought well what the heck, most of them are just the kind Beau described; she didn't think they had been food or shelter for anyone, or there would not need to be so many of them; and so what was she in business for?

"Maybe the thing that has to be found, now, is just the right story of what was lost."

That was Julie who spoke. All of those who had lived around Beau for long had this experience now and then of saying things that they hadn't known they were going to say, and didn't know if they meant, or *what* they meant. Julie knew this. She knew the sadness too that came with his company and didn't pass away when he left, along with the joy of having had him nearby; the sadness that was maybe Beau's sadness though felt as her own, the sadness for which *lost* was the word. And for which *found* was the word as well.

# 3

Pierce that night dreamed that Rose told him how she had escaped, and been rescued.

"I ran away," she told him. "I could see them all, the others, going the wrong way away over the hills, so many of them. I don't know if they were looking for me. I walked a long time alone. Then a band of other people saw me, and pointed, and started calling to me; and I was afraid. But when they came close I could see that they were kind. They talked to me a long time, days maybe, and everything made sense. The weather was so clear and dry. They asked if I wanted to come with them. They told me I would be safe with them, and I knew I would be."

Pierce in his dream both listened to her talk and saw her among her rescuers, not as though he were one of them but still as though he looked on her too. When they had all rested they moved on, with her among them, climbing steadily upward into the clear air. With them she gathered food and firewood, and sometimes helped to carry the children, great-eyed placid kids who would grip her waist with their knees and lay their cheeks on hers. We'll go up along that ridge under the shade of those trees, they said; and all of them, the old people and the kids and the friends she had found, went up under great red-barked trees so calmly tall, and after a time came out into sight of the sea far below.

He awoke in his bed in Littleville, and it was way before dawn, black and cold; he lay in the warmth of the sun he had dreamed of, unmoving for fear of losing what he had found. For he knew how to make this right. He had awakened knowing how to make it and everything wrong come out right from the present backwards. It was a question: a simple question he had to ask her, the question he had not asked.

The morning after the outreach in Conurbana Rose Ryder had driven him back from the city to the Faraways, though *back* did not seem to be where he came to; no matter how superficially familiar his road and his driveway, he knew he had actually only gone farther on. He parted from her in his yard; she wanted to come in no more than he wanted her to, she had clearly had it with him by then. He watched her back out and turn to go, working her wheel with knitted brows. He went into his house as though swallowed by it, and sat down in his overcoat on the daybed in his office, feeling the place around him as though it expected something from him. Into the Invisible Bedroom he would not go. Though he had not slept, still he stayed all that day and well into the night awake, the dark waters lapping at his feet.

Once he leapt up, telling himself aloud that after all he wasn't friendless, he had counsellors. Beau Brachman would know what to do, what to think; he should go out, drive there now; but the darkness and the image in his mind of the rising road defeated him. Well then he'd call. Beau's phone number was not listed, of course, but Pierce thought he had it somewhere, written down on a matchbook or an envelope from last May when Beau and he were making plans to go up to Skytop Farm for the balloon festival.

Green May morning, the great balloons arising from the pasture. Rose Ryder departing in a black one with Mike Mucho, her lover then, and Sam in Mike's arms. Pierce had just that morning finished reading Kraft's manuscript for the first astonished time, this book that lay now on his desk. In the womb of that time had lain already the dark fœtus that had grown into this time, and yet he and all of them had smiled in the sun and kidded and felt delight and hope. He thought probably they still did, those others.

Here was the number.

He dialed, and waited a long time while it rang. The woman who answered told him Oh no Beau wasn't there, he was away (she seemed to think Pierce would know this, as though everybody must) and she didn't know when he would be back. *I hope soon* she said.

He sat again. He would get up now and then to put a log into his little black stove or go to the bathroom or check the flow of water as the temperature dropped after dark; then return to sit. Which didn't mean he was not in motion much of the time, across the wastes to which he had come: he trod on league upon league, in time to the beating of his heart, not knowing the right way back but quite sure this wasn't it; he watched the beauty and interest drain from things, leaving mocking or sullen husks which still had to be dealt with, his shoes, his clothes, his beard, his food; clustering stuff to be pushed aside so he could Think.

They had tempted her, and she had believed them. They had shown her beautiful false faces that had fooled her, and she had allowed them to take her into their dark tower; she was complacent, smiling, greedy for what they had to give her or said they had. And he, he had no sword, no shield; he knew that for her sake or out of his own powerlessness he would eventually surrender too, no matter that he knew that the lovely rewards were false, were false appearances covering up things loathsome, obscene in their true natures.

He thought: my strength and mastery and wisdom and Reason couldn't make a world; but my fear and weakness could, and they did, and this is it. What was it going to be like to live here forever.

No that was crazy, it was literally insane to think in that fashion; everyone knew that. They all knew better, there where they lived, as he had himself known better once, when he too had lived there among them.

He felt as heavy as though cast in bronze, and at the same time evanescent, nothing but one burning eyeball and a clockwork heart. He came to believe that he might die; he thought that if he did not get help, if he were not somehow shaken awake, then by dawn he would certainly have gone too far, and not be able ever to return. But who could help him now? Who would be on his side, who had the strength? Who would not simply dismiss his fears, or share them? He knew of no such person or being.

Well maybe there was one. Her face and name appeared in his consciousness like the ambiguous answers swimming up out of the dark well within the Magic Eight Ball when it was questioned. After a long hour of saying her name to himself like a charm he got to his feet and went to find the telephone book.

As soon as he had finished dialing and heard her phone begin to ring, Pierce realized in horror that it was after midnight; he knew he should hang up, but he knew also that he had already awakened her or her house, the damage done, and before he could muster the cowardice to put down the phone a low voice answered. Male, he thought.

"I'm sorry," Pierce said. "I'm really sorry, I know how late it is, but could I speak to—" The pastor? The minister? "Could I speak to Rhea? Rhea Rasmussen?"

"Well she's asleep," said the voice. "Is this an emergency?"

He hesitated only a moment; once asked, he knew it was. "Yes. Yes it is."

He could hear obscure fumblings, and something fall, the receiver maybe. "Hello?"

"Yes. Hello. My name is Pierce Moffett. It's likely you don't remember me, but . . ."

"Um," she said. "Yes. I think. Rosie Mucho. You helped at her great-uncle's funeral. Yes. We've spoken. Yes."

"Yes. I am truly, truly sorry to have bothered you so late. But I need to talk to somebody, I need to talk to. To you, in your, well your professional capacity."

"My professional capacity."

"I am in really bad trouble," Pierce said. "Something terrible has happened to me that I don't understand."

There was a silence at her end that Pierce thought might be shocked, or puzzled, or thoughtful. Then she said: "Is this about your friend and the Powerhouse?"

"Um yes," Pierce said.

"Is she in trouble, do you think? Is she suffering?"

"I," Pierce said. "I don't. I don't think so. She seems okay. It's me."

"You?"

"I wonder," Pierce said, and closed his eyes in shame, "if I could come see you."

There was a small pause before she answered. "Now?" she asked.

"I hoped," he said.

"Well no," she said, "that would be a disruption, really. But if you need to talk right now . . . Where are you?"

He told her.

"Oh the Winterhalters'. Yes. I know the place. I'm actually close by. I can be over there in a few minutes. If it's not something you feel you can say on the phone."

Awed by her willingness, she knowing nothing of him except what he had said, he almost told her no, forget it. But a hope had opened in his heart. "I'm not sure it's something I can say at all," Pierce said.

"A few minutes," she said. "Leave a light on."

"All right," he said. "Thank you."

And what would he tell her, he thought, after the line went silent and the air of his house again surrounded him. How he had messed with magic for his own delight, to get for himself what he wanted but should not have had, and in consequence had harmed irretrievably the world, "the world," like a kid with a chemistry set who by chance learns to crystallize or liquefy the bonds of space and time, a process beginning at his own Bunsen burner in his own basement and proceeding outward exponentially. Stop oh stop. Horror and wonder.

He hadn't moved when her headlights swept the room.


"That's a remarkable garment," she said when she had taken an assessing look at his house and at him.

It was Sam Oliphant's dressing gown, purple satin side out, belted in leather. He tried to explain it, and himself a little, his work, his ways: he seemed to have forgotten a lot of this, or to have trouble retrieving it. He offered coffee, she refused.

"Well would you," he said, showing her the daybed where she might sit if she liked, noticing that his lair was not fit for any habitation but his own.

She sat, a little gingerly, and by her look invited him to sit there with her. She tried to get his story from him: carefully probing to make sure, he thought, that he wasn't mad, or suicidal; ready, though, it seemed, if he turned out to be. And trying to gauge Rose's predicament too. And why despite his robe he trembled. Did he think she would be harmed by them?

"No no," said Pierce. "No, I know it's not that. I mean I think maybe most of them are sincere. I want to respect, well her—you know, her spiritual strivings. And this is such a small dumb harmless little group really. Bible people, how many thousands are there. But I have had, well a sort of allergic reaction somehow to it, don't ask me why."

He had not ceased trembling, though now he made a conscious effort to do so, let his tensed shoulders fall and his hands cease to wring one another. Watching, she put her hand over his. "It's so hard," she said. "We think we come to know people because of the intensity of our feelings about them. The more intensely we feel, the closer we think we're getting. It's not always so."

"No," he agreed, or protested. The plain frank touch of her hand was nearly unbearable. "No."

"The opposite sometimes. But you know that. Everybody knows that."

He wondered if that were the real horror of madness, to understand that you don't know what everybody knows, and that this is what separates you from them, the more-or-less well. You are gone to a land where what everybody knows is not known.

She talked more. She told him that when you feel you've invested a lot in a relationship, it can be very painful to think you might have to lose that investment, of time and caring. She said that we cherish others in part because of their freedom, but what happens when that freedom threatens commitment? It can be devastating, she said, to think that there's no good way to save the relationship, that the only right thing is to give it up.

"Well," Pierce said, trying to find comfort in these phrases, boxes in which wisdom was surely kept but that he couldn't open. *It* might not give *him* up, was what he feared.

She stood, and clasped her hands behind her, casting her eyes over his shelves of books. He saw the familiar titles as though through her eyes: the *Malleus maleficarum* with lurid cover, the twelve volumes of Thorndyke's *History of Magic and Experimental Science,* the Rosicrucian anthologies of A. E. Waite. After a silent minute or two she turned to him, and he could tell she thought she had learned something new.

"It couldn't be, could it," she said, "that you've been raising some demons yourself."

"I'm a historian," said Pierce. "I don't, I mean those are research. I'm not a believer, or a practitioner."

"Ah." She continued to study him. "It always seems to me that when scholars take up one subject rather than another it's not for no reason. The opposite, actually."

Too much reading. It was the medieval answer. Too much knowledge, not enough wisdom.

"I'll burn my books," he said.

"Aw, now."

She came and sat again beside him on the daybed, close enough that he smelled the wool shirt she wore, and a light perfume or shampoo. "So tell me," she said. "What's the most painful thing in this to you? What is it that threatens you so much?"

"That it's not true," Pierce said.

She inclined her head to him, surprised maybe and interested. "Oh?"

"I can't bear it," he said. "That she could will herself to believe the stuff they tell her. That she could do that." He saw that she was smiling a little, and wondered if he might have offended. "I mean I can believe that these things can be true for people *inside*," he said, and touched his heart. "I see that it makes sense of the world for people. But not outside. I can't *believe* it. I actually never did. I mean not even when I thought I did." He understood this for the first time.

"And you think that separates you. That she believes what you don't."

"That she believes what is not true. What is demonstrably not the case. That they all can do that."

She lowered her eyes. "Well. *Is it true*. You know oddly enough that's not most people's first concern."

He knew. He clutched his brow.

"I think most people think first about help for pain, and certitude, and happiness. About having some power on their side. You know when these stories were first circulating, that's what people saw in them. Not some verifiable news story. You're a historian. You know this."

"Yes."

"The first question wasn't *Is this true*, what I'm hearing? The first question was *What does it mean?* To me, to the world? What does it ask of me, what does it bring me?"

"I guess," he said. He had bent nearly double on the daybed, clutching himself around the middle as though to contain himself. "Yes, I suppose."

"Like prayer," she said. "About one-half of me—maybe two-thirds—doesn't really believe in the power of prayer to alter the world."

"They do," Pierce said bitterly. "They think they can get anything just by asking. Health. Wealth. New cars."

"Yes well," she said, and smiled. "Yes. We often pray for things that I just don't think God supplies. Even people I love and admire do that: knowing maybe that they're really asking these things of themselves. But you know another part of me knows very well that prayer is powerful. You know it too."

"Okay, yes," he said. "Certainly, maybe. Inside."

"Inside is outside," she said.

"Well will you pray for me then?" Pierce cried in grief and surrender. "Will you pray for me? 'Cause I."

"I will," she said, levelly, simply. "I will. And for her too." She embraced him, somehow able to contain his big self in her slight arms, and for a long time said nothing more while he wept.


Whether because of Rhea Rasmussen's prayers or just the touch of her person, or maybe because of the drink he swallowed when she was gone, Pierce slept for a few hours; and now he had awakened calm in the darkness before dawn. He had dreamed the dream of her escaping, finding the right way away. He had been granted, had been *vouchsafed,* the right thing to do, held it now in his heart and hand.

A simple question. And it didn't matter if the answer was yes or no. Somehow even if he never asked it, just knowing it was the right one was enough; he felt a profound relief, like a nearly drowned man's to breathe air and expel it. But what if he really could ask it? Why on earth did the mere thought of asking it restore him in this way?

He believed that what had happened—it was absurd to think this, but so was his present state of dread and littleness—was that *he had tried to become Rose,* here in this room and in the even more secret chambers of his solitude; and in doing so he had slipped out of his own world and into hers, the world she projected around herself and which she believed in just as he had believed in his own. Not *as her,* though, and happy to be there, but still as himself: lost, therefore, comically lost, not knowing the rules by which this world of hers ran and affrighted by the beings there, familiar friends or opponents to her maybe but to him terrifying in their unlikeliness. But if he had a means to bring her back from that land to his own, he would then be able to return himself. And he did have such means. What he had to do was to ask her, humbly and with all his heart, to come back to the Faraways and live with him instead of going to school in Conurbana, they would work it out somehow; to live with him from then on, for good. Impossibly, but yes definitely, he had to ask her—he laughed aloud in the darkness of his bedroom with hopeless understanding—to be his wife.

He would ask her, he would. The strong wine of resolution flooded him. He thought of arising now, right now going to the phone while the world slept, and calling her. But no it was absurd, not yet six in the morning, she would be still wrapped in sleep, the sweet sleep they promised her. Anyway, he obviously couldn't just baldly put his question to her, and especially not over the phone. There was going to have to be some preparation, considering his bizarre, not to say cruel, behavior over the last weeks. He remembered in shame that he had not kissed her, not once during the whole of that time with her in Conurbana. As though she had been in fact the eidolon or demon manufacture that he, standing on her corner in the dawn, had imagined her to be. Instead of merely confused and needy. It was so simple.

He tossed off his blankets and arose in the cold. There had been a little frost, and the windows were silvered. Pierce drew a bath, standing grinning while the funny old tub filled, clutching himself to calm the shudders that tightened his stomach.

He would not ask that she choose between them, no, she would not have to choose, she could have both; the Lord her God was a jealous God, he knew, but he, Pierce, was not jealous: so long as she chose him as well, freely and with all her heart, as he freely offered his to her, that would—it must—place him on an equal footing with the Old One, a footing he would win by this vast gesture. It seemed to him vast.

There was really only one strength you could bring to bear against your enemies, only one strength anyway that someone shaped as he was shaped could bring. And it was the same as the only aid he could bring, to her or to anyone. *Love suffereth long, and is kind; love seeketh not her own, is not easily provoked, thinketh no evil,* heck they said it themselves, didn't they, even if they didn't mean it, or maybe they did, maybe it was all all right, perfectly nice people actually probably most of them, who knew but that they had the compassion, the charity his own cold soul lacked. What they weren't were wizards or the slaves of wizards with magic on their side. They shrank even as he grew by the power of the question he would put, becoming the ordinary size of human acquaintances or strangers; in an imaginary house, his own house in the future, his and hers, which he could just then see with indistinct vividness, he welcomed them, her crowd. A little mystery cult such as the poor humans of this planet have been joining for ages; they just wanted what they wanted, as he did himself, as she did for sure. Happiness. Help for pain. Certitude.

He sank down moaning into his bath. He thought of Rose asleep, ignorant of this new understanding of his, of their new equality; asleep still in the time before he asked her what he would ask her, still in that former condition, or in none at all really, innocent, oblivious. He thought of how she had wept in his bed the night before she had moved to Conurbana, how he had not said then what he should have said, had been unable to do what he ought to have done: the right way, which appeared before him now. Untaken then and maybe too far behind him. And maybe not.

Rose Ryder was actually awake, in her little apartment in Conurbana; she had no reason to be and it was crazy early but she felt she had slept a week; she got up amid the still-unfamiliar odors of her place, and prayed aloud: Holy Spirit be with me and in me.

She turned and looked around herself.

Awake.

They called it walking in the Spirit, this clarity she saw with sometimes, so clear it was hard to put names to what she saw, the veins and blood of leaves, the swim of liquid in her cat's slit eyes, the fluid persistence of the air and the world; the power of her gaze to know and possess it all; this aerial hum or sung note of exaltation, made in her ears or coming from the whole great world at once. She had tried to explain it, or describe it, to Pierce for instance, and never could; to those who knew it no explanation was necessary.

She picked up her kettle and brushed the cat from the stove where it liked to sit on the warmth of the pilot light; she lit the stove with care, holding the blackened and ragged sleeve of her robe out of the way. She would study this morning, she was all caught up but there was no reason not to get ahead. She could nowadays pick up any book she needed to read and read and understand it, instead of drifting away constantly into wishing and fearing as she always once had; the facts of her basically bullshit psychology textbooks walked right off the page in a funny little jostling parade into her head and lodged there, to answer whenever she summoned them. If that's what she needed and wanted it's what she got. Just ask.

And what would he think—Pierce, who had entered her consciousness, had been beside her somehow as she awoke, a black bear just out of eyeshot—if she told him that all the gifts she had been given (of the Spirit but not only those of the Spirit, other things too, amazing luck, finding yourself in the right time and the right place to get what you wanted or needed, a test grade, cash, a parking place even, a wake-up call, there wasn't anything too small that it couldn't be made to go right), that all of it was for the making of that new clarity and certainty and power and for nothing else? What would he think if she told him (she didn't think she ever would) about the day she had come home, a raw and hopeless evening not long ago, and found sitting on the little enamelled kitchen table a small brown box that (she was certain) hadn't been there at morning; how her heart had warmed immediately with a funny warmth and a profound interest to see it there, as though she had discovered a clue, one more left for her to find? She could tell when she picked it up that it was old, something about the printing on the sides or the weakness of the cardboard flaps she pulled open, it wasn't modern in some way; she'd parted the greasy thick paper inside and taken out a small oiled gear or complex toothed wheel, and had known even before she read the box's side what it was: a distributor gear for an Asp of the year and model hers was, the part she needed but could not find.

*It was just sitting there,* she told her group when they were all witnessing that evening around a different kitchen table in a different part of town; each of them having a story to tell, many of them no more than a moment of hope or certainty but some weirdly circumstantial like her own. And they had all smiled when she was done, some shaking their heads in calm awe or softly clucking their tongues, amazing; she studied their faces to see if one of them was going to admit to having found the car part somewhere and brought it to her house when she wasn't there (no one had then or since) but the most amazing thing was that it *didn't matter* whether God Himself had put an antique car part on her kitchen table (in its original box, with the manufacturer's name and part number on it, just like the stuff Santa supposedly made in his shop at the North Pole that always came complete with cellophane-windowed box and famous brand name) or if finally somebody (Mike?) confessed he'd brought it to her—she could see or imagine the warmth of his smile, the laugh they would have over it—because the joy, the kindness, in it would be the same, and that was the whole point and the whole gift: and now her car ran too, and what could she say except that faith in God and his power and willingness to do anything, anything at all for her, had brought that about? And how could she tell Pierce that?

She made tea and sat at her table, the cat materializing silently there on the Formica to be given a pellet of bread she rolled in her fingers. Winter light in a place that was hers, a life at last her own or becoming her own. Because she had given it away, this time though for real.

Who loses his life shall have it.

For so long, since some time in college maybe, she had come to lose great stretches of time, nights and days but mostly nights, unable to describe them to herself or replay them except as you might memories of what you had heard someone else had done once. Waking up beside people she did not remember meeting, listening to them talk and not understanding them, searching in memory through night streets for the moment or the place she had met or chosen them. She told herself, she told them, that it was the beer, but it wasn't really the beer, she thought, it was the night.

She believed that she had collaborated in this forgetting, so as to deny what she had done even to her most inward awareness, though she could not imagine how she could do this without knowing it still in an even deeper part of herself; psychology said you could successfully deny reality, and she believed it was so just as she believed other things she didn't know or that seemed impossible to her, things said in the group, things Pierce had told her, that the universe was made of nothing but electricity or that the peepers of spring nights weren't bugs but frogs. Frogs! Yes! Tiny frogs! She thought this surely couldn't be so, and she'd studied his face for signs that he knew it wasn't, that he was mocking her or himself in that way he was always doing: as though someone else were listening, to whom the joke would be funny, and funnier because she didn't get it or even get that it was a joke.

Was that cruel, or what? She laughed, forgiving him, laughing because it was so easy to forgive. So easy. She could remember, and she could forgive: forgive because she could remember, and thus be forgiven herself for all that she had once denied. Everything, everything she had done and believed she had not done, all able to be opened and studied, like the cooked books of some shady enterprise, transparent to God, and so to her at last.

Mr. Cichy, Mal, his tinted glasses and pointy beard. Reading what paper in his train seat across the aisle from her, she could almost even at this distance see the name of it. See-shee he pronounced his name but she had already heard it differently in her inward ear when he wrote it and his phone number on a page torn from his leather notebook; Mal Cichy, the man she had set out to meet apparently and could not refuse once she had come across him. Into the tunnel under the river, down into the city toward which she had bent her soul. *Mal sent me* she was to say when they opened the apartment door, where, a palatial building somewhere; in its windows the high city gleamed and glittered ceaselessly. Mal was there already. It was there at that party, or later, another place or party, that she had been asked to be in the film, the Japanese film; a producer or director she met, they were all producers or directors or something, had bought a Japanese film and wanted to add some scenes. She would be masked. A loft somewhere, black-velvet hangings, naked men and other women in masks too. Tenderly, carefully that older woman (the director's lover or friend) had bound the false face on her, just a silk handkerchief really but painted with a Japanese dollface, through which her own face showed faintly, animating it. He paid her at the end of the shoot, counting out fives from a fat wallet. Later he offered her a hundred dollars to let him spank her, and she accepted that money too as she accepted everything else, every assent confirming that there was something inside that could not be reached or soiled.

Somewhere that film must still exist. She had not remembered it or Mal's name or his newspaper (*Observer!*) or the mirrored elevator in which she had arisen to go to that party or the other party. Now she did.

She wondered if it was possible to be possessed from the outside in. When she thought of possession, when they talked about it in the group, she thought of something entering you and taking, yes, possession of your inmost self, something which then drives your outside actions and your speech and whatever. But if something possessed her, and maybe it did or had, it had not crept within her like a germ but had fallen upon her and covered her over, thereupon going on doing things that she herself did not do, herself staying still, amazed at what she could bear, alone insidemost.

And if that was possession, and if it could be lifted, then it would not be the casting out of something that was rooted deep within like a carcinoma, the way some of them talked about it; no the outside one would crack or peel like a shell or a skin or a suit of armor, and then the one inside, the one that nothing had reached, would be the outside: the hidden patent and the inside out.

The phone rang, strange in the half-light, and she went to it slowly, tugging her robe around her protectively. But it wasn't Pierce; it was Mike Mucho.

"Yes I'm awake," she answered his first question, happy to hear his voice. "Yes Mike. Awake."

"Just thought I'd call."

"Yes. Thanks."

"Busy day today?"

"Oh sort of. Studying."

"Okay. No trouble sleeping?"

"No, Mike. None." She laughed as though they shared a secret, which they did, though not the one Pierce thought they shared (which made it even funnier and sweeter) and which wasn't even a secret, she'd tell anybody: that she had no trouble sleeping, and no trouble waking. It had been promised.

"We have to talk later," he said. "Will you be at Dynamo tonight?"

"Yes sure." The cute name for group meetings shamed her a little, and worse were the names beginners in the group bore, dynamen and dynamettes, it was worth studying hard just to go up a level and shed them.

"Some amazing things are happening," he said. "Fast, too. We were talking about you, about what might be next, and where you might fit in."

"Sure," she said, feeling a hot surge of pleasure and anxiety beneath her breastbone.

"So we'll talk," Mike said. "See you."

She hung up and couldn't remember what she had been thinking.

Oh right. Oh yes. Forgiveness: the bugs and frogs that had inhabited her, all made to come forth and be dismissed, so unimportant. Walking in the Spirit: she had only found herself able to do it infrequently so far, but she knew that if she asked and if she practiced she would be in it longer and longer and then at last maybe forever.

Forever.

Pins and needles in her fingertips and a constriction in her throat, as though she sensed a predator somewhere near about to leap.

On the windowsill lay her father's Zippo, which she had stolen from his coat pocket the day she left home, and her pack of Merits. One of those would end this mood for a time: quell it, snuff it. As though it had already done so merely in the thinking of the thought, she could feel the Spirit depart from her.

What had Mike meant, what did they want from her? She had given a bad answer when Ray had talked to her about moving up to the next level of training, she had seen it in his eyes, though he nodded and took her hand and was as kind as ever. She hadn't assented with all her heart. She would, she would, but they had to see it would take time. When you've been a certain way for a long while.

There were probably still a lot of things she could not yet remember, lost like dreams. Or maybe they *were* dreams. She dreamed sometimes that she could remember distinctly things that in waking life she had never done: as though there was a world in there with more than just unreal experiences: with unreal memories too, unreal histories, unreal beginnings, unreal destinies.

She could remember if she tried. She didn't *right now* want to, that's all.

She picked up the pack of cigarettes, slid her thumb tip over the slick cellophane, shook one out and lit it. Smoke eaters: that's what the group called those who hadn't yet given up cigarettes. Dog returning to its vomit. Every time when with Pierce she had lit one she had seen in Pierce's eyes a small triumph, told you so.

Some cult, she thought, feeling a coldness moving from the outside in, familiar coldness, she shrank from its advance. Aren't they supposed to be here, manipulating my mind? Where the hell are they? They give you all this stuff and then leave you alone with it. Do it if you can.

Suddenly, surprising herself, she arose as though yanked upright, walked swiftly over the cold floor to the sink, turned on the tap and thrust the half-filled pack under it. There. There. Better, more final, than throwing them in the trash, that only meant you would be searching there later, pushing through the Tampax and tissues and hair combings to find them. She stood looking down at what she had done, and a wave of longing and loss swept over her so intense she thought she might faint.

The phone rang again. She knew who it was.


"I'm sorry if it's early," Pierce said. At the sound of the connection made he had felt instantly uncertain, as though the phone line had tapped him into a well of alien energy. His heart, which for an hour or two had been so placid, rising and falling like blue sea swells, shrank and began again to drum.

"I was up," she said. "How are you? Are you all right?"

"Well basically. It's just that I had something to say, and I didn't think it could wait. To apologize first, though, and . . ."

"Yes well listen, Moffett, I think you'd better be careful. Some very strange and bad things are happening. I almost set myself on fire yesterday."

"O my God."

"I was boiling water. I was going to put the kettle on. I got this awful feeling, and then I saw that the sleeve of my robe was burning. I mean flames." She waited, and when she heard nothing she said: "I got it out okay. But just imagine if it had reached my hair."

"O my God." More faintly than before.

"It's okay," she said. "The bad stuff can't hurt me. But I worry about you, Moffett. Listen. When I was driving back from your house, the window of my car—and there was no wind blowing or anything, and I wasn't even driving fast—it exploded. It just exploded. On your side."

Silence. Rose waited for a reply, but none came.

"Now you can say it's just coincidence," she said. "You can go ahead and say that if you want, but . . ."

"No," he said. "No, no I won't say that."

"Well." Pause. "I had a talk with Ray," she said. "About us."

Pierce in Littleville, throat thick with panic, thought: Now it comes. What they had all along been planning.

"And what he said was, that if seeing you was making this harder for me, if you were throwing me off, then maybe I might think about not seeing you."

"Uh-huh." A wind blew away his skin and flesh. "Hm."

"For a while."

"Uh-huh."

"He was very kind."

Rose on her end paused again to measure his reaction to this, hidden though from her by blindness and distance. "It's what anybody would say, Pierce," she said. "About somebody having as much trouble as we are."

"So is that what you intend to do?" he said at last.

"No. It's what he said I might want to do. For a while."

"The reason I ask," Pierce said, "is I wondered if you still want to come here for the Ball. On the river."

"If you still want me to."

"I do."

"Well sure. I really do want to. I do."

"Come as you aren't," he said. "That's the rule."

She pondered that till it made sense. "Oh. Okay."

"It could be anything."

"Yep," she said. "There's a lot of things I'm not."

Nothing.

"So what was it you wanted to say?" she said. "You said it couldn't wait." She listened to another and even longer pause, as though maybe something were coming so hard to say that it could not easily pass down the phone's throat and long gullet from there to her; but then Pierce only said "Oh. Oh gosh." And then: "Well." And then: "I'll tell you when I see you. It wasn't anything really. I'm sorry."

# 4

Next it was Rosie Rasmussen who, late that morning, turned in at the stone gateposts looking for Pierce's cottage; ghostly and maybe invented childhood memories of the Winterhalters' house had led her to it. "Okay," she said to Sam. "I think it's someplace down there. A little house by the river." She turned the Bison away from the drive up to the big house, and took the less trodden way down to the fields and the river.

"He should live there," Sam said, pointing to the tall chimneys of the big house. She wore last year's winter coat, rabbit fur matted around the hood and too small, but the warm weather and living in two households had caused the need for a new one to be missed. She clutched her plastic backpack in her arms, for some reason unwilling to sling it in the back as she usually did when going to Mike's.

"That must be it," Rosie said.

"It's little," said Sam.

"Now you're okay with this?" Rosie said. "It's just for a visit. I'll be back really soon."

Sam said nothing.

In the little house Pierce was wearing his own winter coat, he too needing a new one; he had been out going up to do his duty and look into the Winterhalters' house, and on his return had sat again without removing it, safer somehow inside it. He heard Rosie's car approach, rising growling sound that almost until it was upon him he did not recognize for what it was, afraid to get up and look out to see. His door then was flung open suddenly, and he started, clutching the chair's arms; a small child came in, and looked at him frankly in summons or command. No it was just Rosie's daughter Samantha. Rosie too right after her, calling to him.

"Hi," he said, unmoving.

They stood before him, making cheerful greetings, the cold air they had brought in swirling gaily through the place. Sam turned to slam shut the door with awful force. Rosie, arms akimbo, looked around Pierce's house, where she had not been before, and at Pierce himself, who had not risen from his chair.

"You don't look so hot," she said. "Did you sleep in that coat?"

"I don't really sleep."

"Are you okay?"

He wanted badly to tell her that he was not, so badly that the heart within him seemed to vault painfully toward her, and tears came to his eyes; but he only felt his unshaven jaw, and said "Coming down with something."

"Are you eating?"

"Certainly."

"What?"

"Food."

He rose and followed her through the tiny rooms as she toured the place. She peeked through the bathroom into the bedroom beyond with its two beds, the little and the big, but made no remark on them. In the office she ran her long hand over the blue bosom of his typewriter; she lifted the top page of his typescript, and put it down. She noted Kraft's, too, in its box. "You were supposed to copy that," she said.

"Yes," he said. "I will. I haven't. I will."

"I mean what if this place burns down." She lifted the box's cover, and Pierce had an impulse to warn her, warn her away, as from a chasm's lip or a loaded cigar. "Listen," she said. "This is kind of weird, but I have a favor to ask. I have to go talk to a lawyer, in the Jambs, and it might take a while; I thought I could leave Sam at Beau's place, but it's not one of my usual days, and Beau's gone."

"Yes," Pierce said. "I know."

"So I was wondering if Sam could stay and visit for a while. An hour or two."

Sam herself was looking at him over the edge of the table, only her curls and her eyes visible. Pierce paid her a smile.

"Do you believe in God?" she asked him, mildly.

"Um," he said. "Gee. Why do you ask?"

"Sam," said her mother, a warning or a plea.

"Are you a Jew or a Christian?" Sam asked Pierce.

"It's Mike," Rosie said. "She's getting it from him."

After a moment Pierce saw what Rosie had meant: not that Sam had been sent by Mike to ask him these things. "Neither," he said. "There's not just the two."

"So would that be okay?" Rosie asked. "Just for an hour or two?"

"Sure," Pierce said. "If you're okay with me."

"*Mom,*" said Sam. "What if I have a seizure?" She said this to her mother in her own mom voice, her arms akimbo just like Rosie's.

"You won't, hon," Rosie said. "You took your medicine. Right? Right." She pointed upward to a shelf. "Is that," she asked Pierce, "one of those Russian dolls?"

"It is," he said, and took it down, and gave it to Sam. She shook it, heard its interior make sounds; Pierce showed her how it opened. An old crone, and inside her a red-cheeked peasant mom, and inside her a heavy-braided bride, and inside her. Rosie seeing Sam absorbed took Pierce's arm and led him to the kitchen.

"It'll really be all right?" Pierce asked. "About the seizures?"

"What the doctor told me," Rosie answered, "is that you have to live as though one will never happen again. Just live as though. Even though they will. I can't keep her home in bed. Or me either."

"No," said Pierce. "No. But suppose if this morning . . ."

"It's not dangerous," Rosie said. "It's not like a medical emergency. It's just her."

"Uh-huh."

"It lasts a second. A few seconds. Just don't let her head hit the floor. Even then it's okay; she has an amazingly hard head. She'll sleep afterwards. But Pierce it won't happen. I promise."

Being raised in a doctor's house had imbued Pierce, as it had his cousins, with an unalarmed directness in medical matters, spurious mostly, but he listened to Rosie calmly and nodded, I see. Okay.

"So now tell me what's the matter," Rosie said, sitting at the kitchen table. "Something is."

"Well," Pierce said. He drew the unshed overcoat more tightly around him. "You know Rose."

"Yes, Pierce. I know Rose."

"Well the Powerhouse." This name he extruded or secreted only after a struggle. "The Powerhouse International, you know?"

"Oh no," Rosie said.

"The bunch that, you know . . ."

"I know."

"Yes. Well she seems to have. You know."

"Oh my Lord."

She looked over at him where he huddled in his chair, seemingly sightless or seeing something elsewhere. "Pierce," she said in sudden fear. "You're not, not . . ."

"No, no oh no."

"No. But she is?"

"She seems to be." He told her in a low voice all about Conurbana, Mike, Pitt, the glossolalia, the rain; she listened as to a fairy tale or war story, mouth ajar and eyes wide. Oh Lord. Oh my God.

"So," Pierce said. Rosie pondered. He would not tell her about calling Rhea in the midnight; nor about how the Devil broke the windshield of Rose's car. Nor how he had wept.

"So is he living there now? Mike?" she asked.

"I don't know. I guess." He had no idea where they hid during the day, Ray and Pitt and Mike, he had thought of them as vanishing, hadn't tried to imagine them at their breakfast or bath.

"If he is," Rosie said. "If he moved there and didn't tell me. Then that was illegal. Strictly speaking." She pressed her fist against her lips in thought. Then she reached out to touch his hand. "Oh man," she said. "Where's this going to end."

"A little angel was last," said Sam, standing in the doorway. "Inside the baby."

"Right," said Pierce. "Nothing inside her."

"Nothing," said Sam.


What Rosie needed to talk to Allan about was the submission of her quarterly report to the board of the Rasmussen Foundation in New York, a simple enough document that Rosie worried long over, she had typed several drafts on Boney's huge Remington and now Allan said his own secretary would take it and do it right. They had delicately skirted the issue of Rosie's hearing next week, but talked of the Powerhouse and its plans to buy the bankrupt Woods.

"Listen," Allan said. "If a community doesn't want something like this to happen, they have resources. You understand me? There are very many perfectly legal and acceptable ways of countering an unwanted buyer. It doesn't even need to be public."

"Like what ways."

"If you didn't want them to buy it you could buy it yourself. I mean the Foundation could. It might take some doing to convince the board, but I think the asking price is about a million. Suppose you offered a million and a half."

"What are you talking about. The whole Foundation's hardly worth that much."

"You don't pay that much. You take an option to buy for a million and a half. It costs you, say, fifty thousand. The option's good for three years. Eventually the other prospects get bored or their resources dry up. They go away."

"What if they don't?"

"You think of something else. A lot can happen in three years."

"The horse could learn to talk," Rosie said, not quite aloud.

"The Foundation could even inspire a joint community action to raise the option money," Allan said. He gazed thoughtfully out the window, hands linked behind his head, enjoying this, she thought. "Some people are already nervous about this bunch. To say nothing of the fact that having it bought by a nonprofit takes it off the tax rolls."

"Well gee," Rosie said. "I'd help with that. Where do I sign."

"Well let's think this through," Allan said, swivelling toward her. "The Foundation yes could have a lot of influence in keeping these people out. But it could also help make a case for them in the community. It could offer to try to swing opinion in their favor."

"But why would I. Oh. Oh yes." She perceived Allan's train of thought just as it went out of sight. Yes. Then she thought of herself going to them, to Mike; sitting with them around some table somewhere, and making these deals. The Foundation's help in swinging the Woods deal—in exchange for permanent custody of Sam. The nerve it would take, the lies she would have to tell. Maybe she wouldn't have to do it herself; Allan might do it, he might be able to make it sound reasonable and proper, the way some people can offer bribes or tips for favors and make it sound just like business as usual. "But I don't *want* them here," she said. "I don't."

"Well then," Allan said. "You go and try your best on their behalf. And you don't succeed."

Rosie shuddered profoundly, not knowing why. "It's just too weird to think about," she said. "I can't."

Allan shrugged, somewhat theatrically.

"He's not a bad guy," Rosie said. "I do know him. He isn't, really."

Meanwhile Sam showed Pierce how to lie back on a bed and hang your head down almost to the floor, so that you could see the house upside down, the floor as the ceiling, the dusty empty rooms where lamps sprouted, the furniture stuck up above you, all the same but different.

"See?" she said.

"Yes," said Pierce. "Wow."

When lunchtime came he gave her tomato soup with chunks of cheese in it, food he had come to know in Kentucky and still sometimes ate when he needed comfort; after a first hesitant bite she ate it willingly.

"My daddy has a new house," she said as she ate.

"I heard that," he said.

"I have my same ode house."

"Yes. Lucky." He wanted to say that when his parents separated he lost his old house, and all Brooklyn too. "Are you going to his new house today?"

She shrugged, eating. Pierce tried to remember what it had been like to be suddenly parted from his father, but what he mostly remembered about it was the one thing that was most unlike now: that it couldn't be spoken of.

He put Oreo cookies before her, and she marvelled, reaching out for them in slow awe as though for spilled treasure; Pierce suddenly thought maybe he was flouting a family food rule.

"Do you love God?" she said, after scraping the white innards from one with her teeth.

"Um sure," Pierce said.

"I love God. He can cure everything. Like epsa lepsy."

"Ah," Pierce said. "Tell me something. Is it after lunch you take your nap?"

"*You* sually," she said. "But. First I have a story."

"Oh. Okay."

"Do you have any stories?"

"Well I know some."

"I'd rather have a real story," she said. "From a book."

"Oh. Well see I don't have kids, so my books are. Well you know the kind."

"Let's see," she said. She slipped from her tall chair (why don't we remember living in a world where everything was absurdly outsize, tables and chairs and spoons, doorknobs too high to reach, too fat to grasp?) and went to look.

Maybe because it happened to be one she could both reach and take hold of: she drew out a ragged paperback, saw that at least it had pictures, and held it out to Pierce.

"This one?" Pierce said. It was the bound edition of the once well-known comic strip *Little Enosh: Lost Among the Worlds,* for the year 1952. Pierce used to receive these every year on his birthday, sent to Kentucky from his father in Brooklyn, at least so he thought at the time; it was actually his mother who had bought and wrapped them. In Brooklyn at the beginning of his life Axel used to read Enosh to him nightly, in the *New York World.* He accepted this one from Sam, remembering immediately its contents and the times too when he had read it and the others (he saved them all, spine-broken and held together with rubber bands) for comfort and delight from that year down to this.

"You'll like it," he said; but she would make no such assumption, only waited till they sat side by side and he had opened the book to the middle.

"Start at the beginning," she said.

"It doesn't matter where you start," he said. "It's been going on so long."

So here's Little Enosh in his lenticular starship, as usual hurtling over a planet's pocked surface; behind him the planet's sleepy sun goes down. *Dok dok nite* says Enosh, a little fearish (his eyes rolled up and leftwards, what danger might come from there, the Uthras maybe in their own starships bristling with weapons). He lands. *Wherein have I been thrown*? he wonders, though this desolate surface, these random stars, this crescent moon just climbing over the horizon with knowing hooded eyes, and the hints of mushroom-shaped cities or villages far away that Enosh never reaches—these are always there wherever Enosh lands, and he is always surprised; above his round head and round clear helmet floats the eternal Enosh question mark, which sometimes sets off on adventures of its own.

He showed her how you could follow a different thing every time you read an Enosh adventure. The small creatures who (unnoticed by anybody, least of all Enosh) clamber out of the ground or evolve from the eternal stones, grow faces and characters, change and disperse or are absorbed into other parts of the drawing, the stars, the planets. Or the moon, whose commentary on things below is mostly contained in his bored yawns and sly sleepy smiles, who at dawn disappears over the horizon with his towel and toothbrush (*Boyo boy*) leaving Enosh in his predicaments. Or how words and notions—shadows, reflections, predicaments, thoughts (or *tots* in Enosh's strange baby talk)—take on independent life as soon as they are named or pictured.

"See," said Pierce to Sam, as Axel had once to him, "see, here's Enosh trying to rescue Snoopie Sophie from the Inn of the Worlds where she's caught. He calls her the Kurious Kid. Ha ha."

"Ha ha."

Sophie keeps opening doors and climbing to windows to see within rooms that contain great blobby people, fat-fingered men and women in voluminous skirts just barely able to fit inside, shocked or amused at Sophie's peeking. Only years and years later did Pierce come to see that the Inn of the Worlds is a whore-house, and that Sophie's curiosity is about sex, or *is* sex. Sophie forever on the point of losing her shoes, Mary Janes hanging by a toe, their neatly drawn straps a-dangle.

"Who's they?"

"Uthras," Pierce said in a sinister bass. Sam laughed. "Bad guys."

The wicked Uthras have got Enosh drunk, foisting on him a foaming cup of something whose bubbles hover from then on over his own head, sometimes be-coming tiny faces. He is falling asleep, again, again. *Wen U come to the N of a perf-ikday,* he muses, cheek on hand and elbow in liquor-spill, *+ UR left alone wit your Tot.* In the next panel his Tot, a mirror-image Enosh, is beside him, also asleep.

"He has to wake up."

"Yep. He's going to get a letter from his mother. The letter will wake him up."

"It will?"

"It'll say *Wake up,*" Pierce said, and Sam laughed again.

"Does he?"

"Well, see?"

Pierce had forgotten how much of the story was always left out, intentions and announcements often standing for deeds, which in the next day's panels have already been done, or forgotten. Here was Enosh awake, going down the circular stair of the Inn of the Worlds toward the deepmost Lockup for panel af-ter panel (his little bun feet never quite touching them though, their shadows are clearly visible upon the treads; the most moving thing about Enosh is that he can suffer and be brave and at the same time never actually be touched at all; Pierce beside Sam thought this thought for the first time).

"Why is he sad?"

"Well see, he's looking into the cell where Sophie is. See, she's in jail."

Relentless Rutha, Queen of the Uthras, has shackled Snoopie Sophie in the dark well of the Inn of the Worlds; one tiny star only visible through the high thick-barred window, a star like the tear on Sophie's cheek. She's glad to have So-phie there because she knows it will bring Enosh, and after Enosh his mother and protector Amanda de Haye, setting out from the Realms of Light to find and rescue him (*4 the 10² time* admits Enosh). And with the three of them bound up and immobilized (the brutal Uthras laugh and toast one another) then the stars will go out at last and Rutha's awful Boss (who's never ever seen) will never have to hear the word *Light* again. And the plot will work, too; it always does.

"*She* looks like *her,*" Sam said, pointing to Snoopy Sophie and to Amanda de Haye. The same flyaway ringlets and mobile nose, the same puppetlike articula-tion.

"Yup," Pierce says. "See, Enosh thinks so too. What he *doesn't* know, and never does figure out, is that she's his sister. Long-lost."

"Why doesn't his mother tell him?"

"She's sort of forgotten," Pierce said. He wiped tears from his own cheek. "And besides, if she told him, the story would be over."

"Are you sad?" Sam asked him.

"No," said Pierce, "No, oh no," as though surprised by her question. "No no. Listen. Is it time for you to lie down?"

She shrugged, it was up to him, she was not yet a clock person. Pierce showed her the bedroom, how it was reached through the bathroom, which didn't amuse her as much as he thought it would; she resisted this place, a little chilly and weird, and Pierce too after a moment decided no, and instead showed her the daybed by the stove, oh yes sure, she liked this one. She lay down and let him cover her and her rag doll with a blanket, watching him with interest and perhaps caution.

"Okay?"

"Okay," she said. "I *am* a little scared."

"Yes," said Pierce. "I can understand. Without mom or dad. Your first nap here and all. I," he said, "am going to take my nap too."

She looked at him. "You could take Brownie," she said. "I don't mind."

"Oh no," said Pierce. "I will be happy alone wit my Tot."

"Okay."

"Okay."

In his own bed his thought was of her, Sam; and of Rosie, and Rosie's life. To act every day as though you believed your child was safe and okay, while knowing she wasn't; to live knowing you could lose her, or see her hurt. How could you bear that. Well he would never have such a being, so valuable and so vulnerable, in his own life, they inhabited a sphere that he (he thought) did not. The only child of his person there would ever be he had constructed by himself in his own workshop, like Geppetto; had prayed then to the smiling powers that he might be made into a real little boy. And—like that lonely old puppeteer—he had got a sort of conditional yes. Real *to you:* as real as unreal can be: as real as the gods' gifts ever are.

And what had he done with his new son then? What had he imagined he had done with him then?

His heart struck loudly within him like a door slamming shut upon him. Did he really know of no other way to love except that, was it so?

He heard Sam stir, and speak a word, but then no more. Pierce had never seen her asleep, yet he saw her now with clarity, the curve of her open mouth, the curve too of her closed blond-lashed lids.

Could he be sure he knew the difference between a real child and one who could not suffer, one he could pretend even took delight in what he imagined they did together? He had told himself that his son, his phantasm, could not be hurt; whom then had he hurt, in what realm, by what he had pretended to do? It seemed suddenly certain to him that he had caused harm to someone somewhere: that it mattered what he had done in the hollow of his heart and hand.

Just a game. He thought of his cousin Hildy, one night home from the novitiate: they had stayed up late over coffee talking about Last Things, and about that dread moment (Michelangelo in his Judgment in the Sistine Chapel had pictured a damned soul experiencing it) when you realize that you knew this all along, knew what you were doing and what it meant, but pretended you didn't know. That's Damnation, Hildy had said: that moment, lasting forever.

"I'm just afraid for her," Mike Mucho said. "She's only a little kid. It breaks my heart. I've tried to talk to her mother about how I feel, but she won't even talk to me anymore about it. She's just—'here, give her this medicine.' "

Ray Honeybeare pondered this, or did not.

"Well," he said at last. "The medical condition isn't what I'm afraid of. If God doesn't want that child to suffer those fits she won't. And if it's not just ordinary seizures that's bothering her, then the medicine isn't helping anyway."

Mike and he were on the road, going up to the Faraways to meet Rosie Rasmussen to pick up Sam from Rosie. Mike's weekend to have her would begin at sundown on Friday, like a Sabbath. The talk was of her, Sam, though Mike (who was driving) wasn't always clear where Ray's thought was running.

"Let me ask you this," Ray said. "Does your little girl watch television?"

"Well she did. I mean, not the cartoons and, like the violence. She watched the educational channel."

Ray nodded as though this was what he feared he would hear. "And did she attend a little school there?"

"The Sun School," Mike said.

"The one most of the progressive parents send their kids to."

"Well I guess."

"Yes. And what was the one thing that they both taught? That they both put the emphasis on?"

Nothing Mike could think of seemed to be what Ray was thinking of (letters and numbers? Colors and shapes?).

"They teach them to *imagine*," Ray said. "They teach them that it's a wonderful thing to imagine. You pretend to be something, anything, and you are that thing. Pretend to be anywhere and you are there. *Just imagine*."

He regarded Mike with a smile of complicity, or irony, and Mike nodded, though he didn't feel included exactly.

"We want them to open their minds wide, don't we?" Ray said. "And believe that in imagination all power is theirs. But do you see what word is there at the root of *imagine*? It's *magic*, isn't it? We're teaching children to imagine they can have whatever they want, we make them *practice doing it* all day long, and what we're teaching them is the first principle of magic."

Mike began to say something, ask at least for elucidation, thinking of all those children, thinking how he had believed (and thought Ray and all of them also surely believed) in that sense of possibility, in that childlike, that that, but before he could say so much Ray spoke his name.

"Mike. I'll tell you what I'm concerned about, and it's not a small thing. What happens to the *imaginer* who trusts in his own power? I want you to think about this. Right into that wide-open mind can step a being much more powerful than any human person. Right into that mind. And we can call that insanity, if we want, or dysfunction, or seizures, there's a lot of medical names for it. But we recognize it. Don't we."

This was a question or a demand to which Mike was to respond, and he understood that. *Don't we.* If he couldn't see it in his own daughter he could see it in no one, and had been lying to himself and to Ray and to God when he had said that he could. It was a lie to say he believed that Ray could help anyone and not to believe he could help Sam.

"Yes," he said.

"We've been fighting magic for two thousand years, Mike. Remember Simon Magus, a *magus* is a magician, that Peter contended with. He thought the Word of God was some kind of magic, and he tried to buy the power off Peter. Peter said it wasn't for sale. Well in history we can read that this Simon believed himself to be the Power of God Incarnate, and he paraded around a whore he'd picked up in a brothel somewhere, who he called the Lost Wisdom of God. He got people to believe that." Ray chuckled, deeply, and his belly shook with it. "Sure. Here she is, ain't she beautiful. Just use your imaginations, folks."

Peter: that's who Ray was, coarse and big and truthful and plain, whom no evil could approach without his seeing it first for what it was. Safe with him, safe. "Didn't that guy think he could fly?"

"He did. He had a trick he played on people, to make them think he could; and then he convinced himself he really could."

Mike remembered the movie, the red-robed mage climbing to the top of his tower to jump off, what scary hawk-faced actor had played him. He wondered for a moment if Ray was remembering it too, and calling it history.

"If Sam's to beat this thing, Mike, you've got to be strong on her behalf. So very strong."

Mike took the exit toward the Faraways. It had begun to rain lightly again.

"We need to have Sam with us, Mike," Ray said. "We need her right with us from now on. We're going to put all the resources we have into this for you. I promise."


In Pierce's house Sam drew her plastic backpack closer to her. Without climbing out from under the shaggy and smoky-smelling blanket he had wrapped her in, she turned so that she could open it. She thrust her arm into the darkness inside, dug past her clothes till she came upon the glass ball that she had put in, that no one knew was in here but she. Her fingers touched it and then closed around it as though it crept into her hand, cold and round and brown, and greeted her: a living thing underneath all the things that weren't alive. Not even Brownie was alive really. But this was.

She had taken it from the commode in the living room at Arcady, because her mother and her father were going to court and it might be (they wouldn't say so but she had said it to herself, and had seen that it could be said) that she might go and live with him in another house, and she didn't want to leave it alone behind. She brought it out and lifted it into the window light. If she moved her head to one side the dart of light in the center of the ball moved the other way.

Why are they gone? she wondered. Where did they go? Maybe out of these rooms, into rooms she couldn't see.

She thought of the rooms inside mirrors: as far as you can see into them, they are just like your own, except backwards; you can see through their door and down their hall, but then it must go farther, farther than you can see, and you can't be sure it stays the same always, or that the outdoors if there is an outdoors would be the same and not different. Or even if the house really *doesn't* go on but comes to an end and wraps up, smaller than you thought, too small inside to hold you, narrowing like a throat.

# 5

ohn Dee put away the globe of moleskin-colored quartz, the first
of the stones that Edward Kelley had seen into, the last that he
would himself look into. He wrapped it in wool and opened an
ironbound trunk to put it in, only to find that mice had nested there while he
was away, amid the papers: four no five minute pink babes smaller than his finger's end, squirming blindly together, their bed made of his scumbled writings.
Poor naked babes. He must think how he would live now. He had left Prague
city a rich man and arrived in England with nothing but his wife and children,
hungry mouths that he could no longer feed on spirits' promises.

After crossing Germany duchy by duchy in his sail-coach—horseless, for
he had given his fine Hungarian team as a gift to the Landgrave of Hesse in
exchange for a passport through his lands; and by night largely, so his passage
might not alarm the people, already so afraid of what they did not understand; with his children asleep and the sails snapping lowly in the chastened
wind—he had taken a house in Bremen. For the next months he paid his rent
and read and wrote and met with many learned doctors, Heinrich Khunrath
among them, and to all of them he said that yes there was a new age to make,
and it would be made by no powers but their own; let them, therefore, take up
their tools. They could have of him what they wanted, he was dispersing his
estate, if they could find anything of use in his fripper's shop they should take
it away.

No word came from Kelley in Prague. At last Dee hired passage across the
narrow sea, and brought his family home to a cold Christmas: his house broken
into and his library taken away—for its safety's sake, the Queen's officers said—
and Germans and magic not to be talked of. A play written by a mad university
wit about a German magician's awful fall held the stage in London, showing how
he signed a compact with the Devil, was granted invisibility, teased the Pope and
the Emperor: and it was said that real brimstone could sometimes be smelled

when the overreaching mage was dragged down to Hell, and an extra imp or two perceived among the squib-tossing actors in black skins. *I'll burn my books*. The magician of the play was meant for Agrippa, with his staff and his *schwarze Pudel;* but it touched John Dee too.

Yet old friends came to lend him money—one of them Edward Kelley's brother, who did not say how he had come by the ten pounds gold he gave Dee, nor why he could spare it. And the old Queen was kind to him, when she remembered him; she intimated that when the right post fell vacant—it was to be the Chancellery of St. Paul's, or the advowson of St. Cross at Winchester—it would be his. Nothing happened. Come summer, he and Jane presented themselves to the Queen at Sion House with all seven of their children, from Arthur the oldest to baby Frances; Jane Dee, who had once sat among the ladies waiting upon the Queen, was permitted to kiss her hand, and gave her a petition in her husband's name. The Queen took it with her own hand, and put it by her on her pillow, and on the long way back home the family talked of these signs and noted them again and again; and yet nothing came of that either. Next Christmas they were still living on the gifts of friends, and the Queen called Dee to Richmond, and said she would send him a hundred angels—she meant those gold coins whose name the poets loved to quibble with, she too, but not he. *There was never promise made but it was broken or kept,* she said.

One office at last appeared: the wardenship of Manchester College, far to the north. It was not anything he had ever envisioned or wanted, such a distance from London and his home. The chief business of the old warden had been the persecution of Catholic believers, many of whom still lay in Manchester prisons. In the dark of winter, water hard as iron in the streams, he started north with his family, the new baby whom John Dee named Madimia, their lastborn, swaddled like the Christ-child. In February he was installed. His diary, so full an accounting of every visit, every hope and disappointment, every honor paid him, does not describe the ceremony.

He met his duties, cared for his College and the people of his city. They came to borrow his books, as they had in London; many dozens he had brought to Manchester College, and the Lancashiremen came and browsed with their hands clasped behind their backs. Justices of the peace came to ask for help in the cases of witchcraft being brought always before them in those days, a woman seen milking an axe handle and filling two hogsheads with good milk, or contrariwise drying up her neighbor's cow, or things more dreadful, so dreadful that unless men were much more wicked even than Scripture saith, must be the Devil's work. Dee lent them the *Malleus maleficarum* when they asked for it (how could he say no?) but gave them John Wier's *De præstigiis dæmonum* too, that urged mercy for old women fooled by the Devil.

Midwinter again; Dee's curate came to bring him to a widow's house whose seven children had become possessed, lay shivering in their beds unable to speak or sleep as the demon passed from one to another of them.

—I went in their house, said Matthew the curate as they hurried thither, and what did I see but the woman in a fit, and standing over her the man Hartley.

Hartley had a reputation for conjuring. John Dee had been careful never to speak to him. Matthew, panting along with John Dee, told his tale.

—What do you here, says I. Praying, quoth he. Thou pray! says I, why what prayer canst thou say? None but the Lord's prayer, saith he. Well say it, says I. The which he could not do.

The house was small and mean, a broken door and a cloth against the wind. Tall John Dee stooped to enter. Dark as a sepulcher, the one window not glazed but only set in with horn. Children moaning under foot, the bed filled with three or four squirmers. The man Hartley a lump kneeling amid them, a little candle quivering in his hand.

—*Exorciso te immunde spiritus,* the man breathed in a whisper, as though almost afraid he might really be heard. *Ex abi ea.* Go away from her, begone.

—Cease this, Dee said.

Hartley, so occupied he had not heard Dee enter, turned to see the Doctor, and the bright fear in his eyes was the same as the fear in the mother's: who had passed it to whom?

—Put down thy bell and candle, Dee said. Go away from this place. Call down no more powers.

—I will send for the watch, Matthew the curate said to Doctor Dee. It is he himself that has let these wicked spirits in, he.

—No, said John Dee. Let him be gone.

Hartley was harder to remove than that, by turns disputing with Doctor Dee and his curate and continuing to fuss over the children and mutter his formulæ; but at length he was put out, and the charged air calmed, and the children ceased their crying.

—Have no more to do with him, Dee told the mother, who was weeping and clinging to her beads and looked ready to chase after her protector and tormentor. Mind now. Seek a godly preacher, and with him appoint prayers and a fast. Do no more.

He went out into the cold clean air.

—Why do you linger? his curate asked him when he hesitated at the gate.

—I am an old man, John Dee said. Superannuated.

Once in Mortlake he had had a serving maid, poor Isabel Lister, troubled by a wicked spirit. She had tried to drown herself in the well, and John Dee had himself pulled her out near dead. After that he had prayed with her many nights, twice anointed her breast with holy oil to expel the wicked one, and put a woman of the house to watch her always; but not long after *suddenly and very quickly rising from prayer and going toward her chamber, as the mayden her keeper thought, but indede straight way down the stayrs behind the door, most miserably did cut her own throte.*

Had he done that which he should have done for her? All that he could have done? He knelt later that night in humility before the glass with Edward Kelley and asked the angel if he had done aright. What should he have done, what should he now do? And the answer came, the wisdom of their compassion and fearful gaiety: *It is not of thy charge.*

Poor wretch, poor wretches. He had wanted to win help for man's hurts and lacks from God's holy angels, and had won only passage into the world for powers he did not understand, whose natures were not like his.

He found suddenly he could go no farther. Not of thy charge. He sat down on the stones of a wall and put his trembling hands upon his knees. It is not of thy charge.

—That man will be hanged within the year, said Matthew the curate. I doubt not.

—God have mercy on him then. On our souls too.

We must not call down the powers from their spheres, John Dee thought, lest they answer us. For they never will be conformable to our wills, and their own wills are no more bent on helping us than is the sea's, or the wind's. Job asked God for help and understanding, and in answer God showed him the greatness of his creatures, and the strength of his arm, and told him to be silent.

Out of long habit, John Dee went on keeping a record of his daily doings, the books he lent, his children's illnesses, his dreams. *I had the vision and shew of many bokes in my dream, new printed, of very strange arguments.* The entries grow shorter as his life grew long; then they begin to cease. They say nothing of his wife's death of the plague: she whom he thought would long outlive him. The people of Manchester called on God to reveal whose sins had brought the plague upon them, the Papists or the worshippers of Satan; Dee buried his wife, and said nothing.

Visitors came now and then, and are noted in a phrase, and letters too, with news of Edward Kelley. He is in the Emperor's prisons; he has fallen from favor, has been restored to favor; newly married to a Bohemian lady of rank; imprisoned again. In March of '93 Dee dreams of him *two nights running, as if he wer in my howse, familiar, with his wife and brother.* Dee records a letter from Kelley himself, not in Kelley's hand though, inviting Dee to come again to Prague and enter the Emperor's service; all is forgiven. Then on November 25, 1595, Dee enters in his diary a single line: *newes that Sir Edward Kelley was slayne.*

Three tales the people of Prague like to tell visitors: the story of the doomed magician Jan Faust, whose house they can point out, sometimes it's this one in this part of town and sometimes a different one somewhere else; and the Golem made by the Great Rabbi Loewe, who saved the Jews in time of peril, or who imperilled them itself, or both; and the story of the Irish knight-alchemist Kelley, who lived on Gold-maker's street with his beautiful Bohemian wife, Joana, and who fell to his death attempting to escape from the White Tower or another prison when he failed to make gold, or enough gold, for the Emperor.

But Faust never lived in Prague; all his magic was done elsewhere. There is no knowing what the Great Rabbi was capable of, but in fact the Golem was really made by a rabbi in Chelm, fifty years before the Great Rabbi of Prague was born. Edward Kelley was indeed brought after many adventures to the high tower a prisoner of the Imperial guard: but there his fate broke in pieces.

There was one fate where he escaped from the tower and ran; changed his name, vanished, lived somehow somewhere a long time by his wits, an unchanged man.

Or he fell, having got partway down the tower, fell and broke one or both of his legs, the bone coming through the flesh, and was not found till he had bled almost to death, or to death.

Or he was put to his task again there in the tower, like the girl in the story who was put before the pile of straw and told to spin it into gold, and he did it: what he had said he could do, what he knew he could do. He even wrote a rhyming treatise on his methods while in prison, and that has actually come down from that time to this. *Go burn your Bookes and come and learne of me.*

Or he tried but failed. In a sweat of terror trying night after night to insert himself again into the play of those powers, and unable to make them live, make the play begin.

Or Oswald Kroll came to him in the tower, and talked long with him, putting to him again the plea or offer that the Emperor's *sapientes* wished to make to him. The long box and its engine and its uses. Talked at first gently and with elaborate politeness, making a dreadful kind of sense. Kelley huddled on his pallet, more afraid than he had been before any of the spirits whom he had summoned and discoursed with, and said nothing, only shook his head. Kroll came again, and then again. At last he said that there was but one way Kelley could refuse the offer made him: and he began to talk of that *hypothegm* or notion of Alcindus—Kelley had read Alcindus, had he not? *De Radii?*—that the net of rays in which we have our beings, the net of time and space and quality and form, may be escaped, or transcended for a moment. And how? Alcindus says the reason the ancients practiced animal sacrifice was that in the sudden extinguishing of a life a sort of hole was for a moment torn in that net, that net so light yet so strong; and through that hole the priest, the operator, might look or even step, to see the twistings that had tied this bleeding being to the ladder or web of all being—perhaps even, the hole being large enough, to move himself through it as though down a chute or up a ladder, to a far time or place. For a moment.

He said (still speaking with cool politeness, Kelley wide-eyed in the corner, arms wrapped tight around his knees listening) that any blood sacrifice could cause such an opportunity, but that the sacrifice (made with all solemn preparation) of a being of great worth and fullness, one whose nature and fate were bound in a hundred thousand ways to the whole, a being poised halfway between the worms and the angels, a soul that had itself ranged far over time and space and still retained the knottings and knittings that such journeys create: well, who knew how great a hole his sudden passing might open?

Had Sir Edward understood him, Kroll wished to know. Did he understand that they would not let him refuse the offer they made him, and go his way? If he would not be *agent,* and take up his burden and bear it to the future, then he would be *patient,* and suffer otherwise. He must see that it was not for their own sakes or even for the sake of the present age that they asked this of him.

—Not for my sake either, Kelley said; it was all he said.

—You have no sake now, Kroll said. You are not your own. Whose you are, or may be, is the last motion your will can make.

But that was the night that, with the help of the turnkey's daughter, Kelley let himself down from the high window on twisted sheets, and fled, or fell. Or it was the night he was strangled in his cell on the Emperor's orders—"almost a common Practice in the Empire," one later report of him says.

Or they really did put him by, like the cordial a housewife puts by, a whole summer's fruits distilled and bottled with a cork, to sit on a shelf dusty and neglected, but still potent within. On that very night, or possibly another, John Dee awoke alone in his bed in the midnight, and sought a light, and his paper and his pen.

> Dream of EK dead. Methought I saw *in chrystallo* that he was dead, and in a great black Coffin seeled and carried by many into a caverne in a Mountayne, there a Stone being rowled across the entrance to close it. Whereupon I saw no more.

John Dee had said that the one who achieves knowledge of the Monas is rarely seen after by mortal eyes; and he was not much seen in his last years. After Jane's death he gave up his duties in Manchester to curates, and came back to Mortlake, cared for by his daughter Katherine; there he lived almost forgotten. John Aubrey, collecting stories of the old wizard late in the century, has mostly the tales of old Goody Faldo, whose mother tended him in his last illness; she told Aubrey how by skrying the Doctor once recovered a basket of clothes that she and Dee's daughter Madimia lost when they were children together, and how he laid a storm, or started one.

Long before the old Queen died she had ceased to remember him, and the new Scottish King feared witches above all things. John Dee had no means of making a living except to sell his books. By two and three he let them go for a few copper coins, or sometimes for much more to those who thought them to be worth more, whose eyes lit at a title or an *incipit* in the way that Doctor Dee's had too, once, in his youth. Trithemius his *Steganographia.* Agrippa his twelve books of magic. They were to John Dee so much lumber; he would never open them again.

He sold Marsilius, *Libri de vita,* and his *Theologia platonica,* and the books of Mercurius Trismegistus put into Latin by him.

He sold the *Hierogliphica* of Valerianus, and other works of Ægypt, Iamblichus and Porphyry.

He sold his Black Books too, his *Picatrix* and his *Clavis salmonis* and the others, and his alchemies. The actors came and bought his Holinshed and his Cooper and his Stowe and the other histories and travels. He sold his *Copernici revolutiones,* Nuremberg 1543; let the true go with the false, it was not of his charge.

When his best books were gone he sold his pewter, and when his daughter wept he said it mattered not much, they could eat on tin as well. Tin tastes, she said. Wood then, he said, and be glad we have victuals to put on them.

He said it was no matter, that none of it mattered, but he couldn't bear the great house's emptiness, and left it to his daughters; he lived with a few books and tools in a cottage he had bought years before with a plan to add it to the house. He had practically stopped eating, as an old cat or dog does, seeming to live by consuming the last of his life itself, day by day, till it was all gone. Still now and then a dealer in old things came calling; his name was John Clerkson, and more than twenty years before he had brought Edward Kelley to Mortlake, thinking an advantage might come to him from making the introduction, and it had; from certain books given to him for that service then, he had learned a profitable line in spell-lifting and the finding of lost or stolen goods, and had even kept a tame demon for a while.

—Those were good days, Doctor.

—They are gone now.

—They are. It's a new world, and not a better one.

He fingered the things John Dee had brought out for him, a bound Bible, some glassware he had cast himself long ago, a vial of *Mercurius solis.* Caught between his need to have them cheap and the claim that the past and the great Doctor had on him.

—Here is a fine thing, he said.

He took out from the old ironbound trunk a little globe of brown glass and lifted it so that the light pierced it. Not perfect: it had a ray of bubbles that rose from a star or tear of lighter stone, not quite at its heart.

—Pretty, said John Dee.

Clerkson turned it in his fingers, which protruded from a worn glove's. He did not recognize it as the same one before which John Dee had seated young Edward Kelley on that March night in 1582, the night Clerkson had brought him hither.

—You may have it, said Dee; it is no good to me. It is crystal, though not of the best.

Clerkson named a figure larger than he had intended to name. John Dee nodded, nearly imperceptibly, and drew his old robe more tightly around him. After he had watched Clerkson count out the small coins, and had put them away, he said he had no drink to offer his guest. Clerkson said it was no matter. He talked a while with the old man, reluctant to leave him. He thought that he would not sell the stone he had paid for; not with the new Act against Witchcraft. This season the King's Men played a Scottish play full of witches, to please the King. The great fear raged on unabated. No one but those who had used those Arts great and small for many decades knew that all the true sorcerers, both the wicked and the wise, were dead, and what they had once done could be done no more.

.    .    .

No one knows on what day he died, though it was near the winter solstice. He was buried in the chancel of Mortlake church, and must have had a stone above his head, for Goody Faldo remembered how the children used to use it for a marker in their games, and dare one another to run to the wizard's grave. But in Cromwell's time the chancel steps were levelled, and children stopped playing in churches, and the stone was removed, for no reason that's known.

Anyway he had long since set out. *Happy is he that hath his skirts tied up, and is prepared for a journey:* so the angels had told them, himself and Kelley, speaking to them out of the glass in Cracow, the many, the sweet smiling unforgiving faces. *For the way shall be open unto him, and in his joynts shall there dwell no wearinesse. His meat shall be as the tender dew, as the sweetness of the bullock's cud. For unto them that have shall be given, and from them that have not shall be taken away; the burr cleaveth to the willow stem, but on the sands it is tossed as a feather without dwelling.*

But who said those things? Who spoke?

Across the Narrow Seas in Bremen town, John Dee's great coach lay long in a stable, dismasted and shut up. It hadn't been forgotten, though. Twenty years after, men and women were still telling how they had heard it pass their shuttered houses—had heard the sound of its iron-shod wheels on the road or on the cobbles, and no sound of hooves, as though it rolled unhitched downhill. It was seen too; scholars in their towers, out watching the Bear with Thrice-great Hermes, saw from their high windows a sight they might themselves have conjured by their deep studies: either the silvered moonlit road that coiled below had turned river, or. *Moreover there was no wind, not a breath,* one wrote in his book: it moved as though by memory of some other night, a night when the wind really had blown. Too fast to catch, always gone when they set out after it.

And another few years later, in the very lands through which it had passed—like the sound of a far-off gun arriving long after its smoke has been seen—there arose that furor over the sudden appearance of the Rose Cross knights (*Rosenkreutzer*) announcing a Universal Reformation of the Whole Wide World. Just after the Emperor Rudolf died in 1612, while Europe waited to see what would happen next, there appeared at Cassel (the city where John Dee had parted with his horses) a little book with a big title: *Allgemeine und General Reformation, der gantzen weiten Welt. Beneben der Fama Fraternitatis, des Loblichen Ordens des Rosenkreutzes,* etc. etc., telling of the "famous Fraternity" no one had ever heard of, how it had been growing in secret, its members travelling and healing the sick (an art to which their founder, called "Frater C.R.C." or "Christian Rosencreutz," had committed them); in appearance no different from their neighbors, for they were commanded to wear the dress of whatever land they came into; speaking their own secret language, using their own signs by which to recognize one another. Now, however, there was to be a revelation, a sudden advance in all arts and sciences, so that "man might understand his own nobility, and why he is called Microcosmus, and how far his knowledge reaches into Nature": for in a secret place far away the door to the vault where Father Christian Rosencreutz had been buried long ago had been found and opened. No sun had ever shone in there, but it shone with an inner sun! And the good old man (his skin golden and his beard white) was found to be clutching in his hands—a book! The Book M, in fact. And inscribed all around were the names of all the brothers who had ever been and would ever be. So the *Fama Fraternitatis* asserted.

Who were these people? Pamphlets appeared begging them to show themselves, asking for their help now, now before all was lost; begging to be granted membership, or hinting that the writer was himself a brother but not at liberty to say so. Or were they not benevolent but subversive, were they Deists, Socinians, Jesuits in disguise? Some people were certain they were, or worse. Invisible brothers? Working among us with magic arts, doing good *they say,* and supported by powers they are unwilling to name? Catch them, hang them, break them on the wheel.

And Dee? Yes: that "Book M." In another year another Rosicrucian manifesto was published, continuing the astonishing story; and that tract (a *Confessio*) was combined with a "brief consideration of more secret history" by one Philip á Gabella, of whom no one has ever heard before or since, and what was this brief consideration but a version of John Dee's *Monas hieroglyphica* laid out as a language of signs?

John Dee was dead by then; buried in Mortlake church in hopes of the Resurrection. His legendary carriage was no more. But what then was a certain Theophilus Schweighardt (so he called himself ) thinking when in 1618 he published a book—always another book—called *Speculum sophicum Rhodo-Stauroticum,* in praise of the Fraternity, and bound with it a little print, a picture of the *Collegium fraternitatis,* that shows a large building on wheels, moved by its own outstretched and beating wings?

The Invisible College, it was named, moving among us unseen. In the building's windows can be seen the Brothers at their holy work of searching Nature through Art, though what exactly they're doing is less clear. Messages—little folded letters—fly to and from it on their own wings; the Tetragrammaton blesses it from above; citizens, prayerful or confused or unaware, observe its passage, and then perhaps forget all about it, or do not quite forget.

Never forgotten, never remembered exactly: the print of Schweighardt's College, whatever he thought it meant, passed out of his hands, became detached from his (by now cold, by now unreadable) book and in due course it appeared in a cheap compendium of myth and fable put together in the 1920s and signed by a name no more embodied than "Theophilus Schweighardt" or "Philip á Gabella": *A Dictionary of the Deities, Devils and Dæmons of Mankind* by Alexis Payne de St.-Phalle. And one day in 1952 the librarian of the Kentucky State Library in Lexington sent this buckram-bound folio to the tiny town of Bondieu, in response to a request, or maybe in advance of one, from a family there. And a boy living in that house, displaced from his home in the far North, read it and reread it; and he found in it a name for the society he himself belonged to, which he had invented, into which he had initiated all his cousins so that he would not be alone there in those mountains: the Invisible College. The entry was illustrated by this print. In that book he found his College's sign too, John Dee's sign, with which thereafter he marked his schoolbooks and himself and his cousins. He already knew (from this book) that he and his Invisibles were exiles here, travellers, wanderers: that though they wore its dress and spoke its tongue almost like natives, their home country was not this one of ragged hills and coalsmoke and spoliation but a far one, not on any map, not any longer.

Ægypt.

Now twenty-five years later, Pierce stood in the Religion section of the little Carnegie library in Blackbury Jambs in the Faraway Hills—having returned to that section to search for more on the Powerhouse—and looked down at the same picture in the same book, *Deities, Devils and Dæmons of Mankind*. He hadn't known the book was here in this library, a copy not bound in maroon buckram like the one he had known but in its original leather or leatherette, worn and decaying somewhat repulsively around the folds and corners, on its spine blind-stamped the Monas, the little horned one, geometrical infant Pan or Omniform or Pantomorph, son and father of all things.

That was what had drawn him to the book, that sign. He had taken it out from its place in Oversize Books and lifted it into the lamplight, knowing even as he opened it that it would ask of him or offer him something. He could almost hear the whir of gears, the clicking into place of works long stopped, like the man in a dozen movies (Lou Costello one of them certainly) trapped or locked up in the great library, fingering helplessly the spines of old books until by chance the right one is pulled out, and the shelves swing open smoothly; behind them a stone passage and a stair, down which he must go.

A few yards down from the library is the small nineteenth-century office block called the Ball Building. Inside, the halls are wide and the ceilings are high; there is an elevator with a rackety gate and a beautiful brass handle to make it go, and the janitor will sometimes be available to run it. Most people just take the stairs, as Rosie Rasmussen was just then doing; she went two at a time, holding on to the banister and making a soft moaning sound of anguish under her breath, a sound she had not ever heard herself make before.

Some of the varnished doors still have frosted glass in them lettered in gold, and transoms above them that open and shut; some have been changed for modern steel-clads, like Allan Butterman's. Rosie tore it open.

"Is he here?" she cried to the secretary at her desk.

The secretary, maybe not unused to seeing people who looked as Rosie did, leapt up, pulling her headphones from her head, and without a word but holding her index finger up, wait a sec, opened the door to Allan's office. He was out before Rosie could reach his door.

"Allan they took her away."

"Rosie. What."

"They took her away. I lost custody."

"No you didn't. No."

"I did."

"No no. Rosie come inside. Come in and sit."

She came in, but couldn't sit. She had taken a wound, one of those wounds whose first symptom is certainty that what has happened can't really have happened, that the world and time have made a mistake, a dreadful mistake that has to be made right and can't be: those wounds can take a long time to heal.

"Tell me."

"I missed it."

"You didn't go? You forgot?" He was unable, even he, not to express astonished horror. Rosie's hands went to her face.

"I didn't forget. I was there. But I missed it. Oh Allan."

She had gone that morning, wearing the same sober suit and heels she had worn for Boney's funeral and carrying her papers and her beating heart; it was clear to her by then that she had pulled a Rosie and leapt in where fools fear to tread or whatever the saying is, that taking this on and throwing Allan aside was one of those big sudden gestures she had now and then made in her life, those ones that sometimes took years to make up for. She no more wanted to face a judge and lawyers than. And the closer the hour and the place came, the clearer and deeper these convictions grew.

But she was there, not only on time but early, walking into the old Cascadia courthouse with its familiar smell of floor polish and contention, and asked the aged uniformed man at his little desk where Room Two was, where she had been directed to appear; he pointed a thumb down the hall, and almost immediately she had come upon a door marked with that number, and gone in.

"Oh no," Allan said. "Rosie."

The hearing before hers seemed to be running late. The big room looked like the room she had been in before with Mike; she supposed they all looked about like this, these rooms, nationwide. She sneaked into a seat in the back, looking around for Mike and not seeing him or the crowd of suited lawyers she expected him to have with him. Maybe they knew what she didn't, that there was no reason to show up on time. She rehearsed, again, the talk she would have with Sam, if arrangements got changed, or even if. Sam sometimes when mommies and daddies don't live together. She listened to the proceedings, though she couldn't follow them; she wondered how people could bear to live their lives, as Allan did, as Mike seemed not afraid to do, in the struggle to get from others and not to give. No she must not think that way, she had to fight, she had to. And she had to pee. What was the delay, anyway?

"This is my fault," Allan said. "This is entirely my fault."

"No, Allan, no."

The hearing stopped at last, nothing apparently resolved, and people began to leave, noting incuriously or with interest Rosie sitting there with her legs crossed; the judge or magistrate too, before he slipped offstage like an actor, through a back door. And the place was empty. Rosie sat in the silence for a moment before she opened her papers once more to look, to be absolutely sure. And the old man in uniform who had directed her here came in the door and looked at her in mute puzzlement.

"*Part* Two was where you were supposed to go," Allan said. "*Part* Two of Family Court. Upstairs. Not Room Two, whatever that is."

When she did reach Part Two of Family Court she already knew that something irremediable had happened. And she found the room empty. Everything over and decided, all in a minute, by default, in her absence, because of her absence.

Gone.

"They were there, you weren't," Allan said. "First requirement in making your case. Show up."

That, in other terms, was what the judge told her when Rosie found her, just leaving for lunch: a stern lean rouged old woman, rings on nearly every finger and a white silk blouse whose costly beauty Rosie registered even as the woman told her that her ex-husband now had custody of their child.

"You told her, didn't you?" Allan asked. Rosie sat now and Allan shut the door to the outer office and the secretary. "You told her it was a mistake, that you, that . . ."

"Of course I did. Of *course*."

But she hadn't. The woman had regarded Rosie with the remote pity or censure of a being of some different moral order from her, and in her few words passed a judgment on Rosie that Rosie seemed to have been expecting to hear for a very long time, all her life, and to which she could not respond. She heard laughter far down the hall, people departing that way, triumphant; and a voice— her own, actually, though she heard it as someone else's, the voice of someone who wasn't going to surrender—said *maybe they're not gone yet.* And Rosie broke her gaze from the judge's face and began to run.

To the parking lot, first, where Mike wasn't, nor the van from The Woods he had been using. The halls again, empty, all the doors shut, lunchtime. Then to her own car, and back to the Jambs at a speed the old station wagon hadn't ever hit on this stretch of road before, to Beau's house on Maple Street. Beau still wasn't there. Neither was Sam. It's okay, the woman in the kitchen said, her dad just came and picked her up.

Then here.

"This won't stand up," Allan said. "Obviously justice was not served here. I mean that's the point. Even that woman must see that."

Rosie leapt to her feet. "Mike," she said. "He must have *known*." She had been returned in spirit for an awful moment to the courthouse and its halls and people (the judge, the guard, the people in the hearing room), as she would be returned over and over in the next months, awake and asleep; and there she perceived for the first time this fact, that Mike must have known. "He must have known I wouldn't just not show up. That something had happened."

Allan looked at her, those deep dark sympathetic eyes, and he nodded. "Sure. He must have known. And he didn't say anything. Not a word."

While she had sat like a dope in that other room, the wrong room, where other people's lives were changed, Mike had stood before that judge and said not a word, hadn't asked for time, hadn't asked for. Mercy.

"We can get this reopened," Allan said. "This is a travesty." She could see him choosing the moral ground he would fight on, his head lowered and the corners of his mouth down-drawn. "A travesty." His eyes focussed elsewhere, thinking; he patted his inner coat pockets for his glasses or his pen or something, and checked his tie knot. As though arming. A painful gratitude swept Rosie.

"Allan," she said. "I was really stupid."

"It doesn't matter, Rosie. What matters is what we do now."

"It matters. I was really stupid and I can't be anymore." She met his look. "Listen, I want to say. I'm going to take the job. The directorship. I've changed my mind."

"You don't have to say that, Rosie."

"Don't you think," Rosie said, "it might help? A real job? Wouldn't it look good? Not to mention that what the Foundation does is important to them. Isn't it? Isn't that true?"

"Well they did have some funding at one time. Who knows now. But those aren't good reasons for committing to the position. I was wrong to suggest anything like that."

"Those aren't the reasons." She rose and smoothed her skirt, her gabardine business suit. "Really they aren't."

"No?"

"No," she said. "Actually no. I think I'd be good at it. I ought to do it. I want to." She felt enter her, last thing she would have expected, a steely resolve; it was the unfairness, the stupid cruelty, that did it, for she knew now she couldn't plead or beg or even make deals with that, that mercilessness; everything in her had wanted to, and would have too if she had come into the room with Mike and he had shown any kindness, any love, but that was impossible now, and she wouldn't weep, she wouldn't weep again till this was over.

She didn't, either, not for the remainder of the morning as she and Allan planned and Allan made calls, and not for the days that followed; only when she left Allan's office that day and went down to her car again, and on the floor of the front seat was a shoe of Sam's and an apple half turned brown and odorous, she did. If because of what she had done or failed to do she lost Sam to them and they took her away with them, then her heart, which had just begun to awaken and grow again, would die forever within her and never be able to be resuscitated, she would carry it from then on, a cold cinder in her breast.

And that wasn't even the worst part. *Just don't let them hurt her* she begged someone, not Mike, not anyone; *just please don't let them hurt her.* She wept and wept, and the gods drank up her tears, as they have always drunk up our tears, yours and mine and everyone's, and by their sweetness were sustained for another day.

# 6

BADDON is Hebrew for the black angel called in Greek APOLLYON
(*q.v.*); ABA is an angelic luminary concerned in human sexuality,
who ministers to SARABOTES (*q.v.*) who rules the angels on Friday;
but ABBA is a name for God, "in Aramaic the equivalent of *papa*."

Pierce Moffett had had two fathers, a first and a second. The one in Brooklyn where he had been born (that was poor queer Axel, whom Pierce had not
seen in months) and the other in the country to which the first had sent him
away or allowed him to be carried away, northeastern Kentucky. That was his
uncle Sam, into whose big house filled with cousins Pierce had entered as
haughty and frightened as a prince in exile. In Sam's own bedroom, at the top of
that square gray house, Pierce had concealed the girl-child he and his cousins
had found.

Where had his uncle been that Pierce had dared to commit this outrage?
Gone. He had been gone. He must have been.

She was a little sharp-faced girl of about Pierce's own age then, ten or nine,
but far smaller, quick and stringy. He remembered (just then remembered them,
lifted them as from an archæological dig, brushed away the dust) her cracked
patent-leather shoes, and the way she had walked her socks down beneath her
heels, her dirty white anklets; the gray cold hard tendons of her ankles. What
though had her name been; what had they done to her there, he and his cousins;
tormented her somehow or overcome her, used her, saved her. Not saved her.

She had no mother. He remembered that. His cousins did not either. Pierce
had a mother, Axel's wife, Winnie: Axel's wife still, though they had not lived together for decades, hadn't since the time Axel had been arrested during a police
raid on a dark little bar in Greenwich Village, the year moon-faced Ike first ran
for president. And maybe Axel could have talked his way out of that, gosh some
dreadful mistake, for Winnie was always willing to be convinced that everything
was okay; but because Axel loved her—he still did—and because it had been a

frightful night and he seemed to himself flayed and without a skin, he wanted Winnie to know him at last for real, to know what he was: what he was to himself, inside. And because she sat so calmly listening to his story he decided he could tell her more. And the next day she began to think how she could get away from him and from Sodom, and get her son Pierce away too.

It was to Kentucky she fled. Sam's wife, radiant Opal, had died the year before—the former worst thing that had ever happened in Winnie's life—and Winnie determined to go there, and to help him and the children if she could. Not to stay the rest of her life or her brother's, she had not thought so far ahead as that; but there she would still be when he died twenty years later.

*Don't let them make you hate me,* Axel had begged his son in tears the day he had been taken away from Brooklyn. *O don't.*

Of course Pierce was told nothing then, for this was in the Age of Not Saying Things; secrets enough to power a hundred melodramas accumulated in every village, every city block, needless secrets, cruel secrets that sometimes killed their possessors as pearls do oysters. Not knowing gave Pierce (and not him alone) a lifelong thing for secrets, for knowing them, fearing them, sensing their presence, seeking them: not usually in the damp folds of actual lives so much, no he was his mother's son in that regard, but elsewhere, in books, inside.

She was his secret too, little what's-her-name, she and what they did; the first of that kind of secret he had ever entered into, Rose Ryder being the last or latest.

As though he climbed a spiral track up a mountain, he saw that he had come to the same place where he had once stood, only one turn higher up. He could see himself, down there on the former turn, in that past, in his own room in that house, bent over a book, this book or another; he could look with pity down upon himself, at the back of his big shorn head, the vulnerable tendons of his neck. When we can look at ourselves thus in the past, as though we were spirit revenants, chances are we are inventing. Pierce knew that. He only didn't know which way he ought to step, which sight he ought to see. For he was under a compunction to invent the past that had indeed occurred, the one that led to this present, its original and its *imago;* unless he could do that he would never exit from this, would never sleep again.

So:

It's late in a bleak dry winter, evening coming on quickly. Pierce's mother and his uncle Sam have gone away somewhere for a long time, where? Anyway Pierce and his cousins have been left with a housekeeper, a local woman (what now was *her* name), and earlier that day the housekeeper was visited by a little girl, kin of hers, who seemed to have run away from home (the cousins, spying, couldn't quite tell) but the housekeeper wouldn't let her in, drove her off like a stray dog.

Pierce and his girl cousins (Hildy and Bird) slept by themselves in a little four-room bungalow separate from the main house, built by a former owner to keep his married daughter in. So no grown-up knew that the three of them later found the girl at their back door and let her in.

We take actions that maybe we can't help taking, can't help taking because our natures are generous and our hearts not closed, not yet, and then the consequences are ours ever after. Maybe that's what they know, the three of them sitting in the glow of the gas heater with her, feeding her food that Pierce has stolen from the main house; maybe that's why they feel this awe, this quickening. They've never known someone who's really run away from home; they know almost none of the children of this place; they can hardly understand her when she speaks. (Pierce from Brooklyn thinks of his cousins as Kentuckians but actually they've spent much of their lives on suburban Long Island, to which Sam once went to try to establish a practice and a life.) They look at her small feral teeth and the broken nails of her hands, the dull glow of her eyeballs moving in her head from one to another of them, the pulsebeat in her hollow temple. Her body isn't as theirs are. They smell her, not only her musty coat but some other odor that's hers alone, that makes their nostrils open and their heads bend toward her to learn more.

Why can't he hear what they say to one another, hear her tell her name to them? He can see but not hear.

They vow to keep her there and not give her up or send her back to her father, or is he her grandfather, far up the mountain, from whom she fled.

They hide her in different places. During the day their tutor comes up from the hospital (Our Lady of the Way) and in the kitchen of the bungalow gives lessons for half the day: Sister Mary Philomel, a tall nun in black serge and white linen. While the children fill in workbooks, cut out paper valentines, and pray, they think about the found child they have put up in the old chicken house, in the attic, in Dr. Oliphant's own bedroom.

In Dr. Oliphant's bedroom she looks into the closets and opens the drawers and finds a little box containing the diamond ring that the children's dead mother wore. She watches the tiny stone gather the light and disperse it in drops of blue, red, green, and gold.

Did she steal that stone? Or did he? Something happened to it that caused Pierce to be bound over to Sam and punished. It was for her sake that he did it, if he did, and even under duress and suffering he had not told; he had not told.

**SHEKHINA,**    according to Kabbalah the spark of divinity present in the world, sometimes conceived of as identical to the HOLY SPIRIT or WISDOM. In alchemy it is most often a stone or a jewel, the *lapis exulis,* stone of our exile, to be found or made by the perfect philosopher. See also GRAIL.

All they do is read, and she can't read at all. They conceive of a plan to teach her to read, and to make her a Catholic. Mostly this is Hildy's plan, but it can't be argued with.

That was a land bound up in religion, sunken or suspended in it; there were seven churches in the town of Bondieu, whose population hadn't reached four digits by the time Pierce left. Religion there was like whiskey: either you did it or didn't; if you did it, you did a lot of it, and if you didn't you never touched it. Drunk on God.

She tells him that some of her kin handle snakes to prove that no harm can come to them 'cause they accepted Christ. Her father knows that the world's about to end, and all the dead to get up out of their graves where they lie asleep. Her father has struggled with the DEVIL too (she points him out in the big maroon book, amid his own naked WITCHES contorted with pain or glee). There's witches up the mountain too.

That's in the big closet on the second floor of the house, smelling of mothballs and fur. She turns the pages, he reads the words. It's not only the WITCHES and the DEVIL who are naked (his hooked or corkscrew penis displayed) but all the GODS too, a calm Hindu DEVA lifting her orbed breasts, APOLLO and HERMES and the SATYR, and APHRODITE holding her hand delicately over the mound, showing and hiding at once. Outside the closet door his cousin Bird is whispering urgently through the keyhole to them, what are you doing, what are you doing.

On Saturday in the afternoon the Invisible College sometimes goes down to the hospital, to the nun's chapel on the second floor where the priest (he is the nuns' priest as well as the parish priest) is hearing confessions. Other parishioners have their confessions heard in the church down the holler but the Medical Director's children come to this little candy-box chapel now and then if they've missed the regular hours. They go in the hospital, through the foyer past the tall long ovoid statue of the Virgin in her blue and white, the crown of all the stars on her head, the moon under one bare foot and a Serpent perishing in blissful agony beneath the other. Past the Infant of Prague, her divine Son, red-cheeked Kewpie in lace and red velvet, crowned and with his orb and scepter. Outside the chapel is the long black box, carved with unreadable figures, wormholed and beeswaxed, that Sister said was hundreds of years old and came with the Sisters from Prague where their order was formed, and where they had once taught the children of dukes and princes. What was in it? The key is lost. Why had they brought it so far? Sister didn't know; it was before her time.

They don't mention the lost child in their confessions.

BAPTISM.   In all her ceremonies, the Church never fails to notice the presence and possible danger of demons, and has included exorcisms on every page of the liturgy. Baptism is one long exorcism; the infant is born possessed, its entry into the world made under the auspices of a demon, and the sacrament is intended first of all to rout it from the little body.

She got sick and seemed near death, and Pierce stole holy water from the font in the church on a day when he served Mass there, and with it they baptized her, in the dark of the bungalow while the grown-ups slept. She knelt before Pierce and he poured the fluid over her head and read in Latin from his missal.

It seemed it would be easy to save her. She hated her grandfather. She did not have to believe the things she believed, about the Devil in the woods and the end of the world and the things her grandfather told her; they taught her other things she could choose to believe instead. Hildy gave her her favorite holy card of the Little Flower. Pierce showed her his fossil trilobite, and told her about Evolution. She could have chosen them and not her grandfather, if only the grown-ups had offered her that choice, but when they returned and found her there in the house they had not, and the children didn't know why.

Her grandfather came to the house and took her away with him. Sam and Winnie were not afraid of this man, with his long knobby black-haired wrists and his great Adam's apple from which black hairs also sprang; they weren't afraid but they did not contest with him. It seemed the girl hadn't believed the children anyway when they told her that the choice was hers. She went back to her grandfather's house, bearing the sacramental mark they had put upon her in secret, but really not theirs or his at all.

Who was it who had been caught, and who was it who was freed? Who was lost and who was rescued? Who pursued, who fled? Pierce had made that child kneel before him, and taken her soul for his own for a moment: had done magic for the first time, with water and words and the power he invoked. But it was he who had been baptized; on his soul was the mark that couldn't be erased.


In the spring Pierce convinced the Invisibles to go up the mountain and find her, to try again to rescue her, to bring her back with them, save her from her cruel false father. Sam and Winnie weren't told of it, and never would find out: how they packed lunches and went up to Hogback where she lived. It seemed to him now startlingly brave, so brave as to be not credible, yet he could not have invented it: the one great deed the Invisible College was ever called upon to do (the Kentucky branch anyway that Pierce had founded), the one real deed among all the imaginary ones they did every day.

And they couldn't do it. She wouldn't run away with them, and they had had to return without her. Their magic wasn't strong enough, or their faith was too weak; in the wrong from the start, no doubt, whatever their intentions; unwise, however generous. They, or he, had thought she needed rescuing, as his littlest cousin Warren thought the feral dogs who lived in the holler needed rescuing: tempting them home with a bone from the garbage, tying twine around their necks, leading them through the house where they growled and shat till they escaped. *Better off where they came from* Winnie told him.

After they came back without her he had sat on the steps of his house looking toward her mountain, which lay beyond where he could see; sat for days, living in the world he thought *she* lived in, under the curse he thought she bore: God, and her grandfather, and the Devil, and the End of the World. Trying to think what he could do, what she had done.

As he sat now today, still; or once again.

What if he were to arise now and go, go down there. He had not been across the borders of that state since his uncle had died six years before; he had not looked around himself then, had left as soon as he could. He might learn at least what had become of her; her fate, whatever it had been, still hanging in the balance maybe.

No it was crazy, there was no picking up that trail now, no pursuit was possible. And what would he say to her. That what he had done he should not have done; what he should have done he had not done. And that once again now today.

Sam Oliphant's dead wife's diamond ring, in its tiny box of convolute rose velvet. Its empty box.

A task, his task, begun in the past and left undone, that must or might be completed in the present, in another form, for another's sake. Not for his own sake, no, he didn't think so: not something buried in his flesh and needing to be removed, like the wounds that psychiatrists say we go on licking all our lives until we heal them in the remembering of them: not for his sake, nor for that girl's, for whom he had actually done his best maybe possibly, anyway had done what he had done. No not for her sake, or even for Rose's.

For whose sake?

How was the spell to be reversed?

Now afternoon was fading, another brief winter day Pierce had not seen pass. At this gray hour sometimes, as at dawn, he had been able to sleep for a time, but only if he forbore his bed, sat up in his chair in his clothes as though awake. He lost consciousness briefly, but dreamed only of the room he sat in, and the book he held in his lap; and found it still there when he awoke.

It was the lights of a car that had awakened him, and a dog's bark, and the thud of its door. He struggled upright, to meet what he had to meet, whatever it was; and the door was knocked on.

"Pierce, it's Rosie," Rosie called at the door. "Can I come in?"

# 7

I was out, that's all," Rosie said. "Out and about. Paying calls. If you hadn't been here I'd have gone over to Val's maybe. Or."

She wore a rumpled raincoat over a woolly shirt not probably her own originally, and a crocheted hat from some other era of her life. It occurred to Pierce that she did not herself look so hot, but he didn't know if he could trust his perceptions; almost everything he looked at was getting uglier steadily, or sadder, or weaker.

"So," she said. On the floor she spied the *Dictionary of Deities, Dæmons and Devils of Mankind,* and bent to pick it up. "Hey, I know this book."

"Oh yes?"

"Val's taken it out before. She read to me out of it. About—I forget exactly. Plato and love. About Eros, who's a little boy, he says."

"Yes."

"Wasn't it Plato who said we're originally one being, male and female, and then get separated in two?"

"Well. Self and beloved other. Not necessarily male and female."

"Ah-ha," she said, flipping pages. "It was in that stupid poem you found. Which I actually read." She sampled the air, as her dog had done. "You know, you need to do your laundry," she said.

"It's far. The one in Stonykill finally closed. Nasty place, good riddance, but still."

"Come on over to the house. We have this machine you won't believe. The kind where you can watch the wash go around through a little porthole. Sam loves squatting in front of it; she says it's like TV."

"I'm not good company, Rosie. I don't know if I'm up to driving."

"I'll take you. And bring you back soon. You can tell me what you've been thinking. Tell me all about devils and angels."

"I'm swearing off thinking."

"Aw come on," she said, and he saw urgency in her drawn face, she hadn't been sleeping either maybe, the whole world awake. "Come play. Commonna my house-a, my house."

His windows were black, and the alarm clock's short hand had not even crossed out of the left hemisphere, twelve hours and more of dark to go. A small daring awoke in him. It was only his inwardness that had been devastated, burnt-over country where no one dwelt; his exterior was whole, and needed a chat, and maybe a drink, and why not. He nodded thoughtfully, not immediately taking steps, but nodding.

So soon enough she had got him into her car with Alf and Ralph the dogs, and tossed his pillowcase of clothes in back; and heading toward Stonykill and Arcady she told him what had happened to her that morning: how she had lost her court case, and lost Sam to Mike, and to them.

"Oh no Rosie," Pierce said or keened; "oh my Lord." He grasped the top of his head, as though to keep this knowledge from cracking or splitting it.

She told him what Allan had said, that they weren't going to get away with it, and her voice trembled with doubt or maybe (he thought) it was only fierce resolve, and he listened intently and wrote Allan's name inwardly as an ally though he didn't believe in his powers now as he might have once, law and argument and reason. He saw Sam, reft away from her mother, and from him; from the world. The last light went out. Oh those bastards. The way ahead, lit fitfully by the walleyed headlights, seemed suddenly unfamiliar, as though he'd never travelled it before. Houses went by, dark or cheerily lit, that knew nothing of Rosie or Pierce or what had happened to them.

"If you told him," Pierce said helplessly. "Asked him, asked him . . ."

"He won't even talk about it. He already said: he can't have her raised outside his faith. He couldn't bear it. He said he'd do anything." She blotted her eyes on the sleeve of her shirt. "I know Sam loves him a lot," she said. "Probably more than she loves me. And he's gotten to be a better father lately than he was." The gateposts of Arcady appeared, the big house, one light lit.

"No I bet not," Pierce said.

"He has. Nicer. Milder. Less, I don't know, selfish."

Pierce wanted to contradict her, but he couldn't; Rose had grown not less selfish maybe but milder somehow, happier, there was no doubt of it.

"It's not the end of the world," Rosie said, coming to a stop. The wagon began the shuddering spasms it always went through when she turned it off. "People get out of these things. A lot of them do. I read in a magazine."

"Yes. I heard that too."

From somewhere nearby Pierce heard a sound like mocking laughter.

"They come to, sort of," Rosie said. "Snap out of it."

Again, a weird snigger, even closer. Pierce sat upright, looking into the dark.

"Just the sheep," Rosie said. "Spofford's sheep."

Spofford's sheep. Pierce remembered again the sunlit summer afternoon, a year ago August, when the bus he was riding from New York City had broken

down in Fair Prospect, not ten miles from here; he had been on his way to
Conurbana to apply for a job at Peter Ramus College, there where she now was
earning a degree, a *degree,* another mask no doubt for them to do their work behind.

"I'm boarding them for him, you know. They do that all night."

"Are they really hungry?" Pierce asked in sudden pity. "Are they okay without him? Are they? Where is he now, is he coming back, is he all right?"

Rosie told him it was okay, they were okay, and her dog Ralph barked from
the back, and was answered by Spofford's dog out in the darkness; but it was too
late, Pierce was releasing strange sobs, grasping himself around the waist and
brow, and she could only pat his arm and wait.

"I need," she said. "I think I need a drink."


"You asked her to the party?" Rosie asked him in amazement. "At the castle?"

She had found Boney's bottle of Scotch in the bottom of the living-room cabinet, and after some hunting for something she preferred had settled for this stuff
too, top of the line Pierce said but tasting to her of burning leaves. From the
basement came the faint sound of almost all of Pierce's clothes being thumped
and tumbled.

"Yes."

"Oh man," Rosie said. "Pierce you got it bad. I didn't know. Oh Lord."

"Yes."

"One sick puppy."

"I didn't mean for this to happen," Pierce said. "I didn't believe that it would.
I still don't believe it. It is just so foolish."

"She's not good enough for you, Pierce. Oh I don't mean that, that's not it,
but she's not worth this. She's. She's just somebody."

"Well. So am I."

"You know what I mean."

He bent his head. He knew.

"So what's that like?" Rosie asked after a moment. "To feel that so intensely."
Her smile had altered and her gaze grown more inquiring. "I never have. Really,
ever."

"Love 'em and leave 'em, huh, Rosie?"

"Well I just never did."

"It's not so good." He drank. "There used to be a disease," he said, "that people don't seem to suffer from anymore. A disease of love. It was called *amor
hereos.* Crazy Love."

"Oh they still have that. But you don't have it. Come on."

"It was a disease that some people actually tried to catch. The knights of
Provençal, or anyway the poets who wrote about them, thought there was nothing more glorious. *Un Dieu en ciel, en terre une Déesse.*"

Rosie worked this out. "A god in heaven, a goddess on earth."

"*One* God in Heaven," Pierce said. "*One* Goddess on earth."

"Oh really."

"Sometimes those knights died of it. Really. There are cases."

"I thought you at least went out and did good deeds," Rosie said. "In her name."

"Sure."

"She sends you forth."

"Sure." A painful warmth started in his limbs and his breast. "My old teacher said, Frank Walker Barr," and here Pierce intoned somewhat, "that 'in the picture-language of mythology, Woman represents all that can be known; Man is the hero who comes to know it.' "

"To know what."

"What can be known."

"And what if she's not there by the time you get there to know her? What if she's decided to be a hero herself, and go find what's to be known?"

She drank, regarding him, so frank and interested that Pierce lowered his eyes. "Well he wasn't talking about real men and women," Pierce said. "He was talking about *stories*. Allegories in a way. He says Woman *stands for*."

"Pierce," Rosie said. "You think you can go on telling stories like that, where men come looking for women to know them, for a thousand years, and people don't think *This is about me*?"

She crunched ice in her teeth. Another moment arrived in which Pierce knew that he had been wrong, all wrong, and why, and how simple it all was; and again it passed, leaving him bereft and ignorant of why he felt bereft.

"So," she said. "What did you come to know? By the way."

"Oh. Oh, well. Oh jeez." He lifted one bare foot and rubbed it in his hands, cold as a corpse's. "You know," he said. "One thing those old knights always had. When you were lost in the thorny wood, and didn't know what to do next, there would always be a hermit, or a friar of orders gray, who would appear, and take you in, and tell you what to do. Give you a tablet, or a rhyme, or a sword or a prayer. Heal your wounds." He felt his eyes fill.

"Tell you what," Rosie said, and Pierce saw that her eyes too shone, on account of his absurd dilemma he thought but surely not only his. "I'll be your hermit if you'll be mine."

"Okay," he said. "I will if ever I can."

"Me too." She rose and found the bottle again, and splashed more amber fluid in each of their glasses. "It's a deal."

While they drank Rosie made sandwiches and they ate them in the big comfortless kitchen, designed for help to use. Pierce tried to eat, tried to explain to Rosie about Rose Ryder.

"She needed to be swept away," he said. "She needed it not to be up to her; she needed to be. Taken I guess. Rushed in upon."

"By God."

"Well ultimately."

"By you." She ate a warty pickle. "Like how."

"Well I was supposed to *know* how; that was the deal. She trusted me to know."

"Did you?"

"I picked it up."

Rosie studied him smiling. "This was in bed."

"Yes."

"How far did this go?"

"Oh." He lifted his eyes, as though to think or ponder, maybe to avoid Rosie's. "Oh pretty far."

"Come on," she said. "How far."

He tried to tell her, laying down only low cards at first, as she regarded him chin in hand. He told her more. Sometimes she laughed, or nodded in recognition.

"Yeah," she said. "Yup. Old Rose."

"The thing I know is," Pierce said. "That she's like that really. Deep deep. I'm not, but she is."

"Yeah," Rosie said. "Yeah she is." She was nodding rhythmically in a yes-sirree way that made Pierce stop talking and regard her wondering, until Rosie caught his look.

"What."

"You know this?" Pierce asked.

"Hey," Rosie said, and got to her feet. "I've been to bed with her too. Oh yeah. I've *had* her." She grinned broadly at Pierce's face and leaned over as though to embrace him, put one hand on his shoulder and extracted his cigarettes from his pocket.

"You have?" Pierce said. "Rosie, you . . ."

"Yeah. She's got a cute body."

She held her smoke out for a light. Her turn to talk. How last spring, not *last* spring but the spring before. Did Pierce know that Rose and Mike were lovers? Yes sure because that was when Pierce had first come to the county. But he'd had an old lech for her going way back, when Rosie was still Mrs. Mucho; and one night.

"What he said was, what he thought was, that this was supposed to make the marriage stronger. Make a bond between us. That we had shared this. A *bond.*"

She was still grinning dopily, though she wasn't dopey; she turned the cigarette inexpertly in her fingers, enjoying it, enjoying Pierce.

"It didn't work," Pierce guessed.

"It's funny," Rosie said. "The one thought I'd never had before that night was to get a divorce. Never like considered it or toyed with the idea. But after that night—well I never even had to really think about it, it was just obvious."

"It was that bad?"

"No. It wasn't bad. It was"—she made a small, careless gesture with the smoking butt—"kind of fun. Kind of sweet in a creepy way."

"Uh-huh."

"It didn't push me over the edge anyway. No nothing like that. It's more like what I did instead of making a decision, or thinking things through. I mean it *was* making a decision, only in another—medium." She squinted inquiringly at Pierce, are you getting this? And then, "It's as though," she said (or maybe thought; later on she wouldn't remember if she'd said it aloud, if she could have), "as though our bodies and their feelings live a different life from us, that we only partly share, that we only get to look into sometimes when they do something that amazes us. Like that, getting it on with Rose, which meant it was over with Mike even though it didn't seem to *me* to mean that at all. Like that. Or like finding out you love somebody enough to die, being surprised that you do. Or then not loving them anymore, and not being able to a second longer. It seems so sudden. But maybe it's not sudden at all."

Pierce had not spoken, Rosie became aware, in some time.

"So whatcha think of that? Dumb idea?"

"I," said Pierce. The work of pulling his cored and splintered self together enough to ponder such a notion and answer was overwhelming. Nothing he had ever known was turning out to be so, why not this notion of Rosie's? Maybe to-morrow or the next day his thing too would be over, as suddenly as it came on; maybe it was over already, and he just didn't yet realize it.

"Yeah well," Rosie said, and laughed, what do I know.

"No no," said Pierce. "It's. An idea."

Rosie picked up the bottle, and between filling her glass and his she lifted her hooded laughing eyes to him. "I've got an even dumber one," she said. "You want to hear it?"


The disease or *melancholia* called *amor hereos* was formerly believed to have a treatment; not a very certain or reliable one, not a *cure* really but an ameliora-tive, or rather a list of them, which if applied judiciously over a long time might save the sufferer. Exercise and travel and a plain diet of bland and light-colored foods; prayer of course; if these fail, whipping and fasting; then *coitus* with a will-ing and openhearted woman or women, cheerful reminders of the flesh, which paradoxically the sufferer has forgotten in the awful infection of his spirit.

Pierce in Rosie's bed (she led him to it like a child, by the hand) was awed, unmanned almost, by the strangeness, wholly other, of her person and her body when they were disclosed to him, her body actually strange and not strange, as though once familiar but long forgotten, oh I remember; he realized then that all he really remembered was this disclosure, itself always the same, the freckles of her breastbone and the taste of her breath actually altogether new.

"What about," he said.

"Pill," she said.

Still he nearly failed when he embraced her, no longer knowing what would be enough either for her or for him, afraid that his own thermostat was now set so high that no common acts or words could start his fires, and for a moment he turned his face away from hers and wept because he thought now all ordinary tenderness had been taken away from him for good, sold to buy what he was hooked on.

"What," she asked, and smiling made him turn to face her. He wouldn't answer and tried to rise, offering some broken apology, but she pressed him back against the pillows and made him suffer her attentions. Though he covered his face she did to him what everyone knows or says all men like to have done, to be dandled and handled and suckled, and though he went on weeping or shaking with odd sobs he began laughing too, and so did she at his absurdity.

"This the first time you ever did this?" she said when he squirmed.

"No no," he said. "No no. No no."

Just afterward she too wept a little, or only panted maybe, victorious or defeated athlete, wet and wrung. A while after that she spoke: "I thought that went really well," she said. "Actually."

"Should we," Pierce said, "talk about Spofford?"

"No," she said. She was near sleep. "Spofford got eaten by wolves."

The first night Pierce had ever been in these imaginary mountains he had nearly seduced Spofford's Rose, or maybe been seduced by her, in a river cabin, actually now his own house in imaginary Littleville: but of course that was Rose Ryder, Pierce had made a mistake, a simple mistake.

"He's had her too," Rosie said. "You knew that, right?"

"No."

"Oh."

She did sleep then, what she had looked forward to as much as any of it, in the cave of his curled body, anybody's body as far as her own sleeping one knew or cared. Pierce even slept, though not for long. He was one of that quadrant of humanity that can't sleep when touched by a fellow human, no matter how familiar or beloved, and Rosie pressed close and warm and grateful; but mostly he awoke because his eyes were still unsatisfied. In its terminal stages *amor hereos* withers all the body, except the eyes, which of course grow stronger, but cease to shut: the sufferer sleeps no more, or too little to heal. He guessed he should have long ago noticed this symptom, and the hectic creativity or false *afflatus* that had accompanied it, for what they were, but he hadn't.

*En ciel un Dieu,* he repeated, a little charm, a hypnotic; *en ciel un Dieu, en terre une Déesse.* Quixote, befuddled by stories, wrong about everything except the one thing that matters most; not knowing who he was, wherein he had been thrown, who his enemies were, but setting his lance, kicking up his horse in the name of his lady, the wrong lady. What if that really were Pierce's own madness, one sick puppy. His would be just the reverse though of course: deluded by a brain-drying melancholy into thinking he was not a knight, that there were no giants, that there was nothing that mattered.

Rosie woke again when he turned away from her. She touched him, knowing he was awake. "You know something?" she said.

"What."

"You should get married. Have kids." She heard him make a small sound, the smallest possible sound of the purest possible grief; maybe actually no sound at all. "Get out of your head. Get down in the shit and the blood."

"Yes?"

"Oh I don't know. Good night, you dope."

"Good night, Rosie."

# 8

At dawn Beau Brachman, driving back from the City and down the interstate, having gone past the exits that would have led him back to the Faraway Hills and those who waited for him on Maple Street in Blackbury Jambs and every night set a place for him at dinner, turned off onto other roads, the older roads whose numbers had once been codes for escape or pursuit. The Python was going backwards along the ways that long-time past his Olds 88 had borne him forward—his former car, that was: the Double Worm, the black *ouroboros* in which he had crossed and recrossed the country twice in a long loop, a loop that still connected a network or union of souls, the finding or creating of which was Beau's only surety now of where he had come from. It was they of whom Julie had spoken, those whom Beau could call, or call on, to say *Are you seeing this too? I think I see this, I don't know, I'm asking; do you see it?* If he could have brought them all together in one room (he never would or could, it would amount to a category error, it would be a *zoo* almost literally) they wouldn't know one another, would look around themselves in dismay even to find who they were included among. Without them or the thought of their existence Beau felt that his overextended soul would collapse like a circus tent whose poles and guys were let fall. Still, gassing up the Python when evening came at a neon station somewhere on the rim of the Great Central Basin he almost asked if this cup might not pass from him: it was a long way around, and he wondered if he really had to do it all.

Outside Harrisburg, pressing the Wonder Bar in search of human voices, Beau caught what he thought was the far tall transmitter of WIAO, wherever exactly it was, he had never known, hadn't heard the unmistakable sound of it since the last time he had crossed these flatlands; the distant dashed line of a freight train then too, going the same way he went, under a low winter sky.

Up, there it was again. And gone again. Country music swamping it as though in Karo syrup with warm sweet bitterness. Then again back.

*Radio WIAO! Comn at you through the ozone, it's IAO, yow! The cry of the peacock is the name-a God! Where have you been that you couldn't hear, where have you lain asleep? We can reach you throughout these lands, Egyptland where we are imprisoned. Let every ear be open and every heart awaken. Now the news.*

Whatever unimaginable news the great lost station was prepared to retail Beau couldn't pick up. He tuned delicately, a safecracker, as back then he had tuned and sought, when he had roamed with the placid herds of great American cars, feeding with them at places whose ruined shells he was maybe now passing, these spaceship or amœba shapes whose lights were out and broad windows boarded.

*The beautiful immortal Wisdoma God! The last and youngest child of the perfect infinite immobile ones! They were the All, and they searched for Him from Whom they had come forth, He Whom they were within. And she the last and youngest, she leapt the farthest! And and and*

Gone.

That was Her again, though, Her being spoken of: as it had been Her on the streets of New York. So he was on the right way still. He remembered the days he had first begun hearing or collecting this story, learning that it had always been known and told, alongside or underneath the other American stories, an American story too but not American in being so sad.

*And she said Father! I want to know You! I want to love You! Father I want to come closer to You, and do a work like the works You have done! And leaving her Consort she moved, in a motion toward the Father. And oh my what troubles there was then. For this Movement of love and seeking of hers threatened the All with its passion. And that passion was thrust outside the Awful Fullnessa God! Put out and set to wander! O grief! O happy fault!*

In the story as Beau knew it and told it, there was nothing and nowhere then for the fallen Passion of Sophia to fall into: nothing existed except the Pleroma, the Fullness of God's expression of himself. What happened was that her exile itself, the catastrophe or disaster of it, made a place into which she could be exiled: a world of darkness for her to wander in, a place made by her wandering. Not a place outside God or abandoned by him, for there could be no such place, no but deepmost inside him, a hollow in his heart from which he withdrew. At the sight of this Abyss, and at the thought of what she had done and what she had lost, she felt *grief,* and her grief became the first element, water; and she felt *fear,* that she might cease to be, and *bewilderment,* and *ignorance,* and these became elements too; but when she thought of the Light that she had left, it cheered her and caused her *laughter,* which is the stars and the sun.

*It was this world:* the one we know, which hadn't existed till then; this world in its infinitudes, and in its brief lives and hopes as well, made of her suffering, made of her hope. This one Beau crossed now and had crossed then, this story that had become the world: he had heard different chapters or versions of it in bars and diner booths and nighttime drugstores as well as in the cloud castles and tent cities and jingling caravans he had also passed through in those years, finding and losing it again like the rays of WIAO. He was this story too, it was his both to be and to tell. Beau remembered where he had come *to* along it better than where he had come *from* to get there.

He remembered following the No Name River up into the mountains of eastern Kentucky in search of the last of the more perfect gospel bearers, but did not remember what he had heard, on what coast or among what believers, that had set him off to find them. Remembered arriving at dawn or evening in towns named for the coal companies that had once created them, Carbon Glow, Neon, High Hat, Good Luck, each with its railhead, its tall breakers and washers and the water tower marked with the company's sign, some abandoned and rusting; each with its slagheap, accumulated defecation of the long consumption of the land and people; each with its half dozen churches alight at dawn and evening when folks could come, the hand-lettered sign put up outside an ill-made shed no finer than the houses they lived in. Inside they sang:

> *Where the Godhead dwelleth*
> *Temple there is none*
> *Naught that country needeth*
> *Of those aisles of stone.*

> *All the saints that ever*
> *In such courts have stood*
> *Are but babes and feeding*
> *On children's food.*

It was the Old Holiness people who had at last told him how to reach the more perfect gospel bearers. For a long time after he had come to the Old Holiness church they pretended not to know or even to hear when he asked, but he was patient; he knew they knew. And if they did not, then the story that Beau had been following, faint as a mountain track, was really not true, or no longer true.

Old Holiness handled snakes, but not as Holiness or New Holiness did: not as a victory over evil. In their board-and-batten church when the snake was brought out, shook from its sack, the gathered sang in clanging shape-note harmony:

> *In Paradise did Adam sleep*
> *The Serpent woke him, he did weep*
> *Awakened Man he wept full sore*
> *And begged that he might sleep once more.*

After Beau served beside them for a summer, toting and picking corn and minding children and sitting to watch by the side of sick old ones, they began to speak to him of what they knew, usually attributing it to someone else or to dream or rumor: that there were ones who know a truth beyond preaching, a surprise even to the holiest heart. Up in the pineclads, far off the gullied roads, he would need somebody to take him there, and the reason they were hid so fast is that the more perfect gospel bearers know what the law does not want them to know, or to pass on, or certainly to practice: a practice more forbidden than the handling of snakes, which often enough they had the sheriff or the state police on them about.

At last they set him guides (a boy of twelve and his older brother) and they drove and then walked a trail following the river. A *fastness* such as Beau hadn't climbed up into since he had followed his Hmong guides into the clouds to cross from the nation, imaginary to them, of Vietnam into the also imaginary nation of Cambodia. His Kentucky guides barefoot as the Hmong had been. At evening they brought him to a string of cabins and tents along the stream, trucks too turned into dwellings with a cap and a fly and a couple of aluminum chairs. And a small trailer, somehow occupying the center of the encampment, an aqua and cream Voyager dotted with rust at the joints and with fiberglass awnings over the miniature windows. It had been dragged up here with awful effort to be the place where Plato Goodenough the more perfect gospel bearer could lie in his last days. In there now Plato Goodenough was starving himself to death. Once before he had been rescued by the social worker, and taken to doctors; here he wouldn't be found.

In the trailer an ancient smell of mildewed linoleum. On the sheetless mattress Plato lay motionless, propped on pillows, cadaverous already except for the flush of his cheeks and the bright tip of his nose. A clean white shirt buttoned to the neck, where his Adam's apple bobbed, sprouting gray hairs; his body slack and thin as a dropped puppet's. Beau hat in hand came in among the few gathered in the minuscule bedroom and its doorway. Plato Goodenough was talking. He had strength only for a few words each day, and spoke almost too low to be heard.

What Plato Goodenough had done was to refuse the Devil's domination; he had chosen not to put into this body any more of the nourishment it needed to stave off its dissolution. He had begun years before by refusing butcher's meat, though he ate fish for it had no blood. Then he ate no fish; then no food produced through sex congress, milk and eggs and cheese. Now nothing. All the sustenance he had now was branch water and the Last Supper, printed on a black-velvet cloth hung opposite him on the wall; to the apostles gathered at that table he sometimes spoke as familiarly as to those around his bed.

"You see the stars and the planets, the sun and moon," Beau heard him say, only his jaw moving. "Well I tell you all them was angels once, and for their sins was put in bodies, and those are them. And if you think it's a fine thing to have for a body a bright star, well I tell you that to the angels the bodies they have are as burdensome and as hateful as this one of mine is to me, and as much as I do they long to escape them, when as it says, the stars will cease to shine, and fall upon the earth."

Beau wanted to speak, to ask, but could not; and was answered anyway. As evening came on, he withdrew from his side with the others, though one or two watched through the night. In the morning in their cabins along the track they stirred up their fires and made beaten biscuits and red gravy, and at noon they heated cans of tomato soup with Pet milk or chunks of Well Far cheese and ate it with crumbled saltines and boiled coffee. No meat though, no ham fried in lard or Swanson's chicken slid whole and greasy from the can to cook with dumplings, they wouldn't want to be eating flesh through which the souls of their parents and ancestors and dead children had cycled. They ate their food as silently and ravenously as if they had stolen it, their heads bent together and their spoons and jaws going, and were hungry again soon after, ever hungrier as Plato waned. Beau among them knew that their suffering was perhaps greater even than Plato's, and as exemplary, and as necessary. From then on, Beau watching people eat would sometimes see not the familiar humans nourishing themselves and their loved ones but instead, in revulsion and pity, would perceive strange unconscious machines laboring at some automatic work, steam robots grinding and processing, the caught spirit sometimes looking out the hungry eyes. That would be his to bear.

At each dawn some of them went up to the trailer to sit by Plato Goodenough's side, to listen to him, to watch him dissolve for their sakes, because he could do it and they couldn't; then perhaps in their next journey they too could refuse the Devil's domination, his false gifts, and so not have to sweat and toil and suffer here below any longer.

Are you at peace, Plato? they would ask him. Are you satisfied?

I'm at peace, he would answer. But I ain't satisfied. I never will be satisfied here below.

When he ceased to speak, they didn't cease to put their questions; they dribbled water between his lips and watched his chin tremble. They thought he might tell of what he saw, just as he set out, that shore; but he said nothing at the last.

When he was finally altogether shet of it, they burned Plato Goodenough's body. He had asked them to leave it on the stony mountaintop for the buzzards to pick at (Beau thought of Parsi towers he had seen, the desiccated dead atop them and the black birds) but they were afraid for the law. They sang the hymn called "White" while the oily smoke arose:

> I'm a long time trav'ling here below
> I'm a long time trav'ling from my home
> I'm a long time trav'ling here below
> To lay this body down.

Coming up or down out of the Appalachians in the 88 after a year spent there, out into the grid again: into a Movement running through sudden vast congregations of people like wind through standing grain, where lights and shadows came and went. Beau kept on westward through those days as though beating against the current, for the current was hopeful and eager and hungry and happy and Beau was queasy and doubtful and afraid. They believed that the System was coming to an end, that Power could be tamed or expunged, first from their own hearts and then from the world, replaced by Love; that Evolution would bring this about even if it was resisted worldwide at first, or even for a long time. Beau came to know the cosmo-Marxists who remembered what Karl said, that all philosophers heretofore had tried to describe the world, when the point was to change it; but who also knew that these things were the same. That was the Revolution. And it looked easy right then, unless you saw that above the teem of people in motion, which seemed so great from within, were only further levels of the System, the Domination System, like rising levels of cumulus in a squally sky, passing right from the top levels of human power to the lowest levels of other powers.

He wanted to defy them, as Plato Goodenough had done. Over the years between that time and now he had often wanted to, had felt a limitless desire for an end to desire. But the way out in that direction was as closed to him as the way downward that led through MM and Mal Cichy's temptations. It was escape; and escape was what was forbidden to him. He thought of the animals he had seen around the world who, hitched to a stone or a wheel, walked in circles, treading in their own dusty or muddy footprints till they died: beasts without whom the villagers would not survive.

*The beautiful young foolish Wisdoma God! She had a partner now, and the partner was her own Anguish. And with that partner she brought forth a son! The lion-shaped lion-headed one, Jove Jehovah Jaldaboth, the maker and ruler of the heavens that we see and that we labor under.*

There it was again, Radio WIAO, still emitting its rays, the stronger the farther west, the same ceaseless unwearied hectoring as he had heard in that past time, when he had wept to pass on, and known that he could not.

*Oh brothers and sisters! The holy suffering Wisdoma God caught in the pitchy dark of the World Underneath! Waiting in the prison of the Lion-headed One for Jesus to come and strike off her shackles! Oh how many times has it happened, in how many ages of ages! In our hearts too, brothers and sisters, in our own hearts, in the secret prisons made there and maintained there by the heavenly Powers within us!*

They are all her children, all the Powers are: for she's mother as well as lost child, and her restlessness and her smart mouth are the source of our miseries, but also the source of our saving consciousness of them; mother yes of the ones who oppress us, but always our help against them too, teaching us how to evade or defeat them, like the giant's wife helping Jack. Her tricks and techniques being what we call Human Life on Earth. She herself is the source of our knowledge that she must be rescued, source too of our knowledge that we can do that: rescue her.

We can do that: he, Beau himself, any of us.

*Apostle Peter! He spoke to Simon the Magus and he said to him: How can you say what Jesus never said, that you are the embodiment of the Entire Holy Power and Lighta God? And Simon answered him saying: Because every soul on earth is. And Peter asked him again: How can you say that this woman Helen, this this this woman of ill repute, is the present incarnation of the holy beautiful suffering Wisdoma God? And Simon answered: Because there is no woman that is not.*

Beau lifted his eyes to the green signs and the stern choices they offered in stark white letters, on front or back, upward or down, and he slowed, and exited. He was between East and West. Rain was falling, and up ahead, illuminated in their separate small booths, were the two people, a man on one side and a woman on the other, who admit those who go travelling and take the fare from those who have travelled.

Beau stopped his car there where you were not permitted to stop unless overtaken by some emergency, or were yourself a servant of the highway.

He thought: the thing to be found and fought for has come into being. The thing without which the new age could not be made different from the old, the thing that is also nothing but a kitten saved from drowning maybe, or a cocoon on a milkweed pod taken indoors to open in the warmth. Not an age or even a year from now but now.

Right in his own backyard too, waiting for his return. He hoped he hadn't gone too far in reaching this certainty, that he would not be too late getting back. For even if he had allies, and his allies had allies that he knew nothing of, and so on out to spheres he had never travelled to, he thought that this was his alone to do, just as it was each of theirs. It always is.

Beau made a U-turn.

# 9

osie Rasmussen drove Pierce home in the morning, and though Pierce almost wanted to slip away from her into his unwelcoming little house, she made him stop and give her a hug, rough skin of his cheek against her smooth one. They had already said to one another that the night before hadn't of course actually meant anything, and that that was the sad part actually, that it didn't and couldn't; anyway *she* said that, and Pierce assented.

But that night she called him anyway.

"I talked to Mike finally," she said.

"Yes?"

"Just on the phone."

"Oh."

"I told him I thought what he had done was so unjust. I told him that if he had done that because his religion said it was the right thing then his religion was fake and so was he. I said that if he or any of those people put her in danger I'd."

Pierce gripping his phone listened to smoldering silence. It lasted for a time, and then she said:

"I didn't really say any of that stuff."

"No?"

"No. Just, like, when could I see her again. How to get some things to her. How to get her prescription refilled. Stuff like that. That I was asking for a new hearing."

"Yes."

"You know what he said? He said that unless the rules are changed he doesn't have to let me see her at all. He said that. He said he would though."

"Oh boy. Oh, Rosie."

"I talked to her. For a minute."

"Yes?"

"A minute. That's all."

Silence again, long and bleak.

"So whatcha doing?" she asked him.

"Making my costume. For the Ball."

"Oh yeah? What is it?"

"Can't tell you."

"Aw come on."

"I'll tell you this," he said. "It's what I'm not."


His conception had been a chess knight's horse head, like the helmet of the good White Knight who guides Alice through the wood of no names. But he was unskilled in mask-making; having no idea how to begin, he had first built an armature of cardboard and tape, referring to an encyclopedia volume still open there on the table, to an article on Sculpture, where Cellini's huge equestrian statue of Montefeltro was analyzed. He had got the great arch of the neck pretty well, but the delicate length of temple and nose had come out blunt and ignoble; probably the old mouton cap he had found in The Persistence of Memory Shoppe and cut up for hair and mane had been a bad idea, too woolly and thick; and the ears, lovingly crafted and successful in themselves, were just too big, grossly big, no time to change them or make new ones, and a sense grew within Pierce as he contemplated them that none of it was his choice anyway: or all of it was, and this was it.

> **ASS:**   The most famous Ass in literature is the "Golden Ass" of Lucius
> Apuleius. While visiting a far country, Apuleius becomes infatuated with
> Fotis, a slave girl, servant of an enchantress. Fotis procures from the witch
> a potion to increase her lover's manly powers, but by her error the potion
> transforms him instead into an Ass. In this condition he suffers and labors
> long, is beaten and abused, and is returned to his human state only after
> he has a vision of the Goddess Isis (*q.v.*) Isis rises from the sea dressed in
> the night sky and the stars, and tells him she is all goddesses, all gods
> too. He becomes her devotée, and is cured at last by feeding, at her
> behest, upon a rose. See ALLEGORY.

Gross buck teeth of wadded *papier-mâché* painted yellow. In the *Hieroglyphics* of Valerian, the Ass is the symbol of the Scholar, humbly chewing his dry diet of texts, laboring mightily for Learning. The lacquered eyeballs moist, though, intelligent maybe, but a little cocked, not easy to make them both look in the same direction. Left side the wackier one, mad and errant; right side patient and mild.

> An Ass bore Jesus to Jerusalem, and peasants still see a Cross in the
> markings of the Ass's back; in the Golden Legend it is said that the Ass
> who bore the Savior was the same one that stood by His manger at

Christmas. Because of this, the Pyx bearing the consecrated Host was often carried in procession on the back of an ass: *asinus portans mysterium,* they said, the lowly servant unable to understand higher things.

Time to try it out. Despite what he had said to her, he feared that he had actually violated the rule that Rosie had laid down, that what he would become inside this head smelling of *papier-mâché* and his own hot breath—he hoped it was what he was not, but felt pretty sure that this hope was vain.

Bruno is pleased to mock the pedants by naming the Ass as the steed of **MERCURY** (*q.v.*), but classically he is Priapus's beast; indeed **PRIAPUS** (*q.v.*) was at first an ass, and asses were sacrificed to him; but he belongs to **SATURN** (*q.v.*) also; and in ancient Europe at the Saturnalia, the Ass was slain by the New Year. He still appears at Christmas in French mumming, his ears transformed to a long-eared cap: a Fool, slain only to be reborn.

When it was given its last touches, feathery lashes of curled paper and a last painting, he placed it to dry and cure there on the kitchen table, ogling the wall with its cockeyes; he had another drink, and went to sleep or at least recline upon the daybed in the office; from there though he could still see the creature's snout, and the teeth.

After a time he could hear its voice too, quite clearly, telling its life story. *Once,* it began, *I was a real Ass.*

Pierce was actually asleep then, of course. Or maybe this conceit is from a later time: a "false memory" of himself on that daybed, plaid blanket pulled up to his nose and his own eyes wide in horror hearing the empty paste-and-paper thing discourse. Or it's neither of those things, it's a *ludibrium,* the one about the ass that saves the world, whose name is or was *Onorio.*

I grew to maturity in the neighborhood of Thebes, where on a certain day, as I was grazing at the edge of a steep ravine, I saw a nice thistle I longed to get my teeth into. I was sure I could stretch my long neck far enough, and, ignoring both my Wit and my natural Reason (for I was after all an Ass) I leaned farther, and farther, till I couldn't lean anymore; and I fell. And my master looking down saw he had bought me just to feed the crows.

I myself meanwhile, freed from the prison of the body, became a wandering spirit without corporeal parts; and I saw right away that I was no different from all other spirits, who upon the dissolution of their animal or compound bodies immediately set out to Transmigrate. For Fate erases the differences not only between the body of a dead Ass and a dead Human, but between their bodies and the bodies of things thought to be inanimate. Not only that: also erased is the difference between the Asinine and the Human soul, and indeed the soul of all things. All spirits return into Amphitrite, who is all spirits; thence they come back again.

I did so; I skipped over the Elysian Fields amid the multitudes
guided there by Mercury. And I drank—no rather I *pretended* to drink
from swift-flowing Lethe, just dipping my chinny-chin-chin so that the
Watchers would be deceived. Back down then through the Gate of Horn I
came, but—choosing my own destination this time—I headed for the
purest air and not the lower depths, and alighted at that famous
Hippocrene spring on that famous Mount Parnassus; and there, though
Fate ordained I must still be an Ass, yet by my great strength I grew from
my flanks two wings more than strong enough to bear me. I was the
Flying Ass, or Pegasean Steed!

Yes it's the *Cabala del Caballo Pegaseo,* Bruno's story or kabal of the Universal Ass,
patient/mocking, shiftless/hardworking, wise/stupid, stubborn/willing little gray
Onorio, the Pegasean Steed of every age; returning again and again after his life
on earth to be swallowed up in Amphitrite or Fullness, and spat out again.

It was I who carried out old Jove's orders, served Bellerophon when he
saved the maid Andromeda from her bondage on the Rock, which
without my help he could not have done; I had a hundred other
adventures, died and was reborn as a hundred heroes and pedants,
Aristotle not the least famous. Unlike my brother written of by Apuleius,
the Man made an Ass, I was the Ass made Man. At last I was assumed
into Heaven right there by Andromeda, to one side of Cygnus, near Pisces
and Aquarius.

His work still not done though; Hermes-Mercurius has always further tasks for
him; in every age there is plenty of scope for an Ass. Braying and kicking, or
mild and patient, Onorio again and again is turned back from Heaven's cool
shores and the prospect of green fields, to embody down on earth the *coniunctio
oppositorum,* the best and worst, and to show us what it means to know and suffer. Or to laugh and refuse to suffer, same thing.

Among those who will listen, speak [so Mercurius directs him]. Among
mathematicians, measure and weigh; among students of Nature ask,
teach, affirm, determine. Go everywhere, among all, dispute with all, be
brother to all, be One with the Many, win over everybody, be everything.

Bruno in the dungeons of the Venetian Inquisition told the whole story of Onorio to his fellow prisoners. (He cast their fortunes for them too, writing phrases
from Psalms inside circles he drew in the dirt.) He said to them: Samson killed
a thousand Philistines with an ass's jawbone; what could he have done with a
whole, living ass? He told them—we know this from the prisoners themselves,
a couple of whom were spies put in with him to record his sayings—that the
Pope was a great Ass, that the friars (of whom he had been one) were asses, and
the teachings of Holy Church *dottrini d'asini.* Of course Bruno knew that what he

said would be reported. He supposed that the Venetian inquisitors would get the joke, and ponder it.

The Venetians certainly wrote it all down, and perhaps they did ponder it. When the Roman Inquisition demanded that Bruno be turned over to them (they had been waiting twenty years to have a talk with him about his opinions) the Venetians, who usually resisted such requests, gave in. Bruno was sent to Rome.

*He seems to think that iron bars and stone walls are as nothing,* the Venetians wrote to the Romans. *He comports himself as though he were an honored guest, and when he is questioned he trims and with a smile makes little of his beliefs, not out of fear but as though he wished not to offend us, his hosts. He has sought, he says, an audience with the Most Holy Father, for whom he has news of great importance, and with a bow thanks us for transporting him thither.* And lastly they added this note concerning the strange man they had kept for a time without fathoming: *If he is proven to be mad, we ask that all mercies be shown him.*

Now all over the Faraways, men and women were dressing up as persons, places and things they were not, laughing at themselves in mirrors, as the day died and the shadows lengthened.

"Sybil," said Val to Rosie. "She's a character I read about. In that book I showed you."

"The *Dictionary*," Rosie said. "I just saw that book at Pierce's house."

"No wonder I couldn't get it. I had to do this from memory."

Val was vast, swathed in white sheets over pink long underwear, gold rope crossing between her breasts and cinching her waist, cape and hood of red velvet, and a long golden curly wig. In her arms a big loose book or folder, full of paper burned around the edges.

"So okay," said Rosie. "What."

"Sybil. She was a fortune-teller; she knew the secrets of the future. An oracle."

Rosie laughed. "Right. Good choice."

" 'Come as you aren't,' right?"

"Right."

"She had this book, full of prophecies about this family. And she brought it to the mother of the clan, the matriarch. And says, Pay me like a hundred gold pieces."

"Right."

"The mother is ripped. A hundred? No no. Too much. So the Sybil takes a page out of the book—a *leaf,* that's a page, right?"

"I think."

"And tosses it in the fire. What the hell are you *doing*? Okay, says the Sybil, the price is now two hundred. *Two* hundred? For *less*? She's not paying more for less. So the Sybil rips off another leaf, and tosses it in too."

Rosie laughed, getting it.

"Now the price is three hundred." Val held up three fingers. "And the mother is going nuts, watching her burn up the future. She's raging. Too much? Okay another page goes. Price goes up."

"And?"

"At a thousand, with one page left, she still refuses. In the fire. But before it goes, the mother shouts *Wait I'll pay*! Sybil snatches it out. Half a burnt page left." Val grinned wickedly. "And she pays."

"Is this a warning? To your customers?"

"Customers?" Val said, offended. "And so what about you?" She pointed to Rosie's old jeans and sweater. "You're just you. No?"

"I know. I've got to think of something."

"Rosie! It's about two hours from now!"

"Right. Well let's see."

She looked around herself at the living room and hall of Arcady where they stood, as though a ball gown or fairy wings might be hanging on the hall tree or the back of the closet door.

"I've been so crazy," she said. "Sam. Mike. I mean you've given this a lot of thought."

She went to the basement door beneath the stairs, opened it a crack, thought of the clothes turning in the washing machine down there, thought of Sam, thought of Pierce, thought of Boney's old housekeeper Mrs. Pisky. Shut the door again.

"Okay," she said.

She went to the stairs up, and Val followed her, who had never been taken up the stairs here before, would not have asked to be, would have sneered at the offer of a tour. What broad dark stairs upward. The light in Rosie's eye was alarming, as though she were seeing something unseeable except to her, and just ahead.

"This is his room?" Val said at the door of the room Rosie went into.

"Yep."

The old-man smell not quite dispersed from it, the dent in the big bed's middle where it had borne him. Val entered cautiously.

"He really was a son of a bitch," Rosie said. "But he was kind to me."

She opened the mirrored folding doors of the closet and the room they reflected was shattered and flung about. Rosie had stood here six months before, choosing a suit for Boney's dead body to wear.

"Okay you'll have to help me with this," Rosie said. "Here." She took out and handed to Val a vested suit of Harris tweed.

"Oh no," said Val.

"I like this room," Rosie said. Like a train that has pulled away from the station and is at last getting its long load rolling, she was aglow and picking up speed. "I like these big windows, and the closets. My closet is." She made a quick gesture meaning zilch, nothing, insignificant. She pulled open Boney's drawers, and took out a white shirt from among those still folded there, Mrs. Pisky's work; she snapped it open like a flag. "Think I should make this room mine?"

"Well hell," said Val.

Rosie doffed her sweater, and slipped Boney's rag-soft shirt on.

"You've got it on wrong," Val said.

"Help me here," said Rosie.

Val stepped to where Rosie stood with Boney's shirt on back to front. Boney had liked his shirts generous at neck and breast, and this one could be buttoned easily up Rosie's back. "O my God," Val said.

"French cuffs," Rosie said, holding out her arms. "We'll need cuff links."

A big tie next; Val chose a wine-dark one with an obscure pattern, looped it like a hangman's noose around Rosie's neck and pondered how to tie it. Rosie made suggestions, facing the other way and describing loops in the air with her hands. "Over and around and back up and down through."

Good enough if not Boney's own Windsor four-in-hand. The vest then, woolly side to the back, silky side to the front, Rosie cinched its little belt as Val buttoned.

"I think I will take it," Rosie said. "This room. I think I will. It's got to be painted though. White."

"Off-white," said Val.

"All this stuff can go," Rosie said. The blackish etchings, she meant, Old World churches or monuments; the slipper chair and the somber drapes. She might sleep in his bed, though. She might.

The pants were difficult, more carefully engineered than Rosie would have thought and unwilling to be reversed, besides being a good deal too long. Laughing now giddily like bad girls, they got scissors and cut away at the fine fabric. "But what about," Val said, turning Rosie's wrong-way head in her hands, as though it might swivel, like a doll's.

"Ah!" said Rosie. She waddled from the room, Val shrieking with laughter to see her go; she had an idea. Downstairs somewhere, in some crowded never-sorted drawer of this and that—she could see the drawer and almost examine its contents but could not place it in space.

Down here too she'd make changes, she thought. Pull down those ivory-lace curtains, like mummy's cerements, and their heavy drapes; change the wallpaper. Okay. All right. The leather couches would go too, that one on which Sam had had her first seizure.

"Here," Rosie said, heading for the old commode or chest in the living room, the one atop which the little casket of wood held the glass ball in its bag, knowing before she reached it that she was right. The doors she opened revealed closed drawers, why so secret. She pulled open the lower one (when had she done this before, so that she knew where to look? Anyway here she was again) and rooted through the stuff there, postcards and old journals and a big pocket watch and a calendar. She picked up and for a moment studied a little photograph: a tintype, she guessed, only a few inches square, a boy in an autumn garden dressed in Elizabethan costume. Who and where? Toss it back. And here, what she wanted: a white mask. A white sad delicate human face, its broad upper lip like a jawless skull's but its fine nose and brow somehow beautiful.

"Here," she said.

A label pasted on the inside said *La Zanze Venexiana Maschere espressive. Neutrie larve.*

She lifted it and by its ribbons hung it on the back of her head, so that its white nose pointed back, toward where we've been, and its long Venetian lip hung just above the tie-knot. Rosie heard Val behind her utter a low shuddery gasp. She walked backwards toward Val, reaching at her with wrong-way hands. Even spookier though was when she walked forward, like a movie running in reverse, the old-man puppet she had become bent all wrong.

"There," Rosie said. "All done."

Almost all done. Boney Rasmussen himself, within whose hearing they stood, waited with what would have been tears in his eyes if he had had eyes that could weep, tears of rage and longing, rage at himself and his powerlessness, longing which he tried to turn upon them like a lamp or flare so that they could see his need. *He* could see nothing but the door he stood before, which had seemed to come ajar.

"Or should I sell it?" Rosie asked, the question and its answer just then blooming within her. "Sell it and just get an office somewhere. What do you think?"

"O my God," cried Val, aghast; she who had had her own place up for sale for years. And she thought: Sell, yes sell, why not. A cold wind of possibility blew through her breast, and she remembered—as we do sometimes in the course of the day, our waking brains or souls jogged by something we happen to see or taste—that last night (wasn't it last night?) she dreamed a dream. She dreamed she had gone out under the stars, down by the river, and looked up; and for the first time she knew them all, the Zodiac and all the others, their faces as familiar to her as their names: she had known them all her life. Pointing to them one after the other she had said their common names aloud: there was the Pot and Pan, the Wedding Dress, the twins Cosmo and Otto, the Boy Barber, Harold the Great, the Red Man, Omphalos, Wednesday Mensday Womensday, the Big Bug. And the bright planets round as marbles rolled among them. She had awakened still knowing every stupid name, though she couldn't think of them all now; and as she had lain abed, she'd thought a thought she had not thought before: that maybe Mama was wrong.

Maybe Mama was wrong. It could be that what gratified Mama so much to believe, and that had caused Val such pain to know, was just not so. There was actually too little in the story, when you thought about it, to make it so for certain; you could, if you wanted, decide it wasn't so. Her father? Knowledge not worth paying for: let it burn.

Now Rosie in the hall put on over her curls the tweed cap Boney had never gone outdoors without between October and May, backwards, of course, and standing backwards tried to glimpse herself in the pier glass. Val, who had started to laugh at her own abnegation or refusal laughed louder to see Rosie, a lot louder. Rosie saw the impossibility within the glass: for the first and only time, she and the one in there were facing the same way.

And at that the door before Boney opened (though the front door of Arcady stayed firmly shut) and like a thin curtain drawn out an open window by a sudden outpouring gust or breath he escaped.

O thank you child. O thank God or time. Freed from Una Knox, great Archon of oblivion: he would not after all (as he had so much feared) dissolve in her embrace forever. Which didn't mean that he had no others to contend with: Boney Rasmussen had done nothing to ready himself for this journey, nothing but yearn; all the spheres remained before him to be crossed, and he could be stopped before he climbed even to the moon's. On the path upward there are as many dangerous beings to meet as on the dark path downward, and almost everyone who sets out is stopped and turned back, not once but many times; they won't give up the things they've brought along, or their throats are dry as gravedust and they're happy to drink there at the silver river, and drift with the multitudes forgetful toward the Gate in Cancer to be returned. If in the sphere of Fire Boney had no good answer to the hard questions that would be put to him, he could be stuck there with the many souls who inhabit that sphere, the ones we can see squirm and dart when we stare up into a bright sky, stuck raging until he entirely consumes himself and is returned to earth to animate slugs and snails and oysters.

He knew nothing of all this yet. He only set out, taking long quick steps, going (he thought) along the road toward Fellowes Kraft's house not far away, toward which he had been setting out that night in July when. There was something there he wanted to see or collect, but then no he was not headed there, not onward but upward, climbing a stair in the air.

Val had not meant to accomplish any of this, nor had Rosie, though they each felt a sudden chill at his passage, and looked around to see if the door to the basement or something had been left open. No, Rosie had meant only to get herself going right-way at last, to come or go as she wasn't, or hadn't been. For she was under the same obligation as everyone she had invited, in fact it had been she who had laid the obligation on them all, come as you aren't, and she couldn't exempt herself: nor would she have wanted to.

"I gotta start all over," she said.

"What!"

"Well I need some long johns or something on under this," Rosie said. "I'll freeze my buns."

"Who are you?" Pierce Moffett asked the figure who stood at his open door in the lamplight.

"Night," she said.

"No stars?"

She drew some out from within her sable wrappings, and showed them to him in her black-gloved hand: rhinestones all a-glitter, chokers and bracelets.

"No moon?" he asked.

"I'm Night, not light," she answered. "Who are you?"

"Night too," he said, "or Knight rather; at least that's what I started out to be; but something went wrong."

He took her hand—she was a little unsteady in her heels and gown of black, high-collared opera cape, hat and muff of gleaming fur—and helped her up his steps and into his house. He had lit every lamp. His head, all done, stood on the table.

"Oh yeah I see," she said, and turned to smile on him. "Uh-huh. It's cute."

"It is cute," he said. "But not a Knight."

"No, maybe not."

"I knew a young girl in Madras," Pierce quoted. "Who allowed me to fondle her ass . . ."

Rose laughed, getting it.

"It was not round and pink," Pierce said, "or cleft as you'd think . . ."

"It was gray," Rose guessed.

"Had long ears, and ate grass." He wore evening clothes, a set chosen from the rack at The Persistence, the only coat and trousers large enough, and mis-matched; in the night and the darkness no one would know. To the great head he had affixed a paper bat-wing collar and a grosgrain ribbon tie. He lifted it, and placed it over his head. Rose made a small cry, startled or touched, universal and ancient response to a mask, upon which all visits from the gods and the dead had once depended. LARVA, a mask; also, a GHOST (*q.v.*) or SPECTER. Man made god, or the reverse; possessor and possessed in one.

It is said that he who rides an Ass to Hell will not be subject to the power of the DEVIL (*q.v.*) but just how this is to be done is nowhere made apparent.

"Where's this one from?" he asked when they went out into the moonlight, and he saw her car. "Another loaner?"

"A friend," Rose said, and patted it. "A Tomcat."

"The car, not the friend," Pierce guessed.

"Mine really can't be driven. The window. I told you."

"Yes."

She seemed to pause a moment, as though herself remembering something, or changing her mind about being here where she had perhaps just now found herself.

"I have to leave early," she said. "Don't let me, you know. Stay up late. You know?"

"I won't," said the Ass. "I promise."

# 10

**E**veryone said they had never seen Butterman's look like this, bright banners hanging and flags flying from the towers, all alight. Some remembered when they were kids swimming or rowing out to the island, to drink beer or make out or plink at rats with a .22. Only the oldest remembered it when it was open, and the docks were busy and band music could be heard from the riverbanks.

The marina had an excursion boat that Rosie had hired, a flat-bottomed paddle-wheel craft like a little bus, and all that night it plied the waters between the castle and the shore. Groups of guests gathered at the dock, breathing frost in the dock's light and greeting one another as they waited to board, then laughing as the boat departed, pulling for the island. Allan Butterman had worked out the guest list with Rosie: those who had to be invited, and if those were, which others also had to be. Many of the dignitaries were people whose family names Rosie remembered from childhood, from that old big world that resembled this smaller one in so many respects, that was caught or contained inside it; some were the very kids that Rosie had known, others she knew from Boney's funeral in July; they were lawyers and businesspeople who sat on the school committees and the town council, sold real estate or did plumbing and heating, and they were bluff or shy or both at once—glad to meet her at last and to study her, fabulous being just emerged from a hole or den they'd been watching with interest for some time, and deeply grateful (they said) for what she had done: this is quite a place, quite a place.

Allan in a borrowed judge's robe and curly white wig introduced her to those he knew as Rosie walked among them, hearing laughter behind her wherever she went and wondering if people guessed it was a suit of Boney's that she wore, his tie and cap. She felt now a little foolish and impertinent and wished somewhat she had adopted the strategy so many of the women had—just dress to the teeth in gown and jewels, long gloves and *décolletage*. Come as you aren't, a queen or movie star or Marie Antoinette. Their men tended to be clowns or bums or big babies with suckers, why. Like these two now entering, she gorgeous and sinister in black taffeta and sequined cat's-eye mask and a sable wrap, he as a donkey following her.

"You've got my book," Val said to Pierce, the first of the mummers to approach him. "I need it. Bring it back."

Pierce stared at her, not knowing if these words belonged to the character she was dressed as, or were spoken to the character he was dressed as, or were a real communication. "Book?"

"The *Dictionary*."

"Oh yes." He felt stupid, and stubborn too. "Hey, it's not yours."

"Not yours either, ass." Val turned to look Rose over, and winked conspiratorially at her, suddenly in her rouge and golden curls looking like a gross and dissolute bawd.

"I took it out," Pierce said.

"Well nobody'd taken it out for years before me. Since Kraft."

"Kraft?"

"Fellowes Kraft. Yes. Didn't you notice his name on the card? Just above mine? About six times?"

Pierce could see it now, but he hadn't seen it then: the yellowed ticket and its purple stamped dates, and on it Val's pencil scrawl, and yes Kraft's blue-black fountain-pen ink, neat and antique, his earliest signatures (from years ago, this one card had lasted for two decades and more) already fading.

"Oh yes," he said.

"Oh yes," Val said. She tossed her goldilocks. "Oh yes."

Oh yes. Pierce thought of the apparent unlikelihood of that old bad book showing up here in this town to which he had come; thought too of Kraft's great pile of paper on his desk, and of the astonishing coincidence, as he had supposed it to be, of its tales with those he had himself known and journeyed in when he was a kid, and he saw that it was certainly not coincidence at all but causation and consequence, only reversed, running from this moment backwards, to. Well to the starting point wherever that was or is. He had been fooled, deeply and profoundly fooled, the extent of it was not even yet evident to him but he knew that too at least. He saw how it might be possible, if you were blinded or in deep darkness, to take what seemed like a very long journey in a very small place; you might by chance return not once but many times to the same suite of rooms, the same walled garden or forest glade, and (for a good while anyway) think you were always farther on.

"I have," he said, "a great desire to a bottle of hay."

"Cash bar," said Val. "All proceeds to the rehab."

From inside the ass's head it was somewhat hard to see; Pierce caught only glimpses of the other guests in the throng around them. There was JOVE or maybe JEHOVAH in great beard and robe, paper lightning bolts in his hand, he laughed with Rhea Rasmussen swathed in red satin as a Cardinal or INQUISITOR; there was APOLLO with his bays and lyre, PANDORA the robot temptress whom the GODS manufactured to degrade us, with her box of evils and her CROW of hopeless hope (this was actually just a SORCERESS, Pierce had overinterpreted her); a SANTA, a WOLF-MAN and a MUMMY wrapped in unravelling cerements, more than one ANGEL, the FOUR BEASTS of the Gospels, Bull, Eagle, Lion and Man, who was apparently a woman; a CRONE or WITCH or ILL-FAVORED LADY, who was certainly a man, and the DEVIL too, who waved familiarly to Pierce and waggled his long tongue at Rose. Somebody she knew from before, probably.

He brought her a beer, and then another, the homely brown bottles assorting ill with her spangled blackness, loosening her tongue and her spirit.

"I'll tell you something," he said, because she had asked about *your work* in her good-girl voice. "I'm not going to finish that book, Rose. I'm done with it."

"Well in a way that's good," she said, and struck a match for the cigarette that she held between her fingers, deb style. "Because actually it was all sort of falsehoods, I mean." She let smoke issue softly from her mouth. "Didn't they pay you though? Would you have to give it back?"

"I'll burn that bridge when I come to it." He held out his hand to her. "Would you," he said, "like to dance?"

The band Rosie had hired, the Orphics, were a local bunch that had had a couple of minor hits ("Don't Turn Back," "All the Birds and Beasts"); reversing the usual arrangement, the lead singer was a gorgeous and narcissistic male and the rest of the band female. They had been setting up on the stage of the Keep and tuning up for a long time, trying out a pile of strange instruments (electric lute, sackbutt, hurdy-gurdy) and now swung into their signature tune:

> Don't Turn Back
> There ain't no city left to see
> Don't Turn Back
> Just go on ahead, say Follow me
> Follow where your shadow points and maybe so will he.
>
> Maybe he burned his bridges down, yeah maybe so
> Maybe he burned his boats, to go where you wanna go;
> But maybe he's not behind you, and baby if that's so
> You don't want to know.
> [Chorus: Don't turn back, etc.]

The noise and the thunder of many feet shook the dust from the rafters of the Keep; the music spread out to the courtyards and belvederes and towers, and people joined the dance as though catching it like a medieval plague, and laughing passed it on. There wasn't a breath of wind to stir the banners or ruffle the pinnaces of the towers, but the longer the dance went on the more the dancers felt themselves stirred, as though by one of those movie winds that ruffle the clothes and hair of characters to whom something large or romantic or life-changing is about to happen: less a wind though than a free-floating certainty not attached to any consciousness, a wild guess or suggestion seeming to pass from person to person by means of the Orphics or the dance or Rosie Rasmussen moving effectually backwards among them: a sense that the important things have been neglected or have not been noticed, or seen for what they are, which was an odd feeling for people to feel who were just then occupied with being who they were not.

Most of them would just drink and dance it away and not remember it to-morrow; but some of them would get the idea that there was something to be done, something to be looked for or looked out for, and when they woke they would climb into their attics to find perhaps nothing but the unfamiliar long view from the small high windows, or they would pull down their photo albums, lives led in the Faraways, and turn the pages with a sense that some people or events that ought to be there were missing, as though taken out to be saved or stored elsewhere, and others newly inserted in their places; just as old though, the same humpbacked cars and wedding parties on Mount Randa, veils blown in the wind, shy smiles of people now dead, a cigarette in their fingers. *What was it I was to remember or foresee, what have I forgotten to recall, from where did I begin that led me here?*

When Boney that summer had lain dying, Rosie had found herself sometimes thinking—except that *thinking* was too definite a word for it, it was something she only caught just as it exited from her head or heart, "gone as soon as it came" and not to be believed—but thinking, anyway, that her little county, which from an early time had been her family's fiefdom practically, was like a town in a story where everyone lay fast asleep; or rather *not* fast but restlessly, unwillingly, sleepwalking and murmuring, while some evil power or gang of thieves moved among them unseen, lifting the jewels from their bodies or rifling the safes: to be *under a spell,* in fact, which it was up to her to break, if she could awaken herself. She hadn't thought of this when she had decided to have this party, and didn't think it as she spoke her brief welcome to all of them through the roaring, abashing mike that the lead singer of the Orphics handed to her; but she remembered it as she went among them, the ones Allan had introduced her to, and waved to them and smiled; and to some of them she came and spoke into their ears, shouting over the Orphics' racket, but what she said was only *Listen can I come see you? Can we talk sometime? There's something I wanted to ask you about, can we set a time? I wonder if you can help me, it's important for the area, can we talk?* And they cupped their hands behind their ears and nodded and took her elbow to ask or hear more.

And she kept thinking as she went among them: if only Sam were here. If only.

She had asked Mike, but as soon as he heard the word *masked* he'd refused, and she wouldn't beg him. She stood momentarily alone in the busy courtyard. A group of young moms, some she knew, chased or fed their children, and Rosie remembered the solitude she had felt long ago looking at moms, not being one herself. She turned so that her masked and clothed self faced toward the kids, and walked backwards recklessly and blindly toward where she thought they were. She flapped up her hand (encased in a pink rubber household glove, right one on her left hand, the final touch) and waved, listening for their laughter, but instead a silence seemed to gather, and she turned her face to them again.

From out of their midst Sam came. They parted for her, children and grown-ups, though Sam didn't notice them; she was asleep, maybe asleep, in an old white nightgown with a dreadful stain on it, her feet bare. And Rosie knew that Sam was lost to her: all that Rosie had done and would do was for her sake, and yet Sam in her suffering had never been hers at all, or was, now and forever, more than hers.

No it wasn't Sam at all, how stupid. A child wholly different, with little an-gel wings on her back and ice-cream spill down her robe. She stared at Rosie's backwards front and turned away unmoved.

Rosie hearing nothing but her heartbeat felt a touch on her shoulder.

"Beau."

"Changing direction, Rosie?"

"Facing front, Beau." She wanted to take him in her arms, safe, but her arms wouldn't lift that high. "God where have you *been*?"

"Travelling. Thanks for inviting me."

"Well hey. How come you didn't dress up?"

"How come I didn't?"

"The invitation *said*. Come as you aren't."

Beau, smiling, opened his arms like welcoming Jesus. "Ta daa," he said.

"Oh you."

"Where's Sam?" Beau asked. "She'd like this."

"Oh Christ," Rosie said. "Beau. You haven't heard."

She had called him and called him, to tell him what had happened; she had wanted to tell him, to ask him what now, and yet had been afraid. As though—like that judge—he held some power of reproach or condemnation over her. Now seeing him she knew it wasn't so, and with the guests passing around her and the boom and keening feedback of the band sounding in the smoky air she told him.

"Where is she now?" Beau asked.

"With Mike."

"Where's Mike?"

"He said he's between places. I think he's not living here anymore but he won't admit it. He said he had to go out to Indiana for some reason."

Beau had turned away, alarming Rosie by the deep thought in his face, as though he were trying to remember something or envision something.

"What. Beau, what."

"I think you have to find out where they are," he said. "And I don't think you should let him take her out to Indiana."

"He said only a little while."

Beau was shaking his head. "Not just for her sake," he said. "It's for more than that."

Rosie felt the breath leave her body, as though she'd fallen from a height and struck earth. She tried to inhale. "He's got her medicine," she said. "He's. He wouldn't hurt her."

"He loves her a lot," Beau said. "He does. It ought to keep her safe. But the people she's with. They believe, they really believe that no harm can come to them."

Rosie thought of Mike: *Do you think I'd let harm come to her?*

"My lawyer says go easy," she said. "He said these things take time. He's trying to get her back. He is."

Beau nodded, listening. Then he said: "I don't think you should let him take her out there." He put his hand on her shoulder, on Boney's tweed. "I mean are you comfortable with that?"

"No. No."

"No. I'm not either." He was smiling again. "I mean you don't go to Indiana unless you can't get out of it. Right?"

"But how," Rosie said.

"We'll talk," Beau said. "There's help. We'll do what we need to. Let me look and think." He drew her to him. "You do too," he said.

She watched him go, hearing her name called from elsewhere, duties to do. *Not just for her sake.* She tried to see Sam again, that vision of Sam among the children, but couldn't summon it, could see in her mind only the other child, a human child, paper wings on her back and tinsel in her hair.


Beau Brachman sat down beside Pierce, out of the way of the Orphics. "So how's the world-changing coming?" he asked. His hand indicated the revels, the transformed people and magic beasts; he patted Pierce's woolly head. "Have you been practicing?"

Pierce couldn't imagine what Beau meant. He stared stupidly. Rose had been swept away by other, more tireless dancers, and his drink was empty.

"Changing the world. You remember we talked. Getting what you need or want. Practicing on dreams."

Pierce remembered: the night of the big wind, the night—wasn't it?—where this began. "Aha," he said. "Yes. You said."

"Yes."

In his dreams he had faced them, but he had only fled, or frightened himself awake; or he was an eye and an ear only, not present, not acting; wishing and hoping only. Which was maybe why he was so helpless now. "You know," he said, "I don't know if you remember, that night. The night Rose flipped her car."

"I remember," Beau said.

"She was in trouble then, real trouble. I didn't realize how much. I don't mean with the law. She." He hesitated, knowing what a dreadful secret he was on the point of revealing; before he could make up his mind to reveal it, he saw that Beau was regarding the floor solemnly; and he knew that Beau already knew, and had known all along.

"Well," Pierce said. "Anyway. You know she's a Christian now."

"The Powerhouse," Beau said.

"You know them?"

"Oh sure. Some of the people who've stayed at the place have gotten in with them. And some people have come to us from them too. To get away." He smiled. "You know Rose stayed at the house once."

"She did?"

"A long while ago. It was when she first came from the City. She was pretty confused by what happened to her there. So she stayed with us. A few weeks, I guess."

"How did she, I mean how did you . . ."

Beau shrugged. "We met," he said.

Pierce remembered the first time—the first moment, actually—that he him-self had seen Beau: at Spofford's Full Moon party, by this same Blackbury River a year and a half ago, not ten minutes before he saw Rose for the first time. *I don't belong here,* he'd confessed to Beau, Beau with his satyr's smile, playing on a pan-pipe to a sleepy child. *I'm actually from somewhere else.*

He took the mask from his head and put it beside him. Beau neither laughed nor ceased smiling. An awful hope arose in Pierce, that if he dared finally to ask he might be answered.

"Beau," he said. "What is it? Why have I come into this darkness? What am I doing here? Why has the world turned into this kind of place?"

"What kind of place?"

Pierce lifted his hand and his eyes, to the night sky obscured by the fire's smoke and the lights; and then to Beau. "I," he said. "I feel like I've somehow uncovered an awful secret evil that pervades the world," Pierce said. "Don't ask me why."

"Maybe because you have."

Pierce stared at him, trying to see past his smile, the mask Beau wore.

"That night on the road," Beau said. "When Rose flipped her car. She was running away from the powers."

"Powers?"

"We all try to. The trouble was she ran from the powers right into the arms of other powers."

"She says now her power's from, you know. God."

"All the powers are the same," Beau said. "Each inside all the others."

"No no Beau, don't say stuff like that." He donned his head again. "The worst thing is how it seems to be my fault somehow." He tried another little laugh. "I mean of course I know it's not."

"It's not," Beau said. "But that doesn't mean you're not supposed to fix it."

Pierce only stared.

"Oh it's not just you," Beau said. "It's the same for everybody. For me too. For everybody. Well except for some guys."

The music arose overpoweringly for a moment, amid whoops and cries of appreciation. Then Beau said, as though changing the subject: "I bet she's got a lot more beautiful lately."

He lifted his gaze then, for Rose had come up behind Pierce, flushed and panting, and Pierce leapt up. He saw, behind her black mask, her liquid eyes pass over Beau without recognition, she being who she was not, and unknown to him; and his smile didn't alter.

"Listen, Moffett," she said. "Aren't you supposed to be looking out for me?"

"Yes. I am."

"Well I think I need a coffee. Pretty quick."


Partly maybe because they are essentially fake, the towers and ramparts of the castle are unexpectedly complicated, stairs and doorways and arches multiplying. Pierce pressed through the crowd of phantasts on his errand, and got around somehow to the less finished service side of the place, or so he imagined. These doors led, he thought, either to the johns or back into the Keep where the food and dancing were; he chose one and opened it.

Yes he was seemingly now in the backstage area, and just as he perceived this the Orphics ceased, taking a break, and a busy quiet followed through which the ghosts of their chords flitted. Pierce tried to part the dusty and moth-eaten velvets, like an old mad courtesan's gown; the head he wore made it hard to see.

"Teasers and tormentors," said a soft voice near him.

Pierce saw that sitting on a bentwood chair in the dark of the wings was a partygoer, lost or drunk or both. "Come again?" he said.

"The names of stage curtains," the person said. His voice a delicate and slightly affected whine. A generous drink in his hand. "Teasers are those. Tormentors are those. They keep the audience from peeking backstage. Destroying the illusion."

"I was looking for coffee," Pierce said. "I think it's best to go back."

"Oh no, no. Always best to go straight on."

"Ha ha," said Pierce. Masks always make us oracular. The one this fellow wore was a realistic human face, a pleasant tired older fellow with crinkly eyes and a shock of molded white rubber hair. Pierce supposed he ought to know the face, politician or movie star or.

"It's a pretty little theater," the mask said. "I always thought it could be used for something."

"Sure." Pierce raised his eyes to the darkness of the flies.

"Once I tried to produce Marlowe's *Doctor Faustus* here. A huge flop. We got almost to dress rehearsals."

"It's a hard one," Pierce said.

"Lucky," the fellow said. " 'Faustus,' I mean. It means lucky in Latin."

"So it does." He hadn't thought of that. He supposed Marlowe had.

"I came to believe," the man said, and crossed his legs, ready for a chat, "that Marlowe must have been an awful shit."

"Oh?"

"Yes. I think of him as a totally amoral person who liked to arouse people, just because he knew he could. Get them to riot and go on rampages. His plays did, you know. Against Jews. Catholics. Whomever he could turn a crowd against."

"Magicians."

"Oh yes. Poor old Doctor Dee. And I don't think for a minute he cared anything about the Devil or God's justice. He was like a punk rock star today, with a swastika tattooed on his forehead, getting kids to go mad and commit suicide." He lifted his drink to his mouth, and drank, or pretended to. "A genius, though. Unlike your rockers. There's the difference."

Who was that mask? Pierce knew he had seen the face it was modelled on, in some special context; the boyish snub nose, the hair that had once been sandy. "What happened?" he asked. "To your production?"

The man sighed hugely, and for a long moment looked around himself, the expression on his false face altering as the light took it differently. Then he said:

"Well I've failed. I failed. Yes I think that's evident now." He said this with what seemed great anguish. "The conception was just too huge, the parts too many. No matter how long it was let to go on, it got no closer to being done."

"It's a corrupted text," Pierce said. "I believe." There was, he now saw, another bentwood chair beside the man, exactly like the one he sat in.

"I so much wanted it to *knit*," the other said. He interlaced his own fingers. "Past and present, then and now. The story of the thing lost, and how it was found. More than anything I wanted it to *resolve*. And all it does is *ramify*.

"You take this party, or ball," he said, lifting his glass as though to toast it. "I mean it's hardly the *Walpurgisnacht* that was promised for so long."

"Well," Pierce said. "I mean."

"The all-purged-night; the all-perjurers'-night. The transmuting revels, the night machinery out of which we all come different. Wasn't that the idea? 'Where nothing is but what is not.' What is not yet, or is not any longer."

"Ah," said Pierce, feeling a last bass-drum thump from the Orphics in his breast, or was that only his own heart. "Ah yes."

The masked man pointed at Pierce with a yellow-nailed smoker's forefinger. "And take yourself, for another instance," he said. "How are you to be understood now? The Golden Ass? Dionysus? There's Bottom, of course. Whose dream hath no bottom."

"Well it wasn't what I planned," Pierce said. And suddenly weary he sat down where he was so obviously meant to sit. "Not at all what I intended."

"No. No. Not at all. I'm so sorry. Well at a certain point invention flags, you see; you begin to repeat, helplessly. You keep coming upon the same few conceptions over and over, greeting each one with glad cries, yes! Yes! The way on! Until you realize what it is, oh here I go again, the same story again, as ever. And you feel so damned."

So damned what? Pierce wished he had a nice drink like this guy's, who didn't seem to be drinking his.

"I just hope," he said, "we won't all be in here forever, and none of us able to move up, or down."

Pierce's heart shrank. "Oh don't worry," he said. "No party lasts that long."

"You," the fellow said. Somehow his voice had lost the delicate affected whine it had begun with, as though that had been part of the mask, and this was his own, a flatter voice, with an angry irony in it. "It'll have to be you that does it. Somehow, I don't know how. If you don't make a contribution, haven't I labored in vain? Not to speak of your own sufferings."

"I," Pierce said. "I was supposed to be getting coffee." And he rose, feeling the sudden dream horror of having forgotten for a fatal length of time the mission you've set out on, too late, too long. "Gotta run."

"You'll have to do it," the man called after him. "I'm so sorry." By the sound of his voice Pierce could tell he had removed his mask, but nothing would have induced him to look back to see who was beneath it.


Meanwhile, the Orphics have set up a theremin, a black box surmounted by a slim antenna; the women play this antenna with their hands, running delicately up and down inches from it, as though it were the central nerve of an invisible phallus they stroke, from whose possessor they draw eerie wails of bliss or agony. Night, turning and turning to the music, is being touched by strangers whose hands she slips away from, till the red DEVIL whispers in her ear and makes her laugh.

"Gotcha," he says, and "Hello, Mal," she says back to him. "Knew it was you."

"Let's go up on the battlements," he says to her, "and look see how far down it is."

"Oh no," she says. "I know that one, Mal."

"I'll buy you a drink," he says. "Whatcha drinking?"

"Not what you can get," she says, and her tireless feet have left the paving stones.

"Come on," he says, "for old times' sake."

"You can't catch me," she says.

"Later," he says, "later," as she spins away from his touch and from them all to turn and turn in a circle of her own. The lead singer, pale hair streaming, sings:

*We gotta live, Lesbia*
*We gotta love*
*So let the cold old men rave on, it's all right*

*Kiss me one time, Lesbia*
*Kiss me ten times*
*Now square that number, girl, then multiply't*

*Just keep on kissing, Lesbia*
*Don't stop your counting*
*Till way past a thousand the number's out of sight*

*Keep the sun from setting, Lesbia*
*Make it rise back up*
*'Cause when our sun's gone down it's one long mother of a night.*

"*Vivamus, mea Lesbia, et amemus,*" Pierce muttered inside his ass's head. "Let's live and love. We can, we could."

"What language are you speaking?" Val asked him, with whom Pierce found himself gravely waltzing to the tune. Where was Rose again?

"Latin," he said. "Catullus. It's the song they're singing, don't ask me why."

"They're singing in English."

"*Una est perpetua nox dormienda,*" Pierce said. "One endless night's sleep. Una. Nox. Perpetua."

Val suddenly stopped still. Pierce saw that he had spoken a name, and that it was the name of someone she knew, the name of someone *he* knew even though he couldn't think who it was or how he knew her.

"Una Knox," Val said. "Oh my God." She turned away from the throng in consternation, and gripped her brow. A last firework was lofted into the air with a long suspenseful whisper, and then popped lazily. "Then. Oh my God it was just some kind of joke. She's not real."

"She isn't? *Who* isn't?" Pierce called after her.

"Rosie! Rosie!" Val cried, catching sight of Rosie's back, or front. But when the person turned to Val, Pierce saw it was a different old gent, a real one, who had just come as he was. Val went off looking side to side. And Pierce remembered who Una Knox was: she was the woman Boney Rasmussen said he was leaving all that he had to, the woman who had puzzled everyone, Rosie Rasmussen and the lawyers and all his relatives.

Well she was real enough, Pierce guessed: Una P. Knox, great Uthra of the end, third of the three great ones, everyone's mother and heir. Rosie Rasmussen had often told him that Boney had refused to admit that he, just like everybody, was bound for that endless night. He had believed or hoped that someone, Kraft or Pierce even, might find for him the thing that no one yet has found. But Boney had known all right, he had only resisted; his resistance had of course been futile but he'd known that too. So one last small joke in the face of it or her: he had left her everything.

He looked up. On the ramparts above appeared Night herself in sable furs. Rose Ryder came down toward him weaving unsteadily, a top slowing down.

"See," she said, "you let me stay too late. I knew you would."

"No," Pierce said. "No we'll go. It's over anyway."

No it was not Boney Rasmussen who would not honor Death; it was Ray Honeybeare and Mike Mucho and the rest of them, Dr. Retlaw O. Walter; it was they who denied her. *O Death where is thy sting.* Rose Ryder could come here dressed as her, as Night, just because it was not who she was. It was who she was fleeing from, Beau said: but she had fled her in the wrong direction, right into the arms of other powers, and all those powers were the same, all the way down or out; and now Pierce thought she was deeper in than before, and he didn't know how to reach her, and would not dare go there if he did.

"So tell me," he asked her as he helped her toward the boat. "How long were you living in the City?"

"Oh not long. A few months."

"And when you were there," Pierce said. "What did you do? Who did you, what."

"I don't remember."

"And when was this? I was there then. Was this after you ran away from Wesley?"

"Who?"

"Wesley. Wes. Your first husband. The one who."

"Him?" She opened her eyes in surprise and amusement, holding his arm. "Well you tell me," she said, and laughed. "It was you who made him up."


But did she come at last to the party, Una Knox, she herself and not another dressed as her? For wasn't she invited, or at least expected? Well that could be her disembarking from the paddleboat now, hugely tall in a drape of sight-drowning black, a head above stark white bone, not a skull exactly or not a human skull but certainly something from which the flesh has fallen and which the sun has bleached, anyone who's lived on earth would recognize it; and bony sockets within which no eye can be seen or imagined.

It's very late now and the revellers are actually shedding bits of their getups as inconvenient or already falling apart, not who they ever were; more people now are going out than in. The band's about to quit, and does quit just as this personage comes to stand in the doorway. Everyone, not everyone at once but each group as it is passed, turns to look and wonder, and stops talking for a moment, the braver ones calling out greetings or acknowledgment, not returned except by a look. Up at the back on the dais, Rosie stands to see this dark eminence, the last dignitary to be greeted, the one she's waited for.

Coming in behind, exciting almost as much awe or interest, a spindly wraith in sheepskins, long white hair floating on the heaters' airs, eyes so pale they must be sightless yet they look left and right and seem to smile. The bony dark one stops before Rosie and puts out a big plain human hand. Tattooed on the back— tattooed so long ago it's grown obscure, though Rosie knows it instantly—is a blue fish. The hand opens and shows or proffers a large ugly tooth, a canine tooth, a wolf's tooth.

"For you. All I brought."

"Oh you," Rosie says.

Spofford lifts for a moment the mask from his head (not a skull but a lamb's pelvic bone, sun-whitened and still smelling inside of the high plains where he found it) and is seen to be grinning broadly, pleased with himself. The dead tooth in the middle of his own mouth has come out on this trip somehow at last, leaving a comic hole.

"Oh you bastard," Rosie says, weeping and laughing at once into his black cloak, holding him tight. "Oh you."

From down below, where not only spectral Cliff but everyone else has been watching, it looks as though great Death has taken another elderly victim from behind, wrenching the man's poor limbs all out of bent: and they all laugh, for of course it's not Death at all, not at all.

"But what *happened*?" she says. The big tooth is hard in her hand. "What the hell happened?"

"I'll never tell," Spofford says. A glance Cliff's way. "It can't be told." But he's still grinning, and it seems that one day—maybe long after it's not true any-more—he might.

"See, Moffett," Rose Ryder said to Pierce. "The difference was. In our relation-ship. You were mostly interested in the sex."

Pierce registered the past tense. "Yes?"

"To me there were other things. Things that meant more."

"There were?"

"Sure."

What other things had there been, he wondered, had things happened be-tween them that he had had no knowledge of or was she forgetting how every night, every single night. What would she rather have been doing?

Her black mask was on a chair beside his broad bed where she lay, pretty drunk and grinning blissfully, moving slowly as though sunk in clear syrup. The ass's head was on the floor and yet still affixed to Pierce's shoulders, where it was to remain for a long time.

"To *me*," she said, and raked her long hair with both her hands. "To me there were other things."

Well he had been wrong so far about everything else, so maybe what she said was so. It seemed likely, suddenly, certain even, self-evident. It hadn't been he serving her, laboring to bring her to awareness of her own nature and forcing her assent to it: no. Out of her own generosity or curiosity or awesome acquies-cence, whatever it had been (love, no not love) she had bent herself to fill needs that *she* had uncovered or recognized in *him,* latent till then.

Sure. All along. He had not touched her, probably at all. Probably she had fooled him into thinking the necessity was hers, because she knew he wanted it that way. Maybe she was glad for him, glad to do it, it being so obvious what he needed and wanted, so badly needed. Like a strong nurse able to put up with excretions and cryings-out of any kind, her job or role, until it grew at last too onerous.

*But did you like it?* she had asked him, shivering and weeping in his arms after his exactions. *Did you, did you really like it, did you?*

"Well I have to tell you," he said, and the lump in his throat hurt as though the words themselves scored it in their passage. "I. I never, you know. I never did those things with anyone else. Never with anyone before."

"Oh?" she said, smiling. "Hard to believe."

"I'm not really," he said, "I mean I don't really," and then nothing more, for he could see even despite her unfocussed forgetful eyes that she did not believe him at all, and never would or could; not that or anything else he said on that score. And he had taught her that.

"Say listen," she said, and rose a little on her elbow. "Hic. When you called me before. You said you had something really important to say. Hic. Then you never said it."

"Oh ah," said Pierce, and sat on the end of the bed. Why was it that every day, every hour that passed seemed to fly into remote antiquity almost instantly, to become so hard to remember, positively conjectural, before it could be acted on or its consequences grasped? "Well it was crazy, in a way. A crazy idea." She only waited, still smiling. "Well. I thought. I thought that there was a way out, or maybe through, our difficulties."

"What difficulties?"

"I was going to ask you," and he dove, "to marry me."

But she had drifted off, to sleep or elsewhere, and returned too late to hear. "What did you say?"

"I was going to ask you," he said, and a burble of weird laughter arose in him to reiterate it, it was just so god damn stupidly sad, "to marry me."

"Oh."

"Kids," Pierce said. "Maybe."

"Oh. Jeez. God that is just so hic sweet." Even through the blur of alcohol clouding her face he could see her eyes aglow. "Pierce."

"I thought: if you did, if you would, then I."

"Aw," she said. "You know though really. I couldn't marry anyone who didn't share my faith."

Now he did laugh, gently, at himself as much as at her, but certainly at her: her abstracted drunken serious certainty, immemorial seemingly but only adopted a month or so ago, he wondered what it would be like to be able to speak a new language with such conviction. "Sure," he said. "Sure, I see."

"Hic," she said.

"I just thought it up. Wild hair up my ass. You know."

"Hic," she said again, and looking appalled she tried to rise. "Oh hic no. I've got the hic hiccups. I hate that. I'll have them now for hours. Hic. I always do."

"Drink water backwards. Breathe into a bag."

"I tried that once and hic passed out."

"What I thought was," Pierce said, "that if you could say Yes to that question, then I could put up with. With anything." He folded his hands, and hung them between his knees. "Anything. I don't know why I thought it. Why don't you pray?"

She looked on him, and then turned to lay her head in his lap. He felt the small spasm of her next hiccup.

"What," Pierce said. "It wouldn't work on hiccups?"

"Of course it would 'work,' " she said, laughing. "Of course."

"If it be possible let this hiccup pass from me," Pierce said. "But not my will but thine be done."

"Pierce."

"Well."

She closed her eyes. "Holy Spirit be with me and in me," she said. "Please let these hiccups stop. I ask this in Jesus' name. Amen."

Her head in his lap was heavy. So small in compass, so huge inside, infinite actually. She breathed in and out. There were no more hiccups; the hiccups were gone. In a few moments she was asleep.


"I remembered I'd been there before," Rosie Rasmussen was just then saying to Spofford. By her bed, her own old one still and not Boney's former one, lay all of Boney's clothes in a heap, as though Boney had dropped them there. "When I was thirteen or so. I was sent there for a cough that wouldn't stop. The girl in the bed next to mine died. I was there when she died in the night."

Spofford's long bare body like a dark god's was arrayed on the bed, his head supported by his arm and fist, one knee raised and his other hand resting languidly on it: a river god, Bernini's or Tiepolo's, Rosie was thinking these things with a part of her mind unenlisted for the telling of what she told or the feeling of what she felt. She wiped her tears with a corner of the sheet. She had thought she could tell about what she had learned in the hospital, not back then but now, about illness and being alive and patience and chance, about the odds and how they are different from fate: the odds aren't fate at all even though you can be fooled into thinking they are, that the terrible thing or the illness or the wonderful recovery is not just the odds but something that had been waiting there all along to happen; it's not. She believed this still but she was too frightened and drunk and depleted to make it sound true, and she let it pass through her and be lost; but it wasn't lost, it would return, it was part of her now.

"I found out then in the hospital, that first time," she said, "that I didn't want to die; that I wanted to be in the world. I hadn't been before but I wanted to be. Maybe that's how I got better. I got better when that girl died. Isn't that strange to think. Like a trade. But it wasn't."

"No," Spofford said. "It wasn't."

"Well it's not easy for me. Being in the world. It still isn't."

"No," said Spofford, who knew. "It isn't."

"You have to learn it over and over. Like finding something you lost again and again."

"How can I help?" Spofford said.

Rosie thought of the knights Pierce and she talked about, who went out and did things women told them to do, if they could. She thought it wouldn't matter if they did it because they had to, or for reasons of their own; it happened at least. When there was no other way it could.

"I want you to help me take her back," Rosie said. "It could be weeks till I can do it. But I'm so afraid that if I wait . . . I can't wait."

"What," Spofford said. "Snatch her?"

Rosie made no answer. They both listened to the winter night and the silence of the house where Sam was not.

"It's not just for me or her," Rosie said, thinking of what Beau had said. "It's more. I can't explain." She couldn't explain because she hadn't understood what Beau had meant, but she was willing to say it anyway, on the chance that it might move him, as it had her; but she didn't need to, he would have done it for her, he would have done it for Sam alone, which was the only motive that could actually succeed. But what was it, exactly, that he was to do?

"I just want her back," Rosie said. "I want you to get her back."

# 11

I t was actually some years, several years, before Pierce saw Rose Ryder again, and they were very different people by then. It was in the Midwest, actually, which turned out to be quite unlike the place he had imagined it to be; he had never had occasion to visit there. They walked and talked together by the side of a wide brown river; it was night, but the water seemed to illuminate it with a glow it possessed, and there were lights too, far off where the river made a sweeping bend, toward which they went.

He wanted to know first of all if she was all right, of course, and it seemed she was; she talked of those days with a tolerant humor, it was a long time ago now. Pierce marvelled at the strength of human desire and aspiration, a hunger profound beyond all these schemes, greater than anything proposed to fill it. She shook her head, and flicked the end of her cigarette with her thumbnail (never had quit apparently) and told him how she had come through.

"I can't complain," she said. "Never complain, never explain. That's my motto."

What surprised him most about her now was that she had cut her hair short, he didn't know when or why and was shy to ask; had cut it short and yes lightened its color too, it was almost blond, a tawny complex color he could not resolve in the night and the river light. He lifted his hand to touch it, and she suffered him.

"There's just a lot you don't know, Pierce," she said, and he thought that yes so there was, and he thought without fear that he wanted to know it, he did: and in his thinking this his heart seemed to return again into his bosom.

They walked the dim towpath. This river, he knew, was a tributary of the same great river into which the river that received the waters of the Shadow and the Blackbury far away flowed. You could set out on this one and go back and back until you reached the juncture of those.

"I mostly wanted to say," he said, "that I'm sorry I was such a. That I managed everything I was given to do so badly. That I failed. That I was so stupidly unkind."

"Don't apologize," she said. "Anyway it wasn't a bad experience. They taught me a lot." A smile of remembrance or anticipation bloomed in her face, and she seemed to grow young. "Know what I can still do?" she asked. "Watch."

She had taken out a match, a kitchen match of the largest kind, and held it up in the dark between them, and looked fixedly at its red head. He knew the look: he had just time in which to recognize it (hieroglyph of his damned state) when the match, untouched, burst into flame.

The furious hiss and flare of it woke him, mouth open and gulping, heart striking hard. Beau Brachman stood in his living room, holding a small paper bag and looking at him with interest.

"You guys left that party quick," Beau said. "I never caught up with Rose again."

"She wanted to get some sleep," Pierce said. He pulled out the makings for a pot of coffee. "She left pretty early. She had to be back for something."

"What something?" Beau asked.

"I don't know."

Beau put the paper bag he carried on Pierce's kitchen table. "You need something to go with that coffee," he said.

"I'm not really hungry."

"Ah," said Beau. "Rosie says you're not eating right."

Once again Pierce was surprised, disbelieving actually, to hear that others thought about him, talked about him to one another. "No no," he said. "No no."

Beau had opened the paper bag he had brought and was considering its contents. "Granola," he said. "We make this. It's sold all over. Well all over the county anyway. This kind is . . ." He sniffed it. "This is Gone Nuts granola, I think. Or Totally Spirit."

"Gee," Pierce said. "Either would do." He had in fact never eaten granola. He finished making his bitter brew.

"There's something we've got to find out," Beau said. "We need to know where Sam is."

"You think Rose would know?"

"I hoped she was still here."

"I can call her later. I guess. I'm not sure she'd, she'd . . ."

"No. That's not good." He opened a cabinet and found a bowl suitable for cereal; examined it as though for flaws; and set it down beside the bag. "When were you going to see her again?"

"I think," Pierce said, "I'm not going to. At all ever. That's kind of my plan. I mean maybe someday, when . . . well."

"You've told her this?"

"No." She had genuinely delighted in the great Ball, in his attentions, in the fireworks, everything, drinking it in as though it were distilled just for her. And Pierce knew he would die if he didn't break off with her.

"Beau, at the party you said," Pierce began, and then paused, unsure whether Beau really had said this, in so-called waking life anyway. "You said that it wasn't my fault. This. All this."

"Yes."

"But that it still might be mine to fix."

"Yes."

"I think that too. I don't believe it but I think it."

"The story's about you," Beau said.

"But why would I be so important, why me and not somebody else?" he cried. "It's crazy to think that. It's crazy to *think* something you don't *believe*."

"Look," Beau said. "Why did you think it was, that you happened to appear here? Just here, in the Faraways? That day when you did, last summer, a summer ago. Didn't you think it was strange how you came into this story?"

"Everything's strange," Pierce said. "Or nothing is." But he thought of it, how he had come into the Faraways, how on a noontime he had got off the bus on his way to the city of Conurbana; how he had sat in the shade of a great tree, a huge living thing, whose leaves had lifted in a breeze that passed through the valley then; a Little Breeze that stirred his hair and his heart. He thought he had been escaping, escaping at last.

"The world is made from stories," Beau said, as though imparting a simple truth to a child, who was hearing it for the first time, first of the many times it would take to become a truth. "And right now it's this one. And will be till it's told."

"One story," Pierce said. "That's what *she* says. What they say. I won't believe it."

"You're not required to finish it," Beau said. "But you're not supposed to give it up either."

"See this is what's crazy," Pierce said wildly. "This is the craziness of thinking that the world is a plot, a game, something to be figured out or solved. Exactly the kind of sick, the kind of. No. No."

"The world *is* a game," Beau said. "And it's also a world too."

"I can't go back there," Pierce said. "Not to that city. I can't."

"I'm not saying it's not hard," Beau said. "Dangerous even. Even if it's only you who thinks so."

"I can't," Pierce said. "I disagree in principle."

Beau rose, and came to where Pierce stood. For a moment Pierce thought that Beau meant to embrace him, and he waited in dread and hope for this, whatever it might mean, whatever it would impart. But Beau only slipped his arm through Pierce's, as though he thought Pierce might fall; he turned his hand, and took Pierce's hand in a strong backwards grip.

"Well if you do go," Beau said, "see if you can learn about Sam."

.     .     .

When Beau was gone Pierce sat before the bowl and bag.

He supposed you ate this stuff with milk. It was all he had to eat. He got up and looked in the fridge, milk, how about that, and unsoured.

Sugar too, totally spirit, white as white.

He mixed all these things and lifted a heaping, dripping spoonful toward his mouth. *It's a game, and it's a world too.* What Rose had said: *That was only a game.* No matter; they had played for keeps. And now see. Not required to finish it, can't give it up either.

He bit down. Instantly his mouth was flooded with a taste that was the exact cognate of a smell, one that for a brief time somewhen had ruled his life with an awful power but that he had not smelled since; now it, and all that time with it, rushed into his sensorium, he could see, taste, smell nothing else, though he could give it no name or place.

He bit again, shifting the awful bolus in his mouth, and there arose within him in all its detail the summer camp to which once, at age nine or even eight, he had been remanded by his mother and father, who somehow knew no better, thought maybe to get him out of the apartment and the city and his books for a while anyway; and the utter exile he had experienced there. Axel had not reckoned, and Winnie couldn't have understood, that he didn't know the first thing about ordinary boyhood, did not know even the rules of baseball in any but a general way, did not know how to do the Australian crawl or paddle a canoe; he had not dared to speak to anyone lest these shortcomings be discovered, had hidden and skulked, had not even been able to ask where the bathrooms were and had *peed his pants* for the first days of his captivity there (earning the utter scorn and rejection of every other boy who came near him, but Pierce was too terrorized to regret or even to notice this, even now no single face was brought back to him of all those happy lads) until at last and by chance he had come upon the noisome outhouses, and realized nearly fainting with relief and revulsion what they were: and it was the odor of that row of shacks, their pits, their lime buckets, their soiled paper, whatever exactly constituted it, that overwhelming acrid odor, that had been released in this bite of granola that Pierce still held between his teeth, able for a long moment neither to swallow nor expel it.

He stood, gulping, brimful of self-pity. How could they have, how could they. How could he, but he only a little kid after all, ah poor little son of a bitch. He realized he was to weep again, and the rage not to weep, to weep no more, made the sobs when they came out the more awful.

Oh that place. The dreadful company of his fellows, the penitential meals, the round of meaningless activity that could not be refused, rarely avoided. He had not ever after felt so whittled away, so at a loss, so subject to inescapable and unfeeling others, not until the Army, which that camp resembled in every respect, down to the burr haircuts and the noise level.

No he had not gone into the Army, what was he thinking. He lifted his head. He had not been a soldier, had made himself appear undesirable, undraftable according to the standards of the day, by what should have been a transparent ruse, but that he had made convincing maybe by his apparently frank cooperation— he had actually asked the recruiting officer if it were possible to appeal their decision to reject him.

Had he even gone to that camp? It seemed impossible that he could have. He looked down at his inoffensive bowl of grains, but didn't dare take another bite. A horrid thought fled through him: that *Beau had given him the stuff for a reason.* A pawn in a game of Beau's own, caught now, captured. No now *that* was crazy for sure. What reason, anyway.

He sat again. He remembered how he had left the Army Recruiting Station on Whitehall Street in bottommost Manhattan and been unable to go more than a block, just out of their sight, before he had to sit down on the curb amid the crowds and weep in relief and gratitude. Out.

Unthinking he ate more of the granola. One bite, another.

Assent and escape. That had been his gambit with powerful figures of every kind, hadn't it, not only with the Army, the Church, but with teachers and employers too, with his advisor Frank Walker Barr, his agent Julie Rosengarten: being too timid to deny, to dismiss, to fight back, Pierce had only assented, finding no reason not to assent. As he had to his uncle Sam's commandments too, under whose rule he found himself without his choosing and yet without any reasonable grounds on which to protest; *seeming* to assent anyway, trying to assent, crafting the absolute dissent of his heart into something that looked like assent: cunningly, out of motherwit and doubletalk, metaphysical quibbles, extended metaphors and evasive anagogies, until it was convincing even to himself. And by that means escaping the judgment of those to whom he must seem to assent.

Of course there was One who could not be escaped by those means; and that One had taken his beloved, and embraced her, and now she was His, and beckoned Pierce too to assent; and he couldn't, no more, not this time. And so he must turn away and hide, or stand and fight. Fight or flight. That was all.

Was he going to have to believe that?

It apparently didn't matter what he believed, only what he did.

Well he would do it then. In the face of its impossibility and asininity, which was the very point. *A fool's errand,* the only kind he would ever be sent on or chosen for; if he did not accept it he would be chosen for none.

So he went and washed and dressed warmly and put some whiskey in his flask, his silver flask, and left his house early that afternoon. He went out to his old Steed, spavined Rosinante, and took his place behind the wheel. Then he got out again, and went back to the house, for he had forgotten his car key.

The *front path* of my house is beaten by my own footsteps, there is no other. The guardian *trees* are long gone if they were ever there. The *cup* I find is plain and much-used, and through it runs a dreadful crack; it is the one I asked might pass from me; I drink from it still, last thing before I go. The *key* is on the desk among my papers, and it is this one, the key to my car, that I need for the journey. Outside my back door is another *path,* the path we first came up together, going the wrong way; the *water* that is there is the endless river, it wells up amid the rocks and flows through the pumps and hoses of my house, the same river that runs far under the earth and in the heavens too.

He had not gone very far toward the highway when he chanced to look down at the gauges displayed on the dashboard before him, which he was not in the habit of consulting very often, and saw that the needle of the gas gauge was prostrate, pointing at E; he had no idea how long it had been lying there. There was, he knew, only one gas station between here and the strip beyond the Jambs, where there were several: a decrepit one-man operation just then coming into sight. Wolfram's.

Gray and unpainted, Wolfram's seemed as much junkyard as gas station; old cars and parts of cars, fenders, tires and radiators rusting, but a couple of refrigerators too and a weather-flayed Naugahyde couch. The brand of gas advertised on the big round sign was one not sold elsewhere, and Wolfram was rarely there; he trusted his customers to help themselves, and drop their money through a slot in his door.

Pierce had never pumped his own gas before. He had often seen it done though; had stopped here once with Spofford and once with Rosie and watched them. He could do it; he had to.

He drew the Steed up to one of the two pumps, aligning as best he could its rear end with the handle; got out filled with apprehension and dusted his hands together, ashamed at how little he knew, who was it that should have taught him and had not, or was it (of course it was) that he had himself assiduously avoided learning these things, as he had all sports and manly arts whatever, and now see; and thinking these thoughts, which he had thought before, he unscrewed the silver cap of his tank (newer cars had theirs hidden behind small doors). Warning himself not to forget to screw that cap back on again, he pulled the hose from the pump. He remembered that what you did next was flick the handle on the pump's side upright, which yes started the pump and reset the numbers on the front. He pumped; he finished, shut it off, gratified, remembered too to put the cap back on; went and put his money in the slot. Peeked through the dirty glass to see if perhaps Wolfram were after all in that den, observing; but could see nothing alive within.

Anyway he'd done it. The Steed however started sluggishly, as though its throat were clogged with phlegm. Pierce turned out onto the road; a terrible odor arose around him, black, burned, wrong. Something was wrong. Pierce had only power enough, foot to the floor, to get off the road, sat stalled then and gripping the wheel in bafflement. He raised his eyes to the mirror and looked back at Wolfram's. He could see the two pumps, that they were mismatched, and realized that he had noticed this even as he had pulled up; and now saw that there was a sign hanging over one, the one colored red. When he got out of his car and walked back a ways toward the station, he could read it. It said DIESEL.

He had filled his car with diesel fuel. He stared at the little scene down at the turn of the road, the shabby shop and the two pumps, seeming to be shrugging and looking askance, not their fault. He thought it likely that no one had ever before done what he had just done, no one; he may have destroyed his car; he thought of abandoning it there forever. Walk home, never leave. He had not understood that there had been a choice to make, and he had made the wrong one. He thought *This could not have happened.*

And it had not; no it hadn't happened. At the last second, as he stood at the pump holding the dripping nozzle (arm, nose and penis in one), before penetration occurred Pierce had noticed that the pump he had chosen was red and the other one blue, and had stopped, wondering why. Looked up to see that sign. And now, his tank replete, he and his Steed went down the valley of the Blackbury, past the Jambs and out onto the highway; Pierce watched the speedometer rise past fifty, toward sixty, and after a time of straining ease off and coast, inertia carrying him forward.

Now the land on either side of the road was deepest country, brown fields rising to pine forests and blue distance. Traffic was thickening, cars and trucks pouring past him on both sides as though he were immobile, a humpbacked rock in midstream. He was, however, his speedometer told him, going nearly at the speed limit. For some time he had been glancing frequently at it and at the other gauges and controls before him, as though ready to do whatever he learned from them was necessary, but in fact mostly just passing his eyes over them in anxious repetition. On one such pass he noticed a control he had not seen before, or had not pondered, a thick lever far down on the left-hand side. What's that do, he wondered, and the next time he came to it on his tour, and before he could caution himself to wait a second, he had pulled it. Several things then happened at the same time. One was that Pierce regretted he had pulled the lever, was able in that moment not only to reconsider but to prophesy that the consequences weren't going to be good. Another was that there was a sudden gasp of wind, and then a horrendous noise, as something large and dark rushed upon him from nowhere and slammed against his windshield, blinding him and instantly crazing the glass from edge to edge.

And Pierce, not knowing what had happened and looking into blank darkness, pressed hard on the brake—fortunately there was no one close behind him—then twisted the wheel and turned the car off the road onto the shoulder, slowing to a stop as he came to understand what he had done, which was to release the hood, which then had caught the wind of his forward motion, been lifted like an unbraced sail, and banged into his windshield.

For a long time he sat immobile, his heart firing steadily like a gun and his hands still on the wheel. The windshield had actually held, but there was a fine litter of glass crumbs in his lap and across the seat. He thought of Rose in the night, when she had flipped the Terrier; how stupid she had felt, and how afraid of herself.

He got out. The force of the wind, fifty-five miles an hour, had flung the hood back so hard that the hinges had ruptured; it lay now at a terrible arm-busted back-broken angle against the windshield. Pierce took hold of it and tried to force it down again but it wouldn't move through more than half the arc.

Now what.

*You'd better be careful* she had said to him on the phone, telling him how her windshield had been smashed as she drove this road, it must have been this one, right along here maybe. Smash Corridor. The Devil's Hammer.

He turned to the vast road (much vaster when you stood beside it than it seemed as you drove along it) and wondered how to get help. Trucks approached, hurtled past—the air of their passage thudding against him and his car—and receded with a cry that sank fast from whine to growl, Doppler effect. Someone would soon stop, he supposed, a truck or car or farmer's pickup, and ask what had happened. Or a cop, alerted by some trucker's CB radio; they all had them he heard.

And he would explain himself to their puzzled faces, kindly or remote, amused or censorious; maybe one of them, some big-bellied male, would know what to do, would have tools. Or he would be given a ride, or a wrecker might be called. He could not imagine, could not, what would happen next; it was probably evident to every person in every car that passed, and saw him there, but not to him.

The white sky was opening to the south and the west, and a late sun shone as though through prison bars. No he would not wait, would not try to hail help, it was just too embarrassing. *I have stood sufficient:* what Little Enosh used to say. He looked upward, turning, turning the world.

Beyond the road's shoulder where he stood the ground rose; tall trees walked along the ridge, their slender trunks leading his eyes upward to solemn crowns, brown but not unleaved. As soon as he began climbing to them he ceased to hear the cars on the freeway. When he reached the ridge he found that a tall chain-link fence arose amid the briars and tangled bracken, marking the limit of the state's property maybe; dogs or children had tunnelled beneath it but big Pierce could not. He went along it, unwilling to quit, and for some reason it ended, and let him pass around it and through the screen of trees.

Pastures shorn and bronzed, gentle swells going on upward and down, seamed with streams where willows grew. Sheep country, he thought, and even as he thought it saw sheep in numbers arise over the breast of a far brown hill and clothe it, then hurry away, goaded by busy dogs. Pierce stood for a while, tasting the breeze, and then started downward. Soon he found himself amid more sheep, shepherded by a boy and an old man. They greeted Pierce, the boy's smile guileless, maybe even foolish, and the old one's broad; he held the stump of a pipe in his teeth, his cheeks were russet and his hair white and woolly like his sheep's.

Pierce walked and talked with them. Other shepherds could be seen on the hills, marshalling their sheep like untidy armies. Why were they all gathering here? It was time for the move down from the mountains, he was told, to the warmer valleys to the west and south, where they would spend the winter. *Trans-humance,* Pierce thought: a big change, mountains to valleys, summer to winter; but the same change, one that herders have been making yearly for centuries, millennia even. He noted the ocher identifying marks on the sheep's wool and how it differed from flock to flock, some marked on the hindquarters, some on the shoulders, and he remembered the name of the stuff they were marked with: it was redding.

And so because night was coming on Pierce stayed with them in their encampment in the yellow willows by the stream. All through the night more shepherds and sheep came in. Pierce wondered if Spofford might be among them. He lay long awake listening to the dogs and to the voices of the excited sheep, needful and silly; but toward dawn they slept. Pierce slept. Before day came they began to move, all as one, and Pierce went with them.

Going down the long passes through the forested hills they kept together, and were careful not to let their lambs stray; they never saw any of the packs that went the same way they did, but they were there. They could be heard sometimes at night, not a howling but a faint yipping, like puppies: the dogs heard, and pricked up their ears. Pierce took his turn walking the perimeter of the flock, sleepy but not weary, no not weary, glad. Glad that he had happened to be wearing good strong boots when he left home; glad, too, to be no longer among those condemned to pursue. What he had wanted or sought, whatever it had been, he would learn to do without. He could remember why he had come out from the City to these solitudes in the first place, and why he had left behind all that he had left behind. He walked on behind the flocks toward the valleys and the west.

Or no he did not, of course he did not, did not climb up from the highway and pass through those trees; though he did wonder, looking up at their tops, at the clearing sky beyond them, what lay that way, and did think that if he were offered some way to pass on and away from this he might take it. But then he just got back behind the wheel and started the Steed (no he had not shattered the windshield, at the last moment a fleeting caution had caught up with him and he had not pulled that lever; he had pulled off the road for a moment, though, already exhausted and feeling a worrisome flutter in his bowels, what if he were seized with some dreadful urgency while caught in the midst of a jockeying flotilla or making a tough hill; okay after all though it seemed). He rolled along the shoulder for a moment waiting for the traffic to thin, and then tramped down the accelerator, teeth bared and hands tight on the wheel. Be definite and fearless, she had told him, when entering a stream of traffic.


Hardest of all, to do and to tell of, was the going down into the city of Conurbana when at last it was brought before him by the unfolding road; to go off where the signs said "Downtown" and circle down half-constructed ramps through temporary concrete chutes barely one car wide, where yellow and even orange signs warned him away, some set around with little flaming lamps. But

he did all that too, gripping his wheel so tightly that he felt his fingertips growing numb; searching the streets for familiar sights, that vast plaza and its mono-
lith maybe. Surely he would remember her corner, where he had stood
bewildered and afraid, but once he was out of the downtown city center every
corner looked like that one. Until—this never happens—he came to a stop at a
red light, and the street was Mechanic, wide and poor, and he remembered it,
and turned wholly by chance the right way on it and it soon intersected hers, he
caught the street sign out of the corner of his eye and turned the right way down
that one too, even odds really but not for Pierce, and after a fearful string of
blocks saw her red car, actually saw it parked on the street before a nondescript
building, hers. So it really had all happened, here in this city. He parked behind
it; when he got out he saw that one of its tires was flat.

Not only that. Its windshield was intact, but the roll-down window on the
passenger's side was gone, replaced by a panel of ragged and milky plastic. *The
window shattered,* she'd said, *but only on your side.*

Well hell. *That* window was the one he had compulsively tried to close, jam-
ming its little handle over and over. And all her other passengers too no doubt.
And from the tension it just finally.

Not the Devil anyway. Or rather only the devil that is in things, in built
things especially, the physics devil who does only what he must, nothing personal. Pierce might have laughed (he had long been troubled himself by that one
after all) but didn't.

Inside the front door of her building there was a buzzer to press, her last
name beside it in peacock-green ink, and a single discreet initial. After a pause
long enough to make him think with awful gratitude that there was no one there,
it rang back, and the door he was holding opened. A stair to go up, one flight, and
a door to knock on. A woman not Rose opened it, and Pierce, startled, looked behind himself to find the door he apparently should have knocked on, no that
wasn't it, this was; the woman watched him do that, and then said "Looking for
Rose?"

"Yes. Sorry."

"She's gone."

Gone. "Oh."

"I mean not for good. She'll be back I think, but she's gone for a while. They
didn't tell her how long."

The woman's thin dark hair was partially wrapped around great pink rollers,
he could guess from their disposition what kind of a look she was aiming for,
and how far she would get toward it.

"She's let me stay here," she said. "I lost my place."

"Oh. Uh-huh." He stood, wavering like a candle flame.

"Did you want to come in?" the woman said. "Make a phone call or something? I'm sorry she ain't here. You come a long way?"

"Oh," he said, and shook his head, and shrugged.

"Was this business?"

"Um no."

At last she took his arm and drew him in, since it had become evident that he could do nothing definite himself. "Gets cold with the door open."

"Where," he said, trying to remember this room and these furnishings, cognates of the ones he had recently seen and touched but not necessarily the same ones. "Where was it she went?"

"West," the woman said. "Indiana."

"Oh."

"I'm sorry she didn't tell you. If she knew you was coming."

"She didn't."

"Oh."

"Mexico," he said. "Mexico, Indiana. Is that right?"

"Well yeah," she said warily. Pierce realized he was looming and staring in a way that would surely cause her to stop talking, she was one of them herself certainly.

"I'm a, a friend of hers," he said, and smiled a smile that probably wasn't reassuring; she smiled back, though. From within the bedroom he heard a child call: *Bobby. Bobby Bobby.*

"He can't say Mommy," the woman said. "It's his ear."

"Do you mind," he said, "if I sit down?"

"No sure."

She watched him sit carefully and tentatively on a kitchen chair, as though unsure it would hold him, or if his legs would bend. Then went to see her child, who was shaking a playpen's bars in rage or passion. On the kitchen table was a Testament, not Rose's white one, this woman's doubtless, new-looking yet already stuck full of place markers.

"Do you," he asked when she returned, "know when she's coming back? What her plans were?"

"Well I *guess* she's coming back," the woman said. "I mean all her stuff is here. She didn't know just when."

"Okay well," Pierce said. "Sorry to bother you."

She sat down beside him, as though to keep him from rising. "You know her real well?" she asked.

Pierce said nothing.

"You're not Powerhouse," she said, sure of that.

"No."

"And you come from far away?"

"Well. A hundred miles, or actually more, I guess."

"She was real excited about this chance to go out there. Excited and I guess a little scared. How they kinda sprang it on her."

With exactly Rose's gesture, the woman picked up a pack of cigarettes, toyed with it a moment, and put it curtly down.

"Did she go out there alone?" Pierce asked.

"No, no. There was Pitt Thurston, and let's see. Ray I know was going." Like a child telling a story she made reference to several people he could not be expected to know.

"Mike Mucho?" Pierce said.

"Yes. They ast me to come too. 'Cause of his little daughter, poor thing. I couldn't 'cause I just got *him* back." And she looked toward the playpen.

Pierce hadn't removed his overcoat, and was suddenly overwhelmed by the heat, why do people like this woman always want it so hot. "Well I guess I," he said, and rose, and looked at his watch.

She watched him walk the linoleum irresolutely. Then she spoke. "Can you tell me somethn?" she asked. "Why'd you come lookn for her? Does she need you?"

The reasons were not this woman's business, and he tried to make a face that said that, and knew that he had failed. She continued to regard him, in scrutiny or maybe supplication, something, something that made him look away. "Well she and I were. Have been. Sort of. Well close. And I was worried for her." He studied the child in its little jail. "How far is it, do you guess?"

"Don't know. I never been there."

"Dr. Walter," Pierce said. "Retlaw O. Walter."

"Listen," the woman said, in a voice that made Pierce turn to her. "You ought to keep agoin. Long as you started, long as you got this far."

She reached out and put her hand on the sleeve of his coat.

"Don't stop following her," she said. "Don't stop. The kind she is. She needs you to keep on."

"If she needed me," Pierce said, "she wouldn't have gone. Not that way. Not so far."

"You don't know," the woman said, and stood up. "Maybe she couldn't say. Maybe she doesn't know."

He stood unmoving, his car key in his hand. He thought of his little house by the river. He thought of Rosie Rasmussen, and Sam lost to her.

"Look," she said, trying to guide him to sit again. "You need something to eat? Let me get you something."

"No," said Pierce. "No no."

But she had already opened the refrigerator, scaring from its top the graymalkin, who had stayed behind, and starting her son's wails of desire.

"Ain't got much," she said.

"Please," he begged, but could not for some reason refuse; she gave him Velveeta cheese and Wonder bread and strawberry pop and even that did not enlighten him as to who she was and why she knew what she knew; but when he had eaten it he felt it strengthen and vivify him. He had been hungry, he guessed. Hungry yes, hungry as hell.

"You cain't stop now," she said. "You never did before."

"But," he said.

"We'll steal the world if you let us," she said. "Don't let us. Don't."

She stood then, and quick before he could speak again she pointed. "You go west on 6," she said. "That's all. West on 6, then take 66."

"Six," he said, "six six."

"Bobby," said the child. "Bobby."

She could see he didn't really know what he had to do, so she found a pencil and a scrap of paper, receipt for a turnpike ticket, and on its back drew him a little map, the rights and lefts he must make. She licked the pencil before she started to write. He had not, he thought, ever seen anyone actually do that; but once, long ago, he had.

# 12

S o he went on. The western ramps lifted his car up out of the city center and above the river. He joined the multicolored traffic hurrying home or toward some other destiny or none. By that time the sun was setting, a lurid bloody smear crossed by the white plumes of falling or escaping planes. Such sunsets had once been rare, but they were common now, caused by the clouds of gas and smoke that he and others were making, from here to out there where he was headed and far beyond. To the south on the long river island below the city he could see, as he travelled on, the great parabolic towers of the nuclear power plant, the one that Metatron had made to power the whole of this quadrant of the megalopolis; above their tops formless beings of steam stood up as tall again as they, and gestured slowly.

They were armed, supposedly, the supposed adherents of the supposed cult or religion. Who knew, but out there in the boonies where he had never been anything was possible. Night fell. He thought how there is but one road, one dark wood, one hill to climb, one river to cross; one city to come to, one night, one dawn. Each one is only encountered again and again, apprehended, understood, recounted, forgotten, lost and found again. And yet at the same time and for everyone the universe stretches out infinitely in every direction you can look in or think about, at every instant. He had thought this thought before, not once, more than once, but he had long forgotten all those other instances, and he soon forgot this one too.

Ahead of him by many hours went the black van with smoked windows (once the property of The Woods Center for Psychotherapy) driven by Pitt Thurston; Pitt leaned over the big wheel, his nose pointed eagerly toward the west, and now and then his lips drew back a little in a smile that revealed the tips of his canines. Ray Honeybeare beside him seemed asleep. In the seat behind them were Mike Mucho and Rose Ryder, erect and alert even after the long miles; silent though, nothing to say. Between them, Sam, silent too, knowing for the first time the melancholy of rainy winter highways at nightfall; and—hiding its light in the plastic backpack in her lap, unknown so far to anyone but her—the globe of moleskin-colored quartz she had taken from the big commode in the living room of Arcady. The road straightened itself, pointing ahead, the long dashes that marked its hide appearing one after another out of the darkness to slide beneath the tires and be lost.

No that could not have been or there would have been no end to it; there *is* no end to it that way and we can never have found ourselves here doing this if we had gone that way and done that.

What happened was that as soon as Pierce started off from the street where Rose had lived he immediately lost himself, his earlier luck having run out; he found he could not both read the little map the woman had drawn and drive the car, and he took one wrong turn and then another. After a long anxious time he came upon signs for Route 6 and entered doubtfully upon it (a more confident car behind him honking at him to prod him along) and set out. Only after dark, when he had seen no promised signs for the westward road, did he recall or consider that he had seen the awful sun go down on his left (hadn't he?) and that therefore it was certain (wasn't it?) that he was going north not south, back the way he had come; but still he went on, unwilling to get off again for fear he would set off in another direction entirely and never find his way either there or back, and anyway shedding with every mile his conviction and his courage. Sometimes he wept.

Long after dark he turned in again at the Winterhalter gateposts, uncertain what he had done and what he had not done but only seemed to have done. Of one thing he was certain, though: that he had failed again, this time utterly; and that when he came to this same place on the next turn of the rising or falling spiral he would doubtless fail again, and then again, forever.

In his own house everything was as it had been, though seeming to have just hurried into place seconds before he arrived, and looking a little harried and disordered; he thought he heard a faint settling rattle from the crowded drawers of kitchen implements, a rustle from his papers in their piles. He went to the phone and lifted it warily, but the familiar tone was produced almost instantly. He thought with sick sadness of the news he must give. He dialed. No one answered at Arcady.

Meanwhile at The Woods Center for Psychotherapy (which according to the laws of the state had actually ceased to exist in the previous month, its assets being sold to satisfy its creditors), the lights were coming on. The black bulk of it was pierced by a few windows blinking open like eyes one or two at a time, starting with a string along the west basement where the laundry is, whose door was the only one to which the new possessors had been given a key.

It was Ray Honeybeare, and Mike Mucho and Sam, and a group of the others whom Ray had picked out to help make a thorough inventory of the place and its contents pursuant to a purchase and sale agreement.

Ray had asked Mike to come along at the last minute, even as Mike arrived at the Bypass Inn ready to go west. Mike, seeing Ray so preoccupied and distant, had made no argument. Ray also suggested that Mike bring Sam along, her situation too new and unsettling, no reason to make her feel abandoned; and Ray had touched Sam's hair with his big hand.

They went up floor by floor, switching on banks of lights as they went, finding the switches with a big red flashlight the vanguard carried. Laughing at their own voices echoing in the darkness, picking out spooky shapes with the lantern before resolving them with the overheads into timid inanimate objects, furniture and piled boxes. Mike Mucho lifted Sam to switch on some lights, click, lovely simple cause and effect. Ray Honeybeare came last, who as it happened had an unreasoning fear of the dark.

As though the sleeping pile awoke, startled and displeased, a dull rumble began all around them: the group in the basement had got the furnace going. The radiators were few and weak, never having been needed much; the heating system was high on the list of things that would need redoing. Ray had told them to bring sleeping bags and expect to be cold even in the daytime while the work of inventory and assessment was done.

They had intended to get here a lot earlier, and after a while Ray suggested that it was now so late that maybe they should start bedding down, and get an early start in the morning. Most of them elected to lay out their sleeping bags in the main-floor lounge, a big sleepover, and there was more hilarity as the bathrooms were shared and nightclothes divulged, until Ray took out his small Testament and began looking for a passage he wanted to read; and then they grew quiet.

Mike was still in the bathroom, helping Sam get ready, watching her brush her teeth with great enthusiasm and flair and then sit on the pot, cheek in hand waiting.

"So that's it?" Mike asked her. "All ready?"

"Well," she said, and raised a forefinger. "I have to take my medicine."

"Do you always take it?"

"*You*-sually," Sam said. "If I need to I can cancel."

"You don't like it."

"Daddy," she said, letting him know he was being obtuse.

"Because it's way down in the van," Mike said. "I left it. I don't know why I didn't remember it. And we want to hear Ray read. Don't we."

"If I don't take it Mommy cries."

"Does she?"

"Sometimes. What I don't like," she said, "is the *taste*." She made a face of tried patience and disgust, eyes crossed and lifted and her remarkable big pink tongue, long enough to touch her nose with, hanging down. Mike laughed and clasped her.

"Listen," he said. "I don't think you have to take that medicine tonight. I don't want you to have to take it. I think—I think there's a way for you to never have to take it again."

"Yay," Sam said calmly, as though she had long expected this announcement, and it was overdue.

"Mommy doesn't need to cry, Sam," Mike said, and he bent and took her by the shoulders. Sam saw little starry tears inside his own eyes. "Nobody ever needs to cry."

She took his hand and they went out into the big lounge, and the young people applauded her in her jammies; she wiggled into her sleeping bag, lined in flannel on which were printed cartoon people, Ray had shaken his head over them, smiling in something that was not quite amusement or even tolerance. After a few moments she got out again and dragged her plastic backpack near her, and got back in again.

Mike thought she would fall asleep while Ray read, but she didn't. *There was war in heaven; Michael and his angels fought against the Dragon; and the Dragon fought, and his angels; and prevailed not.* After Ray had shut the book and prayed a while in silence, Mike went to him in sock feet to consult with him, and when he looked back he could see Sam's open eyes. Ray took his shoulder, and motioned with his great head toward the door.

"Be back in a minute, sweetie," he whispered to Sam; he followed Ray out of the lounge and down the dim wood-panelled hall toward the director's office.

"There's a reason why this has happened to this child," Ray said. "I don't know exactly what the reason is and it may be, Mike, that you don't know the reason either."

He had pointed Mike to a chair. He himself remained standing, leaning against the former director's broad desk, his slippered feet crossed and his tartan robe tied loosely around him. Mike realized that he was sitting in the same chair, in the same room, where he had first applied for a job at The Woods.

"But maybe," Ray said, "you *do* know it, or knew it once, and don't remember it now."

"I don't know it, Ray," Mike said. "I don't."

"This trouble that she's experiencing now," Ray said, as though he hadn't heard Mike speak. "It was let into her at some past time somehow. This evil."

"How do you mean, let into her." A kind of internal noise like a rising wind was filling Mike's ears, he thought at first that it was the roar of the far-off furnace, then knew it was not. "What time, when."

"Well," Ray said, and now he turned to look directly at him, "Mike, whenever it was—and maybe it was more than one time, I don't know—it's perhaps still giving strength to this thing. We don't know that. But we know that something which can make such a little child so sick has got to have once been well fed. Do you understand? Got to have."

"What are you saying, Ray. That I."

As soon as these words left his mouth they seemed to Mike to be a lie, a form of lying, even though the words said nothing in themselves. Ray didn't respond, but for a long time didn't look away: as though Mike had not spoken, but might. Then he pushed his great body from the desk's edge, and tightened his robe. "Throw away that medicine, Mike," he said. "She's not going to be helped by anything you put in her. There's been enough of that."

The phone's ring in the midnight lifted Pierce bodily from his bed like a cartoon animal.

"Hi Pierce. This is Rose Ryder."

Cheery, as though she were in the neighborhood, just down the road or over the hill. But she could not be.

"Where are you?" he asked.

"I'm," she said, and seemed to study her surroundings, he could hear nothing, the swish maybe of a passing car. "I'm in Millstone."

"In where?"

"Millstone, Ohio. Near Zanesville. The far side."

"Rose," he said.

"I'm sorry I didn't tell you about this," she said. "I really meant to, last night."

He couldn't think for a moment what she meant, last night, then understood that yes it had been only twenty-four hours, less, since she had been with him here in this house.

"I'm going out to Indiana," she said. "It happened really fast."

"I know," he said. "Indiana. I knew that." There was a silence on her end that might have been wonderment or suspicion. "I went to your house today," he said. "To your apartment."

"Why?" she asked.

He couldn't say, couldn't remember; or what he remembered could not be said. "Are you all right?" he asked. "Do you need me to come get you?"

"I'm fine."

"I will. I can. I can leave now."

"Pierce. I'm fine."

He heard another car go past. He saw her, for a moment, at a public phone, her eyes lowered and her hair falling over the instrument, a hand over her other ear to hear. "When will you come back?" he said. "Will you come back?"

"I don't know," she said. "Maybe when they finish the deal with The Woods and it reopens. They're up there now, Ray and Mike and those. It's all going so fast. So fast."

"Mike's not with you?"

"He's coming soon," she said. "Pierce, I've gotta go. Goodbye."

"No."

"I just wanted to tell you where I was," she said. "Where I'm going. It wasn't fair not to tell you."

"Wait," he cried; but Rose didn't hear him, she had hung up, for the van's horn had already sounded twice; the van waited rain-slick and already exhaling whitely at the pumps. She'd told them she was only going to pee.

She wept a little, but in the rain no one would notice the wetness she wiped from her cheeks. All she wanted was what she wanted, and out there she would know, maybe, what that really was; and knowing it would not be different from having it. The side door of the van slid open for her as she approached. It was still many hours more.

The world is, or was then, a figuration, a cipher, an equation to be solved, a seal to be completed. It was also (as it is now) just a world, full of this and that in billions, unresolvable, both entire and infinite. Rose Ryder hadn't remembered exactly what Pierce said about marriage on the night of the ball, but what he told her had touched her, and left in her heart the conviction that after all he had not tried to use her awakening to God as a means of shedding her, the way most men would do, the way you would expect. It was for that reason that she thought she ought to give him a call from the road, to say goodbye. And because Pierce was someone who had never been able to tell left from right, and never would, he had been there in his house in Littleville to answer.

Pierce called Arcady again. This time the phone was picked up. It was Brent Spofford.

"Hi, it's Pierce."

"Hi."

"Is Rosie there?"

"She's asleep," said the shepherd, sounding wary and distant, which brought a furious blush to Pierce's cheek and a corresponding icy grip to his heart; but there was no way to speak of what had occurred between himself and Rosie, supposing that something actually had.

"Well don't get her," Pierce said, but Spofford had already left the phone, and soon Pierce heard Rosie's voice, and for a moment couldn't speak, overcome with something, compassion or humility or grief.

"Pierce?" she said. "You okay?"

"Yes."

"Where are you?"

"Home." He gathered himself, cleared his throat of the coagulated tears and fears that had collected there. "I don't know how long I'll be here, but. I wanted to tell you. I think I know where Sam is."

# 13

Far up on the slopes of Mount Randa, tallest of the hills that form the Faraways, there stands on an easterly bluff a monument, put up some years ago to honor that locally famous autodidact and visionary Hurd Hope Welkin, "the educated shoemaker," naturalist, reformer, philosopher, divine. The original plan for this monument had been a statue of the old man himself, not set up on a pedestal or pointing the way east, but just standing on the earth, bent and white-bearded, wearing the old checked suit and wide-awake hat he always went botanizing in; he would be caught having just spied a specimen in the mountain grasses, *Silene virginica Hurdii,* and bending to it: the moment before he heard what he afterward called "this loud though yet gentle noise," on that "fair day in summer, the sun shining clear, and no wind stirring": that noise that awakened him.

The path upward to the monument from the valley below follows old cowpaths and loggers' ways, coming and going on its traverses, disappearing into a slough or a woods and appearing again, marked occasionally with round rocks painted white. It was now dawn of the following day, once again mild in the Faraways, and from where the monument stood the sun could be seen beginning to rise, still molten and uncollected. On the path, far down, able to be discerned only by the hawks awakening on the heights, Pierce Moffett walked, climbing upward. Now and then he paused and lifted his head, confused or alarmed, as though he too heard a loud though gentle noise; once he started back down again, only to stop, seeming to remember something, and turn to climb once more.

That there was a path upward to this place had been mentioned to Pierce on the first day he had come to the Faraways. Brent Spofford amid his sheep had pointed upward, and they had talked of one day going all the way up to the spot. And on this day when Pierce found himself long before dawn still awake, he decided that rather than dispute further with the demons gathered around his bed he would get up, throw on some clothes, and go for a walk. A good long walk. Past the Littleville post office, not a mile from the Winterhalters', he came across a small road he had not noticed before, an enamelled sign pointing upward, with the symbol of the shoemaker's last on it; and he turned up that way. His disputants had not been left behind, but went along with him, and he told and re-told his story to them, or refuted theirs; they charged him with his sins, and he denied or admitted them. Then he began again. Now and then he stopped, looked around himself in wonder to find himself here, the world too; tried to judge how far he had walked, and failed; told himself to go back, and instead went on.

The long view from the monument on the heights had formerly been even longer, before the mountain farms were given up and their pastures filled up with quaking aspen, sumac, balm-of-Gilead poplars, firs and pine. You could have seen then all the way down to where the Shadow River joins the Blackbury, and runs to pour over the curve of the earth. Down there now, in the wooded hills, were the lights of Blackbury Jambs still lit, the all-night gas station blue, the streetlights yellow.

Lights were lit too in Allan Butterman's office, where the counsellor was already at work though nobody else in the Ball Building was. He had court appearances today and felt unready, had come in in his sweats to look over the papers his secretary had prepared last night and left neatly flagged and tabbed. On the hat rack his black suit and white shirt hung like armor waiting to be donned.

"Well it's not theirs yet," he said to Rosie Rasmussen. "Maybe it never will be." Rosie had tracked him here, and though he had tried to ignore the call, on the fourth ring he had given in.

"No?" Rosie said. "It's where they are right now. Moving in."

"Well we've found some things out," Allan said. "In the first place they are not a registered nonprofit, as they have listed themselves as being."

"They aren't?"

"Not in this state. Maybe somewhere. Indiana or Iowa or wherever. Not here. They can't buy it under the conditions they propose until they are. And that's not all." He switched his phone to the left ear, and lifted his feet to his desk. "There's a story. A young woman named Flora Fasti, I think it was Flora, who became a convert to this organization. She was an heiress, I didn't learn where the money came from but there was a lot of it, and she was also very ill. She was starving to death. Have you ever heard of this? She wouldn't eat, not that there was anything wrong with her physically. She just wouldn't. Or not enough anyway."

"I've heard of it. It has a name, I forget what, Mike told me. I've known people, girls."

"All girls, yes," said Allan. "So she became a convert, and they claimed they could cure her, get her out from under this. And she made over to them her entire fortune. It came to well over a million. Gave them control over it. A gift. Just like that."

"So that's where the money is."

"It goes on," Allan said. "Apparently they don't have the pull with God that they claim to have, because she died. Flora died. In their center or headquarters. It was hushed up for a time but has now come out. And the state is very interested in this, and so are her collateral relatives. Who tend to think that maybe Flora was deceived and robbed."

"Oh my God."

"Anyway, the money now is in dispute to say the least. No one knows how this will turn out. Maybe they'll win. They certainly have been on a streak. But you never know."

For a long time Rosie said nothing more. Dawn gathered in Allan Butterman's window.

"Allan, I have to see you this morning," she said. "I have to."

"I'm going to be in court."

"I mean right now. In a little while. I'm, well I have to do something today that I want your advice on. I wasn't sure I had to do it but now I am. It won't take long. Please."

"You can't ask?"

"I have to see you. When I tell you you'll know why. Allan, it might be the last thing you'll ever want to hear from me, and if it is I'll understand."

There are multitudes of spirits, Giordano Bruno taught, rank on rank, more kinds of spirits than there are kinds of material things like dogs, stars, stones and roses. They are mortal, though many live fabulously long lives; some are good, some bad, some neither good nor bad; they can be shy, weak and flighty, fierce and terrible, placid and inert, stupid or wise. Of those who clustered around Pierce as he went up Mount Randa he might have distinguished several of these kinds. There are demons who can hear and understand our voices and demons that cannot; there are fiery great gods who need nothing from us and demons who live with us companionably; there are some who love us, some who shun us, like the "light-fleers, throwers of stones whose impact is however harmless" who had often thrown stones at young Bruno and his friends back in Nola, up near the ruined temple of Portus on Mount Cicala, a mountain like this one.

You never know in what form you might encounter one. Travelling spirits can house themselves in plants, in gemstones, in animals. And in fact Pierce, just then sensing something behind him to be afraid of, half turned to see a large black dog, just steps away, following him silently, *dogging* him: red tongue awag, and eyes like coals.

MEPHISTO. *Schwarze Pudel*, uncommonest of his shapes. You can only know this, in these latter days, if you've read it somewhere, and Pierce had, and how does it happen that such a notion can so startle the heart, intellectual Meaning translated into physiological Dread in a single beat? For upon seeing the hound so near, Pierce drew the big breath of a startled mammal who might need the air in the coming fight, elbows jutting and claws at the ready; and he bared his own canines. He did this all in an instant, without a choice, poor beast. The dog (just a dog, it was obvious in a moment) only tilted his head quizzically at him, and wagged his tail. *Everyman I will go with thee.*

They walked on together. Pierce thought of the little she-wolf that once, long ago, Sam and Winnie being absent, he and his cousins had taken in, to tame or try to tame. He began to tell this story to his interlocutors, only to realize it had not happened. Soon thereafter he found himself speaking to a new person, one he hadn't known to be present to him before: not Pitt Thurston or spectral Rose or Mike Mucho, not Robbie or any other phantasmic offspring, not the Kentucky girl either, she-wolf cub whom he still couldn't name, but a girl. A nine-year-old girl, about; a girl in knee socks and a plaid kilt fastened with a silver safety pin, large wise glasses maybe, a tender broad brow. He had been talking to her, and listening to her answer, for some while before she came clear to him.

If it really all was up to me, he said to her, I would hope it would be different.

Different how, she asked.

Not so dark, Pierce said. Not all the time.

And? she asked.

I would like, Pierce said, and the hard lump in his throat hurt just as though he spoke aloud; I would like the earth back. I would like it to be first, not last. I would like it to be final. Just earth.

How so? she asked, so grown-up, but perhaps understanding less than she seemed. He wanted to say that if it was up to him, well he wanted it to be *not* up to him. He wanted to come last, he and all his kind, latest children of a billion ancestors; he wanted not to have come from elsewhere but to know he arose here, where he would lie down at last. That's all. He wanted to resign his commission or decline his duty. This sick plague of Meaning he was caught in, or of no meaning, which seemed to be the same thing, a world of no meaning but many acts, where intentions had random effects unrelated to desire or need and yet produced by them, like the dishes a madman breaks trying to fight off his pursuers: he wanted it to stop. That's all.

If that's what you want, she said, that's what you'll have to make.

I did what I thought I was supposed to do, he said, and I failed. I would like to be freed.

Up to you, she said. *Nunc dimittis.* Tomorrow to fresh woods, and pastures new.

But what about Sam? he cried to her, or the brightening air. What about Rose? Will they all be all right? Will she be all right?

It is not of thy charge, she said.

Sometimes the gods are as amused by releasing the caught soul like an undersized trout as by reeling it in once more. Or maybe it was only that the sun arose fully just then, warming earth and Pierce's cheek, making the world real, and real to him; or maybe it was that the accumulation of sleepless nights, the stresses of hopeless effort, and the long breakfastless climb upward now caused, or "triggered," a release of endorphins in Pierce's brain like those which give the flagging athlete a sudden superb calm strength, the world bright and the goal near and easy: a neurochemical process coming to be understood just then in far-off labs, just at the turning of the age. Whatever it was, in that moment they all fled away.

All of them, the staring demons, the name-callers and rock-throwers, Pitt and Ray and the dynamen and dynamettes, he actually saw them turning tail, growing small and scattering. All the powers, not only those who had afflicted him but those who had aided him as well; even she herself who had just now answered him. *They folded into 10ths like the Arabs and quietly stolaway* said Enosh, who was one himself.

Pierce took another step, and then stopped, and lifted his eyes to the heights, blinking. Then he turned and looked back down the way he had come. He realized he didn't know how he had got here so high; remembered setting out from his house and turning upward but not the rest. He looked down to see that he was wearing two different shoes, a black one and a brown one, pulled on in his ignorance in the darkness of his bedroom. He had walked miles without noticing.

Oh you dope, he thought. What are you, nuts?

Wake up, he said, as though to another, and then again: Wake up. And, blinking with mouth ajar as though in fact awaking, he looked upon a roadside tangle of bittersweet, the black branches frosted and the berries orange and red; for a long time he looked at it. He felt his cloudy breath issuing; and he heard a clamor of crows assuring one another they were there, and the day begun. That's all.

He turned to walk back down the mountain. The black dog (who himself lived up that way) watched him go. With his two different shoes, like one of those heroes who goes to the Happy Isles or the land of the dead to find the flower or the fleece, and comes back up onto the surface of the earth with one foot shod and the other bare, one hoofed or cloven and the other human. His own hands though, he thought, were empty. So was the sky.

When he got back to his house, he thought, he would call his mom in Florida. He would go see her; go and get some answers from her, make her tell him; ask her, get her to tell him, to tell him

Bobby.

That was the name. Bobby what, Bobby. As though a stubborn stone now gave way at last under a lifting bar and rolled aside, Pierce without surprise found her name: *Bobby Shaftoe.*

Bobby Shaftoe's gone to sea Silver buckles at her knee She'll come back and marry me Pretty Bobby Shaftoe. That was her name. And inside her name, he saw, was the name of his imaginary son.

He felt lighter than he had in days and weeks. It wouldn't last, of course, for his tasks were not yet done or even recognized for what they were; he knew it, too, and tried to memorize the things he saw as he came down again to the river road and its habitations—the sun in the brown bracken, melting the frost and making it glisten; the long body of mist prone over the supine river, pierced with the same light; old green truck in that driveway, tailpipe breathing whitely, waiting for its master—so that he could, when it was lost, recall that at least for this moment he had known better. He would not forget. Yet even before night came again he would be helplessly picking up his burdens, *asinus portans mysterium,* and he would go on carrying them far longer than everyone else thought he should, or could.

At The Woods Center for Psychotherapy Sam Mucho was now awake. It was six in the morning, which happened to be the hour at which the big clock in the main lounge had stopped after it had ceased to be wound. She didn't wonder why she was wide awake so far before everyone else. It had now been sixteen hours since her last dose of medicine.

The light had been left on in the bathroom, a little one, and the door was almost shut, just a thin L of light around its edge. It was far away out the entrance of the lounge and a little down the hall but she could see it.

*Tinkle* was what Mrs. Pisky always said. Sam got out of the bag and on her hands and knees looked around at those sleeping, unable to tell which of the rolls of darkness was her father. She went on all fours through and around them, and one stirred and then was still; and when she was past them all she stood, and went out into the hall and down to the bathroom. She could begin to taste the taste of immensity but didn't recognize it, confusing it with the strangeness of the big building and the dark. Then she did recognize it.

It was one of the young people from Conurbana who witnessed Sam's seizure. She heard Sam call *Daddy* softly from the bathroom in the hall, in a voice that awakened her but not Mike; she couldn't at first figure out just where the call had come from, and when she reached the bathroom Sam was falling.

The woman cried out *Oh my God.* Then Mike's name.

He stumbled up, feet caught in the entangling sleeping bag, and several others got up too, who beat him to the bathroom to look in but let him pass when he got there. Sam was in the young woman's arms rigid and grimacing, the young woman rigid too, mouth corners drawn down in fear and horror.

"Okay," Mike said. "Okay. It's okay."

He gathered Sam up. She had lost bladder control and her nightgown was wet; she was on fire; then spasms shook her as though the rigid structure she had become were being torn apart.

"She'll swallow her tongue," somebody said. "You got to get her mouth open."

"No," Mike said. "No she's okay."

Someone began to pray, and then the others too, as though remembering to do so, and just as they did that Sam in Mike's arms suddenly softened and turned again into a human child. She opened her eyes.

"Okay hon," Mike said. "It's okay."

She didn't answer; she pulled a wisp of hair from her mouth with a pinky, her eyelids fluttered, she regarded Mike as though she had never seen him before; then she curled against him and in a moment was deep asleep.

Mike looked up at the faces of those gathered at the bathroom door, looking down at him and his daughter concerned or shocked or curious, like the faces of people at an accident. He thought of Sam looked at in this way all her life; he knew that he would not be able to protect her because he could never tell when she would need him, he would always be looking the other way or doing something else. He bent to kiss her brow, and his lips touched the cool sweat. Ray Honeybeare was now among those looking down at him and his daughter, and the others looked to Ray.

# 14

On the carriage drive at Arcady were parked Val's Beetle and Spofford's Dodge Ram, beside them the old Bison station wagon and the Python sedan that Beau Brachman drove. A motorcycle too, resting canted on its kickstand as though taking a sharp turn at speed.

"Mike will be very afraid," Beau was saying. They all sat on the floor of the great living room as though around a campfire; only Val chose to remain in the depths of the leather couch. "He won't have understood how much he was being asked to give up, and now that he does understand he's going to be confused and empty and afraid. He wants to get to the other side of this quickly, where it will be all better. Anything could be asked of him now and he won't know how to refuse. That's what I think."

He looked around the circle, and at last to Cliff, who considered Beau's face or his words for a moment, and then assented, with a little nod. Spofford, who had been watching Cliff with care, now turned his gaze again on Beau. Rosie took his hand.

"I think it has to be done," Beau said. "I think it's important, and I don't think we can wait at all." It was the most important thing that could be done, and everything depended on it from here forward; at the same time it was just one act on one winter day and only one child at risk. Beau knew that. "I should have known earlier," he said, "and I didn't."

"How many people are up there?" Cliff asked. "Are any of them people we know, besides what's this guy, Mike? Anybody we can go calling on?"

"They'll let us in," Beau said. "The getting in won't be hard. Where Sam is, maybe yes."

Cliff seemed uncomfortable. "I want there to be somebody I know. Somebody I can ask for."

"Ask," Beau said, "for Bobby."

No one spoke, or asked Beau how he knew this name, or why he suggested it. Cliff could be admitted there or almost anywhere if he had someone he could ask after, someone whose name he knew, toward whom he could open himself in honest inquiry. It was a thing he could do. Spofford knew it. Beau knew it.

"But the main one?" Rosie asked. She had seen him, the one she wouldn't now name, at Boney's funeral, where he had only appeared seemingly to make himself known to her, and to the Foundation; she had since looked up the grant proposals submitted by The Woods for the program in healing, and seen his weird name on them. She had dreamed of him too: she just then realized that.

"I know Ray Honeybeare," Beau said. "I know him." His face was as clear as it always was; it was the others who felt a dark chill, or a tense resolve.

"One thing I want to know," Val asked. "Is anybody going to jail for this. I mean that's not going to do the kid any good."

Rosie fetched a huge sigh, and hugged herself. Allan hadn't answered when she asked him what would happen, waving his hand by his ear as though to brush away the incoming words. If she genuinely believed Sam was at risk? If she was open with Mike for as long as she could be before she acted, if there was no coercion at all, none? But Allan had stopped listening, was already denying that he was hearing what she said. So she couldn't answer Val.

"Mike would have to press charges somehow," Spofford said, and lifted his brows and looked around the circle, am I right?

"He won't," Beau said.

Spofford did not nod satisfied. He took Rosie's hand again.

"We'll wait till it's dark," Beau said. "There's a funny reason for that I won't tell you." His smile was unchanged, Beau's smile that they all knew, abashing and cheering and mystifying all at once. "Anyway that's not long from now. Rosie. Do you have a room I could sit in for a while? Just sit."

She got up, looking around the circle to see if others understood this any better than she did, and saw that they did not, but felt no need to ask; she took Beau first to Boney's office, but once he was in it he laughed, looking around, and shook his head No. No not here. He liked the kitchen better, sat down at the old wooden table in a hard chair and was still even before Rosie backed away out the swinging door.


Night falls so fast in December at the latitude of the Faraway Hills; it had hardly been day at all, and the lights had long been lit at The Woods. Through the building and the garages and the sheds and over the grounds the young men and women of the Powerhouse had gone in twos and threes, finding excuses not to be alone but not knowing why they should be afraid to be, and then excuses to end their surveying and return into the big main building and the lounge. Yes that was where Ray and the others were, and there was the reason: Mike sat with his daughter on the ottoman in the center of the room, and Ray with his Testament on a hard chair. By twos and threes they entered quietly and took seats.

Ray explained to them what he was going to try to do, and why he thought it was necessary, and he looked around at their faces as though to garner their assent. He asked them for their prayers. Then he got up, with some effort, and Sam watched him grow big and come to stand over her.

"Sam's not going to understand everything that happens here tonight," he said to them, looking down on Sam, "but it's going to make a very big difference to her, I think, if God wills." He said this in that masking way grown-ups have of smiling and looking into a child's eyes and at the same time saying things the child is assumed not to get or even really to hear. "We have to be prepared for some difficult manifestations. But we know no real harm can come to us, or to this child."

They moved in their chairs or in their places, and some made soft noises. Sam, understanding that she was the sole focus of their attention, became alarmed.

"Daddy."

Mike held her shoulders and bent to kiss her head. Ray put his hand over Mike's.

"Daddy's going to go out for a while now, honey," he said. "Because we want to talk a little alone. You and I."

Mike raised his head, but didn't release Sam.

"No," he said. "Of course I'll stay." He said it to Ray, not to Sam. "Of course."

"Mike, this is something I don't think you can witness. Mike." The soft iteration of his name silenced Mike. No one there in the lounge was looking at him but Ray: he saw that.

"Well is there a reason?" he asked, trying for a voice as low and firm as Ray's, where had all his strength gone, where.

"Yes there's a reason," Ray said. "We've talked about this."

Mike took his hands from Sam's body.

"Mike, I want to work with you on this," Ray said. "There's nothing that can't be lifted from you, from your soul: nothing. And I want to help you to ask for that. But this child's need is more urgent now."

Sam had begun to shudder intermittently, the cold in the lounge intense. Mike wanted to take off his own down vest, wrap her in it, but he couldn't.

"He can stay," Sam said. "I don't mind."

"Mike," Ray said.

They all waited, and Mike looked at none of them; he wanted to say to Sam *I'll be right outside honey* but he couldn't do that either, if it was he who had once hurt her so dreadfully he couldn't say that, it would sound like a threat or a warning, it sounded like that to him even as he heard himself think of saying it.

He couldn't touch her. He couldn't say he loved her.

"You'll be all right," he said. "Ray loves you. You listen." He stood, pulling away from her hand that reached for him, but not able to avoid Ray, who moved to him more nimbly than Mike would have thought he could, and took him in a big embrace, and holding him laughed a small and kindly laugh, these things aren't so important; but Mike knew they were; then Ray let him go, and turned to Sam.

"Daddy?"

"It's okay," Mike said, and half looked back but not so far as to see her, putting out his hand toward her as he went away. He went out through the big arched door and down past the bathroom where Sam had had her seizure and down the hall to the window that looked out to the golf course and the hills. He could hear voices from the lounge, prayer maybe, but not the words.

It seemed to Mike that only as Ray spoke of them did the things he referred to (*whenever it was, maybe more than one time*) come into being; and that when they came into being they came into being as Mike's own secret, things that no one knew but he. It wasn't so, he knew it hadn't been so before, but he felt it now coming to be so: and therefore to have always been so.

*Like wishes come true, huh,* Rosie had mocked him once when Mike had tried to tell her about prayer, tried to tell her that the physics isn't final, that maybe we can have what we want.

He thought these thoughts, but could hardly attend to them; the voice was his own and what it said was true but at the same time had nothing to do with him, like the voice in a train station announcing trains when you know your own has already gone, already long gone, and there is nothing to be done.

*You don't have to wait till Judgment Day to go to Hell,* Ray had once told him. *You can start right now if you want to.*

He had been there a long time, maybe, when a voice spoke, very near him, he had heard no one approach:

"Mike, man."

He turned. A wraithlike person was coming to touch him, a person entirely white, a human person. The remains of Mike Mucho nearly flew apart in terror, but the touch when it came was annealing.

"Mike, can we talk, man? It's important."

Something caught Mike's eye down at the broad hall's other end, a mouse maybe crossing the floor or a bat awakened by the furnace's heat and flitting at eye level down and into the lounge, no it was nothing. He thought of Beau Brachman's mocking smile.

"What about?" he asked.

What those gathered in the lounge saw—ceasing to pray and rising—was a small man in an Afghan shepherd's coat, long Jesus hair and a face like his too (they had seen it in prayer, all of them, not all the same face but always with this smile, this dread calm and beauty) who asked Ray too a quiet question.


"Why am I here?" Val asked.

The moon was faintly gibbous now, and there was nothing else for Spofford and Val to look at. Beau had told her she was necessary to the thing he had devised with Rosie, but he couldn't tell her why, and only from Beau would she accept such an assignment, on such terms; usually by this time of year she had already ceased to leave her rooms above the Faraway Lodge except for groceries and cartons of Kents when the supplies ran low. "Why am I here?"

"So I don't go nuts," Spofford said calmly.

Beau, Cliff and Rosie had gone up the hill to The Woods in Beau's car, leaving Val and Spofford at the point where the road up Mount Whirligig became The Woods's private way, and a big rustic but grand sign stood in the middle of the road, obstructing and welcoming at once: The Woods Center for Psychotherapy. *Wait here,* Beau had said, and rolled his window up.

Now he and Val sat in the truck together looking at the sign. More than one such place Brent Spofford had spent time in in the bad years after Vietnam, places of compassion and help, so fearsome and repellent he didn't like being so close to one. The Beetle was beside the truck, but its heater was, of course, useless; Val's breath was as white as cigarette smoke.

"You," Val said. "Nimrod the mighty hunter. Ice water in the veins."

"That's what it feels like right now." He turned up his collar. "Well. They also serve."

He too did not understand what had been asked of him in Beau's plan; there was nowhere else he would have wanted to be now but here, and he thought that if he were in some sense too late and had not done for Rosie and for Sam what he could have or should have done, then. Then what? He wouldn't answer even to himself. He was no hunter; but he knew darkness, that was true, and he knew waiting in the cold for what you didn't understand, or couldn't quite believe in. He had done a lot of that this year.

He thought all that, and was quiet for a while; but then he pulled on his cap and opened the truck door. "I'm going to walk a ways up there," he said.

"No. Beau said we wait here."

"I can't."

"Listen," Val said, starting to climb out too. "You're not leaving me alone in this woods."

"Just a few steps up the road," Spofford said. "To anticipate what's coming. I won't get out of sight."

But he hadn't gone more than a few yards upward when he saw, and Val from inside the truck also saw, a person coming down the road: only a progressive distortion of the moonshadows of naked trees, but definitely a person. Soon Spofford could hear footsteps on the dirt.

Two people: Rosie, with Sam in her arms wrapped in a sleeping bag.


Distances walked are greater than distances driven; walked in the winter woods at night carrying a frightened five-year-old much greater; Rosie kept putting her feet one in front of the other without seeming to get any farther, expecting to see headlights or hear pursuit. As though entirely disconnected from her circumstances her brain went on buzzing along about its own concerns, going through its files; Rosie noticed it—she had nothing else to do—but she paid no attention. Plot, she thought: she had once, right after she split from Mike, reading the novels of Fellowes Kraft, wondered if some lives, her life maybe, had plots in the same way books do: courses that turn halfway or two-thirds to the end and proceed back through the events or conjunctions that formed them, reversing each one in turn, or most of them, to bring about an ending. How far can you go into the woods? Halfway: then you start coming out again. No, no plot: you never got halfway; astonishing things or nothing or new things would go on and on, never returning you ever to resolve or tie up the threads, tie up the beasts once let loose. You just went on.

How far? Way beyond here; beyond death maybe. She thought of Sam grown, grown old, dead, past death. She saw Spofford coming up the road toward her at last, at last.

"Cliff brought her to me. And told me to go on, not wait."

Spofford took Sam from her, who cried aloud in delight to see him, climbed up to his neck to circle it with her arms cooing and laughing. Val laughed too. Spofford carried Sam to the truck, bundled her into the cab, and Rosie climbed in too.

"Val, you got to go on," she said. "You go on in your car. Drive all over hell. If you see somebody sticking behind you, just keep driving. Then go home. Don't go to Boney's."

"Where's Beau?" Val said.

"Beau said to go on," Rosie said, and now in the light of the truck's instrument panel coming on Val could see she wept, or had wept. "He said he won't be coming back. He said he'll be all right, and don't look for him. He won't be coming back."

None of them believed that, not even Rosie who had heard him say it. But they said nothing more. Spofford doused his own lights and turned around in the roadway, and by the moon's light set off ahead of Val; at the first road he turned down again, not certain where it led but sure it led somewhere.

"Mike put up no fight?" he said at last. Rosie hadn't spoken. "What happened in there?"

"We went up in Beau's car," Rosie said. "They wanted me to wait. They said they didn't think it would be long. They told me to lock the car doors till I saw Cliff again. And Beau said." She wiped her face with the flannel of Sam's sleeping bag. "Beau said he could win her back, he said he thought he could, but might not be able to come back himself. That's all. A while later Cliff came out with Sam."

"That's all?"

"That's all."

The small bundle of Sam between them on the seat. She put out an arm and made a soft gesture in the air. "Beau made the lights go out," she said. "Do you know Beau?"

# 15

When the world ends it ends differently for each person then alive to see it, each person who chances to see it among all the other things to be seen and felt and understood around us all the time; and then very soon it begins again. And almost everyone persists, almost unchanged, into the new world, which is exactly like the old in almost every respect, or seems to be in the brief moment when the old world can still be remembered.

Almost everyone.

The creatures of the passage time do not persist, who only came into existence for the length of time the world wavered undecided over what shape it would take next; they dissolve or are dismembered like the Golem, or they vacate their bodies and leave only bones, like the beings of the night sky who have left only bright dotted lines to show where once they were. And there are those who cannot persist because the new age was made out of their substance; the world ended in their knowledge that it would, and the new world was born of their ignorance of what it could be.

When the West was endless, a sea reaching into the sunset, that was where the beasts and heroes of an old age went at last, stepping aboard a ship restless at anchor, the sign of Cancer painted on their sails. *After it had all been swept into the unrecoverable again, Rosicrucian brothers fleeing, the Stone, the Cup, the Rose all blown away again like leaves* (so Pierce on a May morning had once imagined the unwritten end of Kraft's last book); *under a fuliginous and pitchy sky (dawn due to come, but otherwhere and elsewhen than there and then) they would be gathered up, the heroes of that age that would already be growing imaginary, gathered up one by one by an old man, his beard white as milk and a star on his forehead. Gathered up. Come along now, for our time is past.*

So now too.

Beau Brachman unfolded his map. No West any longer for the heroes and beings of the old age to depart into? There is always a West. There will be room enough in the 88 for them all, all those whose time is now past or passing: the huntress-spirit Bobby and her spirit-father Floyd, drawn from the land they have gone into; and Plato Goodenough the more perfect gospel bearer; leontocephalic Retlaw O. Walter and his animal angels; Mal Cichy and his: the creatures of the passage time, some of whom will persist into the time to come but will not be who they have been, will not remember even what they did and suffered there, or where they journeyed. Overcoming insuperable ontological difficulties, Beau must separate those persons who will continue from the very same persons who will not, and then *turn back* with the ones who will not, away from the what-is-to-be, toward the what-has-been. There they will be hidden, unable to be discovered even by those who knew them, for when the passage time is over, there is no passage time; when the next age has settled and begun to unfold there are no "ages," and those who never believed in them are right.

So they are for Adocentyn, white city in the West, in a country once more without a name. *Come along now for our time is past.* It may take long, it may be years still, but Beau will gather them all up, as leaves are gathered: as leaves, or pages, for *as the generation of leaves so is that of men*, and of the making of books there really is "when all is said and done" an end.

# 16

On the green table of turned and pierced wood in Pierce Moffett's dining room in Littleville, atop a staggered pile of other books, humped slightly by a pencil he had closed up inside it marking the last page he had used, there lay a tall ledger bound in gray cloth with leatherette corners. Impressed on the cover of this book was a net of geometrical decoration, and the word RECORD in attenuated capitals.

Inside, the number of every page was stamped—not printed but stamped— on its upper right-hand corner. What sort of stamper did that work? Why had it been easier to stamp them than to print them? How did the three spider-shaped splotches come to be on the pages stamped ten and eleven, liquid of some sort that fell there and melted the ink away to unreadability before the spots dried to permanence themselves? Where is this book now, did it pass over or was it lost in the last world?

It was on a spring day when he had first moved from New York City to Blackbury Jambs that Pierce went into the little variety store and soda fountain on River Street (the store from which the daily busses departed for New York and Conurbana far away) and found there, to his delight and astonishment (everything about his new life astonished him then) all the things he would need to carry on his new career as a writer of books: typewriter ribbons and long yellow pencils and sharpeners for them, erasers for his errors, pads for his drafts. And amid these things this ledger that seemed to have escaped unsold from some former business era. A book already, needing only to be written. He bought it.

The first pages record, or did, the gleanings of his reading, and notes to himself sometimes so cryptic as to be useless, sometimes returning a jolt of *Oh yes* every time he passed them. Here he had put down his plan to arrange his book according to the twelve houses of the Zodiac, four Books, three Parts to a Book, Spring Summer Autumn Winter, Air Fire Water Earth.

Astonishing the crust he was then capable of, the nerve.

Here also he copied out possible epigraphs, for chapters, for parts, for the whole book. Pierce loved collecting these, seeming to himself to have done a good day's work when he found an aptly gnomic one, and he was ready to write or rewrite a chapter if needed just to reveal its compact meaning, wrapped suggestively in italics. The last one entered was from Isaiah (though not found there, found quoted in some other book, which one? He would not remember):

Behold: the former things have come to pass, and new things do I
declare: before they spring forth I tell you of them.

A bit farther on are the pages where Robbie is recorded; how Pierce believed he had discovered, after years of pondering, what he really wanted from the world, and that the discovery was not different from its fulfillment. How he opened his door to find his phantasmic son standing on his doorstep, his son having found out about him too and set out to find him. And all that followed is there, Pierce's pen skirling across the spread-eagled pages unashamed, and perhaps it will be there when Pierce can no longer bear to read about it.

Rose too, more cryptically: needing fewer words, because present otherwise to Pierce, in her flesh, and he quite sure he could not ever forget what his rows of exclamation points and brief ejaculations signified, what acts, what initiations. He was already beginning to.

He had just returned from his mother's house in Florida, had not unpacked, nor did he think he would. He shivered and jigged where he stood looking down at the open book, and from his nostrils came plumes of condensing breath. The radiators of his little house were cold iron, the steam that should animate them unproduceable; the wood and paper he had fed into the stove had not yet heated even the stove itself, and the little potbelly would never get the whole house warm. His bedroom beyond the frozen bath was a Yukon where he would not go.

Lying misstacked doggo and dangerous beside the journal or record book on the green table was the pile of his writings, appearing to him as strange and unlikely there as the droppings of some huge intruding animal, moose or rhino. He felt a deep reluctance to touch any of it; if he picked up a page and brought it before his eyes and saw what it said, heard in his ear the voice he had laid down there begin to speak, he might faint in dread and disgust, as though a corpse's jaw were to begin to wag, its gray tongue to make words. That sudden strange spasm of production, he could see it now for what it had been, the unreal phosphorescence of an ignited firework spending itself, dying in its spending. A show, a logorrhea, always pretend and over now.

Well so what. He would get a job, pay back the money somehow. He was unfitted for much but maybe if he humbled himself he could use what he knew for someone's benefit somewhere, teach high-school kids maybe to write a decent sentence or parse one. Almost he imagined himself in such a circumstance, his patient class, the chalkdust on his fingers, the diagrammed sentence on the greenboard; but he quelled it. No more imaginings, never ever. Do it first, then imagine it.

He was going to have to find somewhere else to live, too.

The long drought was over, and the land was deep in snow. The first big snowfall had come while Pierce was in Florida, he had watched it fall on the TV at his mother's house; more was beginning to fall now, he could see it in the windows, a few messenger flakes come calling, the big army on the way. It would fall and fall, thicken into a great white pelt over all the county; in the spring it would melt from the mountains and feed the brooks and streams that fed the Shadow and the Blackbury, and the water meadows would flood and the vegetables grow. But it hadn't fallen soon enough to swaddle Pierce's water pipe; either that or the temperature had fallen sooner. His water, his alone in the neighborhood, was frozen fast.


At the Littleville post office, to which Pierce made his way on foot along the glistening highway, there was a letter from Rose Ryder, postmarked Indiana on the same day Pierce left for Florida.

This post office is something of a local attraction, often pointed out to tourists; there is even a postcard of it itself on sale inside it. A puddingstone pile with fairy-tale peaked roofs covered in varicolored shingles, it was created to be a trolley stop on an interurban rail line that was never built; the station was too pretty to tear down, and the Postal Service was at length persuaded to buy it. Pierce, standing at the cage with the letter in his hand and the rest of his (valueless, unintelligible) mail in his arm, asked the postmistress if he might, please, use the john.

She looked at him somewhat doubtfully; there was a glittering chain on her glasses. "Well it's not really a public, um. Is this a."

"Yes it is. It really is."

On the cold seat, his clothes unsoiled thank God or chance, Pierce held the letter before him.

*Pierce I have to apologize first for running out like that so suddenly but I got a sudden call to come out here and I really couldn't say no. I don't really understand why they have to make things so mysterious and everything but anyway here I am in a place in Indiana and there is so much to say. I won't have time to really explain. This is the center of this group here and it's rather unimpressive in some ways compared to what I thought, but the buildings and things aren't what's important and they say that bigger and better headquarters are in the offing and you wouldn't believe how fast things are growing. Well the weirdest thing I've found out, and again I don't quite understand the reason for the secrecy, it turns out that Dr. Walter is* [here there was a line heavily marked out, one or maybe two rejected ways of saying what *needed to be said] is not alive now. I don't exactly know when he passed into sleep, as they say, but it wasn't like yesterday. I don't get it exactly why they don't want everybody to know but they don't. Here everybody knows. I guess that makes me some kind of insider. Well I don't really feel like one and I know I've got so far to go. But the real thing I need to say is. For a while I'm leaving the country. I am going, you won't believe this, to Peru. The Powerhouse International you know, is opening a they don't say a mission but an outreach there, and I speak Spanish (it all came back to me, just rushed out of me) and so. Pierce I never expected this and I'm afraid and I'm happy. Of course I won't be alone.*

There were, Pierce noticed, bars on the miniature window of the toilet, but why. The place happened to be (and Pierce would remember this when he saw it) just the size and warm buff color of Giordano Bruno's cell in the Castel St. Angelo in Rome. There are a thousand prisons to be stuck in, a thousand deaths after death; and for each one a liberty.

*I hope you'll write to me, Pierce. You've been so important to me this year, which was quite a year for me. Whatever happens you've got to admit it was interesting.*

At the bottom of the page, below her rapid signature:

*PS I gave up smoking here, really this time.*

He walked home, the cuffs of his pants snow-wet, her letter crushed in his pocket. He supposed that there would come a day when her name on an envelope would not have the power to loosen his bowels; when he would see that the saddest thing was not her capitulation to the Powerhouse, but that she had never had power over the world, and still didn't; and neither did they.

He took a pot from his kitchen, scooped snow with it, took it inside and set it on the stove. Fire versus water. He would have coffee at least.

A weary wanderer who had lost his way in a part of the world strange to him came at last to a great house, and asked the lord of that place for shelter in exchange for labor. Yes, the lord said, you may stay in this small house here as long as you like. There is only one thing you must be sure to do: you must keep the water flowing in the freezing weather. But how am I to do that? asked the wanderer. The lord explained how a certain key had to be turned to exactly the right degree, and the water would flow and not freeze.

All went well. When winter came the lord told the wanderer: I am going away on a long journey to the South. I won't return until the winter is over. Remember what I have told you about the life-giving spring and how it flows, for if you do not tend to it there will be no water for you to drink . . .

Pierce laughed aloud, skirts of his coat parted and his rump toasting at his stove. King Winter had fooled him, patient and gullible ass, and lashed him to this unworkable system, no it had never worked and never would.

We live in tales, he thought, and tales have endings but no exits, except into their frame tales. He *had* failed; and yet there was no right thing he could have done, not with his water, not about Rose, not with anything, that was beyond or different from his attempts to do the right thing; there is no right way for stories to come out, only our struggles to make them come out right. Well he wasn't going to stick around to see how this one came out. He exited now into the unimaginable frame tale of this tale, which held who knew what, another city and another dawn. He wondered what he should write to the Winterhalters. He felt, like Rose, afraid and happy.

Of course frame tales too have endings, endings of their own; but from them, too, you can exit, only into further frame tales. Yes, Pierce thought: yes, so we figure that out, maybe, finally, about our tales; and maybe we conceive the ambition to make our way—to think or hope our way—out from the tale we find ourselves into the frame tale of that tale, where its terms were first set and its reasons for being told were given; and not to stop there, either, but to make it all the way out, tale into frame tale into frame tale to the authorial origin, the first once-upon-a-time of all.

Well fine. But to believe you really *have* made it all the way out is an illusion; for the tale has no author.

Rose it is authorless. The outermost one too if there even is an outermost one. That's Ray's arrogance with his little black book, to believe that there is an outermost one and that he knows what it is. To believe he can stand outside the story, with the Author, the book in his hand. In the beginning was the Word.

All right. But the greater error was the one that had tempted Pierce himself, to believe that we ourselves are the authors of the tales we live within. That's the ultimate arrogance of power, the arrogance of the gods: for all the gods believe themselves self-created, and believe themselves to be issuing their own strong stories, news to us.

Well we don't create them, those stories. They are uncreated; they come to us without our willing it, "from a region of awareness beyond our ken," beyond even where the Powers are at war: countless tales or the same few tales in countless varieties, enough to go around, enough for each of us to have his own, only to learn it's not his own at all. We have not created them—but we can learn compassion for those who are living and suffering alongside us within them (within the old tales, the old old tales) and trying to make them come out right, or to come out at all; maybe, after many adventures and much suffering, to exit to the frame.

You're not required to finish it, Beau said; but you're not to give it up either.

*Oh I see,* he thought or breathed, his Sagittarian verb, the heart pierced by its own arrow: *I see.*

He picked up his pen, and on the unfinished page of his journal he wrote a new epigraph, not someone else's this time but his own, for a book not yet written and maybe unwriteable:

Will we not, then, find what we seek at last? Will we not be saved? Will
we not awaken? Yes, we will; surely we will; and not once either but
many times: time after time.

Far down inside the night lands that are Death, down in the dark where Little
Enosh is in Rutha's prison, there is an infinitesimal bright spark of knowing that
could dissolve all the worlds, if it were ever to be released. But it might never be
released. And just as far outward—farthestmost, out beyond the enclosing circles, where Beau longs to go for good—is the same knowing, a knowing that
could fold the great sad mistaken dark to its breast like a small child and close
it up at last in grateful nothingness, the same nothingness from which it came at
first; but that might never happen either.

Meanwhile, no matter what, "deer walk on our mountains," up on Mount
Randa for instance nosing in the snow for the withered apples of abandoned or-
chards, near where Spofford's new cellar-hole is smothered up; meanwhile
flamingoes in their hundreds rise from the waters of the salt marshes in Florida
and Africa too, all startled or moved at once by something none of them alone
could have perceived; and the stars turn unseen behind the sun, only seeming
to be changeless; and Sam and Rosie watch the tiger cubs roll and bite on TV at
Arcady, and Rosie waits to hear the phone ring.

It was only Pierce calling, this time anyway, and not the law, or vengeful cultists:
just calling to say he was homeless now and so was ready to go do his duty and
use his fellowship, or be a fellow, or however it was to be termed. He said he
supposed he could sleep there in his house for one night on the floor by the fire,
drink bottled water and piss outdoors in the snow, but he couldn't do it long, so
he had to get going; and Rosie said not to be silly and come stay with them for
a while.

Spofford went out to bring him back (the Steed was deep in the snow of his
yard, for Pierce had taken the plane and the bus to his mother's and had made
no provision for it; when just out of curiosity he forced open its door and turned
the key in the ignition nothing happened anyway; he would never, though he
didn't know this yet, ride in it again). When Spofford drove up, Pierce was
standing in his overcoat and galoshes at the stone gateposts with a large duffel
in his hand and a cardboard box clutched to his breast. Behind him a long line
of footprints in the snow, going in and then back out.

"You didn't have to come all the way out here," Spofford said. "I'd of got in."

"Well."

"Chains," said Spofford. "Four-wheel drive."

"Anyway thanks."

They went out onto the river road; Pierce listened to the chink of the chains
and squinted his eyes against the awful innocence of the snow in the sun. "Spofford," he said.

"Yes."

"Can I ask you something?"

"The answer's yes," Spofford said. "I know all about it. She told me." He looked over at Pierce with what Pierce, only daring to catch his eye for a moment, thought to be amusement. "Happens," he said. "Fortunately she still likes me best. Surprising. But she does. So that's okay."

Pierce said nothing. This was not in fact what he had meant to ask his old friend about. Spofford had long ago warned him that the round dance that went on in these parts would eventually lead almost everybody to almost everybody else. His breast filled hugely, and rested. In the rearview mirror he saw the chimneys of the Winterhalters' mansion, and then their road and the town of Littleville, pass backwards away.

"Do you remember," he said after a time, "the day I came here, the day the bus broke down?"

"Sure. A year ago. Summer before last."

"Do you remember anything unusual about that day?"

"Only that. Your arrival. Buswrecked."

"I remember sitting there," Pierce said, "in front of the store in Fair Prospect. I remember sitting there and drinking a Coke. I remember that a little breeze sprang up."

Spofford once again glanced at him. Only after a moment did he realize that Pierce desired to have this detail corroborated. "Uh-huh," he said.

"You remember?"

"No."

"A little breeze," Pierce said. He had sat there and thought of his Three Wishes, the three everyone deserves, and how he would treat them; how he would wish for health or wealth or love and the third wish would be to forget he had ever been granted any wishes. And he had thought that if that were to happen right then at the moment of his sitting there, then he wouldn't know it; and yet everything that followed would follow from them, from those wishes, whatever they were. Or had been.

"Just after that," Pierce said, "you and your sheep came out onto the main road. You with a straw hat on your head and your crook."

"My what?"

"Crook," said Pierce, and drew one in the air. "The thing shepherds use."

But Spofford was already shaking his head, amused. "No. No way. Never owned one."

"Yes sure," Pierce said. "It's one of your attributes. *Il Pastor fido*. You. It's what I know about you."

"You got quite the head," Spofford said. "A thing I have always admired. It's a privilege to know you, man, in many ways. But you know sometimes a sheep is just a sheep. Most times, in fact."


Arcady was almost comically appealing, its chimneys and fancywork all capped with sugar snow, the winter-woolly sheep milling at the fence. A fire too burning in the study fireplace. There Pierce put down the box containing the type-script. On the big desk were laid out all of the letters that Fellowes Kraft had sent to Boney Rasmussen over several years, but most particularly from the last trip that Kraft had taken to Europe, on Boney's nickel, ten years before: the trip that now Pierce would retake.

"I don't know what to tell you," Rosie said. "How you're supposed to wrap this up."

The day of Boney's funeral she told Pierce that Boney had intended him to have this research grant, that Pierce would know what it was for and how to pur-sue what was to be pursued; what it was that Boney wanted so badly to know. And how to put it into an application.

"Well you know the basic idea," he said. "Kraft's idea. That the world—you know, reality, all this—goes through changes. Every now and then it enters a sort of period of indeterminism, anything possible; and it stays in that passage time until, well until."

He picked up from the desk a sepia postcard, sent from Prague in 1968, a picture of the Charles Bridge that seemed to date from much earlier.

"Until what."

"Until a certain thing is found. A certain thing that only exists, or comes to be, in that time. It's the stone, or the elixir, or the thing that Boney wanted found. If it's not found the world stops changing, or never stops changing, and dies. But it's always found. So far."

"Kraft believed this?"

"I don't know. He didn't exactly make it up. Something like this is in stories all over the world. Sometimes the thing has been lost, sometimes it's hidden. Sometimes it can only be found by a pure fool."

"Hey. There's the job for you."

"I'm a fool," Pierce said. "But I'm not pure."

He turned the card over:

*Intourist has given me a room in a former convent of the Infantines, a won-derful Baroque building built by the great Bohemian magnate Peter of Rosm-berk (sp?). I have my own cell. I imagine myself in black, Pure, and subsumed in prayer.*

"Well," Rosie said. "Isn't one way of finding it just to find out it can't be found?"

"Sure. Or to find out that 'it' is nothing but the journey undertaken to find it. And the story of the journey told afterward."

"Then you're on," said Rosie.

Pierce had been looking with deep reluctance on the piles of pale blue let-ters flimsy as ashes. He picked one up, the second page of one, no date, no place.

*this Croll or Kroll, by the way (author of the* Basilica Chymica) *had a famous chest or trunk of some kind, containing I am not sure what, which after his sudden death (sudden for an iatrochemist) was sought for fiercely by the Em-*

*peror, who fought off the great noble Peter von Rosemberk, who also desper-*
*ately wanted it. No mention of this trunk or chest after that. Where is it now?*
*Where for that matter is the Perspective Lute, invented by Cornelius Drebbel;*
*where is the Perpetual Motion Machine he made for the Emperor in 1610?*
*Where is the Prophetic Automaton built in this city by Kepler's friend Jost*
*Bürgi, the clockmaker who invented the second? And what exactly did it*
*prophesy?*

"You can have this to take with you too," Rosie said. She gave him an old leather-bound guidebook of a kind now passé: onionskin pages nearly pictureless, tiny type picked out with stars, arrows, bullets, and other *notæ*.

"Gee," said Pierce.

"It's full of Kraft's writing," Rosie said. And so it was, fine spidery blue-black annotations that Pierce would need better light to read, much better light.

"And *this*," Rosie said, with a gesture of what-the-hell generosity. A little book, also of an old-fashioned kind, privately printed. "His life."

Written by himself, for who to read? It was called *Sorrow, Sit Down.* For a moment Pierce's eyes filled; but they did that now every day, at something or at nothing; every day. He opened to the pictures. Three young men in an open truck or jeep on a mountain track: *On expedition in the Giant Mountains,* it said. *1935.*

"Anything else?" Pierce asked, holding these.

"Well," Rosie said, and looked around herself. "Oh sure. You should see this."

She led him out into the living room, to a polished cabinet or commode, he had noted its workmanship before, what was the name of that art whereby pictures were made of bits of different veneers. A violin with a curly ribbon tied to its neck, a peacock, a pen, a book, an hourglass. Rosie reached up to turn the key in the little casket that surmounted it.

"I'm not going to give it to you," she said, "because I'm pretty sure it belongs here."

"Good," said Pierce. "Fine."

"I've told you about it," she said. "You know all about it already." She put her hand in, but after a moment's puzzled groping she took out nothing but a velvet bag, black and empty, limp as a dead kitten.

"It's gone," she said.

"Gone?"

"It was right here," Rosie said.

Gone, thought Pierce, well sure.

Gone, Rosie thought too, wondering.

Gone, dreamed Sam, asleep upstairs in her bed; *gone,* she dreamed she said, watching it roll purposefully across her bedroom floor and out across the hall and down the stair.

—Gone, said Doctor John Dee. Gone. Over the hills and far away.

*Gone,* Fellowes Kraft had written on the last page he would finish of the yellow typescript that lay now in the lamplight on Boney Rasmussen's desk; *gone once more, gone to hide her head where no one knows, until someday somewhere* And then no more.


Pierce Moffett was not cured, no: for he was awake and thinking in the gulf of darkness after midnight, his eyes open and his heart alert. Thinking about Jesus. It was Solstice Night; the snow falling steadily outside could be sensed more than seen or heard, perhaps lightening the darkness a little, perhaps making a sound in all its soundless alightings.

Such a funny contradictory moment in the calendar (the old circular one, not the straight-on one of datebooks and newspapers, though the abstracted members and limbs of the older one could of course still be found in those). For it's the end of autumn and the first day of winter, which in this northern zone has already well begun, and which stretches on from there deep and crisp and even for many weeks and months: and yet it's the birthday of the Sun, the day after his long decline and death are over and he begins, weak as an infant, to grow and flourish again; and so we celebrate, in the cold and the dark.

Maybe that's why Jesus is a solar myth, or so easily could become one, or attract to himself the properties of one. Born, to the rejoicing of the whole cosmos; but little and weak and obscure, in a poor part of town.

Rose had told him that *they* didn't celebrate Christmas the usual way, that *they* made no big deal about its annual recurrence, and why? Because most people act as though it happens every year, the birth of Jesus, and it doesn't: it happened once, a long time ago. Once and for all.

In Kentucky once near Christmas Pierce and his family gathered to listen to that radio priest, elsewhere he could already be seen on TV but not yet in that fastness, what was his name, so perfectly unctuous and shallow; Uncle Sam liked him for his jokes and his paradoxes and because he was the only one of *ours* on the airwaves amid all the Baptists. And that Christmas he asked them to imagine with him, to imagine Jesus, *picture* Him to ourselves, God becoming incarnate, on His way down to earth, passing through all the starry waste cold and dark that lay between His home in Heaven and that womb He would inhabit, that stable in Palestine. Oh Beloved what a long long journey for our sakes.

Fulton Sheen: yes.

And Pierce for that one moment, the only one he remembered, had been held and shaken by the story that he had all his life assented to; grateful and appalled by God's great painful goodness at Christmas.

The journey we all take, down through the spheres, gathering our human natures around us as we come; Pierce had told Val and Spofford and Rosie about it in the yard of the Faraway Lodge. But He the one father's son who didn't need to take it; and did anyway.

He wondered if Beau would say that He too got ensnared by the Archons and the princes of this world, as every messenger always does. Well sure, by the

Pope and the Powerhouse, sure. So that He has to keep setting out, every year; every year arriving here small and bare and wailing in the dark of the sun.

Pierce turned over on the bed he had been given, which had been Rosie's, and which smelled of her too; his ear pressed against it, he listened to the mattress's ticks and tocks, another country down deep. What'll I do, he asked. O what'll I do.

After a time he got up. He pulled on his pants and sweater in the dark, and went out into the hall, the house silent and unstirring and his footsteps making no sound, solid old oak floors and long runners. He thought he had turned in the direction of the bathroom, but the door he opened was a stair, leading down, a light at the bottom, and he took it. It came out in the kitchen, where a light had been left on over the stove, and last night's glasses and dishes squatted unwashed by the sink.

In the study at the end of the hall another light left burning, nobody paying attention, too much to think about. In there he had sat once with Boney Rasmussen and told him about finding the unfinished manuscript of Kraft's last book. *Maybe you should finish it,* Boney had said. Well now?

With Hermes Mercurius, Messenger and Trickster, Shepherd of men into the land of death. At the end of every age he comes to ingather the gods and heroes of that age, who won't survive its dissolution, to his City, which will at that time come to be in the westernmost limit of his disappearing land. Come along now it's time.

That's how Pierce used to think he would end the book, if he were to end it, if it could be ended.

One of their number though left behind in the storm of the world. They seal him in a boat and set him afloat on the years, to be both the message and the messenger. Like Jor-El amid the vastation of Krypton, sealing his son within the capsule that will carry him into the far future and another world, to grow up not knowing his name or nature, the only one of his kind.

One time it was the man-king Hermes himself, the Thrice-great, self-interred or maybe helped into bed by his even greater progenitor, ibis-headed Theuth. Found centuries later, the Smaragdine Tablet gripped in his white hands. In a cave or something supposedly. And then there's the Rosicrucians' story of their founder, discovered in a tomb in a room in a cave.

Kraft should have put that stuff in. Maybe he meant to. If Pierce were writing it, he would. Set it in Prague maybe, where whatever it was that was supposed to happen was supposed to happen; where Dee and Bruno and the others were for a moment gathered.

Where Pierce this winter was to journey.

If he were to finish it, he would put that in: the depths of Rudolf's castle, the Brotherhood gathered, all those magicians with their weird but real names, Drebbel and Bragadino and de Boodt. Oswald Kroll and his black box. Yes and in the box perhaps the.

Yes.

An actual box or trunk or chest which actually could play that part appeared just then to Pierce, a chest that had yes indeed survived and been carried from that very city, yes! To the New World for no good reason or maybe a real good one, yes, still freighted with its freight, maybe, which was in Pierce's telling to be who or what? And opened when?

Now. If he, Pierce, were to finish it, it would end not then but now.

Pierce in the house where all but he were asleep sat down on the chaise longue of buttoned leather where Boney had spent his last days, and pulled over his lap the afghan that Boney had vainly tried to warm himself with.

Far down the snowy night then, above the town of Pikeville in eastern Kentucky, in the creepy Victorian mansion that the Infantine sisters had turned into a boarding school called Queen of the Angels, the Supervisor, Sister Mary Philomel, knelt before that very box, long black and beeswaxed, which had once resided in the Bondieu hospital but had been moved here (Sister too) when that hospital was renovated. Often in this autumn, not every night but many nights, Sister had come down the stairs at hours like this, unable to rest; had come here to listen, ear against the cold slick wood, to the sounds inside. For on the night of the Equinox, that September night when the wind had blown so hard, she had discovered that she herself possessed the key to this box, and on that night had gone and turned the key in the lock, which didn't open the thing but seemed to set something inside in motion: a series of noises like clockwork or machinery, faint but distinct, altering in rhythm and tenor over time and reminding Sister of the model machines she saw as a child in exhibits at the World's Fair, which at the end of their whirrings and clankings and tickings turned out a pretend car, or cigarette, or breadloaf, or cement block. And then another and another. She told no one what she had done and what she heard, bearing the secret within her like the worst sin she had ever committed, or like the awful knowledge that she had stomach cancer (since cured by the grace of God); but she kept coming to this hall in the silence of the night and kneeling and listening to the sounds, and she could not deny (as she could in the busy bright day) that they were there, and changing too: moving—definitely, obviously—to their end.

So Pierce at Arcady dreamed it, afloat on Boney's chaise longue, and so it was: so it will come to have been.

But then *No no,* Pierce thought, and sat upright. No not that box; not *him,* of course not. *He* is not the one to tell the future, this present, what it needs to hear. It wasn't he who walked across Europe bringing Ægypt into being around him, and the Ægyptians too who met him and helped him everywhere, his brothers all, though indistinguishable from their countrymen and neighbors.

Yes he. Jordanus Brunus Nolanus. Who would somehow have to be got out of prison at the end of the story (*Carcer*), plucked from the burning to be reserved to a different fate, another tomb. *The Jonah that the fish spat out, the brand to be plucked from the burning,* said the angels to John Dee and Edward Kelley, when first they showed them Bruno in the glass; *the stone rejected by the builders that has become the corner of the house. Our pretty rose. Our Bruin sleeping in a cave through the winter.*

Yes.

By his bare feet was his bag, right where he had left it last evening; and in the bag the book called RECORD, and also (he rooted deeper) a pencil, no a pen.

Just then in the dark front hallway of Queen of the Angels School (smelling, at this time of the year, of pine branches and candle smoke) Sister Mary Philomel heard the sounds within the old carved chest come to a stop; and she knew that the heavy lid could be lifted now, if she chose to lift it, though in fact she seemed hardly to have a choice. She did lift it (see her long clean pale hands, Pierce and his cousins had marvelled at them, much older now though and the blue veins prominent, the gold wedding band sunk deep in the *pronubis,* Bride of Christ) and with all her strength heaved it back against the wall. Heart thudding from effort and expectation, she looked inside.

Pierce thought: But who will be chosen in *this* passage time, our own? And into what box shall he or she or it be put? And in what future open her eyes?

A small ghost flitted across his peripheral vision, down at the end of the hall, a white child.

There was after all nothing in the chest in Pikeville; nothing but—what? A few common nouns maybe: a cup, a key, a stone, a book.

Pierce waited and watched, guessing whom he had seen, and in a moment Sam reappeared, bare-armed in a white nightgown: sleepwalking maybe or confused. She stood in the high hall for a time, and lifted the pale curls of her hair with one hand, looking around herself as though she expected to see something that she did not see; but then she turned toward the light in the study, and walked right down and in.

"Hi."

"Hi, Sam."

"Are you up?" she asked.

"Yep."

"The snow woke me up," Sam said. She looked up at him frankly, smiling a little.

"Sam, you should be in bed," Pierce said. "You need your sleep."

"It's okay," she said. "I'm strong, see?" She made a strongman's arm, and Pierce took it delicately in his fingers; light as a bird's wing, warm to his touch. "Wow," he said. He felt salt fluid burn the orbits of his eyes, oh please no more. He thought again how easily harm could come to your children, you would never rest; and yet with Sam near him he did rest, as he hadn't before.

"My ode house is gone," she said.

"Yes?"

"This is my house now."

"Oh. Good."

"Where's your house?"

"I don't think I have one."

She sat down on the chaise beside him and folded her hands in the lap of her thin gown; Pierce wondered if she shouldn't be dressed more warmly, though she didn't shiver; her bare feet hung down. "We should sing," she said.

"We should?"

"Sing 'Silent Night,'" Sam said.

"Oh Sam," Pierce said. He knew he could not do this, could not even begin. "You sing it. Please."

She composed herself in rapt solemnity and sang:

*Silent night*
*Holy night*
*All is gone*
*All is bright*

—and then collapsed in embarrassed giggles.

"Now you sing," she said.

"What song."

"Sing my favorite," Sam said, and when Pierce didn't respond, she said its name with both hands displayed, as though it was obvious: "'Three Kings.'"

"Oh," Pierce said. "Right. Sure. I knew that."

They sang it together sitting on the chaise.

*We three kings of ory and tar*
*Bearing gifts we travelled a far*
*Field and fountain moor and mountain*
*Following yonder star.*

*O Star of wonder, star of night*
*Star with royal beauty bright*
*Ever leading still proceeding*
*Lead us with thy, to thy*

Neither could quite remember the last words, it wasn't "endless night" or "loving light" or "purple plight" but they hummed a sound that rhymed. As they sang, rays or waves of quicksilver *pneuma,* the spirit-stuff that enwrapped their souls, were carried out in the song or as the song, tentative and soiled (his) and pure and clear (hers); and journeyed outward, endlessly. When the song was over, they looked at each other, bass and treble, and smiled, pleased with their effort. It was not long till dawn, the twenty-second of December, 1979. When Sam was Pierce's age, it would be ten years into a new century, no a new *millennium,* and the world would be as it was coming to be: it would not be the way it had all along been, nor yet what we then thought it would become. It is really, the old alchemists always said, so simple.

On the eighth day of the first February of a new century (1600), Giordano Bruno was taken from his small cell high up in the Castel St. Angelo and brought before a consistory of Cardinals and Inquisitors General at the Church of St. Agnes in Agony to hear sentence pronounced on him.

For eight years the Fathers had struggled with the man to convince him to recant the obvious heresies he was guilty of. For eight years he had variously denied he had said these things, or denied that they were heretical, and insisted on putting his case before the Pope. All that was now done; now he was pressed to his knees before the Holy Fathers, and his sentence read. He was firstly to be "degraded," stripped of all his priestly attributes and privileges; he would then be handed over to the Governor of Rome, who the Fathers of course prayed would have mercy on him and spare him the full rigor of the law. They also ordered all his writings to be burned in the Square of St. Peter and placed forever on the Index of Forbidden Books. *And thus we say, pronounce, sentence, declare, degrade, command and ordain, we chase forth and we deliver and we pray, in this and in every other better method that we reasonably can and should.*

A young German named Gaspar Schopp or Scioppius, a recent convert from Lutheranism to Catholicism of whom the Vatican was very proud, witnessed this final arraignment and what followed; and he wrote home how when Bruno had heard all this, and when he was allowed to stand, he said loudly and clearly to the gathered Cardinals that he was sure it frightened them more to pronounce this sentence than it did him to hear it.

Perhaps it did.

Bruno was taken, then, to an old fortress by Tiber-side belonging to the city, the Tor di Nona, crowds already gathering and the city news-sheets talking up the coming events. Yet again there was a postponement, ten days, the Governor falling into paralysis for no known reason or his servants unable to act; and the Pope in his chambers fought back an impulse to read Bruno's petition, which he somehow kept stumbling on wherever he went, like a cat that brushed up against his legs; its ribbons had actually come undone as it lay on his table, and the leaves opened.

Then Time shook himself alert. At two in the morning on the eighteenth, brothers of the Headless John Society assembled at St. Ursula in the depths of night, as was their habit, and proceded to the Tor to awaken the prisoner, to "offer up the winter-prayers" and give comfort and correction, maybe even snatch the man back from the abyss at the last instant. But no, he stayed up through the night with them talking and disputing, "setting his brain and mind to a thousand errors and vaingloryings" (but what were these really? What did he say at the last?) until the Servants of Justice came to take him.

There was a little gray donkey tied up outside in the dawnlight, where the crowds were being held back by the Servants; Giordano Bruno clothed only in a white shroud emblazoned at the corners with Andrew crosses (and maybe little devils and hell flames too, some observers saw them) was led out. What is that on his head and breast? An iron brace that keeps his jaws tight shut, no more talking ever, and when his books are burned that will be that. He was mounted backward on his steed to cheers of loathing, and a tall white paper hat put on his head, a fool as well as a devil.

The crowds along the way were vast; it was a Jubilee Year, the first Jubilee Year in which the Papacy could feel sure, really sure, that it was not about to come to an end and be lost in the sudden ending of the world; all around, the city was being renewed, just as the Holy Catholic Church itself was. Fifty Cardinals from all over Christendom were assembled here, there were processions, high masses, new churches dedicated daily. The little ceremony at the square of the flower-sellers was not even the best attended.

He was stripped naked after being tied to the stake. At the inn La Vacca at the piazza's end the guests looked out the upper-story windows. Gaspar Schopp says a cross was held out to Bruno at the last moment, but he turned away from it.

After many years had passed, the Vatican authorities would begin to claim that they hadn't burned Giordano Bruno at the stake at all, that what was burned that day on the square was a *simulacrum* or effigy. As all the papers relating to the trial and the execution had disappeared into deep and unbreachable archives, those who wished to believe this could.

Something burned for sure, for a long time.

The little ass that had borne the man stood by the scaffold; after the man had been dragged from his back the ass had been forgotten about, his rope not even tied. Jostled by those pushing forward to have a better look, and those pushing back who had seen enough, the beast kicked once, and pranced away. No one stopped him, no one noticed him. He left the Campo di Fiori (not pausing even at the unattended stalls where winter vegetables were sold, whose greens hung down temptingly) and entered the narrow streets beyond, Hatmakers' Street, Locksmiths' Street, Crossbow-makers' Street, Trunk-makers' Street, out beneath the high walls of palaces and churches, skirting the crowds that filled the Piazza Navona, finding another way, north, always north. Now and then boys or shopkeepers chased after him, housewives tried to snatch his lead, but he kicked out and brayed, and they laughed and fell behind, none could catch him. Some noticed the sacred Cross on his shaggy back, the Cross that all asses still bear in honor of Our Lord, Whom one of their kind once carried; but this Cross was not the same, no not the same.

Next day a news-sheet, *Avvisi*, noted that "the wicked Dominican Brother from Nola we gave news of before has been burned alive in the Campo di Fiori; he said that he died willingly as a martyr, and that his soul would ascend in the smoke to Paradise. Today he knows if he was right or not."

But he didn't say that. He couldn't speak. No one heard anything.

*One certainty consoled me then in my darkest hour,* says Lucius Apuleius the Golden Ass, *that the new year was here at last, and the wildflowers would soon be coming out to color the meadows; and in the gardens the rosebuds long imprisoned in their thorny stocks would appear, and open, and breathe out their indescribable odor; and I would eat and eat, and become once again myself.*

# AUTHOR'S NOTE

T o the many authors cited as sources in the preceding volumes of this series, the author wishes to add the following: Nuccio Ordine, *Giordano Bruno and the Philosophy of the Ass*; Angelo Maria Ripellino, *Magic Prague*; Brian P. Levack, *The Witch-hunt in Early Modern Europe*; Ioan Culiano, *The Tree of Gnosis*; Carlo Ginzburg, *Ecstasies*; Deborah Vansau Mc-Cauley, *Appalachian Mountain Religion: A History*; Helen Reisner (ed.), *Children with Epilepsy: A Parent's Guide*. Translations from ancient authors, Apuleius to Bruno, are the work of the present author or have been adapted by him from the translations of others; almost all conform in most respects to the originals. Likewise, all extracts from the diaries, works, and letters of John Dee are quoted more or less *verbatim* except for those that are fictitious, or are not now as they once were.

The author's profound thanks are due to Harold Bloom; to Laurie Block and Paul Park for their critiques; and to Ron Drummond for his help.